AF520775

The yellowbacks... classics of popular fiction

The yellowjackets or yellowbacks were a great series of bestselling adventure and crime thrillers that had its origins in the mid to late 19th century following on from the 'penny dreadfuls'. They virtually began the mass market revolution of the early 20th century with a clear standard format and imprint/series livery (what would today be called branding). Hodder & Stoughton published the yellow jackets in two main series with series run dates of: 1923-1939 and later 1949-1957.

As the tagline ('where thrillers really began') on the back cover implies, the imprint and series focused on thrillers that were the bestsellers of their time. This current reissue or retro revival if you will, brings back many of these masterpieces, now classics in their own way and extends it further by including key titles from that period that were either great crime or thriller or even general commercial fiction (including sub-genres of noir, horror, gothic, romance, westerns etc) influences of their time. There are some perennial favourites and many rarities either lost or not easily available. being revived in the current series. Writers and characters ranged from adventure heroes like Bulldog Drummond, Allan Quatermain, Richard Hannay or the Saint through thriller grandmasters Edgar Wallace and E. Phillips Oppenheim, crime and mystery maestros like Patricia Wentworth, GK Chesterton, Agatha Christie and the Detection club, to western and swashbucklers like Zane Grey, Max Brand, Captain Blood and even romance or general fiction classics like Hermina Black, Denise Robins, Marie Corelli or Stella Morton. These were books that had storytelling at their heart and always entertained.

The yellowbacks had both hardback (with varying design elements) and paperback (which built the series look) versions with the latter still carrying the imprint 'yellowjacket'. The current reissues pay tribute to both and use an amalgam of elements from both editions while retaining the complete yellow (or 'mustard-plaster') livery with the author's name in blue beveled type with a 'simulated emboss' effect and a white outer 'outline', and the book title in black. These reissues retain the distinctive size of the original mass market paperback and follow the three main category variations—the thrillers (crime, westerns, mystery, adventure) had blue lettering for the author's name, while Romance and 'softer general fiction had red; and other categories like humour had green.

For more detail and a full list of titles visit https://www.hachetteindia.com/home/yellowbacks

THE COMPLETE RAFFLES

THE COMPLETE RAFFLES

E.W. Hornung (1866–1921) was an English author and poet known for writing the A.J. Raffles series of stories about a gentleman thief in late nineteenth-century London. Hornung was educated at Uppingham School. In 1898 he wrote 'In the Chains of Crime', which introduced Raffles and his sidekick, Bunny Manders; the characters were based partly on his friends Oscar Wilde and his lover, Lord Alfred Douglas, and also on the characters of Sherlock Holmes and Dr Watson, created by his brother-in-law, Arthur Conan Doyle. The series of Raffles short stories were collected for sale in book form in 1899, and two further books of Raffles short stories followed. Aside from these, Hornung was a prodigious writer of fiction, publishing numerous books from 1890 to 1914.

THE COMPLETE RAFFLES

E.W. Hornung

The Amateur Cracksman
The Black Mask
A Thief in the Night
Mr Justice Raffles

hachette

The Complete Raffles
The first of the series, *The Amateur Cracksman*, was published in 1899 by Methuen Publishing in the United Kingdom; This was followed by *The Black Mask*, published in 1901 by Grant Richards in the United Kingdom; Then came *A Thief in the Night* published in 1905 by Chatto & Windus in the United Kingdom; And the final book, *Mr. Justice Raffles*, was published in 1909 by Smith, Elder & Co. in the United Kingdom.

1

The texts in these editions in most cases have been reprinted as is, with minimal editorial changes and by and large no bowdlerizing for political correctness; though in some editions, a few words and phrases considered archaic, or those considered offensive now, along with archaic punctuation may have been modified in places to make the text more accessible to today's readers. The narratives, language, beliefs, social mores and/or cultural depictions, in these volumes are a reflection of their times and must be viewed as such. They may also contain certain cultural, racial and gender prejudices and stereotypes that may be outdated or clearly wrong then and wrong today; but their removal would be tantamount to claiming these prejudices never existed. The Publisher does not endorse or support those depictions or stereotypes; and these books have been made available for a discerning audience that will read it for entertainment value and a chronicle/record of popular fiction of past times.

Cover design by Priya Singh adapted from the original classic yellowjacket by Hodder & Stoughton.

Cover illustration by Ishan Trivedi.

Series note: Some of the books in the series (unless otherwise credited) may have cover or inside illustrations from the original yellowbacks or early editions, and while full restoration has been attempted, some images may be grainy or faded due to the condition of the original material. The end notes or bonus material or blurb details may have been sourced from the public domain or free use publications such as Wikipedia and attribution is hereby made also allowing similar free use reproduction from here. Sources requiring further specific attribution may write in and further detailing and/or corrections shall be made in subsequent printings/editions.

Reprint specifications may be subject to change including but not limited to finishes, paper, colour sections.

ISBN: 978-93-5731-234-9

Hachette Book Publishing India Pvt. Ltd.
4th & 5th Floors, Corporate Centre,
Plot No. 94, Sector 44, Gurugram - 122 003, India

Typeset in Electra LT STD 10/12.5 pt by Manipal Technologies Limited, Manipal

Printed and bound in India by Manipal Technologies Limited, Manipal

CONTENTS

The Amateur Cracksman 1
1. The Ides of March 3
2. A Costume Piece 26
3. Gentlemen and Players 44
4. Le Premier Pas 65
5. Wilful Murder 83
6. Nine Points of the Law 99
7. The Return Match 117
8. The Gift of the Emperor 134

The Black Mask 161
Narrator's Note 163
1. No Sinecure 165
2. A Jubilee Present 187
3. The Fate of Faustina 203
4. The Last Laugh 224
5. To Catch a Thief 243
6. An Old Flame 267
7. The Wrong House 292
8. The Knees of the Gods 307

A Thief in the Night 329
1. Out of Paradise 331
2. The Chest of Silver 351
3. The Rest Cure 368
4. The Criminologists' Club 387
5. The Field of Philippi 409
6. A Bad Night 431

7. A Trap to Catch a Cracksman 449
8. The Spoils of Sacrilege 469
9. The Raffles Relics 489
10. The Last Word 509

Mr Justice Raffles
1. An Inaugural Banquet 519
2. "His Own Familiar Friend" 527
3. Council of War 537
4. "Our Mr Shylock" 546
5. Thin Air 556
6. Camilla Belsize 567
7. In Which We Fail to Score 578
8. The State of the Case 587
9. A Triple Alliance 595
10. "My Raffles Right or Wrong" 610
11. A Dash in the Dark 621
12. A Midsummer Night's Work 630
13. Knocked Out 641
14. Corpus Delicti 650
15. Trial by Raffles 663
16. Watch and Ward 680
17. A Secret Service 695
18. The Death of a Sinner 705
19. Apologia 719

Appendix : Essay by George Orwell :
'Raffles and Miss Blandish' 725

THE AMATEUR CRACKSMAN

"To A. C. D. This Form of Flattery"

Doyle was flattered and was the sort of unofficial editor of Hornung's work but had one reservation about the stories.

"I think I may claim that his famous character Raffles was a kind of inversion of Sherlock Holmes, Bunny playing Watson. He admits as much in his kindly dedication. I think there are few finer examples of short-story writing in our language than these, though I confess I think they are rather dangerous in their suggestion. I told him so before he put pen to paper, and the result has, I fear, borne me out. You must not make the criminal a hero".—Arthur Conan Doyle

1

THE IDES OF MARCH

It was about half-past twelve when I returned to the Albany as a last desperate resort. The scene of my disaster was much as I had left it. The baccarat-counters still strewed the table, with the empty glasses and the loaded ash-trays. A window had been opened to let the smoke out, and was letting in the fog instead. Raffles himself had merely discarded his dining-jacket for one of his innumerable blazers. Yet he arched his eyebrows as though I had dragged him from his bed.

'Forgotten something?' said he, when he saw me on the mat.

'No,' said I, pushing past him without ceremony. And I led the way into his room with an impudence amazing to myself.

'Not come back for your revenge, have you. Because I'm afraid I can't give it you single-handed. I was sorry myself that the others – '

We were face to face by his fireside, and I cut him short.

'Raffles,' said I, 'you may well be surprised at my coming back in this way and at this hour. I hardly know you. I was never in your rooms before tonight. But I fagged for you at school, and you said you remembered me. Of course that's no excuse; but will you listen to me – for two minutes?'

In my emotion I had at first to struggle for every word; but his face reassured me as I went on, and I was not mistaken in its expression.

'Certainly my dear fellow,' said he, 'as many minutes as you like. Have a Sullivan and sit down.' And he handed me his silver cigarette-case.

'No,' said I, finding a full voice as I shook my head; 'no, I won't smoke, and I won't sit down, thank you. Nor will you ask me to do either when you've heard what I have to say.'

'Really?' said he, lighting his own cigarette with one clear blue eye upon me. 'How do you know?'

'Because you will probably show me the door,' I cried bitterly; 'and you'll be justified in doing it! But it's no good beating about the bush. You know I dropped over two hundred just now?'

He nodded.

'I hadn't the money in my pocket.'

'I remember.'

'But I had my cheque-book, and I wrote each of you a cheque at that desk.'

'Well?'

'Not one of them was worth the paper it was written on, Raffles. I am overdrawn already at my bank!'

'Surely only for the moment?'

'No. I have spent everything.'

'But somebody told me you were so well off. I heard you had come in for money?'

'So I did. Three years ago. It has been my curse; now it's all gone – every penny! Yes, I've been a fool; there never was nor will be such a fool as I've been... Isn't this enough for you? Why don't you turn me out?' He was walking up and down with a very long face instead.

'Couldn't your people do anything?' he asked at length.

'Thank God,' I cried, 'I have no people! I was an only child. I came in for everything there was. My one comfort is that they're gone, and will never know.'

I cast myself into a chair and hid my face. Raffles continued to pace the rich carpet that was of a piece with everything else in his rooms. There was no variation in his soft and even footfalls.

'You used to be a literary little cuss,' he said at length; 'didn't you edit the mag before you left? Anyway I recollect fagging you to do my verses; and literature of sorts is the very thing nowadays; any fool can make a living at it.'

I shook my head. 'Any fool couldn't write off my debts,' said I.

'Then you have a flat somewhere?' he went on.

'Yes, in Mount Street.'

'Well, what about the furniture?'

I laughed aloud in my misery. 'There's been a bill of sale on every stick for months!' And at that Raffles stood still, with raised eyebrows and stem eyes that I could meet the better now that he knew the worst; then, with a shrug, he resumed his walk, and for some minutes neither of us spoke. But in his handsome unmoved face I read my fate and death-warrant; and with every breath I cursed my folly and my cowardice in coming to him at all. Because he had been kind to me at school, when he was captain of the eleven, and I his fag, I had dared to look for kindness from him now; because I was ruined, and he rich enough to play cricket all the summer, and do nothing for the rest of the year, I had fatuously counted on his mercy, his sympathy, his help! Yes, I had relied on him in my heart, for all my outward diffidence and humility; and I was rightly served. There was as little of mercy as of sympathy in that curling nostril, that rigid jaw, that cold blue eye which never glanced my way. I caught up my hat. I blundered to my feet. I would have gone without a word, but Raffles stood between me and the door.

'Where are you going?' said he.

'That's my business,' I replied. 'I won't trouble you any more.'

'Then how am I to help you?'

'I didn't ask your help.'

'Then why come to me?'

'Why, indeed!' I echoed. 'Will you let me pass?'

'Not until you tell me where you are going and what you mean to do.'

'Can't you guess?' I cried. And for many seconds we stood staring in each other's eyes.

'Have you got the pluck?' said he, breaking the spell in a tone so cynical that it brought my last drop of blood to the boil.

'You shall see,' said I, as I stepped back and whipped the pistol from my overcoat pocket. 'Now, will you let me pass or shall I do it here?'

The barrel touched my temple, and my thumb the trigger. Mad with excitement as I was, ruined, dishonoured, and now finally determined to make an end of my mis-spent life, my only surprise to this day is that I did not do so then and there. The despicable satisfaction of involving another in one's destruction added its miserable appeal to my baser egoism; and had fear or horror flown to my companion's face, I shudder to think I might have died diabolically happy with that look for my last impious consolation. It was the look that came instead which held my hand. Neither fear nor horror were in it; only wonder, admiration, and such a measure of pleased expectancy as caused me after all to pocket my revolver with an oath.

'You devil!' I said. 'I believe you wanted me to do it!'

'Not quite,' was the reply, made with a little start, and a change of colour that came too late. 'To tell you the truth, though, I half thought you meant it, and I was never more fascinated in my life. I never dreamt you had such stuff in you, Bunny! No, I'm hanged if I let you go now. And you'd better not try that game again, for you won't catch me stand and look on a second time. We must think of some way out of the mess. I had no idea you were a chap of that sort! There, let me have the gun.'

One of his hands fell kindly on my shoulder, while the other slipped into my overcoat pocket, and I suffered him to deprive me of my weapon without a murmur. Nor was this simply because Raffles had the power of making himself irresistible at will. He was beyond comparison the most masterful man whom I have ever known; yet my acquiescence was due to more than the mere subjection of the weaker nature to the stronger. The forlorn hope which had brought me to the Albany was turned as by magic into an almost staggering sense of safety. Raffles would help me after all! A.J. Raffles would be my friend! It was as though all the world had come round suddenly to my side; so far, therefore, from resisting his action, I caught and clasped his hand with a fervour as uncontrollable as the frenzy which had preceded it.

'God bless you!' I cried. 'Forgive me for everything. I will tell you the truth. I did think you might help me in my extremity, though I well knew that I had no claim upon you. Still – for the old school's sake – the sake of old times – I thought you might give me another chance. If you wouldn't, I meant to blow out my brains – and will still if you change your mind.'

In truth I feared that it was changing, with his expression, even as I spoke, and in spite of his kindly tone and kindlier use of my old school nickname. His next words showed me my mistake.

'What a boy it is for jumping to conclusions! I have my vices, Bunny, but backing and filling is not one of them. Sit down, my good fellow, and have a cigarette to soothe your nerves. I insist. Whisky? The worst thing for you; here's some coffee that I was brewing when you came in. Now listen to me. You speak of "another chance". What do you mean? Another chance at baccarat? Not if I know it. You think the luck must turn; suppose it didn't. We should only have made bad worse. No, my dear chap, you've plunged enough. Do you put yourself in my hands or do you not? Very well then, you plunge no more, and I undertake not to present my cheque. Unfortunately, there are the other men; and still more unfortunately, Bunny, I'm as hard up at this moment as you are yourself!'

It was my turn to stare at Raffles. 'You?' I vociferated. 'You hard up? How am I to sit here and believe that?'

'Did I refuse to believe it of you?' he returned, smiling. 'And, with your own experience, do you think that because a fellow has rooms in this place, and belongs to a club or two, and plays a little cricket, he must necessarily have a balance at the bank? I tell you, my dear man, that at this moment I'm as hard up as ever you were. I have nothing but my wits to live on – absolutely nothing else. It was as necessary for me to win some money this evening as it was for you. We're in the same boat, Bunny, we'd better pull together.'

'Together!' I jumped at it. 'I'll do anything in this world for you, Raffles,' I said, 'if you really mean that you won't give me away. Think of anything you like and I'll do it! I was a desperate man when I came here, and I'm just as desperate now. I don't mind what I do if only I can get out of this without a scandal.'

Again I see him, leaning back in one of the luxurious chairs with which his room was furnished. I see his indolent, athletic figure; his pale, sharp, clean-shaven features; his curly black hair; his strong unscrupulous mouth. And again I feel the clear beam of his wonderful eye, cold and luminous as a star, shining into my brain – sifting the very secrets of my heart.

'I wonder if you mean all that!' he said at length. 'You do in your present mood; but who can back his mood to last? Still, there's hope when a chap takes that tone. Now I think of it, too, you were a plucky little devil at school; you once did me rather a good turn, I recollect. Remember it, Bunny? Well, wait a bit, and perhaps I'll be able to do you a better one. Give me time to think.'

He got up, lit a fresh cigarette, and fell to pacing the room once more, but with a slower and more thoughtful step, and for a much longer period than before. Twice he stopped at my chair as though on the point of speaking, but each time he checked himself and resumed his stride in silence. Once he threw up the window, which he had shut some time since, and stood for some moments leaning out into the fog which filled the Albany courtyard. Meanwhile a clock on the chimneypiece struck one, and one again for the half-hour, without a word between us.

Yet I not only kept my chair with patience, but I acquired an incongruous equanimity in that half-hour. Insensibly I had shifted my burden to the broad shoulders of this splendid friend, and my thoughts wandered with my eyes as the minutes passed. The room was the good-sized, square one, with the folding doors, the marble mantelpiece, and the gloomy, old-fashioned distinction peculiar to the Albany. It was charmingly furnished and arranged with the right amount of negligence and the right amount of taste. What struck me most, however, was the absence of the usual insignia of a cricketer's den. Instead of the conventional rack of war-worn bats, a carved oak bookcase, with every shelf in a litter, filled the better part of one wall; and where I looked for cricketing groups, I found reproductions of such works as 'Love and Death' and 'The Blessed Damozel', in dusty frames and different parallels. The man might have been a minor poet instead of an athlete of the first water. But there had always been a fine streak of aestheticism in his complex composition; some of these very pictures I had myself dusted in his study at school; and they set me thinking of yet another of his many sides – and of the little incident to which he had just referred.

Everybody knows how largely the tone of a public school depends on that of the eleven, and on the character of the captain of cricket in particular; and I have never heard it denied that in A.J. Raffles's time our tone was good, or that such influence as he troubled to exert was on the side of the angels. Yet it was whispered in the school that he was in the habit of parading the town at night in loud checks and a false beard. It was whispered, and disbelieved. I alone knew it for a fact; for night after night had I pulled the rope up after him when the rest of the dormitory was asleep, and kept awake by the hour to let it down again on a given signal. Well, one night he was over-bold, and within an ace of ignominious expulsion in the hey-day of his fame. Consummate daring and extraordinary nerve on his part, aided, doubtless, by some little presence of mind on mine, averted that untoward result; and no more need be said of a discreditable incident. But I cannot pretend to have forgotten it in throwing myself on this man's mercy in my desperation. And I was wondering how much of his leniency was owing to the fact that Raffles had not forgotten it either, when he stopped and stood over my chair once more.

'I've been thinking of that night we had the narrow squeak,' he began. 'Why do you start?'

'I was thinking of it too.'

He smiled, as though he had read my thoughts.

'Well, you were the right sort of little beggar then, Bunny; you didn't talk and you didn't flinch. You asked no questions and you told no tales. I wonder if you're like that now?'

'I don't know,' said I, slightly puzzled by his tone. 'I've made such a mess of my own affairs that I trust myself about as little as I'm likely to be trusted by anybody else. Yet I never in my life went back on a friend. I will say that; otherwise perhaps I mightn't be in such a hole tonight.'

'Exactly,' said Raffles, nodding to himself, as though in assent to some hidden train of thought; 'exactly what I remember of you, and I'll bet it's as true now as it was ten years ago. We don't alter, Bunny. We only develop. I suppose neither you nor I are really altered since you used to let down that rope and I used to come up it hand over hand. You would stick at nothing for a pal – what?'

'At nothing in this world,' I was pleased to cry.

'Not even at a crime?' said Raffles, smiling.

I stopped to think, for his tone had changed, and I felt sure he was chaffing me. Yet his eye seemed as much in earnest as ever, and for my part I was in no mood for reservations.

'No, not even at that,' I declared; 'name your crime, and I'm your man.'

He looked at me one moment in wonder, and another moment in doubt; then turned the matter off with a shake of his head, and the little cynical laugh that was all his own.

'You're a nice chap, Bunny! A real desperate character – what? Suicide one moment, and any crime I like the next! What you want is a drag, my boy, and you did well to come to a decent law-abiding citizen with a reputation to lose. None the less we must have that money tonight – by hook or crook.'

'Tonight, Raffles?'

'The sooner the better. Every hour after ten o'clock tomorrow morning is an hour of risk. Let one of those cheques get round to your own bank, and you and it are dishonoured together. No, we must raise the wind tonight and re-open your account first thing tomorrow. And I rather think I know where the wind can be raised.'

'At two o'clock in the morning?'

'Yes.'

'But how – but where – at such an hour?'

'From a friend of mine here in Bond Street.'

'He must be a very intimate friend.'

'Intimate's not the word. I have the run of his place and a latchkey all to myself.'

'You would knock him up at this hour of the night?'

'If he's in bed.'

'And it's essential that I should go in with you?'

'Absolutely.'

'Then I must; but I'm bound to say I don't like the idea, Raffles.'

'Do you prefer the alternative?' asked my companion, with a sneer. 'No, hang it, that's unfair!' he cried apologetically in the same breath. 'I quite understand. It's a beastly ordeal. But it would never do for you to stay outside. I tell you what, you shall have a peg before we start – just one. There's the whisky, here's the syphon, and I'll be putting on an overcoat while you help yourself.'

Well, I daresay I did so with some freedom, for this plan of his was not the less distasteful to me from its apparent inevitability. I must own, however, that it possessed fewer terrors before my glass was empty. Meanwhile Raffles rejoined me, with a covert-coat over his blazer, and a soft felt hat set carelessly on the curly head he shook with a smile as I passed him the decanter.

'When we come back,' said he. 'Work first, play afterwards. Do you see what day it is?' he added, tearing a leaflet from a Shakespearean calendar as I drained my glass. 'March 15th. "The Ides of March, the Ides of March, remember." Eh, Bunny, my boy? You won't forget them, will you?'

And, with a laugh, he threw some coals on the fire before turning down the gas like a careful householder. So we went out together as the clock on the chimneypiece was striking two.

II

Piccadilly was a trench of raw white fog, rimmed with blurred street-lamps, and lined with a thin coating of adhesive mud. We met no other wayfarers on the deserted flagstones, and were ourselves favoured with a very hard stare from the constable of the beat, who, however, touched his helmet on recognising my companion.

'You see, I'm known to the police,' laughed Raffles as we passed on. 'Poor devils, they've got to keep their weather eye open on a night like this! A fog may be a bore to you and me, Bunny, but it's a perfect godsend to the criminal classes, especially so late in their season. Here we are, though – and I'm hanged if the beggar isn't in bed and asleep after all!'

We had turned into Bond Street, and had halted on the kerb a few yards down on the right. Raffles was gazing up at some windows across the road, windows barely discernible through the mist, and without the glimmer of a light to throw them out. They were over a jeweller's shop, as I could see by the peep-hole in the shop door, and the bright light burning within. But the entire 'upper part', with the private street door next to the shop, was black and blank as the sky itself.

'Better give it up for tonight,' I urged. 'Surely the morning will be time enough!'

'Not a bit of it,' said Raffles. 'I have his key. We'll surprise him. Come along.'

And seizing my right arm, he hurried me across the road, opened the door with his latchkey, and in another moment had shut it swiftly but softly behind us. We stood together in the dark. Outside, a measured step was approaching; we had heard it through the fog as we crossed the street; now, as it drew nearer, my companion's fingers tightened on my arm.

'It may be the chap himself,' he whispered. 'He's the devil of a night-bird. Not a sound, Bunny! We'll startle the life out of him. Ah!'

The measured step had passed without a pause. Raffles drew a deep breath, and his singular grip of me slowly relaxed.

'But still, not a sound,' he continued in the same whisper; 'we'll take a rise out of him, wherever he is! Slip off your shoes and follow me.'

Well, you many wonder at my doing so, but you can never have met A.J. Raffles. Half his power lay in a conciliating trick of sinking the commander in the leader. And it was impossible not to follow one who led with such a zest. You might question, but you followed first. So now, when I heard him kick off his own shoes, I did the same, and was on the stairs at his heels before

I realised what an extraordinary way was this of approaching a stranger for money in the dead of night. But obviously Raffles and he were on exceptional terms of intimacy, and I could not infer but that they were in the habit of playing practical jokes on each other.

We groped our way so slowly upstairs that I had time to make more than one note before we reached the top. The stair was uncarpeted. The spread fingers of my right hand encountered nothing on the damp wall: those of my left trailed through a dust that could be felt on the banisters. An eerie sensation had been upon me since we entered the house. It increased with every step we climbed. What hermit were we going to startle in his cell?

We came to a landing. The banisters led us to the left, and to the left again. Four steps more, and we were on another and a longer landing, and suddenly a match blazed from the back. I never heard it struck. Its flash was blinding. When my eyes became accustomed to the light, there was Raffles holding up the match with one hand, and shading it with the other, between bare boards, stripped walls, and the open doors of empty rooms.

'Where have you brought me?' I cried. 'The house is unoccupied!'

'Hush! Wait!' he whispered, and he led the way into one of the empty rooms. His match went out as we crossed the threshold, and he struck another without the slightest noise. Then he stood with his back to me, fumbling with something that I could not see. But, when he threw the second match away, there was some other light in its stead, and a slight smell of oil. I stepped forward to look over his shoulder, but before I could do so he had turned and flashed a tiny lantern in my face.

'What's this?' I gasped. 'What rotten trick are you going to play?'

'It's played,' he answered, with his quiet laugh.

'On me?'

'I'm afraid so, Bunny.'

'Is there no one in the house, then?'

'No one but ourselves.'

'So it was mere chaff about your friend in Bond Street who could let us have that money?'

'Not altogether. It's quite true that Danby is a friend of mine.'

'Danby?'

'The jeweller underneath.'

'What do you mean?' I whispered, trembling like a leaf as his meaning dawned upon me. 'Are you going to get the money from the jeweller?'

'Well, not exactly.'

'What then?'

'The equivalent — from his shop.'

There was no need for another question. I understood everything but my own density. He had given me a dozen hints, and I had taken none. And there I stood staring at him, in that empty room; and there he stood with his dark lantern, laughing at me.

'A burglar!' I gasped. 'You – you!'

'I told you I lived by my wits.'

'Why couldn't you tell me what you were going to do? Why couldn't you trust me? Why must you lie?' I demanded, piqued to the quick for all my horror.

'I wanted to tell you,' said he. 'I was on the point of telling you more than once. You may remember how I sounded you about crime, though you have probably forgotten what you said yourself. I didn't think you meant it at the time, but I thought I'd put you to the test. Now I see you didn't, and I don't blame you. I only am to blame. Get out of it, my dear boy, as quick as you can; leave it to me. You won't give me away, whatever else you do!'

Oh, his cleverness! His fiendish cleverness! Had he fallen back on threats, coercion, sneers, all might have been different even then. But he set me free to leave him in the lurch. He would not blame me. He did not even bind me to secrecy; he trusted me. He knew my weakness and my strength, and was playing on both with his master's touch.

'Not so fast,' said I. 'Did I put this into your head, or were you going to do it in any case?'

'Not in any case,' said Raffles. 'It's true I've had the key for days, but when I won tonight I thought of chucking it; for, as a matter of fact, it's not a one-man job.'

'That settles it. I'm your man.'

'You mean it?'

'Yes – for tonight.'

'Good old Bunny,' he murmured, holding the lantern for one moment to my face; the next he was explaining his plans, and I was nodding, as though we had been fellow cracksmen all our days.

'I know the shop,' he whispered, 'because I've got a few things there. I know this upper part too; it's been to let for a month, and I got an order to view, and took a cast of the key before using it. The one thing I don't know is how to make a connection between the two; at present there's none. We may make it up here, though I rather fancy the basement myself. If you wait a minute I'll tell you.'

He set his lantern on the floor, and crept to a back window, and opened it with scarcely a sound; only to return shaking his head, after shutting the window with the same care.

'That was our one chance,' said he, 'a back window above a back window; but it's too dark to see anything, and we daren't show an outside light. Come down after me to the basement; and remember, though there's not a soul on the premises, you can't make too little noise. There – there – listen to that!'

It was the measured tread that we had heard before on the flagstones outside. Raffles darkened his lantern, and again we stood motionless till it had passed.

'Either a policeman,' he muttered, 'or a watchman that all these jewellers run between them. The watchman's the man for us to watch; he's simply paid to spot this kind of thing.'

We crept very gingerly down the stairs, which creaked a bit in spite of us, and we picked up our shoes in the passage; then down some narrow stone steps, at the foot of which Raffles showed his light, and put on his shoes once more, bidding me do the same in rather a louder tone than he had permitted himself to employ overhead. We were now considerably below the level of the street, in a small space with as many doors as it had sides. Three were ajar, and we saw through them into empty cellars; but in the fourth a key was turned and a bolt drawn; this one presently let us out into the bottom of a deep square well of fog. A similar door faced it across this area, and Raffles had the lantern close against it, and was hiding the light with his body, when a short and sudden crash made my heart stand still. Next moment I saw the door wide open, and Raffles standing within and beckoning me with a jemmy.

'Door number one,' he whispered. 'Deuce knows how many more there'll be, but I know of two at least. We won't have to make much noise over them, either; down here there's less risk.'

We were now at the bottom of the exact fellow to the narrow stone stair which we had just descended; the yard, or well, being the one part common to both the private and the business premises. But this flight led to no open passage; instead, a singularly solid mahogany door confronted us at the top.

'I thought so,' muttered Raffles, handing me the lantern, and pocketing a bunch of skeleton keys, after tampering for a few minutes with the lock. 'It'll be an hour's work to get through that!'

'Can't you pick it?'

'No. I know these locks. It's no use trying. We must cut it out, and it'll take us an hour.'

It took us forty-seven minutes by my watch; or rather it took Raffles, and never in my life have I seen anything more deliberately done. My part was simply to stand by with the dark lantern in one hand, and a small bottle of rock-oil in the other. Raffles had produced a pretty embroidered case, intended obviously for his razors, but filled instead with the tools of his secret trade, including the rock-oil. From this case he selected a bit, capable of drilling a hole an inch in diameter, and fitted it to a small but very strong steel brace. Then he took off his covert-coat and his blazer, spread them neatly on the top step – knelt on them – turned *up his* shirt- cuffs – and went to work with brace-and-bit near the keyhole. But first he oiled the bit to minimise the noise, and this he did invariably before beginning a fresh hole, and often in the middle of one. It took thirty-two separate borings to cut round that lock.

I noticed that through the first circular orifice Raffles thrust a forefinger; then, as the circle became an ever-lengthening oval, he got his hand through up to the thumb, and I heard him swear softly to himself.

'I was afraid so!'

'What is it?'

'An iron gate on the other side!'

'How on earth are we to get through that?' I asked in dismay.

'Pick the lock. But there may be two. In that case they'll be top and bottom, and we shall have two fresh holes to make, as the door opens inwards. It won't open two inches as it is.'

I confess I did not feel sanguine about the lock-picking, seeing that one lock had baffled us already; and my disappointment and impatience must have been a revelation to me had I stopped to think. The truth is that I was entering into our nefarious undertaking with an involuntary zeal of which I was myself quite unconscious at the time. The romance and the peril of the whole proceeding held me spellbound and entranced. My moral sense and my sense of fear were stricken by a common paralysis. And there I stood, shining my light and holding my phial with a keener interest than I had ever brought to any honest avocation. And there knelt A.J. Raffles, with his black hair tumbled, and the same watchful, quiet, determined half-smile with which I have seen him send down over after over in a county match!

At last the chain of holes was complete, the lock wrenched out bodily, and a splendid bare arm plunged up to the shoulder through the aperture, and through the bars of the iron gate beyond.

'Now,' whispered Raffles, 'if there's only one lock it'll be in the middle. Joy! Here it is! Only let me pick it, and we're through at last.'

He withdrew his arm, a skeleton key was selected from the bunch, and then back went his arm to the shoulder. It was a breathless moment. I heard the heart throbbing in my body, the very watch ticking in my pocket, and ever and anon the tinkle-tinkle of the skeleton key. Then – at last – there came a single unmistakable click. In another minute the mahogany door and the iron gate yawned behind us, and Raffles was sitting on an office table, wiping his face, with the lantern throwing a steady beam by his side.

We were now in a bare and roomy lobby behind the shop, but separated therefrom by an iron curtain, the very sight of which filled me with despair. Raffles, however, did not appear in the least depressed, but hung up his coat and hat on some pegs in the lobby before examining this curtain with his lantern.

'That's nothing,' said he, after a minute's inspection; 'we'll be through that in no time, but there's a door on the other side which may give us trouble.'

'Another door!' I groaned. 'And how do you mean to tackle this thing?'

'Prise it up with the jointed jemmy. The weak point of these iron curtains is the leverage you can get from below. But it makes a noise, and this is where you're coming in, Bunny; this is where I couldn't do without you. I must have you overhead to knock through when the street's clear. I'll come with you and show a light.'

Well, you may imagine how little I liked the prospect of this lonely vigil; and yet there was something very stimulating in the vital responsibility which it involved. Hitherto I had been a mere spectator. Now I was to take part in the game. And the fresh excitement made me more than ever insensible to those considerations of conscience and of safety which were already as dead nerves in my breast.

So I took my post without a murmur in the front room above the shop. The fixtures had been left for the refusal of the incoming tenant, and fortunately for us they included Venetian blinds, which were already down. It was the simplest matter in the world to stand peeping through the laths into the street, to beat twice with my foot when anybody was approaching, and once when all was clear again. The noises that even I could hear below, with the exception of one metallic crash at the beginning, were indeed incredibly slight; but they ceased altogether at each double rap from my toe, and a policeman passed quite half a dozen times beneath my eyes, and the man whom I took to be the jeweller's watchman oftener still, during the better pan of an hour that I spent at the window. Once, indeed, my heart was in my mouth, but only once. It was when the watchman stopped and peered through the peep-hole into the lighted shop. I waited for his whistle. I waited for the gallows or the gaol! But my signals had been studiously obeyed, and the man passed on in undisturbed serenity. In the end I had a signal in my turn, and retraced my steps with lighted matches down the broad stairs, down the narrow ones, across the area, and up into the lobby where Raffles awaited me with an outstretched hand.

'Well done, my boy!' said he. 'You're the same good man in a pinch, and you shall have your reward. I've got a thousand pounds' worth if I've got a penn'oth. It's all in my pockets. And here's something else I found in this locker; very decent port and some cigars, meant for poor dear Danby's business friends. Take a pull, and you shall light up presently. I've found a lavatory, too, and we must have a wash-and-brush-up before we go, for I'm as black as your boot.'

The iron curtain was down, but he insisted on raising it until I could peep through the glass door on the other side and see his handiwork in the shop beyond. Here two electric lights were left burning all night long, and in their cold white rays I could at first see nothing amiss. I looked along an orderly lane, an empty glass counter on my left, glass cupboards of untouched silver on my right, and facing me the filmy black eye of the peep-hole that shone like a stage moon on the street. The counter had not been emptied by Raffles; its contents were in the Chubb's safe, which he had given up at a glance; nor had he looked at the silver, except to choose a cigarette-case for me. He had confined himself entirely to the shop window. This was in three compartments, each secured for the night by removable panels with separate locks. Raffles had removed them a few hours before their time, and the electric light shone on a corrugated shutter bare as the ribs of an empty carcase. Every article of value was gone from the one place which was invisible from the little window in the door; elsewhere all was as it had been left overnight. And but for a train of mangled doors behind the iron curtain, a bottle of wine and a cigar-box with which liberties had been taken, a rather black towel in the lavatory, a burnt match here and there, and our finger-marks on the dusty banisters, not a trace of our visit did we leave.

'Had it in my head for long?' said Raffles, as we strolled through the streets towards dawn, for all the world as though we were returning from a dance. 'No, Bunny, I never thought of it till I saw that upper part empty about a month ago, and bought a few things in the shop to get the lie of the land. That reminds me that I never paid for them; but, by Jove, I will tomorrow and if that isn't poetic justice, what is? One visit showed me the possibilities of the place, but a second convinced me of its impossibilities without a pal. So I had practically given up the idea, when you came along on the very night and in the very plight for it! But here we are at the Albany, and I hope there's some fire left; for I don't know how you feel, Bunny, but for my part I'm as cold as Keats' owl.'

He could think of Keats on his way from a felony! He could hanker for his fireside like another. Floodgates were loosened within me, and the plain English of our adventure rushed over me as cold as ice. Raffles was a burglar. I had helped to commit one burglary, therefore I was a burglar too. Yet I could stand and warm myself by his fire and watch him empty his pockets, as though we had done nothing wonderful or wicked!

My blood froze. My heart sickened. My brain whirled. How I had liked this villain! How I had admired him! How my liking and admiration must turn to loathing and disgust. I waited for the change. I longed to feel it in my heart. But – I longed and I waited in vain!

I saw he was emptying his pockets; the table sparkled with their hoard. Rings by the dozen, diamonds by the score; bracelets, pendants, aigrettes, necklaces; pearls, rubies, amethysts, sapphires; and diamonds always, diamonds in everything, flashing bayonets of light, dazzling me – blinding me – making me disbelieve because I could no longer forget. Last of all came no gem, indeed, but my own revolver from an inner pocket. And that struck a chord. I suppose I said something – my hand flew out. I can see Raffles now, as he looked at me once more with a high arch over each clear eye. I can see him pick out the cartridges with his quiet, cynical smile, before he would give me my pistol back again.

'You mayn't believe it, Bunny,' said he, 'but I never carried a loaded one before. On the whole I think it gives one confidence. Yet it would be very awkward if anything went wrong; one might use it, and that's not the game at all, though I have often thought that the murderer who has just done the trick must have great sensations before things get too hot for him. Don't look so distressed, my dear chap, I've never had those sensations, and I don't suppose I ever shall.'

'But this much you have done before?' said I, hoarsely.

'Before? My dear Bunny, you offend me! Did it look like a first attempt? Of course I have done it before.'

'Often?'

'Well – no. Not often enough to destroy the charm, at all events; never, as a matter of fact, unless I'm cursedly hard up. Did you hear about the Thimbleby diamonds? Well, that was the last time – and a poor lot of paste they were. Then there was the little business of the Dormer house-boat at Henley last year. That was mine also – such as it was. I've never brought off a really big *coup* yet; when I do I shall chuck it up.'

Yes, I remembered both cases very well. To think that he was their author! It was incredible, outrageous, inconceivable. Then my eyes would fall upon the table, twinkling and glittering in a hundred places, and incredulity was at an end.

'How came you to begin?' I asked, as curiosity overcame mere wonder, and a fascination for his career gradually wove itself into my fascination for the man.

'Ah! that's a long story,' said Raffles. 'It was in the Colonies, when I was out there playing cricket. It's too long a story to tell you now, but I was in much the same fix that you were in tonight, and it was my only way out. I never meant it for anything more; but I'd tasted blood, and it was all over with me. Why should I work when I could steal? Why settle down to some humdrum uncongenial billet, when excitement, romance, danger, and a decent living were all going begging together. Of course, it's very wrong, but we can't all be moralists, and the distribution of wealth is very wrong to begin with. Besides, you're not at it all the time. I'm sick of quoting Gilbert's lines to myself, but they're profoundly true. I only wonder if you'll like the life as much as I do!'

'Like it?' I cried. 'Not I! It's no life for me. Once is enough!'

'You wouldn't give me a hand another time?'

'Don't ask me, Raffles. Don't ask me, for God's sake!'

'Yet you said you would do anything for me! You asked me to name my crime! But I knew at the time you didn't mean it; you didn't go back on me tonight, and that ought to satisfy me, goodness knows! I suppose I'm ungrateful, and unreasonable, and all that. I ought to let it end at this. But you're the very man for me, Bunny, the – very – man! Just think how we got through tonight. Not a scratch – not a hitch! There's nothing very terrible in it, you see; there never would be, while we worked together.'

He was standing in front of me with a hand on either shoulder; he was smiling as he knew so well how to smile. I turned on my heel, planted my elbows on the chimneypiece, and my burning head between my hands. Next instant a still heartier hand had fallen on my back.

'All right, my boy! You are quite right and I'm worse than wrong. I'll never ask it again. Go, if you want to, and come again about midday for the cash. There was no bargain; but, of course, I'll get you out of your scrape – especially after the way you've stood by me tonight.'

I was round again with my blood on fire.

'I'll do it again,' I said through my teeth.

He shook his head. 'Not you,' he said, smiling quite good-humouredly on my insane enthusiasm.

'I will,' I cried with an oath. 'I'll lend you a hand as often as you like! What does it matter now? I've been in it once. I'll be in it again. I've gone to the devil anyhow. I can't go back, and wouldn't if I could Nothing matters another rap! When you want me I'm your man.'

And that is how Raffles and I joined felonious forces on the Ides of March.

2

A COSTUME PIECE

London was just then talking of one whose name is already a name and nothing more. Reuben Rosenthall had made his millions on the diamond fields of South Africa, and had come home to enjoy them according to his lights; how he went to work will scarcely be forgotten by any reader of the halfpenny evening papers, which revelled in endless anecdotes of his original indigence and present prodigality, varied with interesting particulars of the extraordinary establishment which the millionaire set up in St John's Wood. Here he kept a retinue of Kaffirs, who were literally his slaves; and hence he would sally with enormous diamonds in his shirt and on his finger, in the convoy of a prize-fighter of heinous repute, who was not, however, by any means the worst element in the Rosenthall *ménage*. So said common gossip; but the fact was sufficiently established by the interference of the police on at least one occasion, followed by certain magisterial proceedings which were reported with justifiable gusto and huge headlines in the newspapers aforesaid. And this was all one knew of Reuben Rosenthall up to the time when the Old Bohemian Club, having fallen on evil days, found it worth its while to organise a great dinner in honour of so wealthy an exponent of the club's principles. I was not at the banquet myself, but a member took Raffles, who told me all about it that very night.

'Most extraordinary show I ever went to in my life,' said he. 'As for the man himself – well, I was prepared for something grotesque, but the fellow fairly took my breath away. To begin with, he's the most astounding brute to look at, well over six feet, with a chest like a barrel and a great hook-nose, and the reddest hair and whiskers you ever saw. Drank like a fire-engine, but only got drunk enough to make us a speech that I wouldn't have missed for ten pounds. I'm only sorry you weren't there too, Bunny, old chap.'

I began to be sorry myself, for Raffles was anything but an excitable person, and never had I seen him so excited before. Had he been following Rosenthall's example? His coming to my rooms at midnight, merely to tell me about his dinner, was in itself enough to excuse a suspicion which was certainly at variance with my knowledge of A.J. Raffles.

'What did he say?' I inquired mechanically, divining some subtler explanation of this visit, and wondering what on earth it could be.

'Say?' cried Raffles. 'What did he not say! He boasted of his rice, he bragged of his riches, and he blackguarded society for taking him up for his money and dropping him out of sheer pique and jealousy because he had so much. He mentioned names, too, with the most charming freedom, and swore he was as good a man as the Old Country had to show – *pace* the Old Bohemians. To prove it he pointed to a great diamond in the middle of his shirt-front with a little finger loaded with another just like it: which of our bloated princes could show a pair like that? As a matter of fact, they seemed quite wonderful stones, with a curious purple gleam to them that must mean a pot of money. But old Rosenthall swore he wouldn't take fifty thousand pounds for the two, and wanted to know where the other man was who went about with twenty-five thousand in his shirt front, and the other twenty-five on his little finger. He didn't exist. If he did, he wouldn't have the pluck to wear them. But he had – he'd tell us why. And before you could say Jack Robinson he had whipped out a whacking great revolver!'

'Not at the table?'

'At the table! In the middle of his speech! But it was nothing to what he wanted to do. He actually wanted us to let him write his name in bullets on the opposite wall to show us why he wasn't afraid to go about in all his diamonds! That brute Purvis, the prize-fighter who is his paid bully, had to bully his master before he could be persuaded out of it. There was quite a panic for the moment; one fellow was saying his prayers under the table, and the waiters bolted to a man.

'What a grotesque scene!'

'Grotesque enough, but I rather wish they had let him go the whole hog and blaze away. He was as keen as knives to show us how he could take care of his purple diamonds; and, do you know, Bunny, I was as keen as knives to see.'

And Raffles leant towards me with a sly, slow smile that made the hidden meaning of his visit only too plain to me at last.

'So you think of having a try for his diamonds yourself?'

He shrugged his shoulders.

'It is horribly obvious, I admit. But – yes, I have set my heart upon them! To be quite frank, I have had them on my conscience for some time; one couldn't hear so much of the man, and his prize-fighter, and his diamonds, without feeling it a kind of duty to have a go for them; but when it comes to brandishing a revolver and practically challenging the world, the thing becomes inevitable. It is simply thrust upon one. I was fated to hear that challenge, Bunny, and I, for one, must take it up. I was only sorry I couldn't get on my hind legs and say so then and there.'

'Well,' I said, 'I don't see the necessity as things are with us; but, of course, I'm your man.'

My tone may have been half-hearted. I did my best to make it otherwise. But it was barely a month since our Bond Street exploit, and we certainly could have afforded to behave ourselves for some time to come. We had been getting along so nicely; by his advice I had scribbled a thing or two; inspired by Raffles, I had even done an article on our own jewel robbery; and for the moment I was quite satisfied with this sort of adventure. I thought we ought to know when we were well off, and could see no point in our running fresh risks before we were obliged. On the other hand, I was anxious not to show the least disposition to break the pledge that I had given a month ago. But it was not on my manifest disinclination that Raffles fastened.

'Necessity, my dear Bunny? Does the writer only write when the wolf is at the door? Does the painter paint for bread alone? Must you and I be driven to crime like Tom of Bow and Dick of Whitechapel? You pain me, my dear chap; you needn't laugh, because you do. Art for art's sake is a vile catchword, but I confess it appeals to me. In this case my motives are absolutely pure, for I doubt if we shall ever be able to dispose of such peculiar stones. But if I don't have a try for them – after tonight, I shall never be able to hold up my head again.'

His eye twinkled, but it glittered too.

'We shall have our work cut out,' was all I said.

'And do you suppose I should be keen on it if we hadn't?' cried Raffles. 'My dear fellow, I would rob St Paul's Cathedral if I could, but I could no more scoop a till when the shopwalker wasn't looking than I could bag apples out of an old woman's basket. Even that little business last month was a sordid affair, but it was necessary, and I think its strategy redeemed it to some extent. Now there's some credit, and more sport, in going where they boast they're on their guard against you. The Bank of England, for example, is the ideal crib; but that would need half a dozen of us with years to give to the job; and meanwhile Reuben Rosenthall is high enough game for you and me. We know he's armed. We know how Billy Purvis can fight. It'll be no soft thing, I grant you. But what of that, my good Bunny — what of that? A man's reach must exceed his grasp, dear boy, or what the dickens is a heaven for?'

'I would rather we didn't exceed ours just yet,' I answered laughing, for his spirit was irresistible, and the plan was growing upon me, despite my qualms.

'Trust me for that,' was his reply; 'I'll see you through. After all I expect to find that the difficulties are nearly all on the surface. These fellows both drink like the devil, and that should simplify matters considerably. But we shall see, and we've must take our time. There will probably turn out to be a dozen different ways in which the thing might be done, and we shall have to choose between them. It will mean watching the house for at least a week in any case; it may mean lots of other things that will take much longer; but give me a week, and I will tell you more. That's to say if you're really on?'

'Of course I am,' I replied indignantly. 'But why should I give you a week? Why shouldn't we watch the house together?'

'Because two eyes are as good as four, and take up less room. Never hunt in couples unless you're obliged. But don't you look offended, Bunny; there'll be plenty for you to do when the time comes, that I promise you. You shall have your share of the fun, never fear, and a purple diamond all to yourself — if we're lucky.'

On the whole, however, this conversation left me less than lukewarm, and I still remember the depression which came over me when Raffles was gone. I saw the folly of the enterprise to which I had committed myself – the sheer, gratuitous, unnecessary folly of it. And the paradoxes in which Raffles revelled, and the frivolous casuistry which was nevertheless half sincere, and which his mere personality rendered wholly plausible at the moment of utterance, appealed very little to me when recalled in cold blood. I admired the spirit of pure mischief in which he seemed prepared to risk his liberty and his life, but I did not find it an infectious spirit on calm reflection. Yet the thought of withdrawal was not to be entertained for a moment. On the contrary, I was impatient of the delay ordained by Raffles; and, perhaps, no small part of my secret disaffection came of his galling determination to do without me until the last moment.

It made it no better that this was characteristic of the man and of his attitude towards me. For a month we had been, I suppose, the thickest thieves in all London, and yet our intimacy was curiously incomplete. With all his charming frankness, there was in Raffles a vein of capricious reserve which was perceptible enough to be very irritating. He had the instinctive secretiveness of the inveterate criminal. He would make mysteries of matters of common concern; for example, I never knew how or where he disposed of the Bond Street jewels, on the proceeds of which we were both still leading the outward lives of hundreds of other young fellows about town. He was consistently mysterious about that and other details, of which it seemed to me that I had already earned the right to know everything. I could not but remember how he had led me into my first felony, by means of a trick, while yet uncertain whether he could trust me or not. That I could no longer afford to resent, but I did resent his want of confidence in me now. I said nothing about it, but it rankled every day, and never more than in the week that succeeded the Rosenthall dinner. When I met Raffles at the club he would tell me nothing; when I went to his rooms he was out, or pretended to be. One day he told me he was getting on well, but slowly; it was a more ticklish game than he had thought; but when I began to ask questions he would say no more. Then and there, in my annoyance, I took my own decision. Since he would tell me nothing of the result of his vigils, I determined to keep one of my own account, and that very evening found my way to the millionaire's front gates.

The house he was occupying is, I believe, quite the largest in the St John's Wood district. It stands in the angle formed by two broad thoroughfares, neither of which, as it happens, is a bus route, and I doubt if many quieter spots exist within the four-mile radius. Quiet also was the great square house, in its garden of grass-plots and shrubs; the lights were low, the millionaire and his friends obviously spending their evening elsewhere. The garden walls were only a few feet high: In one there was a side door opening into a glass passage; in the other two five-barred grained-and-varnished gates, one at either end of the little semi-circular drive, and both wide open. So still was the place that I had a great mind to walk boldly in and learn something of the premises; in fact, I was on the point of doing so, when I heard a quick, shuffling step on the pavement behind me. I turned round and faced the dark scowl and the dirty clenched fists of a dilapidated tramp.

'You fool!' said he. 'You utter idiot!'

'Raffles!'

'That's it,' he whispered savagely; 'tell all the neighbourhood – give me away at the top of your voice!'

With that he turned his back upon me, and shambled down the road, shrugging his shoulders and muttering to himself as though I had refused him alms. A few moments I stood astounded, indignant, at a loss; then I followed him. His feet trailed, his knees gave, his back was bowed, his head kept nodding; it was the gait of a man eighty years of age. Presently he waited for me midway between two lamp-posts. As I came up he was lighting rank tobacco, in a cutty pipe, with an evil-smelling match, and the flame showed me the suspicion of a smile.

'You must forgive my heat, Bunny, but it really was very foolish of you. Here am I trying every dodge – begging at the door one night – hiding in the shrubs the next – doing every mortal thing but stand and stare at the house as you went and did. It's a costume piece, and in you rush in your ordinary clothes. I tell you they're on the look-out for us night and day. It's the toughest nut I ever tackled!'

'Well,' said I, 'if you had told me so before I shouldn't have come. You told me nothing.'

He looked hard at me from under the broken rim of a battered billycock.

'You're right,' he said at length. 'I've been too close. It's become second nature with me, when I've anything on. But here's an end of it, Bunny, so far as you're concerned. I'm going home now, and I want you to follow me; but for heaven's sake keep your distance, and don't speak to me again till I speak to you. There – give me a start.' And he was off again, a decrepit vagabond, with his hands in his pockets, his elbows squared, and frayed coat-tails swinging raggedly from side to side.

I followed him to the Finchley Road. There he took an omnibus, and I sat some rows behind him on the top, but not far enough to escape the pest of his vile tobacco. That he could carry his character-sketch to such a pitch – he who would only smoke one brand of cigarettes! It was the last, least touch of the insatiable artist, and it charmed away what mortification there still remained in me. Once more I felt the fascination of a comrade who was for ever dazzling one with a fresh and unsuspected facet of his character.

As we neared Piccadilly I wondered what he would do. Surely he was not going into the Albany like that? No, he took another omnibus to Sloane Street, I sitting behind him as before. At Sloane Street we changed again, and were presently in the long lean artery of the King's Road. I was now all agog to know our destination, nor was I kept many more minutes in doubt. Raffles got down. I followed. He crossed the road and disappeared up a dark turning. I pressed after him, and was in time to see his coat-tails as he plunged into a still darker flagged alley to the right. He was holding himself up and stepping out like a young man once more; also, in some subtle way, he already looked less disreputable. But I alone was there to see him, the alley was absolutely deserted, and desperately dark. At the farther end he opened a door with a latchkey, and it was darker yet within.

Instinctively I drew back and heard him chuckle. We could no longer see each other.

'All right, Bunny! There's no hanky-panky this time. These are studios, my friend, and I'm one of the lawful tenants.'

Indeed, in another minute we were in a lofty room with skylight, easels, dressing-cupboard, platform, and every other adjunct save the signs of actual labour. The first thing I saw, as Raffles lit the gas, was its reflection in his silk hat on the pegs beside the rest of his normal garments.

'Looking for the works of art?' continued Raffles, lighting a cigarette and beginning to divest himself of his rags. 'I'm afraid you won't find any, but there's the canvas I'm always going to make a start upon. I tell them I'm looking high and low for my ideal model. I have the stove lit on principle twice a week, and look in and leave a newspaper and a smell of Sullivans – how good they are after shag! Meanwhile I pay my rent and am a good tenant in every way; and it's a very useful little *pied-à-terre* – there's no saying how useful it might be at a pinch. As it is, the billycock comes in and the topper goes out, and nobody takes the slightest notice of either; at this time of night the chances are that there's not a soul in the building except ourselves.'

'You never told me you went in for disguises,' said I, watching him as he cleansed the grime from his face and hands.

'No, Bunny, I've treated you very shabbily all round. There was really no reason why I shouldn't have shown you this place a month ago, and yet there was no point in my doing so, and circumstances are just conceivable in which it would have suited us both for you to be in genuine ignorance of my whereabouts. I have something to sleep on, as you perceive, in case of need, and, of course, my name is not Raffles in the King's Road. So you will see that one might bolt farther and fare worse.'

'Meanwhile you use the place as a dressing-room?'

'It's my private pavilion,' said Raffles. 'Disguises? In some cases they're half the battle, and it's always pleasant to feel that, if the worst comes to the worst, you needn't necessarily be convicted under your own name. Then they're indispensable in dealing with the fences. I drive all my bargains in the tongue and raiment of Shoreditch. If I didn't there'd be the very devil to pay in blackmail. Now, this cupboard's full of all sorts of toggery. I tell the woman who cleans the room that it's for my models when I find 'em. By the way, I only hope I've got something that'll fit you, for you'll want a rig for tomorrow night.'

'Tomorrow night!' I exclaimed. 'Why, what do you mean to do?'

'The trick,' said Raffles. 'I intended writing to you as soon as I got back to my rooms, to ask you to look me up tomorrow afternoon; then I was going to unfold my plan of campaign, and take you straight into action then and there. There's nothing like putting the nervous players in first; it's the sitting with their pads on that upsets their apple cart; that was another of my reasons for being so confoundedly close. You must try to forgive me. I couldn't help remembering how well you played up last trip, without any time to weaken on it beforehand. All I want is for you to be as cool and smart tomorrow night as you were then; though, by Jove, there's no comparison between the two cases!'

'I thought you would find it so.'

'You were right. I have. Mind you, I don't say this will be the tougher job all round; we shall probably get in without any difficulty at all; it's the getting out again that may flummox us. That's the worst of an irregular household!' cried Raffles, with quite a burst of virtuous indignation. 'I assure you, Bunny, I spent the whole of Monday night in the shrubbery of the garden next door looking over the wall, and, if you'll believe me, somebody was about all night long! I don't mean the Kaffirs. I don't believe they ever get to bed at all, poor devils! No, I mean Rosenthall himself, and that pasty-faced beast Purvis. They were up and drinking from midnight when they came in, to broad daylight, when I cleared out. Even then I left them sober enough to slang each other. By the way, they very nearly came to blows in the garden, within a few yards of me, and I heard something that might come in useful and make Rosenthall shoot crooked at a critical moment. You know what an I.D.B. is?'

'Illicit Diamond Buyer?'

'Exactly. Well, it seems that Rosenthall was one. He must have let it out to Purvis in his cups. Anyhow, I heard Purvis taunting him with it, and threatening him with the breakwater at Capetown; and I begin to think our friends are friend and foe. But about tomorrow night: there's nothing subtle in my plan. It's simply to get in while these fellows are out on the loose, and to lie low till they come back, and longer. If possible we must doctor the whisky. That would simplify the whole thing, though it's not a very sporting game to play; still, we must remember Rosenthall's revolver; we don't want him to sign his name on us. With all those Kaffirs about, however, it's ten to one on the whisky, and a hundred to one against us if we go looking for it. A brush with the heathen would spoil everything, if it did no more. Besides, there are the ladies – '

'The deuce there are!'

'Ladies with an "i," and the very voices for raising Cain. I fear, I fear the clamour! It would be fatal to us. *Au contraire*, if we can manage to stow ourselves away unbeknowns, half the battle will be won. If Rosenthall turns in drunk, it's a purple diamond apiece. If he sits up sober, it may be a bullet instead.

We will hope not, Bunny; and all the firing wouldn't be on one side; but it's on the knees of the gods.'

And so we left it when we shook hands in Piccadilly – not by any means as much later as I could have wished. Raffles would not ask me to his rooms that night. He said he made it a rule to have a long night before playing cricket and – other games. His final word to me was framed on the same principle.

'Mind, only one drink tonight, Bunny. Two at the outside – as you value your life – and mine!'

I remember my abject obedience, and the endless, sleepless night it gave me; and the roofs of the houses opposite standing out at last against the blue-grey London dawn. I wondered whether I should ever see another, and was very hard on myself for that little expedition which I had made on my own wilful account.

It was between eight and nine o'clock in the evening when we took up our position in the garden adjoining that of Reuben Rosenthall; the house itself was shut up, thanks to the outrageous libertine next door, who, by driving away the neighbours, had gone far towards delivering himself into our hands. Practically secure from surprise on that side, we could watch our house under cover of a wall just high enough to see over, while a fair margin of shrubs in either garden afforded us additional protection. Thus entrenched we had stood an hour, watching a pair of lighted bow-windows with vague shadows flitting continually across the blinds, and listening to the drawing of corks, the clink of glasses, and a gradual crescendo of coarse voices within. Our luck seemed to have deserted us; the owner of the purple diamonds was dining at home and dining at undue length. I thought it was a dinnerparty. Raffles differed; in the end he proved right. Wheels grated in the drive, a carriage and pair stood at the steps; there was a stampede from the dining-room, and the loud voices died away, to burst forth presently from the porch.

Let me make our position perfectly clear. We were over the wall, at the side of the house, but a few feet from the dining-room windows. On our right, one angle of the building cut the back lawn in two diagonally; on our left, another angle just permitted us to see the jutting steps and the waiting carriage. We saw Rosenthall come out – saw the glimmer of his diamonds before anything. Then came the pugilist; then a lady with a head of hair like a bath sponge; then another, and the party was complete.

Raffles ducked and pulled me down in great excitement.

'The ladies are going with them,' he whispered.

'This is great!'

'That's better still.'

'The Gardenia!' the millionaire had bawled.

'And that's best of all,' said Raffles, standing upright as hoofs and wheels crunched through the gates and rattled off at a fine speed.

'Now what?' I whispered, trembling with excitement.

'They'll be clearing away. Yes, here come their shadows. The drawing-room windows open on the lawn. Bunny, it's the psychological moment. Where's that mask?'

I produced it with a hand whose trembling I tried in vain to still, and could have died for Raffles when he made no comment on what he could not fail to notice. His own hands were firm and cool as he adjusted my mask for me, and then his own.

'By Jove, old boy,' he whispered cheerily, 'you look about the greatest ruffian I ever saw! These masks alone will down a black, if we meet one. But I'm glad I remembered to tell you not to shave. You'll pass for Whitechapel if the worst comes to the worst and you don't forget to talk the lingo. Better sulk like a mule if you're not sure of it, and leave the dialogue to me; but, please our stars, there will be no need. Now, are you ready?'

'Quite.'

'Got your gag?'

'Yes.'

'Shooter?'

'Yes.'

'Then follow me.'

In an instant we were over the wall, in another on the lawn behind the house. There was no moon. The very stars in their courses had veiled themselves for our benefit. I crept at my leader's heels to some French windows opening upon a shallow verandah. He pushed. They yielded.

'Luck again,' he whispered; 'nothing but luck! Now for a light.'

And the light came!

A good score of electric burners glowed red for the fraction of a second, then rained merciless white beams into our blinded eyes. When we found our sight, four revolvers covered us, and between two of them the colossal frame of Reuben Rosenthall shook with a wheezy laughter from head to foot.

'Good evening, boys,' he hiccoughed. 'Glad to see ye at last! Shift foot or finger, you on the left, though, and you're a dead boy. I mean you, you greaser!' he roared out at Raffles. 'I know you. I've been waitin' for you. I've been watching you all this week! Plucky smart you thought yerself, didn't you? One day beggin', next time shammin' tight, and next one o' them old pals from Kimberley what never come when I'm in. But you left the same tracks every day, you buggins', an' the same tracks every night, all round the blessed premises.'

'All right, guv'nor,' drawled Raffles; 'don't excite. It's a fair cop. We don't sweat to know 'ow you brung it orf. On'y don't you go for to shoot, 'cos we 'aint awmed, s'help me Gord!'

'Ah, you're a knowin' one,' said Rosenthall, fingering his triggers. 'But you've struck a knowin'er.'

'Ho, yuss, we know all abaht thet! Set a thief to catch a thief – ho, yuss.'

My eyes had torn themselves from the round black muzzles, from the accursed diamonds that had been our snare, the pasty pig-face of the over-fed pugilist, and the flaming cheeks and hook nose of Rosenthall himself. I was looking beyond them at the doorway filled with quivering silk and plush, black faces, white eye-balls, woolly pates. But a sudden silence recalled my attention to the millionaire. And only his nose retained its colour.

'What d'ye mean?' he whispered with a hoarse oath. 'Spit it out, or, by Christmas, I'll drill you!'

'Whort price thet brikewater?' drawled Raffles coolly.

'Eh?'

Rosenthall's revolvers were describing widening orbits.

'What price thet brikewater – old I.D.B.?'

'Where in hell did you get hold o' that?' asked Rosenthall, with a rattle in his thick neck meant for mirth.

'You may well arst,' says Raffles. 'It's all over the plice w'ere I come from.'

'Who can have spread such rot?'

'I dunno,' says Raffles; 'arst the gen'leman on yer left; p'raps 'e knows.'

The gentleman on his left had turned livid with emotion. Guilty conscience never declared itself in plainer terms. For a moment his small eyes bulged like currants in the suet of his face; the next, he had pocketed his pistols on a professional instinct, and was upon us with his fists.

'Out o' the light – out o' the light!' yelled Rosenthall in a frenzy.

He was too late. No sooner had the burly pugilist obstructed his fire than Raffles was through the window at a bound; while I, for standing still and saying nothing, was scientifically felled to the floor.

I cannot have been many moments without my senses. When I recovered them there was great to-do in the garden, but I had the drawing-room to myself. I sat up. Rosenthall and Purvis were rushing about outside, cursing the Kaffirs and nagging at each other.

'Over that wall, I tell yer!'

'I tell you it was this one. Can't you whistle for the police?'

'Police be damned! I've had enough of the blessed police.'

'Then we'd better get back and make sure of the other rotter.'

'Oh, make sure o' yer skin. That's what you'd better do. Jala, you black hog, if I catch you skulkin' ...'

I never heard the threat. I was creeping from the drawing-room on my hands and knees, my own revolver swinging by its steel ring from my teeth.

For an instant I thought that the hall also was deserted. I was wrong, and I crept upon a Kaffir on all fours. Poor devil, I could not bring myself to deal him a base blow, but I threatened him most hideously with my revolver, and left the white teeth chattering in his black head as I took the stairs three at a time. Why I went upstairs in that decisive fashion, as though it were my only course, I cannot explain. But garden and ground floor seemed alive with men, and I might have done worse.

I turned into the first room I came to. It was a bedroom – empty, though lit up; and never shall I forget how I started as I entered, on encountering the awful villain that was myself at full length in a pier-glass! Masked, armed, and ragged, I was indeed fit carrion for a bullet or the hangman, and to one or the other I made up my mind. Nevertheless, I hid myself in the wardrobe behind the mirror, and there I stood shivering and cursing my fate, my folly, and Raffles most of all – Raffles first and last – for I daresay half an hour. Then the wardrobe door was flung suddenly open; they had stolen into the room without a sound; and I was hauled downstairs, an ignominious captive.

Gross scenes followed in the hall. The ladies were now upon the stage, and at sight of the desperate criminal they screamed with one accord. In truth I must have given them fair cause, though my mask was now torn away and hid nothing but my left ear. Rosenthall answered their shrieks with a roar for silence; the woman with the bath-sponge hair swore at him shrilly in return; the place became a Babel impossible to describe. I remember wondering how long it would be before the police appeared. Purvis and the ladies were for calling them in and giving me in charge without delay. Rosenthall would not hear of it. He swore that he would shoot man or woman who left his sight. He had had enough of the police. He was not going to have them coming there to spoil sport; he was going to deal with me in his own way. With that he dragged me from all other hands, flung me against a door, and sent a bullet crashing through the wood within an inch of my ear.

'You drunken fool! It'll be murder!' shouted Purvis, getting in the way a second time.

'Wha' do I care? He's armed isn't he? I shot him in self-defence. It'll be a warning to others. Will you stand aside, or d'ye want it yourself?'

'You're drunk,' said Purvis, still between us. 'I saw you take a neat tumblerful since you came in, and it's made you drunk as a fool. Pull yourself together, old man. You ain't a-going to do what you'll be sorry for.'

'Then I won't shoot at him, I'll only shoot roun' an' roun' the beggar. You're quite right, ole feller. Wouldn't hurt him. Great mishtake. Roun' an' roun'. There – like that!'

His freckled paw shot up over Purvis's shoulder, mauve lightning came from his ring, a red flash from his revolver, and shrieks from the women as the reverberations died away. Some splinters lodged in my hair.

Next instant the prize-fighter disarmed him; and I was safe from the devil, but finally doomed to the deep sea. A policeman was in our midst. He had entered through the drawing-room window; he was an officer of few words and creditable promptitude. In a twinkling he had the handcuffs on my wrists, while the pugilist explained the situation, and his patron reviled the force and its representative with impotent malignity. A fine watch they kept; a lot of good they did; coming in when all was over and the whole household might have been murdered in their sleep. The officer only deigned to notice him as he marched me off.

'We know all about you, sir,' said he contemptuously, and he refused the sovereign Purvis proffered. 'You will be seeing me again, sir, at Marylebone.'

'Shall I come now?'

'As you please, sir. I rather think the other gentleman requires you more, and I don't fancy this young man means to give much trouble.'

'Oh, I'm coming quietly,' I said.

And I went.

In silence we traversed perhaps a hundred yards. It must have been midnight. We did not meet a soul. At last I whispered:

'How on earth did you manage it?'

'Purely by luck,' said Raffles. 'I had the luck to get clear away through knowing every brick of those back-garden walls, and the double luck to have these togs with the rest over at Chelsea. The helmet is one of a collection I made up at Oxford; here it goes over this wall, and we'd better carry the coat and belt before we meet a real officer. I got them once for a fancy ball – ostensibly – and thereby hangs a yarn. I always thought they might come in useful a second time. My chief crux tonight was getting rid of the cab that brought me back. I sent him off to Scotland Yard with ten bob and a special message to good old Mackenzie. The whole detective department will be at Rosenthall's in about half an hour. Of course I speculated on our gentleman's hatred of the police – another huge slice of luck. If you'd got away, well and good; if not, I felt he was the man to play with his mouse as long as possible. Yes, Bunny, it's been more of a costume piece than I intended, and we've come out of it, with a good deal less credit. But, by Jove, we're jolly lucky to have come out of it at all!'

3

GENTLEMEN AND PLAYERS

Old Raffles may or may not have been an exceptional criminal, but as a cricketer I dare swear he was unique. Himself, a dangerous bat, a brilliant field, and perhaps the very finest slow bowler of his decade, he took incredibly little interest in the game at large. He never went up to Lord's without his cricket-bag, or showed the slightest interest in the result of a match in which he was not himself engaged. Nor was this mere hateful egotism on his part. He professed to have lost all enthusiasm for the game, and to keep it up only from the very lowest motives.

'Cricket,' said Raffles, 'like everything else, is a good enough sport until you discover a better. As a source of excitement it isn't in it with other things you wot of, Bunny, and the involuntary comparison becomes a bore. What's the satisfaction of taking a man's wicket when you want his spoons? Still, if you can bowl a bit your low cunning won't get rusty, and always looking for the weak spot's just the kind of mental exercise one wants. Yes, perhaps there's some affinity between the two things after all. But I'd chuck up cricket tomorrow, Bunny, if it wasn't for the glorious protection it affords a person of my proclivities.'

'How so?' said I. 'It brings you before the public, I should have thought, far more than is either safe or wise.'

'My dear Bunny, that's exactly where you make a mistake. To follow crime with reasonable impunity you simply must have a parallel ostensible career – the more public the better. The principle is obvious. Mr Peace, of pious memory, disarmed suspicion by acquiring a local reputation for playing the fiddle and taming the animals, and it's my profound conviction that Jack the Ripper was a really eminent public man, whose speeches were very likely reported alongside his atrocities. Fill the bill in some prominent part, and you'll never be suspected of doubling it with another of equal prominence. That's why I want you to cultivate journalism, my boy, and sign all you can. And it's the one and only reason why I don't burn my bats for firewood.'

Nevertheless, when he did play there was no keener performer on the field, nor one more anxious to do well for his side. I remember how he went to the nets, before the first match of the season, with his pocket full of sovereigns which he put on the stumps instead of bails. It was a sight to see the professionals bowling like demons for the hard cash, for whenever a stump was hit a pound was tossed to the bowler and another balanced in its stead, while one man took £3 with a ball that spread-eagled the wicket. Raffles's practice cost him either eight or nine sovereigns; but he had absolutely first-class bowling all the time, and he made fifty-seven runs next day.

It became my pleasure to accompany him to all his matches, to watch every ball he bowled, or played, or fielded, and to sit chatting with him in the pavilion when he was doing none of these three things. You might have seen us there, side by side, during the greater part of the Gentlemen's first innings against the Players (who had lost the toss) on the second Monday in July. We were to be seen, but not heard, for Raffles had failed to score, and was uncommonly cross for a player who cared so little for the game. Merely taciturn with me, he was positively rude to more than one member who wanted to know how it had happened, or who ventured to commiserate with him on his luck; there he sat, with a straw hat tilted over his nose and a cigarette stuck between lips that curled disagreeably at every advance. I was, therefore, much surprised when a young fellow of the exquisite type came and squeezed himself in between us, and met with a perfectly civil reception despite the liberty. I did not know the boy by sight, nor did Raffles introduce us; but their conversation proclaimed at once the slightness of acquaintanceship and a licence on the lad's part which combined to puzzle me. Mystification reached its height when Raffles was informed that the other's father was anxious to meet him, and he instantly consented to gratify that whim.

'He's in the Ladies' Enclosure. Will you come round now?'

'With pleasure,' says Raffles. 'Keep a place for me, Bunny.'

And they were gone.

'Young Crowley,' said some voice farther back. 'Last year's Harrow Eleven.'

'I remember him. Worst man in the team.'

'Keen cricketer, however. Stopped till he was twenty to get his colours. Governor made him. Keen breed. Oh, pretty, sir! Very pretty!'

The game was boring me. I only came to see old Raffles perform. Soon I was looking wistfully for his return, and at length I saw him beckoning me from the palings to the right.

'Want to introduce you to old Amersteth,' he whispered, when I joined him. 'They've a cricket week next month, when this boy Crowley comes of age, and we've both got to go down and play.'

'Both!' I echoed. 'But I'm no cricketer!'

'Shut up,' says Raffles. 'Leave that to me. I've been lying for all I'm worth,' he added sepulchrally, as we reached the bottom of the steps. 'I trust to you not to give the show away.'

There was the gleam in his eye that I knew well enough elsewhere, but was unprepared for in those healthy, sane surroundings; and it was with very definite misgivings and surmises that I followed the Zingari blazer through the vast flower-bed of hats that bloomed beneath the ladies' awning.

Lord Amersteth was a fine-looking man with a short moustache and a double chin. He received me with much dry courtesy, through which, however, it was not difficult to read a less flattering tale. I was accepted as the inevitable appendage of the invaluable Raffles, with whom I felt deeply incensed as I made my bow.

'I have been bold enough', said Lord Amersteth, 'to ask one of the Gentlemen of England to come down and play some rustic cricket for us next month. He is kind enough to say that he would have liked nothing better, but for this little fishing expedition of yours, Mr – , Mr – ,' and Lord Amersteth succeeded in remembering my name.

It was, of course, the first I had ever heard of that fishing expedition, but I made haste to say that it could easily, and should certainly, be put off. Raffles gleamed approval through his eyelashes. Lord Amersteth bowed and shrugged.

'You're very good, I'm sure,' said he. 'But I understand you're a cricketer yourself?'

'He was one at school,' said Raffles, with infamous readiness.

'Not a real cricketer,' I was stammering meanwhile.

'In the eleven?' said Lord Amersteth.

'I'm afraid not,' said I.

'But only just out of it,' declared Raffles, to my horror.

'Well, well, we can't all play for the Gentlemen,' said Lord Amersteth slyly. 'My son Crowley only just scraped into the eleven at Harrow, and he's going to play. I may even come in myself at a pinch; so you won't be the only duffer, if you are one, and I shall be very glad if you will come down and help us too. You shall flog a stream before breakfast and after dinner, if you like.'

'I should be very proud,' I was beginning, as the mere prelude to resolute excuses; but the eye of Raffles opened wide upon me; and I hesitated weakly, to be duly lost.

'Then that's settled,' said Lord Amersteth, with the slightest suspicion of grimness. 'It's to be a little week, you know, when my son comes of age. We play the Free Foresters, the Dorsetshire Gentlemen, and probably some local lot as well. But Mr Raffles will tell you all about it, and Crowley shall write. Another wicket! By Jove, they're all out! Then I rely on you both.' And, with a little nod, Lord Amersteth rose and sidled to the gangway.

Raffles rose also, but I caught the sleeve of his blazer.

'What are you thinking of?' I whispered savagely. 'I was nowhere near the eleven. I'm no sort of cricketer. I shall have to get out of this!'

'Not you,' he whispered back. 'You needn't play, but come you must. If you wait for me after half-past six, I'll tell you why.'

But I could guess the reason; and I am ashamed to say that it revolted me much less than did the notion of making a public fool of myself on a cricket field. My gorge rose at this as it no longer rose at crime, and it was in no tranquil humour that I strolled about the ground while Raffles disappeared in the pavilion. Nor was my annoyance lessened by a little meeting I witnessed between young Crowley and his father, who shrugged as he stopped and stooped to convey some information which made the young man look a little blank. It may have been pure self-consciousness on my part, but I could have sworn that the trouble was their inability to secure the great Raffles without his insignificant friend.

Then the bell rang, and I climbed to the top of the pavilion to watch Raffles bowl. No subtleties are lost up there; and if ever a bowler was full of them, it was A.J. Raffles on this day, as, indeed, all the cricket world remembers. One had not to be a cricketer oneself to appreciate his perfect command of pitch and break, his beautifully easy action, which never varied with the varying pace, his great ball on the leg-stump – his dropping head-ball – in a word, the infinite ingenuity of that versatile attack. It was no mere exhibition of athletic prowess, it was an intellectual treat, and one with a special significance in my eyes. I saw the 'affinity between the two things', saw it in that afternoon's tireless warfare against the flower of professional cricket. It was not that Raffles took many wickets for few runs; he was too fine a bowler to mind being hit; and time was short, and the wicket good. What I admired, and what I remember, was the combination of resource and cunning, of patience and precision, of head-work and handiwork, which made every over an artistic whole. It was all so characteristic of that other Raffles whom I alone knew!

'I felt like bowling this afternoon,' he told me later – in the cab. 'With a pitch to help me, I'd have done something big; as it is, three for forty-one, out of the four that fell, isn't bad for a slow bowler on a plumb wicket against those fellows. But I felt venomous! Nothing riles me more than being asked about for my cricket as though I were a pro. myself.'

'Then why on earth go?'

'To punish them, and – because we shall be jolly hard up, Bunny, before the season's over!'

'Ah!' said I. 'I thought it was that.'

'Of course it was! It seems they're going to have the very devil of a week of it – balls – dinner-parties – swagger house-party – general junketings — and, obviously, a houseful of diamonds as well. Diamonds galore! As a general rule nothing would induce me to abuse my position as a guest. I've never done it, Bunny. But in this case we're engaged like the waiters and the band, and by heaven we'll take our toll! Let's have a quiet dinner somewhere and talk it over.'

'It seems rather a vulgar sort of theft,' I could not help saying; and to this, my single protest, Raffles instantly assented.

'It is a vulgar sort,' said he; 'but I can't help that. We're getting vulgarly hard up again, and there's an end on't. Besides, these people deserve it and can afford it. And don't you run away with the idea that all will be plain sailing; nothing will be easier than getting some stuff, and nothing harder than avoiding all suspicion, as, of course, we must. We may come away with no more than a good working plan of the premises. Who knows? In any case there's weeks of thinking in it for you and me.'

But with those weeks I will not weary you further than by remarking that the 'thinking' was done entirely by Raffles, who did not always trouble to communicate his thoughts to me. His reticence, however, was no longer an irritant. I began to accept it as a necessary convention of these little enterprises. And, after our last adventure of the kind, more especially after its *dénouement*, my trust in Raffles was much too solid to be shaken by a want of trust in me, which I still believe to have been more the instinct of the criminal than the judgment of the man.

It was on Monday, August 10, that we were due at Milchester Abbey, Dorset; and the beginning of the month found us cruising about that very county, with fly-rods actually in our hands. The idea was that we should acquire at once a local reputation as decent fishermen, and some knowledge of the country-side, with a view to further and more deliberate operations in the event of an unprofitable week. There was another idea which Raffles kept to himself until he had got me down there. Then one day he produced a cricket-ball in a meadow we were crossing, and threw me catches for an hour together. More hours he spent in bowling to me on the nearest green; and, if I was never a cricketer, at least I came nearer to being one, by the end of that week, than ever before or since.

Incident began early on the Monday. We had sallied forth from a desolate little junction within quite a few miles of

'It's all up!' I gasped, as he turned up the gas and I shut the door. 'We're being watched. We've been followed down from town. There's a detective here on the spot!'

'How do you know?' asked Raffles, turning upon me quite sharply, but without the least dismay. And I told him how I knew.

'Of course,' I added, 'it was the fellow we saw in the inn this afternoon.'

'The detective?' said Raffles. 'Do you mean to say you don't know a detective when you see one, Bunny?'

'If that wasn't the fellow, which is?'

Raffles shook his head.

'To think that you've been talking to him for the last hour in the billiard room, and couldn't spot what he was!'

'The Scotch photographer – '

I paused aghast.

'Scotch he is,' said Raffles, 'and photographer he may be. He is also Inspector Mackenzie of Scotland Yard – the very man I sent the message to that night last April. And you couldn't spot who he was in a whole hour! Oh, Bunny, Bunny, you were never built for crime!'

'But,' said I, 'if that was Mackenzie, who was the fellow you bolted from at Warbeck?'

'The man he's watching.'

'But he's watching us!'

Raffles looked at me with a pitying eye, and shook his head again before handing me his open cigarette-case.

'I don't know whether smoking's forbidden in one's bedroom, but you'd better take one of these and stand tight, Bunny, because I'm going to say something offensive.'

I helped myself with a laugh.

'Say what you like, my dear fellow, if it really isn't you and I that Mackenzie's after.'

'Well, then, it isn't, and it couldn't be, and nobody but a born Bunny would suppose for a moment that it was! Do you seriously think he would sit there and knowingly watch his man playing pool under his nose? Well, he might; he's a cool hand, Mackenzie; but I'm not cool enough to win a pool under such conditions. At least, I don't think I am; it would be interesting to see. The situation wasn't free from strain as it was, though I knew he wasn't thinking of us. Crowley told me all about it after dinner, you see, and then I'd seen one of the men for myself this afternoon. You thought it was a detective who made me turn tail at that inn. I really don't know why I didn't tell you at the time, but it was just the opposite. That loud, red-faced brute is one of the cleverest thieves in London, and I once had a drink with him and our mutual fence. I was an East-ender from tongue to toe at the moment, but you will understand that I don't run unnecessary risks of recognition by a brute like that.'

'He's not alone, I hear.'

'By no means; there's at least one other man with him; and it's suggested that there may be an accomplice here in the house.'

'Did Lord Crowley tell you so?'

'Crowley and the champagne between them. In confidence, of course, just as your girl told you; but even in confidence he never let on about Mackenzie. He told me there was a detective in the background, but that was all. Putting him up as a guest is evidently their big secret, to be kept from the other guests because it might offend them, but more particularly from the servants whom he's here to watch. That's my reading of the situation, Bunny, and you will agree with me that it's infinitely more interesting than we could have imagined it would prove.'

'But infinitely more difficult for us,' said I, with a sigh of pusillanimous relief. 'Our hands are tied for this week, at all events.'

'Not necessarily, my dear Bunny, though I admit that the chances are against us. Yet I'm not so sure of that either. There are all sorts of possibilities in these three-cornered combinations. Set A to watch B, and he won't have an eye left for C. That's the obvious theory, but then Mackenzie's a very big A. I should be sorry to have any boodle about me with that man in the house. Yet it would be great to nip in between A and B and score off them both at once! It would be worth a risk, Bunny, to do that; it would be worth risking something merely to take on old hands like B and his men at their old game! Eh, Bunny? That would be something like a match. Gentlemen and Players at single wicket, by Jove!'

His eyes were brighter than I had known them for many a day. They shone with the perverted enthusiasm which was roused in him only by the contemplation of some new audacity. He kicked off his shoes and began pacing his room with noiseless rapidity; not since the night of the Old Bohemian dinner to Reuben Rosenthall had Raffles exhibited such excitement in my presence; and I was not sorry at the moment to be reminded of the fiasco to which that banquet had been the prelude.

'My dear A. J.,' said I in his very own tone, 'you're far too fond of the uphill game; you will eventually fall a victim to the sporting spirit and nothing else. Take a lesson from our last escape, and fly lower as you value our skins. Study the house as much as you like, but do – not – go and shove your head into Mackenzie's mouth!'

My wealth of metaphor brought him to a standstill, with his cigarette between his fingers and a grin beneath his shining eyes.

'You're quite right, Bunny. I won't. I really won't. Yet – you saw old Lady Melrose's necklace? I've been wanting it for years! But I'm not going to play the fool, honour bright, I'm not; yet –

by Jove! – to get to windward of the professors and Mackenzie too! It would be a great game, Bunny, it would be a great game!'

'Well, you mustn't play it this week.'

'No, no, I won't. But I wonder how the professors think of going to work? That's what one wants to know. I wonder if they've really got an accomplice in the house? How I wish I knew their game! But it's all right, Bunny; don't you be jealous; it shall be as you wish.'

And with that assurance I went off to my own room and so to bed with an incredibly light heart. I had still enough of the honest man in me to welcome the postponement of our actual felonies, to dread their performance, and to deplore their necessity; which is merely another way of stating the too patent fact that I was an incomparably weaker man than Raffles, while every whit as wicked. I had, however, one rather strong point. I possessed the gift of dismissing unpleasant considerations, not intimately connected with the passing moment, entirely from my mind. Through the exercise of this faculty I had lately been living my frivolous life in town with as much ignoble enjoyment as I had derived from it the year before; and similarly, here at Milchester, in the long-dreaded cricket- week, I had after all a quite excellent time.

It is true that there were other factors in this pleasing disappointment. In the first place, *mirabile dictu*, there were one or two even greater duffers than I on the Abbey cricket field. Indeed, quite early in the week, when it was of most value to me, I gained considerable kudos for a lucky catch; a ball, of which I had merely heard the hum, stuck fast in my hand, which Lord Amersteth himself grasped in public congratulation. This happy accident was not to be undone even by me, and, as nothing succeeds like success, and the constant encouragement of the one great cricketer on the field was in itself an immense stimulus, I actually made a run or two in my very next innings. Miss Melhuish said pretty things to me that night at the great ball in honour of Viscount Crowley's majority; she also told me that was the night on which the robbers would assuredly make their raid, and was full of arch tremors when we sat out in the garden, though the entire premises were illuminated all night long. Meanwhile the quiet Scotsman took coundess photographs by day, which he developed by night in a dark room admirably situated in the servants' pan of the house; and it is my first belief that only two of his fellow guests knew Mr Clephane of Dundee for Inspector Mackenzie of Scotland Yard.

The week was to end with a trumpery match on the Saturday, which two or three of us intended abandoning early in order to return to town that night. The match, however, was never played. In the small hours of the Saturday morning a tragedy took place at Milchester Abbey.

Let me tell of the thing as I saw and heard it. My room opened upon the central gallery, and was not even on the same floor as that on which Raffles – and I think all the other men – were quartered. I had been put, in fact, into the dressing room of one of the grand suites, and my two near neighbours were old Lady Melrose and my host and hostess. Now, by the Friday evening the actual festivities were at an end, and, for the first time that week I must have been sound asleep since midnight, when all at once I found myself sitting up breathless. A heavy thud had come against my door, and now I heard hard breathing and the dull stamp of muffled feet.

'I've got ye,' muttered a voice. 'It's no use struggling.'

It was the Scotch detective, and a new fear turned me cold. There was no reply, but the hard breathing grew harder still, and the muffled feet beat the floor to a quicker measure. In sudden panic I sprang out of bed and flung open my door. A light burnt low on the landing, and by it I could see Mackenzie swaying and staggering in a silent tussle with some powerful adversary.

'Hold this man!' he cried, as I appeared. 'Hold the rascal!'

But I stood like a fool until the pair of them backed into me, when, with a deep breath, I flung myself on the fellow, whose face I had seen at last. He was one of the footmen who waited at table; and no sooner had I pinned him than the detective loosed his hold.

'Hang on to him,' he cried. 'There's more of 'em below.'

And he went leaping down the stairs, as other doors opened, and Lord Amersteth and his son appeared simultaneously in their pyjamas. At that my man ceased struggling: but I was still holding him when Crowley turned up the gas.

'What the devil's all this?' asked Lord Amersteth, blinking. 'Who was that ran downstairs?'

'MacClephane!' said I hastily.

'Aha!' said he, turning to the footman. 'So you're the scoundrel, are you? Well done! Well done! Where was he caught?'

I had no idea.

'Here's Lady Melrose's door open,' said Crowley. 'Lady Melrose! Lady Melrose!'

'You forget she is deaf,' said Lord Amersteth. 'Ah! that'll be her maid.'

An inner door had opened; next instant there was a little shriek, and a white figure gesticulated on the threshold.

'Où donc est l'écrin de Madame la Marquise? La fenêtre est ouverte. Il a disparu!'

'Window open and jewel case gone, by Jove!' exclaimed Lord Amersteth. 'Mais comment est Madame la Marquise? Est-elle bien?'

'Oui, milor. Elle dort.'

'Sleeps through it all,' said my lord. 'She's the only one, then!'

'What made Mackenzie – Clephane – bolt?' young Crowley asked me.

'Said there were more of them below.'

'Why the devil couldn't you tell us so before?' he cried, and went leaping downstairs in his turn.

He was followed by nearly all the cricketers, who now burst upon the scene in a body, only to desert it for the chase. Raffles was one of them, and I would gladly have been another, had not the footman chosen this moment to hurl me from him, and to make a dash in the direction from which they had come. Lord Amersteth had hit him in an instant; but the fellow fought desperately, and it took the two of us to drag him downstairs; amid a terrified chorus from half-open doors. Eventually we handed him over to two other footmen who appeared with their night-shirts tucked into their trousers, and my host was good enough to compliment me as he led the way outside.

'I thought I heard a shot,' he added. 'Didn't you?'

'I thought I heard three.'

And out we dashed into the darkness.

I remember how the gravel pricked my feet, how the wet grass numbed them as we made for the sound of voices on an outlying lawn. So dark was the night that we were in the cricketers' midst before we saw the shimmer of their pyjamas, and then Lord Amersteth almost trod on Mackenzie as he lay prostrate in the dew.

'Who's this?' he cried. 'What on earth's happened?'

'It's Clephane,' said a man who knelt over him. 'He's got a bullet in him somewhere.'

'Is he alive?'

'Barely.'

'Good God! Where's Crowley?'

'Here I am,' called a breathless voice. 'It's no good, you fellows. There's nothing to show which way they've gone. Here's Raffles; he's chucked it, too.' And they ran up panting.

'Well, we've got one of them, at all events,' muttered Lord Amersteth. 'The next thing is to get this poor fellow indoors.

Take his shoulders somebody. Now his middle. Join hands under him. Altogether now; that's the way. Poor fellow! Poor fellow! His name isn't Clephane at all. He's a Scotland Yard detective, down here for these very villains!'

Raffles was the first to express surprise; but he had also been the first to raise the wounded man. Nor had any of them a stronger or more tender hand in the slow procession to the house. In a little we had the senseless man stretched on a sofa in the library. And there, with ice on his wound and brandy in his throat, his eyes opened and his lips moved.

Lord Amersteth bent down to catch the words.

'Yes, yes,' said he, 'we've got one of them safe and sound. The brute you collared upstairs.' Lord Amersteth bent lower. 'By Jove! Lowered the jewel-case out of the window, did he? And they've got clean away with it! Well, well! I only hope we'll be able to pull this good fellow through. He's off again.'

An hour passed; the sun was rising.

It found a dozen young fellows on the settees in the billiard-room, drinking whisky and soda-water in their overcoats and pyjamas, and still talking excitedly in one breath. A time-table was being passed from hand to hand: the doctor was still in the library. At last the door opened, and Lord Amersteth put in his head.

'It isn't hopeless,' said he, 'but it's bad enough. There'll be no cricket today.'

Another hour, and most of us were on our way to catch the early train; between us we filled a compartment almost to suffocation. And still we talked all together on the night's event; and still I was a little hero in my way, for having kept my hold on the ruffian who had been taken; and my gratification was subtle and intense. Raffles watched me under lowered lids. Not a word had we had together; not a word did we have until we had left the others at Paddington, and were

4

LE PREMIER PAS

That night he told me the story of his earliest crime. Not since the fateful morning of the Ides of March, when he had just mentioned it as an unreported incident of a certain cricket tour, had I succeeded in getting a word out of Raffles on the subject. It was not for want of trying; he would shake his head, and watch his cigarette smoke thoughtfully; a subtle look in his eyes, half cynical, half wistful, as though the decent honest days that were no more had had their merits after all. Raffles would plan a fresh enormity, or glory in the last, with the unmitigated enthusiasm of the artist. It was impossible to imagine one throb or twitter of compunction beneath those frankly egoistic and infectious transports. And yet the ghost of a dead remorse seemed still to visit him with the memory of his first felony, so that I had given the story up long before the night of our return from Milchester. Cricket, however, was in the air, and Raffles's cricket-bag back where he sometimes kept it, in the fender, with the remains of an old Orient label still adhering to the leather. My eyes had been on this label for some time, and I suppose his eyes had been on mine, for all at once he asked me if I still burned to hear that yarn.

'It's no use,' I replied. 'You won't spin it. I must imagine it for myself.'

'How can you?'

'Oh, I begin to know your methods.'

'You take it I went with my eyes open, as I do now, eh?'

'I can't imagine your doing otherwise.'

'My dear Bunny, it was the most unpremeditated thing I ever did in my life!'

His chair wheeled back into the books as he sprang up with sudden energy. There was quite an indignant glitter in his eyes.

'I can't believe that,' said I craftily. 'I can't pay you such a poor compliment.'

'Then you must be a fool – '

He broke off, stared hard at me, and in a trice stood smiling in his own despite.

'Or a better knave than I thought you, Bunny, and by Jove, it's the knave! Well – I suppose I'm fairly drawn; I give you best, as they say out here. As a matter of fact, I've been thinking of the thing myself; last night's racket reminds me of it in one or two respects. I tell you what, though, this is an occasion in any case, and I'm going to celebrate it by breaking the one good rule of my life. I'm going to have a second drink!'

The whisky tinkled, the syphon fizzed, and ice plopped home; and seated there in his pyjamas, with the inevitable cigarette, Raffles told me the story that I had given up hoping to hear. The windows were wide open; the sounds of Piccadilly floated in at first. Long before he finished, the last wheels had rattled, the last brawler was removed, we alone broke the quiet of the summer night.

'... No, they do you very well indeed. You pay for nothing but drinks, so to speak, but I'm afraid mine were of a comprehensive character. I had started in a hole, I ought really to have refused the invitation; then we all went to the Melbourne Cup, and I had the certain winner that didn't win, and that's not the only way you can play the fool in Melbourne. I wasn't the steady old stager I am now, Bunny: my analysis was a confession in itself. But the others didn't know how hard up I was, and I swore they shouldn't. I tried the Jews, but they're extra fly out there. Then I thought of a kinsman of sorts, a second cousin of my father's whom none of us knew anything about, except that he was supposed to be in one or other of the Colonies. If he were a rich man, well and good, I would work him; if not there would be no harm done. I tried to get on his tracks, and, as luck would have it, I succeeded (or thought I had) at the very moment when I happened to have a few days to myself. I was cut over on the hand, just before the big Christmas match, and couldn't have bowled a ball if they had played me.

'The surgeon who fixed me up happened to ask me if I was any relation of Raffles of the National Bank, and the pure luck of it almost took my breath away. A relation who was a high official in one of the banks, who would finance me on my mere name – could anything be better? I made up my mind that this Raffles was the man I wanted, and was awfully sold to find next moment that he wasn't a high official at all. Nor had the doctor so much as met him, but had merely read of him in connection with a small sensation at the suburban branch which my namesake managed; an armed robber had been rather pluckily beaten off, with a bullet in him, by this Raffles; and the sort of thing was so common out there that this was the first I had heard of it! A suburban branch – my financier had faded into some excellent fellow with a billet to lose if he called his soul his own. Still a manager was a manager, and I said I would soon see whether this was the relative I was looking for, if he would be good enough to give me the name of that branch.

'"I'll do more," says the doctor. 'I'll give you the name of the branch he's been promoted to, for I think I heard they've moved him up one already." And the next day he brought me the name of the township of Yea, some fifty miles north of Melbourne; but, with the vagueness which characterised all his information, he was unable to say whether I should find my relative there or not.

'"He's a single man, and his initials are W. F.," said the doctor, who was certain enough of the immaterial points. "He left his old post several days ago, but it appears he's not due at the new one till the New Year. No doubt he'll go before then to take things over and settle in. You might find him up there and you might not. If I were you I should write."

'"That'll lose two days," said I, "and more if he isn't there," for I'd grown quite keen on this up-country manager, and I felt that if I could get at him while the holidays were still on, a little conviviality might help matters considerably.

'"Then," said the doctor, "I should get a quiet horse and ride. You needn't use that hand."

'"Can't I go by train?"

'"You can and you can't. You would still have to ride. I suppose you're a horseman?"

'"Yes."

'"Then I should certainly ride all the way. It's a delightful road, through Whittlesea and over the Plenty Ranges. It'll give you some idea of the bush, Mr Raffles, and you'll see the sources of the water-supply of this city, sir. You'll see where every drop of it comes from, the pure Yan Yean! I wish I had time to ride with you.'

'"But where can I get a horse?"

The doctor thought a moment.

'"I've a mare of my own that's as fat as butter for want of work," said he. "It would be a charity to me to sit on her back for a hundred miles or so, and then I should know you'd have no temptation to use that hand."

"You're far too good," I protested.

'"You're A.J. Raffles," he said.

'And if ever there was a prettier compliment, or a finer instance of even Colonial hospitality, I can only say, Bunny, that I never heard of either.'

He sipped his whisky, threw away the stump of his cigarette, and lit another before continuing.

'Well, I managed to write a line to W. F. with my own hand, which, as you will gather, was not very badly wounded; it was simply this third finger that was split and in splints; the next morning the doctor packed me off on a bovine beast that would have done for an ambulance. Half the team came up to see me start; the rest were rather sick with me for not stopping to see the match out, as if I could help them to win by watching them. They little knew the game I'd got on myself, but still less did I know the game I was going to play.

'It was an interesting ride enough, especially after passing the place called Whittlesea, a real wild township on the lower slopes of the ranges, where I recollect having a deadly meal of hot mutton and tea with the thermometer at three figures in the shade. The first thirty miles or so was a good metal road, too good to go half round the world to ride on, but after Whittlesea it was a mere track over the ranges, a track I often couldn't see and left entirely to the mare. Now it dipped into a gully and ran through a creek, and all the time the local colour was inches thick: gum trees galore and parrots all colours of the rainbow. In one place a whole forest of gums had been ring-barked, and were just as though they had been painted white, without a leaf or a living thing for miles. And the first living thing I did meet was the sort to give you the creeps; it was a riderless horse coming full tilt through the bush, with the saddle twisted round and the stirrup-irons ringing. Without thinking, I had a shot at heading him with the doctor's mare, and blocked him just enough to allow a man who came galloping after to do the rest.

'"Thank ye, mister," growled the man, a huge chap in a red checked shirt, with a beard like W.G. Grace, but the very devil of an expression.

'"Been an accident?" said I, reining up.

'"Yes," said he, scowling as though he defied me to ask any more.

'"And a nasty one," I said, "if that's blood on the saddle!"

'Well, Bunny, I may be a blackguard myself, but I don't think I ever looked at a fellow as that chap looked at me. But I stared him out, and forced him to admit that it was blood on the twisted saddle, and after that he became quite tame. He told me exactly what had happened. A mate of his had been dragged under a branch, and had his nose smashed, but that was all; had sat tight after it till he dropped from loss of blood, another mate was with him in the bush.

'As I've said already, Bunny, I wasn't the old stager that I am now – in any respect – and we parted good enough friends. He asked me which way was I was going, and when I told him, he said I should save seven miles, and get a good hour earlier to Yea, by striking off the track and making for a peak that we could see through the trees, and following a creek that I should see from the peak. Don't smile, Bunny! I began by saying I was a child in those days. Of course, the short cut was the long way round; and it was nearly dark when that unlucky mare and I saw the single street of Yea.

'I was looking for the bank when a fellow in a white suit ran down from the verandah.

'"Mr Raffles?" said he.

'"Mr Raffles!" said I, laughing, as I shook his hand.

'"You're late."

'"I was misdirected."

'"That all? I'm relieved," he said. "Do you know what they are saying? There are some brand-new bushrangers on the road between Whittlesea and this – a second Kelly gang! They'd have caught a Tartar in you, eh?"

'"They would in you," I retorted, and my *tu quoque* shut him up and seemed to puzzle him. Yet there was much more sense in it than in his compliment to me, which was absolutely pointless.

"I'm afraid you'll find things pretty rough," he resumed, when he had unstrapped my valise, and handed my reins to his man. "It's lucky you're a bachelor like myself."

'I could not quite see the point of this remark either, since, had I been married, I should hardly have sprung my wife upon him in this free-and-easy fashion. I muttered the conventional sort of thing, and then he said I should find it all right when I settled, as though I had come to graze upon him for weeks! "Well," thought I, "these Colonials do take the cake for hospitality!" And, still marvelling, I let him lead me into the private part of the bank.

'"Dinner will be ready in a quarter of an hour," said he, as we entered. "I thought you might like a tub first, and you'll find all ready in the room at the end of the passage. Sing out if there's anything you want. Your luggage hasn't turned up yet, by the way, but here's a letter that came this morning."

'"Not for me?"

'"Yes, didn't you expect one?"

'"I certainly did not!"

'"Well, here it is."

'And, as he lit me to my room, I read my own superscription of the previous day – to W.F. Raffles!

'Bunny, you've had your wind bagged at footer, I daresay; you know what that's like? All I can say is that my moral wind was bagged by that letter as I hope, old chap, I have never yet bagged yours. I couldn't speak. I could only stand with my own letter in my hands until he had the good taste to leave me by myself.

'W.F. Raffles! We had mistaken each other for W.F. Raffles – for the new manager who had not yet arrived! Small wonder we had conversed at cross-purposes; the only wonder was that we had not discovered our mutual mistake. How the other man would have laughed! But I – I could not laugh. By Jove, no, it was no laughing matter for me! I saw the whole thing in a flash, without a tremor, but with the direct depression from my own single point of view. Call it callous if you like, Bunny, but remember that I was in much the same hole as you've since been in yourself, and that I had counted on W.F. Raffles even as you counted on A.J. I thought of the man with the W. G. beard – the riderless horse with the bloody saddle – the deliberate misdirection that had put me off the track and out of the way – and now the missing manager and the report of bushrangers at this end. But I simply don't pretend to have felt any personal pity for a man whom I had never seen; that kind of pity's usually cant; and besides, all mine was needed for myself.

'I was in as big a hole as ever. What the devil was I to do? I doubt if I have sufficiently impressed upon you the absolute necessity of my returning to Melbourne in funds. As a matter of fact it was less the necessity than my own determination which I can truthfully describe as absolute.

'Money I would have – but how – but how? Would this stranger be open to persuasion – if I told him the truth? No; that would set us all scouring the country for the rest of the night. Why should I tell him? Suppose I left him to find out his mistake ... would anything be gained? Bunny, I give you my word that I went to dinner without a definite intention in my head, or one premeditated lie upon my lips. I might do the decent, natural thing, and explain matters without loss of time; on the other hand, there was no hurry, I had not opened the letter, and could always pretend I had not noticed the initials; meanwhile something might turn up. I could wait a little and see. Tempted I already was, but as yet the temptation was vague, and its very vagueness made me tremble.

'"Bad news, I'm afraid," said the manager, when at last I sat down at his table.

'"A mere annoyance," I answered – I do assure you – on the spur of the moment and nothing else. But my lie was told; my position was taken; from that moment onward there was no retreat. By implication, without realising what I was doing, I had already declared myself W.F. Raffles. Therefore, W.F. Raffles I would be, in that bank, for that night. And the devil teach me how to use my lie!'

Again he raised his glass to his lips – I had forgotten mine. His cigarette-case caught the gaslight as he handed it to me. I shook my head without taking my eyes from his.

'The devil played up,' continued Raffles, with a laugh. 'Before I tasted my soup I had decided what to do. I had determined to rob that bank instead of going to bed, and be back in Melbourne for breakfast if the doctor's mare could do it. I would tell the old fellow that I had missed my way and been bushed for hours, as I easily might have been, and had never got to Yea at all. At Yea, on the other hand, the personation and robbery would ever after be attributed to a member of the gang that had waylaid and murdered the new manager with that very object. You are acquiring some experience in such matters, Bunny. I ask you, was there ever a better get-out? Last night's was something like it, only never such a certainty. And I saw it from the beginning – saw to the end before I had finished my soup!

'To increase my chances, the cashier, who also lived in the bank, was away over the holidays, had actually gone down to Melbourne to see us play; and the man who had taken my horse also waited at table; for he and his wife were the only servants, and they slept in a separate building. You may depend I ascertained this before we had finished dinner. Indeed, I was by way of asking too many questions (the most oblique and delicate was that which elicited my host's name, Ewbank), nor was I careful enough to conceal their drift.

'"Do you know," said this fellow Ewbank, who was one of the downright sort, "if it wasn't you, I should say you were in a funk of robbers? Have you lost your nerve?"

'"I hope not," said I, turning jolly hot, I can tell you; "but – well, it's not a pleasant thing to have to put a bullet through a fellow!"

"No?" said he, coolly. "I should enjoy nothing better myself; besides, yours didn't go through."

'"I wish it had!" I was smart enough to cry.

'"Amen!" said he.

'"And I emptied my glass; actually I did not know whether my wounded bank-robber was in prison, dead, or at large!

'But, now that I had had more than enough of it, Ewbank would come back to the subject. He admitted that the staff was small; but as for himself, he had a loaded revolver under his pillow all night, under the counter all day, and he was only waiting for his chance.

'"Under the counter, eh?" I was ass enough to say.

'"Yes; so had you!"

'He was looking at me in surprise, and something told me that to say "of course – I had forgotten!" would have been quite fatal, considering what I was supposed to have done. So I looked down my nose and shook my head.

'"But the papers said you had!" he cried.

'"Not under the counter," said I.

'"But it's the regulation!"

'For the moment, Bunny, I felt stumped, though I trust I only looked more superior than before, and I think I justified my look.

'"The regulation!" I said at length, in the most offensive tone at my command. "Yes, the regulation would have us all dead men! My dear sir, do you expect your bank-robber to let you reach for your gun in the place where he knows it's kept? I had mine in my pocket, and I got my chance by retreating from the counter with all visible reluctance."

'Ewbank stared at me with open eyes and a five-barred forehead, then came down his fist on the table.

'"By God, that was smart! Still," he added, like a man who would not be in the wrong, "the papers said the other thing, you know!"

'"Of course," I rejoined, "because they said what I told them. You wouldn't have had me advertise the fact that I improved upon the bank's regulations, would you?"

'So that cloud rolled over, and by Jove it was a cloud with a golden lining! Not silver – real good Australian gold! For old Ewbank hadn't quite appreciated me till then; he was a hard nut, a much older man than myself, and I felt pretty sure he thought me young for the place, and my supposed feat a fluke. But I never saw a man change his mind more openly. He got out his best brandy, he made me throw away the cigar I was smoking and opened a fresh box. He was a convivial-looking party, with a red moustache, and a very humorous face (not unlike Tom Emmett's), and from that moment I laid myself out to attack him on his convivial flank. But he wasn't a Rosenthall, Bunny; he had a treble-seamed, hand-sewn head, and could have drunk me under the table ten times over.

'"All right," I thought, "you may go to bed sober, but you'll sleep like a timber yard!" And I threw half he gave me through the open window when he wasn't looking.

'But he was a good chap, Ewbank, and don't you imagine he was at all intemperate. Convivial I called him, and I only wish he had been something more. He did, however, become more and more genial as the evening advanced, and I had not much difficulty in getting him to show me round the bank at what was really an unearthly hour for such a proceeding. It was when he went to fetch the revolver before turning in. I kept him out of his bed another twenty minutes, and I knew every inch of the business premises before I shook hands with Ewbank in my room.

'You won't guess what I did with myself for the next hour. I undressed and went to bed. The incessant strain involved in even the most deliberate impersonation is the most wearing thing I know; then how much more so when the impersonation is impromptu! There's no getting your eye in; the next word may bowl you out; it's batting in a bad light all through. I haven't told you of half the tight places I was in during a conversation that ran into hours and became dangerously intimate towards the end. You can imagine them for yourself, and then picture me spread out on my bed, getting my second wind for the big deed of the night.

'Once more I was in luck, for I had not been lying there long before I heard my dear Ewbank snoring like a harmonium, and the music never ceased for a moment; it was as loud as ever when I crept out and closed my door behind me, as regular as ever when I stopped to listen at his. And I have still to hear the concert that I shall enjoy much more. The good fellow snored me out of the bank, and was still snoring when I again stood and listened under his open window.

'Why did I leave the bank first? To catch and saddle the mare and tether her in a clump of trees close by: to have the means of escape nice and handy before I went to work. I have often wondered at the instinctive wisdom of the precaution; unconsciously I was acting on what has been one of my guiding principles ever since. Pains and patience were required; I had to get my saddle without waking the man, and I was not used to catching horses in a horse-paddock. Then I distrusted the poor mare, and I went back to the stables for a hatful of oats, which I left with her in the clump, hat and all. There was a dog, too, to reckon with (our very worst enemy, Bunny); but I had been cute enough to make immense friends with him during the evening; and he wagged his tail, not only when I came downstairs, but when I reappeared at the back door.

'As the *soi-disant* new manager, I had been able, in the most ordinary course, to pump poor Ewbank about anything and everything connected with the working of the bank, especially in those twenty last invaluable minutes before turning in. And I had made a very natural point of asking him where he kept, and would recommend me to keep, the keys at night. Of course, I thought he would take them with him to his room; but no such thing; he had a dodge worth two of that. What it was doesn't much matter, but no outsider would have found those keys in a month of Sundays.

'I, of course, had them in a few seconds, and in a few more I was in the strong-room itself. I forgot to say that the moon had risen and was letting quite a lot of light into the bank. I had, however, brought a bit of candle with me from my room; and in the strongroom, which was down some narrow stairs behind the counter in the banking chamber, I had no hesitation in lighting it. There was no window down there, and though I could no longer hear old Ewbank snoring, I had not the slightest reason to anticipate disturbance from that quarter. I did think of locking myself in while I was at work, but, thank goodness, the iron door had no keyhole on the inside.

'Well, there was heaps of gold in the safe, but I only took what I needed and could comfortably carry, not much more than a couple of hundred altogether. Not a note would I touch, and my native caution came out also in the way I divided the sovereigns between all my pockets, and packed them up so that I shouldn't be like the old woman of Banbury Cross. Well you think me too cautious still, but I was insanely cautious then. And so it was that, just as I was ready to go, whereas I might have been gone ten minutes, there came a violent knocking at the outer door.

'Bunny, it was the outer door of the banking chamber! My candle must have been seen! And there I stood, with the grease running hot over my fingers, in that brick grave of a strong room!

'There was only one thing to be done. I must trust to the sound sleeping of Ewbank upstairs, open the door myself, knock the visitor down, or shoot him with the revolver I had been new chum enough to buy before leaving Melbourne, and make a dash for that clump of trees and the doctor's mare. My mind was made up in an instant, and I was at the top of the strong-room stairs, the knocking still continuing, when a second sound drove me back. It was the sound of bare feet coming along a corridor.

'My narrow stair was stone, I tumbled down it with little noise, and had only to push open the iron door, for I had left the keys in the safe. As I did so I heard a handle turn overhead, and thanked my gods that I had shut every single door behind me. You see, old chap, one's caution doesn't always let one in!

'"Who's that knocking?" said Ewbank, up above.

'I could not make out the answer, but it sounded to me like the irrelevant supplication of a spent man. What I did hear plainly, was the cocking of the bank revolver before the bolts were shot back. Then, a tottering step, a hard, short, shallow breathing, and Ewbank's voice in horror:

'"Good Lord! What's happened to you? You're bleeding like a pig!"

'"Not now," came with a grateful sort of sigh.

'"But you have been! What's done it?"

'"Bushrangers."

'"Down the road?"

'"This and Whittlesea – tied to tree – cock-shots – left me – bleed to death..."

The weak voice failed, and the bare feet bolted. Now was my time – if the poor devil had fainted. But I could not be sure, and there I crouched down below in the dark, at the half-shut iron door, not less spell-bound than imprisoned. It was just as well, for Ewbank wasn't gone a minute.

'"Drink this," I heard him say, and when the other spoke again his voice was stronger.

'"Now I begin to feel alive."

'"Don't talk!"

'"It does me good. You don't know what it was, all those miles alone, one an hour at the outside! I never thought I should come through. You must let me tell you – in case I don't!"

'"Well, have another sip."

'"Thank you... I said bushrangers; of course there are no such things nowadays."

'"What were they, then?"

'"Bank thieves; the one that had the pot-shots was the very brute I drove out of the bank at Coburg, with a bullet in him!" '

'I knew it!'

'Of course you did, Bunny; so did I, down in that strong-room; but old Ewbank didn't, and I thought he was never going to speak again.

'"You're delirious," he says at last. "Who in blazes do you think you are?"

'"The new manager."

'"The new manager's in bed and asleep upstairs!"

'"When did he arrive?"

'"This evening."

'"Call himself Raffles?"

'"Yes."

'"Well, I'm damned!" whispered the real man. "I thought it was just revenge, but now I see what it was. My dear sir, the man upstairs is an imposter – if he's upstairs still! He must be one of the gang. He's going to rob the bank – if he hasn't done so already!"

'"If he hasn't done so already," muttered Ewbank after him; "if he's upstairs still! By God, if he is I'm sorry for him!"

'His tone was quiet enough, but about the nastiest I ever heard. I tell you, Bunny, I was glad I'd brought that revolver.

It looked as though it must be mine against his, muzzle to muzzle.

'"Better have a look down here, first," said the new manager.

'"While he gets through his window? No, no, he's not down here."

'"It's easy to have a look."

'Bunny, if you ask me what was the most thrilling moment of my infamous career, I say it was that moment. There I stood at the bottom of those narrow stone stairs, inside the strong-room, with the door a good foot open, and I didn't know whether it would creak or not. The light was coming nearer – and I didn't know! I had to chance it. And it didn't creak a bit; it was far too solid and well-hung; and I couldn't have banged it if I'd tried, it was too heavy; and it fitted so close that I felt and heard the air squeeze out in my face. Every shred of light went out, except the streak underneath, and it brightened. How I blessed that door!

'"No, he's not down there," I heard, as though through cottonwool; then the streak went out too, and in a few seconds I ventured to open once more, and was in time to hear them creeping to my room.

'Well, now, there was not a fifth of a second to be lost; but I'm proud to say I came up those stairs on my toes and fingers, and out of that bank (they'd gone and left the door open) just as gingerly as though my time had been my own. I didn't even forget to put on the hat that the doctor's mare was eating her oats out of, as well as she could with a bit, or it alone would have landed me. I didn't even gallop away, but just jogged off quietly in the thick dust at the side of the road (though I own my heart was galloping), and thanked my stars the bank was at that end of the township, in which I really hadn't set foot. The very last thing I heard was the two managers raising Cain and the coachman. And now, Bunny – '

He stood up and stretched himself, with a smile that ended in a yawn. The black windows had faded through every shade of indigo; they now framed their opposite neighbours, stark and livid in the dawn; and the gas seemed turned to nothing in the globes.

'But that's not all?' I cried.

'I'm sorry to say it is,' said Raffles apologetically. 'The thing should have ended with an exciting chase, I know, but somehow it didn't. I suppose they thought I had got no end of a start; then they had made up their minds that I belonged to the gang, which was not so many miles away; and one of them had got as much as he could carry from that gang as it was. But I wasn't to know all that, and I'm bound to say that there was plenty of excitement left for me. Lord, how I made that poor brute travel when I got among the trees! Though we must have been well over fifty miles from Melbourne, we had done it at a snail's pace; and those stolen oats had brisked the old girl up to such a pitch that she fairly bolted when she felt her nose turned south. By Jove, it was no joke, in and out among those trees, and under branches with your face in the mane! I told you about the forest of dead gums? It looked perfectly ghostly in the moonlight. And I found it as still as I had left it – so still that I pulled up there, my first halt, and lay with my ear to the ground for two or three minutes. But I heard nothing – not a thing but the mare's bellows and my own heart. I'm sorry, Bunny; but if ever you write my memoirs, you won't have any difficulty in working up that chase. Play those dead gum-trees for all they're worth, and let the bullets fly like hail. I'll turn round in my saddle to see Ewbank coming up hell-for-leather in his white suit, and I'll duly paint it red. Do it in the third person, and they won't know how it's going to end.'

'But I don't know myself,' I complained. 'Did the mare carry you all the way back to Melbourne?'

'Every rod, pole, or perch! I had her well seen to at our hotel, and returned her to the doctor in the evening. He was tremendously tickled to hear I had been bushed; next morning he brought me the paper to show me what I had escaped at Yea!'

'Without suspecting anything?'

'Ah!' said Raffles, as he put out the gas; 'that's a point on which I've never made up my mind. The mare and her colour was a coincidence – luckily she was only a bay – and I fancy the condition of the beast must have told a tale. The doctor's manner was certainly different. I'm inclined to think he suspected something, though not the right thing. I wasn't expecting him, and I fear my appearance may have increased his suspicions.'

I asked him why.

'I used to have rather a heavy moustache,' said Raffles, 'but I lost it the day after I lost my innocence.'

5

WILFUL MURDER

Of the various robberies in which we were both concerned, it is but the few, I find, that will bear telling at any length. Not that the others contained details which even I would hesitate to recount; it is, rather, the very absence of untoward incident which renders them useless for my present purpose. In point of fact our plans were so craftily laid (by Raffles) that the chances of a hitch were invariably reduced to a minimum before we went to work. We might be disappointed in the market value of our haul; but it was quite the exception for us to find ourselves confronted by unforeseen impediments, or involved in a really dramatic dilemma. There was a sameness, even in our spoil; for, of course, only the most precious stones are worth the trouble we took and the risks we ran. In short, our most successful escapades would prove the greatest weariness of all in narrative form; and none more so than the dull affair of the Ardagh emeralds, some eight or nine weeks after the Milchester cricket week. The former, however, had a sequel that I would rather forget than all our burglaries put together.

It was the evening after our return from Ireland, and I was waiting at my rooms for Raffles, who had gone off as usual to dispose of the plunder. Raffles had his own method of conducting this very vital branch of our business, which I was well content to leave entirely in his hands. He drove the bargains, I believe, in a thin but subtle disguise of the flashy-seedy order, and always in the Cockney dialect of which he had made himself a master. Moreover, he invariably employed the same 'fence', who was ostensibly a money-lender in a small (but yet notorious) way, and in reality a rascal as remarkable as Raffles himself. Only lately I also had been to the man, but in my proper person. We had needed capital for the getting of these very emeralds, and I had raised a hundred pounds, on the terms you would expect from a soft-spoken greybeard with an ingratiating smile, an incessant bow, and the shiftiest old eyes that ever flew from rim to rim of a pair of spectacles. So the original sinews and the final spoils of war came in this case from the self-same source – a circumstance which appealed to us both.

But these same final spoils I was still to see, and I waited and waited with an impatience that grew upon me with the growing dusk. At my open window I had played Sister Ann until the faces in the street below were no longer distinguishable. And now I was tearing to and fro in the grip of horrible hypothesis – a grip that tightened when at last the lift-gates opened with a clatter outside – that held me breathless until a well-known tattoo followed on my door.

'In the dark!' said Raffles, as I dragged him in. 'Why, Bunny, what's wrong?'

'Nothing – now you've come,' said I, shutting the door behind him in a fever of relief and anxiety. 'Well? Well? What did they fetch?'

'Five hundred.'

'Down?'

'Got it in my pocket.'

'Good man!' I cried. 'You don't know what a stew I've been in. I'll switch on the light. I've been thinking of you and nothing else for the last hour. I – I was ass enough to think something had gone wrong!'

Raffles was smiling when the white light filled the room, but for the moment I did not perceive the peculiarity of his smile. I was fatuously full of my own late tremors and present relief, and my first idiotic act was to spill some whisky and squirt the soda-water all over in my anxiety to do justice to the occasion.

'So you thought something had happened?' said Raffles, leaning back in my chair as he lit a cigarette, and looking much amused. 'What should you say if something had? Sit tight, my dear chap! It was nothing of the slightest consequence, and it's all over now. A stern chase and a long one, Bunny, but I think I'm well to windward this time.'

And suddenly I saw that his collar was limp, his hair matted, his boots thick with dust.

'The police?' I whispered aghast.

'Oh dear, no; only old Baird.'

'Baird! But wasn't it Baird who took the emeralds?'

'It was.'

'Then how came he to chase you?'

'My dear fellow, I'll tell you if you give me a chance, it's really nothing to get in the least excited about. Old Baird has at last spotted that I'm not quite the common cracksman I would have him think me. So he's been doing his best to run me to my burrow.'

'And you call that nothing!'

'It would be something if he had succeeded; but he has still to do that. I admit, however, that he made me sit up for the time being. It all comes of going on the job so far from home. There was the old brute with the whole thing in his morning paper. He knew it must have been done by some fellow who could pass himself off for a gentleman, and I saw his eyebrows go up the moment I told him I was the man, with the same old twang that you could cut with a paper knife. I did my best to get out of it – swore I had a pal who was a real swell – but I saw very plainly that I had given myself away. He gave up haggling. He paid my price as though he enjoyed doing it. But I felt him following when I made tracks – though, of course, I didn't turn round to see.'

'Why not?'

'My dear Bunny, it's the very worst thing you can do. As long as you look unsuspecting they'll keep their distance, and so long as they keep their distance you stand a chance. Once show that you know you're being followed, and it's flight or fight for all you're worth. I never even looked round; and mind you never do in the same hole. I just hurried up to Blackfriars and booked for High Street, Kensington, at the top of my voice; and as the train was leaving Sloane Square out I hopped, and up all those stairs like a lamplighter, and round to the studio by the back streets. Well, to be on the safe side, I lay low there all the afternoon, hearing nothing in the least suspicious, and only wishing I had a window to look through instead of that beastly skylight. However, the coast seemed clear enough, and thus far it was my mere idea that he would follow me; there was nothing to show he had. So at last I marched out in my proper rig – almost straight into old Baird's arms!'

'What on earth did you do?'

'Walked past him as though I had never set eyes on him in my life, and didn't then; took a cab in the King's Road, and drove like the deuce to Clapham Junction; rushed on to the nearest platform, without a ticket, jumped into the first train I saw, got out at Twickenham, walked full tilt back to Richmond, took the District to Charing Cross, and here I am! Ready for tub and a change, and the best dinner the club can give us. I came to you first, because I thought you might be getting anxious. Come round with me, and I won't keep you long.'

'You're certain you've given him the slip?' I said, as we put on our hats.

'Certain enough; but we can make assurance doubly sure,' said Raffles, and went to my window, where he stood for a minute or two looking down into the street.

'All right?' I asked him.

'All right,' said he; and we went downstairs forthwith, and so to the Albany arm-in-arm.

But we were both rather silent on the way. I, for my part, was wondering what Raffles would do about the studio in Chelsea, whither, at all events, he had been successfully dogged. To me the point seemed one of immediate importance, but when I mentioned it he said there was time enough to think about that. His one other remark was made after we had nodded (in Bond Street) to a young blood of our acquaintance who happened to be getting himself a bad name.

'Poor Jack Rutter!' said Raffles, with a sigh. 'Nothing's sadder than to see a fellow going to the bad like that. He's about mad with drink and debt; did you see his eye? Odd that we should have met him tonight, by the way; it's old Baird who's said to have skinned him. I've a jolly good mind to skin old Baird!'

And his tone took a sudden low fury, made the more noticeable by another long silence, which lasted, indeed, throughout an admirable dinner at the club, and for some time after we had settled down in a quiet corner of the smoking-room with our coffee and cigars. Then at last I saw Raffles looking at me with his lazy smile, and I knew that the morose fit was at an end.

'I daresay you wonder what I've been thinking about all this time?' said he. 'I've been thinking what rot it is to go doing things by halves!'

'Well,' said I, returning his smile, 'that's not a charge that you can bring against yourself, is it?'

'I'm not so sure,' said Raffles, blowing a meditative puff; 'as a matter of fact, I was thinking less of myself than of that poor devil of a Jack Rutter. There's a fellow who does things by halves; he's only half gone to the bad; and look at the difference between him and us! He's under the thumb of a villainous money-lender; we arc solvent citizens. He's taken to drink; we're as sober as we are solvent. His pals are beginning to cut him; our difficulty is to keep the pal from the door. *Enfin*, he begs or borrows, which is stealing by halves; and we steal outright and are done with it. Obviously, ours is the more honest course. Yet I'm not sure, Bunny, but we're doing the thing by halves ourselves!'

'Why? What more could we do?' I exclaimed in soft derision, looking round, however, to make sure that we were not overheard.

'What more?' said Raffles. 'Well, murder – for one thing.'

'Rot!'

'A matter of Opinion, my dear Bunny; I don't mean it for rot. I've told you before that the biggest man alive is the man who's committed a murder, and not yet been found out; at least he ought to be, but he so very seldom has the soul to appreciate himself. Just think of it! Think of coming here and talking to the men, very likely about the murder itself; and knowing you've done it; and wondering how they'd look if they knew! Oh, it would be great, simply great! But, besides all that, when you were caught, there'd be a merciful and dramatic end of you. You'd fill the bill for a few weeks and then snuff out with a flourish of extra-specials; you wouldn't rust with a vile repose for seven or fourteen years.'

'Good old Raffles!' I chuckled. 'I begin to forgive you for being in bad form at dinner.'

'But I was never more earnest in my life.'

'Go on!'

'I mean it.'

'You know very well that you wouldn't commit a murder, whatever else you might do.'

'I know very well I'm going to commit one tonight!'

He had been leaning back in the saddle-bag chair, watching me with keen eyes sheathed by languid lids; now he started forward, and his eyes leapt to mine like cold steel from the scabbard. They struck home to my slow wits; their meaning was no longer in doubt. I, who knew the man, read murder in his clenched hands, and murder in his locked lips, but a hundred murders in those hard blue eyes.

'Baird?' I faltered, moistening my lips with my tongue.

'Of course.'

'But you said it didn't matter about the room in Chelsea?'

'I told a lie.'

'Anyway you gave him the slip afterwards!'

'That was another. I didn't. I thought I had when I came up to you this evening; but when I looked out of your window – you remember? – to make assurance doubly sure – there he was on the opposite pavement down below.'

'And you never said a word about it!'

'I wasn't going to spoil your dinner, Bunny, and I wasn't going to let you spoil mine. But there he was as large as life, and, of course, he followed us to the Albany. A fine game for him to play, a game after his mean old heart; blackmail for me, bribes from the police, the one bidding against the other; but he shan't play it with me, he shan't live to, and the world will have an extortioner the less. Waiter! Two Scotch whiskies and sodas. I'm off at eleven, Bunny; it's the only thing to be done.'

'You know where he lives, then?'

'Yes, out Willesden way, and alone; the fellow's a miser among other things. I long ago found out all about him.'

Again I looked around the room; it was a young man's club, and young men were laughing, chatting, smoking, drinking, on every hand. One nodded to me through the smoke. Like a machine I nodded to him, and turned back to Raffles with a groan.

'Surely you will give him a chance!' I urged. 'The very sight of your pistol should bring him to terms.'

'It wouldn't make him keep them.'

'But you might try the effect?'

'I probably shall. Here's a drink for you, Bunny. Wish me luck.'

'I'm coming too.'

'I don't want you.'

'But I must come!'

An ugly gleam shot from the steel-blue eyes.

'To interfere?' said Raffles.

'Not I.'

'You give me your word?'

'I do.'

'Bunny, if you break it – '

'You may shoot me too!'

'I most certainly should,' said Raffles solemnly. 'So you come at your own peril, my dear man; but if you are coming – well, the sooner the better, for I must stop at my rooms on the way.'

Five minutes later I was waiting for him at the Piccadilly entrance to the Albany. I had a reason for remaining outside. It was the feeling – half hope, half fear – that Angus Baird might still be on our trail – that some more immediate and less cold-blooded way of dealing with him might result from a sudden encounter between the money-lender and myself. I would not warn him of his danger; but I would avert tragedy at all costs. And when no such encounter had taken place, and Raffles and I were fairly on our way to Willesden, that, I think, was still my honest resolve. I would not break my word if I could help it, but it was a comfort to feel that I could break it if I liked, on an understood penalty. Alas! I fear my good intentions were tainted with a devouring curiosity, and overlaid by the fascination which goes hand in hand with horror.

I have a poignant recollection of the hour it took us to reach the house. We walked across St James's Park (I can see the lights now, bright on the bridge and blurred on the water), and we had some minutes to wait for the last train to Willesden. It left at 11.21, I remember, and Raffles was put out to find it did not go on to Kensal Rise. We had to get out at Willesden Junction and walk on through the streets into fairly open country that happened to be quite new to me. I could never find the house again. I remember, however, that we were on a dark foot-path between the woods and fields when the clocks began striking twelve.

'Surely,' said I, 'we shall find him in bed and asleep?'

'I hope we do,' said Raffles grimly.

'Then you mean to break in?'

'What else did you think?'

I had not thought about it at all; the ultimate crime had monopolised my mind. Beside it burglary was a bagatelle, but one to deprecate none the less. I saw obvious objections; the man was *au fait* with cracksmen and their ways, he would certainly have firearms, and might be the first to use them.

'I could wish nothing better,' said Raffles. 'Then it will be man to man, and devil take the worst shot. You don't suppose I prefer foul play to fair, do you? But die he must, by one or the other, or it's a long stretch for you and me.'

'Better that than this!'

'Then stay where you are my good fellow. I told you I didn't want you; and this is the house. So good-night.'

I could see no house at all, only the angle of a high wall rising solitary in the night, with the starlight glittering on battlements of broken glass; and in the wall a tall green gate, bristling with spikes, and showing a front for battering-rams in the feeble rays of an outlying lamp-post cast across the new-made road. It seemed to me a road of building sites, with but this one house built, all by itself, at one end; but the night was too dark for more than a mere impression.

Raffles, however, had seen the place by daylight, and had come prepared for the special obstacles; already he was reaching up and putting champagne corks on the spikes, and in another moment he had his folded covert coat across the corks. I stepped back as he raised himself, and saw a little pyramid of slates snip the sky above the gate; as he squirmed over I ran forward, and had my own weight on the spikes and corks and covert coat when he gave the latter a tug.

'Coming after all?'

'Rather!'

'Take care then; the place is all bell-wires and springs. It's no soft spring this! There – stand still while I take off the corks.'

The garden was very small and new, with a grass-plot still in separate sods, but a quantity of full-grown laurels stuck into the raw clay beds. 'Bells in themselves,' Raffles whispered; 'there's nothing else rustles so – cunning old beast!' And we gave them a wide berth as we crept across the grass.

'He's gone to bed!'

'I don't think so, Bunny. I believe he's seen us.'

'Why?'

'I saw a light.'

'Where?'

'Downstairs, for an instant, when I – – '

His whisper died away; he had seen the light again, and so had I.

It lay like a golden rod under the front door – and vanished. It reappeared like a gold thread under the lintel – and vanished for good. We heard the stairs creak, creak, and cease, also for good. We neither saw nor heard any more, though we stood waiting on the grass till our feet were soaked with the dew.

'I'm going in,' said Raffles at last. 'I don't believe he saw us at all. I wish he had. This way.'

We trod gingerly on the path, but the gravel stuck to our wet soles, and grated horribly in a little tiled verandah with a glass door leading within. It was through this glass that Raffles had first seen the light; and he now proceeded to take out a pane, with the diamond, the pot of treacle, and the sheet of brown paper which were seldom omitted from his impedimenta. Nor did he dispense with my own assistance, though he may have accepted it as instinctively as it was proffered. In any case it was these fingers that helped to spread the treacle on the brown paper, and pressed the latter to the glass until the diamond had completed its circuit and the pane fell gently back into our hands.

Raffles now inserted his long hand, turned the key in the lock, and, by making a long arm, succeeded in drawing the bolt at the bottom of the door; it proved to be the only one, and the door opened, though not very wide.

'What's that?' said Raffles, as something crunched beneath his feet on the very threshold.

'A pair of spectacles,' I whispered, picking them up. I was still fingering the broken lenses and the bent rims when Raffles tripped and almost fell, with a gasping cry that he made no effort to restrain.

'Hush, man, hush!' I entreated under my breath. 'He'll hear you!'

For answer his teeth chattered – even his – and I heard him fumbling with his matches.

'No, Bunny; he won't hear us,' whispered Raffles presently, and he rose from his knees and lit a gas as the match burnt down.

Angus Baird was lying on his own floor, dead, with his grey hairs glued together by his blood; near him a poker with the black end glistening; in a comer his desk, ransacked, littered. A clock ticked noisily on the chimneypiece, for perhaps a hundred seconds there was no other sound.

Raffles stood very still, staring down at the dead, as a man might stare into an abyss after striding blindly to its brink. His breath came audibly through wide nostrils; he made no other sign and his lips seemed sealed.

'That light!' said I hoarsely; 'the light we saw under the door!'

With a start he turned to me.

'It's true. I had forgotten it. It was in here I saw it first!'

'He must be upstairs still!'

'If he is we'll soon rout him out. Come on!'

Instead I laid a hand upon his arm, imploring him to reflect – that his enemy was dead now – that we should certainly be involved – that now or never was our own time to escape. He shook me off in a sudden fury of impatience, a reckless contempt in his eyes, and, bidding me save my own skin if I liked, he once more turned his back upon me, and this time left me half resolved to take him at his word. Had he forgotten on what errand he himself was here? Was he determined that this night should end in black disaster? As I asked myself these questions his match flared in the hall; in another moment the stairs were creaking under his feet, even as they had creaked under those of the murderer; and the human instinct that inspired him in defiance of his risk was borne in also upon my slower sensibilities. Could we let the murderer go? My answer was to bound up the creaking stairs and to overhaul Raffles on the landing.

But three doors presented themselves; the first opened into a bedroom with the bed turned down but undisturbed; the second room was empty in every sense; the third door was locked.

Raffles lit the landing gas.

'He's in there,' said he, cocking his revolver. 'Do you remember how we used to break into the studies at school? Here goes!'

His flat foot crashed over the keyhole, the lock gave, the door flew open, and in the sudden draught the landing gas heeled over like a cobble in a squall; as the flame righted itself I saw a fixed bath, two bath-towels knotted together – an open window – a cowering figure – and Raffles struck aghast on the threshold.

'Jack – Rutter?'

The words came thick and slow with horror, and in horror I heard myself repeating them, while the cowering figure by the bathroom window rose gradually erect.

'It's you!' he whispered, in amazement no less than our own; 'it's you two! What's it mean, Raffles? I saw you get over the gate; a bell rang, the place is full of them. Then you broke in? What's it all mean?'

'We may tell you that, when you tell us what in God's name you've done, Rutter!'

'Done? What have I done?' The unhappy wretch came out into the light with bloodshot, blinking eyes, and a bloody shirt-front. 'You know – you've seen – but I'll tell you if you like. I've killed a robber; that's all. I've killed a robber, a usurer, a jackal, a blackmailer, the cleverest and the cruellest villain unhung. I'm ready to hang for him. I'd kill him again!'

And he looked us fiercely in the face, a fine defiance in his dissipated eyes; his breast heaving, his jaw like a rock.

'Shall I tell you how it happened?' he went passionately on. 'He's made my life a hell these weeks and months past. You may know that. A perfect hell. Well, tonight I met him in Bond Street. Do you remember when I met you fellows? He wasn't twenty yards behind you; he was on your tracks, Raffles; he saw me nod to you, and stopped me and asked me who you were. He seemed as keen as knives to know, I couldn't think why, and didn't care either, for I saw my chance. I said I'd tell him all about you if he'd give me a private interview. He said he wouldn't. I said he should, and held him by the coat; by the time I let him go you were out of sight, and I waited where I was till he came back in despair. I had the whip hand of him then. I could dictate where the interview should be, and I made him take me home with him, still swearing to tell him all about you when we'd had our talk. Well, when we got here I made him give me something to eat, putting him off and off; and about ten o'clock I heard the gate shut. I waited a bit, and then asked him if he lived alone.'

'"Not at all," ' says he; '"did you not see the servant?" '

'I said I'd seen her, but I thought I heard her go; if I was mistaken no doubt she would come when she was called; and I yelled three times at the top of my voice. Of course there was no servant to come. I knew that, because I came to see him one night last week, and he interviewed me himself through the gate, but wouldn't open it. Well, when I had done yelling, and not a soul had come near us, he was as white as that ceiling. Then I told him we could have our chat at last; and I picked the poker out of the fender, and told him how he'd robbed me, but by God he shouldn't rob me any more. I gave him three minutes to write and sign a settlement of all his iniquitous claims against me, or have his brains beaten out over his own carpet. He thought a minute, and then went to his desk for pen and paper. In two seconds he was round like lightning with a revolver, and I went for him bald-headed. He fired two or three times and missed – you can find the holes if you like; but I hit him every time – by God! I was like a savage till the thing was done. And then I didn't care. I went through his desk looking for my own bills, and was coming away when you turned up. I said I didn't care, nor do I; but I was going to give myself up tonight, and shall still; so you see I shan't give you fellows much trouble!'

He was done; and there we stood on the landing of the lonely house, the low, thick, eager voice still racing and ringing through our ears; the dead man below, and in front of us his impenitent slayer. I knew to whom the impenitence would appeal when he had heard the story, and I was not mistaken.

'That's all rot,' said Raffles, speaking after a pause; 'we shan't let you give yourself up.'

'You shan't stop me! What would be the good? The woman saw me; it would only be a question of time; and I can't face waiting to be taken. Think of it; waiting for them to touch you on the shoulder! No, no, no; I'll give myself up and get it over.'

His speech was changed; he faltered, floundered. It was as though a clearer perception of his position had come with the bare idea of escape from it.

'But listen to me,' urged Raffles. 'We're here at our peril ourselves. We broke in like thieves to enforce redress for a grievance like your own. But don't you see? We took out a pane – did the thing like regular burglars. We shall get the credit of all the rest!'

'You mean that I shan't be suspected?'

'I do.'

'But I don't want to get off scot-free,' cried Rutter hysterically. 'I've killed him. I know that. But it was in self-defence; it wasn't murder. I must own up and take the consequences. I shall go mad if I don't.'

His hands twitched; his lips quivered; the tears were in his eyes. Raffles took him roughly by the shoulder.

'Look here, you fool! If the three of us are caught here now, do you know what those consequences would be? We should swing in a row in six weeks' time! You talk as though we were sitting in a club; don't you know it's one o'clock in the morning, and the lights on, and a dead man down below? For God's sake pull yourself together, and do what I tell you, or you're a dead man yourself.'

'I wish I was one!' Rutter sobbed. 'I wish I had his revolver, I'd blow my own brains out. It's somewhere under him! O my God, my God!'

His knees knocked together; the frenzy of reaction was at its height. We had to take him downstairs between us, and so through the front door out into the open air.

All was still outside – all but the smothered weeping of the unstrung wretch upon our hands. Raffles returned for a moment to the house; then all was dark as well. The gate opened from within; we closed it carefully behind us; and so left the starlight shining on broken glass and polished spikes, one and all as we had found them.

We escaped; no need to dwell on our escape. Our murderer seemed set upon the scaffold: drunk with his deed, he was more trouble than six men drunk with wine. Again and again we threatened to leave him to his fate, to wash our hands of him. But incredible and unmerited luck was with the three of us. Not a soul did we meet between that and Willesden; and of those who saw us later, did one think of the two young men with crooked white ties, supporting a third in a seemingly unmistakable condition, when the evening papers apprised the town of a terrible tragedy at Kensal Rise?

We walked to Maida Vale, and thence drove openly to my rooms. But I alone went upstairs; the other two proceeded to the Albany, and I saw no more of Raffles for forty-eight hours. He was not at his rooms when I called in the morning, he had left no word. When he reappeared the papers were full of the murder; and the man who had committed it was on the wide Atlantic, a steerage passenger from Liverpool to New York.

'There was no arguing with him,' so Raffles told me; 'either he must make a clean breast of it or flee the country. So I rigged him up at the studio, and we took the first train to Liverpool. Nothing would induce him to sit tight and enjoy the situation as I should have endeavoured to do in his place; and it's just as well! I went to his diggings to destroy some papers, and what do you think I found? The police in possession; there's a warrant out against him already! The idiots think that window wasn't genuine, and the warrant's out. It won't be my fault if it's ever served!'

Nor, after all these years, can I think it will be mine.

6

NINE POINTS OF THE LAW

'Well,' said Raffles, 'what do you make of it?'

I read the advertisement once more before replying. It was in the last column of the *Daily Telegraph*, and it ran:

'Two Thousand Pounds Reward. – The above sum may be earned by any one qualified to undertake delicate mission and prepared to run certain risk. – Apply by telegram, Security, London.'

'I think,' said I, 'it's the most extraordinary advertisement that ever got into print!'

Raffles smiled.

'Not quite all that, Bunny; still, extraordinary enough, I grant you.'

'Look at the figure.'

'It is certainly large.'

'And the mission – and the risk!'

'Yes; the combination is frank, to say the least of it. But the really original point is requiring applications by telegram to a telegraphic address! There's something in the fellow who thought of that, and something in his game; with one word he chokes off the million who answer an advertisement every day – when they can raise the stamp. My answer cost me five bob; but then I prepaid another.'

'You don't mean to say that you've applied?'

'Rather,' said Raffles. 'I want two thousand pounds as much as any man.'

'Put your own name?'

'Well – no, Bunny, I didn't. In point of fact, I smell something interesting and illegal, and you know what a cautious chap I am. I signed myself Glasspool, care of Hickey, 38 Conduit Street; that's my tailor, and after sending the wire I went round and told him what to expect. He promised to send the reply along the moment it came. I shouldn't be surprised if that's it!'

And he was gone before a double knock on the outer door had done ringing through the rooms, to return next minute with an open telegram and a face full of news.

'What do you think?' said he. 'Security's that fellow Addenbrooke, the police-court lawyer, and he wants to see me instanter!' 'Do you know him then?'

'Merely by repute. I only hope he doesn't know me. He's the chap who got six weeks for sailing too close to the wind in the Sutton-Wilmer case; everybody wondered why he wasn't struck off the rolls. Instead of that he's got a first-rate practice on the seamy side, and every blackguard with half a case takes it straight to Bennett Addenbrooke. He's probably the one man who would have the cheek to put in an advertisement like that, and the one man who could do it without exciting suspicion. It's simply in his line; but you may be sure there's something shady at the bottom of it. The odd thing is that I have long made up my mind to go to Addenbrooke myself if accidents should happen.'

'And you're going to him now?'

'This minute,' said Raffles, brushing his hat; 'and so are you.'

'But I came in to drag you out to lunch.'

'You shall lunch with me when we've seen this fellow. Come on, Bunny, and we'll choose your name on the way. Mine's Glasspool, and don't you forget it.'

Mr Bennett Addenbrooke occupied substantial offices in Wellington Street, Strand, and was out when we arrived; but he had only just gone 'over the way to the court'; and five minutes sufficed to produce a brisk, fresh-coloured, resolute-looking man, with a very confident, rather festive air, and black eyes that opened wide at the sight of Raffles.

'Mr – Glasspool?' exclaimed the lawyer.

'My name,' said Raffles, with dry effrontery.

'Not up at Lord's, however!' said the other, slyly. 'My dear sir, I have seen you take far too many wickets to make any mistake!'

For a single moment Raffles looked venomous; then he shrugged and smiled, and the smile grew into a little cynical chuckle.

'So you have bowled me out in my turn?' said he. 'Well, I don't think there's anything to explain. I am harder up than I wished to admit under my own name, that's all, and I want that thousand pounds reward.'

'Two thousand,' said the solicitor. 'And the man who is not above an alias happens to be just the sort of man I want; so don't let that worry you, my dear sir. The matter, however, is of a strictly private and confidential character. ' And he looked very hard at me.

'Quite so,' said Raffles. 'But there was something about a risk?'

'A certain risk is involved.'

'Then surely three heads will be better than two. I said I wanted that thousand pounds; my friend here wants the other. We are both cursedly hard up, and we go into this thing together or not at all. Must you have his name too? I should give him my real one, Bunny.'

Mr Addenbrooke raised his eyebrows over the card I found for him; then he drummed upon it with his finger-nail, and his embarrassment expressed itself in a puzzled smile.

'The fact is I find myself in a difficulty,' he confessed at last. 'Yours is the first reply I have received; people who can afford to send long telegrams don't rush to the advertisements in the *Daily Telegraph*; but, on the other hand, I was not quite prepared to hear from men like yourselves. Candidly, and on consideration, I am not sure that you are the stamp of men for me – men who belong to good clubs! I rather intended to appeal to the – er – adventurous classes.'

'We are adventurers,' said Raffles gravely.

'But you respect the law?'

The black eyes gleamed shrewdly.

'We are not professional rogues, if that's what you mean,' said Raffles smiling. 'But on our beam-ends we are; we would do a good deal for a thousand pounds apiece, eh, Bunny?'

'Anything,' I murmured.

The solicitor rapped his desk.

'I'll tell you what I want you to do. You can but refuse. It's illegal, but it's illegality in a good cause; that's the risk, and my client is prepared to pay for it. He will pay for the attempt, in case of failure; the money is as good as yours once you consent to run the risk. My client is Sir Bernard Debenham, of Broom Hall, Esher.'

'I know his son,' I remarked.

Raffles knew him too, but said nothing, and his eye drooped disapproval in my direction. Bennett Addenbrooke turned to me.

'Then,' said he, 'you have the privilege of knowing one of the most complete young blackguards about town, and the *fans et origo* of the whole trouble. As you know the son, you may know of the father too, at all events by reputation; and in that case I needn't tell you that he is a very peculiar man. He lives alone in a storehouse of treasures which no eyes but his ever behold. He is said to have the finest collection of pictures in the south of England, though nobody ever sees them to judge; pictures, fiddles, and furniture are his hobby, and he is undoubtedly very eccentric. Nor can one deny that there has been considerable eccentricity in his treatment of his son. For years Sir Bernard paid his debts, and the other day, without the slightest warning, not only refused to do so any more, but absolutely stopped the lad's allowance. Well, I'll tell you what has happened; but first of all you must know, or you may remember, that I appeared for young Debenham in a little scrape he got into a year or two ago. I got him off all right, and Sir Bernard paid me handsomely on the nail. And no more did I hear or see of either of them until one day last week.'

The lawyer drew his chair nearer ours, and leant forward with a hand on either knee.

'On Tuesday of last week I had a telegram from Sir Bernard; I was to go to him at once. I found him waiting for me in the drive; without a word he led me to the picture-gallery, which was locked and darkened, drew up a blind, and stood simply pointing to an empty picture-frame. It was a long time before I could get a word out of him. Then at last he told me that that frame had contained one of the rarest and most valuable pictures in England – in the world – an original Velasquez. I have checked this,' said the lawyer, 'and it seems literally true; the picture was a portrait of the Infanta Maria Teresa, said to be one of the artist's greatest works, second only to another portrait of one of the Popes of Rome – so they told me at the National Gallery, where they had its history by heart. They say there that the picture is practically priceless. And young Debenham has sold it for five thousand pounds!'

'The deuce he has,' said Raffles.

I inquired who had bought it.

'A Queensland legislator of the name of Craggs – the Hon. John Montagu Craggs, M.L.C., to give him his full title. Not that we knew anything about him on Tuesday last; we didn't even know for certain that young Debenham had stolen the picture. But he had gone down for money on the Monday evening, had been refused, and it was plain enough that he had helped himself in this way; he had threatened revenge, and this was it. Indeed, when I hunted him up in town on the Tuesday night, he confessed as much in the most brazen manner imaginable. But he wouldn't tell me who was the purchaser, and finding out took the rest of the week; but I did find out, and a nice time I've had of it ever since! Backwards and forwards between Esher and the Metropole, where the Queenslander is staying, sometimes twice a day; threats, offers, prayers, entreaties, not one of them a bit of good!'

'But,' said Raffles, 'surely it's a clear case? The sale was illegal; you can pay him back his money and force him to give the picture up.'

'Exactly; but not without an action and a public scandal, and that my client declines to face. He would rather lose even his picture than have the whole thing get into the papers; he has disowned his son, but he will not disgrace him; yet his picture he must have by hook or crook, and there's the rub! I am to get it back by fair means or foul. He gives me *carte blanche* in the matter, and, I verily believe, would throw in a blank cheque if asked. He offered one to the Queenslander, but Craggs simply tore it in two; the one old boy is as much a character as the other, and between the two of them I'm at my wits' end.'

'So you put that advertisement in the paper?' said Raffles, in the dry tones he had adopted throughout the interview.

'As a last resort, I did.'

'And you wish us to steal this picture?'

It was magnificently said; the lawyer flushed from his hair to his collar.

'I knew you were not the men!' he groaned. 'I never thought of men of your stamp! But it's not stealing,' he exclaimed heatedly; 'it's recovering stolen property. Besides, Sir Bernard will pay him his five thousand as soon as he has the picture;

and, you'll see, old Craggs will be just as loth to let it come out as Sir Bernard himself. No, no – it's an enterprise, an adventure, if you like – but not stealing.'

'You yourself mentioned the law,' murmured Raffles.

'And the risk,' I added.

'We pay for that,' he said once more.

'But not enough,' said Raffles, shaking his head. 'My good sir, consider what it means to us. You spoke of those clubs; we should not only get kicked out of them, but put in prison like common burglars! It's true we're hard up, but it simply isn't worth it at the price. Double your stakes, and I for one am your man.'

Addenbrooke wavered.

'Do you think you could bring it off?'

'We could try.'

'But you have no – '

'Experience? Well, hardly!'

'And you would really run the risk for four thousand pounds?'

Raffles looked at me. I nodded.

'We would,' said he, 'and blow the odds!'

'It's more than I can ask my client to pay,' said Addenbrooke, growing firm.

'Then it's more than you can expect us to risk.'

'You are in earnest?'

'Yes!'

'Say three thousand if you succeed!'

'Four is our figure, Mr Addenbrooke.'

'Then I think it should be nothing if you fail.'

'Double or quits?' cried Raffles. 'Well, that's sporting. Done!'

Addenbrooke opened his lips, half rose, then sat back in his chair, and looked long and shrewdly at Raffles – never once at me.

'I know your bowling,' said he reflectively. 'I go up to Lord's whenever I want an hour's real rest, and I've seen you bowl again and again – yes, and take the best wickets in England on a plumb pitch. I don't forget the last Gentlemen and Players;

I was there. You're up to every trick – everyone... I'm inclined to think that if anybody could bowl out this old Australian ... Damme, I believe you're my very man!'

The bargain was clenched at the Cafe Royal, where Bennett Addenbrooke insisted on playing host at an extravagant luncheon. I remember that he took his whack of champagne with the nervous freedom of a man at high pressure, and have no doubt I kept him in countenance by an equal indulgence; but Raffles, ever an exemplar in such matters, was more abstemious even than his wont, and very poor company to boot. I can see him now, his eyes in his plate—thinking, thinking. I can see the solicitor glancing from him to me in an apprehension of which I did my best to disabuse him by reassuring looks. At the close Raffles apologised for his preoccupation, called for an A.B.C. time-table, and announced his intention of catching the 3.2 to Esher.

'You must excuse me, Mr Addenbrooke,' said he, 'but I have my own idea, and for the moment I would much prefer to keep it to myself. It may end in fizzle, so I would rather not speak about it to either of you just yet. But speak to Sir Bernard I must, so will you write me one line to him on your card? Of course, if you wish you must come down with me and hear what I say; but I really don't see much point in it.'

And as usual Raffles had his way, though Bennett Addenbrooke showed some temper when he was gone, and I myself shared his annoyance to no small extent. I could only tell him that it was in the nature of Raffles to be self-willed and secretive, but that no man of my acquaintance had half his audacity and determination; that I for my part would trust him through and through and let him gang his own gait every time. More I dared not say, even to remove those chill misgivings with which I knew that the lawyer went his way.

That day I saw no more of Raffles, but a telegram reached me when I was dressing for dinner:

'Be in your rooms tomorrow from noon and keep rest of day clear. – Raffles.'

It had been sent off from Waterloo at 6.42.

So Raffles was back in town; at an earlier stage of our relations I should have hunted him up then and there, but now I knew better. His telegram meant that he had no desire for my society that night or the following forenoon; that when he wanted me I should see him soon enough.

And see him I did, towards one o'clock next day. I was watching for him from my window in Mount Street, when he drove up furiously in a cab, and jumped out without a word to the man. I met him next minute at the lift gates, and he fairly pushed me back into my rooms.

'Five minutes, Bunny!' he cried. 'Not a moment more.'

And he tore off his coat before flinging himself into the nearest chair.

'I'm fairly on the rush,' he panted; 'having the very devil of a time! Not a word till I've told you all I've done. I settled my plan of campaign yesterday at lunch. The first thing was to get in with this man Craggs; you can't break into a place like the Metropole, it's got to be done from the inside. Problem one, how to get at the fellow. Only one sort of pretext would do – it must be something to do with this blessed picture, so that I might see where he'd got it and all that. Well, I couldn't go and ask to see it out of curiosity, and I couldn't go as a second representative of the old chap, and it was thinking how I could go that made me such a bear at lunch. But I saw my way before we got up. If I could only lay hold of a copy of the picture I might ask leave to go and compare it with the original. So down I went to Esher to find out if there was a copy in existence, and was at Broom Hall for one hour and a half yesterday afternoon. There was no copy there, but they must exist, for Sir Bernard himself (there's "copy" there!) has allowed a couple to be made since the picture has been in his possession. He hunted up the painters' addresses, and the rest of the evening I spent in hunting up the painters themselves; but their work had been done on commission; one copy had gone out of the country, and I'm still on the track of the other.'

'Then you haven't seen Craggs yet?'

'Seen him and made friends with him, and if possible he's the funnier old cuss of the two; but you should study 'em both. I took the bull by the horns this morning, went in and lied like Ananias, and it was just as well I did – the old ruffian sails for Australia by tomorrow's boat. I told him a man wanted to sell me a copy of the celebrated Infanta Maria Teresa of Velasquez, that I'd been down to the supposed owner of the picture, only to find that he had just sold it to him. You should have seen his face when I told him that! He grinned all round his wicked old head. 'Did old Debenham admit the sale?' says he; and when I said he had he chuckled to himself for about five minutes. He was so pleased that he did just what I hoped he would do; he showed me the great picture – luckily it isn't by any means a large one – also the case he's got it in. It's an iron map-case in which he brought over the plans of his land in Brisbane; he wants to know who would suspect it of containing an Old Master too? But he's had it fitted with a new Chubb's lock, and I managed to take an interest in the key while he was gloating over the canvas. I had the wax in the palm of my hand, and I shall make my duplicate this afternoon.'

Raffles looked at his watch and jumped up saying he had given me a minute too much.

'By the way,' he added, 'you've got to dine with him at the Metropole tonight!'

'I?'

'Yes; don't look so scared. Both of us are invited – I swore you were dining with me. I accepted for us both; but I shan't be there.'

His clear eye was upon me, bright with meaning and with mischief. I implored him to tell me what his meaning was.

'You will dine in his private sitting-room,' said Raffles; 'it adjoins his bedroom. You must keep him sitting as long as possible, Bunny, and talking all the time!'

In a flash I saw his plan.

'You're going for the picture while we're at dinner?'

'I am.'

'If he hears you!'

'He shan't.'

'But if he does!'

And I fairly trembled at the thought.

'If he does,' said Raffles, 'there will be a collision, that's all. Revolvers would be out of place in the Metropole, but I shall certainly take a life-preserver.'

'But it's ghastly!' I cried. 'To sit and talk to an utter stranger and to know that you're at work in the next room!'

'Two thousand apiece,' said Raffles quietly.

'Upon my soul I believe I shall give it away!'

'Not you, Bunny. I know you better than you know yourself.'

He put on his coat and his hat.

'What time have I to be there?' I asked him, with a groan.

'Quarter to eight. There will be a telegram from me saying I can't turn up. He's a terror to talk, you'll have no difficulty to keep the ball rolling; but head him off his picture for all you're worth. If he offers to show it you, say you must go. He locked up the case elaborately this afternoon, and there's no earthly reason why he should unlock it again in this hemisphere.'

'Where shall I find you when I get away?'

'I shall be down at Esher. I hope to catch the 9.55.'

'But surely I can see you again this afternoon?' I cried in a ferment, for his hand was on the door. 'I'm not half coached up yet! I know I shall make a mess of it!'

'Not you,' he said again, 'but I shall if I waste any more time. I've got a deuce of a lot of rushing about to do yet. You won't find me at my rooms. Why not come down to Esher yourself by the last train? That's it – down you come with the latest news! I'll tell old Debenham to expect you: he shall give us both a bed. By Jove! he won't be able to do us too well if he's got his picture.'

'If!' I groaned as he nodded his adieu; and he left me limp with apprehension, sick with fear, in a perfectly pitiable condition of pure stage-fright.

For, after all, I had only to act my part; unless Raffles failed where he never did fail, unless Raffles the neat and noiseless was for once clumsy and inept, all I had to do was indeed to 'smile and smile and be a villain'. I practised that smile half the afternoon. I rehearsed putative parts in hypothetical conversations. I got up stories. I dipped in a book on Queensland at the club. And at last it was 7.45, and I was making my bow to a somewhat elderly man with a small bald head and a retreating brow.

'So you're Mr Raffles's friend?' said he, overhauling me rather rudely with his light small eyes. 'Seen anything of him? Expected him early to show me something, but he's never come.'

No more, evidently, had his telegram, and my troubles were beginning early. I said I had not seen Raffles since one o'clock, telling the truth with unction while I could; even as we spoke there came a knock at the door; it was the telegram at last, and, after reading it himself, the Queenslander handed it to me.

'Called out of town!' he grumbled. 'Sudden illness of near relative! What near relatives has he got?'

I knew of none, and for an instant I quailed before the perils of invention; then I replied that I had never met any of his people, and again felt fortified by my veracity.

'Thought you were bosom pals?' said he, with (as I imagined) a gleam of suspicion in his crafty little eyes.

'Only in town,' said I. 'I've never been to his place.'

'Well,' he growled, 'I suppose it can't be helped. Don't know why he couldn't come and have his dinner first. Like to see the death-bed I'd go to without my dinner; it's a full-skin billet, if you ask me. Well, must just dine without him, and he'll have to buy his pig in a poke after all. Mind touching that bell? Suppose you know what he came to see me about. Sorry I shan't see him again, for his own sake. I liked Raffles – took to him amazingly. He's a cynic. Like cynics. One myself. Rank bad form of his mother, or his aunt, and I hope she will kick the bucket.'

I connect these specimens of his conversation, though they were doubtless detached at the time, and interspersed with remarks of mine here and there. They filled the interval until dinner was served, and they gave me an impression of the man which his every subsequent utterance confirmed. It was an impression which did away with all remorse for my treacherous presence at his table. He was that terrible type, the Silly Cynic, his aim a caustic commentary on all things and all men, his achievement mere vulgar irreverence and unintelligent scorn. Ill-bred and ill-informed, he had (on his own showing) fluked into fortune on a rise in land; yet cunning he possessed, as well as malice, and he chuckled till he choked over the misfortunes of less astute speculators in the same boom. Even now I cannot feel much compunction for my behaviour to the Hon. J.M. Craggs, M.L.C.

But never shall I forget the private agonies of the situation, the listening to my host with one ear and for Raffles with the other! Once I heard him – though the rooms were not divided by the old-fashioned folding-doors, and though the door that did divide them was not only shut but richly curtained, I could have sworn I heard him once. I spilt my wine and laughed at the top of my voice at some coarse sally of my host's. And

I heard nothing more, though my ears were on the strain. But later, to my horror, when the waiter had finally withdrawn, Craggs himself sprang up and rushed to his bedroom without a word. I sat like stone till he returned.

'Thought I heard a door go,' he said. 'Must have been mistaken ... imagination ... gave me quite a turn. Raffles tell you of the priceless treasure I've got in there?'

It was the picture at last; up to this point I had kept him to Queensland and the making of his pile. I tried to get him back there now, but in vain. He was reminded of his great ill-gotten possession. I said that Raffles had just mentioned it, and that set him off. With the confidential garrulity of a man who has dined too well, he plunged into his darling topic, and I looked past him at the clock. It was only a quarter to ten.

In common decency I could not go yet. So there I sat (we were still at port) and learnt what had originally fired my host's ambition to possess what he was pleased to call a 'real, genuine, twin-screw, double-funnelled, copper-bottomed Old Master'; it was to 'go one better' than some rival legislator of pictorial proclivities. But even an epitome of his monologue would be so much weariness; suffice it that it ended inevitably in the invitation I had dreaded all the evening.

'But you must see it. Next room. This way.'

'Isn't it packed up?' I inquired hastily.

'Lock and key. That's all.'

'Pray don't trouble,' I urged.

'Trouble be hanged!' said he. 'Come along.'

And all at once I saw that to resist him further would be to heap suspicion upon myself against the moment of impending discovery. I therefore followed him into his bedroom without further protest, and suffered him first to show me the iron map-case which stood in one corner; he took a crafty pride in this receptacle, and I thought he would never cease descanting on its innocent appearance and its Chubb's lock. It seemed an interminable age before the key was in the latter. Then the ward clicked, and my pulse stood still.

'By Jove!' I cried the next instant.

The canvas was in its place among the maps!

'Thought it would knock you,' said Craggs, drawing it out and unfolding it for my benefit. 'Grand thing, ain't it? Wouldn't think it had been painted two hundred and thirty years? It has, though, my word! Old Johnson's face will be a treat when he sees it; won't go bragging about his pictures much more. Why, this one's worth all the pictures in Colony o' Queensland put together. Worth fifty thousand pounds, my boy – and I got it for five!'

He dug me in the ribs, and seemed in the mood for further confidences. My appearance checked him, and he rubbed his hands.

'If you take it like that,' he chuckled, 'how will old Johnson take it? Go out and hang himself to his own picture-rods, I hope!'

Heaven knows what I contrived to say at last. Struck speechless first by my relief, I continued silent from a very different cause. A new tangle of emotions tied my tongue. Raffles had failed – could I not succeed? Was it too late? Was there no way?

'So long,' he said, taking a last look at the canvas before he rolled it up – 'so long till we get to Brisbane.'

The flutter I was in as he closed the case!

'For the last time,' he went on, as his keys jingled back into his pocket. 'It goes straight into the strong-room on board.'

For the last time! If I could but send him out to Australia with only its legitimate contents in his precious map-case! If I could but succeed where Raffles had failed!

We returned to the other room. I have no notion how long he talked, or what about. Whisky and soda-water became the order of the hour. I scarcely touched it, but he drank copiously, and before eleven I left him incoherent. And the last train for Esher was the 11.50 out of Waterloo.

I took a cab to my rooms. I was back at the hotel in thirteen minutes. I walked upstairs. The corridor was empty; I stood an instant on the sitting-room threshold, heard a snore within, and admitted myself softly with my gentleman's own key, which it had been a very simple matter to take away with me.

Craggs never moved; he was stretched on the sofa fast asleep. But not fast enough for me. I saturated my handkerchief with the chloroform I had brought, and I laid it gently over his mouth. Two or three stertorous breaths, and the man was a log.

I removed the handkerchief; I extracted the keys from his pocket. In less than five minutes I put them back, after winding the picture about my body beneath my Inverness cape. I took some whisky and soda-water before I went.

The train was easily caught – so easily that I trembled for ten minutes in my first-class smoking carriage, in terror of every footstep on the platform – in unreasonable terror till the end. Then at last I sat back and lit a cigarette, and the lights of Waterloo reeled out behind.

Some men were returning from the theatre. I can recall their conversation even now. They were disappointed with the piece they had seen. It was one of the later Savoy operas, and they spoke wistfully of the days of *Pinafore* and *Patience*. One of them hummed a stave, and there was an argument as to whether the air was out of *Patience* or the *Mikado*. They all got out at Surbiton, and I was alone with my triumph for a few intoxicating minutes. To think that I had succeeded where Raffles had failed! Of all our adventures this was the first in which I had played a commanding part; and, of them all, this was infinitely the least discreditable. It left me without a conscientious qualm; I had but robbed a robber, when all was said. And I had done it myself, single-handed – *ipse egomet!*

I pictured Raffles, his surprise, his delight. He would think a little more of me in future. And that future, it should be different. We had two thousand pounds apiece – surely enough to start afresh as honest men – and all through me.

In a glow I sprang out at Esher, and took the one belated cab that was waiting under the bridge. In a perfect fever I beheld Broom Hall, with the lower storey still lit up, and saw the front door open as I climbed the steps.

'Thought it was you,' said Raffles cheerily. 'It's all right. There's a bed for you. Sir Bernard's sitting up to shake your hand.'

His good spirits disappointed me. But I knew the man; he was one of those who wear their brightest smile in the blackest hour. I knew him too well by this time to be deceived.

'I've got it!' I cried in his ear. 'I've got it!'

'Got what?' he asked, stepping back.

'The picture?'

'What?'

'The picture. He showed it to me. You had to go without it; I saw that. So I determined to have it. And here it is.'

'Let's see,' said Raffles grimly.

I threw off my cape and unwound the canvas from about my body. While I was doing so an untidy old gentleman made his appearance in the hall, and stood looking on with raised eyebrows.

'Looks pretty fresh for an Old Master, doesn't she?' said Raffles.

His tone was strange. I could only suppose that he was jealous of my success.

'So Craggs said. I hardly looked at it myself.'

'Well, look now – look closely. By Jove, I must have faked her better than I thought!'

'It's a copy!' I cried.

'It's the copy,' he answered. 'It's the copy I've been tearing all over the country to procure. It's the copy I faked back and front, so that, on your own showing, it imposed upon Craggs, and might have made him happy for life. And you go and rob him of that!'

I could not speak.

'How did you manage it?' inquired Sir Bernard Debenham.

'Have you killed him?' asked Raffles sardonically.

I did not look at him; I turned to Sir Bernard Debenham, and to him I told my story, hoarsely, excitedly, for it was all that I could do to keep from breaking down. But as I spoke I became calmer, and I finished in mere bitterness, with the remark that another time Raffles might tell me what he meant to do.

'Another time!' he cried instantly. 'My dear Bunny, you speak as though we were going to turn burglars for a living!'

'I trust you won't,' said Sir Bernard smiling, 'for you are certainly two very daring young men. Let us hope our friend from Queensland will do as he said, and not open his map-case till he gets back there. He will find my cheque awaiting him, and I shall be very much surprised if he troubles any of us again.'

Raffles and I did not speak till I was in the room which had been prepared for me. Nor was I anxious to do so then. But he followed me and took my hand.

'Bunny,' said he, 'don't you be hard on a fellow! I was in the deuce of a hurry, and didn't know that I should get what I wanted in time, and that's a fact. But it serves me right that you should have gone and undone one of the best things I ever did. As for your handiwork, old chap, you won't mind my saying that I didn't think you had it in you. In future – '

'Don't talk to me about the future!' I cried. 'I hate the whole thing! I'm going to chuck it up!'

'So am I,' said Raffles, 'when I've made my pile.'

7

THE RETURN MATCH

I had turned into Piccadilly, one thick evening in the following November, when my guilty heart stood still at the sudden grip of a hand upon my arm. I thought – I was always thinking – that my inevitable hour was come at last. It was only Raffles, however, who stood smiling at me through the fog.

'Well met!' said he; 'I've been looking for you at the club.'

'I was just on my way there,' I returned, with an attempt to hide my tremors. It was an ineffectual attempt, as I saw from his broader smile, and by the indulgent shake of his head.

'Come up to my place instead,' said he. 'I've something amusing to tell you.'

I made excuses, for his tone foretold the kind of amusement, and it was a kind against which I had successfully set my face for months. I have stated before, however, and I can but reiterate, that to me, at all events, there was never anybody in the world so irresistible as Raffles when his mind was made up. That we had both been independent of crime since our little service to Sir Bernard Debenham – that there had been no occasion for that masterful mind to be made up in any such direction for many a day – was the undeniable basis of a longer spell of honesty than I had hitherto enjoyed during the term of our mutual intimacy. Be sure I would deny it if I could; the very thing I am to tell you would discredit such a boast. I made my excuses, as I have said. But his arm slid through mine, with his little laugh of light-hearted mastery. And even while I argued we were on his staircase in the Albany.

His fire had fallen low. He poked and replenished it after turning on the lights. As for me, I stood by sullenly in my overcoat until he dragged it off my back.

'What a chap you are!' said Raffles playfully. 'One would really think I had proposed to crack another crib, this blessed night! Well, it isn't that, Bunny; so get into that chair, and take one of these Sullivans and sit tight.'

He held the match to my cigarette; he brought me a whisky and soda. Then he went out in the lobby, and, just as I was beginning to feel happy, I heard a bolt shot home. It cost me an effort to remain in that chair; next moment he was straddling another and gloating over my discomfiture across his folded arms.

'You remember Milchester, Bunny, old boy?'

His tone was as bland as mine was grim when I answered that I did.

'We had a little match there that wasn't down on the card. Gentlemen and Players, if you recollect?'

'I don't forget it.'

'Seeing that you never got an innings, so to speak, I thought you might. Well, the Gentlemen scored pretty freely, but the Players were all caught – '

'Poor devils!'

'Don't be too sure. You remember the fellow we saw in the inn? The florid, overdressed chap who I told you was one of the cleverest thieves in town?'

'I remember him. Crawshay his name turned out to be.'

'Well, it was certainly the name he was convicted under, so Crawshay let it be. You needn't waste any pity on him, old chap; he escaped from Dartmoor yesterday afternoon.'

'Well done!'

Raffles smiled, but his eyebrows had gone up and his shoulders followed suit.

'You are perfectly right; it was very well done indeed. I wonder you didn't see it in the paper. In a dense fog on the moor yesterday good old Crawshay made a bolt for it, and got away without a scratch under heavy fire. All honour to him, I agree; a fellow with that much grit deserves his liberty. But Crawshay has a good deal more. They hunted him all night long; couldn't find him for nuts; and that was all you missed in the morning papers.'

He unfolded a *Pall Mall*, which he had brought in with him.

'But listen to this; here's an account of the escape; with just the addition which puts the thing on a higher level. "The fugitive has been traced to Totnes, where he appears to have committed a peculiarly daring outrage in the early hours of this morning. He is reported to have entered the lodgings of the Rev A.H. Ellingworth, curate of the parish, who missed his clothes on rising at the usual hour; later in the morning those of the convict were discovered neatly folded at the bottom of a drawer. Meanwhile Crawshay had made good his second escape, though it is believed that so distinctive a guise will lead to his recapture during the day." What do you think of that, Bunny?'

'He is certainly a sportsman,' said I, reaching for the paper.

'He's more,' said Raffles; 'he's an artist, and I envy him. The curate, of all men! Beautiful – beautiful! But that's not all. I saw just now on the board at the club that there's been an outrage on the line near Dawlish. Parson found insensible in the six-foot way. Our friend again. The telegram doesn't say so, but it's obvious; he's simply knocked some other fellow out, changed clothes again, and come on gaily to town. Isn't it great? I do believe it's the best thing of the kind that's ever been done!'

'But why should he come to town?'

In an instant the enthusiasm faded from Raffles's face: clearly I had reminded him of some prime anxiety, forgotten in his impersonal joy over the exploit of a fellow criminal. He looked over his shoulder towards the lobby before replying.

'I believe,' said he, 'that the beggar's on my tracks!'

And as he spoke he was himself again – quietly amused – cynically unperturbed – characteristically enjoying the situation and my surprise.

'But look here, what do you mean?' said I. 'What does Crawshay know about you?'

'Not much; but he suspects.'

'Why should he?'

'Because, in his way, he's very nearly as good a man as I am; because, my dear Bunny, with eyes in his head and brains behind them, he couldn't help suspecting. He saw me once in town with old Baird. He must have seen me that day in the pub, on the way to Milchester, as well as afterwards on the cricket field. As a matter of fact, I know he did, for he wrote and told me so before his trial.'

'He wrote to you! And you never told me!'

The old shrug answered the old grievance.

'What was the good, my dear fellow? It would only have worried you.'

'Well, what did he say?'

'That he was sorry he had been run in before getting back to town, as he had proposed doing himself the honour of paying me a call; however, he trusted it was only a pleasure deferred, and he begged me not to go and get lagged myself before he came out. Of course he knew the Melrose necklace was gone, though he hadn't got it; and he said that the man who could take that and leave the rest was a man after his own heart. And so on, with certain little proposals for the far future, which I fear may be the very near future indeed! I'm only surprised he hasn't turned up yet.'

He looked again towards the lobby, which he had left in darkness, with the inner door shut as carefully as the outer one. I asked him what he meant to do.

'Let him knock – if he gets so far. The porter is to say I'm out of town; it will be true, too, in another hour or so.'

'You're going off tonight?'

'By the 7.15 from Liverpool Street. I don't say much about my people, Bunny, but I have the best of sisters married to a country parson in the eastern counties. They always make me welcome, and let me read the lessons for the sake of getting me to church. I'm sorry you won't be there to hear me on Sunday, Bunny. I've figured out some of my best schemes in that parish, and I know of no better port in a storm. But I must pack. I thought I'd just let you know where I was going, and why, in case you cared to follow my example.'

He flung the stump of his cigarette into the fire, stretched himself as he rose, and remained so long in the inelegant attitude that my eyes mounted from his body to his face; a second later they had followed his eyes across the room, and I also was on my legs. On the threshold of the folding doors that divided bedroom and sitting-room, a well-built man stood in ill-fitting broadcloth, and bowed to us until his bullet head presented an unbroken disc of short red hair.

Brief as was my survey of this astounding apparition, the interval was long enough for Raffles to recover his composure; his hands were in his pockets, and a smile upon his face, when my eyes flew back to him.

'Let me introduce you, Bunny,' said he, 'to our distinguished colleague, Mr Reginald Crawshay.'

The bullet head bobbed up, and there was a wrinkled brow above the coarse, shaven face, crimson, also I remember, from the grip of a collar several sizes too small. But I noted nothing consciously at the time. I had jumped to my own conclusion, and I turned on Raffles with an oath.

'It's a trick!' I cried. 'It's another of your cursed tricks. You got him here, and then you got me. You want me to join you, I suppose? I'll see you damned!'

So cold was the stare which met this outburst that I became ashamed of my words while they were yet upon my lips.

'Really, Bunny!' said Raffles, and turned his shoulder with a shrug.

'Lord love yer,' cried Crawshay, ''e knew nothin'. 'E didn't expect me; 'e's all right. And you're the cool canary, you are,' he went on to Raffles. 'I knoo you were, but, do me proud, you're one after my own kidney.' And he thrust out a shaggy hand.

'After that,' said Raffles, taking it, 'what am I to say? But you must have heard my opinion of you. I am proud to make your acquaintance. How the deuce did you get in?'

'Never you mind,' said Crawshay, loosening his collar; 'let's talk about how I'm to get out. Lord love yer, but that's better!' There was a livid ring round his bull-neck, that he fingered tenderly. 'Didn't know how much longer I might have to play the gent,' he explained, 'didn't know who you'd bring in.'

'Drink whisky and soda?' inquired Raffles, when the convict was in the chair from which I had leapt.

'No, I drink it neat,' replied Crawshay, 'but I talk business first. You don't get over me like that, Lor' love yer!'

'Well, then, what can I do for you?'

'You know without me tellin' you.'

'Give it a name.'

'Clean heels, then; that's what I want to show, and I leaves the way to you. We're brothers in arms, though I ain't armed this time. It ain't necessary. You've too much sense. But brothers we are, and you'll see a brother through. Let's put it at that. You'll see me through in your own way. I leaves it all to you.'

His tone was rich with conciliation and concession; he bent over and tore a pair of button boots from his bare feet, which he stretched towards the fire, painfully uncurling his toes.

'I hope you take a larger size than them,' said he. 'I'd have had a see if you'd given me time. I wasn't in long afore you.'

'And you won't tell me how you got in?'

'Wot's the use? I can't teach you nothin'. Besides I want out. I want out of London, an' England, an' bloomin' Europe too. That's all I want of you, mister. I don't arst how you go on the job. You know w'ere I come from, 'cos I heard you say; you know w'ere I want to 'ead for, 'cos I've just told yer; the details I leaves entirely to you.'

'Well,' said Raffles, 'we must see what can be done.'

'We must,' said Mr Crawshay, and leaned back comfortably, and began twirling his stubby thumbs.

Raffles turned to me with a twinkle in his eye; but his forehead was scored with thought, and resolve mingled with resignation in the lines of his mouth. And he spoke exactly as though he and I were alone in the room.

'You seize the situation, Bunny? If our friend here is "copped", to speak his language, he means to "blow the gaff' on you and me. He is considerate enough not to say so in so many words, but it's plain enough, and natural enough for that matter. I would do the same in his place. We had the bulge before; he has it now; it's perfectly fair. We must take on this job; we aren't in a position to refuse it: even if we were, I should take it on. Our friend is a great sportsman; he has got clear away from Dartmoor; it would be a thousand pities to let him go back. Nor shall he; not if I can think of a way of getting him abroad.'

'Any way you like,' murmured Crawshay, with his eyes shut. 'I leaves the 'ole thing to you.'

'But you'll have to wake up and tell us things.'

'All right, mister; but I'm fair on the rocks for a sleep!'

And he stood up blinking.

'Think you were traced to town?'

'Must have been.'

'And here?'

'Not in this fog – not with any luck.'

Raffles went into the bedroom, lit the gas there, and returned next minute.

'So you got in by the window?'

'That's about it.'

'It was devilish smart of you to know which one; it beats me how you brought it off in daylight, fog or no fog! But let that pass. Don't you think you were seen?'

'I don't think it, sir.'

'Well, let's hope you are right. I shall reconnoitre and soon find out. And you'd better come too, Bunny, and have something to eat and talk it over.'

As Raffles looked at me, I looked at Crawshay, anticipating trouble; and trouble brewed in his blank, fierce face, in the glitter of his startled eyes, in the sudden closing of his fists.

'And what's to become of me?' he cried out with an oath.

'You wait here.'

'No, you don't,' he roared, and at a bound had his back to the door. 'You don't get round me like that, you cuckoos!'

Raffles turned to me with a twitch of the shoulders.

'That's the worst of these professors,' said he; 'they never will use their heads. They see the pegs, and they mean to hit 'em; but that's all they do see and mean, and they think we're the same. No wonder we licked them last time!'

'Don't talk through yer neck,' snarled the convict. 'Talk out straight, curse you!'

'Right,' said Raffles. 'I'll talk as straight as you like. You say you put yourself in my hands – you leave it all to me – yet you don't trust me an inch! I know what's to happen if I fail. I accept the risk. I take this thing on. Yet you think I'm going straight out to give you away and make you give me away in turn. You're a fool, Mr Crawshay, though you have broken Dartmoor; you've got to listen to a better man, and obey him. I see you through in my own way, or not at all. I come and go as I like, and with whom I like, without your interference; you stay here and lie just as low as you know how, be as wise as your word, and leave the whole thing to me. If you won't – if you're fool enough not to trust me – there's the door. Go out and say what you like, and be damned to you!'

Crawshay slapped his thigh.

'That's talking!' said he. 'Lord love yer, I know where I am when you talk like that. I'll trust yer. I know a man when he get's his tongue between his teeth; you're all right. I don't say so much about this other gent, though I saw him along with you on the job that time in the provinces; but if he's a pal of yours, Mr Raffles, he'll be all right too. I only hope you gents ain't too stony – '

And he touched his pockets with a rueful face.

'I only went for their togs,' said he. 'You never struck two such stony-broke cusses in yer life.'

'That's all right,' said Raffles. 'We'll see you through properly. Leave it to us, and you sit tight.'

'Rightum!' said Crawshay. 'And I'll have a sleep time you're gone. But no sperrits – no, thank'ee – not yet! Once let me loose on lush, and, Lord love yer, I'm a gone coon!'

Raffles got his overcoat, a long, light driving coat, I remember, and even as he put it on our fugitive was dozing in the chair; we left him murmuring incoherently, with the lights out, and his bare feet toasting.

'Not such a bad chap, that professor,' said Raffles on the stairs; 'a real genius in his way, too, though his methods are a little elementary for my taste. But technique isn't everything; to get out of Dartmoor and into the Albany in the same twenty-four hours is a whole that justifies its parts. Good Lord!'

We had passed a man in the foggy courtyard, and Raffles had nipped my arm.

'Who was it?'

'The last man we want to see! I hope to heaven he didn't hear me!'

'But who is it, Raffles?'

'Our old friend Mackenzie, from the Yard!'

I stood still with horror.

'Do you think he's on Crawshay's track?'

'I don't know. I'll find out.'

And before I could remonstrate he had wheeled me round; when I found my voice he merely laughed, and whispered that the bold course was the safe one every time.

'But it's madness – '

'Not it. Shut up! Is that you, Mr Mackenzie?'

The detective turned about and scrutinised us keenly; and through the gaslit mist I noticed that his hair was grizzled at the temples, and his face still cadaverous, from the wound that had nearly been his death.

'Ye have the advantage o' me, sirs,' said he.

'I hope you're fit again,' said my companion. 'My name is Raffles, and we met at Milchester last year.'

'Is that a fact?' cried the Scotsman, with quite a start. 'Yes, now I remember your face, and yours too, sir. Ay, yon was a bad business, but it ended vera well, an' that's the main thing.'

His native caution had returned to him. Raffles pinched my arm.

'Yes, it ended splendidly, but for you,' said he. 'But what about this escape of the leader of the gang, that fellow Crawshay? What do you think of that, eh?'

'I havena the parteeculars,' replied the Scot.

'Good!' cried Raffles. 'I was only afraid you might be on his tracks once more!'

Mackenzie shook his head with a dry smile, and wished us good evening, as an invisible window was thrown up and a whistle blown softly through the fog.

'We must see this out,' whispered Raffles. 'Nothing more natural than a little curiosity on our part. After him, quick!'

And he followed the detective into another entrance on the same side as that from which we had emerged, the left-hand side on one's way to Piccadilly; quite openly we followed him, and at the foot of the stairs met one of the porters of the place. Raffles asked him what was wrong.

'Nothing, sir,' said the fellow glibly.

'Rot!' said Raffles. 'That was Mackenzie, the detective. I've just been speaking to him. What's he here for? Come on, my good fellow; we won't give you away, if you've instructions not to tell.'

The man looked quaintly wistful, the temptation of an audience hot upon him; a door shut upstairs, and he fell.

'It's like this,' he whispered. 'This afternoon a gen'leman comes arfter rooms, and I sent him to the orfice; one of the clurks, 'e goes round with 'im an' shows 'im the empties, an' the gen'leman's partic'ly struck on the set the coppers is up in now. So he sends the clurk to fetch the manager, as there was one or two things he wished to speak about; an' when they come back, blowed if the gent isn't gone! Beg your pardon, sir, but he's clean disappeared off the face of the premises!' And the porter looked at us with shining eyes.

'Well?' said Raffles.

'Well, sir, they looked about, an' at larst they give him up for a bad job; thought he'd changed his mind an' didn't want to tip the clurk; so they shut up the place and come away. An' that's all till about 'alf an hour ago, when I takes the manager his extry-speshul *Star*; in about ten minutes he comes running out with a note an' sends me with it to Scotland Yard in a hansom. An' that's all I know, sir – straight. The coppers is up there now, and the tec. and the manager, and they think their gent is about the place somewhere still. Least, I reckon that's their idea; but who he is, or what they want him for, I dunno,'

'Jolly interesting!' said Raffles. 'I'm going up to inquire. Come on, Bunny; there should be some fun.'

'Beg your pardon, Mr Raffles, but you won't say nothing about me?'

'Not I; you're a good fellow. I won't forget it if this leads to sport. Sport!' he whispered, as we reached the landing. 'It looks like precious poor sport for you and me, Bunny!'

'What are you going to do?'

'I don't know. There's no time to think. This, to start with.' And he thundered on the shut door; a policeman opened it. Raffles strode past him with the air of a chief commissioner, and I followed before the man had recovered from his astonishment. The bare boards rang under us; in the bedroom we found a knot of officers stooping over the window-ledge with a constable's lantern. Mackenzie was the first to stand upright, and he greeted us with a glare.

'May I ask what you gentlemen want?' said he.

'We want to lend a hand,' said Raffles briskly. 'We lent one once before, and it was my friend here who took over from you and the fellow who split on all the rest and held him tight. Surely that entitles him, at all events, to see any fun that's going? As for myself, well it's true I only helped to carry you to the house; but for old acquaintance I do hope, my dear Mr Mackenzie, that you will permit us to share such sport as there may be. I myself can only stop a few minutes, in any case.'

'Then ye'll not see much,' growled the detective, 'for he's not up here. Constable, go and stand at the foot o' the stairs, and let no other body come up on any conseederation; these gentlemen may be able to help us after all.'

'That's kind of you, Mackenzie!' cried Raffles warmly. 'But what is it all? I questioned a porter I met coming down, but could get nothing out of him, except that somebody had been to see these rooms and not since been seen himself.'

'He's a man we want,' said Mackenzie. 'He's concealed himself somewhere about these premises, or I'm vera much mistaken. D'ye reside in the Albany, Mr Raffles?'

'I do.'

'Will your rooms be near these?'

'On the next staircase but one.'

'Ye'll just have left them?'

'Just.'

'Been in all the afternoon, likely?'

'Not all.'

'Then I may have to search your rooms, sir. I am prepared to search every room in the Albany! Our man seems to have gone for the leads; but unless he's left more marks outside than in, or we find him up there, I shall have the entire building to ransack.'

'I will leave you my key,' said Raffles at once. 'I am dining out, but I'll leave it with the officer down below.'

I caught my breath in mute amazement. What was the meaning of this insane promise? It was wilful, gratuitous, suicidal; it made me catch at his sleeve in open horror and disgust; but, with a word of thanks, Mackenzie had returned to his window-sill, and we sauntered unwatched through the folding doors in the adjoining room. Here the window looked down into the courtyard; it was still open; and as we gazed out in apparent idleness, Raffles reassured me.

'It's all right, Bunny; you do what I tell you and leave the rest to me. It's a tight corner, but I don't despair. What you've got to do is to stick to these chaps, especially if they search my rooms; they mustn't poke about more than necessary, and they won't if you're there.'

'But where will you be? You're never going to leave me to be landed alone?'

'If I do, it will be to turn up trumps at the right moment. Besides, there are such things as windows, and Crawshay's the man to take his risks. You must trust me, Bunny; you've known me long enough.'

'And you're going now?'

'There's no time to lose. Stick to them, old chap, don't let them suspect you, whatever else you do.' His hand lay an instant on my shoulder; then he left me at the window, and recrossed the room.

'I've got to go now,' I heard him say; 'but my friend will stay and see this through, and I'll leave the light on in my rooms – and my key with the constable downstairs. Good luck, Mackenzie; only wish I could stay.'

'Good-bye, sir,' came in a preoccupied voice, 'and many thanks.'

Mackenzie was still busy at his window, and I remained at mine, a prey to mingled fear and wrath, for all my knowledge of Raffles and of his infinite resource. By this time I felt that I knew more or less what he would do in any given emergency; at least I could conjecture a characteristic course of equal cunning and audacity. He would return to his rooms, put Crawshay on his guard, and – stow him away? No – there were such things as windows. Then why was Raffles going to desert us all? I thought of many things – lastly of a cab. These bedroom windows looked into a narrow side-street; they were not very high; from them a man might drop on to the roof of a cab – even as it passed – and be driven away – even under the noses of the police! I pictured Raffles driving that cab, unrecognisable in the foggy night; the vision came to me as he passed under the window, tucking up the collar of his great driving-coat on the way to his rooms; it was still with me when he passed again on his way back, and stopped to hand the constable his key.

'We're on his track,' said a voice behind me. 'He's got up on the leads, sure enough, though how he managed it from yon window is a myst'ry to me. We're going to lock up here and try what like it is from the attics. So you'd better come with us if you've a mind.'

The top floor at the Albany, as elsewhere, is devoted to the servants – a congeries of little kitchens and cubicles, used by many as lumber-rooms – by Raffles among the many. The annexe in this case was, of course, empty as the rooms below; and that was lucky, for we filled it, what with the manager, who now joined us, and another tenant whom he brought with him to Mackenzie's undisguised annoyance.

'Better let in all Piccadilly at a crown a head,' said he. 'Here, my man, out you go on the roof to make one less, and have your truncheon handy.'

We crowded to the little window, which Mackenzie took care to fill; and a minute yielded no sound but the crunch and slither of constabulary boots upon sooty slates. Then came a shout.

'What now?' cried Mackenzie.

'A rope,' we heard, 'hanging from the spout by a hook!'

'Sirs,' purred Mackenzie, 'yon's how he got up from below! He would do it with one o' they telescope sticks, an' I never thocht o't! How long a rope, my lad?'

'Quite short. I've got it.'

'Did it hang over a window? Ask him that!' cried the manager. 'He can see by leaning over the parapet.'

The question was repeated by Mackenzie; a pause, then, 'Yes, it did.'

'Ask him how many windows along!' shouted the manager in high excitement.

'Six, he says,' said Mackenzie the next minute; and he drew in his head and shoulders. 'I should just like to see those rooms, six windows along.'

'Mr Raffles's,' announced the manager after a mental calculation.

'Is that a fact?' cried Mackenzie. "Then we shall have no difficulty at all. He's left me his key down below.'

The words had a dry, speculative intonation, which even then I found time to dislike; it was as though the coincidence had already struck the Scotsman as something more.

'Where is Mr Raffles?' asked the manager, as we all filed downstairs.

'He's gone out to his dinner,' said Mackenzie.

'Are you sure?'

'I saw him go,' said I. My heart was beating horribly. I would not trust myself to speak again. But I wormed my way to a front place in the little procession, and was, in fact, the second man to cross the threshold that had been the Rubicon of my life. As I did so I uttered a cry of pain, for Mackenzie had trod back heavily on my toes; in another second I saw the reason, and saw it with another and a louder cry.

A man was lying at full length before the fire, on his back, with a little wound in the white forehead, and the blood draining into his eyes. And the man was Raffles himself!

'Suicide,' said Mackenzie calmly. 'No – here's the poker – looks more like murder.' He went on his knees and shook his head quite cheerfully. 'An' it's not even murder,' said he, with a shade of disgust in his matter-of-fact voice; 'yon's no more than a flesh- wound, and I have my doubts whether it felled him; but, sirs, he just stinks o' chloryform!'

He got up and fixed his keen grey eyes upon me; my own were full of tears, but they faced him unashamed.

'I understood ye to say ye saw him go out?' said he sternly.

'I saw that long driving-coat; of course I thought he was inside it.'

'And I could ha' sworn it was the same gent when he gave me the key!'

It was the disconsolate voice of the constable in the background; on him turned Mackenzie, white to the lips.

'You'd think anything, some of you damned policemen,' said he. 'What's your number, you rotter? P 34? You'll be hearing more of this, Mr P 34! If that gentleman were dead – instead of coming to himself while I'm talking – do you know what you'd be? Guilty of his manslaughter, you stuck pig in buttons! Do you know who you've let slip, butter-fingers? Crawshay – no less – him that broke Dartmoor yesterday. By the God that made ye, P 34, if I lose him I'll hound ye from the forrce!'

Working face – shaking fist – a calm man on fire. It was a new side of Mackenzie, and one to mark and to digest. Next moment he had flounced from our midst.

'Difficult thing to break your own head,' said Raffles later; 'infinitely easier to cut your own throat. Chloroform's another matter; when you've used it on others, you know the dose to a nicety. So you thought I was really gone? Poor old Bunny! But I hope Mackenzie saw your face?'

'He did,' said I. I would not tell him all Mackenzie must have seen, however.

'That's all right. I wouldn't have had him miss it for worlds; and you mustn't think me a brute, old boy, for I fear that man; and, you know, we sink or swim together.'

'And now we sink or swim with Crawshay too,' said I dolefully.

'Not we!' cried Raffles with conviction. 'Old Crawshay's a true sportsman, and he'll do by us as we've done by him; besides, this makes us quits; and I don't think, Bunny, that we'll take on the professors again!'

8

THE GIFT OF THE EMPEROR

I

When the King of the Cannibal Islands made faces at Queen Victoria, and a European monarch set the cables tingling with his compliments on the exploit, the indignation in England was not less than the surprise, for the thing was not so common as it has since become. But when it transpired that a gift of peculiar significance was to follow the congratulations, to give them weight, the inference prevailed that the white potentate and the black had taken simultaneous leave of their fourteen senses. For the gift was a pearl of price unparalleled, picked aforetime by British cutlasses from a Polynesian setting, and presented by British royalty to the sovereign who seized this opportunity of restoring it to its original possessor.

The incident would have been a godsend to the Press a few weeks later. Even in June there were leaders, letters, large headlines, leaded type; the *Daily Chronicle* devoted half its literary page to a charming drawing of the island capital which the new *Pall Mall*, in a leading article headed by a pun, advised the Government to blow to flinders. I was myself driving a poor but not dishonest quill at the time, and the topic of the hour goaded me into satiric verse which obtained a better place than anything I had yet turned out. I had let my flat in town, and taken inexpensive quarters at Thames Ditton, on a plea of a disinterested passion for the river.

'First-rate, old boy,' said Raffles (who must needs come and see me there), lying back in the boat while I sculled and steered. 'I suppose they pay you pretty well for these, eh?'

'Not a penny.'

'Nonsense, Bunny! I thought they paid so well? Give them time, and you'll get your cheque.'

'Oh, no, I shan't,' said I gloomily. 'I've got to be content with the honour of getting in; the editor wrote to say so, in so many words,' I added. But I gave the gentleman his distinguished name.

'You don't mean to say you've written for payment already?'

No; it was the last thing I had intended to admit. But I had done it. The murder was out; there was no sense in further concealment. I had written for my money because I really needed it; if he must know, I was cursedly hard up. Raffles nodded as though he knew already. I warmed to my woes. It was no easy matter to keep your end up as a raw freelance of letters; for my part, I was afraid I wrote neither well enough nor ill enough for success. I suffered from a persistent ineffectual feeling after style. Verse I could manage; but it did not pay. To personal paragraphs or to baser journalism I could not and I would not stoop.

Raffles nodded again, this time with a smile that stayed in his eyes as he leant back watching me. I knew that he was thinking of other things I had stooped to, and I thought I knew what he was going to say. He had said it before so often; he was sure to say it again. I had my answer ready, but evidently he was tired of asking the same question. His lids fell, he took up the paper he had dropped, and I sculled the length of the old red wall of Hampton Court before he spoke again.

'And they gave you nothing for these! My dear Bunny, they're capital, not only *qua* verses, but for crystallising your subject and putting it in a nutshell. Certainly you've taught me more about it than I knew before. But is it really worth fifty thousand pounds – a single pearl?'

'A hundred, I believe; but that wouldn't scan.

'A hundred thousand pounds!' said Raffles, with his eyes shut. And again I made certain what was coming, but again I was mistaken. 'If it's worth all that,' he cried at last, 'there would be no getting rid of it at all; it's not like a diamond that you can subdivide. But I beg your pardon, Bunny. I was forgetting!'

And we said no more about the emperor's gift; for pride thrives on an empty pocket, and no privation would have drawn from me the proposal which I had expected Raffles to make. My expectation had been half a hope, though I only knew it now. But neither did we touch again on what Raffles professed to have forgotten – my 'apostasy', 'my lapse into virtue', as he had been pleased to call it. We were both a little silent, a little constrained, each preoccupied with his own thoughts. It was months since we had met, and, as I saw him off towards eleven o'clock that Sunday night, I fancied it was for more months that we were saying good-bye.

But as we waited for the train I saw those clear eyes peering at me under the station lamps, and when I met their glance Raffles shook his head.

'You don't look well on it, Bunny,' said he. 'I never did believe in this Thames Valley. You want a change of air.'

I wished I might get it.

'What you really want is a sea voyage.'

'And a winter at St Moritz, or do you recommend Cannes or Cairo? It's all very well, A .J., but you forget what I told you about my funds.'

'I forget nothing. I merely don't want to hurt your feelings. But, look here, a sea voyage you shall have. I want a change myself, and you shall come with me as my guest. We'll spend July in the Mediterranean.'

'But you're playing cricket – '

'Hang the cricket!'

'Well, if I thought you meant it – '

'Of course I mean it. Will you come?'

'Like a shot – if you go.'

And I shook his hand, and waved mine in farewell, with the perfectly good-humoured conviction that I should hear no more of the matter. It was a passing thought, no more, no less. I soon wished it were more; that week found me wishing myself out of England for good and all. I was making nothing. I could but subsist on the difference between the rent I paid for my flat and the rent at which I had sublet it, furnished, for the season. And the season was near its end, and creditors awaited me in town. Was it possible to be entirely honest? I had run no bills when I had money in my pocket, and the more downright dishonesty seemed to me less the ignoble.

But from Raffles, of course, I heard nothing more; a week went by, and half another week; then, late on the second Wednesday night, I found a telegram from him at my lodgings, after seeking him vainly in town, and dining with desperation at the solitary club to which I still belonged.

'Arranged to leave Waterloo by North German Lloyd special,' he wired, '9.25 A.M. Monday next will meet you Southampton aboard *Uhlan* with tickets, am writing.'

And write he did, a light-hearted letter enough, but full of serious solicitude for me and for my health and prospects; a letter almost touching in the light of our past relations, in the twilight of their complete rupture. He said that he had booked two berths to Naples, that we were bound for Capri, which was clearly the Island of the Lotos-eaters, that we would bask there together, 'and for a while forget'. It was a charming letter. I had never seen Italy; the privilege of initiation should be his. No mistake was greater than to deem it an impossible country for the summer. The Bay of Naples was never so divine, and he wrote of 'faery lands forlorn', as though the poetry sprang unbidden to his pen. To come back to earth and prose, I might think it unpatriotic of him to choose a German boat, but on no other line did you receive such attention and accommodation for your money. There was a hint of better reasons. Raffles wrote, as he had telegraphed, from Bremen; and I gathered that the personal use of some little influence with the authorities there had resulted in a material reduction in our fares.

Imagine my excitement and delight! I managed to pay what I owed at Thames Ditton, to squeeze a small editor for a very small cheque, and my tailors for one more flannel suit. I remember that I broke my last sovereign to get a box of Sullivan's cigarettes for Raffles to smoke on the voyage. But my heart was as light as my purse on the Monday morning, the fairest morning of an unfair summer, when the special whirled me through the sunshine to the sea.

A tender awaited us at Southampton. Raffles was not on board, nor did I really look for him till we reached the liner's side. And then I looked in vain. His face was not among the many that fringed the rail; his hand was not of the few that waved to friends. I climbed aboard in a sudden heaviness. I had no ticket, nor the money to pay for one. I did not even know the number of my room. My heart was in my mouth as I waylaid a steward and asked if a Mr Raffles was on board. Thank heaven – he was! But where? The man did not know; was plainly on some other errand, and a-hunting I must go. But there was no sign of him on the promenade deck, and none below in the saloon; the smoking-room was empty but for a little German with a red moustache twisted into his eyes; nor was Raffles in his own cabin, whither I inquired my way in desperation, but where the sight of his own name on the baggage was certainly a further reassurance. Why he himself kept in the background, however, I could not conceive, and only sinister reasons would suggest themselves in explanation.

'So there you are! I've been looking for you all over the ship!'

Despite the graven prohibition, I had tried the bridge as a last resort; and there, indeed, was A.J. Raffles, seated on a skylight, and leaning over one of the officers' long chairs, in which reclined a girl in a white drill coat and skirt – a slip of a girl with a pale skin, dark hair, and rather remarkable eyes. So much I noted as he rose and quickly turned; thereupon I could think of nothing but the swift grimace which preceded a start of well-feigned astonishment.

'Why – Bunny?' cried Raffles. 'Where have you sprung from?'

I stammered something as he pinched my hand.

'And you are coming in this ship? And to Naples too? Well, upon my word! Miss Werner, may I introduce my friend?'

And he did so without a blush, describing me as an old schoolfellow whom he had not seen for months, with wilful circumstance and gratuitous detail that filled me at once with confusion, suspicion, and revolt. I felt myself blushing for us both, and I did not care. My address utterly deserted me, and I made no effort to recover it, to carry the thing off. All I would do was to mumble such words as Raffles actually put into my mouth, and that I doubt not with a thoroughly evil grace.

'So you saw my name in the list of passengers, and came in search of me? Good old Bunny! I say, though, I wish you'd share my cabin? I've got a beauty on the promenade deck, but they wouldn't promise to keep me by myself. We ought to see about it before they shove in some alien. In any case, we shall have to get out of this.'

For a quartermaster had entered the wheel-house, and even while we had been speaking the pilot had taken possession of the bridge; as we descended, the tender left us with flying handkerchiefs and shrill good-byes; and as we bowed to Miss Werner on the promenade deck there came a deep, slow throbbing underfoot, and our voyage had begun.

It did not begin pleasantly between Raffles and me. On deck he had overborne my stubborn perplexity by dint of a forced though forceful joviality; in his cabin the gloves were off.

'You idiot,' he snarled. 'You've given me away again!'

'How have I given you away?'

I ignored the separate insult in his last word.

'How? I should have thought any clod could see that I meant us to meet by chance!'

'After taking both tickets yourself?'

'They know nothing about that on board; besides, I hadn't decided when I took the tickets.'

'Then you should have let me know when you did decide. You lay your plans, and never say a word, and expect me to tumble to them by light of nature. How was I to know you had anything on?'

I had turned the tables with some effect. Raffles almost hung his head.

'The fact is, Bunny, I didn't mean you to know. You – you've grown such a pious rabbit in your old age!'

My nickname and his tone went far to mollify me, other things went further, but I had much to forgive him still.

'If you were afraid of writing,' I pursued, 'it was your business to give me the tip the moment I set foot on board. I would have taken it all right. I am not so virtuous as all that.'

Was it my imagination, or did Raffles look slightly ashamed? If so, it was for the first and last time in all the years I knew him; nor can I swear to it even now.

'That', said he, 'was the very thing I meant to do – to lie in wait in my room and get you as you passed. But – '

'You were better engaged?'

'Say otherwise.'

'The charming Miss Werner?'

'She is quite charming.'

'Most Australian girls are,' said I.

'How did you know she was one?' he cried.

'I heard her speak.'

'Brute!' said Raffles, laughing; 'she has no more twang than you have. Her people are German, she has been to school in Dresden, and is on her way out alone.'

'Money?' I inquired.

'Confound you!' he said, and, though he was laughing, I thought it was a point at which the subject might be changed.

'Well,' I said, 'it wasn't for Miss Werner you wanted us to play strangers, was it? You have some deeper game than that, eh?'

'I suppose I have.'

'Then hadn't you better tell me what it is?'

Raffles treated me to the old cautious scrutiny that I knew so well; the very familiarity of it, after all these months, set me smiling in a way that might have reassured him; for dimly already I divined his enterprise.

'It won't send you off in the pilot's boat, Bunny?'

'Not quite.'

'Then – you remember the pearl you wrote the – '

I did not wait for him to finish his sentence.

'You've got it!' I cried, my face on fire, for I caught sight of it that moment in the state-room mirror.

Raffles seemed taken aback.

'Not yet,' said he; 'but I mean to have it before we get to Naples.'

'Is it on board?'

'Yes.'

'But how – where – who's got it?'

'A little German officer, a whipper-snapper with perpendicular moustaches.'

'I saw him in the smoke-room.'

That's the chap; he's always there. Herr Captain Wilhelm von Heumann, if you look in the list. Well, he's the special envoy of the emperor, and he's taking the pearl out with him!'

'You found this out in Bremen?'

'No, in Berlin, from a newspaper man I know there. I'm ashamed to tell you, Bunny, that I went there on purpose!'

I burst out laughing.

'You needn't be ashamed. You are doing the very thing I was rather hoping you were going to propose the other day on the river.'

'You were hoping it?' said Raffles, with his eyes wide open. Indeed, it was his turn to show surprise, and mine to be much more ashamed than I felt.

'Yes,' I answered, 'I was quite keen on the idea; but I wasn't going to propose it.'

'Yet you would have listened to me the other day?'

Certainly I would, and I told him so without reserve; not brazenly, you understand; not even now with the gusto of a man who savours such an adventure for its own sake, but doggedly, defiantly, through my teeth, as one who had tried to live honestly and had failed. And, while I was about it, I told him much more. Eloquently enough I daresay, I gave him chapter and verse of my hopeless struggle, my inevitable defeat; for hopeless and inevitable they were to a man with my record, even though that record was written only in one's own soul. It was the old story of the thief trying to turn honest man; the thing was against nature, and there was an end of it.

Raffles entirely disagreed with me. He shook his head over my conventional view. Human nature was a board of chequers; why not reconcile one's self to alternate black and white? Why desire to be all one thing or all the other, like our forefathers on the stage or in the old-fashioned fiction? For his part, he enjoyed himself on all squares of the board, and liked the light the better for the shade. My conclusion he considered absurd.

'But you err in good company, Bunny, for all the cheap moralists who preach the same twaddle; old Virgil was the first and worst offender of you all. I back myself to climb out of

Avernus any day I like, and sooner or later I shall climb out for good. I suppose I can't very well turn myself into a Limited Liability Company. But I could retire and settle down and live blamelessly ever after. I'm not sure that it couldn't be done on this pearl alone!'

'Then you don't still think it too remarkable to sell?'

'We might take a fishery and haul it up with smaller fry. It would come after months of ill-luck, just as we were going to sell the schooner; by Jove, it would be the talk of the Pacific!'

'Well, we've got to get it first. Is this von What's-his-name a formidable cuss?'

'More so than he looks; and he has the cheek of the devil!'

As he spoke, a white drill skirt fluttered past the open stateroom door, and I caught a glimpse of an upturned moustache beyond. 'But is he the chap we have to deal with? Won't the pearl be in the purser's keeping?'

Raffles stood at the door, frowning out upon the Solent, but for an instant he turned to me with a sniff.

'My good fellow, do you suppose the whole ship's company knows there's a gem like that aboard? You said that it was worth a hundred thousand pounds; in Berlin they say it's priceless. I doubt if the skipper himself knows that von Heumann has it on him.'

'And he has?'

'Must have.'

'Then we have only him to deal with?'

He answered me without a word. Something white was fluttering past once more, and Raffles, stepping forth, made the promenaders three.

II

I do not ask to set foot aboard a finer steamship than the *Uhlan* of the Norddeutscher Lloyd, to meet a kindlier man than her then commander or better fellows than his officers. This much at least let me have the grace to admit. I hated the voyage. It was no fault of anybody connected with the ship; it was no fault of the weather, which was monotonously ideal. Not even in my own heart did the reason reside; conscience and I were divorced at last, and the decree made absolute. With my scruples had fled all fear, and I was ready to revel between bright skies and sparkling sea with the light-hearted detachment of Raffles himself. It was Raffles himself who prevented me, but not Raffles alone. It was Raffles and that Colonial minx on her way home from school.

What he could see in her – but that begs the question. Of course he saw no more than I did, but to annoy me, or perhaps to punish me for my long defection, he must turn his back on me and devote himself to this chit from Southampton to the Mediterranean. They were always together. It was too absurd. After breakfast they would begin, and go on until eleven or twelve at night; there was no intervening hour at which you might not hear her nasal laugh, or his quiet voice talking soft nonsense into her ear. Of course it was nonsense! Is it conceivable that a man like Raffles, with his knowledge of the world, and his experience of women (a side of his character upon which I have purposely never touched, for it deserves another volume); is it credible, I ask, that such a man could find anything but nonsense to talk by the day together to a giddy young schoolgirl? I would not be unfair for the world. I think I have admitted that the young person had points. Her eyes, I suppose, were really fine, and certainly the shape of the little brown face was charming, so far as mere contour can charm. I admit also more audacity than I cared about, with enviable health, mettle, and vitality. I may not have occasion to report any of this young lady's speeches (they would scarcely bear it), and am therefore the more anxious to describe her without injustice. I confess to some little prejudice against her. I resented her success with Raffles, of whom, in consequence, I saw less and less each day. It is a mean thing to have to confess, but there must have been something not unlike jealousy rankling within me.

Jealousy there was in another quarter – crude, rampant, undignified jealousy. Captain von Heumann would twirl his moustaches into twin spires, shoot his white cuffs over his rings, and stare at me insolently through his rimless eye-glasses; we ought to have consoled each other, but we never exchanged a syllable. The captain had a murderous scar across one of his cheeks, a present from Heidelberg, and I used to think how he must long to have Raffles there to serve the same. It was not as though von Heumann never had his innings. Raffles let him go in several times a day, for the malicious pleasure of bowling him out as he was 'getting set'; those were his words when I taxed him disingenuously with obnoxious conduct towards a German on a German boat.

'You'll make yourself disliked on board!'

'By von Heumann merely.'

'But is that wise when he's the man we've got to diddle?'

'The wisest thing I ever did. To have chummed up with him would have been fatal – the common dodge.'

I was consoled, encouraged, almost content. I had feared Raffles was neglecting things, and I told him so in a burst. Here we were near Gibraltar, and not a word since the Solent. He shook his head with a smile.

'Plenty of time, Bunny, plenty of time. We can do nothing before we get to Genoa, and that won't be till Sunday night. The voyage is still young, and so are we; let's make the most of things while we can.'

It was after dinner on the promenade deck, and as Raffles spoke he glanced sharply fore and aft, leaving me next moment with a step full of purpose. I retired to the smoking-room, to smoke and read in a corner, and to watch von Heumann, who very soon came to drink beer and to sulk in another.

Few travellers tempt the Red Sea at midsummer; the *Uhlan* was very empty indeed. She had, however, but a limited supply of cabins on the promenade deck, and there was just that excuse for my sharing Raffles's room. I could have had one to myself downstairs, but I must be up above. Raffles had insisted that I should insist on the point. So we were together, I think, without suspicion, though also without any object that I could see.

On the Sunday afternoon I was asleep in my berth, the lower one, when the curtains were shaken by Raffles, who was in his shirt-sleeves on the settee.

'Achilles sulking in his bunk!'

'What else is there to do?' I asked him as I stretched and yawned. I noted, however, the good-humour of his tone, and did my best to catch it.

'I have found something else, Bunny.'

'I daresay!'

'You misunderstand me. The whipper-snapper's making his century this afternoon. I've had other fish to fry.'

I swung my legs over the side of my berth and sat forward, as he was sitting, all attention. The inner door, a grating, was shut and bolted, and curtained like the open port-hole.

'We shall be at Genoa before sunset,' continued Raffles. 'It's the place where the deed's got to be done.'

'So you still mean to do it!'

'Did I ever say I didn't?'

'You have said so little either way.'

'Advisedly so, my dear Bunny; why spoil a pleasure trip by talking unnecessary shop? But now the time has come. It must be done at Genoa or not at all.'

'On land?'

'No, on board, tomorrow night. Tonight would do, but tomorrow is better, in case of mishap. If we were forced to use violence we could get away by the earliest train, and nothing be known till the ship was sailing and von Heumann found dead or drugged – '

'Not dead!' I exclaimed.

'Of course not,' assented Raffles, 'or there would be no need for us to bolt; but if we should have to bolt, Tuesday morning is our time when the ship has got to sail, whatever happens. But I don't anticipate any violence. Violence is a confession of terrible incompetence. In all these years how many blows have you known me strike? Not one, I believe; but I have been quite ready to kill my man every time, if the worst came to the worst.'

I asked him how he proposed to enter von Heumann's stateroom unobserved, and even through the curtained gloom of ours his face lighted up.

'Climb into my bunk, Bunny, and you shall see.'

I did so, but could see nothing. Raffles reached across me and tapped the ventilator, a sort of trapdoor in the wall above his bed, some eighteen inches long and half that height. It opened outwards into the ventilating shaft.

'That', said he, 'is our door to fortune. Open it if you like; you won't see much, because it doesn't open far; but loosening a couple of screws will set that all right. The shaft, as you may see, is more or less bottomless; you pass under it whenever you go to your bath, and the top is a skylight on the bridge. That's why this thing has to be done while we're at Genoa, because they keep no watch on the bridge in port. The ventilator opposite ours is von Heumann's. It again will only mean a couple of screws and there's a beam to stand on while you work.'

'But if anybody should look from below?'

'It's extremely unlikely that anybody will be astir below, so unlikely that we can afford to chance it. No, I can't have you there to make sure. The great point is that neither of us should be seen from the time we turn in. A couple of ship's boys do sentry-go on these decks, and they shall be our witnesses; by Jove, it'll be the biggest mystery that ever was made!'

'If von Heumann doesn't resist.'

'Resist! He won't get the chance. He drinks too much beer to sleep light, and nothing is so easy as to chloroform a heavy sleeper; you've even done it yourself on an occasion of which it's perhaps unfair to remind you. Von Heumann will be past sensation almost as soon as I get my hand through his ventilator. I shall crawl in over his body, Bunny, my boy!'

'And I?'

'You will hand me what I want, and hold the fort in case of accidents, and generally lend me the moral support you've made me require. It's a luxury, Bunny, but I found it devilish difficult to do without it after you turned pi!'

He said that von Heumann was certain to sleep with a bolted door, which he, of course, would leave unbolted, and spoke of other ways of laying a false scent while rifling the cabin. Not that Raffles anticipated a tiresome search. The pearl would be about von Heumann's person; in fact, Raffles knew exactly where and in what he kept it. Naturally, I asked how he could have come by such knowledge, and his answer led up to a momentary unpleasantness.

'It's a very old story, Bunny. I really forget in what book it comes: I'm only sure of the Testament. But Samson was the unlucky hero, and one Delilah the heroine.'

And he looked so knowing that I could not be in a moment's doubt as to his meaning.

'So the fair Australian has been playing Delilah?' said I.

'In a very harmless, innocent sort of way.'

'She got his mission out of him?'

'Yes, I've forced him to score all the points he could, and that was his great stroke, as I hoped it would be. He has even shown Amy the pearl.'

'Amy, eh! and she promptly told you?'

'Nothing of the kind. What makes you think so? I had the greatest trouble in getting it out of her.'

His tone should have been a sufficient warning to me. I had not the tact to take it as such. At last I knew the meaning of his furious flirtation, and stood wagging my head and shaking my finger, blinded to his frowns by my own enlightenment.

'Wily worm!' said I. 'Now I see through it all; how dense I've been!'

'Sure you're not still?'

'No; now I understand what has beaten me all the week. I simply couldn't fathom what you saw in that little girl. I never dreamt it was part of the game.'

'So you think it was that and nothing more?'

'You deep old dog – of course I do!'

'You didn't know she was the daughter of a wealthy squatter?'

'There are wealthy women by the dozen who would marry you tomorrow.'

'It doesn't occur to you that I might like to draw stumps, start clean, and live happily ever after – in the bush?'

'With that voice? It certainly does not!'

'Bunny!' he cried so fiercely that I braced myself for a blow.

But no more followed.

'Do you think you would live happily?' I made bold to ask him.

'God knows!' he answered. And with that he left me, to marvel at his look and tone, and, more than ever, at the insufficiently exciting cause.

III

Of all the mere feats of cracksmanship which I have seen Raffles perform, at once the most delicate and most difficult was that which he accomplished between one and two o'clock on the Tuesday morning, aboard the North German steamer *Uhlan*, lying at anchor in Genoa harbour.

Not a hitch occurred. Everything had been foreseen; everything happened as I had been assured everything must. Nobody was about below, only the ship's boys on deck, and nobody on the bridge. It was twenty-five minutes past one when Raffles, without a stitch of clothing on his body, but with a glass phial, corked with cotton-wool, between his teeth, and a tiny screw-driver behind his ear, squirmed feet first through the ventilator over his berth; and it was nineteen minutes to two when he returned, head first, with the phial still between his teeth, and the cotton-wool rammed home to still the rattling of that which lay like a great grey bean within. He had taken screws out and put them in again; he had unfastened von Heumann's ventilator and had left it fast as he had found it – fast as he instantly proceeded to make his own. As for von Heumann, it had been enough to place the drenched wad first on his moustache, and then to hold it between his gaping lips; thereafter the intruder had climbed both ways across his shins without eliciting a groan.

And here was the prize – this pearl as large as a filbert – with a pale pink tinge like a lady's finger-nail – this spoil of the filibustering age – this gift from a European emperor to a South Sea chief. We gloated over it when all was snug. We toasted it in whisky and soda-water laid in overnight in view of the great moment. But the moment was greater, more triumphant, than our most sanguine dreams. All we had now to do was to secrete the gem (which Raffles had prised from its setting, replacing the latter), so that we could stand the strictest search and yet take it ashore with us at Naples; and this Raffles was doing when I turned in. I myself would have landed incontinently, that night, at Genoa, and bolted with the spoil; he would not hear of it, for a dozen good reasons which will be obvious.

On the whole I do not think that anything was discovered or suspected before we weighed anchor; but I cannot be sure.

It is difficult to believe that a man could be chloroformed in his sleep and feel no tell-tale effects, sniff no suspicious odour, in the morning. Nevertheless, von Heumann reappeared as though nothing had happened to him, his German cap over his eyes and his moustaches brushing the peak. And by ten o'clock we were quit of Genoa; the last lean, blue-chinned official had left our decks; the last fruitseller had been beaten off with bucketsful of water and left cursing us from his boat; the last passenger had come aboard at the last moment – a fussy greybeard who kept the big ship waiting while he haggled with his boatman over half a lira. But at length we were off, the tug was shed, the lighthouse passed, and Raffles and I leaned together over the rail, watching our shadows on the pale green, liquid, veined marble that again washed the vessel's side.

Von Heumann was having his innings once more; it was part of the design that he should remain in all day, and so postponed the inevitable hour; and, though the lady looked bored, and was for ever glancing in our direction, he seemed only too willing to avail himself of his opportunities. But Raffles was moody and ill at ease. He had not the air of a successful man. I could but opine that the impending parting at Naples sat heavily on his spirit. He would neither talk to me, nor would he let me go.

'Stop where you are, Bunny. I've things to tell you. Can you swim?'

'A bit.'

'Ten miles?'

'Ten?' I burst out laughing. 'Not one! Why do you ask?'

'We shall be within a ten miles' swim of the shore most of the day.'

'What on earth are you driving at, Raffles?'

'Nothing; only I shall swim for it if the worst comes to the worst. I suppose you can't swim under water at all?'

I did not answer his question. I scarcely heard it; cold beads were bursting through my skin.

'Why should the worst come to the worst?' I whispered. 'We aren't found out, are we?'

'No.'

'Then why speak as though we were?'

'We may be; an old enemy of ours is on board.'

'An old enemy?'

'Mackenzie.'

'Never.'

'The man with the beard who came aboard last.'

'Are you sure?'

'Sure! I was only sorry to see you didn't recognise him too.'

I took my handkerchief to my face; now that I thought of it, there had been something familiar in the old man's gait, as well as something rather youthful for his apparent years; his very beard seemed unconvincing, now that I recalled it in the light of this horrible revelation. I looked up and down the deck, but the old man was nowhere to be seen.

'That's the worst of it,' said Raffles. 'I saw him go into the captain's cabin twenty minutes ago.'

'But what can have brought him?' I cried miserably. 'Can it be a coincidence – is it somebody else he's after?'

Raffles shook his head.

'Hardly, this time.'

'Then you think he's after you?'

'I've been afraid of it for some weeks.'

'Yet there you stand!'

'What am I to do? I don't want to swim for it before I must. I begin to wish I'd taken your advice, Bunny, and left the ship at Genoa. But I've not the smallest doubt that Mac was watching both ship and station till the last moment. That's why he ran it so fine.' He took a cigarette and handed me the case, but I shook my head impatiently.

'I still don't understand,' said I. 'Why should he be after you? He couldn't come all this way about a jewel which was perfectly safe for all he knew. What's your own theory?'

'Simply that he's been on my track for some time, probably ever since friend Crawshay slipped clean through his fingers last November. There have been other indications. I am really not unprepared for this. But it can only be pure suspicion. I'll defy him to bring anything home, and I'll defy him to find the pearl! Theory, my dear Bunny! I know how he's got here as well as though I'd been inside that Scotsman's skin, and I know what he'll do next. He found out I'd gone abroad, and looked for a motive; he found out about von Heumann and his mission, and here was his motive cut and dried. Great chance – to nab me on a new job altogether. But he won't do it, Bunny; mark my words, he'll search the ship and search us all, when the loss is known; but he'll search in vain. And there's skipper beckoning the whipper-snapper to his cabin; the fat will be in the fire in five minutes!'

Yet there was no conflagration, no fuss, no searching of the passengers, no whisper of what had happened in the air; instead of a stir there was portentous peace; and it was clear to me that Raffles was not a little disturbed at the falsification of all his predictions. There was something sinister in silence under such a loss, and the silence was sustained for hours, during which Mackenzie never reappeared. But he was abroad during the luncheon-hour – he was in our cabin! I had left my book in Raffles's berth, and in taking it after lunch I touched the quilt. It was warm from the recent pressure of flesh and blood, and on an instinct I sprang to the ventilator; as I opened it the ventilator opposite was closed with a snap.

I waylaid Raffles. 'All right. Let him find the pearl.'

'Have you dumped it overboard?'

That's a question I shan't condescend to answer.'

He turned on his heel, and at subsequent intervals I saw him making the most of his last afternoon with the inevitable Miss Werner. I remember that she looked both cool and smart in quite a simple affair of brown holland, which toned well with her complexion, and was cleverly relieved with touches of scarlet. I quite admired her that afternoon, for her eyes were really very good, and so were her teeth, yet I had never admired her more directly in my own despite. For I passed them again and again in order to get a word with Raffles, to tell him I knew there was danger in the wind; but he would not so much as catch my eye. So at last I gave it up. And I saw him next in the captain's cabin.

They had summoned him first; he had gone in smiling; and smiling I found him when they summoned me. The stateroom was spacious, as befitted that of a commander. Mackenzie sat on the settee, his beard in front of him on the polished table; but a revolver lay in front of the captain; and, when I had entered, the chief officer, who had summoned me, shut the door and put his back to it. Von Heumann completed the party, his fingers busy with his moustache.

Raffles greeted me.

'This is a great joke!' he cried. 'You remember the pearl you were so keen about, Bunny, the emperor's pearl, the pearl money wouldn't buy? It seems it was entrusted to our little friend here, to take out to Canoodle Dum, and the poor little chap's gone and lost it; *ergo*, as we're Britishers, they think we've got it!'

'But I know ye have,' put in Mackenzie, nodding to his beard.

'You will recognise that loyal and patriotic voice,' said Raffles. 'Mon, 'tis our auld acquaintance Mackenzie, o' Scoteland Yarrd an' Scoteland itsel'!'

'Dat is enought,' cried the captain. 'Have you submid to be searge, or do I vorce you?'

'What you will,' said Raffles, 'but it will do you no harm to give us fair play first. You accuse us of breaking into Captain von Heumann's stateroom during the small hours of this morning, and abstracting from it this confounded pearl. Well, I can prove that I was in my own room all night long, and I have no doubt my friend can prove the same.'

'Most certainly I can,' said I indignantly. 'The ship's boys can bear witness to that.'

Mackenzie laughed, and shook his head at his reflection in the polished mahogany.

'That was vera clever,' said he, 'and like enough it would ha' served ye had I not stepped aboard. But I've just had a look at they ventilators, and I think I know how ye worrked it. Anyway, captain, it makes no matter. I'll just be clappin' the darbies on these young sparks, an' then – '

'By what right?' roared Raffles in a ringing voice, and I never saw his face in such a blaze. 'Search us if you like; search every scrap and stitch we possess; but you dare to lay a finger on us without a warrant!'

'I wouldna' dare,' said Mackenzie gravely, as he fumbled in his breast-pocket, and Raffles dived his hand into his own. 'Haud his wrist!' shouted the Scotsman; and the huge Colt that had been with us many a night, but had never been fired in my hearing, clattered on the table and was raked in by the captain.

'All right,' said Raffles savagely to the mate. 'You can let go now. I won't try it again. Now Mackenzie, let's see your warrant!'

'Ye'll no mishandle it?'

'What good would that do me? Let me see it,' said Raffles, peremptorily, and the detective obeyed. Raffles raised his eyebrows as he perused the document; his mouth hardened, but suddenly relaxed; and it was with a smile and a shrug that he returned the paper.

'Wull that do for ye?' inquired Mackenzie.

'It may. I congratulate you, Mackenzie; it's a strong hand, at any rate. Two burglaries and the Melrose necklace, Bunny!' And he turned to me with a rueful smile.

'An' all easy to prove,' said the Scotsman, pocketing the warrant. 'I've one o' these for you,' he added, nodding to me, 'only not such a long one.'

'To thingk,' said the captain reproachfully, 'that my shib should be made a den of thiefs! It shall be a very disagreeable madder. I have been obliged to pud you both in irons until we ged to Nables.'

'Surely not!' exclaimed Raffles. 'Mackenzie, intercede with him; don't give your countrymen away before all hands! Captain, we can't escape; surely you could hush it up for the night? Look here, here's everything I have in my pockets; you empty yours too, Bunny, and they shall strip us stark if they suspect we've weapons up our sleeves. All I ask is that we are allowed to get out of this without gyves upon our wrists!'

'Webbons, you may not have,' said the captain; 'bud wad about de bearl dat you were sdealing?'

'You shall have it!' cried Raffles. 'You shall have it this minute if you guarantee no public indignity on board!'

'That I'll see to,' said Mackenzie, 'as long as you behave yourselves. There now, where is't?'

'On the table under your nose.'

My eyes fell with the rest, but no pearl was there; only the contents of our pockets – our watches, pocket-books, pencils, penknives, cigarette-cases – lay on the shiny table along with the revolvers already mentioned.

'Ye're humbuggin' us,' said Mackenzie. 'What's the use?'

'I'm doing nothing of the sort,' laughed Raffles. 'I'm testing you. Where's the harm?'

'It's here, joke apart?'

'On that table, by all my gods.'

Mackenzie opened the cigarette-cases and shook each particular cigarette. Thereupon Raffles prayed to be allowed to smoke one, and, when his prayer was heard, observed that the pearl had been on the table much longer than the cigarettes. Mackenzie promptly caught up the Colt and opened the chamber in the butt.

'Not there, not there,' said Raffles; 'but you're getting hot. Try the cartridges.'

Mackenzie emptied them into his palm, and shook each one at his ear without result.

'Oh, give them to me!'

And, in an instant, Raffles had found the right one, had bitten out the bullet, and placed the emperor's pearl with a flourish in the centre of the table.

'After that you will perhaps show me such little consideration as is in your power. Captain, I have been a bit of a villain, as you see, and as such I am ready and willing to lie in irons all night if you deem it requisite for the safety of the ship. All I ask is that you do me one favour first.'

'That shall debend on wad der vafour has been.'

'Captain, I've done a worse thing aboard your ship than any of you know. I have become engaged to be married, and I want to say good-bye!'

I suppose we were all equally amazed; but the only one to express his amazement was von Heumann, whose deep-chested German oath was almost his first contribution to the proceedings. He was not slow to follow it, however, with a vigorous protest against the proposed farewell; but he was overruled, and the masterful prisoner had his way. He was to have five minutes with the girl, while the captain and Mackenzie stood within range (but not earshot), with their revolvers behind their backs. As we were moving from the cabin in a body, he stopped and gripped my hand.

'So I've let you in at last, Bunny – at last and after all! If you knew how sorry I am... But you won't get much – I don't see why you should get anything at all. Can you forgive me? This may be for years, and it may be for ever, you know! You were a good pal always when it came to the scratch; some day or other you mayn't be so sorry to remember you were a good pal at the last!'

There was a meaning in his eye that I understood; and my teeth were set, and my nerves strung ready, as I wrung that strong and cunning hand for the last time in my life.

How that last scene stays with me, and will stay to my death! How I see every detail, every shadow on the sunlit deck! We were among the islands that dot the course from Genoa to Naples; that was Elba falling back on our starboard quarter, that purple patch with the hot sun setting over it. The captain's cabin opened to starboard, and the starboard promenade deck, sheeted with sunshine and scored with shadow, was deserted but for the group of which I was one, and for the pale, slim, brown figure farther aft with Raffles. Engaged? I could not believe it, cannot to this day. Yet there they stood together, and we did not hear a word; there they stood out against the sunset, and the long, dazzling highway of sunlit sea that sparkled from Elba to the *Uhlan*'s plates; and their shadows reached almost to our feet.

Suddenly – an instant – and the thing was done – a thing I have never known whether to admire or to detest. He caught her – he kissed her before us all – then flung her from him so that she almost fell. It was that action which foretold the next. The mate sprang after him, and I sprang after the mate.

Raffles was on the rail, but only just.

'Hold him, Bunny!' he cried. 'Hold him tight!'

And, as I obeyed that last behest with all my might, without a thought of what I was doing, save that he bade me do it, I saw his hands shoot up and his head bob down, and his lithe, spare body cut the sunset as cleanly and precisely as though he had plunged at his leisure from a diver's board!

*

Of what followed on deck I can tell you nothing, for I was not there. Nor can my final punishment, my long imprisonment, my everlasting disgrace, concern or profit you, beyond the interest and advantage to be gleaned from the knowledge that I at least had my desens. But one thing I must set down, believe it who will – one more thing only and I am done.

It was into a second-class cabin, on the starboard side, that I was promptly thrust in irons, and the door locked upon me as though I were another Raffles. Meanwhile a boat was lowered, and the seas scoured to no purpose, as is doubtless on record elsewhere. But either the setting sun, flashing over the waves, must have blinded all eyes, or else mine were victims of a strange illusion.

For the boat was back, the screw throbbing, and the prisoner peering through his port-hole across the sunlit waters that he believed had closed for ever over his comrade's head. Suddenly the sun sank behind the Island of Elba, the lane of dancing sunlight was instantaneously quenched and swallowed in the trackless waste, and in the middle distance, already miles astern, either my sight deceived me or a black speck bobbed amid the grey. The bugle had blown for dinner; it may well be that all save myself had ceased to strain an eye. And now I lost what I had found, now it rose, now sank, and now I gave it up utterly. Yet anon it would rise again, a mere mote dancing in the dim grey distance, drifting towards a purple island, beneath a fading western sky, streaked with dead gold and cerise. And night fell before I knew whether it was a human head or not.

THE BLACK MASK

Narrator's Note

The life of man, according to the Scriptures, is three score years and ten; but who shall measure that of the modern mediocre novel? With luck it may attain as many days. And who remembers even A.J. Raffles, Cricketer and Cracksman, late of the Albany (among other haunts), now that thirty moons have come and gone since the faithful learned the last of him in a book called The Amateur Cracksman? Yet if he, too, has been utterly forgotten, the fault lies not with the subject of all these papers, but with their pseudonymous perpetrator, his sometime accomplice and most unworthy Boswell; and I have the less hesitation in reminding the few aforesaid that we left our Raffles swimming for his life in blue water, while I was put in prison for my crimes. I was far from sure (if they remember) whether or not it was Raffles's head which I saw at the last, 'a mere mote dancing in the dim grey distance, drifting towards a purple island, beneath a fading western sky', as I was pleased to put it at the time; my one conviction (since quashed) was that I never should set eyes on him again. In what wise we did actually meet once more, how we went in together as before, and how I strove yet again to keep up a worthless wicket while my dear old Raffles flogged the bowling, is all set forth (and nothing extenuated) in the following fresh chapters from our common life. But it was no second innings that we played together; it was a new match; and we played no more for love. Take us, then, not as you left but as you find us now, Amateur Cracksmen no longer, but professionals of the deadliest dye; knowing nobody, without a Club between us, doing little in broad daylight and nothing in our own names; but peeping our last upon a law-abiding world, through the narrow eyelets of The Black Mask.

1

NO SINECURE

I

I am still uncertain which surprised me more, the telegram calling my attention to the advertisement or the advertisement itself. The telegram is before me as I write. It would appear to have been handed in at Vere Street at eight o'clock in the morning of May 11, 1897, and received before half-past at Holloway B.O. And in that drab region it duly found me, unwashed but at work before the day grew hot and my attic insupportable.

> 'See Mr Maturin's advertisement *Daily Mail* might suit you earnestly beg try will speak if necessary...'

I transcribe the thing as I see it before me, all in one breath that took away mine; but I leave out the initials at the end, which completed the surprise. They stood very obviously for the knighted specialist whose consulting-room is within a cab-whistle of Vere Street, and who once called me kinsman for his sins. More recently he had called me other names. I was a disgrace, qualified by an adjective which seemed to me another. I had made my bed, and I could go and lie and die in it. If I ever again had the insolence to show my nose in that house, I should go out quicker than I came in. All this, and more, my least distant relative could tell a poor devil to his face; could ring for his man, and give him his brutal instructions on the spot; and then relent to the tune of this telegram! I have no phrase for my amazement. I literally could not believe my eyes. Yet their evidence was more and more conclusive: a very epistle could not have been more characteristic of its sender. Meanly elliptical, ludicrously precise, saving halfpence at the expense of sense, yet paying like a man for 'Mr' Maturin, that was my distinguished relative from his bald patch to his corns. Nor was all the rest unlike him, upon second thoughts. He had a reputation for charity; he was going to live up to it after all. Either that, or it was the sudden impulse of which the most calculating are capable at times; the morning papers with the early cup of tea, this advertisement seen by chance, and the rest upon the spur of a guilty conscience.

Well, I must see it for myself, and the sooner the better, though work pressed. I was writing a series of articles upon prison life, and had my nib into the whole System; a literary and philanthropical daily was parading my 'charges', the graver ones with the more gusto; and the terms, if unhandsome for creative work, were temporary wealth to me. It so happened that my first cheque had just arrived by the eight o'clock post; and my position should be appreciated when I say that I had to cash it to obtain a *Daily Mail*.

Of the advertisement itself, what is to be said? It should speak for itself if I could find it, but I cannot, and only remember that it was a 'male nurse and constant attendant' that was 'wanted for an elderly gentleman in feeble health'. A male nurse! An absurd tag was appended, offering 'liberal salary to University or public- school man'; and of a sudden I saw that I should get this thing if I applied for it. What other 'University or public-school man' would dream of doing so? Was any other in such straits as I? And then my relenting relative; he not only promised to speak for me, but was the very man to do so. Could any recommendation compete with his in the matter of a male nurse? And need the duties of such be necessarily loathsome and repellent? Certainly the surroundings would be better than those of my common lodging-house and own particular garret; and the food; and every other condition of life that I could think of on my way back to that unsavoury asylum. So I dived into a pawnbroker's shop, where I was a stranger only upon my present errand, and within the hour was airing a decent if antiquated suit, but little corrupted by the pawnbroker's moth, and a new straw hat, on the top of a tram.

The address given in the advertisement was that of a flat at Earl's Court, which cost me a cross-country journey, finishing with the District Railway and a seven minutes' walk. It was now past midday, and the tarry wood-pavement was good to smell as I strode up the Earl's Court Road. It was great to walk the civilised world again. Here were men with coats on their backs, and ladies in gloves. My only fear was lest I might run up against one or other whom I had known of old. But it was my lucky day. I felt it in my bones. I was going to get this berth; and sometimes I should be able to smell the wood-pavement on the old boy's errands; perhaps he would insist on skimming over it in his bath-chair, with me behind.

I felt quite nervous when I reached the flats. They were a small pile in a side-street, and I pitied the doctor whose plate I saw upon the palings before the ground-floor windows; he must be in a very small way, I thought. I rather pitied myself as well. I had indulged in visions of better flats than these. There were no balconies. The porter was out of livery. There was no lift, and my invalid on the third floor! I trudged up, wishing I had never lived in Mount Street, and brushed against a dejected individual coming down. A full-blooded young fellow in a frock-coat flung the right door open at my summons.

'Does Mr Maturin live here?' I inquired.

'That's right,' said the full-blooded young man, grinning all over a convivial countenance.

'I – I've come about his advertisement in the *Daily Mail.*'

'You're the thirty-ninth,' cried the blood; 'that was the thirty-eighth you met upon the stairs, and the day's still young. Excuse my staring at you. Yes, you pass your prelim., and can come inside; you're one of the few. We had most just after breakfast, but now the porter's heading off the worst cases, and that last chap was the first for twenty minutes. Come in here.'

And I was ushered into an empty room with a good bay window, which enabled my full-blooded friend to inspect me yet more critically in a good light; this he did without the least false delicacy; then his questions began.

''Varsity man?'

'No.'

'Public school?'

'Yes.'

'Which one?'

I told him, and he sighed relief.

'At last! You're the very first I've not had to argue with as to what is and what is not a public school. Expelled?'

'No,' I said, after a moment's hesitation. 'No, I was not expelled. And I hope you won't expel me if I ask a question in my turn.'

'Certainly not.'

'Are you Mr Maturin's son?'

'No, my name's Theobald. You may have seen it down below.'

'The doctor?' I said.

'His doctor,' said Theobald, with a satisfied eye. 'Mr Maturin's doctor. He is having a male nurse and attendant by my advice, and he wants a gentleman if he can get one. I rather think he'll see you, though he's only seen two or three all day. There are certain questions which he prefers to ask himself, and it's no good going over the same ground twice. So perhaps I had better tell him about you before we get any further.'

And he withdrew to a room still nearer the entrance, as I could hear, for it was a very small flat indeed. But now two doors were shut between us, and I had to rest content with murmurs through the wall until the doctor returned to summon me.

'I have persuaded my patient to see you,' he whispered, 'but I confess I am not sanguine of the result. He is very difficult to please. You must prepare yourself for a querulous invalid, and for no sinecure if you get the billet.'

'May I ask what's the matter with him?'

'By all means – when you've got the billet.'

Dr Theobald then led the way, his professional dignity so thoroughly intact that I could not but smile as I followed his swinging coat-tails to the sick-room. I carried no smile across the threshold of a darkened chamber which reeked of drugs and twinkled with medicine bottles, and in the middle of which a gaunt figure lay abed in the half-light.

'Take him to the window, take him to the window,' a thin voice snapped, 'and let's have a look at him. Open the blind a bit. Not as much as that, damn you, not as much as that!'

The doctor took the oath as though it had been a fee. I no longer pitied him. It was now very clear to me that he had one patient who was a little practice in himself. I determined there and then that he should prove a little profession to me, if we could but keep him alive between us. Mr Maturin, however, had the whitest face that I have ever seen, and his teeth gleamed out through the dusk as though the withered lips no longer met about them; nor did they except in speech; and anything ghastlier than the perpetual grin of his repose I defy you to imagine. It was with this grin that he lay regarding me while the doctor held the blind.

'So you think you could look after me, do you?'

'I'm certain I could, sir.'

'Single-handed, mind! I don't keep another soul. You would have to cook your own grub and my slops. Do you think you could do all that?'

'Yes, sir, I think so.'

'Why do you? Have you any experience of the kind?'

'No, sir, none.'

'Then why do you pretend you have?'

'I only meant that I would do my best.'

'Only meant, only meant! Have you done your best at everything else, then?'

I hung my head. This was a facer. And there was something in my invalid which thrust the unspoken lie down my throat.

'No, sir, I have not,' I told him plainly.

'He, he, he!' the old wretch tittered; 'and you do well to own it; you do well, sir, very well indeed. If you hadn't owned up, out you would have gone, out neck and crop! You've saved your bacon. You may do more. So you are a public-school boy, and a very good school yours is, but you weren't at either University. Is that correct?'

'Absolutely.'

'What did you do when you left school?'

'I came in for money.'

'And then?'

'I spent my money.'

'And since then?'

I stood like a mule.

'And since then, I say!'

'A relative of mine will tell you if you ask him. He is an eminent man, and he has promised to speak for me. I would rather say no more myself.'

'But you shall, sir, but you shall! Do you suppose that I suppose a public-school boy would apply for a berth like this if something or other hadn't happened? What I want is a gentleman of sorts, and I don't much care what sort;

but you've got to tell me what did happen, if you don't tell anybody else. – Dr Theobald, sir, you can go to the devil if you won't take a hint. This man may do or he may not. You have no more to say to it till I send him down to tell you one thing or the other. Clear out, sir, clear out; and if you think you've anything to complain of, you stick it down in the bill!'

In the mild excitement of our interview the thin voice had gathered strength, and the last shrill insult was screamed after the devoted medico, as he retired in such order that I felt certain he was going to take this trying patient at his word. The bedroom door closed, then the outer one, and the doctor's heels were drumming down the common stair. I was alone in the flat with this highly singular and rather terrible old man.

'And a damned good riddance!' croaked the invalid, raising himself on one elbow without delay. 'I may not have much body left to boast about, but at least I've got a lost old soul to call my own. That's why I want a gentleman of sorts about me. I've been too dependent on that chap. He won't even let me smoke, and he's been in the flat all day to see I didn't. You'll find the cigarettes behind the *Madonna of the Chair*.'

It was a steel engraving of the great Raffaelle, and the frame was tilted from the wall; at a touch a packet of cigarettes tumbled down from behind.

'Thanks; and now a light.'

I struck the match and held it, while the invalid inhaled with normal lips; and suddenly I sighed. I was irresistibly reminded of my poor dear old Raffles. A smoke-ring worthy of the great A.J. was floating upward from the sick man's lips.

'And now take one yourself. I have smoked more poisonous cigarettes. But even these are not Sullivans!'

I cannot repeat what I said. I have no idea what I did. I only knew – I only knew – that it was A.J. Raffles in the flesh!

II

'Yes, Bunny, it was the very devil of a swim; but I defy you to sink in the Mediterranean. That sunset saved me. The sea was on fire. I hardly swam under water at all, but went all I knew for the sun itself; when it set I must have been a mile away; until it did I was the invisible man. I figured on that, and only hope it wasn't set down as a case of suicide. I shall get outed quite soon enough, Bunny, but I'd rather be dropped by the hangman than throw my own wicket away.'

'Oh, my dear old chap, to think of having you by the hand again! I feel as though we were both aboard that German liner, and all that's happened since a nightmare. I thought that time was the last!'

'It looked rather like it, Bunny. It was taking all the risks, and hitting at everything. But the game came off, and some day I'll tell you how.'

'Oh, I'm in no hurry to hear. It's enough for me to see you lying there. I don't want to know how you came there, or why, though I fear you must be pretty bad. I must have a good look at you before I let you speak another word!'

I raised one of the blinds, I sat upon the bed, and I had that look. It left me all unable to conjecture his true state of health, but quite certain in my own mind that my dear Raffles was not and never would be the man that he had been. He had aged twenty years; he looked fifty at the very least. His hair was white; there was no trick about that; and his face was another white. The lines about the corners of the eyes and mouth were both many and deep. On the other hand, the eyes themselves were alight and alert as ever; they were still keen and grey and gleaming like finely-tempered steel. Even the mouth, with a cigarette to close it, was the mouth of Raffles and no other; strong and unscrupulous as the man himself. It was only the physical strength which appeared to have departed; but that was quite sufficient to make my heart bleed for the dear rascal who had cost me every tie I valued but the tie between us two.

'Think I look much older?' he asked at length.

'A bit,' I admitted. 'But it is chiefly your hair.'

'Whereby hangs a tale for when we've talked ourselves out, though I have often thought it was that long swim that started it. Still, the island of Elba is a rummy show, I can assure you. And Naples is a rummier.'

'You went there after all?'

'Rather! It's the European paradise for such as our noble selves. But there's no place that's a patch on little London as a non- conductor of heat; it never need get too hot for a fellow here; if it does it's his own fault. It's the kind of wicket you don't get out on, unless you get yourself out. So here I am again, and have been for the last six weeks. And I mean to have another knock.'

'But surely, old fellow, you're not awfully fit, are you?'

'Fit? My dear Bunny, I'm dead – I'm at the bottom of the sea – and don't you forget it for a minute.'

'But are you all right, or are you not?'

'No, I'm half poisoned by Theobald's prescriptions and putrid cigarettes, and as weak as a cat from lying in bed.'

'Then why on earth lie in bed, Raffles?'

'Because it's better than lying in gaol, as I am afraid you know, my poor dear fellow. I tell you I am dead; and my one terror is of coming to life again by accident. Can't you see? I simply dare not show my nose out of doors – by day. You have no idea of the number of perfectly innocent things a dead man daren't do. I can't even smoke Sullivans, because no man was ever so partial to them as I was in my lifetime, and you never know when you may start a clue.'

'What brought you to these mansions?'

'I fancied a flat, and a man recommended these on the boat; such a good chap, Bunny; he was my reference when it came to signing the lease. You see I landed on a stretcher – most pathetic case – old Australian without a friend in old country – ordered Engadine as last chance – no go – not an earthly – sentimental wish to die in London – that's the history of Mr Maturin. If it doesn't hit you hard, Bunny, you're the first. But it hit friend Theobald hardest of all. I'm an income to him. I believe he's going to marry on me.'

'Does he guess there's nothing wrong?'

'Knows, bless you! But he doesn't know I know he knows, and there isn't a disease in the dictionary that he hasn't treated me for since he's had me in hand. To do him justice, I believe he thinks me a hypochondriac of the first water; but that young man will go far if he keeps on the wicket. He has spent half his nights up here, at guineas apiece.'

'Guineas must be plentiful, old chap!'

'They have been, Bunny. I can't say more. But I don't see why they shouldn't be again.'

I was not going to inquire where the guineas came from. As if I cared! But I did ask old Raffles how in the world he had got upon my tracks; and thereby drew the sort of smile with which old gentlemen rub their hands, and old ladies nod their noses. Raffles merely produced a perfect oval of blue smoke before replying.

'I was waiting for you to ask that, Bunny; it's a long time since I did anything upon which I plume myself more. Of course, in the first place, I spotted you at once by these prison articles; they were not signed, but the fist was the fist of my sitting rabbit!'

'But who gave you my address?'

'I wheedled it out of your excellent editor; called on him at dead of night, when I occasionally go afield like other ghosts, and wept it out of him in five minutes. I was your only relative; your name was not your own name; if he insisted I would give him mine. He didn't insist, Bunny, and I danced down his stairs with your address in my pocket.'

'Last night?'

'No, last week.'

'And so the advertisement was yours, as well as the telegram!'

I had, of course, forgotten both in the high excitement of the hour, or I should scarcely have announced my belated discovery with such an air. As it was I made Raffles look at me as I had known him look before, and the droop of his eyelids began to sting.

'Why all this subtlety?' I petulantly exclaimed. 'Why couldn't you come straight away to me in a cab?'

He did not inform me that I was hopeless as ever. He did not address me as his good rabbit. He was silent for a time, and then spoke in a tone which made me ashamed of mine.

'You see, there are two or three of me now, Bunny: one's at the bottom of the Mediterranean, and one's an old Australian desirous of dying in the old country, but in no immediate danger of dying anywhere. The old Australian doesn't know a soul in town; he's got to be consistent, or he's done. This sitter Theobald is his only friend, and has seen rather too much of him; ordinary dust won't do for his eyes. Begin to see? To pick you out of a crowd, that was the game; to let old Theobald help to pick you, better still! To start with, he was dead against my having anybody at all; wanted me all to himself, naturally; but anything rather than kill the goose! So he is to have a fiver a week while he keeps me alive, and he's going to be married next month. That's a pity in some ways, but a good thing in others; he will want more money than he foresees, and he may always be of use to us at a pinch. Meanwhile he eats out of my hand.'

I complimented Raffles on the mere composition of his telegram, with half the characteristics of my distinguished kinsman squeezed into a dozen odd words; and let him know how the old ruffian had really treated me. Raffles was not surprised; we had dined together at my relative's in the old days, and filed for reference a professional valuation of his household gods. I now learnt that the telegram had been posted, with the hour marked for its despatch, at the pillar nearest Vere Street, on the night before the advertisement was due to appear in the *Daily Mail*. This also had been carefully prearranged; and Raffles's only fear had been lest it might be held over despite his explicit instructions, and so drive me to the doctor for an explanation of his telegram. But the adverse chances had been weeded out and weeded out to the irreducible minimum of risk.

His greatest risk, according to Raffles, lay nearest home: bedridden invalid that he was supposed to be, his nightly terror was of running into Theobald's arms in the immediate neighbourhood of the flat. But Raffles had characteristic methods of minimising even that danger, of which something anon; meanwhile he recounted more than one of his nocturnal adventures, all, however, of a singularly innocent type; and one thing I noticed while he talked. His room was the first as you entered the flat. The long inner wall divided the room not merely from the passage but from the outer landing as well. Thus every step upon the bare stone stairs could be heard by Raffles where he lay; and he would never speak while one was ascending, until it had passed his door. The afternoon brought more than one applicant for the post which it was my duty to tell them that I had already obtained. Between three and four, however, Raffles, suddenly looking at his watch, packed me off in a hurry to the other end of London for my things.

'I'm afraid you must be famishing, Bunny. It's a fact that I eat very little; and that at odd hours, but I ought not to have forgotten you. Get yourself a snack outside, but not a square meal if you can resist one. We've got to celebrate this day this night!'

'Tonight?' I cried.

'Tonight at eleven, and Kellner's the place. You may well open your eyes, but we didn't go there much, if you remember, and the staff seems changed. Anyway, we'll risk it for once. I was in last night, talking like a stage American, and supper's ordered for eleven sharp.'

'You made as sure of me as all that!'

'There was no harm in ordering supper. We shall have it in a private room, but you may as well dress if you've got the duds.'

'They're at my only forgiving relative's.'

'How much will get them out, and square you up, and bring you back bag and baggage in good time?'

I had to calculate. 'A tenner, easily.'

'I had one ready for you. Here it is, and I wouldn't lose any time if I were you. On the way you might look up Theobald, tell him you've got it and how long you'll be gone, and that I can't be left alone all the time. And, by Jove, yes! You get me a stall for the Lyceum at the nearest agent's; there are two or three in High Street; and say it was given you when you come in. That young man shall be out of the way tonight.'

I found our doctor in a minute consulting-room and his shirtsleeves, a tall tumbler at his elbow; at least I caught sight of the tumbler on entering; thereafter he stood in front of it, with a futility which had my sympathy.

'So you've got the billet,' said Dr Theobald. 'Well, as I told you before, and as you have since probably discovered for yourself, you won't find it exactly a sinecure. My own part of the business is by no means that; indeed, there are those who would throw up the case, after the kind of treatment that you have seen for yourself. But professional considerations are not the only ones, and one cannot make too many allowances in such a case.'

'But what is the case?' I asked him. 'You said you would tell me if I was successful.'

Dr Theobald's shrug was worthy of the profession he seemed destined to adorn; it was not incompatible with any construction which one chose to put upon it. Next moment he had stiffened. I suppose I still spoke more or less like a gentleman. Yet, after all, I was only the male nurse. He seemed to remember this suddenly, and he took occasion to remind me of the fact.

'Ah,' said he, 'that was before I knew you were altogether without experience; and I must say that I was surprised even at Mr Maturin's engaging you after that; but it will depend upon yourself how long I allow him to persist in so curious an experiment. As for what is the matter with him, my good fellow, it is no use my giving you an answer which would be double Dutch to you; moreover, I have still to test your discretionary powers. I may say, however, that that poor gentleman presents at once the most complex and most troublesome case, which is responsibility enough without certain features which make it all but insupportable. Beyond this I must refuse to discuss my patient for the present; but I shall certainly go up if I can find time.'

He went up within five minutes. I found him there on my return at dusk. But he did not refuse my stall for the Lyceum, which Raffles would not allow me to use myself, and presented to him offhand without my leave.

'And don't you bother any more about me till tomorrow,' snapped the high thin voice as he was off. 'I can send for you now when I want you, and I'm hoping to have a decent night for once.'

III

It was half-past ten when we left the flat, in an interval of silence on the noisy stairs. The silence was unbroken by our wary feet. Yet for me a surprise was in store upon the very landing. Instead of going downstairs, Raffles led me up two flights, and so out upon a perfectly flat roof.

'There are two entrances to these mansions,' he explained between stars and chimney-stacks: 'one to our staircase, and another round the corner. But there's only one porter, and he lives on the basement underneath us, and affects the door nearest home. We miss him by using the wrong stairs, and we run less risk of old Theobald. I got the tip from the postmen, who come up one way and down the other. Now follow me, and look out!'

There was indeed some necessity for caution, for each half of the building had its L-shaped well dropping sheer to the base, the parapets so low that one might easily have tripped over them into eternity. However, we were soon upon the second staircase, which opened on the roof like the first. And twenty minutes of the next twenty-five we spent in an admirable hansom, skimming east.

'Not much change in the old hole, Bunny. More of these magic-lantern advertisements ... and absolutely the worst bit of taste in town, though it's saying something, in that equestrian statue with the gilt stirrups and fixings: why don't they black the buffer's boots and his horse's hoofs while they are about it? ... More bicyclists, of course. That was just beginning, if you remember. It might have been useful to us... And there's the old club, getting put into a crate for the Jubilee; by Jove, Bunny, we ought to be there. I wouldn't lean forward in Piccadilly, old chap. If you're seen I'm thought of, and we shall have to be jolly careful at Kellner's... Ah, there it is! Did I tell you I was a low-down stage Yankee at Kellner's? You'd better be another, while the waiter's in the room.'

We had the little room upstairs; and on the very threshold, I, even I, who knew my Raffles of old, was taken horribly aback. The table was laid for three. I called his attention to it in a whisper.

'Why, yep!' came through his nose. – 'Say, boy, the lady, she's not comin', but you leave that tackle where 'tis. If I'm liable to pay, I guess I'll have all there is to it.'

I have never been in America, and the American public is the last on earth that I desire to insult; but idiom and intonation alike would have imposed upon my inexperience. I had to look at Raffles to make sure that it was he who spoke, and I had my own reasons for looking hard.

'Who on earth was the lady?' I inquired aghast at the first opportunity.

'She isn't on earth. They don't like wasting this room on two, that's all. Bunny – my Bunny – here's to us both!'

And we clinked glasses swimming with the liquid gold of Steinberg, 1868; but of the rare delights of that supper I can scarcely trust myself to write. It was no mere meal, it was no coarse orgy, but a little feast for the fastidious gods, not unworthy of Lucullus at his worst. And I who had bolted my skilly at Wormwood Scrubs, and tightened my belt in a Holloway attic, it was I who sat down to this ineffable repast! Where the courses were few, but each a triumph of its kind, it would be invidious to single out any one dish; but the *jambon de Westphalie au champagne* tempts me sorely. And then the champagne that we drank, not the quantity but the quality! Well, it was Pol Roger, '84, and quite good enough for me; but even so it was not more dry, nor did it sparkle more, than the merry rascal who had dragged me thus far to the devil, but should lead me dancing the rest of the way. I was beginning to tell him so. I had done my honest best since my reappearance in the world; but the world had done its worst by me. A further antithesis and my final intention were both upon my tongue when the waiter with the Chateau Margaux cut me short; for he was the bearer of more than that great wine; bringing also a card upon a silver tray.

'Show him up,' said Raffles, laconically.

'And who is this?' I cried when the man was gone. Raffles reached across the table and gripped my arm in his vice. His eyes were steel points fixed on mine.

'Bunny, stand by me,' said he in the old irresistible voice, a voice both stern and winning. 'Stand by me, Bunny – if there's a row!'

And there was time for nothing more, the door flying open, and a dapper person entering with a bow; a frock-coat on his back, gold *pince-nez* on his nose; a shiny hat in one hand, and a black bag in the other.

'Good-evening, gentlemen,' said he, at home and smiling.

'Sit down,' drawled Raffles in casual response. 'Say, let me introduce you to Mr Ezra B. Martin of Shicawgo. Mr Martin is my future brother-in-law – this is Mr Robinson, Ezra, manager to Sparks and Company, the cellerbrated joolers on Regent Street.'

I pricked up my ears, but contented myself with a nod. I altogether distrusted my ability to live up to my new name and address.

'I figured on Miss Martin bein' right here, too,' continued Raffles, 'but I regret to say she's not feelin' so good. We light out for Parrus on the 9 a.m. train tomorrer mornin', and she guessed she'd be too dead. Sorry to disappoint you, Mr Robinson; but you'll see I'm advertising your wares.'

Raffles held his right hand under the electric light, and a diamond ring flashed upon his little finger. I could have sworn it was not there five minutes before.

The tradesman had a disappointed face, but for a moment it brightened as he expatiated on the value of that ring and on the price his people had accepted for it. I was invited to guess the figure, but I shook a discreet head. I have seldom been more taciturn in my life.

'Forty-five pounds,' cried the jeweller; 'and it would be cheap at fifty guineas.'

'That's right,' assented Raffles. 'That'd be dead cheap, I allow. But then, my boy, you gotten ready cash, and don't you forget it.'

I do not dwell upon my own mystification in all this. I merely pause to state that I was keenly enjoying that very element. Nothing could have been more typical of Raffles and the past. It was only my own attitude that was changed.

It appeared that the mythical lady, my sister, had just become engaged to Raffles, who seemed all anxiety to pin her down with gifts of price. I could not quite gather whose gift to whom was the diamond ring; but it had evidently been paid for; and I voyaged to the moon, wondering when and how. I was recalled to this planet by a deluge of gems from the jeweller's bag. They lay alight in their cases like the electric lamps above. We all three put our heads together over them, myself without the slightest clue as to what was coming, but not unprepared for violent crime. One does not do eighteen months for nothing.

'Right away,' Raffles was saying. 'We'll choose for her, and you'll change anything she don't like. Is that the idea?'

'That was my suggestion, sir.'

'Then come on, Ezra. I guess you know Sadie's taste. You help me choose.'

And we chose – Lord! What did we not choose? There was her ring, a diamond half-hoop. It cost £95, and there was no attempt to get it for £90. Then there was a diamond necklet – two hundred guineas, but pounds accepted. That was to be the gift of the bridegroom. The wedding was evidently imminent. It behoved me to play a brotherly part. I therefore rose to the occasion; calculated she would like a diamond star (£116), but reckoned it was more than I could afford; and sustained a vicious kick under the table for either verb. I was afraid to open my mouth on finally obtaining the star for the round hundred. And then the fat fell in the fire; for pay we could not; though a remittance (said Raffles) was 'overdo from Noo York'.

'But I don't know you, gentlemen,' the jeweller exclaimed. 'I haven't even the name of your hotel!'

'I told you we was stoppin' with friends,' said Raffles, who was not angry, though thwarted and crushed. 'But that's right, sir! Oh, that's dead right, and I'm the last man to ask you to take

Quixotic risks. I'm tryin' to figure a way out. Yes, sir, that's what I'm tryin' to do.'

'I wish you could, sir,' the jeweller said, with feeling. 'It isn't as if we hadn't seen the colour of your money. But certain rules I am sworn to observe; it isn't as if I was in business for myself; and – you say you start for Paris in the morning!'

'On the 9 a.m. train,' mused Raffles; 'and I've heard no-end yarns about the joolers' stores in Parrus. But that ain't fair; don't you take no notice o' that. I'm trying to figure a way out. Yes, sir!'

He was smoking cigarettes out of a twenty-five box; the tradesman and I had cigars. Raffles sat frowning with a pregnant eye, and it was only too clear to me that his plans had miscarried. I could not help thinking, however, that they deserved to do so, if he had counted upon buying credit for all but £400 by a single payment of some 10 per cent. That again seemed unworthy of Raffles, and I, for my part, still sat prepared to spring any moment at our visitor's throat.

'We could mail you the money from Parrus,' drawled Raffles at length. 'But how should we know you'd hold up your end of the string, and mail us the same articles we've selected tonight?'

The visitor stiffened in his chair. The name of his firm should be sufficient guarantee for that.

'I guess I'm no better acquainted with their name than they are with mine,' remarked Raffles, laughing. 'See here, though! I got a scheme. You pack 'em in this!'

He turned the cigarettes out of the tin box, while the jeweller and I joined wondering eyes.

'Pack 'em in this,' repeated Raffles, 'the three things we want, and never mind the boxes; you can pack 'em in cottonwool. Then we'll ring for string and sealing-wax, seal up the lot right here, and you can take 'em away in your grip. Within three days we'll have our remittance, and mail you the money, and you'll mail us this darned box with my seal unbroken! It's no use you lookin' so sick, Mr Jooler; you won't trust us any, and yet we're goin' to trust you some. – Ring the bell, Ezra, and we'll see if they've gotten any sealing-wax and string.'

They had; and the thing was done. The tradesman did not like it; the precaution was absolutely necessary; but since he was taking all his goods away with him, the sold with the unsold, his sentimental objections soon fell to the ground. He packed necklet, ring and star with his own hands, in cottonwool; and the cigarette-box held them so easily that at the last moment, when the box was closed, and the string ready, Raffles very nearly added a diamond bee- brooch at £51 10s. This temptation, however, he ultimately overcame, to the other's chagrin. The cigarette-box was tied up, and the string sealed, oddly enough, with the diamond of the ring that had been bought and paid for.

'I'll chance you having another ring in the store the dead spit of mine,' laughed Raffles, as he relinquished the box, and it disappeared into the tradesman's bag. 'And now, Mr Robinson, I hope you'll appreciate my true hospitality in not offering you anything to drink while business was in progress. That's Chateau Margaux, sir, and I should judge it's what you'd call an eighteen-carat article.'

In the cab which we took to the vicinity of the flat, I was instantly snubbed for asking questions which the driver might easily overhear, and I took the repulse just a little to heart. I could make neither head nor tail of Raffles's dealings with the man from Regent Street, and was naturally inquisitive as to the meaning of it all. But I held my tongue until we had regained the flat in the curious manner of our exit, and even there until Raffles rallied me with a hand on either shoulder and an old smile upon his face.

'You rabbit!' said he. 'Why couldn't you wait till we got home?'

'Why couldn't you tell me what you were going to do?' I retorted as of yore.

'Because your dear old phiz is still worth its sight in innocence, and because you never could act for nuts! You looked as puzzled as the other poor devil; but you wouldn't if you had known what my game really was.'

'And pray what was it?'

'That,' said Raffles, and he smacked the cigarette-box down upon the mantelpiece. It was not tied. It was not sealed. It flew open from the force of the impact. And the diamond ring that cost £95, the necklet for £200, and my flaming star at another £100, all three lay safe and snug in the jeweller's own cottonwool!

'Duplicate boxes!' I cried.

'Duplicate boxes, my brainy Bunny. One was already packed, and weighted, and in my pocket. I don't know whether you noticed me weighing the three things together in my hand? I know that neither of you saw me change the boxes, for I did it when I was nearest buying the bee-brooch at the end, and you were too puzzled, and the other Johnnie too keen. It was the cheapest shot in the game; the dear ones were sending old Theobald to Southampton on a fool's errand yesterday afternoon, and showing one's own nose down Regent Street in broad daylight while he was gone; but some things are worth paying for and certain risks one must always take. Nice boxes, aren't they? I only wished they contained a better cigarette; but a notorious brand was essential; a box of Sullivans would have brought me to life tomorrow.'

'But they oughtn't to open it tomorrow.'

'Nor will they, as a matter of fact. Meanwhile, Bunny, I may call upon you to dispose of the boodle.'

'I'm on for any mortal thing!'

My voice rang true, I swear, but it was the way of Raffles to take the evidence of as many senses as possible. I felt the cold steel of his eye through mine and through my brain. But what he saw seemed to satisfy him no less than what he heard, for his hand found my hand, and pressed it with a fervour foreign to the man.

'I know you are, and I knew you would be. Only remember, Bunny, it's my turn next to pay the shot!'

You shall hear how he paid it when the time came.

2

A JUBILEE PRESENT

The Room of Gold, in the British Museum, is probably well enough known to the inquiring alien and the travelled American. A true Londoner, however, I myself had never heard of it until Raffles casually proposed a raid.

'The older I grow, Bunny, the less I think of your so-called precious stones. When did they ever bring in half their market value in l.s.d.? There was the first little crib we ever cracked together – you with your innocent eyes shut. A thousand pounds that stuff was worth; but how many hundreds did it actually fetch? The Ardagh emeralds weren't much better; old Lady Melrose's necklace was far worse; but that little lot the other night has about finished me. A cool hundred for goods priced well over four; and £35 to come off for bait, since we only got a tenner for the ring I bought and paid for like an ass. I'll be shot if I ever touch a diamond again! Not if it was the Koh-i-noor; those few whacking stones are too well known, and to cut them up is to decrease their value by arithmetical retrogression. Besides, that brings you up against the fence once more, and I'm done with the beggars for good and all. You talk about your editors and publishers, you literary swine. Barabbas was neither a robber nor a publisher, but a six-barred, barbed-wired, spike-topped fence. What we really want is an Incorporated Society of Thieves, with some public-spirited old forger to run it for us on business lines.'

Raffles uttered these blasphemies under his breath, not, I am afraid, out of any respect for my one redeeming profession, but because we were taking a midnight airing on the roof, after a whole day of June in the little flat below. The stars shone overhead, the lights of London underneath, and between the lips of Raffles a cigarette of the old and only brand. I had sent in secret for a box of the best; the boon had arrived that night; and the foregoing speech was the first result. I could afford to ignore the insolent asides, however, where the apparent contention was so manifestly unsound.

'And how are you going to get rid of your gold?' said I, pertinently.

'Nothing easier, my dear rabbit.'

'Is your Room of Gold a roomful of sovereigns?'

Raffles laughed softly at my scorn.

'No, Bunny, it's principally in the shape of archaic ornaments, whose value, I admit, is largely extrinsic. But gold is gold, from Phoenicia to Klondike, and if we cleared the room we should eventually do very well.'

'How?'

'I should melt it down into a nugget, and bring it home from the USA tomorrow.'

'And then?'

'Make them pay up in hard cash across the counter of the Bank of England. And you *can* make them.'

That I knew, and so said nothing for a time, remaining a hostile though a silent critic, while we paced the cool black leads with our bare feet, softly as cats.

'And how do you propose to get enough away', at length I asked, 'to make it worth while?'

'Ah, there you have it,' said Raffles. 'I only propose to reconnoitre the ground, to see what we can see. We might find some hiding-place for a night; that, I am afraid, would be our only chance.'

'Have you ever been there before?'

'Not since they got the one good, portable piece which I believe that they exhibit now. It's a long time since I read of it – I can't remember where – but I know they have got a gold cup of sorts worth several thousands. A number of the immorally rich clubbed together and presented it to the nation; and two of the richly immoral intend to snaffle it for themselves. At any rate we might go and have a look at it, Bunny, don't you think?'

Think! I seized his arm.

'When? When? When?' I asked, like a quick-firing gun.

'The sooner the better, while old Theobald's away on his honeymoon.'

Our medico had married the week before, nor was any fellow-practitioner taking his work – at least not that considerable branch of it which consisted of Raffles – during his brief absence from town. There were reasons, delightfully obvious to us, why such a plan would have been highly unwise in Dr Theobald. I, however, was sending him daily screeds, and both matutinal and nocturnal telegrams, the composition of which afforded Raffles not a little enjoyment.

'Well, then, when – when?' I began to repeat.

'Tomorrow, if you like.'

'Only to look?' The limitation was my one regret.

'We must do so, Bunny, before we leap.'

'Very well,' I sighed. 'But tomorrow it is!'

I saw the porter that night, and, I still think, bought his absolute allegiance for the second coin of the realm. My story, however, invented by Raffles, was sufficiently specious in itself. That sick gentleman, Mr Maturin (as I had to remember to call him), was really, or apparently, sickening for fresh air. Dr

Theobald would allow him none; he was pestering me for just one day in the country while the glorious weather lasted. I was myself convinced that no possible harm could come of the experiment. Would the porter help me in so innocent and meritorious an intrigue? The man hesitated. I produced my half-sovereign. The man was lost. And at half-past eight next morning – before the heat of the day – Raffles and I drove to Kew Gardens in a hired landau which was to call for us at midday and wait until we came. The porter had assisted me to carry my invalid downstairs, in a carrying-chair hired (like the landau) from Harrod's Stores for the occasion.

It was little after nine when we crawled together into the gardens; by half-past my invalid had had enough, and out he tottered on my arm; a cab, a message to our coachman, a timely train to Baker Street, another cab, and we were at the British Museum – brisk pedestrians now – not very many minutes after the opening hour of 10 a.m.

It was one of those glowing days which will not be forgotten by many who were in town at the time. The Diamond jubilee was upon us, and Queen's weather had already set in. Raffles, indeed, declared it was hot as Italy and Australia put together; and certainly the short summer nights gave the channels of wood and asphalt and the continents of brick and mortar but little time to cool. At the British Museum the pigeons were crooning among the shadows of the grimy colonnade, and the stalwart janitors looked less stalwart than usual, as though their medals were too heavy for them. I recognised some habitual readers going to their labour underneath the dome; of mere visitors we seemed among the first.

'That's the room,' said Raffles, who had bought the twopenny guide, as we studied it openly on the nearest bench; 'Number 43, upstairs and sharp round to the right. Come on, Bunny!'

And he led the way in silence, but with a long methodical stride which I could not understand until we came to the corridor leading to the Room of Gold, where he turned to me for a moment.

'A hundred and thirty-nine yards from this to the open street,' said Raffles, 'not counting the stairs. I suppose we *could* do it in twenty seconds, but if we did we should have to jump the gates. No, you must remember to loaf out at slow march, Bunny, whether you like it or not.'

'But you talked about a hiding-place for a night?'

'Quite so – for all night. We should have to get back, go on lying low, and saunter out with the crowd next day – after doing the whole show thoroughly.'

'What! With gold in our pockets – '

'And gold in our boots, and gold up the sleeves and legs of our suits! You leave that to me, Bunny, and wait till you've tried two pairs of trousers sewn together at the foot! This is only a preliminary reconnoitre. And here we are.'

It is none of my business to describe the so-called Room of Gold, with which I, for one, was not a little disappointed. The glass cases, which both fill and line it, may contain unique examples of the goldsmith's art in times and places of which one heard quite enough in the course of one's classical education; but, from a professional point of view, I would as lief have the ransacking of a single window in the West End as the pick of all those spoils of Etruria and of Ancient Greece. The gold may not be so soft as it appears, but it certainly looks as though you could bite off the business ends of the spoons, and stop your own teeth in doing so. Nor should I care to be seen wearing one of the rings; but the greatest fraud of all (from the aforesaid standpoint) is assuredly that very cup of which Raffles had spoken. Moreover, he felt this himself.

'Why, it's as thin as paper,' said he, 'and enamelled like a middle-aged lady of quality! But, by Jove, it's one of the most beautiful things I ever saw in my life, Bunny. I should like to have it for its own sake, by all my gods!'

The thing had a little square case of plate-glass all to itself at one end of the room. It may have been the thing of beauty that Raffles affected to consider it, but I for my part was in no mood to look at it in that light. Underneath were the names of the plutocrats who had subscribed for this national gewgaw, and I fell to wondering where their £8,000 came in, while Raffles devoured his twopenny guidebook as greedily as a school-girl with a zeal for culture.

'Those are scenes from the martyrdom of St Agnes,' said he ... '"translucent on relief ... one of the finest specimens of its kind". I should think it was! Bunny, you Philistine, why can't you admire the thing for its own sake? It would be worth having only to live up to! There never was such rich enamelling on such thin gold; and what a good scheme to hang the lid up over it, so that you can see how thin it is. I wonder if we could lift it, Bunny, by hook or crook?'

'You'd better try, sir,' said a dry voice at his elbow.

The madman seemed to think we had the room to ourselves. I knew better, but, like another madman, had let him ramble on unchecked. And here was a solid constable confronting us, in the short tunic that they wear in summer, his whistle on its chain, but no truncheon at his side. Heavens! how I see him now; a man of medium size, with a broad, good-humoured perspiring face, and a limp moustache. He looked sternly at Raffles, and Raffles looked merrily at him.

'Going to run me in, officer?' said he. 'That *would* be a joke – my hat!'

'I didn't say as I was, sir,' replied the policeman. 'But that's queer talk for a gentleman like you, sir, in the British Museum!' And he wagged his helmet at my invalid, who had taken his airing in frock-coat and top-hat, the more readily to assume his present part.

'What!' cried Raffles, 'simply saying to my friend that I'd like to lift the gold cup? Why, so I should, officer, so I should!

I don't mind who hears me say so. It's one of the most beautiful things I ever saw in all my life.'

The constable's face had already relaxed, and now a grin peeped under the limp moustache. 'I dare say there's many as feels like that, sir,' said he.

'Exactly; and I say what I feel, that's all,' said Raffles airily. 'But seriously, officer, is a valuable thing like this quite safe in a case like that?'

'Safe enough as long as I'm here,' replied the other, between grim jest and stout earnest. Raffles studied his face; he was still watching Raffles; and I kept an eye on them both without putting in my word.

'You appear to be single-handed,' observed Raffles. 'Is that wise?'

The note of anxiety was capitally caught; it was at once personal and public-spirited, that of the enthusiastic savant, afraid for a national treasure which few appreciated as he did himself. And, to be sure, the three of us now had this treasury to ourselves; one or two others had been there when we entered, but now they were gone.

'I'm not single-handed,' said the officer, comfortably. 'See that seat by the door? One of the attendants sits there all day long.'

'Then where is he now?'

'Talking to another attendant just outside. If you listen you'll hear them for yourself.'

We listened, and we did hear them, but not just outside. In my own mind I even questioned whether they were in the corridor through which we had come; to me it sounded as though they were just outside the corridor.

'You mean the fellow with the billiard-cue who was here when we came in?' pursued Raffles.

'That wasn't a billiard-cue! It was a pointer,' the intelligent officer explained.

'It ought to be a javelin,' said Raffles nervously. 'It ought to be a pole-axe! The public treasure ought to be better guarded than this. I shall write to *The Times* about it – you see if I don't!'

All at once, yet somehow not so suddenly as to excite suspicion, Raffles had become the elderly busybody with nerves; why, I could not for the life of me imagine; and the policeman seemed equally at sea.

'Lor' bless you, sir,' said he, 'I'm all right; don't you bother your head about *me*.'

'But you haven't even got a truncheon!'

'Not likely to want one either. You see, sir, it's early as yet; in a few minutes these here rooms will fill up; and there's safety in numbers, as they say.'

'Oh, it will fill up soon, will it?'

'Any minute now, sir.'

'Ah!'

'It isn't often empty as long as this, sir. It's the Jubilee, I suppose.'

'Meanwhile, what if my friend and I had been professional thieves? Why, we could have overpowered you in an instant, my good fellow!'

'That you couldn't; leastways, not without bringing the whole place about your ears.'

'Well, I shall write to *The Times* all the same. I'm a connoisseur in all this sort of thing, and I won't have unnecessary risks run with the nation's property. You said there was an attendant just outside, but he sounds to me as though he were at the other end of the corridor. I shall write today!'

For an instant we all three listened; and Raffles was right. Then I saw two things in one glance. Raffles had stepped a few inches backward, and stood poised upon the ball of each foot, his arms half raised, a light in his eyes. And another kind of light was breaking over the crass features of our friend the constable.

'Then shall I tell you what *I'll* do?' he cried, with a sudden clutch at the whistle-chain on his chest. The whistle flew out, but it never reached his lips. There were a couple of sharp smacks, like double barrels discharged all but simultaneously and the man reeled against me so that I could not help catching him as he fell.

'Well done, Bunny! I've knocked him out – I've knocked him out! Run you to the door and see if the attendants have heard anything, and take them on if they have.'

Mechanically I did as I was told. There was no time for thought, still less for remonstrance or reproach, though my surprise must have been even more complete than that of the constable before Raffles knocked the sense out of him. Even in my utter bewilderment, however, the instinctive caution of the real criminal did not desen me. I ran to the door, but I sauntered through it, to plant myself before a Pompeiian fresco in the corridor; and there were the two attendants still gossiping outside the further door; nor did they hear the dull crash which I heard even as I watched them out of the comer of each eye.

It was hot weather, as I have said, but the perspiration on my body seemed already to have turned into a skin of ice. Then I caught the faint reflection of my own face in the casing of the fresco, and it frightened me into some semblance of myself as Raffles joined me with his hands in his pockets. But my fear and indignation were redoubled at the sight of him, when a single glance convinced me that his pockets were as empty as his hands, and his mad outrage the most wanton and reckless of his whole career.

'Ah, very interesting, very interesting, but nothing to what they have in the museum at Naples or in Pompeii itself. You must go there some day, Bunny. I've a good mind to take you myself. Meanwhile – slow march! The beggar hasn't moved an eyelid. We may swing for him if you show indecent haste!'

'We!' I whispered. 'We!'

And my knees knocked together as we came up to the chatting attendants. But Raffles must needs interrupt them to ask the way to the Prehistoric Saloon.

'At the top of the stairs.'

'Thank you. Then we'll work round that way to the Egyptian part.'

And we left them resuming their providential chat.

'I believe you're mad,' I said bitterly as we went.

'I believe I *was*,' admitted Raffles; 'but I'm not now, and I'll see you through. A hundred and thirty-nine yards, wasn't it? Then it can't be more than a hundred and twenty now — not as much. Steady, Bunny, for God's sake. It's *slow* march – for our lives.'

There was this much management. The rest was our colossal luck. A hansom was being paid off at the foot of the steps outside, and in we jumped, Raffles shouting 'Charing Cross!' for all Bloomsbury to hear.

We had turned into Bloomsbury Street without exchanging a syllable when he struck the trap-door with his fist.

'Where the devil are you driving us?'

'Charing Cross, sir.'

'I said King's Cross! Round you spin, and drive like blazes, or we miss our train! – There's one to York at 10.35,' added Raffles as the trap-door slammed; 'we'll book there, Bunny, and then we'll slope through the subway to the Metropolitan, and so to ground *via* Baker Street and Earl's Court.'

And actually in half an hour he was seated once more in the hired carrying-chair, while the porter and I staggered upstairs with my decrepit charge, for whose shattered strength even one hour in Kew Gardens had proved too much! Then, and not until then, when we had got rid of the porter and were alone at last, did I tell Raffles, in the most nervous English at my command, frankly and exactly what I thought of him of his latest deed. Once started, moreover, I spoke as I have seldom spoken to living man; and Raffles, of all men, stood my abuse without a murmur; or rather he sat it out, too astounded even to take off his hat, though I thought his eyebrows would have lifted it from his head.

'But it always was your infernal way,' I was savagely concluding. 'You make one plan, and you tell me another – '

'Not today, Bunny, I swear!'

'You mean to tell me you really did start with the bare idea of finding a place to hide in for a night?'

'Of course I did.'

'It was to be the mere reconnoitre you pretended?'

'There was no pretence about it, Bunny.'

'Then why on earth go and do what you did?'

'The reason would be obvious to anyone but you,' said Raffles, still with no unkindly scorn. 'It was the temptation of a minute – the final impulse of the fraction of a second, when Roberto saw that I was tempted, and let me see that he saw it. It's not a thing I care to do, and I shan't be happy till the papers tell me the poor devil is alive. But a knock-out shot was the only chance for us then.'

'Why? You don't get run in for being tempted, nor yet for showing that you are!'

'But I should have deserved running in if I hadn't yielded to such a temptation as that, Bunny. It was a chance in a hundred thousand! We might go there every day of our lives, and never again be the only outsiders in the room, with the billiard-marking Johnnie practically out of earshot at one and the same time. It was a gift from the gods; not to have taken it would have been flying in the face of Providence.'

'But you didn't take it,' said I. 'You went and left it behind.' I wish I had had a Kodak for the little smile with which Raffles shook his head, for it was one that he kept for those great moments of which our vocation is not devoid. All this time he had been wearing his hat, tilted a little over eyebrows no longer raised. And now at last I knew where the gold cup was.

It stood for days upon his chimney-piece, this costly trophy whose ancient history and final fate filled newspaper columns even in these days of Jubilee, and for which the flower of Scotland

Yard was said to be seeking high and low. Our constable, we learnt, had been stunned only, and, from the moment that I brought him an evening paper with the news, Raffles's spirits rose to a height inconsistent with his equable temperament, and as unusual in him as the sudden impulse upon which he had acted with such effect. The cup itself appealed to me no more than it had done before. Exquisite it might be, handsome it was, but so light in the hand that the mere gold of it would scarcely have poured three figures out of a melting-pot. And what said Raffles but that he would never melt it at all!

'Taking it was an offence against the laws of the land, Bunny. That is nothing. But destroying it would be a crime against God and Art, and may I be spitted on the vane of St Mary Abbot's if I commit it!'

Talk such as this was unanswerable; indeed, the whole affair had passed the pale of useful comment; and the one course left to a practical person was to shrug his shoulders and enjoy the joke. This was not a little enhanced by the newspaper reports, which described Raffles as a handsome youth, and his unwilling accomplice as an older man of blackguardly appearance and low type.

'Hits us both off rather neatly, Bunny,' said he. 'But what they none of them do justice to is my dear cup. Look at it; only look at it, man! Was ever anything so rich and yet so chaste? St Agnes must have had a pretty bad time, but it would be almost worth it to go down to posterity in such enamel upon such gold. And then the history of the thing. Do you realise that it's five hundred years old and has belonged to Henry the Eighth and to Elizabeth among others? Bunny, when you have me cremated, you can put my ashes in yonder cup, and lay us in the deep-delved earth together!'

'And meanwhile?'

'It is the joy of my heart, the light of my life, the delight of mine eye.'

'And suppose other eyes catch sight of it?'

'They never must; they never shall.'

Raffles would have been too absurd had he not been thoroughly alive to his own absurdity; there was nevertheless an underlying sincerity in his appreciation of any and every form of beauty, which all his nonsense could not conceal. And his infatuation for the cup was, as he declared, a very pure passion, since the circumstances debarred him from the chief joy of the average collector, that of showing his treasure to his friends. At last, however, and at the height of his craze, Raffles and reason seemed to come together again as suddenly as they had parted company in the Room of Gold.

'Bunny,' he cried, flinging his newspaper across the room, 'I've got an idea after your own heart. I know where I can place if after all!'

'Do you mean the cup?'

'I do.'

'Then I congratulate you.'

'Thanks.'

'Upon the recovery of your senses.'

'Thanks galore. But you've been confoundedly unsympathetic about this thing, Bunny, and I don't think I shall tell you my scheme till I've carried it out.'

'Quite time enough,' said I.

'It will mean your letting me loose for an hour or two under cloud of this very night. Tomorrow's Sunday, the Jubilee's on Tuesday, and old Theobald's coming back for it.'

'It doesn't much matter whether he's back or not if you go late enough.'

'I mustn't be late. They don't keep open. No, it's no use your asking any questions. Go out and buy me a big box of Huntley and Palmer's biscuits; any sort you like, only they must be theirs, and absolutely the biggest box they sell.'

'My dear man!'

'No questions, Bunny; you do your part and I'll do mine.'

Subtlety and success were in his face. It was enough for me, and I had done his extraordinary bidding within a quarter of an hour. In another minute Raffles had opened the box and tumbled all the biscuits into the nearest chair.

'Now newspapers!'

I fetched a pile. He bid the cup of gold a ridiculous farewell, wrapped it up in newspaper after newspaper, and finally packed it in the empty biscuit-box.

'Now some brown paper. I don't want to be taken for the grocer's young man.'

A neat enough parcel it made, when the string had been tied and the ends cut loose; what was more difficult was to wrap up Raffles himself in such a way that even the porter should not recognise him if they came face to face at the corner. And the sun was still up. But Raffles would go, and when he did I should not have known him myself.

He may have been an hour away. It was barely dusk when he returned, and my first question referred to our dangerous ally, the porter. Raffles had passed him unsuspected in going, but had managed to avoid him altogether on the return journey, which he had completed by way of the other entrance and the roof. I breathed again.

'And what have you done with the cup?'

'Placed it!'

'How much for? How much for?'

'Let me think. I had a couple of cabs, and the postage was a tanner, with another twopence for registration. Yes, it cost me exactly five-and-eight.'

'*It* cost *you?* But what did you *get* for it, Raffles?'

'Nothing, my boy.'

'Nothing!'

'Not a crimson cent.'

'I am not surprised. I never thought it had a market value. I told you so in the beginning,' I said, irritably. 'But what on earth have you done with the thing?'

'Sent it to the Queen.'

'You haven't!'

Rogue is a word with various meanings, and Raffles had been one sort of rogue ever since I had known him; but now, for once, he was the innocent variety, a great grey-haired child, running over with merriment and mischief.

'Well, I've sent it to Sir Arthur Bigge, to present to her Majesty, with the loyal respects of the thief, if that will do for you,' said Raffles. 'I thought they might take too much stock of me at the GPO if I addressed it to Sovereign herself. Yes, I drove over to St Martin's-le-Grand with it, and I registered the box into the bargain. Do a thing properly if you do it at all.'

'But why on earth,' I groaned, 'do such a thing at all?'

'My dear Bunny, we have been reigned over for sixty years by infinitely the finest monarch the world has ever seen. The world is taking the present opportunity of signifying the fact for all it is worth. Every nation is laying of its best at her royal feet; every class in the community is doing its little level – except ours. All I have done is to remove one reproach from our fraternity.'

At this I came round, was infected with his spirit, called him the sportsman he always was and would be, and shook his daredevil hand in mine; but, at the same time, I still had my qualms.

'Supposing they trace it to us?' said I.

'There's not much to catch hold of in a biscuit-box by Huntley and Palmer,' replied Raffles; 'that was why I sent you for one. And I didn't write a word upon a sheet of paper which could possibly be traced. I simply printed two or three on a virginal postcard – another halfpenny to the bad – which might have been bought at any post-office in the kingdom. No, old chap, the GPO was the one real danger; there was one detective I spotted for myself; and the sight of him has left me with a thirst. Whisky and Sullivans for two, Bunny, if you please.'

Raffles was soon clinking his glass against mine.

'The Queen,' said he. 'God bless her!'

3

THE FATE OF FAUSTINA

Mar – ga – rì,
  e perzo a Salvatore!
Mar – ga – rì'
  Ma l'ommo è cacciatore!
  Mar – ga – rì,
  Nun ce aje corpa tu!
Chello ch' è fatto, è fatto
  un ne parlammo cchieù!

A piano-organ was pouring the metallic music through our open windows, while a voice of brass brayed the words, which I have since obtained, and print above for identification by such as know their Italy better than I. They will not thank me for reminding them of a tune so lately epidemic in that land of aloes and blue skies; but at least it is unlikely to run in their heads as the ribald accompaniment to a tragedy; and it does in mine.

It was in the early heat of August, and the hour that of the lawful and necessary siesta for such as turn night into day. I was therefore shutting my window in a rage, and wondering whether I should not do the same for Raffles, when he appeared in the silk pyjamas to which the chronic solicitude of Dr Theobald confined him from morning to night.

'Don't do that, Bunny,' said he. 'I rather like that thing, and want to listen. What sort of fellows are they to look at, by the way?'

I put my head out to see, it being a primary rule of our quaint establishment that Raffles must never show himself at any of the windows. I remember now how hot the sill was to my elbows, as I leant upon it and looked down, in order to satisfy a curiosity in which I could see no point.

'Dirty-looking beggars,' said I over my shoulder: 'dark as dark; blue chins, oleaginous curls and ear-rings; ragged as they make them, but nothing picturesque in their rags.'

'Neapolitans all over,' murmured Raffles behind me; 'and that's a characteristic touch, the one fellow singing while the other grinds; they always have that out there.'

'He's rather a fine chap, the singer,' said I, as the song ended. 'My hat, what teeth! He's looking up here, and grinning all round his head; shall I chuck them anything?'

'Well, I have no reason to love the Neopolitans; but it takes me back – it takes me back! Yes, here you are, one each.'

It was a couple of half-crowns that Raffles put into my hand, but I had thrown them into the street for pennies before I saw what they were. Thereupon I left the Italians bowing to the mud, as well they might, and I turned to protest against such wanton waste. But Raffles was walking up and down, his head bent, his eyes troubled; and his one excuse disarmed remonstrance.

'They took me back,' he repeated. 'My God, how they took me back!'

Suddenly he stopped in his stride.

'You don't understand, Bunny, old chap; but if you like you shall. I always meant to tell you some day, but never felt worked up to it before, and it's not the kind of thing one talks about for talking's sake. It isn't a nursery story, Bunny, and there isn't a laugh in it from start to finish; on the contrary, you have often asked me what turned my hair grey, and now you are going to hear.'

This was promising, but Raffles's manner was something more. It was unique in my memory of the man. His fine face softened and set hard by turns. I never knew it so hard. I never knew it so soft. And the same might be said of his voice, now tender as any woman's, now flying to the other extreme of equally unwonted ferocity. But this was toward the end of his tale; the beginning he treated characteristically enough, though I could have wished for a less cavalier account of the Island of Elba, where, upon his own showing, he had met with much humanity.

'Deadly, my dear Bunny, is not the word for that glorified snag, or for the molluscs its inhabitants. But they started by wounding my vanity, so perhaps I am prejudiced after all. I sprung myself upon them as a shipwrecked sailor – a sole survivor – stripped in the sea and landed without a stitch – yet they took no more interest in me than you do in Italian organ-grinders. They were decent enough. I didn't have to pick and steal for a square meal and a pair of trousers – it would have been more exciting if I had. But what a place! Napoleon couldn't stand it, you remember, but he held on longer than I did. I put in a few weeks in their infernal mines, simply to pick up a smattering of Italian; then got across to the mainland in a little wooden timber-tramp; and ungratefully glad I was to leave Elba blazing in just such another sunset as the one you won't forget.

'The tramp was bound for Naples, but first it touched at Baiæ, where I carefully deserted in the night. There are too many English in Naples itself, though I thought it would make a first happy hunting-ground when I knew the language better and had altered myself a bit more. Meanwhile I got a billet of several sorts on one of the loveliest spots that ever I struck on all my travels. The place was a vineyard, but it overhung the sea, and I got taken on as tame sailor-man and emergency bottle-washer. The wages were the noble figure of a lira and a half, which is just over a bob, a day, but there were lashings of sound wine for one and all, and better wine to bathe in. And for eight whole months, my boy, I was an absolutely honest man. The luxury of it, Bunny! I out-Heroded Herod, wouldn't touch a grape, and went in the most delicious danger of being knifed for my principles by the thieving crew I had joined.

'It was the kind of place where every prospect pleases – and all the rest of it – especially all the rest. But may I see it in my dreams till I die – as it was in the beginning – before anything began to happen. It was a wedge of rock sticking out into the bay, thatched with vines, and with the rummiest old house on the very edge of all, a devil of a height above the sea: you might have sat at the windows and dropped your Sullivan-ends plumb into blue water a hundred and fifty feet below.

'From the garden behind the house- – such a garden, Bunny – oleanders and mimosa, myrtles, rosemary, and red tangles of fiery untamed flowers – in a corner of this garden was the top of a subterranean stair down to the sea; at least, there were nearly two hundred steps tunnelled through the solid rock; then an iron gate, and another eighty steps in the open air; and last of all a cave fit for pirates a-penny-plain-and-twopence-coloured. This cave gave upon the sweetest little thing in coves, all deep blue water and honest rocks; and here I looked after the vineyard shipping, a pot-bellied tub with a brown sail, and a sort of dinghy. The tub took the wine to Naples, and the dinghy was the tub's tender.

'The house above was said to be on the identical site of a suburban retreat of the admirable Tiberius; there was the old sinner's private theatre with the tiers cut clean to this day, the well where he used to fatten his lampreys on his slaves, and a ruined temple of those ripping old Roman bricks, shallow as dominoes and ruddier than the cherry. I never was much of an antiquary, but I could have become one there if I'd had nothing else to do; but I had lots. When I wasn't busy with the boats I had to trim the vines, or gather the grapes, or even help make the wine itself in a cool, dark, musty vault underneath the temple, that I can see and smell as I jaw. And can't I hear it and feel it too! Squish, squash, bubble; squash, squish, guggle; and your feet as though you had been wading through slaughter to a throne. Yes, Bunny, you mightn't think it, but this good right foot, that never was on the wrong side of the crease when the ball left my hand, has also been known to

'...crush the lees of pleasure
From sanguine grapes of pain.'

He made a sudden pause, as though he had stumbled on a truth in jest. His face filled with lines. We were sitting in the room that had been bare when first I saw it; there were basket-chairs and a table in it now, all meant ostensibly for me; and hence Raffles would slip to his bed, with schoolboy relish, at every tinkle of the bell. This afternoon we felt fairly safe, for Mr Theobald had called in the morning, and Mrs Theobald still took up much of his time. Through the open window we could hear the piano-organ and 'Mar – ga – ri' a few hundred yards further on. I fancied Raffles was listening to it while he paused. He shook his head abstractedly when I handed him the cigarettes; and his tone hereafter was never just what it had been.

'I don't know, Bunny, whether you're a believer in transmigration of souls. I have often thought it easier to believe than lots of other things, and I have been pretty near believing in it myself since I had my being on that villa of Tiberius. The brute who had it in my day, if he isn't still running it with a whole skin, was or is as cold-blooded a blackguard as the worst of the emperors, but I have often thought he had a lot in common with Tiberius. He had the great high sensual

Roman nose, eyes that were sinks of iniquity in themselves, and that swelled with fatness, like the rest of him, so that he wheezed if he walked a yard; otherwise rather a fine beast to look at, with a huge grey moustache, like a flying gull, and the most courteous manners even to his men; but one of the worst, Bunny, one of the worst that ever was. It was said that the vineyard was only his hobby; if so, he did his best to make his hobby pay. He used to come out from Naples for the weekends – in the tub when it wasn't too rough for his nerves – and he didn't always come alone. His very name sounded unhealthy – Corbucci. I suppose I ought to add that he was a Count, though Counts are two-a-penny in Naples, and in season all the year round.

'He had a little English, and liked to air it upon me, much to my disgust; if I could not hope to conceal my nationality as yet, I at least did not want to have it advertised; and the swine had English friends. When he heard that I was bathing in November, when the bay is still as warm as new milk, he would shake his wicked old head and say, 'You are very audashuss – you are very audashuss!' and put on no end of side before his Italians. By God, he had pitched upon the right word unawares, and I let him know it in the end!

'But that bathing, Bunny; it was absolutely the best I ever had anywhere. I said just now the water was like wine; in my own mind I used to call it blue champagne, and was rather annoyed that I had no one to admire the phrase. Otherwise I assure you that I missed my own particular kind very little indeed, though I often wished that *you* were there, old chap; particularly when I went for my lonesome swim; first thing in the morning, when the bay was all rose-leaves, and last thing at night, when your body caught phosphorescent fire! Ah, yes, it was a good enough life for a change; a perfect paradise to lie low in; another Eden until ...

'My poor Eve!'

And he fetched a sigh that took away his words; then his jaws snapped together, and his eyes spoke terribly while he conquered his emotion. I pen the last word advisedly. I fancy it is one which I have never used before in writing of A.J. Raffles, for I cannot at the moment recall any other occasion upon which its use would have been justified. On resuming, however, he was not only calm, but cold; and this flying for safety to the other extreme is the single instance of self-distrust which the present Achates can record to the credit of his impious Æneas.

'I called the girl Eve,' said he. 'Her real name was Faustina, and she was one of a vast family who hung out in a hovel on the inland border of the vineyard. And Aphrodite rising from the sea was less wonderful and not more beautiful than Aphrodite emerging from that hole!

'It was the most exquisite face I ever saw or shall see in this life. Absolutely perfect features; a skin that reminded you of old gold, so delicate was its bronze; magnificent hair, not black but nearly; and such eyes and teeth as would have made the fortune of a face without another point. I tell you, Bunny, London would go mad about a girl like that. But I don't believe there's such another in the world. And there she was wasting her sweetness upon that lovely but desolate little corner of it! Well, she did not waste it upon me. I would have married her, and lived happily ever after in such a hovel as her people's – with her. Only to look at her – only to look at her for the rest of my days – I could have lain low and remained dead even to you! And that's all I'm going to tell you about that, Bunny; cursed be he who tells more! Yet don't you run away with the idea that this poor Faustina was the only woman I ever cared about. I don't believe in all that "only" rot; nevertheless I tell you that she *was* the one being who ever entirely satisfied my sense of beauty; and I honestly believe I could have chucked the world and been true to Faustina for that alone.

'We met sometimes in the little temple I told you about, sometimes among the vines; now by honest accident, now by flagrant design; and found a ready-made *rendezvous*, romantic as one could wish, in the cave down all those subterranean steps. Then the sea would call us – my blue champagne – my sparkling cobalt – and there was the dinghy ready to our hand. Oh, those nights! I never knew which I liked best, the moonlit ones when you sculled through silver and could see for miles, or the dark nights when the fishermen's torches stood for the sea, and a red zigzag in the sky for old Vesuvius. We were happy. I don't mind owning it. We seemed not to have a care between us. My mates took no interest in my affairs, and Faustina's family did not appear to bother about her. The Count was in Naples five nights of the seven; the other two we sighed apart.

'At first it was the oldest story in literature – Eden *plus* Eve. The place had been a heaven on earth before, but now it was heaven itself. So for a little; then one night, a Monday night, Faustina burst out crying in the boat; and sobbed her story as we drifted without mishap by the mercy of the Lord. And that was almost as old a story as the other.

'She was engaged – what! Had I never heard of it? Did I mean to upset the boat? What was her engagement beside our love? "Niente, niente," crooned Faustina, sighing yet smiling through her tears. No, but what did matter was that the man had threatened to stab her to the heart – and would do it as soon as look at her – that I knew.

'I knew it merely from my knowledge of the Neapolitans, for I had no idea who the man might be. I knew it, and yet I took this detail better than the fact of the engagement, though now I began to laugh at both. As if I was going to let her marry anybody else! As if a hair of her lovely head should be touched while I lived to protect her! I had a great mind to row away to blazes with her that very night, and never go near the vineyard again, or let her either. But we had not a lira between us at the time, and only the rags in which we sat barefoot in the boat. Besides, I had to know the name of the animal who had threatened a woman, and such a woman as this.

'For a long time she refused to tell me, with splendid obduracy; but I was as determined as she; so at last she made conditions. I was not to go and get put in prison for sticking a knife, into him – he wasn't worth it – and I did promise not to stab him in the back. Faustina seemed quite satisfied, though a little puzzled by my manner, having herself the racial tolerance for cold steel; and next moment she had taken away my breath. "It is Stefano," she whispered, and hung her head.

'And well she might, poor thing! Stefano, of all creatures on God's earth – for her!

'Bunny, he was a miserable little undersized wretch – ill-favoured – servile – surly – and second only to his master in bestial cunning and hypocrisy. His face was enough for me; that was what I read in it, and I don't often make mistakes. He was Corbucci's own confidential body-servant, and that alone was enough to damn him in decent eyes: always came out first on the Saturday with the *spese*, to have all ready for his master and current mistress, and stayed behind on the Monday to clear and lock up. Stefano! That worm! I could well understand *his* threatening a woman with a knife; what beat me was how any woman could ever have listened to him; above all, that Faustina should be the one! It passed my comprehension. But I questioned her as gently as I could; and her explanation was largely the threadbare one you would expect. Her parents were so poor. They were so many in family. Some of them begged – would I promise never to tell? Then some of them stole – sometimes – and all knew the pains of actual want. She looked after the cows, but there were only two of them, and brought the milk to the vineyard and elsewhere; but that was not employment for more than one; and there were countless sisters waiting to take her place. Then he was so rich, Stefano.

'"Rich?" I echoed. "Stefano?"

'"Si, Arturo mio."

'Yes, I played the game on that vineyard, Bunny, even to going by my own first name.

'"And how comes he to be rich?" I asked, suspiciously.

'She did not know; but he had given her such beautiful jewels; the family had lived on them for months, she pretending an *avocat* had taken charge of them for her against her marriage. But I cared nothing about all that.

'"Jewels! Stefan!" I could only mutter.

'"Perhaps the Count has paid for some of them. He is very kind."

'"To you, is he?"

'"Oh yes, very kind."

'"And you would live in his house afterwards?"

'"Not now, mio caro – not now!"

'"No, by God you don't! said I in English. "But you would have done so, eh?"

'"Of course. That was arranged. The Count is really very kind."

'"Do you see anything of him when he comes here?"

'Yes, he had sometimes brought her little presents, sweetmeats, ribbons, and the like; but the offering had always been made through this toad of a Stefano. Knowing the men, I now knew all. But Faustina, she had the pure and simple heart, and the white soul, by the God who made it, and for all her kindness to a tattered scapegrace who made love to her in broken Italian between the ripples and the stars. She was not to know what I was, remember; and beside Corbucci and his henchman I was the Archangel Gabriel come down to earth.

'Well, as I lay awake that night, two more lines of Swinburne came into my head, and came to stay:

"God said, 'Let him who wins her take
And keep Faustine.'"

'On that couplet I slept at last, and it was my text and watchword when I awoke in the morning. I forget how well you know your Swinburne, Bunny; but don't you run away with the idea that there was anything else in common between his Faustine and mine. For the last time let me tell you that poor Faustina was the whitest and the best I ever knew.

'Well, I was strung up for trouble when the next Saturday came, and I'll tell you what I had done. I had broken the pledge and burgled Corbucci's villa in my best manner during his absence in Naples. Not that it gave me the slightest trouble; but no human being could have told that I had been in when I came out. And I had stolen nothing, mark you, but only borrowed a revolver from a drawer in the Count's desk, with one or two trifling accessories; for by this time I had the measure of these damned Neapolitans. They are spry enough with a knife, but you show them the business end of a shooting-iron, and they'll streak like rabbits for the nearest hole. But the revolver wasn't for my own use. It was for Faustina, and I taught her how to use it in the cave down there by the sea, shooting at candles stuck upon the rock. The noise in the cave was something frightful, but high up above it couldn't be heard at all, as we proved to each other's satisfaction pretty early in the proceedings. So now Faustina was armed with munitions of self-defence; and I knew enough of her character to entertain no doubt as to their spirited use upon occasion. Between the two of us, in fact, our friend Stefano seemed tolerably certain of a warm week-end.

'But the Saturday brought word that the Count was not coming this week, being in Rome on business, and unable to return in time; so for a whole Sunday we were promised peace; and made bold plans accordingly. There was no further merit in hushing this thing up. "Let him who wins her take and keep

Faustine." Yes, but let him win her openly, or lose her and be damned to him! So on the Sunday I was going to have it out with her people – with the Count and Stefano as soon as they showed their noses. I had no inducement, remember, ever to return to surreptitious life within a cab-fare of Wormwood Scrubs. Faustina and the Bay of Naples were quite good enough for me. And the prehistoric man in me rather exulted in the idea of fighting for my desire.

'On the Saturday, however, we were to meet for the last time as heretofore – just once more in secret – down there in the cave – as soon as might be after dark. Neither of us minded if we were kept for hours; each knew that in the end the other would come; and there was a charm of its own even in waiting with such knowledge. But that night I did lose patience: not in the cave but up above, where first on one pretext and then on another the *direttore* kept me going until I smelt a rat. He was not given to exacting overtime, this *direttore*, whose only fault was his servile subjection to our common boss. It seemed pretty obvious, therefore, that he was acting upon some secret instructions from Corbucci himself, and, the moment I suspected this, I asked him to his face if it was not the case. And it was: he admitted it with many shrugs, being a conveniently weak person, whom one felt almost ashamed of bullying as the occasion demanded.

The fact was, however, that the Count had sent for him on finding he had to go to Rome, and had said he was very sorry to go just then, as among other things he intended to speak to me about Faustina. Stefano had told him all about his row with her, and moreover that it was on my account, which Faustina had never told me, though I had guessed as much for myself. Well, the Count was going to take his jackal's part for all he was worth, which was just exactly what I had expected him to do. He intended going for me on his return, but meanwhile I was not to make hay in his absence, and so this tool of a *direttore* had orders to keep me at it night and day. I undertook not to give the poor beast away, but at the same time told him I had not the faintest intention of doing another stroke of work that night.

'It was very dark, and I remember knocking my head against the oranges as I ran up the long, shallow steps which ended the journey between the *direttore*'s lodge and the villa itself. But at the back of the villa was the garden I spoke about, and also a bare chunk of the cliff where it was bored by that subterranean stair. So I saw the stars close overhead, and the fishermen's torches far below, the coastwise lights and crimson hieroglyph that spelt Vesuvius, before I plunged into the darkness of the shaft. And that was the last time I appreciated the unique and peaceful charm of this outlandish spot.

The stair was in two long flights, with an air-hole or two at the top of the upper one, but not another pin-prick till you came to the iron gate at the bottom of the lower. As you may read of an infinitely lighter place, in a finer work of fiction than you are ever likely to write, Bunny, it was "gloomy at noon, dark as midnight at dusk, and black as the ninth plague of Egypt at midnight". I won't swear to my quotation, but I will to those stairs. They were as black that night as the inside of the safest safe in the strongest strongroom in the Chancery Lane Deposit. Yet I had not got far down them with my bare feet before I heard somebody else coming up in boots. You may imagine what a turn that gave me! It could not be Faustina, who went barefoot three seasons of the four, and yet there was Faustina waiting for me down below. What a fright she must have had! And all at once my own blood ran cold; for the man sang like a kettle as he plodded up and up. It was, it must be, the short-winded Count himself, whom we all supposed to be in Rome!

'Higher he came and nearer, nearer, slowly yet hurriedly, now stopping to cough and gasp, now taking a few steps by elephantine assault. I should have enjoyed the situation if it had not been for poor Faustina in the cave; as it was I was filled with nameless fears. But I could not resist giving that grampus Corbucci one bad moment on account. A crazy handrail ran up one wall, so I carefully flattened myself against the other, and he passed within six inches of me, puffing and wheezing like a brass band. I let him go a few steps higher, and then I let him have it with both lungs.

'"Buona sera, eccellenza signori!" I roared after him. And a scream came down in answer – such a scream! A dozen different terrors were in it; and the wheezing had stopped, with the old scoundrel's heart.

'"Chi sta la?" he squeaked at last, gibbering and whimpering like a whipped monkey, so that I could not bear to miss his face, and got a match all ready to strike.

'"Arturo, signori."

'He didn't repeat my name, nor did he damn me in heaps. He did nothing but wheeze for a good minute, and when he spoke it was with insinuating civility, in his best English.

'"Come nearer, Arturo. You are in the lower regions down there. I want to speak with you."

'"No, thanks, I'm in a hurry," I said, and dropped that match back into my pocket. He might be armed, and I was not.

'"So you are in a 'urry!" and he wheezed amusement. "And you thought I was still in Rome, no doubt; and so I was until this afternoon, when I caught train at the eleventh moment and then another train from Naples to Pozzuoli. I have been rowed here now by a fisherman of Pozzuoli. I had not time to stop anywhere in Naples, but only to drive from station to station. So I am without Stefano, Arturo, I am without Stefano."

'His sly voice sounded preternaturally sly in the absolute darkness, but even through that impenetrable veil I knew it for a sham. I had laid hold of the handrail. It shook violently in my hand; he also was holding it where he stood. And these suppressed tremors, or rather their detection in this way, struck a strange chill to my heart, just as I was beginning to pluck it up.

'"It is lucky for Stefano," said I, grim as death.

'"Ah, but you must not be too 'ard on'im," remonstrated the Count. "You have stole his girl, he speak with me about it, and I wish to speak with you. It is very audashuss, Arturo, very audashuss! Perhaps you are even going to meet her now, eh?"

'I told him straight that I was.

'"Then there is no 'urry, for she is not there."

'"You didn't see her in the cave?" I cried, too delighted at the thought to keep it to myself.

'"I had no such fortune," the old devil said.

'"She is there, all the same."

'"I only wish I 'ad known."

'"And I've kept her long enough!"

'In fact, I threw this over my shoulder as I turned and went running down.

'"I 'ope you will find her!" his malicious voice came croaking after me. "I 'ope you will – I 'ope so."

'And find her I did.'

Raffles had been on his feet some time, unable to sit still or to stand, moving excitedly about the room. But now he stood still enough, his elbows on the cast-iron mantelpiece, his head between his hands.

'Dead?' I whispered.

And he nodded to the wall.

There was not a sound in the cave. There was no answer to my voice. Then I went in, and my foot touched hers, and it was colder than the rock... Bunny, they had stabbed her to the heart. She had fought them, and they had stabbed her to the heart!'

'You say "they",' I said gently, as he stood in heavy silence, his back still turned. 'I thought Stefano had been left behind?'

Raffles was round in a flash, his face white-hot, his eyes dancing death.

'He was in the cave!' he shouted. 'I saw him – I spotted him – it was broad twilight after those stairs – and I went for him with my bare hands. Not fists, Bunny; not fists for a thing like that; I meant getting my fingers into his vile little heart and tearing it out by the roots. I was stark mad. But he had the revolver – hers. He blazed it at arm's length, and missed. And that steadied me. I had smashed his funny-bone against the rock before he could blaze again; the revolver fell with a rattle, but without going off; in an instant I had it tight, and the little swine at my mercy at last.'

'You didn't show him any?'

'Mercy? With Faustina dead at my feet? I should have deserved none in the next world if I had shown him any in this! No, I just stood over him, with the revolver in both hands, feeling the chambers with my thumb; and as I stood he stabbed at me; but I stepped back to that one, and brought him down with a bullet in his guts.

'"And I can spare you two or three more," I said, for my poor girl could not have fired a shot. "Take that one to hell with you – and that – and that."

'Then I started coughing and wheezing like the Count himself, for the place was full of smoke. When it cleared my man was very dead, and I tipped him into the sea, to defile that rather than Faustina's cave. And then – and then – we were alone for the last time, she and I, in our own pet haunt; and I could scarcely see her, yet I would not strike a match, for I knew she would not have me see her as she was. I could say good-bye to her without that. I said it; and I left her like a man, and up the first open-air steps with my head in the air and the stars all sharp in the sky; then suddenly they swam, and back I went like a lunatic, to see if she was really dead, to bring her back to life... Bunny, I can't tell you any more.'

'Not of the Count?' I murmured at last.

'Not even of the Count,' said Raffles, turning round with a sigh. 'I left him pretty sorry for himself; but what was the good of that? I had taken blood for blood, and it was not Corbucci who had killed Faustina. No, the plan was his, but that was not part of the plan. They had found out about our meetings in the cave; nothing simpler than to have me kept hard at it overhead and to carry off Faustina by brute force in the boat. It was their only chance, for she had said more to Stefano than she had admitted to me, and more than I am going to repeat about myself. No persuasion would have induced her to listen to him again; so they tried force; and she drew Corbucci's revolver on them, but they had taken her by surprise, and Stefano stabbed her before she could fire.'

'But how do you know all that?' I asked Raffles, for his tale was going to pieces in the telling, and the tragic end of poor Faustina was no ending for me.

'Oh,' said he, 'I had it from Corbucci at his own revolver's point. He was waiting at his window, and I could have potted him at my ease where he stood against the light listening hard enough but not seeing a thing. So he asked whether it was Stefano, and I whispered, "Si, signore"; and then whether he had finished Arturo, and I brought the same shot off again. He had let me in before he knew who was finished and who was not.'

'And did you finish him?'

'No; that was too good for Corbucci. But I bound and gagged him about as tight as man was ever gagged or bound, and I left him in his room with the shutters shut and the house locked up. The shutters of that old place were six inches thick, and the walls nearly six feet; that was on the Saturday night, and the Count wasn't expected at the vineyard before the following Saturday. Meanwhile he was supposed to be in Rome. But the dead would doubtless be discovered next day, and I am afraid this would lead to his own discovery with the life still in him. I believe he figured on that himself, for he sat threatening me gamely till the last. You never saw such a sight as he was, with his head split in two by a ruler tied at the back of it, and his great moustache pushed up into his bulging eyes. But I locked him up in the dark without a qualm, and I wished and still wish him every torment of the damned.'

'And then?'

'The night was still young, and within ten miles there was the best of ports in a storm, and hundreds of holds for the humble stowaway to choose from. But I didn't want to go further than Genoa, for by this time my Italian would wash, so I chose the old Norddeutscher Lloyd, and had an excellent voyage in one of the boats slung inboard over the bridge. That's better than any hold, Bunny, and I did splendidly on oranges brought from the vineyard.'

'And at Genoa?'

'At Genoa I took to my wits once more, and have been living on nothing else ever since. But there I had to begin all over again, and at the very bottom of the ladder. I slept in the streets. I begged. I did all manner of terrible things, rather hoping for a bad end, but never coming to one. Then one day I saw a white-headed old chap looking at me through a shop window – a window I had designs upon – and when I stared at him he stared at me – and we wore the same rags. So I had come to that! But one reflection makes many. I had not recognised myself; who on earth would recognise me? London called me – and here I am. Italy had broken my heart – and there it stays.'

Flippant as a schoolboy one moment, playful even in the bitterness of the next, and now no longer giving way to the feeling which had spoilt the climax of his tale, Raffles needed knowing as I alone knew him for a right appreciation of those last words. That they were no mere words I knew full well. That, but for the tragedy of his Italian life, that life would have sufficed him for years, if not for ever, I did and do still believe. But I alone see him as I saw him then, the lines upon his face, and the pain behind the lines; how they came to disappear, and what removed them, you will never guess. It was the one thing you would have expected to have the opposite effect, the thing indeed that had forced his confidence, the organ and the voice once more beneath our very windows:

Margarita de Parete,
era a' sarta d' e' signore;
se pugneva sempe a ddete
pe penzare a Salvatore!
Mar – ga – rì,
e perzo a Salvatore!
Mar – ga – rì,
Ma l'ommo è cacciatore!
Mar – ga – rì,
Nun ce aje corpa tu!
Chello ch' è fatto, è fatto,
un ne parlammo cchieù!

I simply stared at Raffles. Instead of deepening, his lines had vanished. He looked years younger, mischievous and merry and alert as I remembered him of old in the breathless crisis of some madcap escapade. He was holding up his finger; he was stealing to the window; he was peeping through the blind as though our side street were Scotland Yard itself; he was stealing back again, all revelry, excitement, and suspense.

'I half thought they were after me before,' said he. 'That was why I made you look. I daren't take a proper look myself, but what a jest if they were! What a jest!'

'Do you mean the police?' said I.

'The police! Bunny, do you know them and me so little that you can look me in the face and ask such a question? My boy, I'm dead to them – off their books – a good deal deader than being off the hooks! Why, if I went to Scotland Yard this minute, to give myself up, they'd chuck me out for a harmless lunatic. No, I fear an enemy nowadays, and I go in terror of the sometime friend; but I have the utmost confidence in the dear police.'

'Then whom do you mean?'

'The Camorra!'

I repeated the word with a different intonation. Not that I had ever heard of that most powerful and sinister of secret societies; but I failed to see on what ground Raffles should jump to the conclusion that these everyday organ-grinders belonged to it.

'It was one of Corbucci's threats,' said he. 'If I killed him the Camorra would certainly kill me; he kept on telling me so; it was like his cunning not to say that he would put them on my tracks whether or no.'

'He is probably a member himself!'

'Obviously, from what he said.'

'But why on earth should you think that these fellows are?' I demanded, as that brazen voice came rasping through a second verse.

'I don't think. It was only an idea. That thing is so thoroughly Neapolitan, and I never heard it on a London organ before. Then again, what should bring them back here?'

I peeped through the blind in my turn; and, to be sure, there was the fellow with the blue chin and the white teeth watching our windows, and ours only, as he bawled.

'And why?' cried Raffles, his eyes dancing when I told him. 'Why should they come sneaking back to *us*? Doesn't that look suspicious, Bunny; doesn't that promise a lark?'

'Not to me,' I said, having the smile for once. 'How many people, should you imagine, toss them five shillings for as many minutes of their infernal row? You seem to forget that that's what you did an hour ago!'

Raffles had forgotten. His blank face confessed the fact. Then suddenly he burst out laughing at himself.

'Bunny,' said he, 'you've no imagination, and I never knew I had so much! Of course you're right. I only wish you were not, for there's nothing I should enjoy more than taking on another Neapolitan or two. You see, I owe them something still! I didn't settle in full. I owe them more than ever I shall pay them on this side Styx!'

He had hardened even as he spoke: the lines and the years had come again, and his eyes were flint and steel, with an honest grief behind the glitter.

4

THE LAST LAUGH

As I have had occasion to remark elsewhere, the pick of our exploits from a frankly criminal point of view are of least use for the comparatively pure purposes of these papers. They might be appreciated in a trade journal (if only that want could be supplied) by skilled manipulators of the jemmy and the large light bunch; but, as records of unbroken yet insignificant success, they would be found at once too trivial and too technical, if not sordid and unprofitable into the bargain. The latter epithets, and worse, have indeed already been applied, if not to Raffles and all his works, at least to mine upon Raffles, by more than one worthy wielder of a virtuous pen. I need not say how heartily I disagree with that truly pious opinion. So far from admitting a single word of it, I maintain it is the liveliest warning that I am giving to the world. Raffles was a genius, and he could not make it pay! Raffles had invention, resource, incomparable audacity, and a nerve in ten thousand. He was both strategist and tactician, and we all now know the difference between the two. Yet for months he had been hiding like a rat in a hole, unable to show even his altered face by night or day without risk, unless another risk were courted by three inches of conspicuous crape. Then thus far our rewards had oftener than not been no reward at all. Altogether it was a very different story from the old festive, unsuspected club and cricket days, with their *noctes ambroisianæ* at the Albany.

And now, in addition to the eternal peril of recognition, there was yet another menace of which I knew nothing. I thought no more of our Neapolitan organ-grinders, though I did often think of the moving page that they had torn from me out of my friend's strange life in Italy. Raffles never alluded to the subject again, and for my part I had entirely forgotten his wild ideas connecting the organ-grinders with the Camorra, and imagining them upon his own tracks. I heard no more of it, and thought as little, as I say. Then one night in the autumn – I shrink from shocking the susceptible for nothing – but there was a certain house in Palace Gardens, and when we got there Raffles would pass on. I could see no soul in sight, no glimmer in the windows. But Raffles had my arm, and on we went without talking about it. Sharp to the left on the Notting Hill side, sharper still up Silver Street, a little tacking west and south, a plunge across High Street, and presently we were home.

'Pyjamas first,' said Raffles, with as much authority as though it mattered. It was a warm night, however, though September, and I did not mind until I came in clad as he commanded to find the autocrat himself still booted and capped. He was peeping through the blind, and the gas was still turned down. But he said that I could turn it up, as he helped himself to a cigarette and nothing with it.

'May I mix you one?' said I.

'No, thanks.'

'What's the trouble?'

'We were followed.'

'Never!'

'You never saw it.'

'But *you* never looked round.'

'I have an eye at the back of each ear, Bunny.'

I helped myself, and I feared with less moderation than might have been the case a minute before.

'So that was why – '

'That was why,' said Raffles, nodding; but he did not smile, and I put down my glass untouched.

'They were following us then!'

'All up Palace Gardens.'

'I thought you wound about coming back over the hill.'

'Nevertheless, one of them's in the street below at this moment.'

No, he was not fooling me. He was very grim. And he had not taken off a thing; perhaps he did not think it worth while.

'Plain clothes?' I sighed, following the sartorial train of thought, even to the loathly arrows that had decorated my person once already for a little aeon. Next time they would give me double. The skilly was in my stomach when I saw Raffles's face.

'Who said it was the police, Bunny?' said he. 'It's the Italians. They're only after me; they won't hurt a hair of your head, let alone cropping it! Have a drink, and don't mind me. I shall score them off before I'm done.'

'And I'll help you!'

'No, old chap, you won't. This is my own little show. I've known about it for weeks. I first tumbled to it the day those Neapolitans came back with their organs, though I didn't seriously suspect things then; they never came again, those two; they had done their part. That's the Camorra all over, from all accounts. The Count I told you about is pretty high up in it, by the way he spoke, but there will be grades and grades between him and the organ-grinders. I shouldn't be surprised if he had every low-down Neapolitan ice-creamer in the town upon my tracks! The organisation's incredible. Then do you remember the superior foreigner who came to the door a few days afterwards? You said he had velvet eyes.'

'I never connected him with those two!'

'Of course you didn't, Bunny, so you threatened to kick the fellow downstairs, and only made them keener on the scent. It was too late to say anything when you told me. But the very next time I showed my nose outside I heard a camera click as I passed, and the fiend was a person with velvet eyes. Then there was a lull – that happened weeks ago. They had sent me to Italy for identification by Count Corbucci.'

'But this is all theory,' I exclaimed. 'How on earth can you know?'

'I don't know,' said Raffles, 'but I should like to bet. Our friend the bloodhound is hanging about the comer near the pillar-box; look through my window, it's dark in there, and tell me who he is.'

The man was too far away for me to swear to his face, but he wore a covert-coat of un-English length, and the lamp across the road played steadily on his boots; they were very yellow, and they made no noise when he took a turn. I strained my eyes, and all at once I remembered the thin-soled, low-heeled, splay yellow boots of the insidious foreigner, with the soft eyes and the brown-paper face, whom I had turned from the door as a palpable fraud. The ring at the bell was the first I had heard of him, there had been no warning step upon the stairs, and my suspicious eye had searched his feet for rubber soles.

'It's the fellow,' I said, returning to Raffles, and I described his boots.

Raffles was delighted.

'Well done, Bunny; you're coming on,' said he. 'Now I wonder if he's been over here all the time, or if they sent him over expressly? You did better than you think in spotting those boots, for they can only have been made in Italy, and that looks like the special envoy. But it's no use speculating. I must find out.'

'How can you?'

'He won't stay there all night.'

'Well?'

'When he gets tired of it I shall return the compliment and follow *him*.'

'Not alone,' said I, firmly.

'Well, we'll see. We'll see at once,' said Raffles, rising. 'Out with the gas, Bunny, while I take a look. Thank you. Now wait a bit... yes! He's chucked it; he's off already; and so am I!'

But I slipped to our outer door, and held the passage.

'I don't let you go alone, you know.'

'You can't come with me in pyjamas.'

'Now I see why you made me put them on!'

'Bunny, if you don't shift I shall have to shift you. This is my very own private one-man show. But I'll be back in an hour – there!'

'You swear?'

'By all my gods.'

I gave in. How could I help giving in? He did not look the man that he had been, but you never knew with Raffles, and I could not have him lay a hand on me. I let him go with a shrug and my blessing, then ran into his room to see the last of him from the window.

The creature in the coat and boots had reached the end of our little street, where he appeared to have hesitated, so that Raffles was just in time to see which way he turned. And Raffles was after him at an easy pace, and had himself almost reached the comer when my attention was distracted from the alert nonchalance of his gait. I was marvelling that it alone had, not long ago, betrayed him, for nothing about him was so unconsciously characteristic, when suddenly I realised that Raffles was not the only person in the little lonely street. Another pedestrian had entered from the other end, a man heavily built and clad, with an astrakhan collar to his coat on this warm night, and a black slouch hat that hid his features from my bird's-eye view. His steps were the short and shuffling ones of a man advanced in years and in fatty degeneration, but of a sudden they stopped beneath my very eyes. I could have dropped a marble into the dinted crown of the black felt hat. Then, at the same moment, Raffles turned the comer without looking round, and the big man below raised both his hands and his face. Of the latter I saw only the huge white moustache, like a flying gull, as Raffles had described it: for at a glance I divined that this was his arch-enemy, the Count Corbucci himself.

I did not stop to consider the subtleties of the system by which the real hunter lagged behind while his subordinate pointed the quarry like a sporting dog. I left the Count shuffling onward faster than before, and I jumped into some clothes as though the flats were on fire. If the Count was going to follow Raffles in his turn then I would follow the Count in mine, and there would be a midnight procession of us through the town. But I found no sign of him in the empty street, and no sign in the Earl's Court Road, that looked as empty for all its length, save for a natural enemy standing like a waxwork with a glimmer at his belt.

'Officer,' I gasped, 'have you seen anything of an old gentleman with a big white moustache?'

The unlicked cub of a common constable seemed to eye me the more suspiciously for the flattering form of my address.

'Took a hansom,' said he at length.

A hansom! Then he was not following the others on foot; there was no guessing his game. But something must be said or done.

'He's a friend of mine,' I explained, 'and I want to overtake him. Did you hear where he told the fellow to drive?'

A curt negative was the policeman's reply to that; and if ever I take part in a night assault-at-arms, revolver *versus* baton in the back kitchen, I know which member of the Metropolitan Police Force I should like for my opponent.

If there was no overtaking the Count, however, it should be a comparatively simple matter in the case of the couple on foot, and I wildly hailed the first hansom that crawled into my ken. I must tell Raffles who it was that I had seen; the Earl's Court Road was long, and the time since he vanished in it but a few short minutes. I drove down the length of that useful thoroughfare, with an eye apiece on either pavement, sweeping each as with a brush, but never a Raffles came into the pan. Then I tried the Fulham Road, first to the west, then to the east, and in the end drove home to the flat as bold as brass. I did not realise my indiscretion until I had paid the man and was on the stairs. Raffles never dreamt of driving all the way back; but I was hoping now to find him waiting up above. He had said an hour. I had remembered it suddenly. And now the hour was more than up. But the flat was as empty as I had left it; the very light that had encouraged me, pale though it was, as I turned the corner in my hansom, was but the light that I myself had left burning in the desolate passage.

I can give you no conception of the night that I spent. Most of it I hung across the sill, throwing a wide net with my ears, catching every footstep afar off, every hansom bell farther still, only to gather in some alien whom I seldom even landed in our street. Then I would listen at the door. He might come over the roof; and eventually someone did; but now it was broad daylight, and I flung the door open in the milkman's face, which whitened at the shock as though I had ducked him in his own pail.

'You're late,' I thundered as the first excuse for my excitement.

'Beg your pardon,' said he indignantly, 'but I'm half an hour before my usual time.'

'Then I beg yours,' said I; 'but the fact is, Mr Maturin has had one of his bad nights, and I seem to have been waiting hours for milk to make him a cup of tea.'

This little fib (ready enough for a Raffles, though I say it) earned me not only forgiveness but that obliging sympathy which is a branch of the business of the man at the door. The good fellow said that he could see I had been sitting up all night, and he left me pluming myself upon the accidental art with which I had told my very necessary tarradiddle. On reflection I gave the credit to instinct, not accident, and then sighed afresh as I realised how the influence of the master was sinking into me, and he heaven knew where! But my punishment was swift to follow, for within the hour the bell rang imperiously twice, and there was Dr Theobald on our mat, in a yellow Jaeger suit, with a chin as yellow jutting over the flaps that he had turned up to hide his pyjamas.

'What's this about a bad night?' said he.

'He couldn't sleep, and he wouldn't let me,' I whispered, never loosening my grasp of the door, and standing tight against the other wall. 'But he's sleeping like a baby now.'

'I must see him.'

'He gave strict orders that you should not.'

'I'm his medical man, and I – '

'You know what he is,' I said, shrugging; 'the least thing wakes him, and you will if you insist on seeing him now. It will be the last time, I warn you! I know what he said, and you don't.'

The doctor cursed me under his fiery moustache.

'I shall come up during the course of the morning,' he snarled.

'And I shall tie up the bell,' I said, 'and if it doesn't ring he'll be sleeping still, but I will not risk waking him by coming to the door again.'

And with that I shut it in his face. I was improving, as Raffles had said; but what would it profit me if some evil had befallen him? And now I was prepared for the worst. A boy came up whistling and leaving papers on the mats; it was getting on for eight o'clock, and the whisky and soda of half-past twelve stood untouched and stagnant in the tumbler. If the worst had happened to Raffles, I felt that I would either never drink again, or else seldom do anything else.

Meanwhile I could not even break my fast, but roamed the flat in a misery not to be described, my very linen still unchanged, my cheeks and chin now tawny from the unwholesome night. How long would it go on? I wondered for a time. Then I changed my tune: how long could I endure it?

It went on actually until the forenoon only, but my endurance cannot be measured by the time, for to me every hour of it was an arctic night. Yet it cannot have been much after eleven when the ring came at the bell, which I had forgotten to tie up after all. But this was not the doctor; neither, too well I knew, was it the wanderer returned. Our bell was the pneumatic one that tells you if the touch be light or heavy; the hand upon it now was tentative and shy.

The owner of the hand I had never seen before. He was young and ragged, with one eye blank, but the other ablaze with some fell excitement. And straightaway he burst into a low torrent of words, of which all I knew was that they were Italian, and therefore news of Raffles, if only I had known the language! But dumb-show might help us somewhat, and in I dragged him, though against his will, a new alarm in his one wild eye.

'Non capite?' he cried when I had him inside and had withstood the torrent.

'No, I'm bothered if I do!' I answered, guessing his question from his tone.

'Vostro amico,' he repeated over and over again; and then, Toco tempo, poco tempo, poco tempo!'

For once in my life the classical education of my public-school days was of real value. 'My pal, my pal, and no time to be lost!' I translated freely, and flew for my hat.

'Ecco, signore!' cried the fellow, snatching the watch from my waistcoat pocket, and putting one black thumbnail on the long hand, the other on the numeral twelve. 'Mezzogiomo – poco tempo – poco tempo!' And again I seized his meaning, that it was twenty past eleven, and we must be there by twelve. But where, but where? It was maddening to be summoned like this, and not to know what had happened, nor to have any means of finding out. But my presence of mind stood by me still, I was improving by seven-league strides, and I crammed my handkerchief between the drum and hammer of the bell before leaving. The doctor could ring now till he was black in the face, but I was not coming, and he need not think it.

I half expected to find a hansom waiting, but there was none, and we had gone some distance down the Earl's Court Road before we got one; in fact, we had to run to the stand. Opposite is the church with the clock upon it, as everybody knows, and at sight of the dial my companion had wrung his hands; it was close upon the half- hour.

'Poco tempo – pochissimo!' he wailed. 'Bloom-buree Skewarr,' he then cried to the cabman – 'numero trentotto!'

'Bloomsbury Square,' I roared on my own account. 'I'll show you the house when we get there, only drive like bedamned!'

My companion lay back gasping in his corner. The small glass told me that my own face was pretty red.

'A nice show!' I cried; 'and not a word can you tell me. Didn't you bring me a note?'

I might have known by this time that he had not, still I went through the pantomine of writing with my finger on my cuff. But he shrugged and shook his head.

'Niente,' said he. 'Una quistione di vita, di vita!'

'What's that?' I snapped, my early training coming in again. 'Say it slowly – andante – rallentando.'

Thank Italy for the stage instructions in the songs one used to murder! The fellow actually understood.

'Una – quistione – di – vita.'

'Or mors, eh?' I shouted, and up went the trap-door over our heads.

'Avanti, avanti, avanti!' cried the Italian, turning up his one-eyed face.

'Hell-to-leather,' I translated, 'and double fare if you do it by twelve o'clock.'

But in the streets of London how is one to know the time? In the Earl's Court Road it had not been half-past, and at Barker's in High Street it was but a minute later. A long half-mile a minute, that was going like the wind, and indeed we had done much of it at a gallop. But the next hundred yards took us five minutes by the next clock, and which was one to believe? I fell back upon my own old watch (it was my own), which made it eighteen minutes to the hour as we swung across the Serpentine bridge, and by the quarter we were in the Bayswater Road – not up for once.

'Presto, presto,' my pale guide murmured. 'Affretatevi – avanti!'

'Ten bob if you do it,' I cried through the trap, without the slightest notion of what we were to do. But it was 'una quistione di vita,' and 'vostro amico' must and could only be my miserable Raffles.

What a very godsend is the perfect hansom to the man or woman in a hurry! It had been our great good fortune to jump into a perfect hansom; there was no choice, we had to take the first upon the rank, but it must have deserved its place with the rest nowhere. New tyres, superb springs, a horse in a thousand, and a driver up to every trick of his trade! In and out we went like a fast half-back at the Rugby game, yet where the traffic was thinnest, there were we. And how he knew his way! At the Marble Arch he slipped out of the main stream, and so into

Wigmore Street, then up and in and out and on until I saw the gold tips of the Museum palisade gleaming between the horse's ears in the sun. Plop, plop, plop; ting, ling, ling; bell and horse-shoes, horse-shoes and bell, until the colossal figure of C.J. Fox in a grimy toga spelt Bloomsbury Square with my watch still wanting three minutes to the hour.

'What number?' cried the good fellow overhead.

'Trentotto, trentotto,' said my guide, but he was looking to the right, and I bundled him out to show the house on foot. I had not half a sovereign after all, but I flung our dear driver a whole one instead, and only wished that it had been a hundred.

Already the Italian had his latchkey in the door of 38, and in another moment we were rushing up the narrow stairs of as dingy a London house as prejudiced countryman can conceive. It was panelled, but it was dark and evil-smelling, and how we should have found our way even to the stairs but for an unwholesome jet of yellow gas in the hall, I cannot myself imagine. However, up we went pell-mell, to the right-about on the half-landing, and so like a whirlwind into the drawing-room a few steps higher. There the gas was also burning behind closed shutters, and the scene is photographed upon my brain, though I cannot have looked upon it for a whole instant as I sprang in at my leader's heels.

This room also was panelled, and in the middle of the wall on our left, his hands lashed to a ring-bolt high above his head, his toes barely touching the floor, his neck pinioned by a strap passing through smaller ring-bolts under either ear, and every inch of him secured on the same principle, stood, or rather hung, all that was left of Raffles, for at the first glance I believed him dead. A black ruler gagged him, the ends lashed behind his neck, the blood upon it caked to bronze in the gaslight. And in front of him, ticking like a sledge-hammer, its only hand upon the stroke of twelve, stood a simple, old-fashioned, grandfather's clock – but not for half an instant longer – only until my guide could hurl himself upon it and send the whole thing crashing into the corner. An ear-splitting report accompanied the crash, a white cloud lifted from the fallen clock, and I saw a revolver smoking in a vice screwed below the dial, an arrangement of wires sprouting from the dial itself, and the single hand at once at its zenith and in contact with these.

'Tumble to it, Bunny?'

He was alive; there were his first words; the Italian had the blood-caked ruler in his hand, and with his knife was reaching up to cut the thongs that lashed the hands. He was not tall enough. I seized him and lifted him up, then fell to work with my own knife upon the straps. And Raffles smiled faintly upon us through his blood-stains.

'I want you to tumble to it,' he whispered, 'the neatest thing in revenge I ever knew, and another minute would have fixed it. I've been waiting for it twelve hours, watching the clock round, death at the end of the lap! Electric connection. Simple enough. Hour-hand only – O Lord!'

We had cut the last strap. He could not stand. We supported him between us to a horse-hair sofa, for the room was furnished, and I begged him not to speak, while his one-eyed deliverer was at the door before Raffles recalled him with a sharp word in Italian.

'He wants to get me a drink, but that can wait,' said he in firmer voice; 'I shall enjoy it the more when I've told you what happened. Don't let him go, Bunny; put your back against the door. He's a decent soul, and it's lucky for me I got a word with him before they trussed me up. I've promised to set him up in life, and I will, but I don't want him out of my sight for the moment.'

'If you squared him last night,' I exclaimed, 'why the blazes didn't he come to me till the eleventh hour?'

'Ah, I knew he'd have to cut it fine, though I hoped not quite so fine as all that. But all's well that ends well, and I declare

I don't feel so much the worse. I shall be sore about the gills for a bit – and what do you think?'

He pointed to the long black ruler with the bronze stain; it lay upon the floor; he held out his hand for it, and I gave it to him.

'The same one I gagged him with,' said Raffles, with his still ghastly smile; 'he was a bit of an artist, old Corbucci, after all!'

'Now let's hear how you fell into his clutches,' said I briskly, for I was as anxious to hear as he seemed to tell me, only for my part I could have waited until we were safe in the flat.

'I do want to get it off my chest, Bunny,' old Raffles admitted, 'and yet I hardly can tell you after all. I followed your friend with the velvet eyes. I followed him all the way here. Of course I came up to have a good look at the house when he'd let himself in, and damme if he hadn't left the door ajar! Who could resist that? I had pushed it half open and had just one foot on the mat when I got such a crack on the head as I hope never to get again. When I came to my wits they were hauling me up to that ring-bolt by the hands, and old Corbucci himself was bowing to me, but how *he* got here I don't know yet.'

'I can tell you that,' said I, and told how I had seen the Count for myself on the pavement underneath our windows. 'Moreover,' I continued, 'I saw him spot you, and five minutes after in Earl's Court I was told he'd driven off in a cab. He would see you following his man, drive home ahead, and catch you by having the door left open in the way you describe.'

'Well,' said Raffles, 'he deserved to catch me somehow, for he'd come from Naples on purpose, ruler and all, and the ring-bolts were ready fixed, and even this house taken furnished for nothing else! He meant catching me before he'd done, and scoring off me in exactly the same way that I scored off him, only going one better of course. He told me so himself, sitting where I am sitting now, at three o'clock this morning, and smoking a most abominable cigar that I've smelt ever since.

It appears he sat twenty-four hours when I left *him* trussed up, but he said twelve would content him in my case, as there was certain death at the end of them, and I mightn't have life enough left to appreciate my end if he made it longer. But I wouldn't have trusted him if he could have got the clock to go *twice* round without firing off the pistol. He explained the whole mechanism of that to me; he had thought it all out on the vineyard I told you about; and then he asked if I remembered what he had promised me in the name of the Camorra. I only remembered some vague threats, but he was good enough to give me so many particulars of that institution that I could make a European reputation by exposing the whole show if it wasn't for my unfortunate resemblance to that infernal rascal Raffles. Do you think they would know me at the Yard, Bunny, after all this time? Upon my soul I've a good mind to risk it!'

I offered no opinion on the point. How could it interest me then? But interested I was in Raffles, never more so in my life. He had been tortured all night and half a day, yet he could sit and talk like this the moment we cut him down; he had been within a minute of his death, yet he was as full of life as ever; ill-treated and defeated at the best, he could still smile through his blood as though the boot were on the other leg. I had imagined that I knew my Raffles at last. I was not likely so to flatter myself again.

'But what has happened to these villains?' I burst out, and my indignation was not only against them for their cruelty, but also against their victim for his phlegmatic attitude toward them. It was difficult to believe that this was Raffles.

'Oh,' said he, 'they were to go off to Italy *instanter*; they should be crossing now. But do listen to what I am telling you; it's interesting, my dear man. This old sinner Corbucci turns out to have been no end of a boss in the Camorra – says so himself. One of the *capi paranze*, my boy, no less; and the velvety Johnny a *giovano onorato*, Anglice, fresher. This fellow here was also in it, and I've sworn to protect him from them evermore; and it's just as I said, half the organ-grinders in London belong, and the whole lot of them were put on my tracks by secret instructions. This excellent youth manufactures iced poison on Saffron Hill when he's at home.'

'And why on earth didn't he come to me quicker?'

'Because he couldn't talk to you, he could only fetch you, and it was as much as his life was worth to do that before our friends had departed. They were going by the eleven o'clock from Victoria, and that didn't leave much chance, but he certainly oughtn't to have run it as fine as he did. Still you must remember that I had to fix things up with him in the fewest possible words, in a single minute that the other two were indiscreet enough to leave us alone together.'

The ragamuffin in question was watching us with all his solitary eye, as though he knew that we were discussing him. Suddenly he broke out in agonised accents, his hands clasped, and a face so full of fear that every moment I expected to see him on his knees. But Raffles answered kindly, reassuringly, I could tell from his tone, and then turned to me with a compassionate shrug.

'He says he couldn't find the mansions, Bunny, and really it's not to be wondered at. I had only time to tell him to hunt you up and bring you here by hook or crook before twelve today, and after all he has done that. But now the poor devil thinks you're riled with him, and that we'll give him away to the Camorra.'

'Oh, it's not with him I'm riled,' I said frankly, 'but with those other blackguards, and – and with you, old chap, for taking it all as you do, while such infamous scoundrels have the last laugh, and are safely on their way to France!'

Raffles looked up at me with a curiously open eye, an eye that I never saw when he was not in earnest. I fancied he did not like my last expression but one. After all, it was no laughing matter to him.

'But are they?' said he. 'I'm not so sure.'

'You said they were!'

'I said they should be.'

'I heard nothing but the clock all night. It was like Big Ben striking at the last – striking nine to the fellow on the drop.'

And in that open eye I saw at last a deep glimmer of the ordeal through which he had passed.

'But, my dear old Raffles, if they're still on the premises – '

The thought was too thrilling for a finished sentence.

'I hope they are,' he said grimly, going to the door. 'There's a gas on! Was that burning when you came in?'

Now that I thought of it, yes, it had been.

'And there's a frightfully foul smell,' I added, as I followed Raffles down the stairs. He turned to, me gravely with his hand upon the front-room door, and at the same moment I saw a coat with an astrakhan collar hanging on the pegs.

'They are in here, Bunny,' he said, and turned the handle.

The door would only open a few inches. But a detestable odour came out, with a broad bar of yellow gaslight. 'Raffles put his handkerchief to his nose. I followed his example, signing to our ally to do the same, and in another minute we had all three squeezed into the room.

The man with the yellow boots was lying against the door, the Count's great carcase sprawled upon the table, and at a glance it was evident that both men had been dead some hours. The old Camorrist had the stem of a liqueur-glass between his swollen blue fingers, one of which had been cut in the breakage, and the livid flesh was also brown with the last blood that it would ever shed. His face was on the table, the huge moustache projecting from under either leaden cheek, yet looking itself strangely alive. Broken bread and scraps of frozen macaroni lay upon the cloth and at the bottom of two soup-plates and a tureen; the macaroni had a tinge of tomato; and there was a crimson dram left in the tumblers, with an empty *fiasco* to show whence it came. But near the great grey head upon the table another liqueur-glass stood, unbroken, and still full of some white and stinking liquid; and near that a tiny silver flask, which made me recoil from Raffles as I had not from the dead; for I knew it to be his.

'Come out of this poisonous air,' he said sternly, 'and I will tell you how it has happened.'

So we all three gathered together in the hall. But it was Raffles who stood nearest the street-door, his back to it, his eyes upon us two. And though it was to me only that he spoke at first, he would pause from point to point, and translate into Italian for the benefit of the one-eyed alien to whom he owed his life.

'You probably don't even know the name, Bunny,' he began, 'of the deadliest poison yet known to science. It is cyanide of cacodyl, and I have carried that small flask of it about with me for months. Where I got it matters nothing; the whole point is that a mere sniff reduces flesh to clay. I have never had any opinion of suicide, as you know, but I always felt it worth while to be forearmed against the very worst. Well, a bottle of this stuff is calculated to stiffen an ordinary roomful of ordinary people within, five minutes; and I remembered my flask when they had me as good as crucified in the small hours of this morning. I asked them to take it out of my pocket. I begged them to give me a drink before they left me. And what do you suppose they did?'

I thought of many things but suggested none, while Raffles turned this much of his statement into sufficiently fluent Italian. But when he faced me again his face was still flaming.

'That beast Corbucci!' said he – 'how can I pity him? He took the flask; he would give me none; he flicked me in the face instead. My idea was that he, at least, should go with me – to sell my life as dearly as that – and a sniff would have settled us both. But no, he must tantalise and torment me; he thought it brandy; he must take it downstairs to drink to my destruction! Can you have any pity for a hound like that?'

'Let us go,' I at last said hoarsely, as Raffles finished speaking in Italian, and his second listener stood open-mouthed.

'We will go,' said Raffles, 'and we will chance being seen; if the worst comes to the worst this good chap will prove that I have been tied up since one o'clock this morning, and the medical evidence will decide how long those dogs have been dead.'

But the worst did not come to the worst, more power to my unforgotten friend the cabman, who never came forward to say 'what manner of men he had driven to Bloomsbury Square at top speed on the very day upon which the tragedy was discovered there, or whence he had driven them. To be sure, they had not behaved like murderers, whereas the evidence at the inquest all went to show that the defunct Corbucci was little better. His reputation, which transpired with his identity, was that of a libertine and a renegade, while the infernal apparatus upstairs revealed the fiendish arts of the anarchist to boot. The inquiry resulted eventually in an open verdict, and was chiefly instrumental in killing such compassion as is usually felt for the dead who die in their sins.

But Raffles would not have passed this title for this tale.

5

TO CATCH A THIEF

I

Society persons are not likely to have forgotten the series of audacious robberies by which so many of themselves suffered in turn during the brief course of a recent season. Raid after raid was made upon the smartest houses in town, and within a few weeks more than one exalted head had been shorn of its priceless tiara. The Duke and Duchess of Dorchester lost half the portable pieces of their historic plate on the very night of their Graces' almost equally historic costume ball. The Kenworthy diamonds were taken in broad daylight, during the excitement of a charitable meeting on the ground floor, and the gifts of her belted bridegroom to Lady May Paulton while the outer air was thick with a prismatic shower of confetti. It was obvious that all this was the work of no ordinary thief, and perhaps inevitable that the name of Raffles should have been dragged from oblivion by callous disrespecters of the departed and unreasoning apologists for the police. These wiseacres did not hesitate to bring a dead man back to life because they knew of no living one capable of such feats; it is their heedless and inconsequent calumnies that the present paper is partly intended to refute. As a matter of fact, our joint innocence in this matters was only exceeded by our common envy, and for a long time, like the rest of the world, neither of us had the slightest clue to the identity of the person who was following in our steps with such irritating results.

'I should mind less', said Raffles, 'if the fellow were really playing my game. But abuse of hospitality was never one of my strokes, and it seems to be the only shot he's got. When we took old Lady Melrose's necklace, Bunny, we were not staying with the Melroses, if you recollect.'

We were discussing the robberies for the hundredth time, but for once under conditions more favourable to animated conversation than our unique circumstances permitted in the flat. We did not often dine out. Dr Theobald was one impediment, the risk of recognition was another. But there were exceptions, when the doctor was away or the patient defiant, and on these rare occasions we frequented a certain unpretentious restaurant in the Fulham quarter, where the cooking was plain but excellent, and the cellar a surprise. Our bottle of '89 champagne was empty to the label when the subject arose, to be touched by Raffles in the reminiscent manner indicated above. I can see his clear eye upon me now, reading me, weighing me. But I was not so sensitive to his scrutiny at the time. His tone was deliberate, calculating, preparatory; not as I heard it then, through a head full of wine, but as it floats back to me across the gulf between that moment and this.

'Excellent fillet!' said I grossly. 'So you think this chap is as much in society as we were, do you?'

I preferred not to think so myself. We had cause enough for jealousy without that. But Raffles raised his eyebrows an eloquent half-inch.

'As much, my dear Bunny? He is not only in it, but of it; there's no comparison between us there. Society is in rings like a target, and we never were in the bull's-eye, however thick you may lay on the ink! I was asked for my cricket. I haven't forgotten it yet. But this fellow's one of themselves, with the right of *entree* into houses which we could only "enter" in a professional sense. That's obvious unless all these little exploits are the work of different hands, which they as obviously are not. And it's why I'd give five hundred pounds to put salt on him tonight!'

'Not you,' said I, as I drained my glass in festive incredulity.

'But I would, my dear Bunny Waiter! another half-bottle of this,' and Raffles leant across the table as the empty one was taken away. 'I never was more serious in my life,' he continued below his breath. 'Whatever else our successor may be, he's not a dead man like me, or a marked man like you. If there's any truth in my theory, he's one of the last people upon whom suspicion is ever likely to rest; and oh, Bunny, what a partner he would make for you and me!'

Under less genial influences the very idea of a third partner would have filled my soul with offence; but Raffles had chosen his moment unerringly, and his arguments lost nothing by the flowing accompaniment of the extra pint. They were, however, quite strong in themselves. The gist of them was that thus far we had remarkably little to show for what Raffles would call 'our second innings'. This even I could not deny. We had scored a few 'long singles', but our 'best shots' had gone 'straight to hand', and we were 'playing a deuced slow game'. Therefore we needed a new partner – and the metaphor failed Raffles. It had served its turn. I already agreed with him. In truth I was tired of my false position as hireling attendant, and had long fancied myself an object of suspicion to that other impostor the doctor. A fresh, untrammelled start was a fascinating idea to me, though two was company, and three in our case might be worse than none. But I did not see how we could hope, with our respective handicaps, to solve a problem which was already the despair of Scotland Yard.

'Suppose I have solved it,' observed Raffles, cracking a walnut in his palm.

'How could you?' I asked, without believing for an instant that he had.

'I have been taking the *Morning Post* for some time now.'

'Well?'

'You have got me a good many odd numbers of the less base society papers.'

'I can't for the life of me see what you're driving at.'

Raffles smiled indulgently as he cracked another nut.

'That's because you've neither observation nor imagination, Bunny – and yet you try to write! Well, you wouldn't think it, but I have a fairly complete list of the people who were at the various functions under cover of which these different little *coups* were brought off.'

I said very stolidly that I did not see how that could help him. It was the only answer to his good-humoured but self-satisfied contempt; it happened also to be true.

Think,' said Raffles, in a patient voice.

'When thieves break in and steal,' said I, 'upstairs, I don't see much point in discovering who was downstairs at the time.'

'Quite,' said Raffles – 'when they do break in.'

'But that's what they have done in all these cases. An upstairs door found screwed up, when things were at their height below; thief gone and jewels with him before alarm could be raised. Why, the trick's so old that I never knew you condescend to play it.'

'Not so old as it looks,' said Raffles, choosing the cigars and handing me mine. 'Cognac or Benedictine, Bunny?'

'Brandy,' I said coarsely.

'Besides,' he went on 'the rooms were not screwed up; at Dorchester House, at any rate, the door was only locked, and the key missing, so that it might have been done on either side.'

'But that was where he left his rope-ladder behind him!' I exclaimed in triumph; but Raffles only shook his head.

'I don't believe in that rope-ladder, Bunny, except as a blind.'

'Then what on earth do you believe?'

'That every one of these so-called burglaries has been done from the inside, by one of the guests; and what's more, I'm very much mistaken if I haven't spotted the right sportsman.'

I began to believe that he really had, there was such a wicked gravity in the eyes that twinkled faintly into mine. I raised my glass in convivial congratulation, and still remember the somewhat anxious eye with which Raffles saw it emptied.

'I can only find one likely name,' he continued, 'that figures in all these lists, and it is anything but a likely one at first sight. Lord Ernest Belville was at all those functions. Know anything about him, Bunny?'

'Not the Rational Drink fanatic?'

'Yes.'

That's all I want to know.'

'Quite,' said Raffles; 'and yet what could be more promising? A man whose views are so broad and moderate, and so widely held already (saving your presence, Bunny), does not bore the world with them without ulterior motives. So far so good. What are this chap's motives? Does he want to advertise himself? No, he's somebody already. But is he rich? On the contrary, he's as poor as a rat for his position, and apparently without the least ambition to be anything else; certainly he won't enrich himself by making a public fad of what all sensible people are agreed upon as it is. Then suddenly one gets one's own old idea – the alternative profession! My cricket – his Rational Drink! But it is no use jumping to conclusions. I must know more than the newspapers can tell me. Our aristocratic friend is forty, and unmarried. What has he been doing all these years? How the devil was I to find out?'

'How did you?' I asked, declining to spoil my digestion with a conundrum, as it was his evident intention that I should.

'Interviewed him!' said Raffles, smiling slowly on my amazement.

'You – interviewed him?' I echoed. 'When – and where?'

'Last Thursday night, when, if you remember, we kept early hours, because I felt done. What was the use of telling you what I had up my sleeve, Bunny? It might have ended in fizzle, as it still may. But Lord Ernest Belville was addressing the meeting at Exeter Hall; I waited for him when the show was over, dogged him home to King John's Mansions, and interviewed him in his own rooms there before he turned in.'

My journalistic jealousy was piqued to the quick. Affecting a scepticism I did not feel (for no outrage was beyond the pale of his impudence), I inquired dryly which journal Raffles had pretended to represent. It is unnecessary to report his answer. I could not believe him without further explanation.

'I should have thought', he said, 'that even you would have spotted a practice I never omit upon certain occasions. I always pay a visit to the drawing-room and fill my waistcoat pocket from the card-tray. It is an immense help in any little temporary impersonation. On Thursday night I sent up the card of a powerful writer connected with a powerful paper; if Lord Ernest had known him in the flesh I should have been obliged to confess to a journalistic ruse; luckily he didn't – and I had been sent by my editor to get the interview for next morning. What could be better for the alternative profession?'

I inquired what the interview had brought forth.

'Everything,' said Raffles. 'Lord Ernest has been a wanderer these twenty years. Texas, Fiji, Australia. I suspect him of wives and families in all three. But his manners are a liberal education. He gave me some beautiful whisky, and forgot all about his fad. He is strong and subtle, but I talked him off his guard. He is going to the Kirkleathams' tonight – I saw the card stuck up. I stuck some wax into his keyhole as he was switching off the lights.'

And, with an eye upon the waiters, Raffles showed me a skeleton key, newly twisted and filed; but my share of the extra pint (I am afraid no fair share) had made me dense. I looked from the key to Raffles with puckered forehead – for I happened to catch sight of it in the mirror behind him.

'The Dowager Lady Kirkleatham', he whispered, 'has diamonds as big as beans, and likes to have 'em all on – and goes to bed early – and happens to be in town!'

And now I saw.

'The villain means to get them from her!'

'And I mean to get them from the villain,' said Raffles; 'or, rather, your share and mine.'

'Will he consent to a partnership?'

'We shall have him at our mercy. He daren't refuse.'

Raffles's plan was to gain access to Lord Ernest's rooms before midnight; there we were to lie in wait for the aristocratic rascal, and if I left all details to Raffles, and simply stood by in case of a rumpus, I should be playing my part and earning my share. It was a part that I had played before, not always with a good grace, though there had never been any question about the share. But tonight I was nothing loath. I had had just champagne enough – how Raffles knew my measure! – and I was ready and eager for anything. Indeed, I did not wish to wait for the coffee, which was to be especially strong by order of Raffles. But on that he insisted, and it was between ten and eleven when at last we were in our cab.

'It would be fatal to be too early,' he said as we drove; 'on the other hand, it would be dangerous to leave it too late. One must risk something. How I should love to drive down Piccadilly and see the lights! but unnecessary risks are another story.'

II

King John's Mansions, as everybody knows, are the oldest, and ugliest, and the tallest block of flats in all London. But they are built upon a more generous scale than has since become the rule, and with a less studious regard for the economy of space. We were about to drive into the spacious courtyard when the gatekeeper checked us in order to let another hansom drive out. It contained a middle-aged man of the military type, like ourselves in evening dress. That much I saw as his hansom crossed our bows, because I could not help seeing it, but I should not have given the incident a second thought if it had not been for its extraordinary effect upon Raffles. In an instant he was out upon the kerb, paying the cabby, and in another he was leading me across the street, away from the mansions.

'Where on earth are you going?' I naturally exclaimed.

'Into the park,' said he. 'We are too early.'

His voice told me more than his words. It was strangely stern.

'Was that him – in the hansom?'

'It was.'

'Well, then, the coast's clear,' said I comfortably. I was for turning back, then and there, but Raffles forced me on with a hand that hardened on my arm.

'It was a nearer thing than I care about,' said he. 'This seat will do; no, the next one's farther from a lamp-post. We will give him a good half-hour, and I don't want to talk.'

We had been seated some minutes when Big Ben sent a languid chime over our heads to the stars. It was half-past ten, and a sultry night. Eleven had struck before Raffles awoke from his sullen reverie, and recalled me from mine with a slap on the back. In a couple of minutes we were in the lighted vestibule at the inner end of the courtyard of King John's Mansions.

'Just left Lord Ernest at Lady Kirkleatham's,' said Raffles. 'Gave me his key and asked us to wait for him in his rooms. Will you send us up in the lift?'

In a small way, I never knew old Raffles do anything better. There was not an instant's demur. Lord Ernest Belville's rooms were at the top of the building, but we were in them as quickly as lift could carry and page-boy conduct us. And there was no need for the skeleton key after all; the boy opened the outer door with one of his own, and switched on the lights before leaving us.

'Now that's interesting,' said Raffles, as soon as we were alone; 'they can come in and clean when he is out. What if he keeps his swag at the bank? By Jove, that's an idea for him! I don't believe he's getting rid of it; it's all lying low somewhere, if I'm not mistaken, and he's not a fool.'

While he spoke he was moving about the sitting-room, which was charmingly furnished in the antique style, and making as many remarks as though he were an auctioneer's clerk with an inventory to prepare and a day to do it in, instead of a cracksman who might be surprised in his crib at any moment.

'Chippendale of sorts, eh, Bunny? Not genuine, of course; but where can you get genuine Chippendale now, and who knows it when they see it? There's no merit in mere antiquity. Yet the way people pose on the subject! If a thing's handsome and useful, and good cabinet-making it's good enough for me.'

'Hadn't we better explore the whole place?' I suggested nervously. He had not even bolted the outer door. Nor would he when I called his attention to the omission.

'If Lord Ernest finds his rooms locked up he'll raise Cain,' said Raffles; 'we must let him come in and lock up for himself before we corner him. But he won't come yet; if he did it might be awkward, for they'll tell him down below what I told them. A new staff comes on at midnight. I discovered that the other night.'

'Supposing he does come in before?'

'Well, he can't have us turned out without first seeing who we are, and he won't try it on when I've had one word with him. Unless my suspicions are unfounded, I mean.'

'Isn't it about time to test them?'

'My good Bunny, what do you suppose I've been doing all this while? He keeps nothing in here. There isn't a lock to the

Chippendale that you couldn't pick with a penknife, and not a loose board in the floor, for I was treading for one before the boy left us. Chimneys no use in a place like this where they keep them swept for you. Yes, I'm quite ready to try his bedroom.'

There was but a bathroom besides; no kitchen, no servant's room; neither is necessary in King John's Mansions. I thought it as well to put my head inside the bathroom while Raffles went into the bedroom, for I was tormented by the horrible idea that the man might all this time be concealed somewhere in the flat. But the bathroom blazed void in the electric light. I found Raffles hanging out of the starry square which was the bedroom window, for the room was still in darkness. I felt for the switch at the door.

'Put it out again!' said Raffles fiercely. He rose from the sill, drew blinds and curtains carefully, then switched on the light himself. It fell upon a face creased more in pity than in anger, and Raffles only shook his head as I hung mine.

'It's all right, old boy,' said he; 'but corridors have windows too, and servants have eyes; and you and I are supposed to be in the other room, not in this. But cheer up, Bunny! this is *the* room; look at the extra bolt on the door; he's had that put on, and there's an iron ladder to his window in case of fire! Way of escape ready against the hour of need; he's a better man than I thought him, Bunny, after all. But you may bet your bottom dollar that if there's any boodle in the flat it's in this room.'

Yet the room was very lightly furnished; and nothing was locked. We looked everywhere, but we looked in vain. The wardrobe was filled with hanging coats and trousers in a press, the drawers with the softest silk and finest linen. It was a camp bedstead that would not have unsettled an anchorite; there was no place for treasure there. I looked up the chimney, but Raffles told me not to be a fool, and asked if I ever listened to what he said. There was no question about his temper now. I never knew him in a worse.

'Then he's got it in the bank,' he growled. 'I'll swear I'm not mistaken in my man!'

I had the tact not to differ with him there. But I could not help suggesting that now was our time to remedy any mistake we might have made. We were on the right side of midnight still.

"Then we'll stultify ourselves downstairs,' said Raffles. 'No, I'll be shot if I do! He may come in with the Kirkleatham diamonds; You do what you like, Bunny, but I don't budge.'

'I certainly shan't leave you,' I retorted, 'to be knocked into the middle of next week by a better man than yourself.'

I had borrowed his own tone, and he did not like it. They never do. I thought for a moment that Raffles was going to strike me – for the first and last time in his life. He could if he liked. My blood was up. I was ready to send him to the devil. And I emphasised my offence by nodding and shrugging towards a pair of very large Indian clubs that stood in the fender, on either side of the chimney up which I had presumed to glance.

In an instant Raffles had seized the clubs, and was whirling them about his grey head in a mixture of childish pique and puerile bravado which I should have thought him altogether above. And suddenly as I watched him his face changed, softened, lit up, and he swung the clubs gently down upon the bed.

'They're not heavy enough for their size,' said he rapidly; 'and I'll take my oath they're not the same weight!'

He shook one club after the other, with both hands, close to his ear; then he examined their butt-ends under the electric light. I saw what he suspected now, and caught the contagion of his suppressed excitement. Neither of us spoke. But Raffles had taken out the portable tool-box that he called a knife, and always carried, and as he opened the gimlet he handed me the club he held. Instinctively I tucked the small end under my arm and presented the other to Raffles.

'Hold him tight,' he whispered, smiling. 'He's not only a better man than I thought him, Bunny; he's hit upon a better dodge than ever I did, of its kind. Only I should have weighed them evenly – to a hair.'

He had screwed the gimlet into the circular butt, close to the edge, and now we were wrenching in opposite directions. For a moment or more nothing happened. Then all at once something gave, and Raffles swore an oath as soft as any prayer. And for the minute after that his hand went round and round with the gimlet, as though he were grinding a piano-organ, while the end wormed slowly out on its delicate thread of fine hard wood.

The clubs were as hollow as drinking-horns, the pair of them, for we went from one to the other without pausing to undo the padded packets that poured out upon the bed. These were deliciously heavy to the hand, yet thickly swathed in cotton-wool, so that some stuck together, retaining the shape of the cavity, as though they had been run out of a mould. And when we did open them – but let Raffles speak.

He had deputed me to screw in the ends of the clubs, and to replace the latter in the fender where we had found them. When I had done the counterpane was glittering with diamonds where it was not shimmering with pearls.

'If this isn't the tiara that Lady May was married in,' said Raffles, 'and that disappeared out of the room she changed in, while it rained confetti on the steps, I'll present it to her instead of the one she lost... It was stupid to keep these old gold spoons, valuable as they are; they made the difference in the weight... Here we have probably the Kenworthy diamonds... I don't know the history of these pearls... This looks like one family of rings – left on the basin-stand, perhaps – alas! poor lady! And that's the lot.'

Our eyes met across the bed.

'What's it all worth?' I asked hoarsely.

'Impossible to say. But more than all we ever took in all our lives. That I'll swear to.'

'More than all – '

My tongue swelled with the thought.

'But it'll take some turning into cash, old chap!'

'And – must it be a partnership?' I asked, finding a lugubrious voice at length.

'Partnership be damned!' cried Raffles heartily. 'Let's get out quicker than we came in.'

We pocketed the things between us, cotton-wool and all, not because we wanted the latter, but to remove all immediate traces of our really meritorious deed.

'The sinner won't dare to say a word when he does find out,' remarked Raffles of Lord Ernest; 'but that's no reason why he should. And out before he must. Everything's straight in here, I think; no, better leave the window open as it was, and the blind up. Now out with the light. One peep at the other room. That's all right, too. Out with the passage light, Bunny, while I open – '

His words died away in a whisper. A key was fumbling at the lock outside.

'Out with it – out with it!' whispered Raffles in an agony; and as I obeyed he picked me off my feet and swung me bodily but silently into the bedroom, just as the outer door opened, and a masterful step strode in.

The next five were horrible minutes. We heard the apostle of Rational Drink unlock one of the deep drawers in his antique sideboard, and sounds followed suspiciously like the splash of spirits and the steady stream from a syphon. Never before or since did I experience such a thirst as assailed me at that moment, nor do I believe that many tropical explorers have known its equal. But I had Raffles with me, and his hand was as steady and as cool as the hand of a trained nurse. That I know because he turned up the collar of my overcoat for me, for some reason, and buttoned it at the throat. I afterwards found that he had done the same to his own, but I did not hear him doing it. The one thing I heard in the bedroom was a tiny metallic click, muffled and deadened in his overcoat pocket, and it not only removed my last tremor, but strung me to a higher pitch of excitement than ever. Yet I had then no conception of the game that Raffles was deciding to play, and that I was to play with him in another minute.

It cannot have been longer before Lord Ernest came into his bedroom. Heavens, but my heart had not forgotten how to thump! We were standing near the door, and I could swear he touched me; then his boots creaked, there was a rattle in the fender – and Raffles switched on the light.

Lord Ernest Belville crouched in its glare with one Indian club held by the end, like a footman with a stolen bottle. A good- looking, well-built, iron-grey, iron-jawed man; but a fool and a weakling at that moment, if he had never been either before.

'Lord Ernest Belville,' said Raffles, 'it's no use. This is a loaded revolver, and if you force me I shall use it on you as I would on any other desperate criminal. I am here to arrest you for a series of robberies at the Duke of Dorchester's, Sir John Kenworthy's, and other noblemen's and gentlemen's houses during the present season. You'd better drop what you've got in your hand. It's empty.'

Lord Ernest lifted the club an inch or two, and with it his eyebrows – and after it his stalwart frame as the club crashed back into the fender. And as he stood at his full height, a courteous but ironic smile under the cropped moustache, he looked what he was, criminal or not.

'Scotland Yard?' said he.

'That's our affair, my lord.'

'I didn't think they'd got it in them,' said Lord Ernest. 'Now I recognise you. You're my interviewer. No, I didn't think any of you fellows had got all that in you. Come into the other room, and I'll show you something else. Oh, keep me covered by all means. But look at this!'

On the antique sideboard, their size doubled by reflection in the polished mahogany, lay a coruscating cluster of precious stones, that fell in festoons about Lord Ernest's fingers as he handed them to Raffles with scarcely a shrug.

'The Kirkleatham diamonds,' said he. 'Better add 'em to the bag.'

Raffles did so without a smile, with his overcoat buttoned up to the chin, his tall hat pressed down to his eyes, and between the two, his incisive features and his keen, stern glance, he looked the ideal detective of fiction and the stage. What *I* looked God knows, but I did my best to glower and show my teeth at his side. I had thrown myself into the game, and it was obviously a winning one.

'Wouldn't take a share, I suppose?' Lord Ernest said casually.

Raffles did not condescend to reply. I rolled back my lips like a bull-pup.

'Then a drink, at least!'

My mouth watered, but Raffles shook his head impatiently.

'We must be going, my lord, and you will have to come with us.'

I wondered what in the world we should do with him when we had got him.

'Give me time to put some things together? Pair of pyjamas and toothbrush, don't you know?'

'I cannot give you many minutes, my lord, but I don't want to cause a disturbance here, so I'll tell them to call a cab if you like. But I shall be back in a minute, and you must be ready in five. Here, Inspector, you'd better keep this while I am gone.'

And I was left alone with that dangerous criminal! Raffles nipped my arm as he handed me the revolver, but I got small comfort out of that.

'Sea-green Incorruptible?' inquired Lord Ernest, as we stood face to face.

'You don't corrupt me,' I replied through naked teeth.

'Then come into my room. I'll lead the way. Think you can hit me if I misbehave?'

I put the bed between us without a second's delay. My prisoner flung a suit-case upon it, and tossed things into it with a dejected air; suddenly, as he was fitting them in, without raising his head (which I was watching), his right hand closed over the barrel with which I covered him.

'You'd better not shoot,' he said, a knee upon his side of the bed; 'if you do it may be as bad for you as it will be for me!'

I tried to wrest the revolver from him.

'I will if you force me,' I hissed.

'You'd better not,' he repeated, smiling; and now I saw that if I did I should only shoot into the bed or my own legs. His hand was on the top of mine, bending it down, and the revolver with it. The strength of it was as the strength of ten of mine; and now both his knees were on the bed; and suddenly I saw his other hand, doubled into a fist, coming up slowly over the suit-case.

'Help!' I called feebly.

'Help, forsooth! I begin to believe *you are* from the Yard,' he said – and his uppercut came with the 'yard'. It caught me under the chin. It lifted me off my legs. I have a dim recollection of the crash that I made in failing.

III

Raffles was standing over me when I recovered consciousness. I lay stretched upon the bed across which that blackguard Belville had struck his knavish blow. The suit-case was on the floor, but its dastardly owner had disappeared.

'Is he gone?' was my first faint question.

"Thank God you're not, anyway!" replied Raffles with what struck me then as mere flippancy. I managed to raise myself upon one elbow.

'I meant Lord Ernest Belville,' said I with dignity. 'Are you quite sure that he's cleared out?'

Raffles waved a hand towards the window, which stood wide open to the summer stars.

'Of course,' said he, 'and by the route I intended him to take; he's gone by the iron ladder, as I hoped he would. What on earth should we have done with him? My poor dear Bunny, I thought you'd take a bribe! But it's really more convincing as it is, and just as well for Lord Ernest to be convinced for the time being.'

'Are you sure he is?' I questioned, as I found a rather shaky pair of legs.

'Of course!' cried Raffles again, in the tone to make one blush for the least misgiving on the point. 'Not that it matters one bit,' he added, airily, 'for we have him either way; and when he does tumble to it, as he may any minute, he won't dare to open his mouth.'

'Then the sooner we clear out the better,' said I, but I looked askance at the open window, for my head was spinning still.

'When you feel up to it,' returned Raffles, 'we shall *stroll* out, and I shall do myself the honour of ringing for the lift. The force of habit is too strong in you, Bunny. I shall shut the window and leave everything exactly as we found it. Lord Ernest will probably tumble before he is badly missed; and then he may come back to put salt on us; but I should like to know what he can do even if he succeeds! Come, Bunny, pull yourself together, and you'll be a different man when you're in the open air.'

And for a while I felt one, such was my relief at getting out of those infernal mansions with unfettered wrists; this we managed easily enough; but once more Raffles's performance of a small part was no less perfect than his more ambitious work upstairs, and something of the successful artist's elation possessed him as we walked arm-in-arm across St James's Park. It was long since I had known him so pleased with himself, and only too long since he had had such reason.

'I don't think I ever had a brighter idea in my life,' he said; 'never thought of it till he was in the next room; never dreamt of its coming off so ideally even then, and didn't much care, because we had him all ways up. I'm only sorry you let him knock you out. I was waiting outside the door all the time, and it made me sick to hear it. But I once broke my own head, Bunny, if you remember, and not in half such an excellent cause!'

Raffles touched all his pockets in his turn, the pockets that contained a small fortune apiece, and he smiled in my face as we crossed the lighted avenues of the Mall. Next moment he was hailing a hansom – for I suppose I was still pretty pale – and not a word would he let me speak until we had alighted as near as was prudent to the flat.

'What a brute I've been, Bunny!' he whispered then; 'but you take half the swag, old boy, and right well you've earned it. No, we'll go in by the wrong door and over the roof; it's too late for old Theobald to be still at the play, and too early for him to be safely in his cups.'

So we climbed the many stairs with cat-like stealth, and like cats crept out upon the grimy leads. But tonight they were no blacker than their canopy of sky; not a chimney-stack stood out against the starless night; one had to feel one's way in order to avoid tripping over the low parapets of the L-shaped wells that ran from roof to basement to light the inner rooms. One of these wells was spanned by a flimsy bridge with iron handrails that felt warm to the touch as Raffles led the way across; a hotter and a closer night I have never known.

'The flat will be like an oven,' I grumbled, at the head of our own staircase.

'Then we won't go down,' said Raffles, promptly; 'we'll slack it up here for a bit instead. No, Bunny, you stay where you are! I'll fetch you a drink and a deck-chair, and you shan't come down till you feel more fit.'

And I let him have his way, I will not say as usual, for I had even less than my normal power of resistance that night. That villainous uppercut! My head still sang and throbbed, as I seated myself on one of the aforesaid parapets, and buried it in my hot hands. Nor was the night one to dispel a headache; there was distinct thunder in the air. Thus I sat in a heap, and brooded over my misadventure, a pretty figure of a subordinate villain, until the step came for which I waited; and it never struck me that it came from the wrong direction.

'You have been quick,' said I, simply.

'Yes,' hissed a voice I recognised; 'and you've got to be quicker still! Here, out with your wrists; no, one at a time; and if you utter a syllable you're a dead man.'

It was Lord Ernest Belville; his close-cropped, iron-grey moustache gleamed through the darkness, drawn up over his set teeth. In his hand glittered a pair of handcuffs, and before I knew it one had snapped its jaws about my right wrist.

'Now come this way,' said Lord Ernest, showing me a revolver also, 'and wait for your friend. And, recollect, a single syllable of warning will be your death!'

With that the ruffian led me to the very bridge I had just crossed at Raffles's heels, and handcuffed me to the iron rail midway across the chasm. It no longer felt warm to my touch, but icy as the blood in all my veins.

So this high-born hypocrite had beaten us at our game and his, and Raffles had met his match at last! That was the most intolerable thought, that Raffles should be down in the flat on my account, and that I could not warn him of his impending fate; for how was it possible without making such an outcry as should bring the mansions about our ears? And there I shivered on that wretched plank, chained like Andromeda to the rock, with a black infinity above and below; and before my eyes, now grown familiar with the peculiar darkness, stood Lord Ernest Belville, waiting for Raffles to emerge with full hands and unsuspecting heart! Taken so horribly unawares, even Raffles must fall an easy prey to a desperado in resource and courage scarcely second to himself, but one whom he had fatally underrated from the beginning. Not that I paused to think how the thing had happened; my one concern was for what was to happen next.

And what did happen was worse than my worst foreboding, for first a light came flickering into the sort of companion-hatch at the head of the stairs, and finally Raffles – in his shirt-sleeves! He was not only carrying a candle to put the finishing touch to him as a target; he had dispensed with coat and waistcoat downstairs, and was at once full-handed and unarmed.

'Where are you, old chap?' he cried softly, himself blinded by the light he carried; and he advanced a couple of steps towards Belville. 'This isn't you, is it?'

And Raffles stopped, his candle held on high, a folding-chair under the other arm.

'No, I am not your friend,' replied Lord Ernest, easily; 'but kindly remain standing exactly where you are, and don't lower that candle an inch, unless you want your brains blown into the street.'

Raffles said never a word, but for a moment did as he was bid; and the unshaken flame of the candle was testimony alike to the stillness of the night and to the finest set of nerves in Europe. Then, to my horror, he coolly stooped, placing candle and chair on the leads, and his hands in his pockets, as though it were but a pop-gun that covered him.

'Why didn't you shoot?' he asked insolently, as he rose. 'Frightened of the noise? I should be, too, with an old-pattern machine like that. All very well for service in the field – but on the housetops at dead of night!'

'I shall shoot, however,' replied Lord Ernest, as quietly in his turn, and with less insolence, 'and chance the noise, unless you instantly restore my property. I am glad you don't dispute the last word,' he continued after a slight pause. 'There is no keener honour than that which subsists, or ought to subsist, among thieves; and I need hardly say that I soon spotted you as one of the fraternity. Not in the beginning, mind you! For the moment I did think you were one of these smart detectives jumped to life from some sixpenny magazine but to preserve the illusion you ought to provide yourself with a worthier lieutenant. It was he who gave your show away,' chuckled the wretch, dropping for a moment the affected style of speech which seemed intended to enhance our humiliation; 'smart detectives don't go about with little innocents to assist them. You needn't be anxious about him, by the way; it wasn't necessary to pitch him into the street; he is to be seen though not heard, if you look in the right direction. Nor must you put all the blame upon your friend; it was not he, but you, who made so sure that I had got out by the window. You see, I was in my bathroom all the time – with the door open.'

'The bathroom, eh?' Raffles echoed with professional interest. 'And you followed us on foot across the park?'

'Of course.'

'And then in a cab?'

'And afterwards on foot once more.'

'The simplest skeleton would let you in down below.'

I saw the lower half of Lord Ernest's face grinning in the light of the candle set between them on the ground.

'You follow every move,' said he; 'there can be no doubt you are one of the fraternity; and I shouldn't wonder if we had formed our style upon the same model. Ever know A.J. Raffles?'

The abrupt question took my breath away; but Raffles himself did not lose an instant over his answer.

'Intimately,' said he.

'That accounts for you, then,' laughed Lord Ernest, 'as it does for me, though I never had the honour of the master's acquaintance. Nor is it for me to say which is the worthier disciple. Perhaps, however, now that your friend is handcuffed in mid-air, and you yourself are at my mercy, you will concede me some little temporary advantage?'

And his face split in another grin from the cropped moustache downward, as I saw no longer by candle-light, but by a flash of lightning which tore the sky in two before Raffles could reply.

'You have the bulge at present,' admitted Raffles; 'but you have still to lay hands upon your, or our, ill-gotten goods. To shoot me is not necessarily to do so; to bring either one of us to a violent end is only to court a yet more violent and infinitely more disgraceful one for yourself. Family considerations alone should rule that risk out of your game. Now, an hour or two ago, when the exact opposite – '

The remainder of Raffles's speech was drowned from my ears by the belated crash of thunder which the lightning had foretold. So loud, however, was the crash when it came, that the storm was evidently approaching us at a high velocity; yet as the last echo rumbled away, I heard Raffles talking as though he had never stopped.

'You offered us a share,' he was saying; 'unless you mean to murder us both in cold blood, it will be worth your while to repeat that offer. We should be dangerous enemies; you had far better make the best of us as friends.'

'Lead the way down to your flat,' said Lord Ernest, with a flourish of his service revolver, 'and perhaps we may talk about it. It is for me to make the terms, I imagine, and in the first place I am not going to get wet to the skin up here.'

The rain was beginning in great drops, even as he spoke, and by a second flash of lightning I saw Raffles pointing to me.

'And what about my friend?' said he.

And then came the second peal.

'Oh, *he's* all right,' the great brute replied; 'do him good! You don't catch me letting myself in for two to one!'

'You will find it equally difficult', rejoined Raffles, 'to induce me to leave my friend to the mercy of a night like this. He has not recovered from the blow you struck him in your own rooms. I am not such a fool as to blame you for that, but you are a worse sportsman than I take you for if you think of leaving him where he is. If he stays, however, so do I.'

And, just as it ceased, Raffles's voice seemed distinctly nearer to me; but in the darkness and the rain, which was now as heavy as hail, I could see nothing clearly. The rain had already extinguished the candle. I heard an oath from Belville, a laugh from Raffles, and for a second that was all; Raffles was coming to me, and the other could not even see to fire; that was all I knew in the pitchy interval of invisible rain before the next crash and the next flash.

And then!

This time they came together, and not till my dying hour shall I forget the sight that the lightning lit and the thunder applauded. Raffles was on one of the parapets of the gulf that my foot-bridge spanned, and in the sudden illumination he stepped across it as one might across a garden path. The width was scarcely greater, but the depth! In the sudden flare I saw to the concrete bottom of the well, and it looked no larger than the hollow of my hand. Raffles was laughing in my ear; he had the iron railing fast; it was between us, but his foothold was as secure as mine. Lord Ernest Belville, on the contrary, was the fifth of a second late for the light, and half a foot short in his spring. Something struck our plank bridge so hard as to set it quivering like a harp-string; there was half a gasp and half a sob in mid-air beneath our feet; and then a sound far below that I prefer not to describe. I am not sure that I could hit upon the perfect simile; it is more than enough for me that I can hear it still. And with that sickening sound came the loudest clap of thunder yet, and a great white glare that showed us our enemy's body far below, with one white hand spread like a starfish, but the head of him mercifully twisted underneath.

'It was his own fault, Bunny. Poor devil! May he and all of us be forgiven; but pull yourself together for your own sake. Well, you can't fall; stay where you are a minute.'

I remember the uproar of the elements while Raffles was gone; no other sound mingled with it; not the opening of a single window, not the uplifting of a single voice. Then came Raffles with soap and water, and the gyve was wheedled from one wrist, as you withdraw a ring for which the finger has grown too large. Of the rest, I only remember shivering till morning in a pitch-dark flat, whose invalid occupier was for once the nurse, and I his patient.

And that is the true ending of the episode in which we two set ourselves to catch one of our own kidney, albeit in another place I have shirked the whole truth. It is not a grateful task to show Raffles as completely at fault as he really was on that occasion; nor do I derive any subtle satisfaction from recounting my own twofold humiliation, or from having assisted never so indirectly in the death of a not uncongenial sinner. The truth, however, has after all a merit of its own, and the great kinsfolk of poor Lord Ernest have but little to lose by its divulgence. It would seem that they knew more of the real character of the apostle of Rational Drink than was known at Exeter Hall. The tragedy was indeed hushed up, as tragedies only are when they occur in such circles. But the rumour that did get abroad, as to the class of enterprise which the poor scamp was pursuing when he met his death, cannot be too soon exploded, since it breathed upon the fair fame of some of the most respectable flats in Kensington.

6

AN OLD FLAME

I

The square shall be nameless, but if you drive due west from Piccadilly the cabman will eventually find it on his left, and he ought to thank you for two shillings. It is not a fashionable square, but there are few with a finer garden, while the studios on the south side lend distinction of another sort. The houses, however, are small and dingy, and about the last to attract the expert practitioner in search of a crib. Heaven knows it was with no such thought I trailed Raffles thither, one unlucky evening at the latter end of that same season, when Dr Theobald had at last insisted upon the bath-chair which I had foreseen in the beginning. Trees whispered in the green garden aforesaid, and the cool smooth lawns looked so inviting that I wondered whether some philanthropic resident could not be induced to lend us the key. But Raffles would not listen to the suggestion, when I stopped to make it, and what was worse, I found him looking wistfully at the little houses instead.

'Such balconies, Bunny! A leg up, and there you would be!'

I expressed a conviction that there would be nothing worth taking in the square, but took care to have him under way again as I spoke.

'I dare say you're right,' sighed Raffles. 'Rings and watches, I suppose, but it would be hard luck to take them from people who live in houses like these. I don't know, though. Here's one with an extra storey. Stop, Bunny; if you don't stop I'll hold on to the railings! This is a good house; look at the knocker and the electric bell. They've had that put in. There's some money here, my rabbit! I dare bet there's a silver-table in the drawing-room; and the windows are wide open. Electric light, too, by Jove!'

Since stop I must, I had done so on the other side of the road, in the shadow of the leafy palings, and as Raffles spoke the ground-floor windows opposite had flown alight, showing as pretty a little' dinner-table as one could wish to see, with a man at his wine at the far end, and the back of a lady in evening dress toward us. It was like a lantern-picture thrown upon a screen. There were only the pair of them, but the table was brilliant with silver and gay with flowers, and the maid waited with the indefinable air of a good servant. It certainly seemed a good house.

'She's going to let down the blind!' whispered Raffles, in high excitement. 'No, confound them, they've told her not to. Mark down her necklace, Bunny, and invoice his stud. What a brute he looks! But I like the table, and that's her show. She has the taste; but he must have money. See the festive picture over the sideboard? Looks to me like a Jacques Saillard. But that silver-table would be good enough for me.'

'Get on,' said I. 'You're in a bath-chair.'

'But the whole square's at dinner! We should have the ball at our feet. It wouldn't take two twos!'

'With those blinds up, and the cook in the kitchen underneath?'

He nodded, leaning forward in the chair, his hands upon the wraps about his legs.

'You must be mad,' said I, and got back to my handles with the word, but when I tugged the chair ran light.

'Keep an eye on the rug,' came in a whisper from the middle of the road; and there stood my invalid, his pale face in a quiver of pure mischief, yet set with his insane resolve. 'I'm only going to see whether that woman has a silver-table – '

'We don't want it – '

'It won't take a minute – '

'It's madness, madness – '

'Then don't you wait!'

It was like him to leave me with that, and this time I had taken him at his last word, had not my own given me an idea. Mad I had called him, and mad I could declare him upon oath if necessary. It was not as though the thing had happened far from home, They could learn all about us at the nearest mansions. I referred them to Dr Theobald; this was a Mr Maturin, one of his patients, and I was his keeper, and he had never given me the slip before. I heard myself making these explanations on the doorstep, and pointing to the deserted bath-chair as the proof, while the pretty parlourmaid ran for the police. It would be a more serious matter for me than for my charge. I should lose my place. No, he had never done such a thing before, and I would answer for it that he never should again.

I saw myself conducting Raffles back to his chair, with a firm hand and a stern tongue. I heard-him thanking me in whispers on the way home. It would be the first tight place I had ever got him out of, and I was quite anxious for him to get into it, so sure was I of every move. My whole position had altered in the few seconds that it took me to follow this illuminating train of ideas; it was now so strong that I could watch Raffles without much anxiety. And he was worth watching.

He had stepped boldly but softly to the front door, and there he was still waiting, ready to ring if the door opened or a face appeared in the area, and doubtless to pretend that he had rung already. But he had not to ring at all; and suddenly I saw his foot in the letter-box, his left hand on the lintel overhead. It was thrilling, even to a hardened accomplice with an explanation up his sleeve! A tight grip with that left hand of his, as he leant backward with all his weight upon those five fingers; a right arm stretched outward and upward to its last inch; and the base of the low, projecting balcony was safely caught.

I looked down and took breath. The maid was removing the crumbs in the lighted room, and the square was empty as before. What a blessing it was the end of the season! Many of the houses remained in darkness. I looked up again, and Raffles was drawing his left leg over the balcony railing. In another moment he had disappeared through one of the French windows which opened upon the balcony, and in yet another he had switched on the electric light within. This was bad enough, for now I, at least, could see everything he did; but the crowning folly was still to come. There was no point in it; the mad thing was done for my benefit, as I knew at once and he afterwards confessed; but the lunatic reappeared on the balcony, bowing like a mountebank – in his crape mask!

I set off with the empty chair, but I came back. I could not desert old Raffles, even when I would, but must try to explain away his mask as well, if he had not the sense to take it off in time. It would be difficult, but burglaries are not usually committed from a bath-chair, and for the rest I put my faith in Dr Theobald. Meanwhile Raffles had at least withdrawn from the balcony, and now I could only see his head as he peered into a cabinet at the other side of the room. It was like the opera of *Aida*, in which two scenes are enacted simultaneously, one in the dungeon below, the other in the temple above. In the same fashion my attention now became divided between the picture of Raffles moving stealthily about the upper room and that of the husband and wife at table underneath. And all at once, as the man replenished his glass with a shrug of the shoulders, the woman pushed back her chair and sailed to the door.

Raffles was standing before the fireplace upstairs. He had taken one of the framed photographs from the chimney-piece, and was scanning it at suicidal length through the eye-holes in the hideous mask which he still wore. He would need it after all. The lady had left the room below, opening and shutting the door for herself; the man was filling his glass once more. I would have shrieked my warning to Raffles, so fatally engrossed overhead, but at this moment (of all others) a constable (of all men) was marching sedately down our side of the square. There was nothing for it but to turn a melancholy eye upon the bath-chair, and to ask the constable the time. I was evidently to be kept there all night, I remarked, and only realised with the words that they disposed of my other explanations before they were uttered. It was a horrible moment for such a discovery. Fortunately the enemy was on the pavement, from which he could scarcely have seen more than the drawing-room ceiling, had he looked; but he was not many houses distant when a door opened and a woman gasped so that I heard both across the road. And never shall I forget the subsequent tableaux in the lighted room behind the low balcony and the French windows.

Raffles stood confronted by a dark and handsome woman whose profile, as I saw it first in the electric light, is cut like a cameo in my memory. It had the undeviating line of brow and nose, the short upper lip, the perfect chin, that are united in marble oftener than in the flesh; and like marble she stood, or rather like some beautiful pale bronze; for that was her colouring, and she lost none of it that I could see, neither trembled; but her bosom rose and fell, and that was all. So she stood without flinching before a masked ruffian, who, I felt, would be the first to appreciate her courage; to me it was so superb that I could think of it this way even then, and marvel how Raffles himself could stand unabashed before so brave a figure. He had not to do so long. The woman scorned him, and he stood unmoved, a framed photograph still in his hand. Then, with a quick, determined movement she turned, not to the door or to the bell, but to the open window by which Raffles had entered; and this with that accursed policeman still in view. So far no word had passed between the pair. But at this point Raffles said something, I could not hear what, but at the sound of his voice the woman wheeled. And Raffles was looking humbly in her face, the crape mask snatched from his own.

'Arthur!' she cried; and that might have been heard in the middle of the square garden.

Then they stood gazing at each other, neither umoved any more, and while they stood the street-door opened and banged. It was the husband leaving the house, a fine figure of a man, but a dissipated face, and a step even now distinguished by the extreme caution which precedes unsteadiness. He broke the spell. His wife came to the balcony, then looked back into the room, and yet again along the road, and this time I saw her face. It was the face of one glancing indeed from Hyperion to a satyr. And then I saw the rings flash, as her hand fell gently upon Raffles's arm.

They disappeared from the window. Their heads showed for an instant in the next. Then they dipped out of sight, and an inner ceiling flashed out under a new light; they had gone into the back drawing-room beyond my ken. The maid came up with coffee; her mistress hastily met her at the door, and once more disappeared. The square was as quiet as ever. I remained some minutes where I was. Now and then I thought I heard their voices in the back drawing-room. I was seldom sure.

My state of mind may be imagined by those readers who take an interest in my personal psychology. It does not amuse me to look back upon it. But at length I had the sense to put myself in Raffles's place. He had been recognised at last, he had come to life. Only one person knew as yet, but that person was a woman, and a woman who had once been fond of him, if the human face could speak. Would she keep his secret?

Would he tell her where he lived? It was terrible to think we were such neighbours, and with the thought that it was terrible came a little enlightenment as to what could still be done for the best. He would not tell her where he lived. I knew him too well for that. He would run for it when he could, and the bath-chair and I must not be there to give him away. I dragged the infernal vehicle round the nearer corner. Then I waited – there could be no harm in that – and at last he came.

He was walking briskly, so I was right, and he had not played the invalid to her; yet I heard him cry out with pleasure as he turned the corner, and he flung himself into the chair with a long-drawn sigh that did me good.

'Well done, Bunny – well done! I am on my way to Earl's Court; she's capable of following me, but she won't look for me in a bath-chair. Home, home, home, and not another word till we get there!'

Capable of following him? She overtook us before we were past the studios in the south side of the square, the woman herself, in a hooded opera-cloak. But she never gave us a glance, and we saw her turn safely in the right direction for Earl's Court, and the wrong one for our humble mansions, Raffles thanked his gods in a voice that trembled, and five minutes later we were in the flat. Then for once it was Raffles who filled the tumblers and found the cigarettes, and for once (and once only in all my knowledge of him) did he drain his glass at a draught.

'You didn't see the balcony scene?' he asked at length; and they were his first words since the woman passed us on his track.

'Do you mean when she came in?'

'No, when I came down.'

'I didn't.'

'I hope nobody else saw it,' said Raffles devoutly. 'I don't say that Romeo and Juliet were brother and sister to us. But you might have said so, Bunny!'

He was staring at the carpet with as wry a face as lover ever wore.

'An old flame?' said I, gently.

'A married woman,' he groaned.

'So I gathered.'

'But she always was one, Bunny,' said he, ruefully. 'That's the trouble. It makes all the difference in the world!'

I saw the difference, but said I did not see how it could make any now. He had eluded the lady, after all; had we not seen her off upon a scent as false as scent could be? There was occasion for redoubled caution in the future, but none for immediate anxiety. I quoted the bedside Theobald, but Raffles did not smile. His eyes had been downcast all this time, and now, when he raised them, I perceived that my comfort had been administered to deaf ears.

'Do you know who she is?' said he.

'Not from Eve.'

'Jacques Saillard,' he said, as though now I must know.

But the name left me cold and stolid. I had heard it, but that was all. It was lamentable ignorance, I am aware, but I had specialised in Letters at the expense of Art.

'You must know her pictures,' said Raffles, patiently; 'but I suppose you thought she was a man. They would appeal to you, Bunny; that festive piece over the sideboard was her work. Sometimes they risk her at the Academy, sometimes they fight shy. She has one of those studios in the same square; they used to live up near Lord's.'

My mind was busy brightening a dim memory of nymphs reflected in woody pools. 'Of course!' I exclaimed, and added something about 'a clever woman.' Raffles rose at the phrase.

'A clever woman!' echoed he scornfully; 'if she were only that I should feel safe as houses. Clever women can't forget their cleverness, they carry it as badly as a boy does his wine, and are about as dangerous. I don't call Jacques Saillard clever outside her art, but neither do I call her a woman at all. She does man's work over a man's name, has the will of any ten men I ever knew, and I don't mind telling you that I fear her more than any person on God's earth. I broke with her once,' said Raffles grimly, 'but I know her. If I had been asked to name the one person in London by whom I was keenest *not* to be bowled out, I should have named Jacques Saillard.'

That he had never before named her to me was as characteristic as the reticence with which Raffles spoke of their past relations, and even of their conversation in the back drawing-room that evening; it was a question of principle with him, and one that I like to remember. 'Never give a woman away, Bunny,' he used to say and he said it again tonight, but with a heavy cloud upon him, as though his chivalry was sorely tried.

'That's all right,' said I, 'if you're not going to be given away yourself.'

'That's just it, Bunny! That's just – '

The words were out of him, it was too late to recall them. I had hit the nail upon the head.

'So she threatened you,' I said, 'did she?'

'I didn't say so,' he replied coldly.

'And she is mated with a clown!' I pursued.

'How she ever married him,' he admitted, 'is a mystery to me.'

'It always is,' said I, the wise man for once, and rather enjoying the *rôle*. 'Southern blood?'

'Spanish.'

'She'll be pestering you to run off with her, old chap,' said I.

Raffles was pacing the room. He stopped in his stride for half a second. So she had begun pestering him already! It is wonderful how acute any fool can be in the affairs of his friend. But Raffles resumed his walk without a syllable, and I retreated to safer ground.

'So you sent her to Earl's Court,' I mused aloud; and at last he smiled.

'You'll be interested to hear, Bunny,' said he, 'that I'm now living in Seven Dials, and Bill Sykes couldn't hold a farthing dip to me. Bless you, she had my old police record at her fingers' ends, but it was fit to frame compared with the one I gave her. I had sunk as low as they dig. I divided my nights between the open parks and a thieves' kitchen in Seven Dials. If I was decently dressed it was because I had stolen the suit down the Thames Valley beat the night before last. I was on my way back when first that sleepy square, and then her open window, proved too much for me. You should have heard me beg her to let me push on to the devil in my own way; there I spread myself, for I meant every word; but I swore the final stage would be a six-foot drop.'

'You did lay it on,' said I.

'It was necessary, and that had its effect. She let me go. But at the last moment she said she didn't believe I was so black as I painted myself, and then there was the balcony scene you missed.'

So that was all. I could not help telling him that he had got out of it better than he deserved for ever getting in. Next moment I regretted the remark.

'If I have got out of it,' said Raffles, doubtfully. 'We are dreadfully near neighbours, and I can't move in a minute, with old Theobald taking a grave view of my case. I suppose I had better lie low, and thank the gods again for putting her off the scent for the time being.'

No doubt our conversation was carried beyond this point, but it certainly was not many minutes later, nor had we left the subject, when the electric bell thrilled us both to a sudden silence.

'The doctor?' I queried, hope fighting with my horror.

'It was a single ring.'

'The last post?'

'You know he knocks, and it's long past his time.'

The electric bell rang again, but now as though it never would stop.

'You go, Bunny,' said Raffles, with decision. His eyes were sparkling. His smile was firm.

'What am I to say?'

'If it's the lady let her in.'

It was the lady, still in her evening cloak, with her fine dark head half hidden by the hood, and an engaging contempt of appearances upon her angry face. She was even handsomer than I had thought, and her beauty of a bolder type, but she was also angrier than I had anticipated when I came so readily to the door. The passage into which it opened was an exceedingly narrow one, as I have often said, but I never dreamt of barring this woman's way, though not a word did she stoop to say to me. I was only too glad to flatten myself against the wall, as the rustling fury strode past me into the lighted room with the open door.

'So this is your thieves' kitchen!' she cried, in high-pitched scorn.

I was on the threshold myself, and Raffles glanced toward me with raised eyebrows.

'I have certainly had better quarters in my day,' said he, 'but you need not call them absurd names before my man.'

'Then send your "man" about his business,' said Jacques Saillard, with an unpleasant stress upon the word indicated.

But when the door was shut I heard Raffles assuring her that I knew nothing, that he was a real invalid overcome by a sudden mad temptation, and all he had told her of his life a lie to hide his whereabouts, but all he was telling her now she could prove for herself without leaving that building. It seemed, however, that she had proved it already by going first to the porter below stairs. Yet I do not think she cared one atom which story was the truth.

'So you thought I could pass you in your chair,' she said, 'or ever in this world again, without hearing from my heart that it was you!'

II

'Bunny,' said Raffles, 'I'm awfully sorry, old chap, but you've got to go.'

It was some weeks since the first untimely visitation of Jacques Saillard, but there had been many others at all hours of the day, while Raffles had been induced to pay at least one to her studio in the neighbouring square. These intrusions he had endured at first with an air of humorous resignation which imposed upon me less than he imagined. The woman meant well, he said, after all, and could be trusted to keep his secret loyally. It was plain to me, however, that Raffles did not trust her, and that his pretence upon the point was a deliberate pose to conceal the extent to which she had him in her power. Otherwise there would have been little point in hiding anything from the one person in possession of the cardinal secret of his identity. But Raffles thought it worth his while to hoodwink Jacques Saillard in the subsidiary matter of his health, in which Dr Theobald lent him unwitting assistance, and, as we have seen, to impress upon her that I was actually his attendant, and as ignorant of his past as the doctor himself. 'So you're right, Bunny,' he had assured me; 'she thinks you knew nothing the other night. I told you she wasn't a clever woman outside her work. But hasn't she a will!' I told Raffles it was very considerate of him to keep me out of it, but that it seemed to me like tying up the bag when the cat had escaped. His reply was an admission that one must be on the defensive with such a woman and in such a case. Soon after this, Raffles, looking far from well, fell back upon his own last line of defence, namely, his bed; and now, as always in the end, I could see some sense in his subtleties, since it was comparatively easy for me to turn even Jacques Saillard from the door, with Dr Theobald's explicit injunctions, and with my own honesty unquestioned. So for a day we had peace once more. Then came letters, then the doctor again and again, and finally my dismissal in the incredible words which have necessitated these explanations.

'Go?' I echoed. 'Go where?'

'It's that ass Theobald,' said Raffles. 'He insists.'

'On my going altogether?'

He nodded.

'And you mean to let him have his way?'

I had no language for my mortification and disgust, though neither was as yet quite so great as my surprise. I had foreseen almost every conceivable consequence of the mad act which brought all this trouble to pass, but a voluntary division between Raffles and me had certainly never entered my calculations. Nor could I think that it had occurred to him before our egregious doctor's last visit, this very morning. Raffles had looked irritated as he broke the news to me from his pillow, and now there was some sympathy in the way he sat up in bed, as though he felt the thing himself.

'I am obliged to give in to the fellow,' said he. 'He's saving me from my friend, and I'm bound to humour him. But I can tell you that we've been arguing about you for the last half-hour, Bunny. It was no use; the idiot has had his knife in you from the first; and he wouldn't see me through on any other conditions.'

'So he is going to see you through, is he?'

'It tots up to that,' said Raffles, looking at me rather hard. 'At all events he has come to my rescue for the time being, and it's for me to manage the rest. You don't know what it has been, Bunny, these last few weeks; and gallantry forbids that I should tell you even now. But would you rather elope against your will, or have your continued existence made known to the world in general and the police in particular? That is practically the problem which I have had to solve, and the temporary solution was to fall ill. As a matter of fact I am ill; and now what do you think? I owe it to you to tell you, Bunny, though it goes against the grain. She would take me "to the dear, warm underworld, where the sun really shines", and she would "nurse me back to life and love"! The artistic temperament is a fearsome thing, Bunny, in a woman with the devil's own will!'

Raffles tore up the letter from which he had read these piquant extracts, and lay back on the pillow, with the tired air of the veritable invalid which he seemed able to assume at will. But for once he did look as though bed was the best place for him; and I used the fact as an argument for my own retention in defiance of Dr Theobald. The town was full of typhoid, I said, and certainly that autumnal scourge was in the air. Did he want me to leave him at the very moment when he might be sickening for a serious illness?

'You know I don't, my good fellow,' said Raffles, wearily; 'but Theobald does, and I can't afford to go against him now. Not that I really care what happens to me now that that woman knows I'm in the land of the living; she'll let it out, to a dead certainty, and at the best there'll be a hue and cry, which is the very thing I have escaped all these years. Now, what I want you to do is to go and take some quiet place somewhere, and then let me know, so that I may have a port in the storm when it breaks.'

'Now you're talking!' I cried, recovering my spirits. 'I thought you meant to go and drop a fellow altogether!'

'Exactly the sort of thing you would think,' rejoined Raffles, with a contempt that was welcome enough after my late alarm. 'No, my dear rabbit, what you've got to do is to make a new burrow for us both. Try down the Thames, in some quiet nook that a literary man would naturally select. I've often thought that more use might be made of a boat, while the family are at dinner, than there ever has been yet. If Raffles is to come to life, old chap, he shall go a-Raffling for all he's worth! There's something to be done with a bicycle, too. Try Ham Common or Roehampton, or some such sleepy hollow a trifle off the line; and say you're expecting your brother from the Colonies.'

Into this arrangement I entered without the slightest hesitation, for we had funds enough to carry it out on a comfortable scale, and Raffles placed a sufficient share at my disposal for the nonce. Moreover, I for one was only too glad to seek fresh fields and pastures new – a phrase which I determined to interpret literally in my choice of fresh surroundings. I was tired of our submerged life in the poky little flat, especially now that we had money enough for better things. I myself had of late had dark dealings with the receivers, with the result that poor Lord Ernest Belville's successes were now indeed ours. Subsequent complications had been the more galling on that account, while the wanton way in which they had been created was the most irritating reflection of all. But it had brought its own punishment upon Raffles, and I fancied the lesson would prove salutary when we again settled down.

'If ever we do, Bunny!' said he, as I took his hand and told him how I was already looking forward to the time.

'But of course we will,' I cried, concealing the resentment at leaving him which his tone and appearance renewed in my breast.

'I'm not so sure of it,' he said, gloomily. 'I'm in somebody's clutches, and I've got to get out of them first.'

'I'll sit tight until you do.'

'Well,' he said, 'if you don't see me in ten days you never will.'

'Only ten days?' I echoed. 'That's nothing at all.'

'A lot may happen in ten days,' replied Raffles, in the same depressing tone, so very depressing in him; and with that he held out his hand a second time, and dropped mine suddenly after as sudden a pressure for farewell.

I left the flat in considerable dejection after all, unable to decide whether Raffles was really ill, or only worried as I knew him to be. And at the foot of the stairs the author of my dismissal, that confounded Theobald, flung open his door and waylaid me.

'Are you going?' he demanded.

The traps in my hands proclaimed that I was, but I dropped them at his feet to have it out with him then and there.

'Yes,' I answered fiercely, 'thanks to you!'

'Well, my good fellow,' he said, his full-blooded face lightening and softening at the same time as though a load were off his mind, 'it's no pleasure to me to deprive any man of his billet, but you never were a nurse, and you know that as well as I do.'

I began to wonder what he meant, and how much he did know, and my speculations kept me silent. 'But come in here a moment,' he continued, just as I decided that he knew nothing at all. And leading me into his minute consulting-room, Dr Theobald solemnly presented me with a sovereign by way of compensation, which I pocketed as solemnly, and with as much gratitude as if I had not fifty of them distributed over my person as it was. The good fellow had quite forgotten my social status, about which he himself had been so particular at our earliest interview; but he had never accustomed himself to treat me as a gentleman, and I do not suppose he had been improving his memory by the tall tumbler which I saw him poke behind a photograph-frame as we entered.

'There's one thing I should like to know before I go,' said I, turning suddenly on the doctor's mat, 'and that is whether Mr Maturin is really ill or not!'

I meant, of course, at the present moment, but Dr Theobald braced himself like a recruit at the drill-sergeant's voice.

'Of course he is,' he snapped – 'so ill as to need a nurse who can nurse, by way of a change.'

With that his door shut in my face, and I had to go my way, in the dark as to whether he had mistaken my meaning, and was telling me a lie, or not.

But for my misgivings upon this point I might have extracted some very genuine enjoyment out of the next few days. I had decent clothes to my back, with money, as I say, in most of the pockets, and more freedom to spend it than was possible in the constant society of a man whose personal liberty depended on a universal supposition that he was dead. Raffles was as bold as ever, and I as fond of him, but whereas he would run any risk in a professional exploit, there were many innocent recreations still open to me which would have been sheer madness in him. He could not even watch a match, from the sixpenny seats, at Lord's Cricket Ground, where the Gentlemen were every year in a worse way without him. He never travelled by rail, and dining out was a risk only to be run with some ulterior object in view. In fact, much as it had changed, Raffles could no longer show his face with perfect impunity in any quarter or at any hour. Moreover, after the lesson he had now learnt, I foresaw increased caution on his part in this respect. But I myself was under no such perpetual disadvantage, and, while what was good enough for Raffles was quite good enough for me, so long as we were together, I saw no harm in profiting by the present opportunity of 'doing myself well'.

Such were my reflections on the way to Richmond in a hansom cab. Richmond had struck us both as the best centre of operations in search of the suburban retreat which Raffles wanted, and by road, in a well-appointed, well-selected hansom, was certainly the most agreeable way of getting there. In a week or ten days Raffles was to write to me at the Richmond post-office, but for at least a week I should be 'on my own'. It was not an unpleasant sensation as I leant back in the comfortable hansom, and rather to one side, in order to have a good look at myself in the bevelled mirror that is almost as great an improvement in these vehicles as the rubber tyres. Really I was not an ill-looking youth, if one may call oneself such at the age of thirty. I could lay no claim either to the striking cast of countenance or to the peculiar charm of expression which made the face of Raffles like no other in the world. But this very distinction was in itself a danger, for its impression was indelible, whereas I might still have been mistaken for a hundred other young fellows at large in London. Incredible as it may appear to the moralists, I had sustained no external hallmark by my term of imprisonment, and I am vain enough to believe that the evil which I did had not a separate existence in my face. This afternoon, indeed, I was struck by the purity of my fresh complexion, and rather depressed by the general innocence of the visage which peered into mine from the little mirror. My straw-coloured moustache, grown in the flat after a protracted holiday, again, preserved the most disappointing dimensions, and was still invisible in certain lights without wax. So far from discerning the desperate criminal who has 'done time' once, and deserved it over and over again, the superior but superficial observer might have imagined that he detected a certain element of folly in my face.

At all events, it was not the face to shut the doors of a first-class hotel against me, without accidental evidence of a more explicit kind, and it was with no little satisfaction that I directed the man to drive to the Star and Garter. I also told him to go through Richmond Park, though he warned me that it would add considerably to the distance and fare. It was autumn, and it struck me that the tints would be fine. And I had learnt from Raffles to appreciate such things, even amid the excitement of an audacious enterprise.

If I dwell upon my appreciation of this occasion it is because, like most pleasures, it was exceedingly short-lived. I was very comfortable at the Star and Garter, which was so empty that I had a room worthy of a prince, where I could enjoy the finest of all views (in patriotic opinion) every morning while I shaved. I walked many miles through the noble park, over the commons of Ham and Wimbledon, and one day as far as that of Esher, where I was forcibly reminded of a service we once rendered to a distinguished resident in this delightful locality. But it was on Ham Common, one of the places which Raffles had mentioned as specially desirable, that I actually found an almost ideal retreat. This was a cottage where I heard, on inquiry, that rooms were to be let in the summer. The landlady, a motherly body, of visible excellence, was surprised indeed at receiving an application for the winter months; but I have generally found that the title of 'author', claimed with an air, explains every little innocent irregularity of conduct or appearance, and even requires something of the kind to carry conviction to the lay intelligence. The present case was one in point, and when I said that I could only write in a room facing north, on mutton chops and milk, with a cold ham in the wardrobe in case of nocturnal inspiration, to which I was liable, my literary character was established beyond dispute. I secured the rooms, paid a month's rent in advance at my own request, and moped in them dreadfully until the week was up and Raffles due any day. I explained that the inspiration would not come, and asked abruptly if the mutton was New Zealand.

Thrice had I made fruitless inquiries at the Richmond post-office; but on the tenth day I was in and out almost every hour. Not a word was there for me up to the last post at night. Home I trudged to Ham with horrible forebodings, and back again to Richmond after breakfast next morning. Still there was nothing. I could bear it no more. At ten minutes to eleven I was climbing the station stairs at Earl's Court.

It was a wretched morning there, a weeping mist shrouding the long straight street, and clinging to one's face in clammy caresses. I felt how much better it was down at Ham, as I turned into our side street, and saw the flats looming like mountains, the chimney-pots hidden in the mist. At our entrance stood a nebulous conveyance, that I took at first for a tradesman's van;

to my horror it proved to be a hearse; and all at once the whole breath ceased upon my lips.

I had looked up at our windows, and the blinds were down!

I rushed within. The doctor's door stood open. I neither knocked nor rang, but found him in his consulting-room with red eyes and a blotchy face. Otherwise he was in solemn black from head to heel.

'Who is dead?'

The red eyes looked redder than ever as Dr Theobald opened them at the unwarrantable sight of me; and he was terribly slow in answering. But in the end he did answer, he did not kick me out as he evidently had a mind.

'Mr Maturin,' he said, and sighed like a beaten man.

I said nothing. It was no surprise to me. I had known it all these minutes. Nay, I had dreaded this from the first, had divined it at the last, though to the last also I had refused to entertain my own conviction. Raffles dead! A real invalid after all! Raffles dead, and on the point of burial!

'What did he die of?' I asked, unconsciously drawing on that fund of grim self-control which the weakest of us seem to hold in reserve for real calamity.

'Typhoid,' he answered. 'Kensington is full of it.'

'He was sickening for it when I left, and you knew it, and could get rid of me then!'

'My good fellow, I was obliged to have a more experienced nurse for that very reason.'

The doctor's tone was so conciliatory that I remembered in an instant what a humbug the man was, and became suddenly possessed with the vague conviction that he was imposing upon me now.

'Are you sure it was typhoid at all?' I cried fiercely to his face. 'Are you sure it wasn't suicide – or murder?'

I confess that I can see little point in this speech as I write it down, but it was what I said in a burst of grief and of wild suspicion; nor was it without effect upon Dr Theobald, who turned bright scarlet from his well-brushed hair to his immaculate collar.

'Do you want me to throw you out into the street?' he cried; and all at once I remembered that I had come to Raffles as a perfect stranger, and for his sake might as well preserve that character to the last.

'I beg your pardon,' I said brokenly. 'He was so good to me – I became so attached to him. You forget I am originally of his class.'

'I did forget it,' replied Theobald, looking relieved at my new tone, 'and I beg *your* pardon for doing so. Hush! They are bringing him down. I must have a drink before we start, and you'd better join me.'

There was no pretence about his drink this time, and a pretty stiff one it was, but I fancy my own must have run it hard. In my case it cast a merciful haze over much of the next hour, which I can truthfully describe as one of the most painful of my whole existence. I can have known very little of what I was doing. I only remember finding myself in a hansom, suddenly wondering why it was going so slowly, and once more awaking to the truth. But it was to the truth itself more than to the liquor that I must have owed my dazed condition. My next recollection is of looking down into the open grave, in a sudden passionate anxiety to see the name for myself. It was not the name of my friend, of course, but it was the one under which he had passed for many months.

I was still stupefied by a sense of inconceivable loss, and had not raised my eyes from that which was slowly forcing me to realise what had happened, when there was a rustle at my elbow, and a shower of hothouse flowers passed before them, falling like huge snowflakes where my gaze had rested. I looked up, and at my side stood a majestic figure in deep mourning. The face was carefully veiled, but I was too close not to recognise the masterful beauty whom the world knew as Jacques Saillard. I had no sympathy with her; on the contrary, my blood boiled with the vague conviction that in some way she was responsible for this death. Yet she was the only woman present – there were not half a dozen of us altogether – and her flowers were the only flowers.

The melancholy ceremony was over, and Jacques Saillard had departed in a funereal brougham, evidently hired for the occasion. I had watched her drive away, and the sight of my own cabman, making signs to me through the fog, had suddenly reminded me that I had bidden them to wait. I was the last to leave, and had turned my back upon the grave-diggers already at their final task, when a hand fell lightly but firmly upon my shoulder.

'I don't want to make a scene in a cemetery,' said a voice, in a not unkindly, almost confidential whisper. 'Will you get into your own cab and come quietly?'

'Who on earth are you?' I exclaimed.

I now remembered having seen the fellow hovering about during the funeral, and subconsciously taking him for the undertaker's head man. He had certainly that appearance, and even now I could scarcely believe that he was anything else.

'My name won't help you,' he said, pityingly. 'But you will guess where I come from when I tell you I have a warrant for your arrest.' My sensations at this announcement may not be believed, but I solemnly declare that I have seldom experienced so fierce a satisfaction. Here was a new excitement in which to drown my grief; here was something to think about; and I should be spared the intolerable experience of a solitary return to the little place at Ham. It was as though I had lost a limb and someone had struck me so hard in the face that the greater agony was forgotten. I got into the hansom without a word, my captor following at my heels, and giving his own directions to the cabman before taking his seat. The word 'station' was the only one I caught, and I wondered whether it was to be Bow Street again. My companion's next words, however, or rather the tone in which he uttered them, destroyed my capacity for idle speculation.

'Mr Maturin!' said he. 'Mr Maturin indeed!'

'Well,' said I, 'what about him?'

'Do you think we don't know who he was?'

'Who was he?' I asked defiantly.

'You ought to know,' said he. 'You got locked up through him the other time, too. His favourite name was Raffles, then.'

'It was his real name,' I said indignantly. 'And he has been dead for years.'

My captor simply chuckled.

'He's at the bottom of the sea, I tell you.'

But I do not know why I should have told him with such spirit, for what could it matter to Raffles now? I did not think; instinct was still stronger than reason, and, fresh from his funeral, I had taken up the. cudgels for my dead friend as though he were still alive. Next moment I saw this for myself, and my tears came nearer the surface than they had been yet; but the fellow at my side laughed outright.

'Shall I tell you something else?' said he.

'As you like.'

'He's not even at the bottom of that grave! He's no more dead than you or I, and a sham burial is his latest piece of villainy!'

I doubt whether I could have spoken if I had tried. I did not try. I had no use for speech. I did not even ask him if he was sure, I was so sure myself. It was all as plain to me as riddles usually are when one has the answer. The doctor's alarm, his unscrupulous venality, the simulated illness, my own dismissal, each fitted in its obvious place, and not even the last had power as yet to mar my joy in the one central fact to which all the rest were as tapers to the sun.

'He is alive!' I cried. 'Nothing else matters – he is alive!'

At last I did ask whether they had got him too; but thankful as I was for the greater knowledge, I confess that I did not much care what answer I received. Already I was figuring out how much we might each get, and how old we should be when we came out. But my companion tilted his hat to the back of his head, at the same time putting his face close to mine, and compelling my scrutiny. And my answer, as you have already guessed, was the face of Raffles himself, superbly disguised (but less superbly than his voice), and yet so thinly that I should have known him in a trice had I not been too miserable in the beginning to give him a second glance.

Jacques Saillard had made his life impossible, and this was the one escape. Raffles had bought the doctor for a thousand pounds, and the doctor had bought a 'nurse' of his own kidney, on his own account; me, for some reason, he would not trust; he had insisted upon my dismissal as an essential preliminary to his part in the conspiracy. Here the details were half humorous, half gruesome, each in turn as Raffles told me the story. At one period he had been very daringly drugged indeed, and, in his own words, 'as dead as a man need be'; but he had left strict instructions that nobody but the nurse and 'my devoted physician' should 'lay a finger on me' afterwards; and by virtue of this proviso a library of books (largely acquired for the occasion) had been impiously interred at Kensal Green. Raffles had definitely undertaken not to trust me with the secret, and, but for my untoward appearance at the funeral (which he had attended for his own final satisfaction), I was assured and am convinced that he would have kept his promise to the letter. In explaining this he gave me the one explanation I desired, and in another moment we turned into Praed Street, Paddington.

'And I thought you said Bow Street!' said I. 'Are you coming straight down to Richmond with me?'

'I may as well,' said Raffles, 'though I did mean to get my kit first, so as to start in fair and square as the long-lost brother from the bush. That's why I hadn't written. The function was a day later than I calculated. I was going to write tonight.'

'But what are we to do?' said I, hesitating, when he had paid the cab. 'I have been playing the Colonies for all they are worth!'

'Oh, I've lost my luggage,' said he, 'or a wave came into my cabin and spoilt every stitch, or I had nothing fit to bring ashore. We'll settle that in the train.'

7

THE WRONG HOUSE

My brother Ralph, who now lived with me on the edge of Ham Common, had come home from Australia with a curious affection of the eyes, due to long exposure to the glare out there, and necessitating the use of clouded spectacles in the open air. He had not the rich complexion of the typical colonist, being indeed peculiarly pale; but it appeared that he had been confined to his berth for the greater part of the voyage, while his prematurely grey hair was sufficient proof that the rigours of bush life had at last undermined an originally tough constitution. Our landlady, who spoilt my brother from the first, was much concerned on his behalf, and wished to call in the local doctor; but Ralph said dreadful things about the profession, and quite frightened the good woman by arbitrarily forbidding her ever to let a doctor inside her door. I had to apologise to her for the painful prejudices and violent language of 'these colonists', but the old soul was easily mollified. She had fallen in love with my brother at first sight, and she never could do too much for him. It was owing to our landlady that I took to calling him Ralph, for the first time in our lives, on her beginning to speak of and to him as 'Mr Raffles'.

'This won't do,' said he to me. 'It's a name that sticks.'

'It must be my fault. She must have heard it from me,' said I self-reproachfully.

'You must tell her it's the short for Ralph.'

'But it's longer.'

'It's the short,' said he; 'and you've got to tell her so.'

Henceforth I heard as much of 'Mr Ralph', his likes and his dislikes, what he would fancy and what he would not, and oh, what a dear gentleman he was, that I often remembered to say 'Ralph, old chap', myself.

It was an ideal cottage, as I said when I found it, and in it our delicate man became rapidly robust. Not that the air was also ideal, for when it was not raining we had the same faithful mist from November to March. But it was something to Ralph to get any air at all, other than night air, and the bicycle did the rest. We taught ourselves, and may I never forget our earlier rides, through Richmond Park when the afternoons were shortest, upon the incomparable Ripley Road when we gave a day to it. Raffles rode a Beeston Humber, a Royal Sunbeam was good enough for me, but he insisted on our both having Dunlop tyres.

'They seem the most popular brand. I had my eye on the road all the way from Ripley to Cobham, and there were more Dunlop marks than any other kind. Bless you, yes, they all leave their special tracks, and we don't want ours to be extra special; the Dunlop's like a rattlesnake, and the Palmer leaves telegraph-wires, but surely the serpent is more in our line.'

That was the winter when there were so many burglaries in the Thames Valley from Richmond upward. It was said that the thieves used bicycles in every case, but what is not said? They were sometimes on foot to my knowledge, and we took a great interest in the series, or rather sequence of successful crimes. Raffles would often get his devoted old lady to read him the latest local accounts, while I was busy with my writing (much I wrote!) in my own room.

We even rode out by night ourselves, to see if we could not get on the tracks of the thieves, and never did we fail to find hot coffee on the hob for our return.

We had indeed fallen upon our feet. Also, the misty nights might have been made for the thieves. But their success was not so consistent, and never so enormous, as people said, especially the sufferers, who lost more valuables than they had ever been known to possess. Failure was often the caitiffs' portion, and disaster once; owing, ironically enough, to that very mist which should have served them. But I am going to tell the story with some particularity, and perhaps some gusto; you will see why who read.

The right house stood on high ground near the river, with quite a drive (in at one gate and out at the other) sweeping past the steps. Between the two gates was a half-moon of shrubs, to the left of the steps a conservatory, and to their right the walk leading to the tradesmen's entrance and the back premises; here also was the pantry window, of which more anon. The right house was the residence of an opulent stockbroker who wore a heavy watch-chain and seemed fair game. There would have been two objections to it had I been the stockbroker. The house was one of a row, though a goodly row, and an army-crammer had established himself next door. There is a type of such institutions in the suburbs; the youths go about in knickerbockers, smoking pipes, except on Saturday nights, when they lead each other home from the last train. It was none of our business to spy upon these boys, but their manners and customs fell within the field of observation. And we did not choose the night upon which the whole row was likely to be kept awake.

The night that we did choose was as misty as even the Thames Valley is capable of making them. Raffles smeared vaseline upon the plated parts of his Beeston Humber before starting, and our dear landlady cosseted us both, and prayed we might see nothing of the nasty burglars, not denying as the reward would be very handy to them that got it, to say nothing of the honour and glory. We had promised her a liberal perquisite in the event of our success, but she must not give other cyclists our idea by mentioning it to a soul. It was about midnight when we cycled through Kingston to Surbiton, having trundled our machines across Ham Fields mournful in the mist as those by Acheron, and so over Teddington Bridge.

I often wonder why the pantry window is the vulnerable point of nine houses out of ten. This house of ours was almost the tenth, for the window in question had bars of sorts, but not the right sort. The only bars that Raffles allowed to beat him were the kind that are let into the stone outside; those fixed within are merely screwed to the woodwork, and you can unscrew as many as necessary if you take the trouble and have the time. Barred windows are usually devoid of other fasteners worthy the name; this one was no exception to that foolish rule, and a push with the penknife did its business. I am giving householders some valuable hints, and perhaps deserving a good mark from the critics. These, in any case, are the points that I would see to, were I a rich stockbroker in a riverside suburb. In giving good advice, however, I should not have omitted to say that we had left our machines in the semicircular shrubbery in front, or that Raffles had most ingeniously fitted our lamps with dark slides, which enabled us to leave them burning.

It proved sufficient to unscrew the bars at the bottom only, and then to wrench them to either side. Neither of us had grown stout with advancing years, and in a few minutes we had both wormed through into the sink, and thence to the floor. It was not an absolutely noiseless process, but once in the pantry we were mice, and no longer blind mice. There was a gas-bracket, but we did not meddle with that. Raffles went armed these nights with a better light than gas; if it were not immoral, I might recommend a dark-lantern which was more or less his patent. It was that handy invention the electric torch, fitted by Raffles with a dark hood to fulfil the functions of a slide. I had held it through the bars while he undid the screws, and now he held it to the keyhole, in which a key was turned upon the other side.

There was a pause for consideration, and in the pause we put on our masks. It was never known that these Thames Valley robberies were all committed by miscreants decked in the livery of crime, but that was because until this night we had never even shown our masks. It was a point upon which Raffles had insisted on all feasible occasions since his furtive return to the world. Tonight it twice nearly lost us everything – but you shall hear.

There is a forceps for turning keys from the wrong side of the door, but the implement is not so easy of manipulation as it might be. Raffles for one preferred a sharp knife and the corner of the panel. You go through the panel because that is thinnest, of course in the corner nearest the key, and you use a knife when you can, because it makes least noise. But it does take minutes, and even I can remember shifting the electric torch from one hand to the other before the aperture was large enough to receive the hand and wrist of Raffles.

He had at such times a motto of which I might have made earlier use, but the fact is that I have only once before described a downright burglary in which I assisted, and that without knowing it at the time. The most solemn student of these annals cannot affirm that he has cut through many doors in our company, since (what was to me) the maiden effort to which I allude. I, however, have cracked only too many a crib in conjunction with A.J. Raffles, and at the crucial moment he would whisper 'Victory or Wormwood Scrubs, Bunny!' or instead of Wormwood Scrubs it might be Portland Bill. This time it was neither one nor the other, for with that very word 'victory' upon his lips they whitened and parted with the first taste of defeat.

'My hand's held!' gasped Raffles, and the white of his eyes showed all round the iris, a rarer thing than you may think.

At the same moment I heard the shuffling feet and the low, excited young voices on the other side of the door, and a faint light shone round Raffles's wrist.

'Well done, Beefy!'

'Hang on to him!'

'Good old Beefy!'

'Beefy's got him!'

'So have I – so have I!'

And Raffles caught my arm with his one free hand. 'They've got me tight,' he whispered. 'I'm done.'

'Blaze through the door,' I urged, and might have done it had I been armed. But I never was. It was Raffles who monopolised that risk.

'I can't – it's the boys – the wrong house!' he whispered. 'Curse the fog – it's done me. But you get out, Bunny, while you can; never mind me; it's my turn, old chap.'

His one hand tightened in affectionate farewell. I put the electric torch in it before I went, trembling in every inch, but without a word. .

Get out! His turn! Yes, I would get out, but only to come in again, for it was my turn – mine – not his. Would Raffles leave me held by a hand through a hole in a door? What he would have done in my place was the thing for me to do now. I began by diving head first through the pantry window and coming to earth upon all fours. But even as I stood up, and brushed the gravel from the palms of my hands and the knees of my knickerbockers, I had no notion what to do next. And yet I was half-way to the front door before I remembered the vile crape mask upon my face, and tore it off as the door flew open and my feet were on the steps.

'He's into the next garden,' I cried to a bevy of pyjamas with bare feet and young faces at either end of them

'Who? Who?' said they, giving way before me.

'Some fellow who came through one of your windows head first.'

'The other Johnny, the other Johnny,' the cherubs chorused.

'Biking past – saw the light – why, what have you there?'

Of course it was Raffles's hand that they had, but now I was in the hall among them. A red-faced barrel of a boy did all the holding, one hand round the wrist, the other palm to palm, and his knees braced up against the panel. Another was rendering ostentatious but ineffectual aid, and three or four others danced about in their pyjamas. After all, they were not more than four to one. I had raised my voice, so that Raffles might hear me and take heart, and now I raised it again. Yet to this day I cannot account for my inspiration, that proved nothing less.

'Don't talk so loud,' they were crying below their breath; 'don't wake 'em upstairs, this is our show.'

'Then I see you've got one of them,' said I as desired. 'Well, if you want the other you can have him too. I believe he's hurt himself.'

'After him, after him!' they exclaimed as one.

'But I think he got over the wall – '

'Come on, you chaps, come on!'

And there was a soft stampede to the hall door.

'Don't all desert me, I say!' gasped the red-faced hero who held Raffles prisoner.

'We must have them both, Beefy!'

'That's all very well – '

'Look here,' I interposed, 'I'll stay by you. I've a friend outside, I'll get him too.'

'Thanks awfully,' said the valiant Beefy. The hall was empty now. My heart beat high.

'How did you hear them?' I inquired, my eye running over him.

'We were down having drinks – game o' nap – in there.'

Beefy jerked his great head towards an open door, and the tail of my eye caught the glint of glasses in the fire-light, but the rest of it was otherwise engaged.

'Let me relieve you,' I said, trembling.

'No, I'm all right.'

'Then I must insist.'

And before he could answer I had him round the neck with such a will that not a gurgle passed my fingers, for they were almost buried in his hot smooth flesh. Oh, I am not proud of it; the act was as vile as act could be; but I was not going to see Raffles taken, my one desire was to be the saving of him, and I tremble even now to think to what lengths I might have gone for its fulfilment. As it was I squeezed and tugged until one strong hand gave way after the other and came feeling round for me, but feebly because they had held on so long. And what do you suppose was happening at the same moment? The pinched white hand of Raffles, reddening with the returning blood, and with a clot of blood upon the wrist, was craning upward and turning the key in the lock without a moment's loss.

'Steady on, Bunny!'

And I saw that Beefy's ears were blue; but Raffles was feeling in his pockets as he spoke. 'Now let him breathe,' said he, clapping his handkerchief over the poor youth's mouth. An empty phial was in his other hand, and the first few stertorous breaths that the poor boy took were the end of him for the time being.

Oh, but it was villainous, my part especially, for he must have been far gone to go the rest of the way so readily. I began by saying I was not proud of this deed, but its dastardly character has come home to me more than ever with the penance of writing it out. I see in myself, at least my then self, things that

I never saw quite so clearly before. Yet let me be quite sure that I would not do the same again. I had not the smallest desire to throttle this innocent lad (nor did I), but only to extricate Raffles from the most hopeless position he was ever in; and after all it was better than a blow from behind. On the whole, I will not alter a word, nor whine about the thing any more.

We lifted the plucky fellow into Raffles's place in the pantry, locked the door on him, and put the key through the panel. Now was the moment for thinking of ourselves, and again that infernal mask which Raffles swore by came near the undoing of us both. We had reached the steps when we were hailed by a voice, not from without but from within, and I had just time to tear the accursed thing from Raffles's face before he turned.

A stout man with a blond moustache was on the stairs, in his pyjamas like the boys.

'What are you doing here?' said he.

'There has been an attempt upon your house,' said I, still spokesman for the night, and still on the wings of inspiration. 'Your sons – '

'My pupils.'

'Indeed. Well, they heard it, drove off the thieves, and have given chase.'

'And where do you come in?' inquired the stout man, descending.

'We were bicycling past, and I actually saw one fellow come head first through your pantry window. I think he got over the wall.'

Here a breathless boy returned.

'Can't see anything of him,' he gasped.

'It's true, then,' remarked the crammer.

'Look at that door,' said I.

But unfortunately the breathless boy looked also, and now he was being joined by others equally short of wind.

'Where's Beefy?' he screamed. 'What on earth's happened to Beefy?'

'My good boys,' exclaimed the crammer, 'will one of you be kind enough to tell me what you've been doing, and what these gentlemen have been doing for you? Come in all, before you get your death. I see lights in the classroom, and more than lights. Can these be signs of a carouse?'

'A very innocent one, sir,' said a well-set-up youth with more moustache than I have yet.

'Well, Olphert, boys will be boys. Suppose you tell me what happened, before we come to recriminations.'

The bad old proverb was my first warning. I caught two of the youths exchanging glances under raised eyebrows. Yet their stout easy-going mentor had given me such a reassuring glance of sidelong humour, as between man of the world and man of the world, that it was difficult to suspect him of suspicion. I was nevertheless itching to be gone.

Young Olphert told his story with engaging candour. It was true that they had come down for an hour's nap and cigarettes; well, and there was no denying that was whisky in the glasses. The boys were now all back in their classroom, I think entirely for the sake of warmth; but Raffles and I were in knickerbockers and Norfolk jackets, and very naturally remained without, while the army-crammer (who wore bedroom slippers) stood on the threshold, with an eye each way. The more I saw of the man the better I liked and the more I feared him. His chief annoyance thus far was that they had not called him when they heard the noise; that they had dreamt of leaving him out of the fun. But he seemed more hurt than angry about that.

'Well, sir,' concluded Olphert, 'we left old Beefy Smith hanging on to his hand, and this gentleman with him, so perhaps he can tell us what happened next?'

'I wish I could,' I cried, with all their eyes upon me, for I had had time to think. 'Some of you must have heard me say I'd fetch my friend in from the road?'

'Yes, I did,' piped an innocent from within.

'Well, and when I came back with him things were exactly as you see them now. Evidently the man's strength was too much for the boy's; but whether he ran upstairs or outside I know ho more than you do.'

'It wasn't like that boy to run either way,' said the crammer, cocking a clear blue eye on me.

'But if he gave chase!'

'It wasn't like him even to let go.'

'I don't believe Beefy ever would,' put in Olphert. 'That's why we gave him the billet.'

'He may have followed him through the pantry window,' I suggested wildly.

'But the door's shut,' put in a boy.

'I'll have a look at it,' said the crammer.

And the key no longer in the lock, and the insensible youth within! They key would be missed, the door kicked in; nay, with the man's eye still upon me, I thought I could smell chloroform; I thought I could hear a moan, and prepared for either any moment. And how he did stare! I have detested blue eyes ever since, and blond moustaches, and the whole stout easy-going type that is not such a fool as it looks. I had brazened it out with the boys, but the first grown man was too many for me, and the blood ran out of my heart as though there was no Raffles at my back. Indeed, I had forgotten him. I had so longed to put this thing through by myself! Even in my extremity it was almost a disappointment to me when his dear cool voice fell like a delicious draught upon my ears. But its effect upon the others is more interesting to recall. Until now the crammer had the centre of the stage, but at this point Raffles usurped a place which was always his at will. People would wait for what he had to say, as these people waited now for the simplest and most natural thing in the world.

'One moment!' he had begun.

'Well?' said the crammer, relieving me of his eyes at last.

'I don't want to lose any of the fun – '

'Nor must you,' said the crammer, with emphasis.

'But we've left our bikes outside, and mine's a Beeston Humber,' continued Raffles. 'If you don't mind we'll bring 'em in before these fellows get away on them.'

And out he went without a look to see the effect of his words, I after him with a determined imitation of his self-control. But I would have given something to turn round. I believe that for one moment the shrewd instructor was taken in, but as I reached the steps I heard him asking his pupils whether any of them had seen any bicycles outside.

That moment, however, made the difference. We were in the shrubbery, Raffles with his electric torch drawn and blazing, when we heard them kicking at the pantry door, and in the drive with our bicycles before man and boys poured pell-mell down the steps.

We rushed our machines to the nearer gate, for both were shut, and we got through and swung it home behind us in the nick of time. Even I could mount before they could reopen the gate, which Raffles held against them for half an instant with unnecessary gallantry. But he would see me in front of him, and so it fell to me to lead the way.

Now, I have said that it was a very misty night (hence the whole thing), and also that these houses were on a hill. But they were not nearly on the top of the hill, and I did what I firmly believe that almost everybody would have done in my place. Raffles, indeed, said he would have done it himself, but that was his generosity, and he was the one man who would not. What I did was to turn in the opposite direction to the other gate, where we might so easily have been cut-off, and to pedal for my life – up-hill!

'My God!' I shouted when I found it out.

'Can you turn in your own length?' asked Raffles, following loyally.

'Not certain.'

Then stick to it. You couldn't help it. But it's the devil of a hill!'

'And here they come!'

'Let them,' said Raffles, and brandished his electric torch, our only light as yet.

A hill seems endless in the dark, for you cannot see the end, and with the patter of bare feet gaining on us, I thought this one could have no end at all. Of course the boys could charge up it quicker than we could pedal, but I even heard the voice of their stout instructor growing louder through the mist.

'Oh, to think I've let you in for this!' I groaned, my head over the handle-bars, every ounce of my weight first on one foot and then on the other. I glanced at Raffles, and in the white light of his torch he was doing it all with his ankles, exactly as though he had been riding in a Gymkhana.

'It's the most sporting chase I was ever in,' said he.

'All my fault!'

'My dear Bunny, I wouldn't have missed it for the world!'

Nor would he forge ahead of me, though he could have done so in a moment, he who from his boyhood had done everything of the kind so much better than anybody else. No, he must ride a wheel's length behind me, and now we could not only hear the boys running, but breathing also. And then of a sudden I saw Raffles on my right striking with his torch; a face flew out of the darkness to meet the thick glass bulb with the glowing wire enclosed; it was the face of the boy Olphert, with his enviable moustache, but it vanished with the crash of glass, and the naked wire thickened to the eye like a tuning-fork struck red-hot.

I saw no more of that. One of them had crept up on my side also; as I looked, hearing him pant, he was grabbing at my left handle, and I nearly sent Raffles into the hedge by the sharp turn I took to the right. His wheel's length saved him. But my boy could run, was overhauling me again, seemed certain of me this time, when all at once the Sunbeam ran easily; every ounce of my weight with either foot once more, and I was over the crest of the hill, the grey road reeling out from under me as I felt for my brake. I looked back at Raffles. He had put up his feet. I screwed my head round still further, and there were the boys in their pyjamas, their hands upon their knees, like so many wicket-keepers, and a big man shaking his fist. There was a lamp-post on the hill-top, and that was the last I saw.

We sailed down to the river, then on through Thames Ditton as far as Esher station, when we turned sharp to the right, and from the dark stretch by Imber Court came to light in Molesey, and were soon pedalling like gentlemen of leisure through Bushey Park, our lights turned up, the broken torch put out and away. The big gates had long been shut, but you can manoeuvre a bicycle through the others. We had no further adventures on the way home, and our coffee was still warm upon the hob.

'But I think it's an occasion for Sullivans,' said Raffles, who now kept them for such. 'By all my gods, Bunny, it's been the most sporting night we ever had in our lives! And do you know which was the most sporting part of it?'

'That up-hill ride!'

'I wasn't thinking of it.'

'Turning your torch into a truncheon?'

'My dear Bunny! A gallant lad – I hated hitting him.'

'I know,' I said. 'The way you got us out of the house!'

'No, Bunny,' said Raffles, blowing rings. 'It came before that, you sinner, and you know it!'

'You don't mean anything I did?' said I, self-conciously, for I began to see that this was what he did mean. And now at last it will also be seen why this story has been told with undue and inexcusable gusto; there is none other like it for me to tell; it is my one ewe-lamb in all these annals. But Raffles had a ruder name for it.

'It was the Apotheosis of the Bunny,' said he, but in a tone I never shall forget.

'I hardly knew what I was doing or saying,' I said. 'The whole thing was a fluke.'

'Then,' said Raffles, 'it was the kind of fluke I always trusted you to make when runs were wanted.'

And he held out his dear old hand.

8

THE KNEES OF THE GODS

I

'The worst of this war,' said Raffles, 'is the way it puts a fellow off his work.'

It was, of course, the winter before last, and we had done nothing dreadful since the early autumn. Undoubtedly the war was the cause. Not that we were among the earlier victims of the fever. I took disgracefully little interest in the Negotiations, while the Ultimatum appealed to Raffles as a sporting flutter. Then we gave the whole thing till Christmas. We still missed the cricket in the papers. But one russet afternoon we were in Richmond, and a terrible type was shouting himself hoarse with 'Eavy British lorsses! – Orful slorter o' the Bo-wers! Orful slorter! Orful slorter! 'Eavy British lorsses!' I thought the terrible type had invented it, but Raffles gave him more than he asked, and then I held the bicycles while he tried to pronounce Eland's Laagte. We were never again without our sheaf of evening papers, and Raffles ordered three morning ones, and I gave up mine in spite of its literary page. We became strategists. We knew exactly what Buller was to do on landing, and, still better, what the other Generals should have done. Our map was the best that could be bought, with flags that deserved a better fate than standing still. Raffles woke me to hear *The Absent-Minded Beggar* on the morning it appeared; he was one of the first substantial subscribers to the fund. By this time our dear landlady was more excited than we. To our enthusiasm for Thomas she added a personal bitterness against the Wild Boars, as she persisted in calling them, each time as though it were the first. I could linger over our landlady's attitude in the whole matter. That was her only joke about it, and the true humorist never smiled at it herself. But you had only to say a syllable for a venerable gentleman, declared by her to be at the bottom of it all, to hear what she could do to him if she caught him. She could put him in a cage and go on tour with him, and make him howl and dance for his food like a debased bear before a fresh audience every day. Yet a more kind-hearted woman I have never known. The war did not uplift our landlady as it did her lodgers.

But presently it ceased to have that precise effect upon us. Bad was being made worse and worse; and then came more than Englishmen could endure in that black week across which the names of three African villages are written for ever in letters of blood. 'All three pegs,' groaned Raffles on the last morning of the week; 'neck-and-crop, neck-and-crop!' It was his first word of cricket since the beginning of the war.

We were both depressed. Old schoolfellows had fallen, and I know Raffles envied them; he spoke so wistfully of such an end. To cheer him up I proposed to break into one of the many more or less royal residences in our neighbourhood; a tough crib was what he needed; but I will not trouble you with what he said to me. There was less crime in England that winter than for years past; there was none at all in Raffles. And yet there were those who could denounce the war!

So we went on for a few of those dark days, Raffles very glum and grim, till one fine morning the Yeomanry idea put new heart into us all. It struck me at once as the glorious scheme it was to prove, but it did not hit me where it hit others. I was not a fox-hunter, and the gentlemen of England would scarcely have owned me as one of them. The case of Raffles was in that respect still more hopeless (he who had even played for them at Lord's), and he seemed to feel it. He would not speak to me all the morning; in the afternoon he went for a walk alone. It was another man who came home, flourishing a small bottle packed in white paper.

'Bunny,' said he, 'I never did lift my elbow; it's the one vice I never had. It has taken me all these years to find my tipple, Bunny; but here it is, my panacea, my elixir, my magic philtre!'

I thought he had been at it on the road, and asked him the name of the stuff.

'Look and see, Bunny.'

And if it wasn't a bottle of ladies' hair-dye, warranted to change any shade into the once fashionable yellow within a given number of applications!

'What on earth', said I, 'are you going to do with this?'

'Dye for my country,' he cried, swelling. '*Dulce et decorum est*, Bunny, my boy!'

'Do you mean that you're going to the Front?'

'If I can without coming to it.'

I looked at him as he stood in the firelight, straight as a dart, spare but wiry, alert, laughing, flushed from his wintry walk; and as I looked, all the years that I had known him, and more besides, slipped from him in my eyes. I saw him captain of the eleven at school. I saw him running with the muddy ball on days like this, running round the other fifteen as a sheep-dog round a flock of sheep. He had his cap on still, and but for the grey hairs underneath – but here I lost him in a sudden mist. It was not sorrow at his going, for I did not mean to let him go alone. It was enthusiasm, admiration, affection, and also, I believe, a sudden regret that he had not always appealed to that part of my nature to which he was appealing now. It was a little thrill of penitence. Enough of it.

'I think it great of you,' I said, and at first that was all.

How he laughed at me! He had had his innings; there was no better way of getting out. He had scored off an African millionaire, the Players, a Queensland Legislator, the Camorra, the late Lord Ernest Belville, and again and again off Scotland Yard. What more could one man do in one lifetime? And at the worst it was the death to die: no bed, no doctor, no temperature – and Raffles stopped himself.

'No pinioning, no white cap,' he added, 'if you like that better.'

'I don't like any of it,' I cried cordially; 'you've simply got to come back.'

'To what?' he asked, a strange look on him. And I wondered – for one instant – whether my little thrill had gone through him. He was not a man of little thrills.

Then for a minute I was in misery. Of course I wanted to go too – he shook my hand without a word – but how could I? They would never have me, a branded jail-bird, in the Imperial Yeomanry! Raffles burst out laughing; he had been looking very hard at me for about three seconds.

'You rabbit,' he cried, 'even to think of it! We might as well offer ourselves to the Metropolitan Police Force. No, Bunny, we go out to the Cape on our own, and that's where we enlist. One of these regiments of irregular horse is the thing for us; you spent part of your pretty penny on horse-flesh, I believe, and you remember how I rode in the bush! We're the very men for them, Bunny, and they won't ask to see our birth-marks out there. I don't think even my hoary locks would put them off, but it would be too conspicuous in the ranks.'

Our landlady first wept on hearing our determination, and then longed to have the pulling of certain whiskers (with the tongs, and they should be red-hot); but from that day, and for as many as were left to us, the good soul made more of us than ever. Not that she was at all surprised; dear brave gentlemen who could look for burglars on their bicycles at dead of night, it was only what you might expect of them, bless their lion hearts. I wanted to wink at Raffles, but he would not catch my eye. He was a ginger-headed Raffles by the end of January, and it was extraordinary what a difference it made. His most elaborate disguises had not been more effectual than this simple expedient, and, with khaki to complete the subdual of his individuality, he had every hope of escaping recognition in the field. The man he dreaded was the officer he had known in old days; there were ever so many of him at the Front; and it was to minimise this risk that we went out second class at the beginning of February.

It was a weeping day, a day in a shroud, cold as clay, yet for that very reason an ideal day upon which to leave England for the sunny Front. Yet my heart was heavy as I looked my last at her; it was heavy as the raw thick air, until Raffles came and leant upon the rail at my side.

'I know what you are thinking, and you've got to stop,' said he. 'It's on the knees of the gods, Bunny, whether we do or we don't, and thinking won't make us see over their shoulders.'

II

Now I made as bad a soldier (except at heart) as Raffles made a good one, and I could not say a harder thing of myself. My ignorance of matters military was up to that time unfathomable, and is still profound. I was always a fool with horses, though I did not think so at one time, and I had never been any good with a gun. The average Tommy may be my intellectual inferior, but he must know some part of his work better than I ever knew any of mine. I never even learnt to be killed. I do not mean that I ever ran away. The South African Field Force might have been strengthened if I had.

The foregoing remarks do not express a pose affected out of superiority to the usual spirit of the conquering hero, for no man was keener on the war than I, before I went to it. But one can only write with gusto of events (like that little affair at Surbiton) in which one has acquitted oneself without discredit, and I cannot say that of my part in the war, of which I now loathe the thought for other reasons. The battlefield was no place for me, and neither was the camp. My ineptitude made me the butt of the looting, cursing, swash-buckling lot who formed the very irregular squadron which we joined; and it would have gone hard with me but for Raffles, who was soon the darling devil of them all, but never more loyally my friend. Your fireside fire-eater does not think of these things. He imagines all the fighting to be with the enemy. He will probably be horrified to hear that men can detest each other as cordially in khaki as in any other wear, and with a virulence seldom inspired by the bearded dead-shot in the opposite trench. To the fireside fire-eater, therefore (for you have seen me one myself), I dedicate the story of Corporal Connal, Captain Bellingham, the General, Raffles, and myself.

I must be vague, for obvious reasons. The troop is fighting as I write; you will soon hear why I am not; but neither is Raffles nor Corporal Connal. They are fighting as well as ever, those other hard-living, harder-dying sons of all soils; but I am not going to say where it was that we fought with them. I believe that no body of men of equal size has done half so much heroic work. But they have got themselves a bad name off the field, so to speak; and I am not going to make it worse by saddling them before the world with Raffles and myself, and that ruffian Connal.

The fellow was a mongrel type, a Glasgow Irishman by birth and upbringing, but he had been in south Africa for years, and he certainly knew the country very well. This circumstance, coupled with the fact that he was a very handy man with horses, as all colonists are, had procured him the first small step from the ranks which facilitates bullying if a man be a bully by nature, and is physically fitted to be a successful one. Connal was a hulking ruffian, and in me had ideal game. The brute was offensive to me from the hour I joined. The details are of no importance, but I stood up to him at first in words, and finally for a few seconds on my feet. Then I went down like an ox, and Raffles came out of his tent. Their fight lasted twenty minutes, and Raffles was marked, but the net result was dreadfully conventional, for the bully was a bully no more.

But I began gradually to suspect that he was something worse. All this time we were fighting every day, or so it seems when I look back. Never a great engagement, and yet never a day when we were wholly out of touch with the enemy. I had thus several opportunities of watching the other enemy under fire, and had almost convinced myself of the systematic harmlessness of his own shooting, when a more glaring incident occurred.

One night three troops of our squadron were ordered to a certain point whither they had patrolled the previous week; but our own particular troop was to stay behind, and in charge of no other than the villainous corporal, both our officer and sergeant having gone into hospital with enteric. Our detention, however, was very temporary, and Connal would seem to have received the usual vague orders to proceed in the early morning to the place where the other three companies had camped. It appeared that we were to form an escort to two squadron waggons containing kits, provisions, and ammunition.

Before daylight Connal had reported his departure to the commanding officer, and we passed the outposts at grey dawn. Now, though I was perhaps the least observant person in the troop, I was not the least wide awake where Corporal Connal was concerned, and it struck me at once that we were heading in the wrong direction. My reasons are not material, but as a matter of fact our last week's patrol had pushed its khaki tentacles both east and west; and eastward they had met with resistance so determined as to compel them to retire; yet it was eastward that we were travelling now. I at once spurred alongside Raffles, as he rode, bronzed and bearded, with war-worn wide-awake over eyes grown keen as a hawk's, and a cutty-pipe sticking straight out from his front teeth. I can see him now, so gaunt and grim and *débonnaire*, yet already with much of the nonsense gone out of him, though I thought he only smiled on my misgivings.

'Did he get the instructions, Bunny, or did we? Very well, then; give the devil a chance.'

There was nothing further to be said, but I felt more crushed than convinced; so we jogged along into broad daylight, until Raffles himself gave a whistle of surprise.

'A white flag, Bunny, by all my gods!' I could not see it; he had the longest sight in all our squadron; but in a little the fluttering emblem, which had gained such a sinister significance in most of our eyes, was patent even to mine. A little longer, and the shaggy Boer was in our midst upon his shaggy pony, with a half-scared, half-incredulous look in his deep set-eyes. He was on his way to our lines with some missive and had little enough to say to us, though frivolous and flippant questions were showered upon him from most saddles.

'Any Boers over there?' asked one, pointing in the direction in which we were still heading.

'Shut up!' interjected Raffles in crisp rebuke.

The Boer looked stolid but sinister.

'Any of our chaps?' added another.

The Boer rode on with an open grin.

And the incredible conclusion of the matter was that we were actually within their lines in another hour; saw them as large as life within a mile and a half on either side of us; and must every man of us have been taken prisoner had not every man but Connal refused to go one inch further, and had not the Boers themselves obviously suspected some subtle ruse as the only conceivable explanation of so madcap a manoeuvre. They allowed us to retire without firing a shot; and retire you may be sure we did, the Kaffirs flogging their teams in a fury of fear, and our precious corporal sullen but defiant.

I have said this was the conclusion of the matter, and I blush to repeat that it practically was. Connal was indeed wheeled up before the colonel, but his instructions were not written instructions, and he lied his way out with equal hardihood and tact.

'You said "over there", sir,' he stoutly reiterated; and the vagueness with which such orders were undoubtedly given was the saving of him for the time being.

I need not tell you how indignant I felt, for one.

'The fellow is a spy!' I said to Raffles, with no nursery oath, as we strolled within the lines that night.

He merely smiled in my face.

'And have you only just found it out, Bunny? I have known it almost ever since we joined; but this morning I did think we had him on toast.'

'It's disgraceful that we had not,' cried I. 'He ought to have been shot like a dog.'

'Not so loud, Bunny, though I quite agree; but I don't regret what has happened as much as you do. Not that I'm less bloodthirsty than you are in this case, but a good deal more so! Bunny, I'm mad-keen oh bowling him out with my own unaided hand – though I may ask you to take the wicket. Meanwhile, don't wear all your animosity upon your sleeve; the fellow has friends who still believe in him; and there is no need for you to be more openly his enemy than you were before.'

Well, I can only vow that I did my best to follow this sound advice; but who but a Raffles can control his every look? It was never my forte, as you know, yet to this day I cannot conceive what I did to excite the treacherous corporal's suspicions. He was clever enough, however, not to betray them, and lucky enough to turn the tables on us, as you shall hear.

III

Bloemfontein had fallen since our arrival, but there was plenty of fight in the Free Staters still, and I will not deny that it was these gentry who were showing us the sport for which our corps came in. Constant skirmishing was our portion, with now and then an action that you would know at least by name, did I feel free to mention them. But I do not, and indeed it is better so. I have not to describe the war even as I saw it, I am thankful to say, but only the martial story of us two and those others of whom you wot. Corporal Connal was the dangerous blackguard you have seen. Captain Bellingham is best known for his position in the batting averages a year or two ago, and for his subsequent failure to obtain a place in any of the five Test Matches. But I only think of him as the officer who recognised Raffles.

We had taken a village, making quite a little name for it and for ourselves, and in the village our division was reinforced by a fresh brigade of the Imperial troops. It was a day of rest, our first for weeks, but Raffles and I spent no small part of it seeking high and low for a worthy means of quenching the kind of thirst which used to beset Yeomen and others who had left good cellars for the veldt. The old knack came back to us both, though I believe that I alone was conscious of it at the time; and we were leaving the house, splendidly supplied, when we almost ran into the arms of an infantry officer, with a scowl upon his red-hot face, and an eyeglass flaming at us in the sun.

'Peter Bellingham!' gasped Raffles, under his breath, and then we saluted and tried to pass on, with the bottles ringing like church bells under our khaki. But Captain Bellingham was a hard man.

'What have you men been doin'?' drawled he.

'Nothing, sir,' we protested like innocence with an injury.

'Lootin's forbidden,' said he. 'You had better let me see those bottles.'

'We are done,' whispered Raffles, and straightway we made a sideboard of the stoop across which we had crept at so inopportune a moment. I had not the heart to raise my eyes again, yet it was many moments before the officer broke silence.

'Uam Var!' he murmured reverentially at last. 'And Long John of Ben Nevis! The first drop that's been discovered in the whole psalm-singing show! What lot do you two belong to?'

I answered.

'I must have your names.'

In my agitation I gave my real one. Raffles had turned away, as though in heart-broken contemplation of our lost loot. I saw the officer studying his half-profile with an alarming face.

'What's *your* name?' he rapped out at last.

But his strange, low voice said plainly that he knew, and Raffles faced him with the monosyllable of confession and assent. I did not count the seconds until the next word, but it was Captain Bellingham who uttered it at last.

'I thought you were dead.'

'Now you see I am not.'

'But you are at your old games!'

'I am not!' cried Raffles, and his tone was new to me. I have seldom heard one more indignant. 'Yes,' he continued, 'This is loot, and the wrong 'un will out. That's what you're thinking, Peter – I beg your pardon – sir. But he isn't let out in the field. We're playing the game as much as you are, old – sir.'

The plural number caused the captain to toss me a contemptuous look. 'Is this the fellah who was taken when you swam for it?' he inquired, relapsing into his drawl. Raffles said I was, and with that took a passionate oath upon our absolute rectitude as volunteers. There could be no doubting him; but the officer's eyes went back at the bottles on the stoop.

'But look at those,' said he; and as he looked himself the light eye melted in his fiery face. 'And I've got Sparklets in my tent,' he sighed. 'You make it in a minute!'

Not a word from Raffles, and none, you may be sure, from me. Then suddenly Bellingham told me where his tent was, and, adding that our case was one for serious consideration, strode in its direction without another word until some sunlit paces separated us.

'You can bring that stuff with you,' he then flung over a shoulder-strap, 'and I advise you to put it where you had it before.'

A trooper saluted him some yards further on, and looked evilly at us as we followed with our loot. It was Corporal Connal of ours, and the thought of him takes my mind off the certainly gallant captain who only that day had joined our division with the reinforcements. I could not stand the man myself. He added soda-water to our whisky in his tent, and would only keep a couple of bottles when we came away. Softened by the spirit, to which disuse made us all a little sensitive, our officer was soon convinced of the honest part that we were playing for once, and for fifty minutes of the hour we spent with him he and Raffles talked cricket without a break. On parting they even shook hands; that was Long John in the captain's head; but the snob never addressed a syllable to me.

And now to the gallows-bird who was still corporal of our troop ; it was not long before Raffles was to have his wish and the traitor's wicket. We had resumed our advance, or rather our humble part in the great surrounding movement then taking place, and were under pretty heavy fire once more, when Connal was shot in the hand. It was a curious casualty in more than one respect, and nobody seems to have seen it happen. Though a flesh-wound, it was a bloody one, and that may be why the surgeon did not at once detect those features which afterwards convinced him that the injury had been self-inflicted. It was the right hand, and until it healed the man could be of no further use in the firing-line; nor was the case serious enough for admission to a crowded field-hospital; and

Connal himself offered his services as custodian of a number of our horses which we were keeping out of harm's way in a donga. They had come there in the following manner. That morning we had been heliographed to reinforce the C.M.R., only to find that the enemy had the range to a nicety when we reached the spot. There were trenches for us men, but no place of safety for our horses nearer than this long and narrow donga which ran from within our lines towards those of the Boers. So some of us galloped them thither, six-in-hand, amid the whine of shrapnel and the whistle of shot. I remember the man next to me being killed by a shell with all his team, and the tangle of flying harness, torn horse-flesh, and crimson khaki that we left behind us on the veldt; also that a small red flag, ludicrously like those used to indicate a putting-green, marked the single sloping entrance to the otherwise precipitous donga, which I for one was duly thankful to reach alive.

The same evening Connal, with a few other light casualties to assist him, took over the charge for which he had volunteered, and for which he was so admirably fitted by his knowledge of horses and his general experience of the country; nevertheless, he managed to lose three or four fine chargers in the course of the first night; and, early in the second, Raffles shook me out of a heavy slumber in the trenches where we had been firing all day.

'I have found the spot, Bunny,' he whispered; 'we ought to out him before the night is over,'

'Connal?'

Raffles nodded.

'You know what happened to some of his horses last night? Well, he let them go himself.'

'Never!'

'I'm as certain of it,' said Raffles, 'as though I'd seen him do it; and if he does it again I shall see him. I can even tell you how it happened. Connal insisted on having one end of the donga to himself, and of course his end is the one nearest the Boers. Well, then, he tells the other fellows to go to sleep at their end – I have it direct from one of them – and you bet they don't need a second invitation. The rest I hope to see tonight.'

'It seems almost incredible,' said I.

'Not more so than the Light Horseman's dodge of poisoning the troughs; that happened at Ladysmith before Christmas; and two kind friends did for that blackguard what you and I are going to do for this one, and a firing-party did the rest. Brutes! A mounted man's worth a file on foot in this country, and well they know it. But this beauty goes one better than the poison; that was wilful waste; but I'll eat my wide awake if our loss last night wasn't the enemy's double gain! What we've got to do, Bunny, is to catch him in the act. It may mean watching him all night, but was ever game so well worth the candle?'

One may say in passing that, at this particular point of contact, the enemy were in superior force, and for once in a mood as aggressive as our own: They were led with a dash, and handled with a skill which did not always characterise their commanders at this stage of the war. Their position was very similar to ours, and indeed we were to spend the whole of next day in trying with an equal will to turn each other out. The result will scarcely be forgotten by those who recognise the occasion from these remarks. Meanwhile it was the eve of battle (most evenings were), and there was that villain with the horses in the donga, and here were we two upon his track.

Raffles's plan was to reconnoitre the place, and then take up a position from which we could watch our man and pounce upon him if he gave us cause. The spot that we eventually chose and stealthily occupied was behind some bushes through which we could see down into the donga; there were the precious horses; and there, sure enough, was our wounded corporal, sitting smoking in his cloak, some glimmering thing in his lap.

'That's his revolver, and it's a Mauser,' whispered Raffles. 'He shan't have a chance of using it on us; either we must be on him before he knows we are anywhere near, or simply report. It's easily proved once we are sure; but I should like to have the taking of him too.'

There was a setting moon. Shadows were sharp and black. The man smoked steadily, and the hungry horses did what I never saw horses do before; they stood and nibbled at each other's tails. I was used to sleeping in the open, under the jewelled dome that seems so much vaster and grander in these wide spaces of the earth. I lay listening to the horses, and to the myriad small strange voices of the veldt, to which I cannot even now put a name, while Raffles watched. 'One head is better than two,' he said, 'when you don't want it to be seen.' We were to take watch and watch about, however, and the other might sleep if he could; it was not my fault that I did nothing else; it was Raffles who could trust nobody but himself. Nor was there any time for recriminations when he did rouse me in the end.

But a moment ago, as it seemed to me, I had been gazing upward at the stars and listening to the dear minute sounds of peace; and in another the great grey slate was clean, and every bone of me set in plaster of Paris, and sniping beginning between pickets with the day. It was an occasional crack, not a constant crackle, but the whistle of a bullet as it passed us by, or a tiny transitory flame for the one bit of detail on a blue hillside, was an unpleasant warning that we two on ours were a target in ourselves. But Raffles paid no attention to their fire; he was pointing downward through the bushes to where Corporal Connal stood with his back to us, shooing a last charger out of the mouth of the donga towards the Boer trenches.

'That's his third,' whispered Raffles, 'But it's the first I've seen distinctly, for he waited for the blind spot before the dawn. It's enough to land him, I fancy, but we mustn't lose time. Are you ready for a creep?'

I stretched myself, and said I was; but I devoutly wished it was not quite so early in the morning.

'Like cats, then, till he hears, and then into him for all we're worth. He's stowed his iron safe away, but he mustn't have time even to feel for it. You take his left arm, Bunny, and hang on to that like a ferret, and I'll do the rest. Ready? Then now!'

And in less time than it would take to tell, we were over the lip of the donga and had fallen upon the fellow before he could turn his head; nevertheless, for a few instants he fought like a wild beast, striking, kicking, and swinging me off my feet as I obeyed my instructions to the letter, and stuck to his left like a leech. But he soon gave that up, and, panting and blaspheming, demanded explanations in his hybrid tongue that had half a brogue and half a burr. What were we doing? What had he done? Raffles at his back, with his right wrist twisted round and pinned into the small of it, soon told him that, and I think the words must have been the first intimation that he had as to who his assailants were.

'So it's you two!' he cried, and a light broke over him. He was no longer trying to shake us off, and now he dropped his curses also, and stood chuckling to himself instead. 'Well,' he went on, 'you're bloody liars both, but I know something else that you are, so you'd better let go.'

A coldness ran through me, and I never saw Raffles so taken aback. His grip must have relaxed for a fraction of time, for our captive broke out in a fresh and desperate struggle, but now we pinned him tighter than ever, and soon I saw him turning green and yellow with the pain.

'You're breaking my wrist!' he yelled at last.

'Then stand still and tell us who we are.'

And he stood still and told us our real names. But Raffles insisted on hearing how he found us out, and smiled as though he had known what was coming when it came. I was dumbfounded. The accursed hound had followed us that evening to Captain Bellingham's tent, and his undoubted cleverness in his own profession of spy had done the rest.

'And now you'd better let me go,' said the master of the situation, as I for one could not help regarding him.

'I'll see you damned,' said Raffles savagely.

'Then you're damned and done for yourself, my cocky criminal. Raffles the burglar! Raffles the society thief! Not dead after all, but 'live and 'listed! Send him home and give him fourteen years, and won't he like 'em, that's all!'

'I shall have the pleasure of hearing you shot first,' retorted Raffles, through his teeth, 'and that alone will make them bearable. Come on, Bunny, let's drive the swine along, and get it over.'

And drive him we did, he cursing, cajoling, struggling, gloating, and blubbering by turns. But Raffles never wavered for an instant, though his face was tragic, and it went to my heart, where that look stays still. I remember at the time, though I never let my hold relax, there was a moment when I added my entreaties to those of our prisoner. Raffles did not even reply to me. But I was thinking of him, I swear. I was thinking of that grey set face that I never saw before or after.

'Your story will be tested,' said the commanding officer, when Connal had been marched to the guard-tent. 'Is there any truth in his?'

'It is perfectly true, sir.'

'And the notorious Raffles has been alive all these years, and you are really he?'

'I am, sir.'

'And what are you doing at the Front?'

Somehow I thought that Raffles was going to smile, but the grim set of his mouth never altered, neither was there any change in the ashy pallor which had come over him in the donga when Connal mouthed his name. It was only his eyes that lighted up at the last question.

'I am fighting, sir,' said he, as simply as any subaltern in the army.

The commanding officer inclined a grizzled head perceptibly, and no more. He was not one of any school, our General; he had his own ways, and we loved both him and them; and I believe that he loved the rough but gallant corps that bore his name. He once told us that he knew something about most of us, and there were things that Raffles had done of which he must have heard. But he only moved his grizzled head.

'Did you know he was going to give you away?' he asked at length, with a jerk of it toward the guard-tent.

'Yes, sir.'

'But you thought it worth while, did you?'

'I thought it necessary, sir.'

The General paused, drumming on his table, making up his mind. Then his chin came up with the decision that we loved in him.

'I shall sift all this,' said he. 'An officer's name was mentioned, and I shall see him myself. Meanwhile you had better go on – fighting.'

IV

Corporal Connal paid the penalty of his crime before the sun was far above the hill held by the enemy. There was abundance of circumstantial evidence against him besides the direct testimony of Raffles and myself, and the wretch was shot at last with little ceremony and less shrift. And that was the one good thing that happened on the day that broke upon us hiding behind the bushes overlooking the donga; by noon it was my own turn.

I have avoided speaking of my wound before I need, and from the preceding pages you would not gather that I am more or less lame for life. You will soon see now why I was in no hurry to recall the incident. I used to think of a wound received in one's country's service as the proudest trophy a man could acquire. But the sight of mine depresses me every morning of my life; it was due for one thing to my own slow eye for cover, in taking which (to aggravate my case) our hardy little corps happened to excel.

The bullet went clean through my thigh, drilling the bone, but happily missing the sciatic nerve; thus the mere pain was less than it might have been, but of course I went over in a light brown heap. We were advancing on our stomachs to take the hill, and thus extend our position, and it was at this point that the fire became too heavy for us, so that for hours (in the event) we moved neither forward nor back. But it was not a minute before Raffles came to me through the whistling scud, and in another I was on my back behind a shallow rock, with him kneeling over me and unrolling my bandage in the teeth of that murderous fire. It was on the knees of the gods, he said, when I begged him to bend lower, but for the moment I thought his tone as changed as his face had been earlier in the morning. To oblige me, however, he took more care; and, when he had done all that one comrade could for another, he did avail himself of the cover he had found for me. So there we lay together on the veldt, under blinding sun and withering fire, and I suppose it is the veldt that I should describe, as it swims and flickers before wounded eyes. I shut mine to bring it back, but all that comes is the keen brown face of Raffles, still a shade paler than its wont, now bending to sight and fire; now peering to see results, brows raised, eyes widened; anon turning to me with the word to set my tight lips grinning. He was talking all the time, but for my sake, and I knew it. Can you wonder that I could not see an inch beyond him? He was the battle to me then; he is the whole war to me as I look back now.

'Feel equal to a cigarette? It will buck you up, Bunny. No, that one in the silver paper, I've hoarded it for this. Here's a light; and so Bunny takes the Sullivan! All honour to the sporting rabbit!'

'At least I went over like one,' said I, sending the only clouds into the blue, and chiefly wishing for their longer endurance. I was as hot as a cinder from my head to one foot; the other leg was ceasing to belong to me.

'Wait a bit,' says Raffles, puckering; 'there's a grey felt hat at deep long-on, and I want to add it to the bag for vengeance... Wait – yes – no, no luck! I must pitch 'em up a bit more. Hallo! magazine empty. How goes the Sullivan, Bunny? Rum to be smoking one on the veldt with a hole in your leg!'

'It's doing me good,' I said, and I believe it was. But Raffles lay looking at me as he lightened his bandolier.

'Do you remember', he said softly, 'the day we first began to think about the war? I can see that pink misty river light, and feel the first bite there was in the air when one stood about; don't you wish we had either here? "Orful slorter, orful slorter"; that fellow's face, I see it too; and here we have the thing he cried. Can you believe it's only six months ago?'

'Yes,' I sighed, enjoying the thought of that afternoon less than he did; 'yes, we were slow to catch fire at first.'

'Too slow,' he said quickly.

'But when we did catch,' I went on, wishing we never had, 'we soon burnt up.'

'And then went out,' laughed Raffles gaily. He was loaded up again. 'Another over at the grey felt hat,' said he; 'by Jove, though, I believe he's having an over at me!'

'I wish you'd be careful,' I urged. 'I heard it too.'

'My dear Bunny, it's on the knees you wot of. If anything's down in the specifications surely that is. Besides – that was nearer!'

'To you?'

'No, to him. Poor devil, he has his specifications too; it's comforting to think that... I can't see where that one pitched; it may have been a wide; and it's very nearly the end of the over again. Feeling worse, Bunny?'

'No, I've only closed my eyes. Go on talking.'

'It was I who let you in for this,' he said, at his bandolier again.

'No, I'm glad I came out.'

And I believe I still was, in a way; for it *was* rather fine to be wounded, just then, with the pain growing less; but the sensation was not to last me many minutes, and I can truthfully say that I have never felt it since.

'Ah, but you haven't had such a good time as I have!'

'Perhaps not.'

Had his voice vibrated, or had I imagined it? Pain-waves and loss of blood were playing tricks with my senses; now they were quite dull, and my leg alive and throbbing; now I had no leg at all, but more than all my ordinary senses in every part of me. And the devil's orchestra was playing all the time, and all around me, on every class of fiendish instrument, which you have been made to hear for yourselves in every newspaper. Yet all that I heard was Raffles talking.

'I have had a good time, Bunny.'

Yes, his voice was sad; but that was all; the vibration must have been in me.

'I know you have, old chap,' said I.

'I am grateful to the General for giving me today. It may be the last. Then I can only say it's been the best – by Jove!'

'What is it?'

And I opened my eyes. His were shining. I can see them now.

'Got him – got the hat! No, I'm hanged if I have; at least he wasn't in it. The crafty cuss, he must have stuck it up on purpose. Another over ... scoring's slow... I wonder if he's sportsman enough to take a hint? His hat-trick's foolish. Will he show his face if I show mine?'

I lay with closed ears and eyes. My leg had come to life again, and the rest of me was numb.

'Bunny!'

His voice sounded higher. He must have been sitting upright.

'Well?'

But it was not well with me; that was all I thought as my lips made the words.

'It's not only been the best time I ever had, old Bunny, but I'm not half sure – '

Of what I can but guess; the sentence was not finished, and never would be in this world.

A THIEF IN THE NIGHT

1

Out of Paradise

If I must tell more tales of Raffles, I can but go back to our earliest days together, and fill in the blanks left by discretion in existing annals. In so doing I may indeed fill some small part of an infinitely greater blank, across which you may conceive me to have stretched my canvas for a first frank portrait of my friend. The whole truth cannot harm him now. I shall paint in every wart. Raffles was a villain, when all is written; it is no service to his memory to gloze the fact; yet I have done so myself before today. I have omitted whole heinous episodes. I have dwelt unduly on the redeeming side. And this I may do again, blinded even as I write by the gallant glamour that made my villain more to me than any hero. But at least there shall be no more reservations, and as an earnest I shall make no further secret of the greatest wrong that even Raffles ever did me.

I pick my words with care and pain, loyal as I still would be to my friend, and yet remembering as I must those Ides of March when he led me blindfold into temptation and crime. That was an ugly office, if you will. It was a moral bagatelle to the treacherous trick he was to play me a few weeks later. The second offence, on the other hand, was to prove the less serious of the two against society, and might in itself have been published to the world years ago. There have been private reasons for my reticence. The affair was not only too intimately mine, and too discreditable to Raffles. One other was involved in it, one dearer to me than Raffles himself, one whose name shall not even now be sullied by association with ours.

Suffice it that I had been engaged to her before that mad March deed. True, her people called it 'an understanding', as well they might. But their authority was not direct; we bowed to it as an act of politic grace; between us, all was well but my unworthiness. That may be gauged when I confess that this was how the matter stood on the night I gave a worthless cheque for my losses at baccarat, and afterwards turned to Raffles in my need. Even after that I saw her sometimes. But I let her guess that there was more upon my soul than she must ever share, and at last I had written to end it all. I remember that week so well! It was the close of such a May as we have never had since, and I was too miserable even to follow the heavy scoring in the papers! Raffles was the only man who could get a wicket up at Lord's, and I never once went to see him play. Against Yorkshire, however, he helped himself to a hundred runs as well; and that brought Raffles round to me, on his way home to the Albany.

'We must dine and celebrate the rare event,' said he. 'A century takes it out of one at my time of life; and you, Bunny, you look quite as much in need of your end of a worthy bottle. Suppose we make it the Cafe Royal, and eight sharp? I'll be there first to fix up the table and the wine.'

And at the Cafe Royal I incontinently told him of the trouble I was in. It was the first he had ever heard of my affair, and I told him all, though not before our bottle had been succeeded by a pint of the same exemplary brand. Raffles heard me out with grave attention. His sympathy was the more grateful for the tactful brevity with which it was indicated rather than expressed.

He only wished that I had told him of this complication in the beginning; as I had not, he agreed with me that the only course was a candid and complete renunciation. It was not as though my divinity had a penny of her own, or I could earn an honest one. I had explained to Raffles that she was an orphan, who spent most of her time with an aristocratic aunt in the country, and the remainder under the repressive roof of a pompous politician in Palace Gardens. The aunt had, I believed, still a sneaking softness for me, but her illustrious brother had set his face against me from the first.

'Hector Carruthers!' murmured Raffles, repeating the detested name with his clear cold eye on mine. 'I suppose you haven't seen much of him?'

'Not a thing for ages,' I replied. 'I was at the house two or three days last year, but they've neither asked me since nor been at home to me when I've called. The old beast seems a judge of men.'

And I laughed bitterly in my glass.

'Nice house?' said Raffles, glancing at himself in his silver cigarette-case.

'Top shelf,' said I. 'You know the houses in Palace Gardens, don't you?'

'Not so well as I should like to know them, Bunny.'

'Well, it's about the most palatial of the lot. The old ruffian is as rich as Crœsus. It's a country place in town.'

'What about the window fastenings?' asked Raffles, casually.

I recoiled from the open cigarette-case that he proffered as he spoke. Our eyes met; and in his there was that starry twinkle of mirth and mischief, that sunny beam of audacious devilment, which had been my undoing two months before, which was to undo me as often as he chose until the chapter's end. Yet for once I withstood its glamour; for once I turned aside that luminous glance with front of steel. There was no need for Raffles to voice his plans. I read them all between the strong lines of his smiling, eager face. And I pushed back my chair in the equal eagerness of my own resolve.

'Not if I know it!' said I. 'A house I've dined in – a house I've seen *her* in – a house where *she* stays by the month together! Don't put it into words, Raffles, or I'll get up and go.'

'You mustn't do that before the coffee and liqueur,' said Raffles, laughing. 'Have a small Sullivan first: it's the royal road to a cigar. And now let me observe that your scruples would do you honour if old Carruthers still lived in the house in question.'

'Do you mean to say he doesn't?'

Raffles struck a match, and handed it first to me. 'I mean to say, my dear Bunny, that Palace Gardens knows the very name no more. You began by telling me you had heard nothing of these people all this year. That's quite enough to account for our little misunderstanding. I was thinking of the house, and you were thinking of the people in the house.'

'But who are they, Raffles? Who has taken the house, if old Carruthers has moved, and how do you know that it is still worth a visit?'

'In answer to your first question – Lord Lochmaben,' replied Raffles, blowing bracelets of smoke towards the ceiling. 'You look as though you had never heard of him; but as the cricket and racing are the only part of your paper that you condescend to read, you can't be expected to keep track of all the peers created in your time. Your other question is not worth answering. How do you suppose that I know these things? It's my business to get to know them, and that's all there is to it. As a matter of fact, Lady Lochmaben has just as good diamonds as Mrs Carruthers ever had; and the chances are that she keeps them where Mrs Carruthers kept hers, if you could enlighten me on that point.'

As it happened, I could, since I knew from his niece that it was one on which Mr Carruthers had been a faddist in his time. He had made quite a study of the cracksman's craft, in a resolve to circumvent it with his own. I remembered myself how the ground-floor windows were elaborately bolted and shuttered, and how the doors of all the rooms opening upon the square inner hall were fitted with extra Yale locks, at an unlikely height, not to be discovered by one within the room. It had been the butler's business to turn and to collect all these keys before retiring for the night. But the key of the safe in the study was supposed to be in the jealous keeping of the master of the house himself. That safe was in its turn so ingeniously hidden that I never should have found it for myself. I well remember how one who showed it to me (in the innocence of her heart) laughed as she assured me that even her little trinkets were solemnly locked up in it every night. It had been let into the wall behind one end of the bookcase, expressly to preserve the barbaric splendour of Mrs Carruthers; without a doubt these Lochmabens would use it for the same purpose; and in the altered circumstances I had no hesitation in giving Raffles all the information he desired. I even drew him a rough plan of the ground floor on the back of my menu-card.

'It was rather clever of you to notice the kind of locks on the inner doors,' he remarked as he put it in his pocket. 'I suppose you don't remember if it was a Yale on the front door as well?'

'It was not,' I was able to answer quite promptly. 'I happen to know because I once had the key when – when we went to a theatre together.'

'Thank you, old chap,' said Raffles, sympathetically. 'That's all I shall want from you, Bunny, my boy. There's no night like tonight!'

It was one of his sayings when bent upon his worst. I looked at him aghast. Our cigars were just in blast, yet already he was signalling for his bill. It was impossible to remonstrate with him until we were both outside in the street.

'I'm coming with you,' said I, running my arm through his.

'Nonsense, Bunny!'

'Why is it nonsense? I know every inch of the ground, and since the house has changed hands I have no compunction. Besides, "I have been there" in the other sense as well: once a thief, you know! In for a penny, in for a pound!'

It was ever my mood when the blood was up. But my old friend failed to appreciate the characteristic as he usually did. We crossed Regent Street in silence. I had to catch his sleeve to keep a hand in his hospitable arm.

'I really think you had better stay away,' said Raffles, as we reached the other kerb. 'I've no use for you this time.'

'Yet I thought I had been so useful up to now?'

'That may be, Bunny, but I tell you frankly I don't want you tonight.'

'Yet I know the ground, and you don't! I tell you what,' said I: 'I'll come just to show you the ropes, and I won't take a pennyweight of the swag.'

Such was the teasing fashion in which he invariably prevailed upon me; it was delightful to note how it caused him to yield in his turn. But Raffles had the grace to give in with a laugh, whereas I too often lost my temper with my point,

'You little rabbit!' he chuckled.'You shall have your share, whether you come or not; but, seriously, don't you think you might remember the girl?'

'What's the use?' I groaned. 'You agree there is nothing for it but to give her up. I am glad to say I saw that for myself before I asked you, and wrote to tell her so on Sunday. Now it's Wednesday, and she hasn't answered by line or sign. It's waiting for one word from her that's driving me mad.'

'Perhaps you wrote to Palace Gardens?'

'No, I sent it to the country. There's been time for an answer, wherever she may be.'

We had reached the Albany, and halted with one accord at the Piccadilly portico, red cigar to red cigar.

'You wouldn't like to go and see if the answer's in your rooms?' he asked.

'No. What's the good? Where's the point in giving her up if I'm going to straighten out when it's too late? It *is* too late, I *have* given her up, and I *am* coming with you!'

The hand that bowled the most puzzling ball in England (once it found its length) descended on my shoulder with surprising promptitude.

'Very well, Bunny! That's finished; but your blood be on your own pate if evil comes of it. Meanwhile we can't do better than turn in here till you have finished your cigar as it deserves, and topped up with such a cup of tea as you must learn to like if you hope to get on in your new profession. And when the hours are small enough, Bunny, my boy, I don't mind admitting I shall be very glad to have you with me.'

I have a vivid memory of the interim in his rooms. I think it must have been the first and last of its kind that I was called upon to sustain with so much knowledge of what lay before me. I passed the time with one restless eye upon the clock, and the other on the tantalus which Raffles ruthlessly declined to unlock. He admitted that it was like waiting with one's pads on; and in my slender experience of the game of which he was a world's master, that was an ordeal not to be endured without a general quaking of the inner man. I was, on the other hand, all right when I got to the metaphorical wicket; and half the surprises that Raffles sprung on me were doubtless due to his early recognition of the fact.

On this occasion I fell swiftly and hopelessly out of love with the prospect I had so gratuitously embraced. It was not only my repugnance to enter that house in that way, which grew upon my better judgment as the artificial enthusiasm of the evening evaporated from my veins. Strong as that repugnance became, I had an even stronger feeling that we were embarking on an important enterprise far too much upon the spur of the moment. The latter qualm I had the temerity to confess to Raffles; nor have I often loved him more than when he freely admitted it to be the most natural feeling in the world. He assured me, however, that he had had my Lady Lochmaben and her jewels in his mind for several months; he had sat behind them at first nights, and long ago determined what to take or to reject; in fine, he had only been waiting for those topographical details which it had been my chance privilege to supply. I now learnt that he had numerous houses in a similar state upon his list; something or other was wanting in each case in order to complete his plans. In that of the Bond Street jeweller it was a trusty accomplice; in the present instance, a more intimate knowledge of the house. And lastly, this was a Wednesday night, when the tired legislator gets early to his bed.

How I wish I could make the whole world see and hear him, and smell the smoke of his beloved Sullivan, as he took me into these the secrets of his infamous trade! Neither look nor language would betray the infamy. As a mere talker, I shall never listen to the like of Raffles on this side of the sod; and his talk was seldom garnished by an oath, never in my remembrance by the unclean word. Then he looked like a man who had dressed to dine out, not like one who had long since dined; for his curly hair, though longer than another's, was never untidy in its length; and these were the days when it was still as black as ink. Nor were there many lines as yet upon the smooth and mobile face; and its frame was still that dear den of disorder and good taste, with the carved bookcase, the dresser and chests of still older oak, and the Wattses and Rossettis hung anyhow on the walls.

It must have been one o'clock before we drove in a hansom as far as Kensington Church, instead of getting down at the gates of our private road to ruin. Constitutionally shy of the direct approach, Raffles was further deterred by a ball in full swing at the Empress Rooms, whence potential witnesses were pouring between dances into the cool deserted street. Instead he led me a little way up Church Street, and so through the narrow passage into Palace Gardens. He knew the house as well as I did. We made our first survey from the other side of the road. And the house was not quite in darkness; there was a dim light over the door, a brighter one in the stables, which stood still further back from the road.

'That's a bit of a bore,' said Raffles. 'The ladies have been out somewhere – trust them to spoil the show! They would get to bed before the stable folk, but insomnia is the curse of their sex and our profession. Somebody's not home yet; that will be the son of the house; but he's a beauty, who may not come home at all.'

'Another Alick Carruthers,' I murmured, recalling the one I liked least of all the household as I remembered it.

'They might be brothers,' rejoined Raffles, who knew all the loose fish about town. 'Well, I'm not sure that I shall want you after all, Bunny.'

'Why not?'

'If the front door's only on the latch, and you're right about the lock, I shall walk in as though I were the son of the house myself.'

And he jingled the skeleton bunch that he carried on a chain as honest men carry their latchkeys.

'You forget the inner doors and the safe.'

'True. You might be useful to me there. But I still don't like leading you in where it isn't absolutely necessary, Bunny.'

'Then let me lead you,' I answered, and forthwith marched across the broad, secluded road, with the great houses standing back on either side in their ample gardens, as though the one opposite belonged to me. I thought Raffles had stayed behind, for I never heard him at my heels, yet there he was when I turned round at the gate.

'I must teach you the step,' he whispered, shaking his head. 'You shouldn't use your heel at all. Here's a grass border for you: walk it as you would the plank! Gravel makes a noise, and flowerbeds tell a tale. Wait – I must carry you across this.'

It was the sweep of the drive, and in the dim light from above the door, the soft gravel, ploughed into ridges by the night's wheels, threatened an alarm at every step. Yet Raffles, with me in his arms, crossed the zone of peril softly as the pard.

'Shoes in your pocket – that's the beauty of pumps!' he whispered on the step: his light bunch tinkled faintly; a couple of keys he stooped and tried, with the touch of a humane dentist; the third let us into the porch. And as we stood together on the mat, as he was gradually closing the door, a clock within chimed a half-hour in fashion so thrillingly familiar to me that I caught Raffles by the arm. My half-hours of happiness had flown to just such chimes! I looked wildly about me in the dim light. Hat-stand and oak settee belonged equally to my past. And Raffles was smiling in my face as he held the door wide for my escape.

'You told me a lie!' I gasped in whispers.

'I did nothing of the sort,' he replied. 'The furniture's the furniture of Hector Carruthers, but the house is the house of Lord Lochmaben. Look here!'

He had stooped, and was smoothing out the discarded envelope of a telegram. 'Lord Lochmaben', I read in pencil by the dim light; and the case was plain to me on the spot. My friends had let their house, furnished, as anybody but Raffles would have explained in the beginning.

'All right,' I said. 'Shut the door.'

And he not only shut it without a sound, but shot a bolt that might have been sheathed in rubber.

In another minute we were at work upon the study door, I with the tiny lantern and the bottle of rock-oil, he with the brace and the largest bit. The Yale lock he had given up at a glance. It was placed high up in the door, feet above the handle, and the chain of holes with which Raffles had soon surrounded it were bored on a level with his eyes. Yet the clock in the hail chimed again, and two ringing strokes resounded through the silent house, before we gained admittance to the room.

Raffles's next care was to muffle the bell on the shuttered window (with a silk handkerchief from the hat-stand) and to prepare an emergency exit by opening first the shutters and then the window itself. Luckily it was a still night, and very little wind came in to embarrass us. He then began operations on the safe, revealed by me behind its folding screen of books, while I stood sentry on the threshold. I may have stood there for a dozen minutes, listening to the loud hall clock and to the gentle dentistry of Raffles in the mouth of the safe behind me, when a third sound thrilled my every nerve. It was the equally cautious opening of a door in the gallery overhead.

I moistened my lips to whisper a word of warning to Raffles. But his ears had been as quick as mine, and something longer. His lantern darkened as I turned my head; next moment I felt his breath upon the back of my neck. It was now too late even for a whisper, and quite out of the question to close the mutilated door. There we could only stand, I on the threshold, Raffles at my elbow, while one carrying a candle crept down the stairs.

The study door was at right angles to the lowest flight, and just to the right of one alighting in the hall. It was thus impossible for us to see who it was until the person was close abreast of us; but by the rustle of the gown we knew that it was one of the ladies, and dressed just as she had come from theatre or ball. Insensibly I drew back as the candle swam into our field of vision: it had not traversed many inches when a hand was clapped firmly but silently across my mouth.

I could forgive Raffles for that, at any rate! In another breath I should have cried aloud: for the girl with the candle, the girl in her ball-dress at dead of night, the girl with the letter for the post, was the last girl on God's wide earth whom I should have chosen thus to encounter – a midnight intruder in the very house where I had been reluctantly received on her account!

I forgot Raffles. I forgot the new and unforgivable grudge I had against him now. I forgot his very hand across my mouth, even before he paid me the compliment of removing it. There was the only girl in all my world: I had eyes and brains for no one and for nothing else. She had neither seen nor heard us, had looked neither to the right nor the left. But a small oak table stood on the opposite side of the hall; it was to this table that she went. On it was one of those boxes in which one puts one's letters for the post; and she stooped to read by her candle the times at which this box was cleared.

The loud clock ticked and ticked. She was standing at her full height now, her candle on the table, her letter in both hands, and in her downcast face a sweet and pitiful perplexity that drew the tears to my eyes. Through a film I saw her open the envelope so lately sealed, and read her letter once more, as though she would have altered it a little at the last. It was too late for that; but of a sudden she plucked a rose from her bosom, and was pressing it in with her letter when I groaned aloud.

How could I help it? The letter was for me: of that I was sure as though I had been looking over her shoulder. She was as true as tempered steel; there were not two of us to whom she wrote and sent roses at dead of night. It was her one chance of writing to me. None would know that she had written. And she cared enough to soften the reproaches I had richly earned with a red rose warm from her own warm heart. And there, there was I, a common thief who had broken in to steal! Yet I was unaware that I had uttered a sound until she looked up, startled, and the hands behind me pinned me where I stood.

I think she must have seen us, even in the dim light of the solitary candle. Yet not a sound escaped her as she peered courageously in our direction; neither did one of us move; but the hall clock went on and on, every tick like the beat of a drum to bring the house about our ears, until a minute must have passed as in some breathless dream. And then came the awakening – with such a knocking and a ringing at the front door as brought all three of us to our senses on the spot.

'The son of the house!' whispered Raffles in my ear, as he dragged me back to the window he had left open for our escape. But as he leaped out first a sharp cry stopped me at the sill. 'Get back! Get back! We're trapped!' he cried; and in the single second that I stood there, I saw him fell one officer to the ground, and dart across the lawn with another at his heels. A third came running up to the window. What could I do but double back into the house? And there in the hall I met my lost love face to face.

Till that moment she had not recognised me. I ran to catch her as she all but fell. And my touch repelled her into life, so that she shook me off, and stood gasping: 'You, of all men! You, of all men!' until I could bear it no more, but broke again for the study window. 'Not that way – not that way!' she cried, in an agony at that. Her hands were upon me now. 'In there, in there,' she whispered, pointing and pulling me to a mere cupboard under the stairs, where hats and coats were hung; and it was she who shut the door on me with a sob.

Doors were already opening overhead, voices calling, voices answering, the alarm running like wildfire from room to room. Soft feet pattered in the gallery and down the stairs about my very ears. I do not know what made me put on my own shoes as I heard them, but I think that I was ready and even longing to walk out and give myself up. I need not say what and who it was that alone restrained me. I heard her name. I heard them crying to her as though she had fainted. I recognised the detested voice of my *bête noir*, Alick Carruthers, thick as might be expected of the dissipated dog, yet daring to stutter out her name. And then I heard, without catching, her low reply; it was in answer to the somewhat stern questioning of quite another voice; and from what followed, I knew that she had never fainted at all.

'Upstairs, miss, did he? Are you sure?'

I did not hear her answer. I conceive her as simply pointing up the stairs. In any case, about my ears once more, there now followed such a patter and tramp of bare and booted feet as renewed in me a base fear for my own skin. But voices and feet passed over my head, went up and up, higher and higher; and I was wondering whether or not to make a dash for it, when one light pair came running down again, and in very despair I marched out to meet my preserver, looking as little as I could like the abject thing I felt.

'Be quick!' she cried in a harsh whisper, and pointed peremptorily to the porch.

But I stood stubbornly before her, my heart hardened by her hardness, and perversely indifferent to all else. And as I stood I saw the letter she had written, in the hand with which she pointed, crushed into a ball.

'Quickly!' She stamped her foot. 'Quickly – *if you ever cared!*'

This in a whisper, without bitterness, without contempt, but with a sudden wild entreaty that breathed upon the dying embers of my poor manhood. I drew myself together for the last time in her sight. I turned, and left her as she wished – for her sake, not for mine. And as I went I heard her tearing her letter into little pieces, and the little pieces falling on the floor.

Then I remembered Raffles, and could have killed him for what he had done. Doubtless by this time he was safe and snug in the Albany: what did my fate matter to him? Never mind; this should be the end between him and me as well; it was the end of everything, this dark night's work! I would go and tell him so. I would jump into a cab and drive there and then to his accursed rooms. But first I must escape from the trap in which he had been so ready to leave me. And on the very steps I drew back in despair. They were searching the shrubberies between the drive and the road; a policeman's lantern kept flashing in and out among the laurels, while a young man in evening clothes directed him from the gravel sweep. It was this young man whom I must dodge, but at my first step in the gravel he wheeled round, and it was Raffles himself.

'Hulloa!' he cried. 'So you've come up to join the dance as well! Had a look inside, have you? You'll be better employed in helping to draw the cover in front here. It's all right, officer – only another gentleman from the Empress Rooms.'

And we made a brave show of assisting in the futile search, until the arrival of more police, and a broad hint from an irritable sergeant, gave us an excellent excuse for going off arm-in-arm. But it was Raffles who had thrust his arm through mine. I shook him off as we left the scene of shame behind.

'My dear Bunny!' he exclaimed. 'Do you know what brought me back?'

I answered savagely that I neither knew nor cared.

'I had the very devil of a squeak for it,' he went on. 'I did the hurdles over two or three garden walls, but so did the flyer who was on my tracks, and he drove me back into the straight and down to High Street like any lamplighter. If he had only had the breath to sing out it would have been all up with me then; as it was I pulled off my coat the moment I was round the corner, and took a ticket for it at the Empress Rooms.'

'I suppose you had one for the dance that was going on,' I growled. Nor would it have been a coincidence for Raffles to have had a ticket for that or any other entertainment of the London season.

'I never asked what the dance was,' he returned. 'I merely took the opportunity of revising my toilet, and getting rid of that rather distinctive overcoat, which I shall call for now. They're not too particular at such stages of such proceedings, but I've no doubt I should have seen some one I knew if I had gone right in. I might even have had a turn, if only I had been less uneasy about you, Bunny.'

'It was like you to come back to help me out,' said I. 'But to lie to me, and to inveigle me with your lies into that house of all houses – that was not like you, Raffles – and I never shall forgive it or you!'

Raffles took my arm again. We were near the High Street gates, of Palace Gardens, and I was too miserable to resist an advance which I meant never to give him an opportunity to repeat.

'Come, come, Bunny, there wasn't much inveigling about it,' said he. 'I did my level best to leave you behind, but you wouldn't listen to me.'

'If you had told me the truth I should have listened fast enough,' I retorted. 'But what's the use of talking? You can boast of your own adventures after you bolted. You don't care what happened to me.'

'I cared so much that I came back to see.'

'You might have spared yourself the trouble! The wrong had been done. Raffles – Raffles – don't you know who she was?'

It was my hand that gripped his arm once more.

'I guessed,' he answered, gravely enough even for me.

'It was she who saved me, not you,' I said. 'And that is the bitterest part of all!'

Yet I told him that part with a strange sad pride in her whom I had lost, through him, for ever. As I ended we turned into High Street; in the prevailing stillness, the faint strains of the band reached us from the Empress Rooms; and I hailed a crawling hansom as Raffles turned that way.

'Bunny,' said he, 'it's no use saying I'm sorry. Sorrow adds insult in a case like this – if ever there was or will be such another! Only believe me, Bunny, when I swear to you that I had not the smallest shadow of a suspicion that *she* was in the house.'

And in my heart of hearts I did believe him; but I could not bring myself to say the words.

'You told me yourself that you had written to her in the country,' he pursued.

'And that letter!' I rejoined, in a fresh wave of bitterness: 'that letter she had written at dead of night, and stolen down to post, it was the one I have been waiting for all these days! I should have got it tomorrow. Now I shall never get it, never hear from her again, nor have another chance in this world or in the next. I don't say it was all your fault. You no more knew that she was there than I did. But you told me a deliberate lie about her people, and that I never shall forgive.'

I spoke as vehemently as I could under my breath. The hansom was waiting at the kerb.

'I can say no more than I have said,' returned Raffles with a shrug. 'Lie or no lie, I didn't tell it to bring you with me, but to get you to give me certain information without feeling a beast about it. But, as a matter of fact, it was no lie about old Hector Carruthers and Lord Lochmaben, and anybody but you would have guessed the truth.'

'What is the truth?'

'I as good as told you, Bunny, again and again.'

'Then tell me now.'

'If you read your paper there would be no need; but if you want to know, old Carruthers headed the list of the Birthday Honours, and Lord Lochmaben is the title of his choice.'

And this miserable quibble was not a lie! My lip curled, I turned my back without a word, and drove home to my Mount Street flat in a new fury of savage scorn. Not a lie, indeed! It was the one that is half a truth, the meanest lie of all, and the very last to which I could have dreamt that Raffles would stoop. So far there had been a degree of honour between us, if only of the kind understood to obtain between thief and thief. Now all that was at an end. Raffles had cheated me. Raffles had completed the ruin of my life. I was done with Raffles, as she who shall not be named was done with me.

And yet, even while I blamed him most bitterly, and utterly abominated his deceitful deed, I could not but admit in my heart that the result was out of all proportion to the intent: he had never dreamt of doing me this injury, or indeed any injury at all. Intrinsically the deceit had been quite venial, the reason for it obviously the reason that Raffles had given me. It was quite true that he had spoken of this Lochmaben peerage as a new creation, and of the heir to it in a fashion only applicable to Alick Carruthers. He had given me hints, which I had been too dense to take, and he had certainly made more than one attempt to deter me from accompanying him on this fatal emprise; had he been more explicit, I might have made it my business to deter him. I could not say in my heart that Raffles had failed to satisfy such honour as I might reasonably expect to subsist between us. Yet it seems to me to require a superhuman sanity always and unerringly to separate cause from effect, achievement from intent. And I, for one, was never quite able to do so in this case.

I could not be accused of neglecting my newspaper during the next few wretched days. I read every word that I could find about the attempted jewel-robbery in Palace Gardens, and the reports afforded me my sole comfort. In the first place, it was only an attempted robbery; nothing had been taken after all. And then – and then – the one member of the household who had come nearest to a personal encounter with either of us was unable to furnish any description of the man – had even expressed a doubt as to any likelihood of identification in the event of an arrest!

I will not say with what mingled feelings I read and dwelt on that announcement. It kept a certain faint glow alive within me until the morning that brought me back the only presents I had ever made her. They were but books; jewellery had been tabooed by the authorities. And the books came back without a word, though the parcel was directed in her hand.

I had made up my mind not to go near Raffles again, but in my heart I already regretted my resolve. I had forfeited love, I had sacrificed honour, and now I must deliberately alienate myself from the one being whose society might yet be some recompense for all that I had lost. The situation was aggravated by the state of my exchequer. I expected an ultimatum from my banker by every post. Yet this influence was nothing to the other. It was Raffles I loved. It was not the dark life we led together, still less its base rewards; it was the man himself, his gaiety, his humour, his dazzling audacity, his incomparable courage and resource. And a very horror of turning to him again in mere need or greed set the seal on my first angry resolution. But the anger was soon gone out of me, and when at length Raffles bridged the gap by coming to me, I rose to greet him almost with a shout.

He came as though nothing had happened; and, indeed, not very many days had passed, though they might have been months to me. Yet I fancied the gaze that watched me through our smoke a trifle less sunny than it had been before. And it was a relief to me when he came with few preliminaries to the inevitable point.

'Did you ever hear from her, Bunny?' he asked.

'In a way,' I answered. 'We won't talk about it, if you don't mind, Raffles.'

'That sort of way!' he exclaimed. He seemed both surprised and disappointed.

'Yes,' I said, 'that sort of way. It's finished. What did you expect?'

'I don't know,' said Raffles. 'I only thought that the girl who went so far to get a fellow out of a tight place might go a little further to keep him from getting into another.'

'I don't see why she should,' said I, honestly enough, yet with the irritation of a less just feeling deep down in my inmost consciousness.

'Yet you did hear from her?' he persisted.

'She sent me back my poor presents, without a word,' I said, 'if you call that hearing.'

I could not bring myself to own to Raffles that I had given her only books. He asked if I was sure that she had sent them back herself; and that was his last question. My answer was enough for him. And to this day I cannot say whether it was more in relief than in regret that he laid a hand upon my shoulder.

'So you are out of Paradise after all!' said Raffles. 'I was not sure, or I should have come round before. Well, Bunny, if they don't want you there, there's a little Inferno in the Albany where you'll be as welcome as ever!'

And still, with all the magic mischief of his smile, there was that touch of sadness which I was yet to read aright.

2

THE CHEST OF SILVER

Like all the tribe of which I held him head, Raffles professed the liveliest disdain for unwieldy plunder of any description; it might be old Sheffield, or it might be solid silver or gold, but if the thing was not to be concealed about the person, he would none whatever of it. Unlike the rest of us, however, in this as in all else, Raffles would not infrequently allow the acquisitive spirit of the mere collector to silence the dictates of professional prudence. The old oak chests, and even the mahogany wine-cooler, for which he had doubtless paid like an honest citizen, were thus immovable with pieces of crested plate, which he had neither the temerity to use, nor the hardihood to melt or sell. He could but gloat over them behind locked doors, as I used to tell him, and at last one afternoon I caught him at it. It was in the year after that of my novitiate, a halcyon period at the Albany, when Raffles left no crib uncracked, and I played second murderer every time. I had called in response to a telegram in which he stated that he was going out of town, and must say good-bye to me before he went. And I could only think that he was inspired by the same impulse towards the bronzed salvers and the tarnished teapots with which I found him surrounded, until my eyes lit upon the enormous silver-chest into which he was fitting them one by one.

'Allow me, Bunny! I shall take the liberty of locking both doors behind you, and putting the key in my pocket,' said Raffles when he had let me in. 'Not that I mean to take you prisoner, my dear fellow; but there are those of us who can turn keys from the outside, though it was never an accomplishment of mine.'

'Not Crawshay again?' I cried, standing still in my hat.

Raffles regarded me with that tantalising smile of his which might mean nothing, yet which often meant so much; and in a flash I was convinced that our most jealous enemy and dangerous rival, the doyen of an older school, had paid him yet another visit.

'That remains to be seen,' was the measured reply; 'and I for one have not set naked eye on the fellow since I saw him off through that window and left myself for dead on this very spot. In fact, I imagined him comfortably back in gaol.'

'Not old Crawshay!' said I. 'He's far too good a man to be taken twice. I should call him the very prince of professional cracksmen.'

'Should you?' said Raffles coldly, with as cold an eye looking into mine. 'Then you had better prepare to repel princes when I'm gone.'

'But gone where?' I asked, finding a corner for my hat and coat, and helping myself to the comforts of the venerable dresser which was one of our friend's greatest treasures. 'Where is it you are off to, and why are you taking this herd of white elephants with you?'

Raffles bestowed the cachet of his smile on my description of his motley plate. He joined me in one of his favourite cigarettes, only shaking a superior head at his own decanter.

'One question at a time, Bunny,' said he. 'In the first place, I am going to have these rooms freshened up with a potful of paint, the electric light, and the telephone you've been at me about so long.'

'Good!' I cried. 'Then we shall be able to talk to each other day and night!'

'And get overheard and run in for our pains? I shall wait till you *are* run in, I think,' said Raffles, cruelly. 'But the rest's a necessity: not that I love new paint or am pining for electric light, but for reasons which I will just breathe in your private ear, Bunny. You must try not to take them too seriously; but the fact is, there is just the least bit of a twitter against me in this rookery of an Albany. It must have been started by that tame old bird, Policeman Mackenzie; it isn't very bad as yet, but it needn't be that to reach my ears. Well, it was open to me either to clear out altogether, and so confirm whatever happened to be in the air, or to go off for a time, under some arrangement which would give the authorities ample excuse for overhauling every inch of my rooms. Which would you have done, Bunny?'

'Cleared out, while I could!' said I, devoutly.

'So I should have thought,' rejoined Raffles. 'Yet you must see the merit of my plan. I shall leave every mortal thing unlocked.'

'Except that,' said I, kicking the huge oak case with the iron bands and clamps, and the baize lining fast disappearing under heavy packages bearing the shapes of urns and candelabra.

'That', replied Raffles, 'is neither to go with me nor to remain here.'

'Then what do you propose to do with it?'

'You have your banking account, and your banker,' he went on. This was perfectly true, though it was Raffles alone who had kept the one open, and enabled me to propitiate the other in moments of emergency.

'Well?'

'Well, pay in this bundle of notes this afternoon, and say you have had a great week at Liverpool and Lincoln; then ask them if they can do with your silver while you run over to Paris for a merry Easter. I should tell them it's rather heavy – a lot of old family stuff that you've a good mind to leave with them till you marry and settle down.'

I winced at this, but consented to the rest after a moment's consideration. After all, and for more reasons than I need enumerate, it was a plausible tale enough. And Raffles had no banker; it was quite impossible for him to explain, across any single counter, the large sums of hard cash which did sometimes fall into his hands; and it might well be that he had nursed my small account in view of the very quandary which had now arisen. On all grounds, it was impossible for me to refuse him, and I am still glad to remember that my assent was given, on the whole, ungrudgingly.

'But when will the chest be ready for me?' I merely asked, as I stuffed the notes into my cigarette-case. 'And how are we to get it out of this, in banking hours, without attracting any amount of attention at this end?'

Raffles gave me an approving nod.

'I'm glad to see you spot the crux so quickly, Bunny. I have thought of your taking it round to your place first, under cloud of night; but we are bound to be seen even so, and on the whole it would look far less suspicious in broad daylight. It will take you some twelve or fifteen minutes to drive to your bank in a growler, so if you are here with one at a quarter to ten tomorrow morning, that will exactly meet the case. But you must have a hansom this minute if you mean to prepare the way with those notes this afternoon!'

It was only too like the Raffles of those days to dismiss a subject and myself in the same breath, with a sudden nod, and a brief grasp of the hand he was already holding out for mine. I had a great mind to take another of his cigarettes instead, for there were one or two points on which he had carefully omitted to enlighten me. Thus, I had still to learn the bare direction of his journey; and it was all that I could do to drag it from him as I stood buttoning my coat and gloves.

'Scotland,' he vouchsafed at last.

'At Easter,' I remarked.

'To learn the language,' he explained. 'I have no tongue but my own, you see, but I try to make up for it by cultivating every shade of that. Some of them have come in useful even to your knowledge, Bunny: what price my Cockney that night in St John's Wood? I can keep up my end in stage Irish, real Devonshire, very fair Norfolk, and three distinct Yorkshire dialects. But my good Galloway Scots might be better, and I mean to make it so.'

'You still haven't told me where to write to you.'

'I'll write to you first, Bunny.'

'At least let me see you off,' I urged at the door. 'I promise not to look at your ticket if you tell me the train!'

'The eleven-fifty from Euston.'

'Then I'll be with you by a quarter to ten.'

And I left him without further parley, reading his impatience in his face. Everything, to be sure, seemed clear enough without that fuller discussion which I loved and Raffles hated. Yet I thought we might at least have dined together, and in my heart I felt just the least bit hurt, until it occurred to me as I drove to count the notes in my cigarette-case. Resentment was impossible after that. The sum ran well into three figures, and it was plain that Raffles meant me to have a good time in his absence. So I told his lie with unction at my bank, and made due arrangements for the reception of his chest next morning. Then I repaired to our club, hoping he would drop in, and that we might dine together after all. In that I was disappointed. It was nothing, however, to the disappointment awaiting me at the Albany, when I arrived in my four-wheeler at the appointed hour next morning.

'Mr Raffles 'as gawn, sir,' said the porter, with a note of reproach in his confidential undertone. The man was a favourite with Raffles, who used him and tipped him with consummate tact, and he knew me only less well.

'Gone!' I echoed aghast. 'Where on earth to?'

'Scotland, sir.'

'Already?'

'By the eleven-fifty lawst night.'

'Last night! I thought he meant eleven-fifty this morning!'

'He knew you did, sir, when you never came, and he told me to tell you there was no such train.'

I could have rent my garments in mortification and annoyance with myself and Raffles. It was as much his fault as mine. But for his indecent haste in getting rid of me, his characteristic abruptness at the end, there would have been no misunderstanding or mistake.

'Any other message?' I inquired morosely.

'Only about the box, sir. Mr Raffles said as you was goin' to take chawge of it time he's away, and I've a friend ready to lend a 'and in getting it on the cab. It's a rare 'eavy 'un, but Mr Raffles an' me could lift it all right between us, so I dessay me an' my friend can.'

For my own part, I must confess that its weight concerned me less than the vast size of that infernal chest, as I drove with it past club and park at ten o'clock in the morning. Sit as far back as I might in the four-wheeler, I could conceal neither myself nor my connection with the huge iron-clamped case upon the roof: in my heated imagination its wood was glass through which all the world could see the guilty contents. Once an officious constable held up the traffic at our approach, and for a moment I put a bloodcurdling construction upon the simple ceremony. Low boys shouted after us – or if it was not after us, I thought it was – and that their cry was 'Stop thief!' Enough said of one of the most unpleasant cab-drives I ever had in life. *Horresco referens.*

At the bank, however, thanks to the foresight and liberality of Raffles, all was smooth water. I paid my cabman handsomely, gave a florin to the stout fellow in livery whom he helped with the chest, and could have pressed gold upon the genial clerk who laughed like a gentleman at my jokes about the Liverpool winners and the latest betting on the Family Plate. I was only disconcerted when he informed me that the bank gave no receipts for deposits of this nature. I am now aware that few London banks do. But it is pleasing to believe that at the time I looked – what I felt – as though all I valued upon earth were in jeopardy.

I should have got through the rest of that day happily enough, such was the load off my mind and hands, but for an extraordinary and most perplexing note received late at night from Raffles himself. He was a man who telegraphed freely, but seldom wrote a letter. Sometimes, however, he sent a scribbled line by special messenger; and overnight, evidently in the train, he had scribbled this one to post in the small hours at Crewe.

''Ware Prince of Professors! *He was in the offing when I left.* If slightest cause for uneasiness about bank, withdraw at once and keep in own rooms like good chap.

A.J.R.

'P.S. – Other reasons, as you shall hear.'

There was a nice nightcap for a puzzled head! I had made rather an evening of it, what with increase of funds and decrease of anxiety, but this cryptic admonition spoilt the remainder of my night. It had arrived by a late post, and I only wished that I had left it all night in my letter-box.

What exactly did it mean? And what exactly must I do? These were questions that confronted me with fresh force in the morning.

The news of Crawshay did not surprise me. I was quite sure that Raffles had been given good reason to bear him in mind before his journey, even if he had not again beheld the ruffian in the flesh. The ruffian and that journey might be more intimately connected than I had yet supposed. Raffles never told me all. Yet the solid fact held good – held better than ever – that I had seen his plunder safely planted in my bank. Crawshay himself could not follow it *there*. I was certain he had not followed my cab: in the acute self-consciousness induced by that abominable drive, I should have known it in my bones if he had. I thought of the porter's friend who had helped with the chest. No, I remembered him as well as I remembered Crawshay; they were quite different types.

To remove that vile box from the bank, on top of another cab, with no stronger pretext and no further instructions, was not to be thought of for a moment. Yet I did think of it, for hours. I was always anxious to do my part by Raffles; he had done more than his by me, not once or twice, today or yesterday, but again and again from the very first. I need not state the obvious reasons I had for fighting shy of the personal custody of his accursed chest. Yet he had run worse risks for me, and I wanted him to learn that he, too, could depend on a devotion not unworthy of his own.

In my dilemma I did what I have often done when at a loss for light and leading. I took hardly any lunch, but went to Northumberland Avenue and had a Turkish bath instead. I know nothing so cleansing to mind as well as body, nothing better calculated to put the finest possible edge on such judgment as one may happen to possess. Even Raffles, without an ounce to lose or a nerve to soothe, used to own a sensuous appreciation of the peace of mind and person to be gained in this fashion when all others failed. For me, the fun began before the boots were off one's feet: the muffled footfalls, the thin sound of the fountain, even the spent swathed forms upon the couches, and the whole clean, warm, idle atmosphere, were so much unction to my simpler soul. The half-hour in the hot-rooms I used to count but a strenuous step to a divine lassitude of limb and accompanying exaltation of intellect. And yet – and yet – it was in the hottest room of all, in a temperature of 270°

Fahrenheit, that the bolt fell from the *Pall Mall Gazette* which I had bought outside the bath.

I was turning over the hot, crisp pages, and positively revelling in my fiery furnace, when the following headlines and leaded paragraphs leapt to my eye with the force of a veritable blow: –

BANK ROBBERS IN THE WEST END

DARING AND MYSTERIOUS CRIME.

An audacious burglary and dastardly assault have been committed on the premises of the City and Suburban Bank in Sloane Street, W. From the details so far to hand, the robbery appears to have been deliberately planned and adroitly executed in the early hours of this morning.

A night-watchman named Fawcett states that between one and two o'clock he heard a slight noise in the neighbourhood of the lower strong-room, used as a repository for the plate and other possessions of various customers of the bank. Going down to investigate, he was instantly attacked by a powerful ruffian, who succeeded in felling him to the ground before an alarm could be raised.

Fawcett is unable to furnish any description of his assailant or assailants, but is of opinion that more than one were engaged in the commission of the crime. When the unfortunate man recovered consciousness, no trace of the thieves remained, with the exception of a single candle which had been left burning on the flags of the corridor.

The strong-room, however, had been opened, and it is feared the raid on the chests of plate and other valuables may prove to have been only too successful, in view of the Easter exodus, which the thieves had evidently taken

> into account. The ordinary banking chambers were not even visited; entry and exit are believed to have been effected through the coal-cellar, which is also situated in the basement. Up to the present the police have effected no arrest.

I sat practically paralysed by this appalling news; and I swear that, even in that incredible temperature, it was a cold perspiration in which I sweltered from head to heel. Crawshay, of course! Crawshay once more upon the track of Raffles and his ill-gotten gains! And once more I blamed Raffles himself: his warning had come too late: he should have wired to me at once not to take the box to the bank at all. He was a madman ever to have invested in so obvious and obtrusive a receptacle for treasure. It would serve Raffles right if that and no other was the box which had been broken into by the thieves.

Yet, when I considered the character of his treasure, I fairly shuddered in my sweat. It was a hoard of criminal relics. Suppose his chest had indeed been rifled, and emptied of every silver thing but one, that one remaining piece of silver, seen of men, was quite enough to cast Raffles into the outer darkness of penal servitude! And Crawshay was capable of it – of perceiving the insidious revenge – of taking it without compunction or remorse.

There was only one course for me. I must follow my instructions to the letter, and recover the chest at all hazards, or be taken myself in the attempt. If only Raffles had left me some address, to which I could have wired some word of warning! But it was no use thinking of that; for the rest, there was time enough up to four o'clock, and as yet it was not three. I determined to go through with my bath and make the most of it. Might it not be my last for years?

But I was past enjoying even a Turkish bath. I had not the patience for a proper shampoo, or sufficient spirit for the plunge. I weighed myself automatically, for that was a matter near my heart; but I forgot to give my man his sixpence until the reproachful intonation of his adieu recalled me to myself. And my couch in the cooling gallery – my favourite couch, in my favourite corner, which I had secured with gusto on coming in – it was a bed of thorns, with hideous visions of a plank-bed to follow!

I ought to be able to add that I heard the burglary discussed on adjacent couches before I left. I certainly listened for it, and was rather disappointed more than once when I had held my breath in vain. But this is the unvarnished record of an odious hour, and it passed without further aggravation from without; only, as I drove to Sloane Street, the news was on all the posters, and on one I read of 'a clue' which spelt for me a doom I was grimly resolved to share.

Already there was something in the nature of a 'run' upon the Sloane Street branch of the City and Suburban. A cab drove away with a chest of reasonable dimensions as mine drove up, while in the bank itself a lady was making a painful scene. As for the genial clerk who had roared at my jokes the day before, he was mercifully in no mood for any more, but, on the contrary, quite rude to me at sight.

'I've been expecting you all the afternoon,' said he. 'You needn't look so pale.'

'Is it safe?'

'That Noah's Ark of yours? Yes, so I hear; they'd just got to it when they were interrupted, and they never went back again.'

'Then it wasn't even opened?'

'Only just begun on, I believe.'

'Thank God!'

'You may; we don't,' growled the clerk. 'The manager says he believes your chest was at the bottom of it all.'

'How could it be?' I asked, uneasily.

'By being seen on the cab a mile off, and followed,' said the clerk.

'Does the manager want to see *me*?' I asked boldly.

'Not unless you want to see him,' was the blunt reply. 'He's been at it with others all the afternoon, and they haven't all got off as cheap as you.'

'Then my silver shall not embarrass you any longer,' said I, grandly. 'I meant to leave it if it was all right, but after all you have said I certainly shall not. Let your man or men bring up the chest at once. I dare say they also have been "at it with others all the afternoon", but I shall make this worth their while.'

I did not mind driving through the streets with the thing this time. My present relief was far too overwhelming as yet to admit of pangs and fears for the immediate future. No summer sun had ever shone more brightly than that rather watery one of early April. There was a green-and-gold dust of buds and shoots on the trees as we passed the park. I felt greater things sprouting in my heart. Hansoms passed with schoolboys just home for the Easter holidays, four-wheelers outward bound with bicycles and perambulators atop; none that rode in them were half so happy as I, with the great load on my cab, but the greater one off my heart.

At Mount Street it just went into the lift; that was a stroke of luck; and the lift-man and I between us carried it into my flat. It seemed a featherweight to me now. I felt a Samson in the exaltation of that hour. And I will not say what my first act was when I found myself alone with my white elephant in the middle of the room; enough that the syphon was still doing its work when the glass slipped through my fingers to the floor.

'Bunny!'

It was Raffles. Yet for a moment I looked about me quite in vain. He was not at the window; he was not at the open door. And yet Raffles it had been, or at all events his voice, and that bubbling over with fun and satisfaction, be his body where it might. In the end I dropped my eyes, and there was his living face in the middle of the lid of the chest, like that of the saint upon its charger.

But Raffles was alive, Raffles was laughing as though his vocal cords would snap, there was neither tragedy nor illusion in the apparition of Raffles. A life-size Jack-in-the-box, he had thrust his head through a lid within the lid, cut by himself between the two iron bands that ran round the chest like the straps of a portmanteau. He must have been busy at it when I found him pretending to pack, if not far into that night, for it was a very perfect piece of work; and even as I stared without a word, and he crouched laughing in my face, an arm came squeezing out, keys in hand; one was turned in either of the two great padlocks, the whole lid lifted, and out stepped Raffles like the conjurer he was.

'So you were the burglar!' I exclaimed at last.'Well, I am just as glad I didn't know.'

He had wrung my hand already, but at this he fairly mangled it in his.

'You dear little brick,' he cried, 'that's the one thing of all things I longed to hear you say! How could you have behaved as you've done if you had known? How could any living man? How could you have acted, as the polar star of all the stages could not have acted in your place? Remember that I have heard a lot, and as good as seen as much as I've heard. Bunny, I don't know where you were greatest: at the Albany, here, or at your bank!'

'I don't know where I was most miserable,' I rejoined, beginning to see the matter in a less perfervid light. 'I know you don't credit me with much finesse, but I would undertake to be in the secret and to do quite as well; the only difference would be in my own peace of mind, which, of course, doesn't count.'

But Raffles wagged away with his most charming and disarming smile; he was in old clothes, rather tattered and torn, and more than a little grimy as to the face and hands, but, on the surface, wonderfully little the worse for his experience. And, as I say, his smile was the smile of the Raffles I loved best.

'You would have done your damnedest, Bunny! There is no limit to your heroism; but you forget the human equation in the pluckiest of the plucky. I couldn't afford to forget it, Bunny; I couldn't afford to give a point away. Don't talk as though I hadn't trusted you! I trusted my very life to your loyal tenacity. What do you suppose would have happened to me if you had let me rip in that strong-room? Do you think I would ever have crept out and given myself up? Yes, I'll have a peg for once; the beauty of all laws is in the breaking, even of the kind we make unto ourselves.'

I had a Sullivan for him, too; and in another minute he was spread out on my sofa, stretching his cramped limbs with infinite gusto, a cigarette between his fingers, a yellow bumper at hand on the chest of his triumph and my tribulation.

'Never mind when it occurred to me, Bunny; as a matter of fact, it was only the other day, when I had decided to go away for the real reasons I have already given you. I may have made more of them to you than I do in my own mind, but at ail events they exist. And I really did want the telephone and the electric light.'

'But where did you stow the silver before you went?'

'Nowhere; it was my luggage – a portmanteau, cricket-bag, and suit-case full of very little else – and by the same token I left the lot at Euston, and one of us must fetch them this evening.'

'I can do that,' said I. 'But did you really go all the way to Crewe?'

'Didn't you get my note? I went all the way to Crewe to post you those few lines, my dear Bunny! It's no use taking trouble if you don't take trouble enough: I wanted you to show the proper set of faces at the bank and elsewhere, and I know you did. Besides, there was an up-train four minutes after mine got in. I simply posted my letter in Crewe station, and changed from one train to the other.'

'At two in the morning!'

'Nearer three, Bunny. It was after seven when I slunk in with the *Daily Mail*. The milk had beaten me by a short can. But even so I had two very good hours before you were due.'

'And to think,' I murmured, 'how you deceived me there!'

'With your own assistance,' said Raffles, laughing. 'If you had looked it up you would have seen there was no such train in the morning, and I never said there was. But I meant you to be deceived, Bunny, and I won't say I didn't – it was all for the sake of the side! Well, when you carted me away with such laudable despatch, I had rather an uncomfortable half-hour, but that was all just then. I had my candle, I had matches, and lots to read. It was quite nice in that strong room until a very unpleasant incident occurred.'

'Do tell me, my dear fellow!'

'I must have another Sullivan – thank you – and a match. The unpleasant incident was steps outside and a key in the lock! I was disporting myself on the lid of the trunk at the time. I had barely time to knock out my light and slip down behind it. Luckily it was only another box of sorts: a jewel-case, to be more precise; you shall see the contents in a moment. The Easter exodus has done me even better than I dared to hope.'

His words reminded me of the *Pall Mall Gazette*, which I had brought in my pocket from the Turkish bath. I fished it out, all wrinkled and bloated by the heat of the hottest room, and handed it to Raffles with my thumb upon the leaded paragraphs.

'Delightful!' said he when he had read them. 'More thieves than one, and the coal-cellar of all places as a way in! I certainly tried to give it that appearance. I left enough candle-grease there to make those coals burn bravely. But it looked up into a blind backyard, Bunny, and a boy of eight couldn't have squeezed through the trap. Long may that theory keep them happy at Scotland Yard!'

'But what about the fellow you knocked out?' I asked. 'That was not like you, Raffles.'

Raffles blew pensive rings as he lay back on my sofa, his black hair tumbled on the cushion, his pale profile as sharp against the light as though slashed out with the scissors.

'I know it wasn't, Bunny,' he said, regretfully. 'But things like that, as the poet will tell you, are really inseparable from victories like mine. It had taken me a couple of hours to break out of that strong-room; I was devoting a third to the harmless task of simulating the appearance of having broken in; and it was then I heard the fellow's stealthy step. Some might have stood their ground and killed him; more would have bolted into a worse corner than they were in already. I left my candle where it was, crept to meet the poor devil, flattened myself against the wall, and let him have it as he passed. I acknowledge the foul blow, but here's evidence that it was mercifully struck. The victim has already told his tale.'

As he drained his glass, but shook his head when I wished to replenish it, Raffles showed me the flask which he had carried in his pocket: it was still nearly full; and I found that he had otherwise provisioned himself over the holidays. On either Easter Day or Bank Holiday, had I failed him, it had been his intention to make the best escape he could. But the risk must have been enormous, and it filled my glowing skin to think that he had not relied on me in vain.

As for his gleanings from such jewel-cases as were spending the Easter recess in the strong-room of my bank, without going into rhapsodies or even particulars on the point, I may mention that they realised enough for me to join Raffles on his deferred holiday in Scotland, besides enabling him to play more regularly for Middlesex in the ensuing summer than had been the case for several seasons. In fine, this particular exploit entirely justified itself in my eyes, in spite of the superfluous (but invariable) secretiveness which I could seldom help resenting in my heart. I never thought less of it than in the present instance; and my one mild reproach was on the subject of the phantom Crawshay.

'You let me think he was in the air again,' I said. 'But it wouldn't surprise me to find that you had never heard of him since the day of his escape through your window.'

'I never even thought of him, Bunny, until you came to see me the day before yesterday, and put him into my head with your first words. The whole point was to make you as genuinely anxious about the plate as you must have seemed all along the line.'

'Of course I see your point,' I rejoined, 'but mine is that you laboured it. You needn't have written me a downright lie about the fellow.'

'Nor did I, Bunny.'

'Not about the "prince of professors" being "in the offing" when you left?'

'My dear Bunny, but so he was!' cried Raffles. 'Time was when I was none too pure an amateur. But after this I take leave to consider myself a professor of the professors. And I should like to see one more capable of skippering their side!'

3

THE REST CURE

I had not seen Raffles for a month or more, and I was sadly in need of his advice. My life was being made a burden to me by a wretch who had obtained a bill of sale over the furniture in Mount Street, and it was only by living elsewhere that I could keep the vulpine villain from my door. This cost ready money, and my balance at the bank was sorely in need of another lift from Raffles. Yet, had he been in my shoes, he could not have vanished more effectually than he had done, both from the face of the town and from the ken of all who knew him.

It was late in August; he never played first-class cricket after July, when a scholastic understudy took his place in the Middlesex eleven. And in vain did I scour my *Field* and my *Sportsman* for the country-house matches with which he wilfully preferred to wind up his season; the matches were there, but never the magic name of A.J. Raffles. Nothing was known of him at the Albany; he had left no instructions about his letters, either there or at the club. I began to fear that some evil had overtaken him. I scanned the features of captured criminals in the illustrated Sunday papers; on each occasion I breathed again; nor was anything worthy of Raffles going on. I will not deny that I was less anxious on his account than on my own. But it was a double relief to me when he gave a first characteristic sign of life.

I had called at the Albany for the fiftieth time, and returned to Piccadilly in my usual despair, when a street sloucher sidled up to me in furtive fashion, and inquired if my name was what it is.

' 'Cause this 'ere's for you,' he rejoined to my affirmative, and with that I felt a crumpled note in my palm.

It was from Raffles. I smoothed out the twisted scrap of paper, and on it were just a couple of lines in pencil –

'Meet me in Holland Walk at dark tonight. Walk up and down till I come.

'A.J.R.'

That was all! Not another syllable, after all these weeks, and the few words scribbled in a wild caricature of his scholarly and dainty hand! I was no longer to be alarmed by this sort of thing; it was all so like the Raffles I loved least; and to add to my indignation, when at length I looked up from the mysterious missive, the equally mysterious messenger had disappeared in a manner worthy of the whole affair. He was, however, the first creature I espied under the tattered trees of Holland Walk that evening.

'Seen 'im yet?' he inquired confidentially, blowing a vile cloud from his horrid pipe.

'No, I haven't; and I want to know where you've seen him,' I replied sternly. 'Why did you run away like that the moment you had given me his note?'

'Orders, orders,' was the reply. 'I ain't such a juggins as to go agen a toff as makes it worf while to do as I'm bid an' 'old me tongue.'

'And who may you be?' I asked, jealously. 'And what are you to Mr Raffles?'

'You silly ass, Bunny, don't tell all Kensington that I'm in town!' replied my tatterdemalion, shooting up and smoothing out into a merely shabby Raffles. 'Here, take my arm – I'm not so beastly as I look. But neither am I in town, nor in England, nor yet on the face of the earth, for all that's known of me to a single soul but you.'

'Then where are you,' I asked, 'between ourselves?'

'I've taken a house near here for the holidays, where I'm going in for a Rest Cure of my own prescription. Why? Oh, for lots of reasons, my dear Bunny; among others, I have long had a wish to grow my own beard: under the next lamp-post you will agree that it's training on very nicely. Then, you mayn't know it, but there's a canny man at Scotland Yard who has had a quiet eye on me longer than I like. I thought it about time to have an eye on him, and I stared him in the face outside the Albany this very morning. That was when I saw you go in, and scribbled a line to give you when you came out. If he had caught us talking he would have spotted me at once.'

'So you are lying low out here!'

'I prefer to call it my Rest Cure,' returned Raffles, 'and it's really nothing else. I've got a furnished house at a time when no one else would have dreamt of taking one in town; and my very neighbours don't know I'm there, though I'm bound to say there are hardly any of them at home. I don't keep a servant, and do everything for myself. It's the next best fun to a desert island. Not that I make much work, for I'm really resting, but I haven't done so much solid reading for years. Rather a joke, Bunny: the man whose house I've taken is one of her Majesty's Inspectors of Prisons and his study's a storehouse of criminology. It has been quite amusing to lie on one's back and have a good look at one's self as others fondly imagine that they see one.'

'But surely you get some exercise?' I asked; for he was leading me at a good rate through the leafy byways of Campden Hill, and his step was as springy and as light as ever.

The best exercise I ever had in my life,' said Raffles, 'and you would never live to guess what it is. It's one of the reasons why I went in for this seedy kit. I follow cabs! Yes, Bunny, I turn out about dusk and meet the expresses at Euston or King's Cross; that is, of course, I loaf outside and pick my cab, and often run my three or four miles for a bob or less. And it not only keeps you in the very pink: if you're good they let you carry the trunks upstairs; and I've taken notes from the inside of more than one commodious residence which will come in useful in the autumn. In fact, Bunny, what with these new Rowton Houses, my beard, and my otherwise well-spent holiday, I hope to have quite a good autumn season before the erratic Raffles turns up in town.'

I felt it high time to wedge in a word about my own far less satisfactory affairs. But it was not necessary for me to recount half my troubles. Raffles could be as full of himself as many a worse man, and I did not like his society the less for these human outpourings. They had rather the effect of putting me on better terms with myself, though bringing him down to my level for the time being. But his egoism was not even skin-deep; it was rather a cloak, which Raffles could cast off quicker than any man I ever knew, as he did not fail to show me now.

'Why, Bunny, this is the very thing!' he cried. 'You must come and stay with me, and we'll lie low side by side. Only remember it really is a Rest Cure. I want to keep literally as quiet as I was without you. What do you say to forming ourselves at once into a practically Silent Order? You agree? Very well, then, here's the street and that's the house.'

It was ever such a quiet little street, turning out of one of those which climb right over the pleasant hill. One side was monopolised by the garden wall of an ugly but enviable mansion standing in its own ground; opposite were a solid file of smaller but taller houses; on neither side were there many windows alight, nor a solitary soul on the pavement or in the road. Raffles led the way to one of the small tall houses. It stood immediately behind a lamp-post, and I could not but notice that a love-lock of Virginia creeper was trailing almost to the step, and that the bow-window on the ground floor was closely shuttered. Raffles admitted himself with his latchkey, and

I squeezed past him into a very narrow hall. I did not hear him shut the door, but we were no longer in the lamplight, and he pushed softly past me in his turn.

'I'll get a light,' he muttered as he went; but to let him pass I had leant against some electric switches, and while his back was turned I tried one of these without thinking. In an instant hall and staircase were flooded with light; in another Raffles was upon me in a fury, and all was dark once more. He had not said a word, but I heard him breathing through his teeth.

Nor was there anything to tell me now. The mere flash of electric light, upon a hall of chaos and uncarpeted stairs, and on the face of Raffles as he sprang to switch it off, had been enough even for me.

'So this is how you have taken the house,' said I, in his own undertone. '"Taken" is good; "taken" is beautiful!'

'Did you think I'd done it through an agent?' he snarled. 'Upon my word, Bunny, I did you the credit of supposing you saw the joke all the time!'

'Why shouldn't you take a house,' I asked, 'and pay for it?'

'Why should I,' he retorted, 'within three miles of the Albany? Besides, I should have had no peace; and I meant every word I said about my Rest Cure.'

'You are actually staying in a house where you've broken in to steal?'

'Not to steal, Bunny! I haven't stolen a thing. But staying here I certainly am, and having the most complete rest a busy man could wish.'

'There'll be no rest for me!'

Raffles laughed as he struck a match. I had followed him into what would have been the back dining-room in the ordinary little London house; the Inspector of Prisons had converted it into a separate study by filling the folding doors with bookshelves, which I scanned at once for the congenial works of which Raffles had spoken. I was not able to carry my examination very far. Raffles had lighted a candle, stuck (by its own grease) in the crown of an opera hat, which he opened the moment the wick caught. The light thus struck the ceiling in an oval shaft, which left the rest of the room almost as dark as it had been before.

'Sorry, Bunny!' said Raffles, sitting on one pedestal of a desk from which the top had been removed, and setting his makeshift lantern on the other. 'In broad daylight, when it can't be spotted from the outside, you shall have as much artificial light as you like. If you want to do some writing, that's the top of the desk on end against the mantelpiece. You'll never have a better chance so far as interruption goes. But no midnight oil or electricity! You observe that their last care was to fix up these shutters; they appear to have taken the top off the desk to get at 'em without standing on it; but the beastly things wouldn't go all the way up, and the strip they leave would give us away to the backs of the other houses if we lit up after dark. Mind that telephone! If you touch the receiver they will know at the exchange that the house is not empty, and I wouldn't put it past the Colonel to have told them exactly how long he was going to be away. He's pretty particular: look at the strips of paper to keep the dust off his precious books!'

'Is he a Colonel?' I asked, perceiving that Raffles referred to the absentee householder.

'Of sappers,' he replied, 'and a V.C. into the bargain, confound him! Got it at Rorke's Drift; prison governor or inspector ever since; favourite recreation, what do you think? Revolver shooting! You can read all about him in his own *Who's Who*. A devil of a chap to tackle, Bunny, when he's at home!'

'And where is he now?' I asked uneasily. 'And how do you know he isn't on his way home?'

'Switzerland,' replied Raffles, chuckling: 'he wrote one too many labels, and was considerate enough to leave it behind for our guidance. Well, hardly any one comes back from

Switzerland at the beginning of September, you know; and nobody ever thinks of coming back before the servants. When they turn up they won't get in. I keep the latch jammed, but the servants will think it's jammed itself, and while they're gone for the locksmith we shall walk out like gentlemen – if we haven't done so already.'

'As you walked in, I suppose?'

Raffles shook his head in the dim light to which my sight was growing inured.

'No, Bunny, I regret to say I came in through the dormer window. They were painting next door but one. I never did like ladder-work, but it takes less time than picking a lock in the broad light of a street lamp.'

'So they left you a latchkey as well as everything else!'

'No, Bunny, I was just able to make that for myself. I am playing at *Robinson Crusoe*, not *The Swiss Family Robinson*. And now, my dear Friday, if you will kindly take off those boots, we can explore the island before we turn in for the night.'

The stairs were very steep and narrow, and they creaked alarmingly as Raffles led the way up, with the single candle in the crown of the Colonel's hat. He blew it out before we reached the halflanding, where a naked window stared upon the backs of the houses in the next road, but lit it again at the drawing-room door. I just peeped in upon a semi-grand swathed in white and a row of water-colours mounted in gold. An excellent bathroom broke our journey to the second floor.

'I'll have one tonight,' said I, taking heart of a luxury unknown in my last sordid sanctuary.

'You'll do no such thing,' snapped Raffles. 'Have the goodness to remember that our island is one of a group inhabited by hostile tribes. You can fill the bath quietly if you try, but it empties under the study window, and makes the very devil of a noise about it. No, Bunny, I bale out every drop, and pour it away through the scullery sink, so you will kindly consult me before you turn a tap. Here's your room; hold the light outside while I draw the curtains; it's the old chap's dressing-room. Now you can bring the glim. How's that for a jolly wardrobe? And look at his coats on their cross-trees inside: dapper old dog, shouldn't you say? Mark the boots on the shelf above, and the little brass rail for his ties! Didn't I tell you he was particular? And wouldn't he simply love to catch us at his kit?'

'Let's only hope it would give him an apoplexy,' said I, shuddering.

'I shouldn't build on it,' said Raffles. 'That's a big man's trouble, and neither you nor I could get into the old chap's clothes. But come into the best bedroom, Bunny. You won't think me selfish if I don't give it up to you? Look at this, my boy, look at this! It's the only one I use in all the house.'

I had followed him into a good room, with ample windows closely curtained, and he had switched on the light in a hanging lamp at the bedside. The rays fell from a thick green funnel in a plateful of strong light upon a table deep in books. I noticed several volumes of the *Invasion of the Crimea*.

'That's where I rest the body and exercise the brain,' said Raffles. 'I have long wanted to read my Kinglake from A to Z, and I manage about a volume a night. There's a style for you, Bunny! I love the punctilious thoroughness of the whole thing; one can understand its appeal to our careful Colonel. His name, did you say? Crutchley, Bunny – Colonel Crutchley, R.E., V.C.'

'We'd put his valour to the test!' said I, feeling more valiant myself after our tour of inspection.

'Not so loud on the stairs,' whispered Raffles. 'There's only one door between us and – '

Raffles stood still at my feet, and well he might! A deafening double-knock had resounded through the empty house; and to add to the utter horror of the moment, Raffles instantly blew out the light. I heard my heart pounding. Neither of us breathed. We were on our way down to the first landing, and for a moment we stood like mice; then Raffles heaved a deep sigh, and in the depths I heard the gate swing home.

'Only the postman, Bunny! He will come now and again, though they have obviously left instructions at the post-office. I hope the old Colonel will let them have it when he gets back. I confess it gave me a turn.'

'Turn!' I gasped. 'I must have a drink, if I die for it.'

'My dear Bunny, that's no part of my Rest Cure.'

'Then good-bye! I can't stand it; feel my forehead; listen to my heart! Crusoe found a footprint, but he never heard a doubleknock at the street door!'

'"Better live in the midst of alarms," ' quoted Raffles, '"than dwell in this horrible place." I must confess we get it both ways, Bunny. Yet I've nothing but tea in the house.'

'And where do you make that? Aren't you afraid of smoke?'

'There's a gas-stove in the dining-room.'

'But surely to goodness,' I cried, 'there's a cellar lower down!'

'My dear good Bunny,' said Raffles, 'I've told you already that I didn't come in here on business. I came in for the Cure. Not a penny will these people be the worse, except for their washing and their electric light, and I mean to leave enough to cover both items.'

'Then,' said I, 'since Brutus is such a very honourable man, we will borrow a bottle from the cellar, and replace it before we go.'

Raffles slapped me softly on the back, and I knew that I had gained my point. It was often the case when I had the presence of heart and mind to stand up to him. But never was little victory of mine quite so grateful as this. Certainly it was a very small cellar, indeed a mere cupboard under the kitchen stairs, with a most ridiculous lock. Nor was this cupboard overstocked with wine. But I made out a jar of whisky, a shelf of Zeltinger, another of claret, and a short one at the top which presented a little battery of golden-leafed necks and corks. Raffles set his hand no lower. He examined the labels, while I held folded hat. and naked light.

'Mumm, '84!' he whispered. 'G.H. Mumm, and A.D. 1884! I am no wine-bibber, Bunny, as you know, but I hope you appreciate the specifications as I do. It looks to me like the only bottle, the last of its case, and it does seem a bit of a shame; but more shame for the miser who hoards in his cellar what was meant for mankind! Come, Bunny, lead the way. This baby is worth nursing. It would break my heart if anything happened to it now!'

So we celebrated my first night in the furnished house; and I slept beyond belief, slept as I never was to sleep there again. But it was strange to hear the milkman in the early morning, and the postman knocking his way along the street an hour later, and to be passed over by one destroying angel after another! I had come down early enough, and watched through the drawing-room blind the cleansing of all the steps in the street but ours. Yet Raffles had evidently been up some time; the house seemed far purer than overnight, as though he had managed to air it room by room; and from the one with the gas-stove there came a frizzling sound that fattened the heart.

I only would I had the pen to do justice to the week I spent indoors on Campden Hill! It might make amusing reading; the reality for me was far removed from the realm of amusement. Not that I was denied many a laugh of suppressed heartiness when Raffles and I were together. But half our time we very literally saw nothing of each other. I need not say whose fault that was. He would be quiet; he was in ridiculous and offensive earnest about his egregious Cure. Kinglake he would read by the hour together, day and night, by the hanging lamp, lying upstairs on the best bed. There was daylight enough for me in the drawing-room below; and there I would sit immersed in criminous tomes, weakly fascinated, until I shivered and shook in my stocking soles. Often I longed to do something hysterically desperate, to rouse Raffles and bring the street about our ears; once I did bring him about mine by striking a single note on the piano, with the soft pedal down. His neglect of me seemed wanton at the time. I have long realised that he was only wise to maintain silence at the expense of perilous amenities, and as fully justified in those secret and solitary sorties which made bad blood in my veins. He was far cleverer than I at getting in and out; but even had I been his match for stealth and wariness, my company would have doubled every risk. I admit now that he treated me with quite as much sympathy as common caution would permit. But at the time I took it so badly as to plan a small revenge.

What with his flourishing beard and the increasing shabbiness of the only suit he had brought with him to the house, there was no denying that Raffles had now the advantage of a permanent disguise. That was another of his excuses for leaving me as he did, and it was the one I was determined to remove. On a morning, therefore, when I awoke to find him flown again, I proceeded to execute a plan which I had already matured in my mind. Colonel Crutchley was a married man; there were no signs of children in the house; on the other hand, there was much evidence that the wife was a woman of fashion. Her dresses overflowed the wardrobe and her room; large flat cardboard boxes were to be found in every corner of the upper floors. She was a tall woman; I was not too tall a man. Like Raffles, I had not shaved on Campden Hill. That morning, however, I did my best with a very fair razor which the Colonel had left behind in my room; then I turned out the lady's wardrobe and the cardboard boxes, and took my choice.

I have fair hair, and at the time it was rather long. With a pair of Mrs Crutchley's tongs, and a discarded hair-net, I was able to produce an almost immodest fringe. A big, black hat with a wintry feather completed a head-dress as unseasonable as my skating skirt and feather boa; of course, the good lady had all her summer frocks away with her in Switzerland. This was all the more annoying from the fact that we were having a very warm September, so I was not sorry to hear Raffles return as I was busy adding a layer of powder to my heated countenance. I listened a moment on the landing, but as he went into the study I determined to complete my toilet in every detail. My idea was first to give him the fright he deserved, and secondly to show him that I was quite as fit to move abroad as he. It was, however, I confess, a pair of the Colonel's gloves that I was buttoning as I slipped down to the study even more quietly than usual. The electric light was on, as it generally was by day, and under it stood as formidable a figure as ever I encountered in my life of crime.

Imagine a thin but extremely wiry man, past middle age, brown and bloodless as any crab-apple, but as coolly truculent and as casually alert as Raffles at his worst. It was, it could only be, the fire-eating and prison-inspecting Colonel himself! He was ready for me, a revolver in his hand, taken, as I could see, from one of those locked drawers in the pedestal desk with which Raffles had refused to tamper; the drawer was open, and a bunch of keys depended from the lock. A grim smile crumpled up the parchment face, so that one eye was puckered out of sight; the other was propped open by an eye-glass, which, however, dangled on its string when I appeared.

'A woman, begad!' the warrior exclaimed. 'And where's the man, you scarlet hussy?'

Not a word could I utter. But, in my horror and my amazement, I have no sort of doubt that I acted the part I had assumed in a manner I never should have approached in happier circumstances.

'Come, come, my lass,' cried the old oak veteran, 'I'm not going to put a bullet through you, you know! You tell me all about it, and it'll do you more good than harm. There, I'll put the nasty thing away, and – God bless me if the brazen wench hasn't squeezed into the wife's kit!'

A squeeze it happened to have been, and in my emotion it felt more of one than ever; but his sudden discovery had not heightened the veteran's animosity against me. On the contrary, I caught a glint of humour through his gleaming glass, and he proceeded to pocket his revolver like the gentleman he was.

'Well, well, it's lucky I looked in,' he continued. 'I only came round on the off-chance of letters, but if I hadn't you'd have had another week in clover. Begad, though, I saw your handwriting the moment I'd got my nose inside! Now just be sensible, and tell me where your good man is.'

I had no man. I was alone, had broken in alone. There was not a soul in the affair (much less the house) except myself. So much I stuttered out in tones too hoarse to betray me on the spot. But the old man of the world shook a hard old head.

'Quite right not to give away your pal,' said he. 'But I'm not one of the marines, my dear, and you mustn't expect me to swallow all that. Well, if you won't say, you won't, and we must just send for those who will.'

In a flash I saw his fell design. The telephone directory lay open on one of the pedestals. He must have been consulting it when he heard me on the stairs; he had another look at it now, and that gave me my opportunity. With a presence of mind rare enough in me to excuse the boast, I flung myself upon the instrument in the corner, and hurled it to the ground with all my might. I was myself sent spinning into the opposite corner at the same instant. But the instrument happened to be a standard of the more elaborate pattern, and I flattered myself that I had put the delicate engine out of action for the day.

Not that my adversary took the trouble to ascertain. He was looking at me strangely in the electric light, standing intently on his guard, his right hand in the pocket where he had dropped his revolver. And I – I hardly knew it – but I caught up the first thing handy for self-defence, and was brandishing the bottle which Raffles and I had emptied in honour of my arrival on this fatal scene.

'Be shot if I don't believe you're the man himself!' cried the Colonel, shaking an armed fist in my face. 'You young wolf in sheep's clothing! Been at my wine, of course! Put down that bottle; down with it this instant, or I'll drill a tunnel through your middle. I thought so! Begad, sir, you shall pay for this! Don't you give me an excuse for potting you now, or I'll jump at the chance! My last bottle of '84 – you miserable blackguard – you unutterable beast!'

He had browbeaten me into his own chair in his own corner; he was standing over me, empty bottle in one hand, revolver in the other, and murder itself in the purple puckers of his raging face. His language I will not even pretend to indicate: his skinny throat swelled and trembled with the monstrous volleys. He could smile at my appearance in his wife's clothes; he would have had my blood for the last bottle of his best champagne. His eyes were not hidden now; they needed no eyeglass to prop them open; large with fury, they started from the livid mask. I watched nothing else. I could not understand why they should start out as they did. I did not try. I say I watched nothing else – until I saw the face of Raffles over the unfortunate officer's shoulder.

Raffles had crept in unheard while our altercation was at its height, had watched his opportunity, and stolen on his man unobserved by either of us. While my own attention was completely engrossed, he had seized the Colonel's pistol-hand and twisted it behind the Colonel's back until his eyes bulged out as I have endeavoured to describe. But the fighting man had some fight in him still; and scarcely had I grasped the situation when he hit out venomously behind with the bottle, which was smashed to bits on Raffles's shin. Then I threw my strength into the scale; and before many minutes we had our officer gagged and bound in his chair. But it was not one of our bloodless victories. Raffles had been cut to the bone by the broken glass; his leg bled wherever he limped; and the fierce eyes of the bound man followed the wet trail with gleams of sinister satisfaction.

I thought I had never seen a man better bound or better gagged. But the humanity seemed to have run out of Raffles with his blood. He tore up table-cloths, he cut down blind-cloths, he brought the dust-sheets from the drawing-room, and multiplied every bond. The unfortunate man's legs were lashed to the legs of his chair, his arms to its arms, his thighs and back fairly welded to the leather. Either end of his own ruler protruded from his bulging cheeks – the middle was hidden by his moustache – and the gag kept in place by remorseless lashings at the back of his head. It was a spectacle I could not bear to contemplate at length, while from the first I found myself physically unable to face the ferocious gaze of those implacable eyes. But Raffles only laughed at my squeamishness, and flung a dust-sheet over man and chair; and the stark outline drove me from the room.

It was Raffles at his worst, Raffles as I never knew him before or after – a Raffles mad with pain and rage, and desperate as any other criminal in the land. Yet he had struck no brutal blow, he had uttered no disgraceful taunt, and probably not inflicted a tithe of the pain he had himself to bear. It is true that he was flagrantly in the wrong, his victim as laudably in the right. Nevertheless, granting the original sin of the situation, and given the unforeseen development, even I failed to see how Raffles could have combined greater humanity with any regard for our joint safety; and had his barbarities ended here, I for one should not have considered them an extraordinary aggravation of an otherwise minor offence. But in the broad daylight of the bathroom, which had a ground-glass window but no blind, I saw at once the serious nature of his wound and of its effect upon the man.

'It will maim me for a month,' said he; 'and if the V.C. comes out alive, the wound he gave may be identified with the wound I've got.'

The V.C.! There, indeed, was an aggravation to one illogical mind. But to cast a moment's doubt upon the certainty of his coming out alive!

'Of course he'll come out,' said I. 'We must make up our minds to that.'

'Did he tell you he was expecting the servants or his wife? If so, of course, we must hurry up.'

'No, Raffles, I'm afraid he's not expecting anybody. He told me, if he hadn't looked in for letters, we should have had the place to ourselves another week. That's the worst of it.'

Raffles smiled as he secured a regular puttee of dust-sheeting. No blood was coming through.

'I don't agree, Bunny,' said he. 'It's quite the best of it, if you ask me.'

'What, that he should die the death?'

'Why not?'

And Raffles stared me out with a hard and merciless light in his clear blue eyes – a light that chilled the blood.

'If it's a choice between his life and our liberty, you're entitled to your decision and I'm entitled to mine, and I took it before I bound him as I did,' said Raffles. 'I'm only sorry I took so much trouble if you're going to stay behind and put him in the way of releasing himself before he gives up the ghost. Perhaps you will go and think it over while I wash my bags and dry 'em at the gas-stove. It will take me at least an hour, which will just give me time to finish the last volume of Kinglake.'

Long before he was ready to go, however, I was waiting in the hall, clothed indeed, but not in a mind which I care to recall.

Once or twice I peered into the dining-room, where Raffles sat before the stove, without letting him hear me. He too was ready for the street at a moment's notice; but a steam ascended from his left leg, as he sat immersed in his red volume. Into the study I never went again; but Raffles did, to restore to its proper shelf this and every other book he had taken out, and so destroy that clue to the manner of man who had made himself at home in the house. On his last visit I heard him whisk off the dust-sheet; then he waited a minute; and when he came out it was to lead the way into the open air as though the accursed house belonged to him.

'We shall be seen!' I whispered at his heels. 'Raffles, Raffles, there's a policeman at the corner!'

'I know him intimately,' replied Raffles, turning, however, the other way. 'He accosted me on Monday, when I explained that I was an old soldier of the Colonel's regiment, who came in every few days to air the place and send on any odd letters. You see, I have always carried one or two about me, re-directed to that address in Switzerland, and when I showed them to him it was all right. But after that it was no use listening at the letter-box for a clear coast, was it?'

I did not answer; there was too much to exasperate in these prodigies of cunning which he could never trouble to tell me at the time. And I knew why he had kept his latest feats to himself: unwilling to trust me outside the house, he had systematically exaggerated the dangers of his own walks abroad; and when to these injuries he added the insult of a patronising compliment on my late disguise, I again made no reply.

'What's the good of your coming with me?' he asked, when I had followed him across the main stream of Notting Hill.

'We may as well sink or swim together,' I answered sullenly.

'Yes? Well, I'm going to swim into the provinces, have a shave on the way, buy a new kit piecemeal, including a cricket-bag (which I really want), and come limping back to the Albany with the same old strain in my bowling leg. I needn't add that I have been playing country-house cricket for the last month under an alias; it's the only decent way to do it when one's county has need of one. That's my itinerary, Bunny; but I really can't see why you should come with me.'

'We may as well swing together,' I growled.

'As you will, my dear fellow,' replied Raffles. 'But I begin to dread your company on the drop!'

I shall hold my pen on that provincial tour. Not that I joined Raffles in any of the little enterprises with which he beguiled the breaks in our journey; our last deed in London was far too great a weight upon my soul. I could see that gallant officer in his chair, see him at every hour of the day and night, now with his indomitable eyes meeting mine ferociously, now a stark outline underneath a sheet. The vision darkened my day and gave me sleepless nights. I was with our victim in all his agony; my mind would only leave him for that gallows of which Raffles had said true things in jest. No, I could not face so vile a death lightly, but I could meet it, somehow, better than I could endure a guilty suspense. In the watches of the second night I made up my mind to meet it half-way, that very morning, while still there might be time to save the life that we had left in jeopardy. And I got up early to tell Raffles of my resolve.

His room in the hotel where we were staying was littered with clothes and luggage new enough for any bridegroom; I lifted the locked cricket-bag, and found it heavier than a cricket-bag has any right to be. But in the bed Raffles was sleeping like an infant, his shaven self once more. And when I shook him he awoke with a smile.

'Going to confess, eh, Bunny? Well, wait a bit; the local police won't thank you for knocking them up at this hour. And I bought a late edition which you ought to see; that must be it on the floor. You have a look in the stop-press column, Bunny.'

I found the place with a sunken heart, and this is what I read: –

WEST END OUTRAGE.

Colonel Crutchley, R.E., V.C., has been the victim of a dastardly outrage at his residence, Peter Street, Campden Hill. Returning unexpectedly to the house, which had been left untenanted during the absence of the family abroad, it was found occupied by two ruffians, who overcame and secured the distinguished officer by the exercise of considerable violence. When discovered through the intelligence of the Kensington police, the gallant victim was gagged and bound hand and foot, and in an advanced stage of exhaustion.

'Thanks to the Kensington police,' observed Raffles, as I read the last words aloud in my horror. 'They can't have gone when they got my letter.'

'Your letter?'

'I printed them a line while we were waiting for our train at Euston. They must have got it that night, but they can't have paid any attention to it till yesterday morning. And when they do, they take all the credit, and give me no more than you did, Bunny!'

I looked at the curly head upon the pillow, at the smiling, handsome face under the curls. And at last I understood.

'So all the time you never meant it!'

'Slow murder? You should have known me better. A few hours' enforced Rest Cure was the worst I wished him.'

'You might have told me, Raffles!'

'That may be, Bunny, but you ought certainly to have trusted me!'

4

THE CRIMINOLOGISTS' CLUB

'But who are they, Raffles, and where's their house? There's no such club on the list in Whitaker.'

'The Criminologists, my dear Bunny, are too few for a local habitation, and too select to tell their name in Gath. They are merely so many solemn students of contemporary crime, who meet and dine periodically at each other's clubs or houses.'

'But why in the world should they ask us to dine with them?'

And I brandished the invitation which had brought me hotfoot to the Albany: it was from the Right Hon the Earl of Thornaby, K.G.; and it requested the honour of my company at dinner, at Thornaby House, Park Lane, to meet the members of the Criminologists' Club. That in itself was a disturbing compliment : judge then of my dismay on learning that Raffles had been invited too.

'They have got it into their heads', said he, 'that the gladiatorial element is the curse of most modern sport. They tremble especially for the professional gladiator. And they want to know whether my experience tallies with their theory.'

'So they say!'

'They quote the case of a league player, *sus per coll.*, and any number of suicides. It really is rather in my public line.'

'In yours, if you like, but not in mine,' said I. 'No, Raffles, they've got their eye on us both, and mean to put us under the microscope, or they would never have pitched on *me*.'

Raffles smiled upon my perturbation.

'I almost wish you were right, Bunny. It would be even better fun than I mean to make it as it is. But it may console you to hear that it was I who gave them your name. I told them you were a far keener criminologist than myself. I am delighted to hear they have taken my hint, and that we are to meet at their gruesome board.'

'If I accept,' said I, with the austerity he deserved.

'If you don't,' rejoined Raffles, 'you will miss some sport after both our hearts. Think of it, Bunny! These fellows meet to wallow in all the latest crimes; we wallow with them as though we knew no more about it than themselves. Perhaps we don't, for few criminologists have a soul above murder; and I quite expect to have the privilege of lifting the discussion into our own higher walk. They shall give their morbid minds to the fine art of burgling, for a change; and while we're about it, Bunny, we may as well extract their opinion of our noble selves. As authors, as collaborators, we will sit with the flower of our critics, and find our own level in the expert eye. It will be a piquant experience, if not an invaluable one; if we are sailing too near the wind, we are sure to hear about it, and can trim our yards accordingly. Moreover, we shall get a very good dinner into the bargain, or our noble host will belie a European reputation.'

'Do you know him?' I asked.

'We have a pavilion acquaintance, when it suits my lord,' replied Raffles, chuckling. 'But I know all about him. He was President one year of the M.C.C., and we never had a better. He knows the game, though I believe he never played cricket in his life. But then he knows most things, and has never done any of them. He has never even married, and never opened his lips in the House of Lords. Yet they say there is no better brain in the august assembly, and he certainly made us a wonderful speech last time the Australians were over. He has read everything, and (to his credit in these days) never written a line. All round he is a whale for theory and a sprat for practice – but he looks quite capable of both at crime!'

I now longed to behold this remarkable peer in the flesh, and with the greater curiosity since another of the things which he evidently never did was to have his photograph published for the benefit of the vulgar. I told Raffles that I would dine with him at Lord Thornaby's, and he nodded as though I had not hesitated for a moment. I see now how deftly he had disposed of my reluctance. No doubt he had thought it all out before: his little speeches look sufficiently premeditated as I set them down at the dictates of an excellent memory. Let it, however, be borne in mind that Raffles did not talk exactly like a Raffles book: he said the things, but he did not say them in so many consecutive breaths. They were punctuated by puffs from his eternal cigarette, and the punctuation was often in the nature of a line of asterisks, while he took a silent turn up and down his room. Nor was he ever more deliberate than when he seemed more nonchalant and spontaneous. I came to see it in the end. But these were early days, in which he was more plausible to me than I can hope to render him to another human being.

And I saw a good deal of Raffles just then; it was, in fact, the one period at which I can remember his coming round to see me more frequently than I went round to him. Of course he would come at his own odd hours, often just as one was dressing to go out and dine, and I can even remember finding him there when I returned, for I had long since given him a key of the flat. It was the inhospitable month of February, and I can recall more than one cosy evening when we discussed anything and everything but our own malpractices; indeed, there were none to discuss just then. Raffles, on the contrary, was showing himself with some industry in the most respectable society, and by his advice I used the club more than ever.

'There is nothing like it at this time of year,' said he. 'In the summer I have my cricket to provide me with decent employment in the sight of men. Keep yourself before the public from morning to night, and they'll never think of you in the still small hours.'

Our behaviour, in fine, had so long been irreproachable that I rose without misgiving on the morning of Lord Thornaby's dinner to the other Criminologists and guests. My chief anxiety was to arrive under the ægis of my brilliant friend, and I had begged him to pick me up on his way; but at five minutes to the appointed hour there was no sign of Raffles or his cab. We were bidden at a quarter to eight for eight o'clock, so after all I had to hurry off alone.

Fortunately, Thornaby House is almost at the end of my street that was; and it seemed to me another fortunate circumstance that the house stood back, as it did and does, in its own august courtyard; for as I was about to knock, a hansom came twinkling in behind me, and I drew back, hoping it was Raffles at the last moment. It was not, and I knew it in time to melt from the porch, and wait one more minute in the shadows, since others were as late as I. And out jumped these others, chattering in stage whispers as they paid their cab.

'Thornaby has a bet about it with Freddy Vereker, who can't come, I hear. Of course, it won't be lost or won tonight. But the dear man thinks he's been invited as a cricketer!'

'I don't believe he's the other thing,' said a voice as brusque as the first was bland. 'I believe it's all bunkum. I wish I didn't, but I do!'

'I think you'll find it's more than that,' rejoined the other, as the doors opened and swallowed the pair.

I flung out limp hands and smote the air. Raffles bidden to what he had well called this 'gruesome board', not as a cricketer, but, clearly, as a suspected criminal! Raffles wrong all the time, and I right for once in my original apprehension! And still no Raffles in sight – no Raffles to warn – no Raffles, and the clocks striking eight!

Well may I shirk the psychology of such a moment, for my belief is that the striking clocks struck out all power of thought and feeling, and that I played my poor part the better for that blessed surcease of intellectual sensation. On the other hand, I was never more alive to the purely objective impressions of any hour of my existence, and of them the memory is startling to this day. I hear my mad knock at the double doors; they fly open in the middle, and it is like some sumptuous and solemn rite. A long slice of silken-legged lackey is seen on either hand; a very prelate of a butler bows a benediction from the sanctuary steps. I breathe more freely when I reach a book-lined library where a mere handful of men do not overflow the Persian rug before the fire. One of them is Raffles, who is talking to a large man with the brow of a demi-god and the eyes and jowl of a degenerate bull-dog. And this is our noble host.

Lord Thornaby stared at me with inscrutable stolidity as we shook hands, and at once handed me over to a tall ungainly man whom he addressed as Ernest, but whose surname I never learnt. Ernest in turn introduced me, with a shy and clumsy courtesy, to the two remaining guests. They were the pair who had driven up in the hansom; one turned out to be Kingsmill, Q.C.; the other I knew at a glance, from his photographs, as Parrington, the back- woods novelist. They were admirable foils to each other, the barrister being plump and dapper, with a Napoleonic cast of countenance, and the author one of the shaggiest dogs I have ever seen in evening clothes. Neither took much stock of me, but both had an eye on Raffles as I exchanged a few words with each in turn. Dinner, however, was immediately announced, and the six of us had soon taken our places round a brilliant little table stranded in a great dark room.

I had not been prepared for so small a party, and at first I felt relieved. If the worst came to the worst, I was fool enough to say in my heart, they were but two to one. But I was soon sighing for that safety which the adage associates with numbers. We were far too few for the confidential duologue with one's neighbour in which I, at least, would have taken refuge from the perils of a general conversation. And the general conversation soon resolved itself into an attack, so subtly concerted, and so artistically delivered, that I could not conceive how Raffles should ever know it for an attack, and that against himself, or how to warn him of his peril. But to this day I am less convinced that I also was honoured by the suspicions of the club; it may have been so, and they may have ignored me for the bigger game.

It was Lord Thornaby himself who fired the first shot, over the very sherry. He had Raffles on his right hand, and the backwoodsman of letters on his left. Raffles was hemmed in by the law on his right, while I sat between Parrington and Ernest, who took the foot of the table, and seemed a sort of feudatory cadet of the noble house. But it was the motley lot of us that my lord addressed, as he sat back blinking his baggy eyes.

'Mr Raffles', said he, 'has been telling me about that poor fellow who suffered the extreme penalty last March. A great end, gentlemen, a great end! It is true that he had been unfortunate enough to strike a jugular vein, but his own end should take its place among the most glorious traditions of the gallows. You tell them, Mr Raffles: it will be as new to my friends as it is to me.'

'I tell the tale as I heard it last time I played at Trent Bridge; it was never in the papers, I believe,' said Raffles, gravely. 'You may remember the tremendous excitement over the Test Matches out in Australia at the time: it seems that the result of the crucial game was expected on the condemned man's last day on earth, and he couldn't rest until he knew it. We pulled it off, if you recollect, and he said it would make him swing happy.'

'Tell 'em what else he said!' cried Lord Thornaby, rubbing his podgy hands.

'The chaplain remonstrated with him on his excitement over a game at such a time, and the convict is said to have replied, "Why, it's the first thing they'll ask me at the other end of the drop!"

'The story was new even to me, but I had no time to appreciate its points. My concern was to watch its effect upon the other members of the party. Ernest, on my left, doubled up with laughter, and tittered and shook for several minutes. My other neighbour, more impressionable by temperament, winced first, and then worked himself into a state of enthusiasm which culminated in an assault upon his shirt-cuff with a joiner's pencil. Kingsmill, Q.C., beaming tranquilly on Raffles, seemed the one least impressed, until he spoke.

'I am glad to hear that,' he remarked in a high bland voice. 'I thought that man would die game.'

'Did you know anything about him, then?' inquired Lord Thornaby.

'I led for the Crown,' replied the barrister, with a twinkle. 'You might almost say that I measured the poor man's neck.'

The point must have been quite unpremeditated; it was not the less effective for that. Lord Thornaby looked askance at the callous silk. It was some moments before Ernest tittered and Parrington felt for his pencil; and in the interim I had made short work of my hock, though it was Johannisberger. As for Raffles, one had but to see his horror to feel how completely he was off his guard.

'In itself, I have heard, it was not a sympathetic case?' was the remark with which he broke the general silence.

'Not a bit.'

'That must have been a comfort to you,' said Raffles, dryly.

'It would have been to me,' vowed our author, while the barrister merely smiled. 'I should have been very sorry to have had a hand in hanging Peckham and Solomons the other day.'

'Why Peckham and Solomons?' inquired my lord.

'They never meant to kill that old lady.'

'But they strangled her in her bed with her own pillow-case!'

'I don't care,' said the uncouth scribe. 'They didn't break in for that. They never thought of scragging her. The foolish old person would make a noise, and one of them tied too tight. I call it jolly bad luck on them.'

'On quiet, harmless, well-behaved thieves,' added Lord Thornaby, 'in the unobtrusive exercise of their humble avocation.'

And, as he turned to Raffles with his puffy smile, I knew that we had reached that part of the programme which had undergone rehearsal: it had been perfectly timed to arrive with the champagne, and I was not afraid to signify my appreciation of that small mercy. But Raffles laughed so quickly at his lordship's humour, and yet with such a natural restraint, as to leave no doubt that he had taken kindly to my own old part, and was playing the innocent inimitably in his turn, by reason of his very innocence. It was a poetic judgment on old Raffles, and in my momentary enjoyment of the novel situation I was able to enjoy some of the good things of this rich man's table. The saddle of mutton more than justified its place in the menu; but it had not spoilt me for my wing of pheasant, and I was even looking forward to a sweet, when a further remark from the literary light recalled me from the table to its talk.

'But, I suppose,' said he to Kingsmill, 'it's "many a burglar *you've* restored to his friends and his relations"?'

'Let us say many a poor fellow who has been charged with burglary,' replied the cheery Q.C. 'It's not quite the same thing, you know, nor is "many" the most accurate word. I never touch criminal work in town.'

'It's the only kind I should care about,' said the novelist, eating jelly with a spoon.

'I quite agree with you,' our host chimed in. 'And of all the criminals one might be called upon to defend, give me the enterprising burglar.'

'It must be the breeziest branch of the business,' remarked Raffles while I held my breath.

But his touch was as light as gossamer, and his artless manner a triumph of even his incomparable art. Raffles was alive to the danger at last. I saw him refuse more champagne, even as I drained my glass again. But it was not the same danger to us both. Raffles had no reason to feel surprise or alarm at such a turn in a conversation frankly devoted to criminology; it must have seemed as inevitable to him as it was sinister to me, with my fortuitous knowledge of the suspicions that were entertained. And there was little to put him on his guard in the touch of his adversaries, which was only less light than his own.

'I am not very fond of Mr Sikes,' announced the barrister, like a man who had got his cue.

'But he was prehistoric,' rejoined my lord. 'A lot of blood has flowed under the razor since the days of Sweet William.'

'True; we have had Peace,' said Parrington, and launched out into such glowing details of that criminal's last moments that I began to hope the diversion might prove permanent. But Lord Thornaby was not to be denied.

'William and Charles are both dead monarchs,' said he. 'The reigning king in their department is the fellow who gutted poor Danby's place in Bond Street.'

There was a guilty silence on the part of the three conspirators – for I had long since persuaded myself that Ernest was not in their secret – and then my blood froze.

'I know him well,' said Raffles, looking up.

Lord Thornaby stared at him in consternation. The smile on the Napoleonic countenance of the barrister looked forced and frozen for the first time during the evening. Our author, who was nibbling cheese from a knife, left a bead of blood upon his beard. The futile Ernest alone met the occasion with a hearty titter.

'What!' cried my lord. '*You know the thief?*'

'I wish I did,' rejoined Raffles, chuckling. 'No, Lord Thornaby, I only meant the jeweller, Danby. I go to him when I want a wedding present.'

I heard three deep breaths drawn as one, before I drew my own.

'Rather a coincidence,' observed our host, dryly, 'for I believe you also know the Milchester people, where Lady Melrose had her necklace stolen a few months afterwards.'

'I was staying there at the time,' said Raffles, eagerly. No snob was ever quicker to boast of basking in the smile of the great.

'We believe it to be the same man,' said Lord Thornaby, speaking apparently for the Criminologists' Club, and with much less severity of voice.

'I only wish I could come across him,' continued Raffles, heartily. 'He's a criminal much more to my mind than your murderers who swear on the drop or talk cricket in the condemned cell!'

'He might be in the house now,' said Lord Thornaby, looking Raffles in the face. But his manner was that of an actor in an unconvincing pan and a mood to play it gamely to the bitter end; and he seemed embittered, as even a rich man may be in the moment of losing a bet.

'What a joke if he were!' cried the Wild West writer.

'*Absit omen!*' murmured Raffles, in better taste.

'Still, I think you'll find it's a favourite time,' argued Kingsmill, Q.C. 'And it would be quite in keeping with the character of this man, so far as it is known, to pay a little visit to the President of the Criminologists' Club, and to choose the evening on which he happens to be entertaining the other members.'

There was more conviction in this sally than in that of our noble host; but this I attributed to the trained and skilled dissimulation of the bar. Lord Thornaby, however, was not to be amused by the elaboration of his own idea, and it was with some asperity that he called upon the butler, now solemnly superintending the removal of the cloth.

'Leggett! Just send upstairs to see if all the doors are open and the rooms in proper order. That's an awful idea of yours, Kingsmill, or of mine!' added my lord, recovering the courtesy of his order by an effort that I could follow. 'We should look fools! I don't know which of us it was, by the way, who seduced the rest from the main stream of blood into this burglarious backwater. Are you familiar with De Quincey's masterpiece on "Murder as a Fine Art", Mr Raffles?'

'I believe I once read it,' replied Raffles, doubtfully.

'You must read it again,' pursued the earl. 'It is the last word on a great subject; all we can hope to add is some baleful illustration or bloodstained footnote, not unworthy of De Quincey's text. Well, Leggett?'

The venerable butler stood wheezing at his elbow. I had not hitherto observed that the man was an asthmatic.

'I beg your lordship's pardon, but I think your lordship must have forgotten.'

The voice came in rude gasps, but words of reproach could scarcely have achieved a finer delicacy.

'Forgotten, Leggett! Forgotten what, may I ask?'

'Locking your lordship's door behind your lordship, my lord,' stuttered the unfortunate Leggett, in the short spurts of a winded man, a few stertorous syllables at a time. 'Been up myself, my lord. Bedroom door – dressing-room door – both locked inside!'

But by this time the noble master was in worse case than the man. His fine forehead was a tangle of livid cords; his baggy jowl filled out like a balloon. In another second he had abandoned his place as our host, and fled the room; and in yet another we had forgotten ours as his guests, and rushed headlong at his heels.

Raffles was as excited as any of us now: he outstripped us all. The cherubic little lawyer and I had a fine race for the last place but one, which I secured, while the panting butler and his satellites brought up a respectful rear. It was our unconventional author, however, who was the first to volunteer his assistance and advice.

'No use pushing, Thornaby!' cried he. 'If it's been done with a wedge and gimlet, you may smash the door, but you'll never force it. Is there a ladder in the place?'

'There's a rope-ladder somewhere, in case of fire, I believe,' said my lord, vaguely, as he rolled a critical eye over our faces. 'Where is it kept, Leggett?'

'William will fetch it, my lord.'

And a pair of noble calves went flashing to the upper regions.

'What's the good of bringing it down?' cried Parrington, who had thrown back to the wilds in his excitement. 'Let him hang it out of the window above your own, and let me climb down and do the rest. I'll undertake to have one or other of these doors open in two twos!'

The fastened doors were at right angles on the landing which we filled between us. Lord Thornaby smiled grimly on the rest of us, when he had nodded and dismissed the author like a hound from the leash.

'It's a good thing we know something about our friend Parrington,' said my lord. 'He takes more kindly to all this than I do, I can tell you.'

'It's grist to his mill,' said Raffles, charitably.

'Exactly! We shall have the whole thing in his next book.'

'I hope to have it at the Old Bailey first,' remarked Kingsmill, Q.C.

'Refreshing to find a man of letters such a man of action too!'

It was Raffles who said this, and the remark seemed rather trite, for him, but in the tone there was a something that just caught my private ear. And for once I understood: the officious attitude of Parrington, without being seriously suspicious in itself, was admirably calculated to put a previously suspected person in a grateful shade. This literary adventurer had elbowed Raffles out of the limelight, and gratitude for the service was what I had detected in Raffles's voice. No need to say how grateful I felt myself. But my gratitude was shot with flashes of unwonted insight. Parrington was one of those who suspected Raffles, or, at all events, one who was in the secret of those suspicions. What if he had traded on the suspect's presence in the house? What if he were a deep villain himself, and *the* villain of this particular piece? I had made up my mind about him, and that in a tithe of the time I take to make it up as a rule, when we heard my man in the dressing-room. He greeted us with an impudent shout; in a few moments the door was open, and there stood Parrington, flushed and dishevelled, with a grimlet in one hand and a wedge in the other.

Within was a scene of eloquent disorder. Drawers had been pulled out, and now stood on end, their contents heaped upon the carpet. Wardrobe doors stood open; empty stud-cases strewed the floor; a clock, tied up in a towel, had been tossed into a chair at the last moment. But a long tin lid protruded from an open cupboard in one corner; and one had only to see Lord Thornaby's wry face behind the lid to guess that it was bent over a somewhat empty tin trunk.

'What a rum lot to steal!' said he, with a twitch of humour at the corners of his canine mouth. 'My peer's robes, with coronet complete!'

We rallied round him in a seemly silence. I thought our scribe would put in his word. But even he either feigned or felt a proper awe.

'You may say it was a rum place to keep 'em,' continued Lord Thornaby. 'But where would you gentlemen stable your white elephants? And these were elephants as white as snow; by Jove, I'll job them for the future!'

And he made merrier over his loss than any of us could have imagined the minute before; but the reason dawned on me a little later, when we all trooped downstairs, leaving the police in possession of the theatre of crime. Lord Thornaby linked arms with Raffles as he led the way. His step was lighter, his gaiety no longer sardonic; his very looks had improved. And I divined the load that had been lifted from the hospitable heart of our host.

'I only wish', said he, 'that this brought us any nearer to the identity of the gentleman we were discussing at dinner; for, of course, we owe it to all our instincts to assume that it was he.'

'I wonder!' said old Raffles, with a foolhardy glance at me.

'But I'm sure of it, my dear sir,' cried my lord. 'The audacity is his and his alone. I look no further than the fact of his honouring me on the one night of the year when I endeavour to entertain my brother Criminologists. That's no coincidence, sir, but a deliberate irony, which would have occurred to no other criminal mind in England.'

'You may be right,' Raffles had the sense to say this time, though I flattered myself it was my face that made him.

'What is still more certain', resumed our host, 'is that no other criminal in the world would have crowned so delicious a conception with so perfect an achievement. I feel sure the Inspector will agree.'

The policeman in command had knocked and been admitted to the library as Lord Thornaby spoke.

'I didn't hear what you said, my lord.'

'Merely that the perpetrator of this amusing outrage can be no other than the swell mobsman who relieved Lady Melrose of her necklace and poor Danby of half of his stock a year or two ago.'

'I believe your lordship has hit the nail on the head.'

'The man who took the Thimblely diamonds and returned them to Lord Thimblely, you know.'

'Perhaps he'll treat your lordship the same.'

'Not he! I don't mean to cry over *my* spilt milk. I only wish the fellow joy of all he had time to take. Anything fresh upstairs, by the way?'

'Yes, my lord: the robbery took place between a quarter-past eight and the half-hour.'

'How on earth do you know?'

'The clock that was tied up in the towel had stopped at twenty past.'

'Have you interviewed my man?'

'I have, my lord. He was in your lordship's rooms until close on the quarter, and all was as it should be when he left it.'

'Then do you suppose the burglar was in hiding in the house?'

'It's impossible to say, my lord. He's not in the house now, for he could only be in your lordship's bedroom or dressing-room, and we have searched every inch of both.'

Lord Thornaby turned to us when the Inspector had retreated, caressing his peaked cap.

'I told him to clear up these points first,' he explained, jerking his head towards the door. 'I had reason to think my man had been neglecting his duties up there. I am glad to find myself mistaken.'

I ought to have been no less glad to see my own mistake. My suspicions of our officious author were thus proved to have been as wild as himself. I owed the man no grudge, and yet in my human heart I felt vaguely disappointed. My theory had gained colour from his behaviour ever since he had admitted us to the dressing-room; it had changed all at once from the familiar to the morose; and only now was I just enough to remember that Lord Thornaby, having tolerated those familiarities as long as they were connected with useful service, had administered a relentless snub the moment that service had been well and truly performed.

But if Parrington was exonerated in my mind, so also was Raffles reinstated in the regard of those who had entertained a far graver and more dangerous hypothesis. It was a miracle of good luck, a coincidence among coincidences, which had whitewashed him in their sight at the very moment when they were straining the expert eye to sift him through and through. But the miracle had been performed, and its effect was visible in every face and audible in every voice. I except Ernest, who could never have been in the secret; moreover, that gay Criminologist was palpably shaken by his first little experience of crime. But the other three vied among themselves to do honour where they had done injustice. I heard Kingsmill, Q.C., telling Raffles the best time to catch him at chambers, and promising a seat in court for any trial he might ever like to hear. Parrington spoke of a presentation set of his books, and in doing homage to Raffles made his peace with our host. As for Lord Thornaby, I did overhear the name of the Athenæum Club, a reference to his friends on the committee, and a whisper (as I verily believed) of Rule II.

The police were still in possession when we went our several ways, and it was all that I could do to drag Raffles up to my rooms, though, as I have said, they were just round the corner. He consented at last as a lesser evil than talking of the burglary in the street; and in my rooms I lost no time in telling him of his late danger and my own dilemma, of the few words I had overheard in the beginning, of the thin ice on which he had cut fancy figures without a crack. It was all very well for him. He had never realised his peril. But let him think of me – listening, watching, yet unable to lift a finger – unable to say one warning word.

Raffles suffered me to finish, but a weary sigh followed the last symmetrical whiff of a Sullivan which he flung into my fire before he spoke.

'No, I won't have another, thank you. I'm going to talk to you, Bunny. Do you really suppose I didn't see through these wiseacres from the first?'

I flatly refused to believe he had done so before that evening. Why had he never mentioned his idea to me? It had been quite the other way, as I indignantly reminded Raffles. Did he mean me to believe he was the man to thrust his head into the lion's mouth for fun? And what point would there be in dragging me there to see the fun?

'I might have wanted you, Bunny. I very nearly did.'

'For my face?'

'It has been my fortune before tonight, Bunny. It has also given me more confidence than you are likely to believe at this time of day. You stimulate me more than you think.'

'Your gallery and your prompter's box in one?'

'Capital, Bunny! But it was no joking matter with me either, my dear fellow; it was touch-and-go at the time. I might have called on you at any moment, and it was something to know I should not have called in vain.'

'But what to do Raffles?'

'Fight our way out and bolt!' he answered, with a mouth that meant it, and a fine gay glitter of the eyes.

I shot out of my chair.

'You don't mean to tell me you had a hand in the job?'

'I had the only hand in it, my dear Bunny.'

'Nonsense! You were sitting at table at the time. No, but you may have taken some other fellow into the show. I always thought you would!'

'One's quite enough, Bunny,' said Raffles dryly; he leant back in his chair and took out another cigarette. And I accepted of yet another from his case; for it was no use losing one's temper with Raffles; and his incredible statement was not, after all, to be ignored.

'Of course,' I went on, 'if you really had brought off this thing on your own, I should be the last to criticise your means of reaching such an end. You have not only scored off a far superior force, which had laid itself out to score off you, but you have put them in the wrong about you, and they'll eat out of your hand for the rest of their days. But don't ask me to believe that you've done all this alone! By George!' I cried, in a sudden wave of enthusiasm, 'I don't care how you've done it, or who has helped you. It's the biggest thing you ever did in your life!'

And certainly I had never seen Raffles look more radiant, or better pleased with the world and himself, or nearer that elation which he usually left to me.

'Then you shall hear all about it, Bunny, if you'll do what I ask you.'

'Ask away, old chap, and the thing's done.'

'Switch off the electric lights.'

'All of them?'

'I think so.'

'There, then.'

'Now go to the back window and up with the blind.'

'Well?'

'I'm coming to you. Splendid! I never had a look so late as this. It's the only window left alight in the house!'

His cheek against the pane, he was pointing slightly downward and very much aslant through a long lane of mews to a little square light like a yellow tile at the end. But I had opened the window and leant out before I saw it for myself.

'You don't mean to say that's Thornaby House?'

I was not familiar with the view from my back windows.

'Of course I do, you rabbit! Have a look through your own race-glass. It has been the most useful thing of all.'

But before I had the glass in focus, more scales had fallen from my eyes; and now I knew why I had seen so much of Raffles these last few weeks, and why he had always come between seven and eight in the evening, and waited at this very window, with these very glasses at his eyes. I saw through them sharply now. The one lighted window pointed out by Raffles came tumbling into the dark circle of my vision. I could not see into the actual room, but the shadows of those within were quite distinct on the lowered blind. I even thought a black thread still dangled against the square of light. It was, it must be, the window to which the intrepid Parrington had descended from the one above.

'Exactly!' said Raffles in answer to my exclamation. 'And that's the window I have been watching these last few weeks. By daylight you can see the whole lot above the ground floor on this side of the house; and by good luck one of them is the room in which the master of the house arrays himself in all his nightly glory. It was easily spotted by watching at the right time. I saw him shaved one morning before you were up. In the evening his valet stays behind to put things straight; and that has been the very mischief. In the end I had to find out something about the man, and wire to him from his girl to meet her outside at eight o'clock. Of course he pretends he was at his post at the time: that I foresaw, and did the poor fellow's work before my own. I folded and put away every garment before I permitted myself to rag the room.'

'I wonder you had time!'

'It took me one more minute, and it put the clock on exactly fifteen. By the way, I did that literally, of course, in the case of the clock they found. It's an old dodge, to stop a clock and alter the time; but you must admit that it looked as though one had wrapped it up all ready to cart away. There was thus any amount of *prima-facie* evidence of the robbery having taken place when we were all at table. As a matter of fact, Lord Thornaby left his dressing-room one minute, his valet followed him the minute after, and I entered the minute after that.'

'Through the window?'

'To be sure. I was waiting below in the garden. You have to pay for your garden in town, in more ways than one. You know the wall, of course, and that jolly old postern? The lock was beneath contempt.'

'But what about the window? It's on the first floor, isn't it?'

Raffles took up the cane which he had laid down with his overcoat. It was a stout bamboo with a polished ferrule. He unscrewed the ferrule, and shook out of the cane a diminishing series of smaller canes, exactly like a child's fishing-rod, which I afterwards found to have been their former state. A double hook of steel was now produced and quickly attached to the tip of the top joint; then Raffles undid three buttons of his waistcoat; and lapped round and round his waist was the finest of Manilla ropes, with the neatest of foot-loops at regular intervals.

'Is it necessary to go any further?' asked Raffles when he had unwound the rope. 'This end is made fast to that end of the hook, the other half of the hook fits over anything that comes its way, and you leave your rod dangling while you swarm up your line. Of course, you must know what you've got to hook on to; but a man who has had a porcelain bath fixed in his dressing-room is the man for me. The pipes were all outside, and fixed to the wall in just the right place. You see I had made a reconnaissance by day in addition to many by night; it would hardly have been worth while constructing my ladder on chance.'

'So you made it on purpose!'

'My dear Bunny,' said Raffles, as he wound the hemp girdle round his waist once more, 'I never did care for ladder-work, but I always said that if I ever used a ladder it should be the best of its kind yet invented. This one may come in useful again.'

'But how long did the whole thing take you?'

'From mother earth to mother earth? About five minutes tonight, and one of those was spent in doing another man's work.'

'What!' I cried. 'You mean to tell me you climbed up and down, in and out, and broke into that cupboard and that big tin box, and wedged up the doors and cleared out with a peer's robes and all the rest of it in five minutes?'

'Of course I don't, and of course I didn't.'

'Then what do you mean, and what did you do?'

'Made two bites at the cherry. Bunny! I had a dress rehearsal in the dead of last night, and it was then I took the swag. Our noble friend was snoring next door all the time, but the effort may still stand high among my small exploits, for I not only took ail I wanted, but left the whole place exactly as I found it, and shut things after me like a good little boy. All that took a good deal longer; tonight I had simply to rag the room a bit, sweep up some studs and links, and leave ample evidence of having boned these rotten robes *tonight*. That, if you come to think of it, was what you writing chaps would call the quintessential Q.E.F. I have not only shown these dear Criminologists that I couldn't possibly have done this trick, but that there's some other fellow who could and did, and whom they've been perfect asses to confuse with me.'

You may figure me as gazing on Raffles all this time in mute and rapt amazement. But I had long been past that pitch. If he had told me now that he had broken into the Bank of England, or the Tower, I should not have disbelieved him for a moment. I was prepared to go home with him to the Albany and find the Regalia under his bed. And I took down my overcoat as he put on his. But Raffles would not hear of my accompanying him that night.

'No, my dear Bunny, I am short of sleep and fed up with excitement. You mayn't believe it – you may look upon me as a plaster devil – but those five minutes you wot of were rather too crowded even for my taste. The dinner was nominally at a quarter to eight, and I don't mind telling you now that I counted on twice as long as I had. But no one came until twelve minutes to, and so our host took his time. I didn't want to be the last to arrive, and I was in the drawing-room five minutes before the hour. But it was a quicker thing than I care about, when all is said.'

And his last word on the matter, as he nodded and went his way, may well be mine; for one need be no criminologist, much less a member of the Criminologists' Club, to remember what Raffles did with the robes and coronet of the Right Hon. the Earl of Thornaby, K.G. He did with them exactly what he might have been expected to do by the gentlemen with whom we had foregathered; and he did it in a manner so characteristic of himself as surely to remove from their minds the last aura of the idea that he and himself were the same person. Carter Paterson was out of the question, and any labelling or addressing to be avoided on obvious grounds. But Raffles stabled the white elephants in the cloak-room at Charing Cross – and sent Lord Thornaby the ticket.

5

THE FIELD OF PHILIPPI

Nipper Nasmyth had been head of our school when Raffles was Captain of Cricket. I believe he owed his nickname entirely to the popular prejudice against a day-boy; and in view of the special reproach which the term carried in my time, as also of the fact that his father was one of the School Trustees, partner in a banking firm of four resounding surnames, and manager of the local branch, there can be little doubt that the stigma was undeserved. But we did not think so then, for Nasmyth was unpopular with high and low, and appeared to glory in the fact. A swollen conscience caused him to see and hear even more than was warranted by his position, and his uncompromising nature compelled him to act on whatsoever he heard or saw: a savage custodian of public morals, he had in addition a perverse enthusiasm for lost causes, loved a minority for its own sake, and untenable tenets for theirs. Such, at all events, was my impression of Nipper Nasmyth, after my first term, which was also his last. I had never spoken to him, but I had heard him speak with extraordinary force and fervour in the school debates. I carried a clear picture of his unkempt hair, his unbrushed coat, his dominant spectacles, his dogmatic jaw. And it was I who knew the combination at a glance, after years and years, when the fateful whim seized Raffles to play once more in the Old Boys' Match, and his will took me down with him to participate in the milder festivities of Founder's Day.

It was, however, no ordinary occasion. The Bicentenary loomed but a year ahead, and a movement was on foot to mark the epoch with an adequate statue of our pious founder. A special meeting was to be held at the School House, and Raffles had been specially invited by the new Head Master, a man of his own standing, who had been in the eleven with him up at Cambridge. Raffles had not been near the old place for years; but I had never gone down since the day I left; and I will not dwell on the emotions which the once familiar journey awakened in my unworthy bosom. Paddington was alive with Old Boys of all ages – but very few of ours – if not as lively as we used to make it when we all landed back for the holidays. More of us had moustaches and cigarettes and 'loud' ties. That was all. Yet of the throng, though two or three looked twice and thrice at Raffles, neither he nor I knew a soul until we had to change at the junction near our journey's end, when, as I say, it was I who recognised Nipper Nasmyth at sight.

The man was own son of the boy we both remembered. He had grown a ragged beard and a moustache that hung about his face like a neglected creeper. He was stout and bent and older than his years. But he spurned the platform with a stamping stride which even I remembered in an instant, and which was enough for Raffles before he saw the man's face.

'The Nipper it is!' he cried. 'I could swear to that walk in a pantomime procession! See the independence in every step: that's his heel on the neck of the oppressor: it's the Nonconformist Conscience in baggy breeches. I must speak to him, Bunny. There was a lot of good in the old Nipper, though he and I did bar each other.'

And in a moment he had accosted the man by the boy's nickname, obviously without thinking of an affront which few would have read in that hearty open face and hand.

'My name's Nasmyth,' snapped the other, drawing himself up to glare.

'Forgive me,' said Raffles, undeterred. 'One remembers a nickname and forgets all it never used to mean. Shake hands, my dear fellow! I'm Raffles. It must be fifteen years since we met.'

'At least,' replied Nasmyth, coldly; but he could no longer refuse Raffles his hand. 'So you are going down', he sneered, 'to this great gathering?' And I stood listening at my distance, as though still in the Middle Fourth.

'Rather!' cried Raffles. 'I'm afraid I have let myself lose touch, but I mean to turn over a new leaf. I suppose that it isn't necessary in your case, Nasmyth?'

He spoke with an enthusiasm rare indeed in him: it had grown upon Raffles in the train: the spirit of his boyhood had come rushing back at fifty miles an hour. He might have been following some honourable calling in town; he might have snatched this brief respite from a distinguished but exacting career. I am convinced that it was I alone who remembered at that moment the life we were really leading at that time. With me there walked this skeleton through every waking hour that was to follow. I shall endeavour not to refer to it again. Yet it should not be forgotten that my skeleton was always there.

'It certainly is not necessary in my case,' replied Nasmyth, still as stiff as any poker. 'I happen to be a Trustee.'

'Of the school?'

'Like my father before me.'

'I congratulate you, my dear fellow!' cried the hearty Raffles – a younger Raffles than I had ever known in town.

'I don't know that you need,' said Nasmyth, sourly.

'But it must be a tremendous interest. And the proof is that you're going down to this show, like all the rest of us.'

'No, I'm not. I live there, you see.'

And I think the Nipper recalled that name as he ground his heel upon an unresponsive flagstone.

'But you're going to this meeting at the School House, surely?'

'I don't know. If I do there may be squalls. I don't know what you think about this precious scheme, Raffles, but *I*...'

The ragged beard stuck out, set teeth showed through the wild moustache, and in a sudden outpouring we had his views. They were narrow and intemperate and perverse as any I had heard him advocate as the firebrand of the Debating Society in my first term. But they were stated with all the old vim and venom. The mind of Nasmyth had not broadened with the years, but neither had its natural force abated, or that of his character either. He spoke with great vigour at the top of his voice; soon we had a little crowd about us; but the tall collars and the broad smiles of the younger Old Boys did not deter our dowdy demagogue. Why spend money on a man who had been dead two hundred years? What good could it do him or the school? Besides, he was only technically our founder. He had not founded a great public school. He had founded a little country grammar school which had pottered along for a century and a half. The great public school was the growth of the last fifty years, and no credit to the pillar of piety. Besides, he was only nominally pious. Nasmyth had made researches, and he knew. And why throw good money after a bad man?

'Are there many of your opinion?' inquired Raffles, when the agitator paused for breath. And Nasmyth beamed on us with flashing eyes.

'Not one to my knowledge, as yet,' said he. 'But we shall see after tomorrow night. I hear it's to be quite an exceptional gathering this year; let us hope it may contain a few sane men. There are none on the present staff, and I only know of one among the Trustees!'

Raffles refrained from smiling as his dancing eye met mine.

'I can understand your view,' he said. 'I am not sure that I don't share it to some extent. But it seems to me a duty to support a general movement like this, even if it doesn't take the direction or the shape of our own dreams. I suppose you yourself will give something, Nasmyth?'

'Give something? I? Not a brass farthing!' cried the implacable banker. 'To do so would be to stultify my whole position. I cordially and conscientiously disapprove of the whole thing, and shall use all my influence against it. No, my good sir, I not only don't subscribe myself, but I hope to be the means of nipping a good many subscriptions in the bud.'

I was probably the only one who saw the sudden and yet subtle change in Raffles – the hard mouth – the harder eye. I, at least, might have foreseen the sequel then and there. But his quiet voice betrayed nothing, as he inquired whether Nasmyth was going to speak at next night's meeting. Nasmyth said he might, and certainly warned us what to expect. He was still fulminating when our train came in.

'Then we meet again at Philippi,' cried Raffles in gay adieu. 'For you have been very frank with us all, Nasmyth, and I'll be frank enough in my turn to tell you that I've every intention of speaking on the other side!'

It happened that Raffles had been asked to speak by his old college friend, the new Head Master. Yet it was not at the School House that he and I were to stay, but at the house that we had both been in as boys. It also had changed hands: a wing had been added, and the double tier of tiny studies made brilliant with electric light. But the quad and the fives-courts did not look a day older; the ivy was no thicker round the study windows; and in one boy's castle we found the traditional print of Charing Cross Bridge which had knocked about our studies ever since a son of the contractor first sold it when he left. Nay, more, there was the bald remnant of a stuffed bird which had been my own daily care when it and I belonged to Raffles. And when we all filed in to prayers, through the green-baize door which still separated the master's part of the house from that of the boys, there was a small boy posted in the passage to give the sign of silence to the rest assembled in the hall, quite identically as in the dim days; the picture was absolutely unchanged; it was only we who were out of it in body and soul.

On our side of the baize door a fine hospitality and a finer flow of spirits were the order of the night. There was a sound representative assortment of quite young Old Boys, to whom ours was a prehistoric time, and in the trough of their modern chaff and chat we old stagers might well have been left far astern of the fun. Yet it was Raffles who was the life and soul of the party, and that not by meretricious virtue of his cricket. There happened not to be another cricketer among us, and it was on their own subjects that Raffles laughed with the lot in turn and in the lump. I never knew him in quite such form. I will not say he was a boy among them, but he was that rarer being, the man of the world who can enter absolutely into the fun and fervour of the salad age. My cares and my regrets had never been more acute, but Raffles seemed a man without either in his life.

He was not, however, the hero of the Old Boys' Match, and that was expected of him by all the school. There was a hush when he went in, a groan when he came out. I had no reason to suppose he was not trying; these things happen to the cricketer who plays out of his class; but when the great Raffles went on to bowl, and was hit all over the field, I was not so sure. It certainly failed to affect his spirits; he was more brilliant than ever at our hospitable board; and after dinner came the meeting at which he and Nasmyth were to speak.

It was a somewhat frigid gathering until Nasmyth rose. We had all dined with our respective hosts, and then repaired to this business in cold blood. Many were lukewarm about it in their hearts; there was a certain amount of mild prejudice, and a greater amount of animal indifference, to be overcome in the opening speech. It is not for me to say whether this was successfully accomplished. I only know how the temperature of that meeting rose with Nipper Nasmyth.

And I dare say, in all the circumstances of the case, his really was a rather vulgar speech. But it was certainly impassioned, and probably as purely instinctive as his denunciation of all the causes which appeal to the gullible many without imposing upon the cantankerous few. His arguments, it is true, were merely an elaboration of those with which he had favoured some of us already; but they were pointed by a concise exposition of the several definite principles they represented, and barbed with a caustic rhetoric quite admirable in itself. In a word, the manner was worthy of the very foundation it sought to shake, or we had never swallowed such matter without a murmur. As it was, there was a demonstration in the wilderness when the voice ceased crying. But we sat in the deeper silence when Raffles rose to reply.

I leant forward not to lose a word. I knew my Raffles so well that I felt almost capable of reporting his speech before I heard it. Never was I more mistaken, even in him! So far from a gibe for a gibe and a taunt for a taunt, there never was softer answer than that which A.J. Raffles returned to Nipper Nasmyth before the staring eyes and startled ears of all assembled. He courteously but firmly refused to believe a word his old friend Nasmyth had said – about himself. He had known Nasmyth for twenty years, and never had he met a dog who barked so loud and bit so little. The fact was that he had far too kind a heart to bite at all. Nasmyth might get up and protest as loud as he liked: the speaker declared he knew him better than Nasmyth knew himself. He had the necessary defects of his great qualities. He was only too good a sportsman. He had a perfect passion for the weaker side. That alone led Nasmyth into such excesses of language as we had all heard from his lips that night. As for

Raffles, he concluded his far too genial remarks by predicting that whatever Nasmyth might say or think of the new fund, he would subscribe to it as handsomely as any of us, like 'the generous good chap' that we all knew him to be.

Even so did Raffles disappoint the Old Boys in the evening as he had disappointed the school by day. We had looked to him for a noble raillery, a lofty and a loyal disdain, and he had fobbed us off with friendly personalities not even in impeccable taste. Nevertheless, this light treatment of a grave offence went far to restore the natural amenities of the occasion. It was impossible even for Nasmyth to reply to it as he might to a more earnest onslaught. He could but smile sardonically, and audibly undertake to prove Raffles a false prophet; and though subsequent speakers were less merciful, the note was struck, and there was no more bad blood in the debate. There was plenty, however, in the veins of Nasmyth, as I was to discover for myself before the night was out.

You might think that in the circumstances he would not have attended the Head Master's ball with which the evening ended; but that would be sadly to misjudge so perverse a creature as the notorious Nipper. He was probably one of those who protest that there is 'nothing personal' in their most personal attacks. Not that Nasmyth took this tone about Raffles when he and I found ourselves cheek by jowl against the ballroom wall; he could forgive his franker critics, but not the friendly enemy who had treated him so much more gently than he deserved.

'I seem to have seen you with this great man Raffles,' began Nasmyth, as he overhauled me with his fighting eye. 'Do you know him well?'

'Intimately.'

'I remember now. You were with him when he forced himself upon me on the way down yesterday. He had to tell me who he was. Yet he talks as though we were old friends.'

'You were in the Upper Sixth together,' I rejoined, nettled by his tone.

'What does that matter? I am glad to say I had too much self-respect, and too little respect for Raffles, ever to be a friend of his then. I knew too many of the things he did,' said Nipper Nasmyth.

His fluent insults had taken my breath. But in a lucky flash I saw my retort.

'You must have had special opportunities of observation, living in the town,' said I; and drew first blood between the long hair and the ragged beard; but that was all.

'So he really did get out at nights?' remarked my adversary. 'You certainly give your friend away. What's he doing now?'

I let my eyes follow Raffles round the room before replying. He was waltzing with a master's wife – waltzing as he did everything else. Other couples seemed to melt before them. And the woman on his arm looked a radiant girl.

'I meant in town, or wherever he lives his mysterious life,' explained Nasmyth, when I told him that he could see for himself. But his clever tone did not trouble me; it was his epithet that caused me to prick my ears. And I found some difficulty in following Raffles right round the room.

'I thought everybody knew what he was doing; he's playing cricket most of his time,' was my measured reply; and if it bore an extra touch of insolence, I can honestly ascribe that to my nerves.

'And is that all he does for a living?' pursued my inquisitor, keenly.

'You had better ask Raffles himself,' said I to that. 'It's a pity you didn't ask him in public, at the meeting!'

But I was beginning to show temper in my embarrassment, and of course that made Nasmyth the more imperturbable.

'Really, he might be following some disgraceful calling, by the mystery you make of it!' he exclaimed. 'And for that matter I call first-class cricket a disgraceful calling, when it's followed by men who ought to be gentlemen, but are really professionals in gentlemanly clothing. The present craze for gladiatorial athleticism I regard as one of the great evils of the age; but the thinly veiled professionalism of the so-called amateur is the greatest evil of that craze. Men play for the Gentlemen and are paid more than the Players who walk out of another gate. In my time there was none of that. Amateurs were amateurs and sport was sport; there were no Raffleses in first-class cricket then. I had forgotten Raffles was a modem first-class cricketer: that explains him. Rather than see my son such another, do you know what I'd prefer to see him?'

I neither knew nor cared: yet a wretched premonitory fascination held me breathless till I was told.

'I'd prefer to see him a thief!' said Nasmyth, savagely; and when his eyes were done with me, he turned upon his heel. So ended that stage of my discomfiture.

It was only to give place to a worse. Was all this accident, or fell design? Conscience had made a coward of me, and yet what reason had I to believe the worst? We were pirouetting on the edge of an abyss; sooner or later the false step must come, and the pit swallow us. I began to wish myself back in London, and I did get back to my room in our old house. My dancing days were already over; there I had taken the one resolution to which I remained as true as better men to better vows; there, the painful association was no mere sense of personal unworthiness. I fell to thinking in my room of other dances... and was still smoking the cigarette which Raffles had taught me to appreciate when I looked up to find him regarding me from the door. He had opened it as noiselessly as only Raffles could open doors and now he closed it in the same professional fashion.

'I missed Achilles hours ago,' said he. 'And still he's sulking in his tent!'

'I have been,' I answered, laughing as he could always make me, 'but I'll chuck it if you'll stop and smoke. Our host doesn't mind; there's an ash-tray provided for the purpose. I ought to be sulking between the sheets, but I'm ready to sit up with you till morning.'

'We might do worse; but, on the other hand, we might do still better,' rejoined Raffles, and for once he resisted the seductive Sullivan. 'As a matter of fact, it's morning now; in another hour it will be dawn; and where could day dawn better than in Warfield Woods, or along the Stockley road, or even on the Upper or the Middle? I don't want to turn in, any more than you do. I may as well confess that the whole show down here has exalted me more than anything for years. But if we can't sleep, Bunny, let's have some fresh air instead.'

'Has everybody gone to bed?' I asked.

'Long ago. I was the last in. Why?'

'Only it might sound a little odd, our turning out again, if they were to hear us.'

Raffles stood over me with a smile made of mischief and cunning; but it was the purest mischief imaginable, the most innocent and comic cunning.

'They shan't hear us at all, Bunny,' said he. 'I mean to get out as I did in the good old nights. I've been spoiling for the chance ever since I came down. There's not the smallest harm in it now; and if you'll come with me I'll show you how it used to be done.'

'But I know,' said I. 'Who used to haul up the rope after you, and let it down again to the minute?'

Raffles looked down on me from lowered lids, over a smile too humorous to offend.

'My dear good Bunny! And do you suppose that even then I had only one way of doing a thing? I've had a spare loophole all my life, and when you're ready I'll show you what it was when I was here. Take off those boots, and carry your tennis-shoes; slip on another coat; put out your light; and I'll meet you on the landing in two minutes.'

He met me with uplifted finger, and not a syllable; and downstairs he led me, stocking soles close against the skirting, two feet to each particular step. It must have seemed child's play to Raffles; the old precautions were obviously assumed for my entertainment; but I confess that to me it was all refreshingly exciting – for once without a risk of durance if we came to grief. With a scarcely a creak we reached the hall, and could have walked out of the street-door without danger or difficulty. But that would not do for Raffles. He must needs lead me into the boys' part, through the green baize door. It took a deal of opening and shutting, but Raffles seemed to enjoy nothing better than these mock obstacles, and in a few minutes we were resting with sharp ears in the boys' hall.

'Through these windows?' I whispered, when the clock over the piano had had matters its own way long enough to make our minds quite easy.

'How else?' whispered Raffles, as he opened the one on whose ledge our letters used to await us of a morning.

'And then through the quad – '

'And over the gates at the end. No talking, Bunny; there's a dormitory just overhead; but ours was in front, you remember, and if they had ever seen me I should have nipped back this way while they were watching the other.'

His finger was on his lips as we got out softly into the starlight. I remember how the gravel hurt as we left the smooth flagged margin of the house for the open quad; but the nearer of two long green seats (whereon you prepared your construe for second-school in the summer term) was mercifully handy; and once in our rubber soles we had no difficulty in scaling the gates beyond the fives- courts. Moreover, we dropped into a very desert of a country road, nor saw a soul when we doubled back beneath the outer study windows, nor heard a footfall in the main street of the slumbering town. Our own fell like the night-dews and the petals of the poet; but Raffles ran his arm through mine, and would chatter in whispers as we went.

'So you and the Nipper had a word – or was it words? I saw you out of the tail of my eye when I was dancing, and I heard you out of the tail of my ear. It sounded like words, Bunny, and I thought I caught my name. He's the most consistent man I know, and the least altered from a boy. But he'll subscribe all right, you'll see, and be very glad I made him.'

I whispered back that I did not believe it for a moment. Raffles had not heard all Nasmyth had said of him. And neither would he listen to the little I meant to repeat to him; he would but reiterate a conviction so chimerical to my mind that I interrupted in my turn to ask him what grounds he had for it.

'I've told you already,' said Raffles. 'I mean to make him.'

'But how?' I asked. 'And when, and where?'

'At Philippi, Bunny, where I said I'd see him. What a rabbit you are at a quotation!

'"And-I think that the field of Philippi,
Was where Caesar came to an end;
But who gave old Brutus the tip I
Can't comprehend!"

'You may have forgotten your Shakespeare, Bunny, but you ought to remember that.'

And I did, vaguely, but had no idea what it or Raffles meant, as I plainly told him.

'The theatre of war,' he answered – 'and here we are at the stage door!'

Raffles had stopped suddenly in his walk. It was the last dark hour of the summer night, but the light from a neighbouring lamp-post showed me the look on his face as he turned.

'I think you also inquired when,' he continued. 'Well, then, this minute – if you'll give me a leg up!'

And behind him, scarcely higher than his head, and not even barred, was a wide window with a wire blind, and the name of Nasmyth among others lettered in gold upon the wire.

'You're never going to break in?'

'This instant, if you'll help me; in five or ten minutes, if you won't.'

'Surely you didn't bring the – the tools?'

He jingled them gently in his pocket.

'Not the whole outfit, Bunny. But you never know when you mayn't want one or two. I'm only thankful I didn't leave the lot behind this time. I very nearly did.'

'I must say I thought you would, coming down here,' I said reproachfully.

'But you ought to be glad I didn't,' he rejoined with his smile. 'It's going to mean old Nasmyth's subscription to the Founder's Fund, and that's to be a big one, I promise you! The lucky thing is that I went so far as to bring my bunch of safe-keys. Now, are you going to help me use them, or are you not? If so, now's your minute; if not, clear out and be – '

'Not so fast, Raffles,' said I testily. 'You must have planned this before you came down, or you would never have brought all those things with you.'

'My dear Bunny, they're a part of my kit! I take them wherever I take my evening clothes. As to this potty bank, I never even thought of it, much less that it would become a public duty to draw a hundred or so without signing for it. That's all I shall touch, Bunny – I'm not on the make tonight. There's no risk in it, either. If I am caught I shall simply sham champagne and stand the racket; it would be an obvious frolic after what happened at that meeting. And they will catch me, if I stand talking here: you run away back to bed – unless you're quite determined to "give old Brutus the tip"!'

Now, we had barely been a minute whispering where we stood, and the whole street was still as silent as the tomb. To me there seemed least danger in discussing the matter quietly on the spot. But even as he gave me my dismissal, Raffles turned and caught the sill above him, first with one hand and then with the other. His legs swung like a pendulum as he drew himself up with one arm, then shifted the position of the other hand, and very gradually worked himself waist-high with the sill. But the sill was too narrow for him; that was as far as he could get unaided; and it was as much as I could bear to see of a feat which in itself might have hardened my conscience and softened my heart. But I had identified his doggerel verse at last. I am ashamed to say that it was part of a set of my very own writing in the school magazine of my time. So Raffles knew the stuff better than I did myself, and yet scorned to press his flattery to win me over! He had won me: in a second my rounded shoulders were a pedestal for those dangling feet. And before many more I heard the old metallic snap, followed by the raising of a sash so slowly and gently as to be almost inaudible to me listening just below.

Raffles went through hands first, disappeared for an instant, then leant out, lowering his hands for me.

'Come on, Bunny! You're safer in than out. Hang on to the sill and let me get you under the arms. Now, all together – quietly does it – and over you come!'

No need to dwell on our proceedings in the bank. I myself had small part in the scene, being posted rather in the wings, at the foot of the stairs leading to the private premises in which the manager had his domestic being. But I made my mind easy about him, for in the silence of my watch I soon detected a nasal note overhead, and it was resonant and aggressive as the man himself. Of Raffles, on the contrary, I heard nothing, for he had shut the door between us, and I was to warn him if a single sound came through. I need scarcely add that no warning was necessary during the twenty minutes we remained in the bank. Raffles afterwards assured me that nineteen of them had been spent in filing one key; but one of his latest inventions was a little thick velvet bag in which he carried the keys; and this bag had two elastic mouths, which closed so tightly about either wrist that he could file away inside, and scarcely hear it himself. As for these keys, they were clever counterfeits of typical patterns by two great safe-making firms. And Raffles had come by them in a manner all his own, which the criminal world may discover for itself.

When he opened the door and beckoned to me, I knew by his face that he had succeeded to his satisfaction, and by experience better than to question him on the point. Indeed, the first thing was to get out of the bank; for the stars were drowning in a sky of ink and water, and it was a comfort to feel that we could fly straight to our beds. I said so in whispers as Raffles cautiously opened our window and peeped out. In an instant his head was in, and for another I feared the worst.

'What was that, Bunny? No, you don't, my son! There's not a soul in sight that I can see, but you never know, and we may as well lay a scent while we're about it. Ready? Then follow me, and never mind the window.'

With that he dropped softly into the street, and I after him, turning to the right instead of the left, and that at a brisk trot instead of the innocent walk which had brought us to the bank. Like mice we scampered past the great schoolroom, with its gable snipping a paler sky than ever, and the shadows melting even in the colonnade underneath. Masters' houses flitted by on the left, lesser landmarks on either side, and presently we were running our heads into the dawn, one under either hedge of the Stockley road.

'Did you see that light in Nab's just now?' cried Raffles as he led.

'No; why?' I panted, nearly spent.

'It was in Nab's dressing-room.'

'Yes?'

'I've seen it there before,' continued Raffles. 'He never was a good sleeper, and his ears reach to the street. I wouldn't like to say how often I was chased by him in the small hours! I believe he knew who it was towards the end, but Nab was not the man to accuse you of what he couldn't prove.'

I had no breath for comment. And on sped Raffles like a yacht before the wind, and on I blundered like a wherry at sea, making heavy weather all the way, and nearer foundering at every stride. Suddenly, to my deep relief, Raffles halted, but only to tell me to stop my pipes while he listened.

'It's all right, Bunny,' he resumed, showing me a glowing face in the dawn. 'History's on its own tracks once more, and I'll bet you it's dear old Nab on ours! Come on, Bunny; run to the last gasp, and leave the rest to me.'

I was past arguing, and away he went. There was no help for it but to follow as best I could. Yet I had vastly preferred to collapse on the spot, and trust to Raffles's resource, as before very long I must. I had never enjoyed long wind, and the hours that we kept in town may well have aggravated the deficiency. Raffles, however, was in first-class training from first-class cricket, and he had no mercy on Nab or me. But the master himself was an old Oxford miler, who could still bear it better than I; nay, as I flagged and stumbled, I heard him pounding steadily behind.

'Come on, come on, or he'll do us!' cried Raffles shrilly over his shoulder; and a gruff sardonic laugh came back over mine. It was pearly morning now, but we had run into a shallow mist that took me by the throat and stabbed me to the lungs. I coughed, and coughed, and stumbled in my stride, until down I went, less by accident than to get it over, and so lay headlong in my tracks. And old Nab dealt me a verbal kick as he passed as he passed.

'You beast!' he growled, as I have known him growl it in form.

But Raffles himself had abandoned the flight on hearing my downfall, and I was on hands and knees just in time to see the meeting between him and old Nab. And there stood Raffles in the silvery mist, laughing with his whole light heart, leaning back to get the full flavour of his mirth; and, nearer me, sturdy old Nab, dour and grim, with beads of dew on the hoary beard that had been lamp-black in our time.

'So I've caught you at last!' said he. 'After more years than I mean to count!'

'Then you're luckier than we are, sir,' answered Raffles, 'for I fear our man has given us the slip.'

'Your man!' echoed Nab. His bushy eyebrows had shot up: it was as much as I could do to keep my own in their place.

'We were indulging in the chase ourselves,' explained Raffles, 'and one of us has suffered for his zeal, as you can see. It is even possible that we, too, have been chasing a perfectly innocent man.'

'Not to say a reformed character,' said our pursuer, dryly. 'I suppose you don't mean a member of the school?' he added, pinking his man suddenly as of yore, with all the old barbed acumen.

But Raffles was now his match.

'That would be carrying reformation rather far, sir. No, as I say, I may have been mistaken in the first instance; but I had put out my light and was looking out of the window when I saw a fellow behaving quite suspiciously. He was carrying his boots and creeping along in his socks – which must be why you never heard him, sir. They make less noise than rubber soles even – that is, they must, you know! Well, Bunny had just left me, so I hauled him out and we both crept down to play detective. No sign of the fellow! We had a look in the colonnade – I thought I heard him – and that gave us no end of a hunt for nothing. But just as we were leaving he came padding past under our noses, and that's where we took up the chase. Where he'd been in the mean time I have no idea; very likely he'd done no harm; but it seemed worth while finding out. He had too good a start, though, and poor Bunny had too bad a wind.'

'You should have gone on, and let me rip,' said I, climbing to my feet at last.

'As it is, however, we will all let the other fellow do so,' said old Nab in a genial growl. 'And you two had better turn into my house, and have something to keep the morning cold out.'

You may imagine with what alacrity we complied; and yet I am bound to confess that I had never liked Nab at school. I still remember my term in his form. He had a caustic tongue and a fine assortment of damaging epithets, most of which were levelled at my devoted skull during those three months. I now discovered that he also kept a particularly mellow Scotch whisky, an excellent cigar, and a fund of anecdote of which a mordant wit was the worthy bursar. Enough to add that he kept us laughing in his study until the chapel bells rang him out.

As for Raffles, he appeared to me to feel far more compunction for the fable which he had been compelled to foist upon one of the old masters than for the immeasurably graver offence against society and another Old Boy. This, indeed, did not worry him at all; and the story was received next day with absolute credulity on all sides. Nasmyth himself was the first to thank us both for our spirited effort on his behalf; and the incident had the ironic effect of establishing an immediate *entente cordiale* between Raffles and his very latest victim. I must confess, however, that for my own part I was thoroughly uneasy during the Old Boys' second innings, when Raffles made a selfish score, instead of standing by me to tell his own story in his own way. There was never any knowing with what new detail he was about to embellish it: and I have still to receive full credit for the tact that it required to follow his erratic lead convincingly. Seldom have I been more thankful than when our train started next morning, and the poor unsuspecting Nasmyth himself waved us a last farewell from the platform.

'Lucky we weren't staying at Nab's,' said Raffles, as he lit a Sullivan and opened his *Daily Mail* at its report of the robbery. 'There was one thing Nab would have spotted like the downy old bird he always was and will be.'

'What was that?'

'The front door must have been found duly barred and bolted in the morning, and yet we let them assume that we came out that way. Nab would have pounced on the point, and by this time we might have been nabbed ourselves.'

It was but a little over a hundred sovereigns that Raffles had taken, and, of course, he had resolutely eschewed any and every form of paper money. He posted his own first contribution of twenty-five pounds to the Founder's Fund immediately on our return to town, before rushing off to more first-class cricket, and I gathered that the rest would follow piecemeal as he deemed it safe. By an odd coincidence, however, a mysterious but magnificent donation of a hundred guineas was almost simultaneously received in notes by the treasurer of the Founder's Fund, from one who simply signed himself 'Old Boy'. The treasurer happened to be our late host, the new man at our old house, and he wrote to congratulate Raffles on what he was pleased to consider a direct result of the latter's speech. I did not see the letter that Raffles wrote in reply, but in due course I heard the name of the mysterious contributor. He was said to be no other than Nipper Nasmyth himself. I asked Raffles if it was true. He replied that he would ask old Nipper point-blank if he came up as usual to the Varsity match, and if they had the luck to meet. And not only did this happen, but I had the greater luck to be walking round the ground with Raffles when we encountered our shabby friend in front of the pavilion.

'My dear fellow,' cried Raffles, 'I hear it was you who gave that hundred guineas by stealth to the very movement you denounced. Don't deny it, and don't blush to find it fame. Listen to me. There was a great lot in what you said; but it's the kind of thing we ought all to back, whether we strictly approve of it in our hearts or not.'

'Exacdy, Raffles, but the fact is – '

'I know what you're going to say. Don't say it. There's not one in a thousand who would do as you've done, and not one in a million who would do it anonymously.'

'But what makes you think I did it, Raffles?'

'Everybody is saying so. You will find it all over the place when you get back. You will find yourself the most popular man down there, Nasmyth!'

I never saw a nobler embarrassment than that of this awkward, ungainly, cantankerous man: all his angles seem to have been smoothed away: there was something quite human in the flushed, undecided, wistful face.

'I never was popular in my life,' he said. 'I don't want to buy my popularity now. To be perfecdy candid with you, Raffles – '

'Don't! I can't stop to hear. They're ringing the bell. But you shouldn't have been angry with me for saying you were a generous good chap, Nasmyth, when you were one all the time. Good-bye, old fellow!'

But Nasmyth detained us a second more. His hesitation was at an end. There was a sudden new light in his face.

'Was I?' he cried. 'Then I'll make it *two* hundred, and damn the odds!'

Raffles was a thoughtful man as we went to our seats. He saw nobody, would acknowledge no remark. Neither did he attend to the cricket for the first half-hour after lunch; instead, he eventually invited me to come for a stroll on the practice ground, where, however, we found two chairs aloof from the fascinating throng.

'I am not often sorry. Bunny, as you know,' he began. 'But I have been sorry since the interval. I've been sorry for poor old

Nipper Nasmyth. Did you see the idea of being popular dawn upon him for the first time in his life?'

'I did; but you had nothing to do with that, my dear man.'

Raffles shook his head over me as our eyes met.

'I had everything to do with it. I tried to make him tell the meanest lie. I made sure he would, and for that matter he nearly did. Then, at the last moment, he saw how to hedge things with his conscience. And his second hundred will be a real gift.'

'You mean under his own name?'

'And with his own free will. My good Bunny, is it possible you don't know what I did with the hundred we drew from that bank?'

'I knew what you were going to do with it,' said I. 'I didn't know you had actually got further than the twenty-five you told me you were sending as your own contribution.'

Raffles rose abruptly from his chair. 'And you actually thought that came out of his money?'

'Naturally.'

'In my name?'

'I thought so.'

Raffles stared at me inscrutably for some moments, and for some more at the great white numbers over the grand stand.

'We may as well have another look at the cricket,' he said. 'It's difficult to see the board from here, but I believe there's another man out.'

6

A BAD NIGHT

There was to be a certain little wedding in which Raffles and I took a surreptitious interest. The bride elect was living in some retirement, with a recently widowed mother, and an asthmatical brother, in a mellow hermitage on the banks of the Mole. The bridegroom was a prosperous son of the same suburban soil, which had nourished both families for generations. The wedding presents were so numerous as to fill several rooms at the pretty retreat upon the Mole, and of an intrinsic value calling for a special transaction with the Burglary Insurance Company in Cheapside. I cannot say how Raffles obtained all this information. I only know that it proved correct in each particular. I was not, indeed, deeply interested before the event, since Raffles assured me that it was 'a one-man-job', and naturally intended to be the one man himself. It was only at the eleventh hour that our positions were inverted by the wholly unexpected selection of Raffles for the English team in the Second Test Match.

In a flash I saw the chance of my criminal career. It was some years since Raffles had served his country in these encounters; he had never thought to be called upon again, and his gratification was only less than his embarrassment. The match was at Old Trafford, on the third Thursday, Friday, and

Saturday in July; the other affair had been all arranged for the Thursday night, the night of the wedding at East Molesey. It was for Raffles to choose between the two diversions, and for once I helped him to make up his mind. I duly pointed out to him that in Surrey, at all events, I was quite capable of taking his place. Nay, more, I insisted at once on my prescriptive right and on his patriotic obligation in the matter. In the country's name and in my own, I implored him to give it and me a chance; and for once, as I say, my arguments prevailed. Raffles sent his telegram – it was the day before the match. We then rushed down to Esher, and over every inch of the ground by that characteristically circuitous route, which he enjoined on me for the next night. And at six in the evening I was receiving the last of my many instructions through a window of the restaurant car.

'Only promise me not to take a revolver,' said Raffles in a whisper. 'Here are my keys; there's an old life-preserver somewhere in the bureau; take that, if you like – though what you take I rather fear you are the chap to use!'

'Then the rope be round my own neck!' I whispered back. 'Whatever else I may do, Raffles, I shan't give you away; and you'll find I do better than you think, and am worth trusting with a little more to do, or I'll know the reason why!'

And I meant to know it, as he was borne out of Euston with raised eyebrows, and I turned grimly on my heel. I saw his fears for me; and nothing could have made me more fearless for myself. Raffles had been wrong about me all these years; now was my chance to set him right. It was galling to feel that he had no confidence in my coolness or my nerve, when neither had ever failed him at a pinch. I had been loyal to him through rough and smooth. In many an ugly corner I had stood as firm as Raffles himself. I was his right hand, and yet he never hesitated to make me his catspaw. This time, at all events, I should be neither one nor the other; this time I was the understudy playing lead at last; and I wish I could think that Raffles ever realised with what gusto I threw myself into his part.

Thus I was first out of a crowded theatre train at Esher next night, and first down the stairs into the open air. The night was close and cloudy; and the road to Hampton Court, even now that the surburban builder has marked much of it for his own, is one of the darkest I know. The first mile is still a narrow avenue, a mere tunnel of leaves at midsummer; but at that time there was not a lighted pane or cranny by the way. Naturally, it was in this blind reach that I fancied I was being followed. I stopped in my stride; so did the steps I made sure I had heard not far behind; and when I went on, they followed suit. I dried my forehead as I walked, but soon brought myself to repeat the experiment, when an exact repetition of the result went to convince me that it had been my own echo all the time. And since I lost it on getting quit of the avenue, and coming out upon the straight and open road, I was not long in recovering from my scare. But now I could see my way, and found the rest of it without mishap, though not without another semblance of adventure. Over the bridge across the Mole, when about to turn to the left, I marched straight upon a policeman in rubber soles. I had to call him 'officer' as I passed, and to pass my turning by a couple of hundred yards, before venturing back another way.

At last I had crept through a garden gate, and round by black windows to a black lawn drenched with dew. It had been a heating walk, and I was glad to blunder on a garden seat, most considerately placed under a cedar which added its own darkness to that of the night. Here I rested a few minutes, putting up my feet to keep them dry, untying my shoes to save time, and generally facing the task before me with a coolness which I strove to make worthy of my absent chief. But mine was a self-conscious quality, as far removed from the original as any other deliberate imitation of genius. I actually struck a match on my trousers, and lit one of the shorter Sullivans. Raffles himself would not have done such a thing at such a moment. But I wished to tell him that I had done it; and in truth I was not more than pleasurably afraid. I had rather that impersonal curiosity as to the issue which has been the saving of me in still more precarious situations. I even grew impatient for the fray, and could not after all sit still as long as I had intended. So it happened that I was finishing my cigarette on the edge of the wet lawn, and about to slip off my shoes before stepping across the gravel to the conservatory door, when a most singular sound arrested me in the act. It was a muffled gasping somewhere overhead. I stood like stone; and my listening attitude must have been visible against the milky sheen of the lawn, for a laboured voice hailed me sternly from a window.

'Who on earth are you?' it wheezed.

'A detective officer,' I replied, 'sent down by the Burglary Insurance Company,'

Not a moment had I paused for my precious fable. It had all been prepared for me by Raffles, in case of need. I was merely repeating a lesson in which I had been closely schooled. But at the window there was pause enough, filled only by the uncanny wheezing of the man I could not see.

'I don't see why they should have sent you down,' he said at length. 'We are being quite well looked after by the local police; they're giving us a special call every hour.'

'I know that, Mr Medlicott,' I rejoined on my own account. 'I met one of them at the corner just now, and we passed the time of night.'

My heart was knocking me to bits. I had started for myself at last.

'Did you get my name from him?' pursued my questioner, in a suspicious wheeze.

'No; they gave me that before I started,' I replied. 'But I'm sorry you saw me, sir; it's a mere matter of routine, and not intended to annoy anybody. I propose to keep a watch on the place all night, but I own it wasn't necessary to trespass as I've done. I'll take myself off the actual premises, if you prefer it.'

This again was all my own; and it met with a success that might have given me confidence.

'Not a bit of it,' replied young Medlicott, with a grim geniality. 'I've just woke up with the devil of an attack of asthma, and may have to sit up in my chair till morning. You'd better come up and see me through, and kill two birds while you're about it. Stay where you are, and I'll come down and let you in.'

Here was a dilemma which Raffles himself had not foreseen! Outside, in the dark, my audacious part was not hard to play; but to carry the improvisation indoors was to double at once the difficulty and the risk. It was true that I had purposely come down in a true detective's overcoat and bowler; but my personal appearance was hardly of the detective type. On the other hand, as the *soi-disant* guardian of the gifts, one might only excite suspicion by refusing to enter the house where they were. Nor could I forget that it was my purpose to effect such entry first or last. That was the casting consideration. I decided to take my dilemma by the horns.

There had been a scraping of matches in the room over the conservatory; the open window had shown for a moment, like an empty picture-frame, a gigantic shadow wavering on the ceiling; and in the next half-minute I remembered to tie my shoes. But the light was slow to reappear through the leaded glasses of an outer door further along the path. And when the door opened, it was a figure of woe that stood within and held an unsteady candle between our faces.

I have seen old men look half their age, and young men look double theirs; but never before or since have I seen a beardless boy bent into a man of eighty, gasping for every breath, shaken by every gasp, swaying, tottering, and choking, as if about to die upon his feet. But even in his throes young Medlicott overhauled me shrewdly, and it was several moments before he would let me take the candle from him.

'I shouldn't have come down – made me worse,' he began whispering in spurts. 'Worse still going up again. You must give me an arm. You will come up? That's right! Not as bad as I look, you know. Got some good whisky, too. Presents are all right; but if they aren't you'll hear of it indoors sooner than out. Now I'm ready – thanks! Mustn't make more noise than we can help – wake my mother.'

It must have taken us minutes to climb that single flight of stairs. There was just room for me to keep his arm in mine; with the other he hauled on the banisters; and so we mounted, step by step, a panting pause on each, and a pitched battle for breath on the half-landing. In the end we gained a cosy library, with an open door leading to a bedroom beyond. But the effort had deprived my poor companion of all power of speech; his labouring lungs shrieked like the wind; he could just point to the door by which we had entered, and which I shut in obedience to his gestures, and then to the decanter and its accessories on the table where he had left them overnight. I gave him nearly half a glassful, and his paroxysm subsided a little as he sat hunched up in a chair.

'I was a fool... to turn in,' he blurted in more whispers between longer pauses. 'Lying down is the devil... when you're in for a real bad night. You might get me the brown cigarettes... on the table in there. That's right ... thanks awfully ... and now a match!'

The asthmatic had bitten off either end of the stramonium cigarette, and was soon choking himself with the crude fumes, which he inhaled in desperate gulps, to exhale in furious fits of coughing. Never was more heroic remedy; it seemed a form of lingering suicide; but by degrees some slight improvement became apparent, and at length the sufferer was able to sit upright, and to drain his glass with a sigh of rare relief. I sighed also, for I had witnessed a struggle for dear life by a man in the flower of his youth, whose looks I liked, whose smile came like the sun through the first break in his torments, and whose first words were to thank me for the little I had done in bare humanity.

That made me feel the thing I was. But the feeling put me on my guard. And I was not unready for the remark which followed a more exhaustive scrutiny than I had hitherto sustained.

'Do you know', said young Medlicott, 'that you aren't a bit like the detective of my dreams?'

'Only too proud to hear it,' I replied. 'There would be no point in my being in plain clothes if I looked exactly what I was.'

My companion reassured me with a wheezy laugh.

'There's something in that,' said he, 'although I do congratulate the insurance people on getting a man of your class to do their dirty work. And I congratulate myself', he was quick enough to add, 'on having you to see me through as bad a night as I've had for a long time. You're like flowers in the depths of winter. Got a drink? That's right! I suppose you didn't happen to bring down an evening paper?'

I said I had brought one, but had unfortunately left it in the train.

'What about the Test Match?' cried my asthmatic, shooting forward in his chair.

'I can tell you that,' said I. 'We went in first – '

'Oh, I know all about that,' he interrupted. 'I've seen the miserable score up to lunch. How many did we scrape altogether?'

'We're scraping them still.'

'No! How many?'

'Over two hundred for seven wickets.'

'Who made the stand?'

'Raffles, for one. He was 62 not out at close of play!'

And the note of admiration rang in my voice, though I tried in my self-consciousness to keep it out. But young Medlicott's enthusiasm proved an ample cloak for mine; it was he who might have been the personal friend of Raffles; and in his delight he chuckled till he puffed and blew again.

'Good old Raffles!' he panted in every pause. 'After being chosen last, and as a bowler-man! That's the cricketer for me, sir; by Jove, we must have another drink in his honour! Funny thing asthma; your liquor affects your head no more than it does a man with a snake-bite; but it eases everything else, and sees you through. Doctors will tell you so, but you've got to ask 'em first; they're no good for asthma! I've only known one who could stop an attack, and he knocked me sideways with nitrite of amyl. Funny complaint in other ways; raises your spirits, if anything. You can't look beyond the next breath. Nothing else worries you. Well, well, here's luck to A.J. Raffles, and may he get his century in the morning!'

And he struggled to his feet for the toast; but I drank it sitting down. I felt unreasonably wroth with Raffles, for coming into the conversation as he had done – for taking centuries in Test Matches as he was doing, without bothering his head about me. A failure would have been in better taste; it would have shown at least some imagination, some anxiety on one's account. I did not reflect that even Raffles could scarcely be expected to picture me in my cups with the son of the house that I had come to rob; chatting with him, ministering to him; admiring his cheery courage, and honestly attempting to lighten his load. Truly it was an infernal position: how could I rob him or his after this? And yet I had thrust myself into it; and Raffles would never, never understand!

Even that was not the worst. I was not quite sure that young Medlicott was sure of me. I had feared this from the beginning, and now (over the second glass that could not possibly affect a man in his condition) he practically admitted as much to me. Asthma was such a funny thing (he insisted) that it would not worry him a bit to discover that I had come to take the presents instead of to take care of them! I showed a sufficiently faint appreciation of the jest. And it was presently punished as it deserved, by the most violent paroxysm that had seized the sufferer yet: the fight for breath became faster and more furious, and the former weapons of no more avail. I prepared a cigarette, hut the poor brute was too breathless to inhale. I poured out yet more whisky, but he put it from him with a gesture.

'Amyl – get me amyl!' he gasped. 'The tin on the table by my bed.'

I rushed into his room, and returned with a little tin of tiny cylinders done up like miniature crackers in scraps of calico; the spent youth broke one in his handkerchief, in which he immediately buried his face. I watched him closely, as a subtle odour reached my nostrils; and it was like the miracle of oil upon the billows. His shoulders rested from long travail; the stertorous gasping died away to a quick but natural respiration; and in the sudden cessation of the cruel contest, an uncanny stillness fell upon the scene. Meanwhile the hidden face had flushed to the ears, and, when at length it was raised to mine, its crimson calm was as incongruous as an optical illusion.

'It takes the blood from the heart,' he murmured, 'and clears the whole show for the moment. If it only lasted! But you can't take two without a doctor; one's quite enough to make you smell the brimstone... I say, what's up? You're listening to something! If it's the policeman we'll have a word with him.'

It was not the policeman; it was no outdoor sound that I had caught in the sudden cessation of the bout for breath. It was a noise, a footstep, in the room below us. I went to the window, and leaned out: right underneath, in the conservatory, was the faintest glimmer of a light from the adjoining room.

'One of the rooms where the presents are!' whispered Medlicott at my elbow. And as we withdrew together, I looked him in the face as I had not done all night.

I looked him in the face like an honest man, for a miracle was to make me one once more. My knot was cut – my course inevitable. Mine, after all, to prevent the very thing that I had come to do! My gorge had long since risen at the deed; the unforeseen circumstances had rendered it impossible from the first; but now I could afford to recognise the impossibility, and to think of Raffles and the asthmatic alike without a qualm. I could play the game by them both, for it was one and the same game. I could preserve thieves' honour, and yet regain some shred of that which I had forfeited as a man!

So I thought as we stood face to face, our ears straining for the least movement below, our eyes locked in a common anxiety. Another muffled footfall – felt rather than heard – and we exchanged grim nods of simultaneous excitement. But by this time Medlicott was as helpless as he had been before; the flush had faded from his face, and his breathing alone would have spoilt everything. In dumb show I had to order him to stay where he was, to leave my man to me. And then it was that in a gusty whisper, with the same shrewd look that had disconcerted me more than once during our vigil, young Medlicott froze and fired my blood by turns.

'I've been unjust to you,' he said, with his right hand in his dressing-gown pocket. 'I thought for a bit – never mind what I thought – I soon saw I was wrong. But – I've had this thing in my pocket all the time!'

And he would have thrust his revolver upon me as a peace-offering, but I would not even take his hand, as I tapped the life-preserver in my pocket, and crept out to earn his honest grip or to fall in the attempt. On the landing I drew Raffles's little weapon, slipped my right wrist through the leathern loop, and held it in readiness? over my right shoulder. Then, downstairs I stole, as Raffles himself had taught me, close to the wall, where the planks are nailed. Nor had I made a sound, to my knowledge; for a door was open, and a light was burning, and the light did not flicker as I approached the door. I clenched my teeth and pushed it open; and there was the veriest villain waiting for me, his little lantern held aloft.

'You blackguard!' I cried, and with a single thwack I felled the ruffian to the floor.

There was no question of a foul blow. He had been just as ready to pounce on me; it was simply my luck to have got the first blow home. Yet a fellow-feeling touched me with remorse, as I stood over the senseless body, sprawling prone, and perceived that I had struck an unarmed man. The lantern only had fallen from his hands; it lay on one side, smoking horribly; and a something in the reek caused me to set it up in haste and turn the body over with both hands.

Shall I ever forget the incredulous horror of that moment?

It was Raffles himself!

How it was possible, I did not pause to ask myself; if one man on earth could annihilate space and time, it was the man lying senseless at my feet; and that was Raffles, without an instant's doubt. He was in villainous guise, which I knew of old, now that I knew the unhappy wearer. His face was grimy, and dexterously plastered with a growth of reddish hair; his clothes were those in which he had followed cabs from the London termini; his boots were muffled in thick socks; and I had laid him low with a bloody scalp that filled my cup of horror. I groaned aloud as I knelt over him and felt his heart. And I was answered by a bronchial whistle from the door.

'Jolly well done!' cheered my asthmatical friend. 'I heard the whole thing – only hope my mother didn't. We must keep it from her if we can.'

I could have cursed him and his mother from my full heart; yet even with my hand on that of Raffles, as I felt his feeble pulse, I told myself that this served him right. Even had I brained him, the fault had been his, not mine. And it was a characteristic, an inveterate fault, that galled me for all my anguish: to trust and yet distrust me to the end, to race through England in the night, to spy upon me at his work – to do it himself after all!

'Is he dead?' wheezed the asthmatic, coolly.

'Not he,' I answered, with an indignation that I dared not show.

'You must have hit him pretty hard,' pursued young Medlicott, 'but I suppose it was a case of getting first knock. And a good job you got it, if this was his,' he added, picking up the murderous little life-preserver which poor Raffles had provided for his own destruction.

'Look here,' I answered, sitting back on my heels. 'He isn't dead, Mr Medlicott, and I don't know how long he'll be as much as stunned. He's a powerful brute, and you're not fit to lend a hand. But that policeman of yours can't be far away. Do you think you could struggle out and look for him?'

'I suppose I am a bit better than I was,' he replied doubtfully. 'The excitement seems to have done me good. If you like to leave me on guard with my revolver, I'll undertake that he doesn't escape me.'

I shook my head with an impatient smile.

'I should never hear the last of it,' said I. 'No, in that case all I can do is to handcuff the fellow and wait till morning if he won't go quietly; and he'll be a fool if he does, while there's a fighting chance.'

Young Medlicott glanced upstairs from his post on the threshold. I refrained from watching him too keenly, but I knew what was in his mind.

'I'll go,' he said hurriedly. 'I'll go as I am, before my mother is disturbed and frightened out of her life. I owe you something, too, not only for what you've done for me, but for what I was fool enough to think about you at the first blush. It's entirely through you that I feel as fit as I do for the moment. So I'll take your tip, and go just as I am, before my poor old pipes strike up another tune.'

I scarcely looked up until the good fellow had turned his back upon the final tableau of watchful officer and prostrate prisoner, and gone out wheezing into the night. But I was at the door to hear the last of him down the path and round the corner of the house. And when I rushed back into the room, there was Raffles sitting cross-legged on the floor, and slowly shaking his broken head as he stanched the blood.

'Et tu, Bunny!' he groaned. 'Mine own familiar friend!'

'Then you weren't even stunned!' I exclaimed. 'Thank God for that!'

'Of course I was stunned,' he murmured, 'and no thanks to you that I wasn't brained. Not to know me in the kit you've seen scores of times! You never looked at me, Bunny; you didn't give me time to open my mouth. I was going to let you run me in so prettily! We'd have walked off arm-in-arm; now it's as tight a place as ever we were in, though you did get rid of old blow-pipes rather nicely. And we shall have the devil's own run for our money!'

Raffles had picked himself up between his mutterings, and I had followed him to the door into the garden, where he stood busy with the key in the dark, having blown out his lantern and handed it to me. But though I followed Raffles, as my nature must, I was far too embittered to answer him again. And so it was for some minutes that might furnish forth a thrilling page, but not a novel one to those who know their Raffles and put up with me. Suffice it that we left a locked door behind us, and the key on the garden wall, which was the first of half-a-dozen that we scaled before dropping into a lane that led to a footbridge higher up the backwater. And when we paused upon the footbridge, the houses along the bank were still in peace and darkness.

Knowing *my* Raffles as I did, I was not surprised when he dived under one end of this bridge, and came up with his Inverness cape and opera hat, which he had hidden there on his way to the house. The thick socks were peeled from his patent leathers, the ragged trousers stripped from an evening pair, bloodstains and Newgate fringe removed at the water's edge, and the whole sepulchre whited in less time than the thing takes to tell. Nor was that enough for Raffles, but he must alter me as well, by wearing my overcoat under his cape, and putting his Zingari scarf about my neck.

'And now,' said he, 'you may be glad to hear there's a 3.12 from Surbiton, which we could catch on all fours. If you like we'll go separately, but I don't think there's the slightest danger now; and I begin to wonder what's happening to old blow-pipes.'

So, indeed, did I, and with no small concern, until I read of his adventures (and our own) in the newspapers. It seemed that he had made a gallant spurt into the road, and there paid the penalty of his rashness by a sudden incapacity to move another inch. It had eventually taken him twenty minutes to creep back to locked doors, and other ten to ring up the inmates. His description of my personal appearance, as reported in the papers, is the only thing that reconciles me to the thought of his sufferings during that half-hour.

But at the time I had other thoughts, and they lay too deep for idle words, for to me also it was a bitter hour. I had not only failed in my self-sought task: I had nearly killed my comrade into the bargain. I had meant well by friend and foe in turn, and I had ended in doing execrably by both. It was not all my fault, but I knew how much my weakness had contributed to the sum. And I must walk with the man whose fault it was, who had travelled two hundred miles to obtain this last proof of my weakness, to bring it home to me, and to make our intimacy intolerable from that hour. I must walk with him to Surbiton, but I need not talk; all through Thames Ditton I had ignored his sallies; nor yet when he ran his arm through mine, on the river front, when we were nearly there, would I break the seal my pride had set upon my lips.

'Come, Bunny,' he said at last, 'I have been the one to suffer most, when all's said and done, and I'll be the first to say that I deserved it. You've broken my head; my hair's all glued up in my gore; and what yarn I'm to put up at Manchester, or how I shall take the field at all tomorrow, I really don't know. Yet I don't blame you, Bunny, and I do blame myself. Isn't it rather hard luck if I'm to go unforgiven into the bargain? I admit that I made a mistake; but, my dear fellow, I made it entirely for your sake.'

'For my sake!' I echoed bitterly.

Raffles was more generous; he ignored my tone.

'I was miserable about you – frankly – miserable!' he went on. 'I couldn't get it out of my head that somehow you would be laid by the heels. It was not your pluck that I distrusted, my dear fellow, but it was your very pluck that made me tremble for you. I couldn't get you out of my head. I went in when runs were wanted, but I give you my word that I was more anxious about you; and no doubt that's why I helped to put on some runs. Didn't you see it in the paper, Bunny? It's the innings of my life, so far.'

'Yes,' I said, 'I saw that you were in at close of play. But I don't believe it was you – I believe you have a double who plays your cricket for you!'

And at the moment that seemed less incredible than the fact.

'I'm afraid you didn't read your paper very carefully,' said Raffles, with the first trace of pique in his tone. 'It was rain that closed play before five o'clock. I hear it was a sultry day in town, but at Manchester we got the storm, and the ground was under water in ten minutes. I never saw such a thing in my life. There was absolutely not the ghost of a chance of another ball being bowled. But I had changed before I thought of doing what I did. It was only when I was on my way back to the hotel, by myself, because I couldn't talk to a soul for thinking of you, that on the spur of the moment I made the man take me to the station instead, and was under way in the restaurant car before I had time to think twice about it. I am not sure that of all the mad deeds I have ever done, this was not the maddest of the lot!'

'It was the finest,' I said in a low voice; for now I marvelled more at the impulse which had prompted his feat, and at the circumstances surrounding it, than even at the feat itself.

'Heaven knows', he went on, 'what they are saying and doing in Manchester! But what can they say? What business is it of theirs? I was there when play stopped, and I shall be there when it starts again. We shall be at Waterloo just after half-past three, and that's going to give me an hour at the Albany on my way to Euston, and another hour at Old Trafford before play begins. What's the matter with that? I don't suppose I shall notch any more, but all the better if I don't; if we have a hot sun after the storm, the sooner they get in the better; and may I have a bowl at them while the ground bites!'

'I'll come up with you,' I said, 'and see you at it.'

'My dear fellow,' replied Raffles, 'that was my whole feeling about you. I wanted to "see you at it" – that was absolutely all. I wanted to be near enough to lend a hand if you got tied up, as the best of us will at times. I knew the ground better than you, and I simply couldn't keep away from it. But I didn't mean you to know that I was there; if everything had gone as I hoped it might, I should have sneaked back to town without ever letting you know I had been up. You should never have dreamt that I had been at your elbow; you would have believed in yourself, and in my belief in you, and the rest would have been silence till the grave. So I dodged you at Waterloo, and I tried not to let you know that I was following you from Esher station. But you suspected somebody was; you stopped to listen more than once; after the second time I dropped behind, but gained on you by taking the short cut by Imber Court and over the footbridge where I left my coat and hat. I was actually in the garden before you were. I saw you smoke your Sullivan, and I was rather proud of you for it, though you must never do that sort of thing again. I heard almost every word between you and the poor devil upstairs. And up to a certain point, Bunny, I really thought you played the scene to perfection.'

The station lights were twinkling ahead of us in the fading velvet of the summer's night. I let them increase and multiply before I spoke.

'And where,' I asked, 'did you think I first went wrong?'

'In going indoors at all,' said Raffles. 'If I had done that, I should have done exactly what you did from that point on. You couldn't help yourself, with that poor brute in that state. And I admired you immensely, Bunny, if that's any comfort to you now.'

Comfort! It was wine in every vein, for I knew that Raffles meant what he said, and with his eyes I soon saw myself in braver colours. I ceased to blush for the vacillations of the night, since he condoned them. I could even see that I had behaved with a measure of decency, in a truly trying situation, now that Raffles seemed to think so. He had changed my whole view of his proceedings and my own, in every incident of the night but one. There was one thing, however, which he might forgive me, but which I felt that I could forgive neither Raffles nor myself. And that was the contused scalp-wound over which I shuddered in the train.

'And to think that I did that,' I groaned, 'and that you laid yourself open to it, and that we have neither of us got another thing to show for our night's work! That poor chap said it was as bad a night as he had ever had in his life; but I call it the very worst that you and I ever had in ours.'

Raffles was smiling under the double lamps of the first-class compartment that we had to ourselves.

'I wouldn't say that, Bunny. We have done worse.'

'Do you mean to tell me you did anything at all?'

'My dear Bunny,' replied Raffles, 'you should remember how long I had been maturing this felonious little plan, what a blow it was to me to have to turn it over to you, and how far I had travelled to see that you did it and yourself as well as might be. You know what I did see, and how well I understood. I tell you again that I should have done the same thing myself, in your place. But I was not in your place, Bunny. My hands were not tied like yours. Unfortunately, most of the jewels have gone on the honeymoon with the happy pair; but these emerald links are all right, and I don't know what the bride was doing to leave this diamond comb behind. Here, too, is the old silver skewer I've been wanting for years – they make the most charming paper-knives in the world – and this gold cigarette-case will just do for your smaller Sullivans.'

Nor were these the only pretty things that Raffles set out in twinkling array upon the opposite cushions. But I do not pretend that this was one of our heavy hauls, or deny that its chief interest still resides in the score of the Second Test Match of that Australian Tour.

7

A TRAP TO CATCH A CRACKSMAN

I was just putting out my light when the telephone rang a furious tocsin in the next room. I flounced out of bed more asleep than awake; in another minute I should have been past ringing up. It was one o'clock in the morning, and I had been dining with Swigger Morrison at his club.

'Hulloa!'

'That you, Bunny?'

'Yes – are you Raffles?'

'What's left of me! Bunny, I want you – quick.'

And even over the wire his voice was faint with anxiety and apprehension.

'What on earth has happened?'

'Don't ask! You never know – '

'I'll come at once. Are you there, Raffles?'

'What's that?'

'Are you there, man?'

'Ye – e – es.'

'At the Albany?'

'No, no, at Maguire's.'

'You never said so. And where's Maguire?'

'In Half-moon Street.'

'I know that. Is he there now?'

'No – not come in yet – and I'm caught.'

'Caught!'

'In that trap he bragged about. It serves me right. I didn't believe in it. But I'm caught at last ... caught ... at last!'

'When he told us he set it every night! Oh, Raffles, what sort of a trap is it? What shall I do? What shall I bring?'

But his voice had grown fainter and wearier with every answer, and now there was no answer at all. Again and again I asked Raffles if he was there; the only sound to reach me in reply was the low metallic hum of the live wire between his ear and mine. And then, as I sat gazing distractedly at my four safe walls, with the receiver still pressed to my head, there came a single groan, followed by the dull and dreadful crash of a human body falling in a heap.

In utter panic I rushed back into my bedroom, and flung myself into the crumpled shirt and evening clothes that lay where I had cast them off. But I knew no more what I was doing than what to do next. I afterwards found that I had taken out a fresh tie, and tied it rather better than usual; but I can remember thinking of nothing but Raffles in some diabolical man-trap, and of a grinning monster stealing in to strike him senseless with one murderous blow. I must have looked in the glass to array myself as I did; but the mind's eye was the seeing eye, and it was filled with this frightful vision of the notorious pugilist known to fame and infamy as Barney Maguire.

It was only the week before that Raffles and I had been introduced to him at the Imperial Boxing Club. Heavy-weight champion of the United States, the fellow was still drunk with his sanguinary triumphs on that side, and clamouring for fresh conquests on ours. But his reputation had crossed the Atlantic before Maguire himself; the grandiose hotels had closed their doors to him; and he had already taken and sumptuously furnished the house in Half-moon Street which does not re-let to this day. Raffles had made friends with the magnificent brute, while I took timid stock of his diamond studs, his jewelled watch-chain, his eighteen-carat bangle, and his six-inch lower jaw. I had shuddered to see Raffles admiring the gewgaws in his turn, in his own brazen fashion, with that air of the cool connoisseur which had its double meaning for me. I for my part would as lief have looked a tiger in the teeth. And when we finally went home with Maguire to see his other trophies, it seemed to me like entering the tiger's lair. But an astounding lair it proved, fitted throughout by one eminent firm, and ringing to the rafters with the last word on fantastic furniture.

The trophies were a still greater surprise. They opened my eyes to the rosier aspect of the noble art, as presently practised on the right side of the Atlantic. Among other offerings, we were permitted to handle the jewelled belt presented to the pugilist by the State of Nevada, a gold brick from the Citizens of Sacramento, and a model of himself in solid silver from the Fisticuff Club in New York. I still remember waiting with bated breath for Raffles to ask Maguire if he were not afraid of burglars, and Maguire replying that he had a trap to catch the cleverest cracksman alive, but flatly refusing to tell us what it was. I could not at the moment conceive a more terrible trap than the heavy-weight himself behind a curtain. Yet it was easy to see that Raffles had accepted the fellow's boast as a challenge. Nor did he deny it later when I taxed him with his mad resolve; he merely refused to allow me to implicate myself in its execution. Well, there was a spice of savage satisfaction in the thought that Raffles had been obliged to turn to me in the end. And, but for the dreadful thud which I had heard over the telephone, I might have extracted some genuine comfort from the unerring sagacity with which he had chosen his night.

Within the last twenty-four hours Barney Maguire had fought his first great battle on British soil. Obviously, he would no longer be the man that he had been in the strict training before the fight; never, as I gathered, was such a ruffian more off his guard, or less capable of protecting himself and his possessions, than in these first hours of relaxation and inevitable debauchery for which Raffles had waited with characteristic foresight. Nor was the terrible Barney likely to be the more abstemious for signal punishment sustained in a far from bloodless victory. Then what could be the meaning of that sickening and most suggestive thud? Could it be the champion himself who had received the *coup de gràce in his* cups? Raffles was the very man to administer it – but he had not talked like that man through the telephone.

And yet – and yet – what else could have happened? I must have asked myself the question between each and all of the above reflections, made partly as I dressed and partly in the hansom on the way to Half-moon Street. It was as yet the only question in my mind. You must know what your emergency is before you can decide how to cope with it; and to this day I sometimes tremble to think of the rashly direct method by which I set about obtaining the requisite information. I drove every yard of the way to the pugilist's very door. You will remember that I had been dining with Swigger Morrison at his club.

Yet at the last I had a rough idea of what I meant to say when the door was opened. It seemed most probable that the tragic end of our talk over the telephone had been caused by the sudden arrival and as sudden violence of Barney Maguire. In that case I was resolved to tell him that Raffles and I had made a bet about his burglar trap, and that I had come to see who had won. I might or might not confess that Raffles had rung me out of bed to this end. If, however, I was wrong about Maguire, and he had not come home at all, then my action would depend upon the menial who answered my reckless ring. But it should result in the rescue of Raffles by hook or crook.

I had the more time to come to some decision, since I rang and rang in vain. The hall, indeed, was in darkness; but when

I peeped through the letter-box I could see a faint beam of light from the back room. That was the room in which Maguire kept his trophies and set his trap. All was quiet in the house: could they have haled the intruder to Vine Street in the short twenty minutes which it had taken me to dress and to drive to the spot? That was an awful thought; but even as I hoped against hope, and rang once more, speculation and suspense were cut short in the last fashion to be foreseen.

A brougham was coming sedately down the street from Piccadilly; to my horror, it stopped behind me as I peered once more through the letter-box, and out tumbled the dishevelled prizefighter and two companions. I was nicely caught in my turn. There was a lamp-post right opposite the door, and I can still see the three of them regarding me in its light. The pugilist had been at least a fine figure of a bully and a braggart when I saw him before his fight; now he had a black eye and a bloated lip, hat on the back of his head, and made-up tie under one ear. His companions were his sallow little Yankee secretary, whose name I really forget, but whom I had met with Maguire at the Boxing Club, and a very grand person in a second skin of shimmering sequins.

I can neither forget nor report the terms in which Barney Maguire asked me who I was and what I was doing there. Thanks, however, to Swigger Morrison's hospitality, I readily reminded him of our former meeting, and of more that I only recalled as the words were in my mouth.

'You'll remember Raffles,' said I, 'if you don't remember me. You showed us your trophies the other night, and asked us both to look you up at any hour of any day or night after the fight.'

I was going on to add that I had expected to find Raffles there before me, to settle a wager that we had made about the man-trap. But the indiscretion was interrupted by Maguire himself, whose dreadful fist became a hand that gripped mine with brute fervour, while with the other he clouted me on the back.

'You don't say!' he cried. 'I took you for some darned crook, but now I remember you purfectly. If you hadn't 've spoke up slick I'd have bu'st your face in, sonny. I would, sure! Come right in, and have a drink to show there's – Jee-hoshaphat!'

The secretary had turned the latchkey in the door, only to be hauled back by the collar as the door stood open, and the light from the inner room was seen streaming upon the banisters at the foot of the narrow stairs.

'A light in my den,' said Maguire in a mighty whisper, 'and the blamed door open, though the key's in my pocket and we left it locked! Talk about crooks, eh? Holy smoke, how I hope we've landed one alive! You ladies and gentlemen, lay round where you are, while I see.'

And the hulking figure advanced on tiptoe, like a performing elephant, until just at the open door, when, for a second we saw his left revolving like a piston and his head thrown back at its fighting angle. But in another second his fists were hands again, and Maguire was rubbing them together as he stood shaking with laughter in the light of the open door.

'Walk up!' he cried, as he beckoned to us three. 'Walk up and see one o' their blamed British crooks laid as low as the blamed carpet, and nailed as tight!'

Imagine my feelings on the mat! The sallow secretary went first, the sequins glittered at his heels, and I must own that for one base moment I was on the brink of bolting through the street door. It had never been shut behind us. I shut it myself in the end. Yet it was small credit to me that I actually remained on the same side of the door as Raffles.

'Reel home-grown, low-down, unwashed Whitechapel!' I had heard Maguire remark within. 'Blamed if our Bowery boys ain't cock-angels to scum like this. Ah, you biter, I wouldn't, soil my knuckles on your ugly face; but if I had my thick boots on I'd dance the soul out of your carcase for two cents!'

After this it required less courage to join the others in the inner room; and for some moments even I failed to identify the truly repulsive object about which I found them grouped. There was no false hair upon the face, but it was as black as any sweep's. The clothes, on the other hand, were new to me, though older and more pestiferous in themselves than most worn by Raffles for professional purposes. And at first, as I say, I was far from sure whether it was Raffles at all; but I remembered the crash that cut short our talk over the telephone; and this inanimate heap of rags was lying directly underneath a wall instrument, with the receiver dangling over him.

'Think you know him?' asked the sallow secretary, as I stopped and peered with my heart in my boots.

'Good Lord, no! I only wanted to see if he was dead,' I explained, having satisfied myself that it was really Raffles, and that Raffles was really insensible. 'But what on earth has happened?' I asked in my turn.

'That's what I want to know,' whined the person in sequins, who had contributed various ejaculations unworthy of report, and finally subsided behind an ostentatious fan.

'I should judge,' observed the secretary, 'that it's for Mr Maguire to say, or not to say, just as he darn pleases.'

But the celebrated Barney stood upon a Persian hearthrug, beaming upon us all in a triumph too delicious for immediate translation into words. The room was furnished as a study, and most artistically furnished, if you consider outlandish shapes in fumed oak artistic. There was nothing of the traditional prizefighter about Barney Maguire, except his vocabulary, and his lower jaw. I had seen over his house already, and it was fitted and decorated throughout by a high-art firm which exhibits just such a room as that which was the scene of our tragedietta. The person in the sequins lay glistening like a landed salmon in a quaint chair of enormous nails and tapestry compact. The secretary leant against an escritoire with huge hinges of beaten metal. The pugilist's own background presented an elaborate scheme of oak and tiles, with ingle-nooks green from the joiner, and a china-cupboard with leaded panes behind his bullet head. And his bloodshot eyes rolled with rich delight from the decanter and glasses on the octagonal table to another decanter in the quaintest and craftiest of revolving spirit-tables.

'Isn't it bully?' asked the prize-fighter, smiling on us each in turn, with his black and bloodshot eyes and his bloated lip. 'To think that I've only to invent a trap to catch a crook, for a blamed crook to walk right into it! You, Mr Man,' and he nodded his great head at me, 'you'll recollect me telling you that I'd gotten one when you come in that night with the other sport? Say, pity he's not with you now; he was a good boy, and I liked him a lot; but he wanted to know too much, and I guess he'd got to want. But I'm liable to tell you now, or else bu'st. See that decanter on the table?'

'I was just looking at it,' said the person in sequins. 'You don't know what a turn I've had, or you'd offer me a little something.'

'You shall have a little something in a minute,' rejoined Maguire. 'But if you take a little anything out of that decanter, you'll collapse like our friend upon the floor.'

'Good Heavens!' I cried out, with involuntary indignation, as his fell scheme broke upon me in a clap.

'Yes, sir!' said Maguire, fixing me with his bloodshot orbs. 'My trap for crooks and cracksmen is a bottle of hocussed whisky, and I guess that's it on the table, with the silver label around its neck. Now look at this other decanter, without any label at all; but for that they're the dead spit of each other. I'll put them side by side, so you can see. It isn't only the decanters, but the liquor looks the same in both, and tastes so you wouldn't know the difference till you woke up in your tracks. I got the poison from a blamed Indian away west, and it's ruther ticklish stuff. So I keep the label around the trap-bottle, and only leave it out nights. That's the idea, and that's all there is to it,' added Maguire, putting the labelled decanter back in the stand. 'But I figure it's enough for ninety-nine crooks out of a hundred, and nineteen out of twenty 'll have their liquor before they go to work.'

'I wouldn't figure on that,' observed the secretary, with a downward glance as though at the prostrate Raffles. 'Have you looked to see if the trophies are all safe?'

'Not yet,' said Maguire, glancing in his turn at the pseudoantique cabinet in which he kept them.

'Then you can save yourself the trouble,' rejoined the secretary, as. he dived under the octagonal table, and came up with a small black bag that I knew at a glance. It was the one that Raffles had used for heavy plunder ever since I had known him.

The bag was so heavy now that the secretary had to use both hands to get it on the table. In another moment he had taken out the jewelled belt presented to Maguire by the State of Nevada, the solid silver statuette of himself, and the gold brick from the Citizens of Sacramento.

Either the sight of his treasures, so nearly lost, or the feeling that the thief had dared to tamper with them after all, suddenly infuriated Maguire to such an extent that he had bestowed a couple of brutal kicks upon the senseless form of Raffles before the secretary and I could interfere.

'Play light, Mr Maguire!' cried the sallow secretary. 'The man's drugged, as well as down.'

'He'll be lucky if he ever gets up, blight and blister him!'

'I should judge it about time to telephone for the police.'

'Not till I've done with him. Wait till he comes to! I guess I'll punch his face into a jam pudding! He shall wash down his teeth with his blood before the coppers come in for what's left!'

'You make me feel quite ill,' complained the grand lady in the chair. 'I wish you'd give me a little something, and not be more vulgar than you can 'elp.'

'Help yourself,' said Maguire, ungallantly, 'and don't talk through your hat. Say, what's the matter with the 'phone?'

The secretary had picked up the dangling receiver.

'It looks to me,' said he, 'as though the crook had rung up somebody before he went off.'

I turned and assisted the grand lady to the refreshment that she craved.

'Like his cheek!' Maguire thundered. 'But who in blazes should *he* ring up?'

'It'll all come out,' said the secretary. 'They'll tell us at the central, and we shall find out fast enough.'

'It don't matter now,' said Maguire. 'Let's have a drink before we rouse him.'

But now I was shaking in my shoes. I saw quite clearly what this meant. Even if I rescued Raffles for the time being, the police would promptly ascertain that it was I who had been rung up by the burglar, and the fact of my not having said a word about it would be directly damning to me, if in the end it did not incriminate us both. It made me quite faint to feel that we might escape the Scylla of our present peril and yet split on the Charybdis of circumstantial evidence. Yet I could see no middle course of conceivable safety, if I held my tongue another moment. So I spoke up desperately, with the rash resolution which was the novel feature of my whole conduct on this occasion. But any sheep would be resolute and rash after dining with Swigger Morrison at his club.

'I wonder if he rang *me* up!' I exclaimed, as if inspired.

'You, sonny?' echoed Maguire, decanter in hand. 'What in hell could he know about you?'

'Or what could you know about him?' amended the secretary, fixing me with eyes like drills.

'Nothing,' I admitted, regretting my temerity with all my heart. 'But some one did ring me up about an hour ago. I thought it was Raffles. I told you I expected to find him here, if you remember.'

'But I don't see what that's got to do with the crook,' pursued the secretary, with his relentless eyes boring deeper and deeper into mine.

"No more do I,' was my miserable reply. But there was a certain comfort in his words, and some simultaneous promise in the quantity of spirit which Maguire splashed into his glass.

'Were you cut off sudden?' asked the secretary, reaching for the decanter, as the three of us sat round the octagonal table.

'So suddenly,' I replied, 'that I never knew who it was who rang me up. No, thank you – not any for me.'

'What!' cried Maguire, raising a depressed head suddenly. 'You won't have a drink in my house? Take care, young man. That's not being a good boy.'

'But I've been dining out,' I expostulated, 'and had my whack. I really have.'

Barney Maguire smote the table with his terrific fist.

'Say, sonny, I like you a lot,' said he. 'But I shan't like you any if you're not a good boy!'

'Very well, very well,' I said hurriedly. 'One finger, if I must.'

And the secretary helped me to not more than two.

'Why should it have been your friend Raffles?' he inquired, returning remorselessly to the charge, while Maguire roared 'Drink up!' and then drooped once more.

'I was half asleep,' I answered, 'and he was the first person who occurred to me. We are both on the telephone, you see. And we had made a bet – '

The glass was at my lips, but I was able to set it down untouched. Maguire's huge jaw had dropped upon his spreading shirt-front, and beyond him I saw the person in sequins fast asleep in the artistic arm-chair.

'What bet?' asked a voice with a sudden start in it. The secretary was blinking as he drained his glass.

'About the very thing we've just had explained to us,' said I, watching my man intently as I spoke. 'I made sure it was a man-trap. Raffles thought it must be something else. We had a tremendous argument about it. Raffles said it wasn't a man-trap. I said it was. We had a bet about it in the end. I put my money on the man-trap. Raffles put his upon the other thing. And Raffles was right – it wasn't a man-trap. But it's every bit as good – every little bit – and the whole boiling of you are caught in it except me!'

I sank my voice with the last sentence, but I might just as well have raised it instead. I had said the same thing over and over again to see whether the wilful tautology would cause the secretary to open his eyes. It seemed to have had the very opposite effect. His head fell forward on the table, with never a quiver at the blow, never a twitch when I pillowed it upon one of his own sprawling arms. And there sat Maguire bolt upright, but for the jowl upon his shirt-front, while the sequins twinkled in a regular rise and fall upon the reclining form of the lady in the fanciful chair. All three were sound asleep, by what accident or by whose design I did not pause to inquire; it was enough to ascertain the fact beyond all chance of error.

I turned my attention to Raffles last of all. There was the other side of the medal. Raffles was still sleeping as sound as the enemy – or so I feared at first. I shook him gently: he made no sign. I introduced vigour into the process: he muttered incoherently. I caught and twisted an unresisting wrist – but it was many and many an anxious moment before his blinking eyes knew mine.

'Bunny!' he yawned, and nothing more until his position came back to him. 'So you came to me,' he went on, in a tone that thrilled me with its affectionate appreciation, 'as I knew you would! Have they turned up yet? They will any minute, you know; there's not one to lose.'

'No, they won't, old man!' I whispered. And he sat up and saw the comatose trio for himself.

Raffles seemed less amazed at the result than I had been as a puzzled witness of the process; on the other hand, I had never seen anything quite so exultant as the smile that broke through his blackened countenance like a light. Obviously it was all no great surprise, and no puzzle at all, to Raffles.

'How much did they have, Bunny?' were his first whispered words.

'Maguire a good three fingers, and the others at least two.'

'Then we needn't lower our voices, and we needn't walk on our toes. Eheu! I dreamt somebody was kicking me in the ribs, and I believe it must have been true.'

He had risen with a hand to his side, and a wry look on his sweep's face.

'You can guess which of them it was,' said I. 'The beast is jolly well served!'

And I shook my fist in the paralytic face of the most brutal bruiser of his time.

'He is safe till the forenoon, unless they bring a doctor to him,' said Raffles. 'I don't suppose we could rouse him now if we tried. How much of the fearsome stuff do you suppose *I* took? About a tablespoonful? I guessed what it was, and couldn't resist making sure; the minute I was satisfied, I changed the label and the position of the two decanters, little thinking I should stay to see the fun; but in another minute I could hardly keep my eyes open. I realised then that I was fairly poisoned with some subtle drug. If I left the house at all in that state, I must leave the spoil behind, or be found drunk in the gutter with my head on the swag itself. In any case I should have been picked up and run in, and that might have led to anything.'

'So you rang me up!'

'It was my last brilliant inspiration – a sort of flash in the brainpan before the end – and I remember very little about it. I was more asleep than awake at the time.'

'You sounded like it, Raffles, now that one has the clue.'

'I can't remember a word I said, or what was the end of it, Bunny.'

'You fell in a heap before you came to the end.'

'You didn't hear that through the telephone?'

'As though we had been in the same room: only I thought it was Maguire who had stolen a march on you and knocked you out.'

I had never seen Raffles more interested and impressed; but at this point his smile altered, his eyes softened, and I found my hand in his.

'You thought that, and yet you came like a shot to do battle for my body with Barney Maguire! Jack-the-Giant-killer wasn't in it with you, Bunny!'

'It was no credit to me – it was rather the other thing,' said I, remembering my rashness and my luck, and confessing both in a breath. 'You know Swigger Morrison?' I added in final explanation. 'I had been dining with him at his club!'

Raffles shook his long old head. And the kindly light in his eyes was still my infinite reward.

'I don't care', said he, 'how deeply you had been dining: *in vino veritas*, Bunny, and your pluck would always out! I have never doubted it, and I never shall. In fact, I rely on nothing else to get us out of this mess.'

My face must have fallen, as my heart sank, at these words. I had said to myself that we were out of the mess already – that we had merely to make a clean escape from the house – now the easiest thing in the world. But as I looked at Raffles, and as Raffles looked at me, on the threshold of the room where the three sleepers slept on without sound or movement, I grasped the real problem that lay before us. It was twofold; and the funny thing was that I had seen both horns of the dilemma for myself, before Raffles came to his senses. But with Raffles in his right mind, I had ceased to apply my own or to carry my share of our common burden another inch. It had been an unconscious withdrawal on my part, an instinctive tribute to my leader; but I was sufficiently ashamed of it as we stood and faced the problem in each other's eyes.

'If we simply cleared out,' continued Raffles, 'you would be incriminated in the first place as my accomplice, and once they had you they would have a compass with the needle pointing straight to me. They mustn't have either of us, Bunny, or they will get us both. And for my part they may as well!'

I echoed a sentiment that was generosity itself in Raffles, but in my case a mere truism.

'It's easy enough for me,' he went on. 'I am a common housebreaker, and I escape. They don't know me from Noah. But they do know you; and how do you come to let me escape? What has happened to you, Bunny? That's the crux. What could have happened after they all dropped off?' And for a minute Raffles frowned and smiled like a sensation novelist working out a plot; then the light broke, and transfigured him through his burnt cork. 'I've got it, Bunny!' he exclaimed. 'You took some of the stuff yourself, though of course not nearly so much as they did.'

'Splendid!' I cried. 'They really were pressing it upon me at the end, and I did say it must be very little.'

'You dozed off in your turn, but you were naturally the first to come to yourself. I had flown; so had the gold brick, the jewelled belt, and the silver statuette. You tried to rouse the others. You couldn't succeed; nor would you if you did try. So what did you do? What's the only really innocent thing you could do in the circumstances?'

'Go for the police,' I suggested dubiously, little relishing the prospect.

'There's a telephone installed for the occasion,' said Raffles. 'I should ring them up, if I were you. Try not to look blue about it, Bunny. They're quite the nicest fellows in the world, and what you have to tell them is a mere microbe to the camels I've made them swallow without a grain of salt. It's really the most convincing story one could conceive; but unfortunately there's another point which will take more explaining away.'

And even Raffles looked grave enough as I nodded.

'You mean that they'll find out you rang me up?'

'They may,' said Raffles. 'I see that I managed to replace the receiver all right. But still – they may.'

'I'm afraid they will,' said I, uncomfortably. 'I'm very much afraid I gave something of the kind away. You see, you had *not* replaced the receiver; it was dangling over you where you lay. This very question came up, and the brutes themselves seemed so quick to see its possibilities that I thought it best to take the bull by the horns and own that I had been rung up by somebody. To be actually honest, I even went so far as to say I thought it was Raffles!'

'You didn't, Bunny!'

'What could I say? I was obliged to think of somebody, and I saw they were not going to recognise you. So I put up a yarn about a wager we had made about this very trap of Maguire's. You see, Raffles, I've never properly told you how I got in, and there's no time now; but the first thing I had said was that I half expected to find you here before me. That was in case they spotted you at once. But it made all that part about the telephone fit in rather well.'

'I should think it did, Bunny,' murmured Raffles, in a tone that added sensibly to my reward. 'I couldn't have done better myself, and you will forgive my saying that you have never in your life done half so well. Talk about that crack you gave me on the head! You have made it up to me a hundredfold by all you have done tonight. But the bother of it is that there's still so much to do, and to hit upon, and so precious little time for thought as well as action.'

I took out my watch, and showed it to Raffles without a word. It was three o'clock in the morning, and the latter end of March. In little more than an hour there would be dim daylight in the streets. Raffles roused himself from a reverie with sudden decision.

'There's only one thing for it, Bunny,' said he. 'We must trust each other, and divide the labour. You ring up the police, and leave the rest to me.'

'You haven't hit upon any reason for the sort of burglar they think you were, ringing up the kind of man they know I am?'

'Not yet, Bunny, but I shall. It may not be wanted for a day or so, and after all it isn't for you to give the explanation. It would be highly suspicious if you did.'

'So it would,' I agreed.

'Then will you trust me to hit on something – if possible before morning – in any case by the time it's wanted? I won't fail you, Bunny. You must see how I can never, never fail you after tonight!'

That settled it. I gripped his hand without another word, and remained on guard over the three sleepers while Raffles stole upstairs. I have since learnt that there were servants at the top of the house, and in the basement a man, who actually heard some of our proceedings! But he was mercifully too accustomed to nocturnal orgies, and those of a far more uproarious character, to appear unless summoned to the scene. I believe he heard Raffles leave. But no secret was made of his exit: he let himself out, and told me afterwards that the first person he encountered in the street was the constable on the beat. Raffles wished him good morning, as well he might; for he had been upstairs to wash his face and hands; and in the prize-fighter's great hat and fur coat he might have marched round Scotland Yard itself, in spite of his having the gold brick from Sacramento in one pocket, the silver statuette of Maguire in the other, and round his waist the jewelled belt presented to that worthy by the State of Nevada.

My immediate part was a little hard after the excitement of those small hours. I will only say that we had agreed that it would be wisest for me to lie like a log among the rest for half an hour, before staggering to my feet and rousing house and police; and that in that half-hour Barney Maguire crashed to the floor, without waking either himself or his companions, though not without bringing my beating heart into the very roof of my mouth.

It was daybreak when I gave the alarm with bell and telephone. In a few minutes we had the house congested with dishevelled domestics, irascible doctors, and arbitrary minions of the law. If I told my story once, I told it a dozen times, and all on an empty stomach. But it was certainly a most plausible and consistent tale, even without that confirmation which none of the other victims was as yet sufficiently recovered to supply. And in the end I was permitted to retire from the scene until required to give further information, or to identify the prisoner whom the good police confidently expected to make before the day was out.

I drove straight to the flat. The porter flew to help me out of my hansom. His face alarmed me more than any I had left in Halfmoon Street. It alone might have spelt my ruin.

'Your flat's been entered in the night, sir,' he cried. 'The thieves have taken everything they could lay hands on.'

'Thieves in my flat!' I ejaculated aghast. There were one or two incriminating possessions up there, as well as at the Albany.

The door's been forced with a jemmy,' said the porter. 'It was the milkman who found it out. There's a constable up there now.'

A constable poking about in my flat of all others! I rushed upstairs without waiting for the lift. The invader was moistening his pencil between laborious notes in a fat pocketbook; he had penetrated no further than the forced door. I dashed past him in a fever. I kept *my* trophies in a wardrobe drawer specially fitted with a Bramah lock. The lock was broken – the drawer void.

'Something valuable, sir?' inquired the intrusive constable at my heels.

'Yes, indeed – some old family silver,' I answered. It was quite true. But the family was not mine.

And not till then did the truth flash across my mind. Nothing else of value had been taken. But there was a meaningless litter in all the rooms. I turned to the porter, who had followed me up from the street; it was his wife who looked after the flat.

'Get rid of this idiot as quick as you can,' I whispered. 'I'm going straight to Scotland Yard myself. Let your wife tidy the place while I'm gone, and have the lock mended before she leaves. I'm going as I am, this minute!'

And go I did, in the first hansom I could find – but not straight to Scotland Yard. I stopped the cab in Piccadilly on the way.

Old Raffles opened his own door to me. I cannot remember finding him fresher, more immaculate, more delightful to behold in every way. Could I paint a picture of Raffles with something other than my pen, it would be as I saw him that bright March morning, at his open door in the Albany, a trim slim figure in matutinal grey, cool and gay and breezy as incarnate spring.

'What on earth did you do it for?' I asked within.

'It was the only solution,' he answered, handing me the cigarettes. 'I saw it the moment I got outside.'

'I don't sec it yet.'

'Why should a burglar call an innocent gentleman away from home?'

'That's what we couldn't make out.'

'I tell you I got it directly I had left you. He called you away in order to burgle you too, of course!'

And Raffles stood smiling upon me in all his incomparable radiance and audacity.

'Buy why me?' I asked. 'Why on earth should he burgle *me*?'

'My dear Bunny, we must leave something to the imagination of the police. But we will assist them with a fact or two in due season. It was the dead of night when Maguire first took us to his house; it was at the Imperial Boxing Club we met him; and you meet other queer fish at the Imperial Boxing Club. You may remember that he telephoned to his man to prepare supper for us, and that you and he discussed telephones and treasure as we marched through the midnight streets. He was certainly bucking about his trophies, and for the sake of the argument you will be good enough to admit that you probably bucked about yours. What happens? You are overheard; you are followed; you are worked into the same scheme, and robbed on the same night.'

'And you really think this will meet the case?'

'I am quite certain of it, Bunny, so far as it rests with us to meet the case at all.'

'Then give me another cigarette, my dear fellow, and let me push on to Scotland Yard.'

Raffles held up both hands in admiring horror.

'Scotland Yard!'

'To give a false description of what you took from that drawer in my wardrobe.'

'A false description! Bunny, you have no more to learn from me. Time was when I wouldn't have let you go there without me to retrieve a lost umbrella. But then I had never seen you retrieve a lost cause!'

And for once I was not sorry for Raffles to have the last unworthy word, as he returned with me to his outer door, and gaily waved me down the stairs.

8

THE SPOILS OF SACRILEGE

There was one deed of those days which deserved a place in our original annals. It is the deed of which I am personally most ashamed. I have traced the course of a score of felonies, from their source in the brain of Raffles to their issue in his hands. I have omitted all mention of the one which emanated from my own miserable mind. But in these supplementary memoirs, wherein I pledged myself to extenuate nothing more that I might have to tell of Raffles, it is only fair that I should make as clean a breast of my own baseness. It was I, then, and I alone, who outraged natural sentiment, and trampled the expiring embers of elementary decency, by proposing and planning the raid upon my own old home.

I would not accuse myself the more vehemently by making excuses at this point. Yet I feel bound to state that it was already many years since the property had passed from our possession into that of an utter alien, against whom I harboured a prejudice which was some excuse in itself. He had enlarged and altered the dear old place out of knowledge; nothing had been good enough for him as it stood in our day. The man was a hunting maniac, and where my dear father used to grow prize peaches under glass, this vandal was soon stabling his hothouse thoroughbreds, which took prizes in their turn at all the county shows. It was a southern county, and I never went down there without missing another greenhouse and noting a corresponding extension to the stables. Not that I ever set foot in the grounds from the day we left; but for some years I used to visit old friends in the neighbourhood, and could never resist the temptation to reconnoitre the scenes of my childhood. And so far as could be seen from the road – which it stood too near – the house itself appeared to be the one thing that the horsy purchaser had left 'much as he found it.

My only other excuse may be none at all in any eyes but mine. It was my passionate desire at this period to 'keep up my end with Raffles in every department of the game felonious. He would insist upon an equal division of all proceeds; it was for me to earn my share. So far I had been useful only at a pinch; the whole credit of any real success belonged invariably to Raffles. It had always been his idea. That was the tradition which I sought to end, and no means could compare with that of my unscrupulous choice. There was the one house in England of which I knew every inch, and Raffles only what I told him. For once I must lead, and Raffles follow, whether he liked it or not. He saw that himself; and I think he liked it better than he liked me for the desecration in view; but I had hardened my heart, and his feelings were too fine for actual remonstrance on such a point.

I, in my obduracy, went to foul extremes. I drew plans of all the floors from memory. I actually descended upon my friends in the neighbourhood, with the sole object of obtaining snapshots over our own old garden wall. Even Raffles could not keep his eyebrows down when I showed him the prints one morning in the Albany. But he confined his open criticisms to the house.

'Built in the late 'sixties, I scc,' said Raffles, 'or else early in the 'seventies.'

'Exactly when it was built,' I replied. 'But that's worthy of a sixpenny detective, Raffles! How on earth did you know?'

'That slate tower bang over the porch, with the dormer windows, and the iron railing and flagstaff atop, makes us a present of the period. You see them on almost every house of a certain size built about thirty years ago. They are quite the most useless excrescences I know.'

'Ours wasn't,' I answered, with some warmth. 'It was my *sanctum sanctorum* in the holidays. I smoked my first pipe up there, and wrote my first verses.'

Raffles laid a kindly hand upon my shoulder.

'Bunny, Bunny, you can rob the old place, and yet you can't hear a word against it!'

'That's different,' said I, relentlessly. 'The tower was there in my time, but the man I mean to rob was not.'

'You really do mean to do it, Bunny?'

'By myself, if necessary!' I averred.

'Not again, Bunny, not again,' rejoined Raffles, laughing, as he shook his head. 'But do you think the man has enough to make it worth our while to go so far afield?'

'Far afield! It's not forty miles on the London and Brighton.'

'Well, that's as bad as a hundred on most lines. And when did you say it was to be?'

'Friday week.'

'I don't much like a Friday, Bunny. Why make it one?'

'It's the night of their Hunt Point-to-Point. They wind up the season with it every year; and the bloated Guillemard usually sweeps the board with his fancy flyers.'

'You mean the man in your old house?'

'Yes; and he tops up with no end of a dinner there', I went on, 'to his hunting pals and the bloods who ride for him. If the festive board doesn't groan under a new regiment of challenge cups, it will be no fault of theirs, and old Guillemard will have to do them top-hole all the same.'

'So it's a case of common pot-hunting,' remarked Raffles, eyeing me shrewdly through the cigarette smoke.

'Not for us, my dear fellow,' I made answer in his own tone. 'I wouldn't ask you to break into the next set of chambers here in the Albany for a few pieces of modem silver, Raffles. Not that we need scorn the cups if we get a chance of lifting them, and if Guillemard does so in the first instance. It's by no means certain that he will. But it *is* pretty certain to be a lively night for him and his pals – and a vulnerable one for the best bedroom!'

'Capital!' cried Raffles, throwing coils of smoke between his smiles. 'Still, if it's a dinner-party, the hostess won't leave her jewels upstairs. She'll wear them, my boy.'

'Not all of them, Raffles; she has far too many for that. Besides, it isn't an ordinary dinner-party; they say Mrs Guillemard is generally the only lady there, and that she's quite charming in herself. Now, no charming woman would clap on all sail in jewels for a roomful of fox-hunters.'

'It depends what jewels she has.'

'Well, she might wear her rope of pearls.'

'I should have said so.'

'And, of course, her rings.'

'Exactly, Bunny.'

"But not necessarily her diamond tiara – '

'Has she got one?'

' – and certainly not her emerald and diamond necklace on top of all!'

Raffles snatched the Sullivan from his lips, and his eyes burned like its end.

'Bunny, do you mean to tell me there are all these things?'

'Of course I do,' said I. 'They are rich people, and he's not quite such a brute as to spend everything on his stable. Her jewels are as much the talk as his hunters. My friends told me all about both the other day when I was down making inquiries. They thought my curiosity as natural as my wish for a few snapshots of the old place. In their opinion the emerald necklace alone must be worth thousands of pounds.'

Raffles rubbed his hands in playful pantomime.

'I only hope you didn't ask too many questions, Bunny! But if your friends are such old friends, you will never enter their heads when they hear what has happened, unless you are seen down there on the night, which might be fatal. Your approach will require some thought: if you like, I can work out the shot for you. I shall go down independently, and the best thing may be to meet outside the house itself on the night of nights. But from that moment I am in your hands.'

And on these refreshing lines our plan of campaign was gradually developed and elaborated into that finished study on which Raffles would rely like any artist of the footlights. None more capable than he of coping with the occasion as it rose, of rising himself with the emergency of the moment, of snatching a victory from the very dust of defeat. Yet, for choice, every detail was premeditated, and an alternative expedient at each finger's end for as many bare and awful possibilities. In this case, however, the finished study stopped short at the garden gate or wall; there, I was to assume command; and though Raffles carried the actual tools of the trade of which he alone was master, it was on the understanding that for once I should control and direct their use.

I had gone down in evening clothes by an evening train, but had carefully overshot old landmarks, and alighted at a small station some miles south of the one where I was still remembered. This committed me to a solitary and somewhat lengthy tramp; but the night was mild and starry, and I marched into it with a high stomach; for this was to be no costume crime, and yet I should have Raffles at my elbow all the night. Long before I reached my destination, indeed, he stood in wait for me on the white highway, and we finished with linked arms.

'I came down early,' said Raffles, 'and had a look at the races. I always prefer to measure my man, Bunny; and you needn't sit in the front row of the stalls to take stock of your friend Guillemard. No wonder he doesn't ride his own horses! The steeplechaser isn't foaled that would carry him round that course. But he's a fine monument of a man, and he takes his troubles in a way that makes me blush to add to them.'

'Did he lose a horse?' I inquired, cheerfully.

'No, Bunny, but he didn't win a race! His horses were by chalks the best there, and his pals rode them like the foul fiend, but with the worst of luck every time. Not that you'd think it, from the row they're making. I've been listening to them from the road – you always did say the house stood too near it.'

'Then you didn't go in?'

'When it's your show? You should know me better. Not a foot would I set on the premises behind your back. But here they are, so perhaps you'll lead the way.'

And I led it without a moment's hesitation, through the unpretentious six-barred gate into the long but shallow crescent of the drive. There were two such gates, one at each end of the drive, but no lodge at either, and not a light nearer than those of the house. The shape and altitude of the lighted windows, the whisper of the laurels on either hand, the very feel of the gravel underfoot, were at once familiar to my senses as the sweet, relaxing, immemorial air that one drank deeper at every breath. Our stealthy advance was to me like stealing back into one's childhood; and yet I could conduct it without compunction. I was too excited to feel immediate remorse, albeit not too lost in excitement to know that remorse for every step that I was taking would be my portion soon enough. I mean every word that I have written of my peculiar shame for this night's work. And it was all to come over me before the night was out. But in the garden I never felt it once.

The dining-room windows blazed in the side of the house facing the road. That was an objection to peeping through the Venetian blinds, as we nevertheless did, at our peril of observation from the road. Raffles would never have led me into danger so gratuitous and unnecessary, but he followed me into it without a word. I can only plead that we both had our reward. There was a sufficient chink in the obsolete Venetians, and through it we saw every inch of the picturesque board. Mrs Guillemard was still in her place, but she really was the only lady, and dressed as quietly as I had prophesied; round her neck was her rope of pearls, but not the glimmer of an emerald nor the glint of a diamond, nor yet the flashing constellation of a tiara in her hair. I gripped Raffles in token of my triumph, and he nodded as he scanned the overwhelming majority of flushed fox-hunters. With the exception of one stripling, evidently the son of the house, they were in evening pink to a man; and as I say, their faces matched their coats. An enormous fellow, with a big bald head and black moustache, occupied my poor father's place; he it was who had replaced our fruitful vineries with his stinking stables; but I am bound to own he looked a genial clod, as he sat in his fat and listened to the young bloods boasting of their prowess, or elaborately explaining their mishaps. And for a minute we listened also, before I remembered my responsibilities, and led Raffles round to the back of the house.

There never was an easier house to enter. I used to feel that keenly as a boy, when, by a prophetic irony, burglars were my bugbear, and I looked under my bed every night in life. The bow-windows on the ground-floor finished in inane balconies to the first-floor windows. These balconies had ornamental iron railings, to which a less ingenious rope-ladder than ours could have been hitched with equal ease. Raffles had brought it with him, round his waist, and he carried the telescopic stick for fixing it in its place. The one was unwound, and the other put together, in a secluded corner of the red-brick walls, where of old I had played my own game of squash-rackets in the holidays. I made further investigations in the starlight, and even found a trace of my original white line along the red wall.

But it was not until we had effected our entry through the room which had been my very own, and made our parlous way across the lighted landing, to the best bedroom of those days and these, that I really felt myself a worm. Twin brass bedsteads occupied the site of the old four-poster from which I had first beheld the light. The doors were the same; my childish hands had grasped these very handles. And there was Raffles securing the landing door with wedge and gimlet, the very second after softly closing it behind us.

'The other leads into the dressing-room, of course? Then you might be fixing the outer dressing-room door,' he whispered at his work, 'but not the middle one, Bunny, unless you want to. The stuff will be in there, you see, if it isn't in here.'

My door was done in a moment, being fitted with a powerful bolt; but now an aching conscience made me busier than I need have been. I had raised the rope-ladder after us into my own old room, and while Raffles wedged his door I lowered the ladder from one of the best bedroom windows, in order to prepare that way of escape which was a fundamental feature of his own strategy. I meant to show Raffles that I had not followed in his train for nothing. But I left it to him to unearth the jewels. I had begun by turning up the gas; there appeared to me no possible risk in that; and Raffles went to work with a will in the excellent light. There were some good pieces in the room, including an ancient tallboy in fruity mahogany, every drawer of which was turned out on the bed without avail. A few of the drawers had locks to pick, yet not one trifle to our taste within. The situation became serious as the minutes flew. We had left the party at its sweets; the solitary lady might be free to roam her house at any minute. In the end we turned our attention to the dressing-room. And no sooner did Raffles behold the bolted door, than up went his hands.

'A bathroom bolt,' he cried below his breath, 'and no bath in the room! Why didn't you tell me, Bunny? A bolt like that speaks volumes; there's none on the bedroom door, remember, and this one's worthy of a strong-room. What if it is their strong-room, Bunny! Oh, Bunny, what if this is their safe!'

Raffles had dropped upon his knees before a carved oak chest of indisputable antiquity. Its panels were delightfully irregular, its angles faultlessly faulty, its one modem defilement a strong lock to the lid. Raffles was smiling as he produced his jemmy. R – r – r – rip went lock or lid in other ten seconds – I was not there to see which. I had wandered back into the bedroom in a paroxysm of excitement and suspense. I must keep busy as well as Raffles, and it was not too soon to see whether the rope-ladder as all right. In another minute...

I stood frozen to the floor. I had hooked the ladder beautifully to the inner sill of wood, and had also let down the extended rod for the more expeditious removal of both on our return to *terra firma*. Conceive my cold horror on arriving at the open window just in time to see the last of hooks and bending rod, as they floated out of sight and reach into the outer darkness of the night, removed by some silent and invisible hand below!

'Raffles – Raffles – they've spotted us and moved the ladder this very instant!'

So I panted as I rushed on tiptoe to the dressing-room. Raffles had the working end of his jemmy under the lid of a leathern jewel-case. It flew open at the vicious twist of his wrist that preceded his reply.

'Did you let them see that you'd spotted that?'

'No.'

'Good! Pocket some of these cases – no time to open them. Which door's nearest the back stairs?'

'The other.'

'Come on, then!'

'No, no, I'll lead the way. I know every inch of it.'

And, as I leant against the bedroom door, handle in hand, while Raffles stooped to unscrew the gimlet and withdraw the wedge, I hit upon the ideal port in the storm that was evidently about to burst on our devoted heads. It was the last place in which they would look for a couple of expert cracksmen with no previous knowledge of the house. If only we could gain my haven unobserved, there we might lie in unsuspected hiding, and by the hour, if not for days and nights.

Alas for that sanguine dream! The wedge was out, and Raffles on his feet behind me. I opened the door, and for a second the pair of us stood still upon the threshold.

Creeping up the stairs before us, each on the tip of his silken toes, was a serried file of pink barbarians, redder in the face than anywhere else, and armed with crops carried by the wrong end. The monumental baldhead with the black moustache led the advance. The fool stood still upon the top step to let out the loudest and cheeriest view-holloa that ever smote my ears.

It cost him more than he may know until I tell him. There was the wide part of the landing between us; we had just that much start along the narrow part with the walls and doors upon our left, the banisters on our right, and the baize door at the end. But if the great Guillemard had not stopped to live up to his sporting reputation, he would assuredly have laid one or other of us by the heels, and either would have been tantamount to both. As I gave Raffles a headlong lead to the baize door, I glanced down the great well of the stairs, and up came the daft yells of these sporting oafs:

'Gone away – gone away!'

'Yoick – yoick – yoick!'

'*Yon*-der they go!'

And gone I had, through the baize door to the back landing, with Raffles at my heels. I held the door for him, and heard him bang it in the face of the spluttering and blustering master of the house. Other feet were already on the lower flight of the back stairs; but the upper flight was the one for me, and in an instant we were racing along the upper corridor with the chuckle-headed pack at our heels. Here it was all but dark – they were the servants' bedrooms that we were passing now – but I knew what I was doing. Round the last corner to the right, through the first door to the left, and we were in the room underneath the tower. In our time a long step-ladder had led to the tower itself. I rushed in the dark to the old corner. Thank God, the ladder was-there still! It leapt under us as we rushed aloft like one quadruped. The breakneck trapdoor was still protected by a curved brass stanchion; this I grasped with one hand, and then Raffles with the other as I felt my feet firm upon the tower floor. In he sprawled after me, and down went the trapdoor with a bang upon the leading hound.

I hoped to feel his deadweight shake the house, as he crashed upon the floor below; but the fellow must have ducked, and no crash came. Meanwhile not a word passed between Raffles and me; he had followed me, as I had led him, without waste of breath upon a single syllable. But the merry lot below were still yelling and belling in full cry.

'Gone to ground!' screamed one.

'Where's the terrier?' screeched another.

But their host of the mighty girth – a man like a soda-water bottle, from my one glimpse of him on his feet – seemed sobered rather than stunned by the crack on that head of his. We heard his fine voice no more, but we could feel him straining every thew against the trapdoor upon which Raffles and I stood side by side. At least I thought Raffles was standing, until he asked me to strike a light, when I found him on his knees instead of on his feet, busy screwing down the trapdoor with his gimlet. He carried three or four gimlets for wedging doors, and he drove them all in to the handle, while I pulled at the stanchion and pushed with my feet.

But the upward pressure ceased before our efforts. We heard the ladder creak again under a ponderous and slow descent; and we stood upright in the dim flicker of a candle-end that I had lit and left burning on the floor. Raffles glanced at the four small windows in turn, and then at me.

'Is there any way out at all?' he whispered, as no other being would or could have whispered to the man who had led him into such a trap. 'We've no rope-ladder, you know.'

'Thanks to me,' I groaned. 'The whole thing's my fault!'

'Nonsense, Bunny; there was no other way to run. But what about these windows?'

His magnanimity took me by the throat; without a word I led him to the one window looking inward upon sloping slates and level leads. Often as a boy I had clambered over them, for the fearful fun of risking life and limb, or the fascination of peering through the great square skylight, down the well of the house into the hall below. There were, however, several smaller skylights, for the benefit of the top floor, through any one of which I thought we might have made a dash. But at a glance I saw we were too late: one of these skylights became a brilliant square before our eyes; opened, and admitted a flushed face on flaming shoulders.'

'I'll give them a fright!' said Raffles through his teeth. In an instant he had plucked out his revolver, smashed the window with its butt, and the slates with a bullet not a yard from the protruding head. And that, I believe, was the only shot that Raffles ever fired in his whole career as a midnight marauder.

'You didn't hit him?' I gasped, as the head disappeared, and we heard a crash in the corridor.

'Of course I didn't, Bunny,' he replied, backing into the tower; 'but no one will believe I didn't mean to, and it'll stick on ten years if we're caught. That's nothing if it gives us an extra five minutes now, while they hold a council of war. Is that a working flagstaff overhead?'

'It used to be.'

'Then there'll be halliards.'

'They were as thin as clothes-lines.'

'And they're sure to be rotten, and we should be seen cutting them down. No, Bunny, that won't do. Wait a bit. Is there a lightning-conductor?'

'There was.'

I opened one of the side windows, and reached out as far as I could.

'You'll be seen from that skylight!' cried Raffles, in a warning undertone.

'No, I won't. I can't see it myself. But here's the lightning-conductor, where it always was.'

'How thick?' asked Raffles, as I drew in and rejoined him.

'Rather thicker than a lead-pencil.'

'They sometimes bear you,' said Raffles, slipping on a pair of white kid gloves, and stuffing his handkerchief into the palm of one. 'The difficulty is to keep a grip; but I've been up and down them before tonight. And it's our only chance. I'll go first, Bunny: you watch me, and do exactly as I do if I get down all right.'

'But if you don't!'

'If I don't,' whispered Raffles, as he wormed through the window feet foremost, 'I'm afraid you'll have to face the music where you are, and I shall have the best of it down in Acheron!'

And he slid out of reach without another word, leaving me to shudder alike at his levity and his peril; nor could I follow him very far by the wan light of the April stars; but I saw his forearms resting a moment in the spout that ran round the tower, between bricks and slates, on the level of the floor; and I had another dim glimpse of him lower still, on the eaves over the very room that we had ransacked. Thence the conductor ran straight to earth in an angle of the façade. And since it had borne him thus far without mishap, I felt that Raffles was as good as down. But I had neither his muscles nor his nerves, and my head swam as I mounted to the window and began to creep out backwards in my turn.

So it was that at the last moment I had my first unobstructed view of the little old tower of other days. Raffles was out of the way; the bit of candle was still burning on the floor, and in its dim light the familiar haunt was cruelly like itself of innocent memory. A lesser ladder still ascended to a tinier trapdoor in the apex of the tower; the fixed seats looked to me to be wearing their old, old coat of grained varnish; nay, the varnish had its ancient smell, and the very vanes outside creaked their message to my ears. I remembered whole days that I had spent, whole books that I had read, here in this favourite fastness of my boyhood. The dirty little place, with the dormer window in each of its four sloping sides, became a gallery hung with poignant pictures of the past. And here was I leaving it with my life in my hands and my pockets full of stolen jewels! A superstition seized me. Suppose the conductor came down with me... suppose I slipped... and was picked up dead, with the proceeds of my shameful crime upon me, under the very windows

...where the sun
Came peeping in at dawn...

I hardly remember what I did, or left undone. I only know that nothing broke, that somehow I kept my hold, and that in the end the wire ran red-hot through my palms, so that both were torn and bleeding when I stood panting beside Raffles in the flower-beds. There was no time for thinking then. Already there was a fresh commotion indoors; the tidal wave of excitement, which had swept all before it to the upper regions, was subsiding in as swift a rush downstairs; and I raced after Raffles along the edge of the drive, without daring to look behind.

We came out by the opposite gate to that by which we had stolen in. Sharp to the right ran the private lane behind the stables, and sharp to the right dashed Raffles, instead of straight along the open road. It was not the course I should have chosen, but I followed Raffles without a murmur, only too thankful that he had assumed the lead at last. Already the stables were lit up like a chandelier; there was a staccato rattle of horseshoes in the stable-yard, and the great gates were opening as we skimmed past in the nick of time. In another minute we were skulking in the shadow of the kitchen- garden wall, while the high-road rang with the dying tattoo of galloping hoofs.

That's for the police,' said Raffles, waiting for me. 'But the fun's only beginning in the stables. Hear the uproar, and see the lights! In another minute they'll be turning out the hunters for the last run of the season!'

'We mustn't give them one, Raffles!'

'Of course we mustn't; but that means stopping where we are.'

'We can't do that!'

'If they're wise they'll send a man to every railway-station within ten miles, and draw every cover inside the radius. I can only think of one that's not likely to occur to them.'

'What's that?'

The other side of this wall. How big is the garden, Bunny?'

'Six or seven acres.'

'Well, you must take me to another of your old haunts, where we can lie low till morning.'

'And then?'

'Sufficient for the night, Bunny! The first thing is to find a burrow. What are those trees at the end of this lane?'

'St Leonard's Forest.'

'Magnificent! They'll scour every inch of that before they come back to their own garden. Come, Bunny, give me a leg up, and I'll pull you after me in two ticks!'

There was indeed nothing better to be done; and, much as I loathed and dreaded entering the place again, I had already thought of a second sanctuary of old days, which might as well be put to the base uses of this disgraceful night. In a far corner of the garden, over a hundred yards from the house, a little ornamental lake had been dug within my own memory; its shores were shelving lawn and steep banks of rhododendrons; and among the rhododendrons nestled a tiny boathouse which had been my childish joy. It was half a dock for the dinghy in which one ploughed these miniature waters, and half a bathing-box for those who preferred their morning tub among the goldfish. I could not think of a safer asylum than this, if we must spend the night upon the premises; and Raffles agreed with me when I had led him by sheltering shrubbery and perilous lawn to the diminutive *chalet* between the rhododendrons and the water.

But what a night it was! The little bathing-box had two doors, one to the water, the other to the path. To hear all that could be heard, it was necessary to keep both doors open, and quite imperative not to talk. The damp night-air of April filled the place, and crept through our evening clothes and light overcoats into the very marrow; the mental torture of the situation was renewed and multiplied in my brain; and all the time one's ears were pricked for footsteps on the path between the rhododendrons. The only sounds we could at first identify came one and all from the stables. Yet there the excitement subsided sooner than we had expected, and it was Raffles himself who breathed a doubt as to whether they were turning out the hunters after all. On the other hand, we heard wheels in the drive not long after midnight; and Raffles, who was beginning to scout among the shrubberies, stole back to tell me that the guests were departing, and being sped, with an unimpaired conviviality which he failed to understand. I said I could not understand it either, but suggested the general influence of liquor, and expressed my envy of their state. I had drawn my knees up to my chin, on the bench here one used to dry oneself after bathing, and there I sat in a seeming stolidity at utter variance with my inward temper. I heard Raffles creep forth again, and I let him go without a word. I never doubted that he would be back again in a minute, and so let many minutes elapse before I realised his continued absence, and finally crept out myself to look for him.

Even then I only supposed that he had posted himself outside in some more commanding position. I took a cat-like stride, and breathed his name. There was no answer. I ventured further, till I could overlook the lawns; they lay like clean slates in the starlight; there was no sign of living thing nearer than the house, which was still lit up, but quiet enough now. Was it a cunning and deliberate quiet, assumed as a snare? Had they caught Raffles, and were they waiting for me? I returned to the boathouse in an agony of fear and indignation. It was fear for the long hours that I sat there waiting for him; it was indignation when at last I heard his stealthy step upon the gravel. I would not go out to meet him. I sat where I was while the stealthy step came nearer, nearer; and there I was sitting when the door opened, and a huge man in riding clothes stood before me in the steely dawn.

I leapt to my feet, and the huge man clapped me playfully on the shoulder.

'Sorry I've been so long, Bunny, but we should never have got away as we were; this riding-suit makes a new man of me, on top of my own, and here's a youth's kit that should do you down to the ground.'

'So you broke into the house again!'

'I was obliged to, Bunny; but I had to watch the lights out one by one, and give them a good hour after that. I went through that dressing-room at my leisure this time; the only difficulty was — to spot the son's quarters at the back of the house; but I overcame it, as you see, in the end. I only hope they'll fit, Bunny. Give me your patent leathers, and I'll fill them with stones and sink them in the pond. I'm doing the same with mine. Here's a brown pair apiece, and we mustn't let the grass grow under them if we're to get to the station in time for the early train while the coast's still clear.'

The early train leaves the station in question at 6.20 a.m.; and that fine spring morning there was a police officer in a peaked cap to see it off; but he was so busy peering into the compartments for a pair of very swell mobsmen, that he took no notice of the huge man in riding clothes, who was obviously intoxicated, or of the more insignificant but not less horsy character who had him in hand. The early train is due at Victoria at 8.28, but these worthies left it at Clap- ham Junction, and changed cabs more than once between Battersea and Piccadilly, and a few of their garments in each four-wheeler. It was barely nine o'clock when they sat together in the Albany, and might have been recognised once more as Raffles and myself.

'And now,' said Raffles, 'before we do anything else, let us turn 'out those little cases that we hadn't time to open when we took them. I mean the ones I handed to you, Bunny. I had a look into mine in the garden, and I'm sorry to say there was nothing in them. The lady must have been wearing their proper contents.'

Raffles held out his hand for the substantial leather cases which I had produced at his request. But that was the extent of my compliance; instead of handing them over, I looked boldly into the eyes that seemed to have discerned my wretched secret at one glance.

'It's no use my giving them to you,' I said. 'They are empty also.'

'When did you look into them?'

'In the tower.'

'Well, let me see for myself.'

'As you like.'

'My dear Bunny, this one must have contained the necklace you boasted about.'

'Very likely.'

'And this one the tiara.'

'I dare say.'

'Yet she was wearing neither, as you prophesied, and as we both saw for ourselves!'

I had not taken my eyes from his.

'Raffles,' I said, 'I'll be frank with you after all. I meant you never to know, but it's easier than telling you a lie. I left both things behind me in the tower. I won't attempt to explain or defend myself; it was probably the influence of the tower, and nothing else; but the whole thing came over me at the last moment, when you had gone and I was going. I felt that I should very probably break my neck, that I cared very little whether I did or not, but that it would be frightful to break it at that house with those things in my pocket. You may say I ought to have thought of all that before; you may say what you like, Raffles, and you won't say more than I deserve. It was hysterical, and it was mean, for I kept the cases to impose on you.'

'You were always a bad liar, Bunny,' said Raffles, smiling. 'Will you think me one when I tell you that I can understand what you felt, and even what you did? As a matter of fact, I have understood for several hours now.'

'You mean what I felt, Raffles?'

'And what you did. I guessed it in the boathouse. I knew that something must have happened or been discovered to disperse that truculent party of sportsmen so soon and on such good terms with themselves. They had not got us; they might have got something better worth having; and your phlegmatic attitude suggested what. As luck would have it, the cases that I personally had collared were the empty ones; the two prizes had fallen to you. Well, to allay my horrid suspicion, I went and had another peep through the lighted Venetians. And what do you think I saw?'

I shook my head. I had no idea, nor was I very eager for enlightenment.

'The two poor people whom it was your own idea to despoil,' quoth Raffles, 'prematurely gloating over these two pretty things!'

He withdrew a hand from either pocket of his crumpled dinner- jacket, and opened the pair under my nose. In one was a diamond tiara, and in the other a necklace of fine emeralds set in clusters of brilliants.

'You must try to forgive me, Bunny,' continued Raffles before I could speak. 'I don't say a word against what you did, or undid; in fact, now it's all over, I am rather glad to think that you did try to undo it. But, my dear fellow, we had both risked life, limb, and liberty; and I had not your sentimental scruples. Why should I go empty away? If you want to know the inner history of my second visit to that good fellow's dressing-room, drive home for a fresh kit and meet me at the Turkish bath in twenty minutes. I feel more than a little grubby, and we can have our breakfast in the cooling gallery. Besides, after a whole night in your old haunts, Bunny, it's Only in order to wind up in Northumberland Avenue.'

9

THE RAFFLES RELICS

It was in one of the magazines for December, 1899, that an article appeared which afforded our minds a brief respite from the then consuming excitement of the war in South Africa. These were the days when Raffles really had white hair, and when he and I were nearing the end of our surreptitious second innings, as professional cracksmen of the deadliest dye. Piccadilly and the Albany knew us no more. But we still operated, as the spirit tempted us, from our latest and most idyllic base, on the borders of Ham Common. Recreation was our greatest want; and though we had both descended to the humble bicycle, a lot of reading was forced upon us in the winter evenings. Thus the war came as a boon to us both. It not only provided us with an honest interest in life, but gave point and zest to innumerable spins across Richmond Park, to the nearest paper-shop; and it was from such an expedition that I returned with inflammatory matter unconnected with the war. The magazine was one of those that are read (and sold) by the million; the article was rudely illustrated on every other page. Its subject was the so-called Black Museum at Scotland Yard; and from the catchpenny text we first learnt that the gruesome show was now enriched by a special and elaborate exhibit known as the Raffles Relics.

'Bunny,' said Raffles, 'this is fame at last! It is no longer notoriety; it lifts one out of the ruck of robbers, into the society of the big brass gods, whose little delinquencies are written in water by the finger of time. The Napoleon Relics we know, the Nelson Relics we've heard about, and here are mine!'

'Which I wish to goodness we could see,' I added longingly. Next moment I was sorry I had spoken. Raffles was looking at me across the magazine. There was a smile on his lips that I knew too well, a light in his eyes that I had kindled.

'What an excellent idea!' he exclaimed quite softly, as though working it out already in his brain.

'I didn't mean it for one,' I answered, 'and no more do you.'

'Certainly I do,' said Raffles. 'I was never more serious in my life.'

'You would march into Scotland Yard in broad daylight?'

'In broad limelight,' he answered, studying the magazine again, 'to set eyes on my own once more. Why, here they all are, Bunny – you never told me there was an illustration. That's the chest you took to your bank with me inside, and those must be my own rope-ladder and things on top. They produce so badly in the twopenny magazines that it's impossible to swear to them. There's nothing for it but a visit of inspection.'

'Then you can pay it alone,' said I grimly. 'You may have altered, but they'd know me at a glance.'

'By all means, Bunny, if you'll get me the pass.'

'A pass!' I cried triumphantly. 'Of course we should have to get one, and of course that puts an end to the whole idea. Who on earth would give a pass for this show, of all others, to an old prisoner like me?'

Raffles addressed himself to the reading of the magazine with a shrug that showed some temper.

'The fellow who wrote this article got one,' said he shortly. 'He got it from his editor, and you could get one from yours if you tried. But pray don't try, Bunny: it would be too terrible for you to risk a moment's embarrassment to gratify a mere whim of mine. And if I went instead of you, and got spotted, which is so likely with this head of hair, and the general belief in my demise, the consequences to you would be too awful to contemplate! Don't contemplate them, my dear fellow. And do let me read my magazine.'

Need I add that I set about the rash endeavour without further expostulation? I was used to such ebullitions from the altered Raffles of these later days, and I could well understand them. All the inconvenience of the new conditions fell on him. I had purged my known offences by imprisonment, whereas Raffles was merely supposed to have escaped punishment in death. The result was that I could rush in where Raffles feared to tread, and was his plenipotentiary in all honest dealings with the outer world. It could not but gall him to be so dependent upon me, and it was for me to minimise the humiliation by scrupulously avoiding the least semblance of an abuse of that power which I now had over him. Accordingly, though with much misgiving, I did his ticklish behest in Fleet Street, where, despite my past, I was already making a certain lowly footing for myself. Success followed, as it will when one longs to fail; and one fine evening I returned to Ham Common with a card from the Convict Supervision Office, New Scotland Yard, which I treasure to this day. I am surprised to see that it was undated, and might still 'Admit Bearer to see the Museum', to say nothing of the bearer's friends, since my editor's name 'and party' is scrawled beneath the legend.

'But he doesn't want to come,' as I explained to Raffles. 'And it means that we can both go, if we both like.'

Raffles looked at me with a wry smile; he was in good enough humour now.

'It would be rather dangerous, Bunny. If they spotted you, they might think of me.'

'But you say they'll never know you now.'

'I don't believe they will. I don't believe there's the slightest risk; but we shall soon see. I've set my heart on seeing, Bunny, but there's no earthly reason why I should drag you into it.'

'You do that when you present this card,' I pointed out. 'I shall hear of it fast enough, if anything happens.'

'Then you may as well be there to see the fun?'

'It will make no difference if the worst comes to the worst.'

'And the ticket is for a party, isn't it?'

'It is.'

'It might even look peculiar if only one person made use of it?'

'It might.'

'Then we're both going, Bunny! And I give you my word,' cried Raffles, 'that no real harm shall come of it. But you mustn't ask to see the Relics, and you mustn't take too much interest in them when you do see them. Leave the questioning to me: it really will be a chance of finding out whether they've any suspicion of one's resurrection at Scotland Yard. And I think I can promise you a certain amount of fun, old fellow, as some little compensation for your pangs and fears.'

The early afternoon was mild and hazy, and unlike winter but for the prematurely low sun struggling through the haze, as Raffles and I emerged from the nether regions at Westminster Bridge, and stood for one moment to admire the infirm silhouettes of Abbey and Houses in flat grey against a golden mist. Raffles murmured of Whistler and of Arthur Severn, and threw away a good Sullivan because the smoke would curl between him and the picture. It is perhaps the picture that I can now see clearest of all the set scenes of our lawless life. But at the time I was filled with gloomy speculation as to whether Raffles would keep his promise of providing an entirely harmless entertainment for my benefit at the Black Museum.

We entered the forbidding precincts; we looked relentless officers in the face, and they almost yawned in ours as they directed us through swing-doors and up stone stairs. There was something even sinister in the casual character of our reception. We had an arctic landing to ourselves for several minutes, which Raffles spent in an instinctive survey of the premises, while I cooled my heels before the portrait of a late Commissioner.

'Dear old gentleman!' exclaimed Raffles, joining me. 'I have met him at dinner, and discussed my own case with him, in the old days. But we can't know too little about ourselves in the Black Museum, Bunny. I remember going to the old place in Whitehall, years ago, and being shown round by one of the tip-top 'tecs. And this may be another.'

But even I could see at a glance that there was nothing of the detective and everything of the clerk about the very young man who had joined us at last upon the landing. His collar was the tallest I have ever seen, and his face was as pallid as his collar. He carried a loose key, with which he unlocked a door a little way along the passage, and so ushered us into that dreadful repository which perhaps has fewer visitors than any other of equal interest in the world. The place was cold as the inviolate vault; blinds had to be drawn up, and glass cases uncovered, before we could see a thing except the row of murderers' death-masks – the placid faces with the swollen necks – that stood out on their shelves to give us ghostly greeting.

'This fellow isn't formidable,' whispered Raffles, as the blinds went up; 'still, we can't be too careful. My little lot are round the corner, in the sort of recess; don't look till we come to them in their turn.'

So we began at the beginning, with the glass case nearest the door; and in a moment I discovered that I knew far more about its contents than our pallid guide. He had some enthusiasm, but the most inaccurate smattering of his subject. He mixed up the first murderer with quite the wrong murder, and capped his mistake in the next breath with an intolerable libel on the very pearl of our particular tribe.

'This revawlver,' he began, 'belonged to the celebrited burgular, Chawles Peace. These are his spectacles, that's his jemmy, and this here knife's the one that Chawley killed the policeman with.'

Now, I like accuracy for its own sake, strive after it myself, and am sometimes guilty of forcing it upon others. So this was more than I could pass.

That's not quite right,' I put in, mildly. 'He never made use of the knife.'

The young clerk twisted his head in its vase of starch.

'Chawley Peace killed two policemen,' said he.

'No, he didn't; only one of them was a policeman; and he never killed anybody with a knife.'

The clerk took the correction like a lamb. I could not have refrained from making it, to save my skin. But Raffles rewarded me with as vicious a little kick as he could administer unobserved.

'Who was Charles Peace?' he inquired, with the bland effrontery of any judge upon the bench.

The clerk's reply came pat and unexpected.

'The greatest burgular we ever had,' said he, 'till good old Raffles knocked him out!'

'The greatest of the pre-Raffleites,' the master murmured, as we passed on to the safer memorials of mere murder. There were misshapen bullets and stained knives that had taken human life; there were lithe, lean ropes which had retaliated after the live letter of the Mosaic law. There was one bristling broadside of revolvers under the longest shelf of closed eyes and swollen throats. There were festoons of rope-ladders – none so ingenious as ours – and then at last there was something that the clerk knew all about. It was a small tin cigarette-box, and the name upon the gaudy wrapper was not the name of Sullivan. Yet Raffles and I knew even more about this exhibit than the clerk.

'There, now,' said our guide, 'you'll never guess the history of that! I'll give you twenty guesses, and the twentieth will be no nearer than the first.'

'I'm sure of it, my good fellow,' rejoined Raffles, a discreet twinkle in his eye. 'Tell us about it, to save time.'

And he opened, as he spoke, his own old twenty-five tin of purely popular cigarettes; there were a few in it still, but between the cigarettes were jammed lumps of sugar wadded with cottonwool. I saw Raffles weighing the lot in his hand with subtle satisfaction. But the clerk saw merely the mystification which he desired to create.

'I thought that'd beat you, sir,' said he. 'It was an American dodge. Two smart Yankees got a jeweller to take a lot of stuff to a private room at Kellner's, where they were dining, for them to choose from. When it came to paying, there was some bother about a remittance; but they soon made that all right, for they were far too clever to suggest taking away what they'd chosen but couldn't pay for. No; all they wanted was that what they'd chosen might be locked up in the safe and considered theirs until their money came for them to pay for it. All they asked was to seal the stuff up in something; the jeweller was to take it away and not meddle with it, nor yet break the seals, for a week or two. It seemed a fair enough thing, now, didn't it, sir?'

'Eminently fair,' said Raffles, sententiously.

'So the jeweller thought,' crowed the clerk. 'You see, it wasn't as if the Yanks had chosen out the half of what he'd brought on appro; they'd gone slow on purpose, and they'd paid for all they could on the nail, just for a blind. Well, I suppose you can guess what happened in the end? The jeweller never heard of those Americans again; and these few cigarettes and lumps of sugar were all he found.'

'Duplicate boxes!' I cried, perhaps a thought too promptly.

'Duplicate boxes!' murmured Raffles, as profoundly impressed as a second Mr Pickwick.

'Duplicate boxes!' echoed the triumphant clerk. 'Artful beggars, these Americans, sir! You've got to crawss the 'Erring Pond to learn a trick worth one o' that!'

'I suppose so,' assented the grave gentleman with the silver hair. 'Unless,' he added, as if suddenly inspired, 'unless it was that man Raffles.'

'It couldn't 've bin,' jerked the clerk from his conning-tower of a collar. 'He'd gone to Davy Jones long before.'

'Are you sure?' asked Raffles. 'Was his body ever found?'

'Found and buried,' replied our imaginative friend. 'Maltar, I think it was; or it may have been Giberaltar. I forget which.'

'Besides,' I put in, rather annoyed at all this wilful work, yet not indisposed to make a late contribution – 'besides, Raffles would never have smoked those cigarettes. There was only one brand for him. It was – let me see – '

'Sullivans!' cried the clerk, right for once. 'It's all a matter of 'abit,' he went on, as he replaced the twenty-five tin box with the vulgar wrapper. 'I tried them once, and I didn't like 'em myself. It's all a question of taste. Now, if you want a good smoke, *ana* cheaper, give me a Golden Gem at quarter of the price.'

'What we really do want', remarked Raffles mildly, 'is to see something else as clever as that last.'

'Then come this way,' said the clerk, and led us into a recess almost monopolised by the iron-clamped chest of thrilling memory, now a mere platform for the collection of mysterious objects under a dust-sheet on the lid. 'These', he continued, unveiling them with an air, 'are the Raffles Relics, taken from his rooms in the Albany after his death and burial, and the most complete set we've got. That's his centre-bit, and this is the bottle of rock-oil he's supposed to have kept dipping it in to prevent making a noise. Here's the revawlver he used when he shot at the gentleman on the roof down Horsham way; it was afterwards taken from him on the P. & O. boat before he jumped overboard.'

I could not help saying I understood that Raffles had never shot at anybody. I was standing with my back to the nearest window, my hat jammed over my brows and my overcoat collar up to my ears.

That's the only time we know about,' the clerk admitted; 'and it couldn't be brought 'ome, or his precious pal would have got more than he did. This empty cawtridge is the one he 'id the Emperor's pearl in, on the Peninsular and Orient. These gimlets and wedges were what he used for fixin' doors. This is his rope-ladder, with the telescope walking-stick he used to hook it up with; he's said to have 'ad it with him the night he dined with the Earl of Thornaby, and robbed the house before dinner. That's his life-preserver; but no one can make out what this little thick velvet bag's for, with the two holes and the elawstic round each. Perhaps you can give a guess, sir?'

Raffles had taken up the bag that he had invented for the noiseless filing of keys. Now he handled it as though it were a tobacco-pouch, putting in finger and thumb, and shrugging over the puzzle with a delicious face; nevertheless, he showed me a few grains of steel-filing as the result of his investigations, and murmured in my ear, 'These sweet police!' I, for my part, could not but examine the life-preserver with which I had once smitten Raffles himself to the ground; actually there was his blood upon it still; and seeing my horror, the clerk plunged into a characteristically garbled version of that incident also. It happened to have come to light among others at the Old Bailey, and perhaps had its share in promoting the quality of mercy which had undoubtedly been exercised on my behalf. But the present recital was unduly trying, and Raffles created a noble diversion by calling attention to an early photograph of himself, which may still hang on the wall over the historic chest, but which I had carefully ignored. It shows him in flannels, after some great feat upon the tented field. I am afraid there is a Sullivan between his lips, a look of lazy insolence in the half-shut eyes. I have since possessed myself of a copy, and it is not Raffles at his best; but the features are clean-cut and regular; and I often wish that I had lent it to the artistic gentlemen who have battered the statue out of all likeness to the man.

'You wouldn't think it of him, would you?' quoth the clerk. 'It makes you understand how no one ever did think it of him at the time.'.

The youth was looking full at Raffles, with the watery eyes of unsuspecting innocence. I itched to emulate the fine bravado of my friend.

'You said he had a pal,' I observed, sinking deeper into the collar of my coat. 'Haven't you got a photograph of him?'

The pale clerk gave such a sickly smile, I could have smacked some blood into his pasty face.

'You mean Bunny?' said the familiar fellow. 'No, sir, he'd be out of place; we've only room for real criminals here. Bunny was neither one thing nor the other. He could follow Raffles, but that's all he could do. He was no good on his own. Even when he put up the low-down job of robbing his old 'ome, it's believed he hadn't the 'eart to take the stuff away, and Raffles had to break in a second time for it. No, sir, we don't bother our heads about Bunny; we shall never hear no more of 'im. He was a harmless sort of rotter, if you awsk me.'

I had not asked him, and I was almost foaming under the respirator that I was making of my overcoat collar. I only hoped that Raffles would say something – and he did.

'The only case I remember anything about', he remarked, tapping the clamped chest with his umbrella, 'was this; and that time, at all events, the man outside must have had quite as much to do as the one inside. May I ask what you keep in it?'

'Nothing, sir.'

'I imagined more relics inside. Hadn't he some dodge of getting in and out without opening the lid?'

'Of putting his head out, you mean,' returned the clerk, whose knowledge of Raffles and his Relics was really most comprehensive on the whole. He moved some of the minor memorials, and with his penknife raised the trapdoor in the lid.

'Only a skylight,' remarked Raffles, deliciously unimpressed.

'Why, what else did you expect?' asked the clerk, letting the trapdoor down again, and looking sorry that he had taken so much trouble.

'A back door, at least!' replied Raffles, with such a sly look at me that I had to turn aside to smile. It was the last time I smiled that day.

The door had opened as I turned, and an unmistakable detective had entered with two more sightseers like ourselves. He wore the hard round hat and the dark thick overcoat which one knows at a glance, as the uniform of his grade; and for one awful moment his steely eye was upon us in a flash of cold inquiry. Then the clerk emerged from the recess devoted to the Raffles Relics, and the alarming interloper conducted his party to the window opposite the door.

'Inspector Druce,' the clerk informed us in impressive whispers, 'who had the Chalk Farm case in hand. He'd be the man for Raffles, if Raffles was alive today!'

'I'm sure he would,' was the grave reply. 'I should be very sorry to have a man like that after me. But what a run there seems to be upon your Black Museum!'

'There isn't reelly, sir,' whispered the clerk. 'We sometimes go weeks on end without having regular visitors like you two gentlemen. I think those are friends of the Inspector's, come to see the Chalk Farm photographs, that helped to hang his man. We've a lot of interesting photographs, sir, if you like to have a look at them.'

'If it won't take long,' said Raffles, pulling out his watch; and as the clerk left our side for an instant, he gripped my arm. 'This is a bit too hot,' he whispered, 'but we mustn't cut and run like rabbits. That might be fatal. Hide your face in the photographs, and leave everything to me. I'll have a train to catch as soon as ever I dare.'

I obeyed without a word, and with the less uneasiness as I had time to consider the situation. It even struck me that Raffles was for once inclined to exaggerate the undeniable risk that we ran by remaining in the same room with an officer whom both he and I knew only too well by name and repute. Raffles, after all, had aged and altered out of knowledge; but he had not lost the nerve that was equal to a far more direct encounter than was at all likely to be forced upon us. On the other hand, it was most improbable that a distinguished detective would know by sight an obscure delinquent like myself; besides, this one had come to the front since my day. Yet a risk it was, and I certainly did not smile as I bent over the album of horrors produced by our guide. I could still take an interest in the dreadful photographs of murderous and murdered men; they appealed to the morbid element in my nature; and it was doubtless with degenerate unction that I called Raffles's attention to a certain scene of notorious slaughter. There was no response. I looked round. There was no Raffles to respond. We had all three been examining the photographs at one of the windows; at another the three newcomers were similarly engrossed; and without one word, or a single sound, Raffles had decamped behind all our backs.

Fortunately the clerk was himself very busy gloating over the horrors of the album; before he looked round I had hidden my astonishment, but not my wrath, of which I had the instinctive sense to make no secret.

'My friend's the most impatient man on earth!' I exclaimed. 'He said he was going to catch a train, and now he's gone without a word!'

'I never heard him,' said the clerk, looking puzzled.

'No more did I; but he did touch me on the shoulder,' I lied, 'and say something or other. I was too deep in this beastly book to pay much attention. He must have meant that he was off. Well, let him be off! I mean to see all that's to be seen.'

And in my nervous anxiety to allay any suspicions aroused by my companion's extraordinary behaviour, I outstayed even the eminent detective and his friends, saw them examine the Raffles Relics, heard them discuss me under my own nose, and at last was alone with the anaemic clerk. I put my hand in my pocket, and measured him with a sidelong eye. The tipping system is nothing less than a minor bane of my existence. Not that one is a grudging giver, but simply because in so many cases it is so hard to know whom to tip and what to tip him. I know what it is to be the parting guest who has not parted freely enough, and that not from stinginess but the want of a fine instinct on the point. I made no mistake, however, in the case of the clerk, who accepted my pieces of silver without demur, and expressed a hope of seeing the article which I had assured him I was about to write. He has had some years to wait for it, but I flatter myself that these belated pages will occasion more interest than offence if they ever do meet those watery eye?

Twilight was falling when I reached the street; the sky behind St Stephen's had flushed and blackened like an angry face; the lamps were lit, and under every one I was unreasonable enough to look for Raffles. Then I made foolishly sure that I should find him hanging about the station, and hung thereabouts myself until one Richmond train had gone without me. In the end I walked over the bridge to Waterloo, and took the first train to Teddington instead. That made a shorter walk of it, but

I had to grope my way through a white fog from the river to Ham Common, and it was the hour of our cosy dinner when I reached our place of retirement. There was only a flicker of firelight on the blinds: I was the first to return after all. It was nearly four hours since Raffles had stolen away from my side in the ominous precincts of Scotland Yard. Where could he be? Our landlady wrung her hands over him; she had cooked a dinner after her favourite's heart, and I let it spoil before making one of the most melancholy meals of my life.

Up to midnight there was no sign of him; but long before this time I had reassured our landlady with a voice and face that must have given my words the lie. I told her that Mr Ralph (as she used to call him) had said something about going to the theatre; that I thought he had given up the idea, but I must have been mistaken, and should certainly sit up for him. The attentive soul brought in a plate of sandwiches before she retired; and I prepared to make a night of it in a chair by the sitting-room fire. Darkness and bed I could not face in my anxiety. In a way I felt as though duty and loyalty called me out into the winter's night: and yet whither should I turn to look for Raffles? I could think of but one place, and to seek him there would be to destroy myself without aiding him. It was my growing conviction that he had been recognised when leaving Scotland Yard, and either taken then and there, or else hunted into some new place of hiding. It would all be in the morning papers; and it was all his own fault. He had thrust his head into the lion's mouth, and the lion's jaws had snapped. Had he managed to withdraw his head in time?

There was a bottle at my elbow, and that night I say deliberately that it was not my enemy but my friend. It procured me at last some surcease from my suspense. I fell fast asleep in my chair before the fire. The lamp was still burning, and the fire red, when I awoke; but I sat very stiff in the iron clutch of a wintry morning. Suddenly I slewed round in my chair. And there was Raffles in a chair behind me, with the door open behind him, quietly taking off his boots.

'Sorry to wake you, Bunny,' said he. 'I thought I was behaving like a mouse; but after a three hours' tramp one's feet are all heels.'

I did not get up and fall upon his neck. I sat back in my chair and blinked with bitterness upon his selfish insensibility. He should not know what I had been through on his account.

'Walk out from town?' I inquired, as indifferently as though he were in the habit of doing so.

'From Scotland Yard,' he answered, stretching himself before the fire in his stocking soles.

'Scotland Yard!' I echoed. 'Then I was right; that's where you were all the time. And yet you managed to escape!'

I had risen excitedly in my turn.

'Of course I did,' replied Raffles. 'I never thought there would be much difficulty about that, but there was even less than I anticipated. I did once find myself on one side of a sort of counter, and an officer dozing at his desk at the other side. I thought it safest to wake him up and make inquiries about a mythical purse left in a phantom hansom outside the Carlton. And the way the fellow fired me out of that was another credit to the Metropolitan Police: it's only in the savage countries that they would have troubled to ask how one had got in.'

'And how did you?' I asked. 'And in the Lord's name, Raffles, when and why?'

Raffles looked down on me under raised eyebrows, as he stood with his coat-tails to the dying fire.

'How and when, Bunny, you know as well as I do,' said he, cryptically. 'And at last you shall hear the honest why and wherefore. I had more reasons for going to Scotland Yard, my dear fellow, than I had the face to tell you at the time.'

'I don't care why you went there,' I cried. 'I want to know why you stayed, or went back, or whatever it was you may have done. I thought they had got you, and you had given them the slip?'

Raffles smiled as he shook his head.

'No, no, Bunny, I prolonged the visit, as I paid it, of my own accord. As for my reasons, they are far too many for me to tell you them all; they rather weighed upon me as I walked out; but you'H see them for yourself if you turn round.'

I was standing with my back to the chair in which I had been asleep; behind the chair was the round lodging-house table; and there, reposing on the cloth with the whisky and sandwiches, was the whole collection of Raffles Relics which had occupied the lid of the silver-chest in the Black Museum at Scotland Yard! The chest alone was missing. There was the revolver that I had only once heard fired, and there the blood-stained life-preserver, brace-and- bit, bottle of rock-oil, velvet bag, rope-ladder, walking-stick, gimlets, wedges, and even the empty cartridge-case which had once concealed the gift of a civilised monarch to a potentate of colour.

'I was a real Father Christmas,' said Raffles, 'when I arrived. It's a pity you weren't awake to appreciate the scene. It was more edifying than the one I found. You never caught *me* asleep in my chair, Bunny!'

He thought I had merely fallen asleep in my chair. He could not see that I had been sitting up for him all night long. The hint of a temperance homily, on top of all I had borne, and from Raffles of all mortal men, tried my temper to its last limit; but a flash of late enlightenment enabled me just to keep it.

'Where did you hide?' I asked grimly.

'At the Yard itself.'

'So I gather; but whereabouts at the Yard?'

'Can you ask, Bunny?'

'I am asking.'

'It's where I once hid before.'

'You don't mean in the chest?'

'I do.'

Our eyes met for a minute.

'You may have ended up there,' I conceded. 'But where did you go first, when you slipped out behind my back, and how the devil did you know where to go?'

'I never did slip out,' said Raffles, 'behind your back. I slipped in.'

'Into the chest?'

'Exactly.'

I burst out laughing in his face.

'My dear fellow, I saw all these things on the lid just afterwards. Not one of them was moved. I watched that detective show them to his friends.'

'And I heard him.'

'But not from the inside of the chest!'

'From the inside of the chest, Bunny. Don't look like that – it's foolish. Try to recall a few words that went before, between the idiot in the collar and me. Don't you remember my asking him if there was anything in the chest?'

'Yes.'

'One had to be sure it was empty, you see. Then I asked if there was a back door to the chest as well as a skylight.'

'I remember.'

'I suppose you thought all that meant nothing?'

'I didn't look for a meaning.'

'You wouldn't; it would never occur to you that I might want to find out whether anybody at the Yard had found out that there *was* something precisely in the nature of a side door – it isn't a back door – to that chest. Well, there is one; there was one soon after I took the chest back from your rooms to mine, in the good old days. You push one of the handles down – which no one ever does – and the whole of that end opens like the front of a doll's house. I saw that was what I ought to have done at first; it's so much simpler than the trap at the top, and one likes to get a thing perfect for its own sake. Besides, the trick had not been spotted at the bank, and I thought I might bring it off again some day; meanwhile, in one's bedroom, with lots of things on top, what a port in a sudden squall!'

I asked why I had never heard of the improvement before, not so much at the time it was made, but in these later days, when there were fewer secrets between us, and this one could avail him no more. But I did not put the question out of pique. I put it out of sheer obstinate incredulity. And Raffles looked at me without replying, until I read the explanation in his look.

'I see,' I said. 'You used to get into it to hide from me!'

'My dear Bunny, I am not always a very genial man,' he answered; 'but when you let me have a key of your rooms, I could not very well refuse you one of mine, although I picked your pocket of it in the end. I will only say that when I had no wish to see you, Bunny, I must have been quite unfit for human society, and it was the act of a friend to deny you mine. I don't think it happened more than once or twice. You can afford to forgive a fellow after all these years!'

'That, yes,' I replied, bitterly; 'but not this, Raffles.'

'Why not? I really hadn't made up my mind to do what I did. I had merely thought of it. It was that smart officer in the same room that made me do it without thinking twice.'

'And we never even heard you!' I murmured, in a voice of involuntary admiration which vexed me with myself. 'But we might just as well!' I was as quick to add in my former tone.

'Why, Bunny?'

'We shall be traced in no time through our ticket of admission.'

'Did they collect it?'

'No; but you heard how very few are issued.'

'Exactly. They sometimes go weeks on end without a regular visitor. It was I who extracted that piece of information, Bunny, and I did nothing rash until I had. Don't you see that with any luck it will be two or three weeks before they are likely to discover their loss?'

I was beginning to see.

'And then, pray, how are they going to bring it home to us? Why should they even suspect us, Bunny? I left early; that's all I did. You took my departure admirably; you couldn't have said more or less if I had coached you myself. I relied on you, Bunny, and you never more completely justified my confidence. The sad thing is that you have ceased to rely on me. Do you really think that I would leave the place in such a state that the first person who came in with a duster would see that there had been a robbery?'

I denied the thought with all energy, though it perished only as I spoke.

'Have you forgotten the duster that was over these things, Bunny? Have you forgotten all the other revolvers and life-preservers that there were to choose from? I chose most carefully, and I replaced my relics with a mixed assortment of other people's which really look just as well. The rope-ladder that now supplants mine is, of course, no patch upon it, but coiled up on the chest it really looks much the same. To be sure, there was no second velvet bag; but I replaced my stick with another quite like it, and I even found an empty cartridge to understudy the setting of the Polynesian pearl. You see the sort of fellow they have to show people round: do you think he's the kind to see the difference next time, or to connect it with us if he does? One left much the same things lying much as he left them, under a dust-sheet which is only taken off for the benefit of the curious, who often don't turn up for weeks on end.'

I admitted that we might be safe for three or four weeks. Raffles held out his hand.

'Then let us be friends about it, Bunny, and smoke the cigarette of Sullivan and peace! A lot may happen in three or four weeks; and what should you say if this turned out to be the last as well as the least of all my crimes? I must own that it seems to me their natural and fitting end, though I might have stopped more characteristically than with a mere crime of sentiment. No, I make no promises, Bunny; now I have got these things, I may be unable to resist using them once more. But with this war one gets all the excitement one requires – and rather more than usual may happen in three or four weeks!'

Was he thinking even then of volunteering for the Front? Had he already set his heart on the one chance of some atonement for his life – nay, on the very death he was to die? I never knew, and shall never know. Yet his words were strangely prophetic, even to the three or four weeks in which those events happened that imperilled the fabric of our Empire, and rallied her sons from the four winds to fight beneath her banner on the veldt. It all seems very ancient history now. But I remember nothing better or more vividly than the last words of Raffles upon his last crime, unless it be the pressure of his hand as he said them, or the rather sad twinkle in his tired eyes.

10

THE LAST WORD

The last of all these tales of Raffles is from a fresher and a sweeter pen. I give it exactly as it came to me, in a letter which meant more to me than it can possibly mean to any other reader. And yet, it may stand for something with those for whom these pale reflections have a tithe of the charm that the real man had for me; and it is to leave such persons thinking yet a little better of him (and not wasting another thought on me) that I am permitted to retail the very last word about their hero and mine.

The letter was my first healing after a chance encounter and a sleepless night; and I print every word of it except the last.

'39, *Campden Grove Court*, W.,
'*June 28, 1900.*

'Dear Harry,

'You may have wondered at the very few words I could find to say to you when we met so strangely yesterday. I did not mean to be unkind. I was grieved to see you so cruelly hurt and lame. I could not grieve when at last I made you tell me how it happened. I honour and envy every man of you – every name in those dreadful lists that fill the papers every day. But I knew about Mr Raffles, and I did not know about you, and there was something I longed to tell you about him, something I could not tell you in a minute in the street, or indeed by word of mouth at all. That was why I asked for your address.

'You said I spoke as if I had known Mr Raffles. Of course I have often seen him playing cricket, and heard about him from you. But I only once met him, and that was the night after you and I met last. I have always supposed that you knew all about our meeting. Yesterday I could see that you knew nothing. So I have made up my mind to tell you every word.

'That night – I mean the next thing – they were all going out to several places, but I stayed behind at Palace Gardens. I had gone up to the drawing-room after dinner, and was just putting on the lights, when in walked Mr Raffles from the balcony. I knew him at once, because I happened to have watched him make his hundred at Lord's only the day before. He seemed surprised that no one had told me he was there, but the whole thing was such a surprise that I hardly thought of that. I am afraid I must say that it was not a very pleasant surprise. I felt instinctively that he had come from you, and I confess that for the moment it made me very angry indeed. Then in a breath he assured me that you knew nothing of his coming, and you would never have allowed him to come, but that he had taken it upon himself as your intimate friend and one who would be mine as well. (I said I would tell you every word.)

'Well, we stood looking at each other for some time, and I was never more convinced of anybody's straightness and sincerity; but he *was* straight and sincere with me, and true to you, that night, whatever he may have been before and after. So I asked him why he had come, and what had happened; and he said it was not what had happened, but what might happen next; so I asked if he was thinking of you, and he just nodded, and told me that I knew very well what you had done. But I began to wonder whether Mr Raffles himself knew, and I tried to get him to tell me what you had done, and he said I knew as well as he did that you were one of the two men who had come to the house the night before. I took some time to answer. I was quite mystified by his manner. At last I asked him how he knew. I can hear his answer now.

'"Because I was the other man," he said quite quietly; "because I led him blindfold into the whole business, and would rather pay the shot than see poor Bunny suffer for it."

'Those were his words, but as he said them he made their meaning clear by going over to the bell, and waiting with his finger ready to ring for whatever assistance or protection I desired. Of course I would not let him ring at all; in fact, at first I refused to believe him. Then he led me out into the balcony, and showed me exactly how he had got up and in. He had broken in for the second night running, and all to tell me that the first night he had brought you with him on false pretences. He had to tell me a great deal more before I could quite believe him. But before he went (as he had come) I was the one woman in the world who knew that A.J. Raffles, the great cricketer, and the so-called 'amateur cracksman' of equal notoriety, were one and the same person.

'He had told me his secret, thrown himself on my mercy, and put his liberty if not his life in my hands, and all for your sake, Harry, to right you in my eyes at his own expense. And yesterday I could see that you knew nothing whatever about it, that your friend had died without telling you of his act of real and yet vain self-sacrifice! Harry, I can only say that now I understand your friendship, and even the lengths to which it carried you. How many, in your place, would not have gone as far for such a friend? Since that night, at any rate, I for one have understood. It has grieved me more than I need try to tell you, Harry, but I have always understood.

'He spoke to me quite simply and frankly of his life. It was wonderful to me then that he should speak of it as he did, and still more wonderful that I should sit and listen to him as I did. But I have often thought about it since, and have long ceased to wonder at myself. There was an absolute magnetism about Mr Raffles which neither you nor I could resist. He had the strength of personality which is a different thing from strength of character; but when you meet both kinds together, they carry the ordinary mortal off his or her feet. You must not imagine you are the only one who would have served and followed him as you did. When he told me it was all a game to him, and the one game he knew that was always exciting, always full of danger and of drama, I could just then have found it in my heart to try the game myself! Not that he treated me to any ingenious sophistries or paradoxical perversities. It was just his natural charm and humour, and a touch of sadness with it all, that appealed to something deeper than one's reason and one's sense of right. Glamour, I suppose, is the word. Yet there was far more in him than that. There were depths, which called to depths; and you will not misunderstand me when I say I think it touched him that a woman should listen to him as I did, and in such circumstances. I know that it touched me to think of such a life so spent, and that I came to myself and implored him to give it all up. I don't think I went on my knees over it. But I am afraid I did cry; and that was the end. He pretended not to notice anything, and then in an instant he froze everything with a flippancy which jarred horribly at the time, but has ever since touched me more than all the rest. I remember that I wanted to shake hands at the end. But Mr Raffles only shook his head, and for one instant his face was as sad as it was gallant and gay all the rest of the time. Then he went as he had come, in his own dreadful way, and not a soul in the house knew that he had been. And even you were never told!

'I didn't mean to write all this about your own friend, whom you knew so much better yourself, yet you see that even you did not know how nobly he tried to undo the wrong he had done you; and now I think I know why he kept it to himself. It is fearfully late – or early – I seem to have been writing all night – and I will explain the matter in the fewest words. I promised Mr Raffles that I would write to you, Harry, and see you if I could. Well, I did write, and I did mean to see you, but I never had an answer to what I wrote. It was only one line, and I have long known you never received it. I could not bring myself to write more, and even those few words were merely slipped into one of the books which you had given me. Years afterwards these books, with my name in them, must have been found in your rooms; at any rate they were returned to me by somebody; and you could never have opened them, for there was my line where I had left it. Of course you had never seen it, and that was all my fault. But it was too late to write again. Mr Raffles was supposed to have been drowned, and everything was known about you both. But I still kept my own independent knowledge to myself; to this day, no one else knows that you were one of the two in Palace Gardens; and I still blame myself more than you may think for nearly everything that has happened since.

'You said yesterday that your going to the war and getting wounded wiped out nothing that had gone before. I hope you are not growing morbid about the past. It is not for me to condone it, and yet I know that Mr Raffles was what he was because he loved danger and adventure, and that you were what you were because you loved Mr Raffles. But, even admitting it was all as bad as bad could be, he is dead, and you are punished. The world forgives, if it does not forget. You are young enough to live everything down. Your part in the war will help you in more ways than one. You were always fond of writing. You have now enough to write about for a literary lifetime. You must make a new name for yourself. You must, Harry, and you will!

'I suppose you know that my aunt, Lady Melrose, died some years ago. She was the best friend I had in the world, and it is thanks to her that I am living my own life now in the one way after my own heart. This is a new block of flats, one of those where they do everything for you; and though mine is tiny, it is more than all I shall ever want. One does just exactly what one likes – and you must blame that habit for all that is least conventional in what I have said. Yet I should like you to understand why it is that I have said so much, and, indeed, left nothing unsaid. It is because I want never to have to say or hear another word about *anything* that is past and over. You may answer that I run no risk. Nevertheless, if you did care to come and see me some day, as such an old friend, we might find one or two new points of contact, for I am rather trying to write myself! You might almost guess as much from this letter; it is long enough for anything; but, Harry, if it makes you realise that one of your oldest friends is glad to have seen you, and will be gladder still to see you again, and to talk of anything and everything *except the past,* I may cease to be ashamed even of its length!

'And so good-bye for the present from

'_______'

I omit her name and nothing else. Did I not say in the beginning that it should never be sullied by association with mine? And yet – even as I write I have a hope in my heart of hearts which is not quite consistent with that sentiment. It is as faint a hope as man ever had, and yet its audacity makes the pen tremble in my fingers. But, if it be ever realised, I shall owe more than I could deserve in a century of atonement, to one who atoned more nobly than I ever can.

And to think that to the very end I never heard one word of it from Raffles!

among the rest, I may cease to be altogether [illegible] Heaven!

And so good-bye for the present from—

VI

[illegible] other name and nothing else. Did [illegible] the beginning that it should never be [illegible] self-mastered? And yet [illegible] [illegible] [illegible] [illegible] [illegible] [illegible] [illegible] a century of [illegible] [illegible] [illegible] And to think that [illegible] [illegible] from Calliest [illegible]

MR JUSTICE RAFFLES

1

AN INAUGURAL BANQUET

Raffles had vanished from the face of the town, and even I had no conception of his whereabouts until he cabled to me to meet the 7.31 at Charing Cross next night. That was on the Tuesday before the Varsity match, or a full fortnight after his mysterious disappearance. The telegram was from Carlsbad, of all places for Raffles of all men! Of course there was only one thing that could possibly have taken so rare a specimen of physical fitness to any such pernicious spot. But to my horror he emerged from the train, on the Wednesday evening, a cadaverous caricature of the splendid person I had gone to meet.

'Not a word, my dear Bunny, till I have bitten British beef!' said he, in tones as hollow as his cheeks. 'No, I'm not going to stop to clear my baggage now. You can do that for me tomorrow, Bunny, like a dear good pal.'

'Any time you like,' said I, giving him my arm. 'But where shall we dine? Kellner's? Neapolo's? The Carlton or the Club?'

But Raffles shook his head at one and all.

'I don't want to dine at all,' he said. 'I know what I want!'

And he led the way from the station, stopping once to gloat over the sunset across Trafalgar Square, and again to inhale the tarry scent of the warm wood-paving, which was perfume to his nostrils as the din of its traffic was music to his ears, before we came to one of those political palaces which permit themselves to be included in the list of ordinary clubs. Raffles, to my surprise, walked in as though the marble hall belonged to him, and as straight as might be to the grill-room where white-capped cooks were making things hiss upon a silver grill. He did not consult me as to what we were to have. He had made up his mind about that in the train. But he chose the fillet steaks himself, he insisted on seeing the kidneys, and had a word to say about the fried potatoes, and the Welsh rarebit that was to follow. And all this was as uncharacteristic of the normal Raffles (who was least fastidious at the table) as the sigh with which he dropped into the chair opposite mine, and crossed his arms upon the cloth.

'I didn't know you were a member of this place,' said I, feeling really rather shocked at the discovery, but also that it was a safer subject for me to open than that of his late mysterious movements.

'There are a good many things you don't know about me, Bunny,' said he wearily. 'Did you know I was in Carlsbad, for instance?'

'Of course I didn't.'

'Yet you remember the last time we sat down together?'

'You mean that night we had supper at the Savoy?'

'It's only three weeks ago, Bunny.'

'It seems months to me.'

'And years to me!' cried Raffles. 'But surely you remember that lost tribesman at the next table, with the nose like the village pump, and the wife with the emerald necklace?'

'I should think I did,' said I; 'you mean the great Dan Levy, otherwise Mr Shylock? Why, you told me all about him, A.J.'

'Did I? Then you may possibly recollect that the Shylocks were off to Carlsbad the very next day. It was the old man's last orgy before his annual cure, and he let the whole room know it. Ah, Bunny, I can sympathise with the poor brute now!'

'But what on earth took you there, old fellow?'

'Can you ask? Have you forgotten how you saw the emeralds under their table when they'd gone, and how *I* forgot myself and ran after them with the best necklace I'd handled since the days of Lady Melrose?'

I shook my head, partly in answer to his question, but partly also over a piece of perversity which still rankled in my recollection. But now I was prepared for something even more perverse.

'You were quite right,' continued Raffles, recalling my recriminations at the time; 'it was a rotten thing to do. It was also the action of a tactless idiot, since anybody could have seen that a heavy necklace like that couldn't have dropped off without the wearer's knowledge.'

'You don't mean to say she dropped it on purpose?' I exclaimed with more interest, for I suddenly foresaw the remainder of his tale.

'I do,' said Raffles. 'The poor old pet did it deliberately when stooping to pick up something else; and all to get it stolen and delay their trip to Carlsbad, where her swab of a husband makes her do the cure with him.'

I said I always felt that we had failed to fulfil an obvious destiny in the matter of those emeralds; and there was something touching in the way Raffles now sided with me against himself.

'But I saw it the moment I had yanked them up,' said he, 'and heard that fat swine curse his wife for dropping them. He told her she'd done it on purpose, too; he hit the nail on the head all right; but it was her poor head, and that showed me my unworthy impulse in its true light, Bunny. I didn't need your reproaches to make me realise what a skunk I'd been all round. I saw that the necklace was morally yours, and there was one clear call for me to restore it to you by hook, crook, or barrel. I left for Carlsbad as soon after its wrongful owners as prudence permitted.'

'Admirable!' said I, overjoyed to find old Raffles by no means in such bad form as he looked. 'But not to have taken me with you, A.J., that's the unkind cut I can't forgive.'

'My dear Bunny, you couldn't have borne it,' said Raffles solemnly. 'The cure would have killed you; look what it's done to me.'

'Don't tell me you went through with it!' I rallied him.

'Of course I did, Bunny. I played the game like a prayer-book.'

'But why, in the name of all that's wanton?'

'You don't know Carlsbad, or you wouldn't ask. The place is squirming with spies and humbugs. If I had broken the rules one of the prize humbugs laid down for me I should have been spotted in a tick by a spy, and bowled out myself for a spy and a humbug rolled into one. Oh, Bunny, if old man Dante were alive today I should commend him to that sink of salubrity for the redraw material of another and a worse Inferno!'

The steaks had arrived, smoking hot, with a kidney apiece and lashings of fried potatoes. And for a divine interval (as it must have been to him) Raffles's only words were to the waiter, and referred to successive tankards of bitter, with the superfluous rider that the man who said we couldn't drink beer was a liar. But indeed I never could myself, and only achieved the impossible in this case out of sheer sympathy with Raffles. And eventually I had my reward, in such a recital of malignant privation as I cannot trust myself to set down in any words but his.

'No, Bunny, you couldn't have borne it for half a week; you'd have looked like that all the time!' quoth Raffles. I suppose my face had fallen (as it does too easily) at his aspersion on my endurance. 'Cheer up, my man; that's better,' he went on, as I did my best. 'But it was no smiling matter out there. No one does smile after the first week; your sense of humour is the first thing the cure eradicates. There was a hunting man at my hotel, getting his weight down to ride a special thoroughbred, and no doubt a cheery dog at home; but, poor devil, he hadn't much chance of good cheer there! Miles and miles on his poor feet before breakfast; mud-poultices all the morning; and not the semblance of a drink all day, except some aerated muck called Gieshübler. He was allowed to lap that up an hour after meals, when his tongue would be hanging out of his mouth. We went to the same weighing machine at cock-crow, and though he looked quite good-natured once when I caught him asleep in his chair, I have known him tear up his weight ticket when he had gained an ounce or two instead of losing one or two pounds. We began by taking our walks together, but his conversation used to get so physically introspective that one couldn't get in a word about one's own works edgeways.'

'But there was nothing wrong with your works,' I reminded Raffles; he shook his head as one who was not so sure.

'Perhaps not at first, but the cure soon sees to that! I closed in like a concertina, Bunny, and I only hope I shall be able to pull out like one. You see, it's the custom of the accursed place for one to telephone for a doctor the moment one arrives. I consulted the hunting man, who of course recommended his own in order to make sure of a companion on the rack. The old arch-humbug was down upon me in ten minutes, examining me from crown to heel, and made the most unblushing report upon my general condition. He said I had a liver! I'll swear I hadn't before I went to Carlsbad, but I shouldn't be a bit surprised if I'd brought one back.'

And he tipped his tankard with a solemn face, before falling to work upon the Welsh rarebit which had just arrived.

'It looks like gold, and it's golden eating,' said poor old Raffles. 'I only wish that sly dog of a doctor could see me at it! He had the nerve to make me write out my own health-warrant, and it was so like my friend the hunting man's that it dispelled his settled gloom for the whole of that evening. We used to begin our drinking day at the same well of German damnably defiled, and we paced the same colonnade to the blare of the same well-fed band. That wasn't a joke, Bunny; it's not a thing to joke about; mud-poultices and dry meals, with teetotal poisons in between, were to be my portion too. You stiffen your lip at that, eh, Bunny? I told you that you never would or could have stood it; but it was the only game to play for the Emerald Stakes. It kept one above suspicion all the time. And then I didn't mind that part as much as you would, or as my hunting pal did; he was driven to fainting at the doctor's place one day, in the forlorn hope of a toothful of brandy to bring him round. But all he got was a glass of cheap Marsala.'

'But did you win those stakes after all?'

'Of course I did, Bunny,' said Raffles below his breath, and with a look that I remembered later. 'But the waiters are listening as it is, and I'll tell you the rest some other time. I suppose you know what brought me back so soon?'

'Hadn't you finished your cure?'

'Not by three good days. I had the satisfaction of a row royal with the Lord High Humbug to account for my hurried departure. But, as a matter of fact, if Teddy Garland hadn't got his Blue at the eleventh hour I should be at Carlsbad still.'

E.M. Garland (Eton and Trinity) was the Cambridge wicketkeeper, and one of the many young cricketers who owed a good deal to Raffles. They had made friends in some country-house week, and foregathered afterward in town, where the young fellow's father had a house at which Raffles became a constant guest. I am afraid I was a little prejudiced both against the father, a retired brewer whom I had never met, and the son whom I did meet once or twice at the Albany. Yet I could quite understand the mutual attraction between Raffles and this much younger man; indeed he was a mere boy, but like so many of his school he seemed to have a knowledge of the world beyond his years, and withal such a spontaneous spring of sweetness and charm as neither knowledge nor experience could sensibly pollute. And yet I had a shrewd suspicion that wild oats had been somewhat freely sown, and that it was Raffles who had stepped in and taken the sower in hand, and turned him into the stuff of which Blues are made. At least I knew that no one could be sounder friend or saner counsellor to any young fellow in need of either. And many there must be to bear me out in their hearts; but they did not know their Raffles as I knew mine; and if they say that was why they thought so much of him, let them have patience, and at last they shall hear something that need not make them think the less.

'I couldn't let poor Teddy keep at Lord's,' explained Raffles, 'and me not there to egg him on! You see, Bunny, I taught him a thing or two in those little matches we played together last August. I take a fatherly interest in the child.'

'You must have done him a lot of good,' I suggested, 'in every way.'

Raffles looked up from his bill and asked me what I meant. I saw he was not pleased with my remark, but I was not going back on it.

'Well, I should imagine you had straightened him out a bit, if you ask me.'

'I didn't ask you, Bunny, that's just the point!' said Raffles. And I watched him tip the waiter without the least *arrière-pensée* on either side.

'After all,' said I, on our way down the marble stair, 'you have told me a good deal about the lad. I remember once hearing you say he had a lot of debts, for example.'

'So I was afraid,' replied Raffles, frankly; 'and between ourselves, I offered to finance him before I went abroad. Teddy wouldn't hear of it; that hot young blood of his was up at the thought, though he was perfectly delightful in what he said. So don't jump to rotten conclusions, Bunny, but stroll up to the Albany and have a drink.'

And when we had reclaimed our hats and coats, and lit our Sullivans in the hall, out we marched as though I were now part-owner of the place with Raffles.

'That,' said I, to effect a thorough change of conversation, since I felt at one with all the world, 'is certainly the finest grill in Europe.'

'That's why we went there, Bunny.'

'But must I say I was rather surprised to find you a member of a place where you tip the waiter and take a ticket for your hat!'

I was not surprised, however, to hear Raffles defend his own caravanserai.

'I would go a step further,' he remarked, 'and make every member show his badge as they do at Lord's.'

'But surely the porter knows the members by sight?'

'Not he! There are far too many thousands of them.'

'I should have thought he must.'

'And I know he doesn't.'

'Well, you ought to know, A.J., since you're a member yourself.'

'On the contrary, my dear Bunny, I happen to know because I never was one!'

2

'HIS OWN FAMILIAR FRIEND'

How we laughed as we turned into Whitehall! I began to feel I had been wrong about Raffles after all, and that enhanced my mirth. Surely this was the old gay rascal, and it was by some uncanny feat of his stupendous will that he had appeared so haggard on the platform. In the London lamplight that he loved so well, under a starry sky of an almost theatrical blue, he looked another man already. If such a change was due to a few draughts of bitter beer and a few ounces of fillet steak, then I felt I was the brewers" friend and the vegetarians" foe for life. Nevertheless I could detect a serious side to my companion's mood, especially when he spoke once more of Teddy Garland, and told me that he had cabled to him also before leaving Carlsbad. And I could not help wondering, with a discreditable pang, whether his intercourse with that honest lad could have bred in Raffles a remorse for his own misdeeds, such as I myself had often tried, but always failed, to produce.

So we came to the Albany in sober frame, for all our recent levity, thinking at least no evil for once in our lawless lives. And there was our good friend Barraclough, the porter, to salute and welcome us in the courtyard.

'There's a gen'leman writing you a letter upstairs,' said he to Raffles. 'It's Mr Garland, sir, so I took him up.'

'Teddy!' cried Raffles, and took the stairs two at a time.

I followed rather heavily. It was not jealousy, but I did feel rather critical of this mushroom intimacy. So I followed up, feeling that the evening was spoilt for me – and God knows I was right! Not till my dying day shall I forget the tableau that awaited me in those familiar rooms. I see it now as plainly as I see the problem picture of the year, which lies in wait for one in all the illustrated papers; indeed, it was a problem picture itself in flesh and blood.

Raffles had opened his door as only Raffles could open doors, with the boyish thought of giving the other boy a fright; and young Garland had very naturally started up from the bureau, where he was writing, at the sudden clap of his own name behind him. But that was the last of his natural actions. He did not advance to grasp Raffles by the hand; there was no answering smile of welcome on the fresh young face which used to remind me of the Phoebus in Guido's Aurora, with its healthy pink and bronze, and its hazel eye like clear amber. The pink faded before our gaze, the bronze turned a sickly sallow; and there stood Teddy Garland as if glued to the bureau behind him, clutching its edge with all his might. I can see his knuckles gleaming like ivory under the back of each sunburnt hand.

'What is it? What are you hiding?' demanded Raffles. His love for the lad had rung out in his first greeting; his puzzled voice was still jocular and genial, but the other's attitude soon strangled that. All this time I had been standing in vague horror on the threshold; now Raffles beckoned me in and switched on more light. It fell full upon a ghastly and a guilty face, that yet stared bravely in the glare. Raffles locked the door behind us, put the key in his pocket, and strode over to the desk.

No need to report their first broken syllables: enough that it was no note young Garland was writing, but a cheque which he was laboriously copying into Raffles's cheque-book, from an old cheque abstracted from a pass-book with A.J. RAFFLES in gilt capitals upon its brown leather back. Raffles had only that year opened a banking account, and I remembered his telling me how thoroughly he meant to disregard the instructions on his cheque-book by always leaving it about to advertise the fact. And this was the result. A glance convicted his friend of criminal intent: a sheet of notepaper lay covered with trial signatures. Yet Raffles could turn and look with infinite pity upon the miserable youth who was still looking defiantly on him.

'My poor chap!' was all he said.

And at that the broken boy found the tongue of a hoarse and quavering old man.

'Won't you hand me over and be done with it?' he croaked. 'Must you torture me yourself?'

It was all I could do to refrain from putting in my word, and telling the fellow it was not for him to ask questions. Raffles merely inquired whether he had thought it all out before.

'God knows I hadn't, A.J.! I came up to write you a note, I swear I did,' said Garland with a sudden sob.

'No need to swear it,' returned Raffles, actually smiling. 'Your word's quite good enough for me.'

'God bless you for that, after this!' the other choked, in terrible disorder now.

'It was pretty obvious,' said Raffles reassuringly.

'Was it? Are you sure? You do remember offering me a cheque last month, and my refusing it?'

'Why, of course I do!' cried Raffles, with such spontaneous heartiness that I could see he had never thought of it since mentioning the matter to me at our meal. What I could not see was any reason for such conspicuous relief, or the extenuating quality of a circumstance which seemed to me rather to aggravate the offence.

'I have regretted that refusal ever since,' young Garland continued very simply. 'It was a mistake at the time, but this week of all weeks it's been a tragedy. Money I must have; I'll tell you why directly. When I got your wire last night it seemed as though my wretched prayers had been answered. I was going to someone else this morning, but I made up my mind to wait for you instead. You were the one I really could turn to, and yet I refused your great offer a month ago. But you said you would be back tonight; and you weren't here when I came. I telephoned and found that the train had come in all right, and that there wasn't another until the morning. Tomorrow morning's my limit, and tomorrow's the match.' He stopped as he saw what Raffles was doing. 'Don't, Raffles, I don't deserve it!' he added in fresh distress.

But Raffles had unlocked the tantalus and found a syphon in the corner cupboard, and it was a very yellow bumper that he handed to the guilty youth.

'Drink some,' he said, 'or I won't listen to another word.'

'I'm going to be ruined before the match begins. I am!' the poor fellow insisted, turning to me when Raffles shook his head. 'And it'll break my father's heart, and – and – '

I thought he had worse still to tell us, he broke off in such despair; but either he changed his mind, or the current of his thoughts set inward in spite of him, for when he spoke again it was to offer us both a further explanation of his conduct.

'I only came up to leave a line for Raffles,' he said to me, 'in case he did get back in time. It was the porter himself who fixed me up at that bureau. He'll tell you how many times I had called before. And then I saw before my nose in one pigeon-hole your cheque-book, Raffles, and your pass-book bulging with old cheques.'

'And as I wasn't back to write one for you,' said Raffles, 'you wrote it for me. And quite right, too!'

'Don't laugh at me!' cried the boy, his lost colour rushing back. And he looked at me again as though my long face hurt him less than the sprightly sympathy of his friend.

'I'm not laughing, Teddy,' replied Raffles kindly. 'I was never more serious in my life. It was playing the friend to come to me at all in your fix, but it was the act of a real good pal to draw on me behind my back rather than let me feel I'd ruined you by not turning up in time. You may shake your head as hard as you like, but I never was paid a higher compliment.'

And the consummate casuist went on working a congenial vein until a less miserable sinner might have been persuaded that he had done nothing really dishonourable; but young Garland had the grace neither to make nor to accept any excuse for his own conduct. I never heard a man more down upon himself, or confession of error couched in stronger terms; and yet there was something so sincere and ingenuous in his remorse, something that Raffles and I had lost so long ago, that in our hearts I am sure we took his follies more seriously than our own crimes. But foolish he indeed had been, if not criminally foolish as he said. It was the old story of the prodigal son of an indulgent father. There had been, as I suspected, a certain amount of youthful riot which the influence of Raffles had already quelled; but there had also been much reckless extravagance, of which Raffles naturally knew less, since your scapegrace is constitutionally quicker to confess himself as such than as a fool. Suffice it that this one had thrown himself on his father's generosity, only to find that the father himself was in financial straits.

'What!' cried Raffles, 'with that house on his hands?'

'I knew it would surprise you,' said Teddy Garland. 'I can't understand it myself; he gave me no particulars, but the mere fact was enough for me. I simply couldn't tell my father everything after that. He wrote me a cheque for all I did own up to, but I could see it was such a tooth that I swore I'd never come on him to pay another farthing. And I never will!'

The boy took a sip from his glass, for his voice had faltered, and then he paused to light another cigarette, because the last had gone out between his fingers. So sensitive and yet so desperate was the blonde young face, with the creased forehead and the nervous mouth, that I saw Raffles look another way until the match was blown out.

'But at the time I might have done worse, and did,' said Teddy, 'a thousand times! I went to the Jews. That's the whole trouble. There were more debts – debts of honour – and to square up I went to the Jews. It was only a matter of two or three hundred to start with; but you may know, though I didn't, what a snowball the smallest sum becomes in the hands of those devils. I borrowed three hundred and signed a promissory note for four hundred and fifty-six.'

'Only fifty per cent!' said Raffles. 'You got off cheap if the percentage was per annum.'

'Wait a bit! It was by way of being even more reasonable than that. The four hundred and fifty-six was repayable in monthly instalments of twenty quid, and I kept them up religiously until the sixth payment fell due. That was soon after Christmas, when one's always hard up, and for the first time I was a day or two late – not more, mind you; yet what do you suppose happened? My cheque was returned, and the whole blessed balance demanded on the nail!'

Raffles was following intently, with that complete concentration which was a signal force in his equipment. His face no longer changed at anything he heard; it was as strenuously attentive as that of any judge upon the bench. Never had I clearer vision of the man he might have been but for the kink in his nature which had made him what he was.

'The promissory note was for four-fifty-six,' said he, 'and this sudden demand was for the lot less the hundred you had paid?'

'That's it.'

'What did you do?' I asked, not to seem behind Raffles in my grasp of the case.

'Told them to take my instalment or go to blazes for the rest!'

'And they?'

'Absolutely drop the whole thing until this very week, and then come down on me for – what do you suppose?'

'Getting on for a thousand,' said Raffles after a moment's thought.

'Nonsense!' I cried. Garland looked astonished too.

'Raffles knows all about it,' said he. 'Seven hundred was the actual figure. I needn't tell you I have given the bounders a wide berth since the day I raised the wind; but I went and had it out with them over this. And half the seven hundred is for default interest, I'll trouble you, from the beginning of January down to date!'

'Had you agreed to that?'

'Not to my recollection, but there it was as plain as a pikestaff on my promissory note. A halfpenny in the shilling per week over and above everything else when the original interest wasn't forthcoming.'

'Printed or written on your note of hand?'

'Printed – printed small, I needn't tell you – but quite large enough for me to read when I signed the cursed bond. In fact I believe I did read it; but a halfpenny a week! Who could ever believe it would mount up like that? But it does; it's right enough, and the long and short of it is that unless I pay up by twelve o'clock tomorrow the governor's to be called in to say whether he'll pay up for me or see me made a bankrupt under his nose. Twelve o'clock, when the match begins! Of course they know that, and are trading on it. Only this evening I had the most insolent ultimatum, saying it was my "dead and last chance."'

'So then you came round here?'

'I was coming in any case. I wish I'd shot myself first!'

'My dear fellow, it was doing me proud; don't let us lose our sense of proportion, Teddy.'

But young Garland had his face upon his hand, and once more he was the miserable man who had begun brokenly to unfold the history of his shame. The unconscious animation produced by the mere unloading of his heart, the natural boyish slang with which his tale had been freely garnished, had faded from his face, had died upon his lips. Once more he was a soul in torments of despair and degradation; and yet once more did the absence of the abject in man and manner redeem him from the depths of either. In these moments of reaction he was pitiful, but not contemptible, much less unlovable. Indeed, I could see the qualities that had won the heart of Raffles as I had never seen them before. There is a native nobility not to be destroyed by a single descent into the ignoble, an essential honesty too bright and brilliant to be dimmed by incidental dishonour; and both remained to the younger man, in the eyes of the other two, who were even then determining to preserve in him all that they themselves had lost. The thought came naturally enough to me. And yet I may well have derived it from a face that for once was easy to read, a clear-cut face that had never looked so sharp in profile, or, to my knowledge, half so gentle in expression.

'And what about these Jews?' asked Raffles at length.

'There's really only one.'

'Are we to guess his name?'

'No, I don't mind telling you. It's Dan Levy.'

'Of course it is!' cried Raffles with a nod for me. 'Our Mr Shylock in all his glory!'

Teddy snatched his face from his hands.

'You don't know him, do you?'

'I might almost say I know him at home,' said Raffles. 'But as a matter of fact I met him abroad.'

Teddy was on his feet.

'But do you know him well enough – '

'Certainly. I'll see him in the morning. But I ought to have the receipts for the various instalments you have paid, and perhaps that letter saying it was your last chance.'

'Here they all are,' said Garland, producing a bulky envelope. 'But of course I'll come with you – '

'Of course you'll do nothing of the kind, Teddy! I won't have your eye put out for the match by that old ruffian, and I'm not going to let you sit up all night either. Where are you staying, my man?'

'Nowhere yet. I left my kit at the club. I was going out home if I'd caught you early enough.'

'Stout fellow! You stay here.'

'My dear old man, I couldn't think of it,' said Teddy gratefully.

'My dear young man, I don't care whether you think of it or not. Here you stay, and moreover you turn in at once. I can fix you up with all you want, and Barraclough shall bring your kit round before you're awake.'

'But you haven't got a bed, Raffles?'

'You shall have mine. I hardly ever go to bed – do I, Bunny?'

'I've seldom seen you there,' said I.

'But you were travelling all last night?'

'And straight through till this evening, and I sleep all the time in a train,' said Raffles. 'I hardly opened an eye all day; if I turned in tonight I shouldn't get a wink.'

'Well, I shan't either,' said the other hopelessly. 'I've forgotten how to sleep!'

'Wait till I learn you!' said Raffles, and went into the inner room and lit it up.

'I'm terribly sorry about it all,' whispered young Garland, turning to me as though we were old friends now.

'And I'm sorry for you,' said I from my heart. 'I know what it is.'

Garland was still staring when Raffles returned with a tiny bottle from which he was shaking little round black things into his left palm.

'Clean sheets yawning for you, Teddy,' said he. 'And now take two of these, and one more spot of whisky, and you'll be asleep in ten minutes.'

'What are they?'

'Somnol. The latest thing out, and quite the best.'

'But won't they give me a frightful head?'

'Not a bit of it; you'll be as right as rain ten minutes after you wake up. And you needn't leave this before eleven tomorrow morning, because you don't want a knock at the nets, do you?'

'I ought to have one,' said Teddy seriously. But Raffles laughed him to scorn.

'They're not playing you for runs, my man, and I shouldn't run any risks with those hands. Remember all the chances they're going to lap up tomorrow, and all the byes they've not got to let!'

And Raffles had administered his opiate before the patient knew much more about it; next minute he was shaking hands with me, and the minute after that Raffles went in to put out his light. He was gone some little time; and I remember leaning out of the window in order not to overhear the conversation in the next room. The night was nearly as fine as ever. The starry ceiling over the Albany Courtyard was only less beautifully blue than when Raffles and I had come in a couple of hours ago. The traffic in Piccadilly came as crisply to the ear as on a winter's night of hard frost. It was a night of wine, and sparkling wine, and the day at Lord's must surely be a day of nectar. I could not help wondering whether any man had ever played in the University match with such a load upon his soul as E.M. Garland was taking to his forced slumbers; and then whether any heavy-laden soul had ever hit upon two such brother confessors as Raffles and myself!

3

COUNCIL OF WAR

Raffles was humming a snatch of something too choice for me to recognise when I drew in my head from the glorious night. The folding-doors were shut, and the grandfather's clock on one side of them made it almost midnight. Raffles would not stop his tune for me, but he pointed to the syphon and decanter, and I replenished my glass. He had a glass beside him also, which was less usual, but he did not sit down beside his glass; he was far too fidgety for that; even bothering about a pair of pictures which had changed places under some zealous hand in his absence, or rather two of Mr Hollyer's fine renderings of Watts and Burne-Jones of which I had never seen Raffles take the slightest notice before. But it seemed that they must hang where he had hung them, and for once I saw them hanging straight. The books had also suffered from good intentions; he gave them up with a shrug. Archives and arcana he tested or examined, and so a good many minutes passed without a word. But when he stole back into the inner room, after waiting a little at the folding-doors, there was still some faint strain upon his lips; it was only when he returned, shutting the door none too quietly behind him, that he stopped humming and spoke out with a grimmer face than he had worn all night.

'That boy's in a bigger hole than he thinks. But we must pull him out between us before play begins. It's one clear call for us, Bunny!'

'Is it a bigger hole than you thought?' I asked, thinking myself of the conversation which I had managed not to overhear.

'I don't say that, Bunny, though I never should have dreamt of his old father being in one too. I own I can't understand that. They live in a regular country house in the middle of Kensington, and there are only the two of them. But I've given Teddy my word not to go to the old man for the money, so it's no use talking about it.'

But apparently it was what they had been talking about behind the folding-doors; it only surprised me to see how much Raffles took it to heart.

'So you have made up your mind to raise the money elsewhere?'

'Before that lad in there opens his eyes.'

'Is he asleep already?'

'Like the dead,' said Raffles, dropping into his chair and drinking thoughtfully; 'and so he will be till we wake him up. It's a ticklish experiment, Bunny, but even a splitting head for the first hour's play is better than a sleepless night; I've tried both, so I ought to know. I shouldn't even wonder if he did himself more than justice tomorrow; one often does when just less than fit; it takes off that dangerous edge of over-keenness which so often cuts one's own throat.'

'But what do you think of it all, A.J.?'

'Not so much worse than I let him think I thought.'

'But you must have been amazed?'

'I am past amazement at the worst thing the best of us ever does, and contrariwise of course. Your rich man proves a pauper, and your honest man plays the knave; we're all of us capable of every damned thing. But let us thank our stars and Teddy's that we got back just when we did.'

'Why at that moment?'

Raffles produced the unfinished cheque, shook his head over it, and sent it fluttering across to me.

'Was there ever such a childish attempt? They'd have kept him in the bank while they sent for the police. If ever you want to play this game, Bunny, you must let me coach you up a bit.'

'But it was never one of your games, A.J.!'

'Only incidentally once or twice; it never appealed to me,' said Raffles, sending expanding circlets of smoke to crown the girls on the Golden Stair that was no longer tilted in a leaning tower. 'No, Bunny, an occasional *exeat* at school is my modest record as a forger, though I admit that augured ill. Do you remember how I left my cheque-book about on purpose for what's happened? To be sinned against instead of sinning, in all the papers, would have set one up as an honest man for life. I thought, God forgive me, of poor old Barraclough or somebody of that kind. And to think it should be "the friend in whom my soul confided"! Not that I ever did confide in him, Bunny, much as I love this lad.'

Despite the tense of that last statement, it was the old Raffles who was speaking now, the incisively cynical old Raffles that I still knew the best, the Raffles of the impudent quotations and jaunty *jeux d'esprit*. This Raffles only meant half he said – but had generally done the other half! I met his mood by reminding him (out of his own *Whitaker*) that the sun rose at 3.51, in case he thought of breaking in anywhere that night. I had the honour of making Raffles smile.

'I did think of it, Bunny,' said he. 'But there's only one crib that we could crack in decency for this money; and our Mr Shylock's is not the sort of city that Caesar himself would have taken *ex itinere*. It's a case for the *testudo* and all the rest of it. You must remember that I've been there, Bunny; at least I've visited his "moving tent," if one may jump from an ancient to an "Ancient and Modern."

And if that was as impregnable as I found it, his permanent citadel must be perched upon the very rock of defence!'

'You must tell me about that, Raffles,' said I, tiring a little of his kaleidoscopic metaphors. Let him be as allusive as he liked when there was no risky work on hand, and I was his lucky and delighted audience till all hours of the night or morning. But for a deed of darkness I wanted fewer fireworks, a steadier light from his intellectual lantern. And yet these were the very moments that inspired his pyrotechnic displays.

'Oh, I shall tell you all right,' said Raffles. 'But just now the next few hours are of more importance than the last few weeks. Of course Shylock's the man for our money; but knowing our tribesmen as I do, I think we had better begin by borrowing it like simple Christians.'

'Then we have it to pay back again.'

'And that's the psychological moment for raiding our "miser's sunless coffers" – if he happens to have any. It will give us time to find out.'

'But he doesn't keep open office all night,' I objected.

'But he opens at nine o'clock in the morning,' said Raffles, 'to catch the early stockbroker who would rather be bled than hammered.'

'Who told you that?'

'Our Mrs Shylock.'

'You must have made great friends with her?'

'More in pity than for the sake of secrets.'

'But you went where the secrets were?'

'And she gave them away wholesale.'

'She would,' I said, 'to you.'

'She told me a lot about the impending libel action.'

'Shylock *v. Fact?*'

'Yes; it's coming on before the vacation, you know.'

'So I saw in some paper.'

'But you know what it's all about, Bunny?'

'No, I don't.'

'Another old rascal, the Maharajah of Hathipur, and his perfectly fabulous debts. It seems he's been in our Mr Shylock's clutches for years, but instead of taking his pound of flesh he's always increasing the amount. Of course that's the whole duty of money-lenders, but now they say the figure runs well into six. No one has any sympathy with that old heathen; he's said to have been a pal of Nana's before the Mutiny, and in it up to the neck he only saved by turning against his own lot in time; in any case it's the pot and the kettle so far as moral colour is concerned. But I believe it's an actual fact that syndicates have been formed to buy up the black man's debts and take a reasonable interest, only the dirty white man always gets to windward of the syndicate. They're on the point of bringing it off, when old Levy inveigles the black into some new Oriental extravagance. *Fact* has exposed the whole thing, and printed blackmailing letters which Shylock swears are forgeries. That's both their cases in a philippine! The leeches told the Jew he must do his Carlsbad this year before the case came on; and the tremendous amount it's going to cost may account for his dunning old clients the moment he gets back.'

'Then why should he lend to you?'

'I'm a new client, Bunny; that makes all the difference. Then we were very good pals out there.'

'But you and Mrs Shylock were better still?'

'Unbeknowns, Bunny! She used to tell me her troubles when I lent her an arm and took due care to look a martyr; my hunting friend had coarse metaphors about heavy-weights and the knacker's yard.'

'And yet you came away with the poor soul's necklace?'

Raffles was tapping the chronic cigarette on the table at his elbow; he stood up to light it, as one does stand up to make the dramatic announcements of one's life, and he spoke through the flame of the match as it rose and fell between his puffs.

'No – Bunny – I did not!'

'But you told me you won the Emerald Stakes!' I cried, jumping up in my turn.

'So I did, Bunny, but I gave them back again.'

'You gave yourself away to her, as she'd given him away to you?'

'Don't be a fool, Bunny,' said Raffles, subsiding into his chair. 'I can't tell you the whole thing now, but here are the main heads. They're at the Savoy Hotel, in Carlsbad I mean. I go to Pupp's. We meet. They stare. I come out of my British shell as the humble hero of the affair at the other Savoy. I crab my hotel. They swear by theirs. I go to see their rooms. I wait till I can get the very same thing immediately overhead on the second floor – where I can even hear the old swine cursing her from under his mud-poultice! Both suites have balconies that might have been made for me. Need I go on?'

'I wonder you weren't suspected.'

'There's no end to your capacity for wonder, Bunny. I took some sweet old rags with me on purpose, carefully packed inside a decent suit, and I had the luck to pick up a foul old German cap that some peasant had cast off in the woods. I only meant to leave it on them like a card; as it was – well, I was waiting for the best barber in the place to open his shop next morning.'

'What had happened?'

'A whole actful of unrehearsed effects; that's why I think twice before taking on old Shylock again. I admire him, Bunny, as a steely foeman. I look forward to another game with him on his own ground. But I must find out the pace of the wicket before I put myself on.'

'I suppose you had tea with them, and all that sort of thing?'

'Gieshübler!' said Raffles with a shudder. 'But I made it last as long as tea, and thought I had located the little green lamps before I took my leave. There was a japanned despatch box in one corner. "That's the Emerald Isle," I thought, "I'll soon have it out of the sea. The old man won't trust 'em to the old lady after what happened in town," I needn't tell you I knew they were there somewhere; he made her wear them even at the tragic travesty of a Carlsbad hotel dinner.'

Raffles was forgetting to be laconic now. I believe he had forgotten the lad in the next room, and everything else but the breathless battle that he was fighting over again for my benefit. He told me how he waited for a dark night, and then slid down from his sitting-room balcony to the one below. And my emeralds were not in the japanned box after all; and just as he had assured himself of the fact, the folding-doors opened 'as it might be these,' and there stood Dan Levy 'in a suit of swagger silk pyjamas.'

'They gave me a sudden respect for him,' continued Raffles; 'it struck me, for the first time, that mud baths mightn't be the only ones he ever took. His face was as evil as ever, but he was utterly unarmed, and I was not; and yet there he stood and abused me like a pickpocket, as if there was no chance of my firing, and he didn't care whether I did or not. So I stuck my revolver nearly in his face, and pulled the hammer up and up. Good God, Bunny, if I had pulled too hard! But that made him blink a bit, and I was jolly glad to let it down again. "Out with those emeralds," says I in low German mugged up in case of need. Of course you realise that I was absolutely unrecognisable, a low blackguard with a blackened face. "I don't know what you mean," says he, "and I'm damned if I care." "*Das halsband*, says I, which means the necklace. "Go to hell," says he. But I struck myself and shook my head and then my fist at him and nodded. He laughed in my face; and upon my soul we were at a deadlock. So I pointed to the clock and held up one finger. "I've one minute to live, old girl," says he through the doors, "if this rotter has the guts to shoot, and I don't think he has. Why the hell don't you get out the other way and alarm the 'ouse?" And that raised the siege, Bunny.

In comes the old woman, as plucky as he was, and shoves the necklace into my left hand. I longed to refuse it. I didn't dare. And the old beast took her and shook her like a rat, until I covered him again, and swore in German that if he showed himself on the balcony for the next two minutes he'd be *ein toter Englander*! That was the other bit I'd got off pat; it was meant to mean "a dead Englishman." And I left the fine old girl clinging on to him, instead of him to her!'

I emptied my lungs and my glass too. Raffles took a sip himself.

'But the rope was fixed to *your* balcony, A.J.?'

'But I began by fixing the other end to theirs, and the moment I was safely up I undid my end and dropped it clear to the ground. They found it dangling all right when out they rushed together. Of course I'd picked the right ball in the way of nights; it was bone-dry as well as pitch-dark, and in five minutes I was helping the rest of the hotel to search for impossible footprints on the gravel, and to stamp out any there might conceivably have been.'

'So nobody ever suspected you?'

'Not a soul, I can safely say; I was the first my victims bored with the whole yarn.'

'Then why return the swag? It's an old trick of yours, Raffles, but in a case like this, with a pig like that, I confess I don't see the point.'

'You forget the poor old lady, Bunny. She had a dog's life before; after that the beans he gave her weren't even fit for a dog. I loved her for her pluck in standing up to him; it beat his hollow in standing up to me; there was only one reward for her, and it was in my gift.'

'But how on earth did you manage that?'

'Not by public presentation, Bunny, nor yet by taking the old dame into my confidence *more cuniculi!*'

'I suppose you returned the necklace anonymously?'

'As a low-down German burglar would be sure to do! No, Bunny, I planted it in the woods where I knew it would be found. And then I had to watch lest it was found by the wrong sort. But luckily Mr Shylock had sprung a substantial reward, and all came right in the end. He sent his doctor to blazes, and had a buck feed and lashings on the night it was recovered. The hunting man and I were invited to the thanksgiving spread; but I wouldn't budge from the diet, and he was ashamed to unless I did. It made a coolness between us, and now I doubt if we shall ever have that enormous dinner we used to talk about to celebrate our return from a living tomb.'

But I was not interested in that shadowy fox-hunter. 'Dan Levy's a formidable brute to tackle,' said I at length, and none too buoyantly.

'That's a very true observation, Bunny; it's also exactly why I so looked forward to tackling him. It ought to be the kind of conflict that the halfpenny press have learnt to call Homeric.'

'Are you thinking of tomorrow, or of when it comes to robbing Peter to pay Peter?'

'Excellent, Bunny!' cried Raffles, as though I had made a shot worthy of his willow. 'How the small hours brighten us up!' He drew the curtains and displayed a window like a child's slate with the sashes ruled across it. 'You perceive how we have tired the stars with talking, and cleaned them from the sky! The mellifluous Heraclitus can have been no sitter up o' nights, or his pal wouldn't have boasted about tiring the sun by our methods. What a lot the two old pets must have missed!'

'You haven't answered my question,' said I resignedly. 'Nor have you told me how you propose to go to work to raise this money in the first instance.'

'If you like to light another Sullivan,' said Raffles, 'and mix yourself another very small and final one, I can tell you now, Bunny.'

And tell me he did.

4

'OUR MR SHYLOCK'

I have often wondered in what pause or phase of our conversation Raffles hit upon the plan which we duly carried out; for we had been talking incessantly, since his arrival about eight o'clock at night, until two in the morning. Yet that which we discussed between two and three was what we actually did between nine and ten, with the single exception necessitated by an altogether unforeseen development, of which the less said the better until the proper time. The foresight and imagination of a Raffles are obviously apt to outstrip his spoken words; but even in the course of speech his ideas would crystallise, quite palpably to the listener, and the sentence that began by throwing out a shadowy idea would culminate in a definite project, as the image comes into focus under the lens, and with as much detail into the bargain.

Suffice it that after a long night of it at the Albany, and but a bath and a cup of tea at my own flat, I found Raffles waiting for me in Piccadilly, and down we went together to the jaws of Jermyn Street. There we nodded, and I was proceeding down the hill when I turned on my heel as though I had forgotten something, and entered Jermyn Street not fifty yards behind Raffles. I had no thought of catching him up. But it so happened that I was in his wake in time to witness a first *contretemps* which did not amount to much at the time; this was merely the violent exit of another of Dan Levy's early callers into the very arms of Raffles. There was a heated apology, accepted with courteous composure, and followed by an excited outpouring which I did not come near enough to overhear. It was delivered by a little man in an aureole of indigo hair, who brushed his great sombrero violently as he spoke and Raffles listened. I could see from their manner that the collision which had just occurred was not the subject under discussion; but I failed to distinguish a word, though I listened outside a hatter's until Raffles had gone in and his new acquaintance had passed me with blazing eyes and a volley of husky vows in broken English.

'Another of Mr Shylock's victims,' thought I; and indeed he might have been bleeding internally from the loss of his pound of flesh; at any rate there was bloodshed in his eyes.

I stood a long time outside that hatter's window, and finally went in to choose a cap. But the light is wicked in those narrow shops, and this necessitated my carrying several caps to the broad daylight of the threshold to gauge their shades, and incidentally to achieve a swift survey of the street. Then they crowned me with an ingenious apparatus like a typewriter, to get the exact shape and measure of my skull, for I had intimated that I had no desire to dress it anywhere else for the future. All this must have taken up the most of twenty minutes, yet after getting as far as Mr Shylock's I remembered that I required what one's hatter (and no one else) calls a 'boater,' and back I went to order one in addition to the cap. And as the next tack fetches the buoy, so my next perambulation (in which, however, I was thinking seriously of a new bowler) brought me face to face with Raffles once more.

We shouted and shook hands; our encounter had taken place almost under the money-lender's windows, and it was so un-English in its cordiality that between our slaps and grasps Raffles managed deftly to insert a stout packet in my breast pocket. I cannot think the most critical pedestrian could have seen it done. But streets have as many eyes as Argus, and some of them are always on one.

'They had to send to the bank for it,' whispered Raffles. 'It barely passed through their hands. But don't you let Shylock spot his own envelope!'

In another second he was saying something very different that anybody might have heard, and in yet another he was hustling me across Shylock's threshold. 'I'll take you up and introduce you,' he cried aloud. 'You couldn't come to a better man, my dear fellow – he's the only honest one in Europe. Is Mr Levy disengaged?'

A stunted young gentleman, who spoke as though he had a hare-lip or was in liquor, neither calamity having really befallen him, said that he thought so, but would see, which he proceeded to do through a telephone, after shifting the indicator from 'Through' to 'Private.' He slid off his stool at once, and another youth, of similar appearance and still more similar peculiarity of speech, who entered in a hurry at that moment, was told to hold on while he showed the gentlemen up-stairs. There were other clerks behind the mahogany bulwark, and we heard the newcomer greeting them hoarsely as we climbed up into the presence.

Dan Levy, as I must try to call him when Raffles is not varnishing my tale, looked a very big man at his enormous desk, but by no means so elephantine as at the tiny table in the Savoy Restaurant a month earlier. His privations had not only reduced his bulk to the naked eye, but made him look ten years younger. He wore the habiliments of a gentleman; even as he sat at his desk his well-cut coat and well-tied tie filled me with that inconsequent respect which the silk pyjamas had engendered in Raffles. But the great face that greeted us with a shrewd and rather scornful geniality impressed me yet more powerfully. In its massive features and its craggy contour it displayed the frank pugnacity of the pugilist rather than the low cunning of the traditional usurer; and the nose in particular, while of far healthier appearance than when I had seen it first and last, was both dominant and menacing in its immensity. It was a comfort to turn from this formidable countenance to that of Raffles, who had entered with his own serene unconscious confidence, and now introduced us with that inimitable air of light-hearted authority which stamped him in all shades of society.

'"Appy to meet you, sir. I hope you're well?' said Mr Levy, dropping one aspirate but putting in the next with care. 'Take a seat, sir, please.'

But I kept my legs, though I felt them near to trembling, and, diving a hand into a breast pocket, I began working the contents out of the envelope that Raffles had given me, while I spoke out in a tone sufficiently rehearsed at the Albany overnight.

'I'm not so sure about the happiness,' said I. 'I mean about its lasting, Mr Levy. I come from my friend, Mr Edward Garland.'

'I thought you came to borrow money!' interposed Raffles with much indignation. The moneylender was watching me with bright eyes and lips I could no longer see.

'I never said so,' I rapped out at Raffles; and I thought I saw approval and encouragement behind his stare like truth at the bottom of the well.

'Who *is* the little biter?' the money-lender inquired of him with delightful insolence.

'An old friend of mine,' replied Raffles, in an injured tone that made a convincing end of the old friendship. 'I thought he was hard up, or I never should have brought him in to introduce to you.'

'I didn't ask you for your introduction, Raffles,' said I offensively. 'I simply met you coming out as I was coming in. I thought you damned officious, if you ask me!'

Whereupon, with an Anglo–Saxon threat of subsequent violence to my person, Raffles flung open the door to leave us to our interview. This was exactly as it had been rehearsed. But Dan Levy called Raffles back. And that was exactly as we had hoped.

'Gentlemen, gentlemen!' said the Jew. 'Please don't make a cockpit of my office, gentlemen; and pray, Mr Raffles, don't leave me to the mercies of your very dangerous friend.'

'You can be two to one if you like,' I gasped valiantly. 'I don't care.'

And my chest heaved in accordance with my stage instructions, as also with a realism to which it was a relief to give full play.

'Come now,' said Levy. 'What did Mr Garland send you about?'

'You know well enough,' said I: 'his debt to you.'

'Don't be rude about it,' said Levy. 'What about the debt?'

'It's a damned disgrace!' said I.

'I quite agree,' he chuckled. 'It ought to 'ave been settled months ago.'

'Months ago?' I echoed. 'It's only twelve months since he borrowed three hundred pounds from you, and now you're sticking him for seven!'

'I am,' said Levy, opening uncompromising lips that entirely disappeared again next instant.

'He borrows three hundred for a year at the outside, and you blackmail him for eight hundred when the year's up.'

'You said "seven" just now,' interrupted Raffles, but in the voice of a man who was getting a fright.

'You also said "blackmailing,"' added Dan Levy portentously. 'Do you want to be thrown downstairs?'

'Do *you* deny the figures?' I retorted.

'No, I don't; have you got his repayment cards?'

'Yes, here in my hands, and they shan't leave them. You see, you're not aware,' I added severely, as I turned to Raffles, 'that this young fellow has already paid up one hundred in instalments; that's what makes the eight; and all this is what'll happen to you if you've been fool enough to get into the same boat.'

The money-lender had borne with me longer than either of us had expected that he would; but now he wheeled back his chair and stood up, a pillar of peril and a mouthful of oaths.

'Is that all you've come to say?' he thundered. 'If so, you young devil, out you go!'

'No, it isn't,' said I, spreading out a document attached to the cards of receipt which Raffles had obtained from Teddy Garland; these I had managed to extract without anything else from the inner pocket in which I had been trying to empty out Raffles's envelope. 'Here,' I continued, 'is a letter, written only yesterday, by you to Mr Garland, in which you say, among other very insolent things: "This is final, and absolutely no excuses of any kind will be tolerated or accepted. You have given ten times more trouble than your custom is worth, and I shall be glad to get rid of you. So you had better pay up before twelve o'clock tomorrow, as you may depend that the above threats will be carried out to the very letter, and steps will be taken to carry them into effect at that hour. This is your dead and last chance, and the last time I will write you on the subject."'

'So it is,' said Levy with an oath. 'This is a very bad case, Mr Raffles.'

'I agree,' said I. 'And may I ask if you propose to "get rid" of Mr Garland by making him "pay up" in full?'

'Before twelve o'clock today,' said Dan Levy, with a snap of his prize-fighting jaws.

'Eight hundred, first and last, for the three hundred he borrowed a year ago?'

'That's it.'

'Surely that's very hard on the boy,' I said, reaching the conciliatory stage by degrees on which Raffles paid me many compliments later; but at the time he remarked, 'I should say it was his own fault.'

'Of course it is, Mr Raffles,' cried the moneylender, taking a more conciliatory tone himself. 'It was my money; it was my three 'undred golden sovereigns; and you can sell what's yours for what it'll fetch, can't you?'

'Obviously,' said Raffles.

'Very well, then, money's like anything else; if you haven't got it, and can't beg or earn it, you've got to buy it at a price. I sell my money, that's all. And I've a right to sell it at a fancy price if I can get a fancy price for it. A man may be a fool to pay my figure; that depends 'ow much he wants the money at the time, and it's his affair, not mine. Your gay young friend was all right if he hadn't defaulted, but a defaulter deserves to pay through the nose, and be damned to him. It wasn't me let your friend in; he let in himself, with his eyes open. Mr Garland knew very well what I was charging him, and what I shouldn't 'esitate to charge over and above if he gave me half a chance. Why should I? Wasn't it in the bond? What do you all think I run my show for? It's business, Mr Raffles, not robbery, my dear sir. All business is robbery, if you come to that. But you'll find mine is all above-board and in the bond.'

'A very admirable exposition,' said Raffles weightily.

'Not that it applies to you, Mr Raffles,' the other was adroit enough to add. 'Mr Garland was no friend of mine, and he was a fool, whereas I hope I may say that you're the one and not the other.'

'Then it comes to this,' said I, 'that you mean him to pay up in full this morning?'

'By noon, and it's just gone ten.'

'The whole seven hundred pounds?'

'Sterling,' said Mr Levy 'No cheques entertained.'

'Then,' said I, with an air of final defeat, 'there's nothing for it but to follow my instructions and pay you now on the nail!'

I did not look at Levy, but I heard the sudden intake of his breath at the sight of my bank-notes, and I felt its baleful exhalation on my forehead as I stooped and began counting them out upon his desk. I had made some progress before he addressed me in terms of protest. There was almost a tremor in his voice. I had no call to be so hasty; it looked as though I had been playing a game with him. Why couldn't I tell him I had the money with me all the time? The question was asked with a sudden oath, because I had gone on counting it out regardless of his overtures. I took as little notice of his anger.

'And now, Mr Levy,' I concluded, 'may I ask you to return me Mr Garland's promissory note?'

'Yes, you may ask and you shall receive!' he snarled, and opened his safe so violently that the keys fell out. Raffles replaced them with exemplary promptitude while the note of hand was being found.

The evil little document was in my possession at last. Levy roared down the tube, and the young man of the imperfect diction duly appeared.

'Take that young biter,' cried Levy, 'and throw him into the street. Call up Moses to lend you a 'and.'

But the first murderer stood nonplussed, looking from Raffles to me, and finally inquiring which biter his master meant.

'That one!' bellowed the money-lender, shaking a lethal fist at me. 'Mr Raffles is a friend o' mine.'

'But 'e'th a friend of 'ith too,' lisped the young man. 'Thimeon Markth come acroth the thtreet to tell me tho. He thaw them thake handth outthide our plathe, after he'd theen 'em arm-in-arm in Piccadilly, 'an he come in to thay tho in cathe – '

But the youth of limited articulation was not allowed to finish his explanation; he was grasped by the scruff of the neck and kicked and shaken out of the room, and his collar flung after him. I heard him blubbering on the stairs as Levy locked the door and put the key in his pocket. But I did not hear Raffles slip into the swivel chair behind the desk, or know that he had done so until the usurer and I turned round together.

'Out of that!' blustered Levy.

But Raffles tilted the chair back on its spring and laughed softly in his face.

'Not if I know it,' said he. 'If you don't open the door in about one minute I shall require this telephone of yours to ring up the police.'

'The police, eh?' said Levy, with a sinister recovery of self-control. 'You'd better leave that to me, you precious pair of swindlers!'

'Besides,' continued Raffles, 'of course you keep an *argumentum ad hominem* in one of these drawers. Ah, here it is, and just as well in my hands as in yours!'

He had opened the top drawer in the right-hand pedestal, and taken therefrom a big bulldog revolver; it was the work of few moments to empty its five chambers, and hand the pistol by its barrel to the owner.

'Curse you!' hissed the latter, hurling it into the fender with a fearful clatter. 'But you'll pay for this, my fine gentlemen; this isn't sharp practice, but criminal fraud.'

'The burden of proof,' said Raffles, 'lies with you. Meanwhile, will you be good enough to open that door instead of looking as sick as a cold mud-poultice?'

The money-lender had, indeed, turned as grey as his hair; and his eyebrows, which were black and looked dyed, stood out like smears of ink. Nevertheless, the simile which Raffles had employed with his own unfortunate facility was more picturesque than discreet. I saw it set Mr Shylock thinking. Luckily, the evil of the day was sufficient for it and him; but so far from complying, he set his back to the locked door and swore a sweet oath never to budge.

'Oh, very well!' resumed Raffles, and the receiver was at his ear without more ado. 'Is that the Exchange? Give me nine-two-double-three Gerrard, will you?'

'It's fraud,' reiterated Levy. 'And you know it.'

'It's nothing of the sort, and *you* know it,' murmured Raffles, with the proper pre-occupation of the man at the telephone.

'You lent the money,' I added. 'That's your business. It's nothing to do with you what he chooses to do with it.'

'He's a cursed swindler,' hissed Levy. 'And you're his damned decoy!'

I was not sorry to see Raffles's face light up across the desk.

'Is that Howson, Anstruther and Martin? – they're only my solicitors, Mr Levy.... Put me through to Mr Martin, please... That you, Charlie?... You might come in a cab to Jermyn Street – I forget the number – Dan Levy's, the money-lender's – thanks, old chap! ... Wait a bit, Charlie – a constable...'

But Dan Levy had unlocked his door and flung it open.

'There you are, you scoundrels! But we'll meet again, my fine swell-mobsmen!'

Raffles was frowning at the telephone.

'I've been cut off,' said he. 'Wait a bit! Clear call for you, Mr Levy, I believe!'

And they changed places, without exchanging another word until Raffles and I were on the stairs.

'Why, the 'phone's not even *through!*' yelled the moneylender, rushing out.

'But *we* are, Mr Levy!' cried Raffles. And down we ran into the street.

5

THIN AIR

Raffles hailed a passing hansom, and had bundled me in before I realised that he was not coming with me.

'Drive down to the club for Teddy's cricket bag,' said he; 'we'll make him get straight into flannels to save time. Order breakfast for three in half-an-hour precisely, and I'll tell him everything before you're back.'

His eyes were shining with the prospect as I drove away, not sorry to escape the scene of that young man's awakening to better fortune than he deserved. For in my heart I could not quite forgive the act in which Raffles and I had caught him overnight. Raffles might make as light of it as he pleased; it was impossible for another to take his affectionately lenient view, not of the moral question involved, but of the breach of faith between friend and friend. My own feeling in the matter, however, if a little jaundiced, was not so strong as to prevent me from gloating over the victory in which I had just assisted. I thought of the notorious extortioner who had fallen to our unscrupulous but not indictable wiles; and my heart tinkled with the hansom bell. I thought of the good that we had done for once, of the undoubted wrong we had contrived to right by a species of justifiable chicanery. And I forgot all about the youth whose battle we had fought and won, until I found myself ordering his breakfast, and having his cricket-bag taken out to my cab.

Raffles was waiting for me in the Albany courtyard. I thought he was frowning at the sky, which was not what it had been earlier in the morning, until I remembered how little time there was to lose.

'Haven't you seen anything of him?' he cried as I jumped out.

'Of whom, Raffles?'

'Teddy, of course!'

'Teddy Garland? Has he gone out?'

'Before I got in,' said Raffles, grimly. 'I wonder where the devil he is!'

He had paid the cabman and taken down the bag himself. I followed him up to his rooms.

'But what's the meaning of it, Raffles?'

'That's what I want to know.'

'Could he have gone out for a paper?'

'They were all here before I went. I left them on his bed.'

'Or for a shave?'

'That's more likely; but he's been out nearly an hour.'

'But you can't have been gone much longer yourself, Raffles, and I understood you left him fast asleep?'

'That's the worst of it, Bunny. He must have been shamming. Barraclough saw him go out ten minutes after me.'

'Could you have disturbed him when you went?'

Raffles shook his head.

'I never shut a door more carefully in my life. I made row enough when I came back, Bunny, on purpose to wake him up, and I can tell you it gave me a turn when there wasn't a sound from in there! He'd shut all the doors after him; it was a second or two before I had the pluck to open them. I thought something horrible had happened!'

'You don't think so still?'

'I don't know what to think,' said Raffles, gloomily; 'nothing has panned out as I thought it would. You must remember that we have given ourselves away to Dan Levy, whatever else we have done, and without doubt set up the enemy of our lives in the very next street. It's close quarters, Bunny; we shall have an expert eye upon us for some time to come. But I should rather enjoy that than otherwise, if only Teddy hadn't bolted in this rotten way.'

Never had I known Raffles in so pessimistic a mood. I did not share his sombre view of either matter, though I confined my remarks to the one that seemed to weigh most heavily on his mind.

'A guinea to a gooseberry,' I wagered, 'that you find your man safe and sound at Lord's.'

'I rang them up ten minutes ago,' said Raffles. 'They hadn't heard of him then; besides, here's his cricket-bag.'

'He may have been at the club when I fetched it away – I never asked.'

'I did, Bunny. I rang them up as well, just after you had left.'

'Then what about his father's house?'

'That's our one chance,' said Raffles. 'They're not on the telephone, but now that you're here I've a good mind to drive out and see if Teddy's there. You know what a state he was in last night, and you know how a thing can seem worse when you wake and remember it than it did at the time it happened. I begin to hope he's gone straight to old Garland with the whole story; in that case he's bound to come back for his kit; and by Jove, Bunny, there's a step upon the stairs!'

We had left the doors open behind us, and a step it was, ascending hastily enough to our floor. But it was not the step of a very young man, and Raffles was the first to recognise the fact; his face fell as we looked at each other for a single moment of suspense; in another he was out of the room, and I heard him greeting Mr Garland on the landing.

'Then you haven't brought Teddy with you?' I heard Raffles add.

'Do you mean to say he isn't here?' replied so pleasant a voice – in accents of such acute dismay – that Mr Garland had my sympathy before we met.

'He has been,' said Raffles, 'and I'm expecting him back every minute. Won't you come in and wait, Mr Garland?'

The pleasant voice made an exclamation of premature relief; the pair entered, and I was introduced to the last person I should have suspected of being a retired brewer at all, much less of squandering his money in retirement as suggested by his son. I was prepared for a conventional embodiment of reckless prosperity, for a pseudo-military type in louder purple and finer linen than the real thing. I shook hands instead with a gentle, elderly man, whose kindly eyes beamed bravely amid careworn furrows, and whose slightly diffident yet wholly cordial address won my heart outright.

'So you've lost no time in welcoming the wanderer!' said he. 'You're nearly as bad as my boy, who was quite bent on seeing Raffles last night or first thing this morning. He told me he should stay the night in town if necessary, and he evidently has.'

There was still a trace of anxiety in the father's manner, but there was also a twinkle in his eyes, which kindled with genial fires as Raffles gave a perfectly truthful account of the young man's movements (as distinct from his words and deeds) overnight.

'And what do you think of his great news?' asked Mr Garland. 'Was it a surprise to you, Raffles?'

Raffles shook his head with a rather weary smile, and I sat up in my chair. What great news was this?

'This son of mine has just got engaged,' explained Mr Garland for my benefit. 'And as a matter of fact it's his engagement that brings me here; you gentlemen mustn't think I want to keep an eagle eye upon him; but Miss Belsize has just wired to say she is coming up early to go with us to the match, instead of meeting at Lord's, and I thought she would be so disappointed not to find Teddy, especially as they are bound to see very little of each other all day.'

I for my part was wondering why I had not heard of Miss Belsize or this engagement from Raffles. He must himself have heard of it last thing at night in the next room, while I was star-gazing here at the open window. Yet in all the small hours he had never told me of a circumstance which extenuated young Garland's conduct if it did nothing else. Even now it was not from Raffles that I received either word or look of explanation. But his face had suddenly lit up.

'May I ask,' he exclaimed, 'if the telegram was to Teddy or to you, Mr Garland?'

'It was addressed to Teddy, but of course I opened it in his absence.'

'Could it have been an answer to an invitation or suggestion of his?'

'Very easily. They had lunch together yesterday, and Camilla might have had to consult Lady Laura.'

'Then that's the whole thing!' cried Raffles. 'Teddy was on his way home while you were on yours into town! How did you come?'

'In the brougham.'

'Through the Park?'

'Yes.'

'While he was in a hansom in Knightsbridge or Kensington Gore! That's how you missed him,' said Raffles confidently. 'If you drive straight back you'll be in time to take him on to Lord's.'

Mr Garland begged us both to drive back with him; and we thought we might; we decided that we would, and were all three under way in about a minute. Yet it was considerably after eleven when we bowled through Kensington to a house that I had never seen before, a house since swept away by the flowing tide of flats, but I can still see every stone and slate of it as clearly as on that summer morning more than ten years ago. It stood just off the thoroughfare, in grounds of its own out of all keeping with their metropolitan environment; they ran from one side-street to another, and further back than we could see. Vivid lawn and towering tree, brilliant beds and crystal vineries, struck one more forcibly (and favourably) than the mullioned and turreted mansion of a house. And yet a double stream of omnibuses rattled incessantly within a few yards of the steps on which the three of us soon stood nonplussed.

Mr Edward had not been seen or heard of at the house. Neither had Miss Belsize arrived; that was the one consolatory feature.

'Come into the library,' said Mr Garland; and when we were among his books, which were somewhat beautifully bound and cased in glass, he turned to Raffles and added hoarsely: 'There's something in all this I haven't been told, and I insist on knowing what it is.'

'But you know as much as I do,' protested Raffles. 'I went out leaving Teddy asleep and came back to find him flown.'

'What time was that?'

'Between nine and half-past when I went out. I was away nearly an hour.'

'Why leave him asleep at that time of morning?'

'I wanted him to have every minute he could get. We had been sitting up rather late.'

'But why, Raffles? What could you have to talk about all night when you were tired and it was Teddy's business to keep fresh for today? Why, after all, should he want to see you the moment you got back? He's not the first young fellow who's got rather suddenly engaged to a charming girl; is he in any trouble about it, Raffles?'

'About his engagement – not that I'm aware.'

'Then he is in some trouble?'

'He was, Mr Garland,' answered Raffles. 'I give you my word that he isn't now.'

Mr Garland grasped the back of a chair.

'Was it some money trouble, Raffles? Of course, if my boy has given you his confidence, I have no right simply as his father – '

'It is hardly that, sir,' said Raffles, gently; 'it is I who have no right to give him away. But if you don't mind leaving it at that, Mr Garland, there is perhaps no harm in my saying that it *was* about some little temporary embarrassment that Teddy was so anxious to see me.'

'And you helped him?' cried the poor man, plainly torn between gratitude and humiliation.

'Not out of my pocket,' replied Raffles, smiling. 'The matter was not so serious as Teddy thought; it only required adjustment.'

'God bless you, Raffles!' murmured Mr Garland, with a catch in his voice. 'I won't ask for a single detail. My poor boy went to the right man; he knew better than to come to me. Like father, like son!' he muttered to himself, and dropped into the chair he had been handling, and bent his head over his folded arms.

He seemed to have forgotten the untoward effect of Teddy's disappearance in the peculiar humiliation of its first cause. Raffles took out his watch, and held up the dial for me to see. It was after the half-hour now; but at this moment a servant entered with a missive, and the master recovered his self-control.

'This'll be from Teddy!' he cried, fumbling with his glasses. 'No; it's for him, and by special messenger. I'd better open it. I don't suppose it's Miss Belsize again.'

'Miss Belsize is in the drawing room, sir,' said the man. 'She said you were not to be disturbed.'

'Oh, tell her we shan't be long,' said Mr Garland, with a new strain of trouble in his tone. 'Listen to this – listen to this,' he went on before the door was shut: '"What has happened? Lost toss. Whipham plays if you don't turn up in time. – J.S."'

'Jack Studley,' said Raffles, 'the Cambridge skipper.'

'I know! I know! And Whipham's reserve man, isn't he?'

'And another wicket-keeper, worse luck!' exclaimed Raffles. 'If he turns out and takes a single ball, and Teddy is only one over late, it will still be too late for him to play.'

'Then it's too late already,' said Mr Garland, sinking back into his chair with a groan.

'But that note from Studley may have been half-an-hour on the way.'

'No, Raffles, it's not an ordinary note; it's a message telephoned straight from Lord's – probably within the last few minutes – to a messenger office not a hundred yards from this door!'

Mr Garland sat staring miserably at the carpet; he was beginning to look ill with perplexity and suspense. Raffles himself, who had turned his back upon us with a shrug of acquiescence in the inevitable, was a monument of discomfiture as he stood gazing through a glass door into the adjoining conservatory. There was no actual window in the library, but this door was a single sheet of plate-glass into which a man might well have walked, and I can still see Raffles in full-length silhouette upon a panel of palms and tree-ferns. I see the silhouette grow tall and straight again before my eyes, the door open, and Raffles listening with an alert lift of the head. I, too, hear something, an elfin hiss, a fairy fusillade, and then the sudden laugh with which Raffles rejoined us in the body of the room.

'It's raining!' he cried, waving a hand above his head. 'Have you a barometer, Mr Garland?'

'That's an aneroid under the lamp-bracket.'

'How often do you set the indicator?'

'Last thing every night. I remember it was between Fair and Change when I went to bed. It made me anxious.'

'It may make you thankful now. It's between Change and Rain this morning. And the rain's begun, and while there's rain there's hope!'

In a twinkling Raffles had regained all his own irresistible buoyancy and assurance. But the older man was not capable of so prompt a recovery.

'Something has happened to my boy!'

'But not necessarily anything terrible.'

'If I knew what, Raffles – if only I knew what!'

Raffles eyed the pale and twitching face with sidelong solicitude. He himself had the confident expression which always gave me confidence; the rattle on the conservatory roof was growing louder every minute.

'I intend to find out,' said he; 'and if the rain goes on long enough, we may still see Teddy playing when it stops. But I shall want your help, sir.'

'I am ready to go with you anywhere, Raffles.'

'You can only help me, Mr Garland, by staying where you are.'

'Where I am?'

'In the house all day,' said Raffles firmly. 'It is absolutely essential to my idea.'

'And that is, Raffles?'

'To save Teddy's face, in the first instance. I shall drive straight up to Lord's, in your brougham if I may. I know Studley rather well; he shall keep Teddy's place open till the last possible moment.'

'But how shall you account for his absence?' I asked.

'I shall account for it all right,' said Raffles darkly. 'I can save his face for the time being, at all events at Lord's.'

'But that's the only place that matters,' said I.

'On the contrary, Bunny, this very house matters even more as long as Miss Belsize is here. You forget that they're engaged, and that she's in the next room now.'

'Good God!' whispered Mr Garland. 'I had forgotten that myself.'

'She is the last who must know of this affair,' said Raffles, with, I thought, undue authority. 'And you are the only one who can keep it from her, sir.'

'I?'

'Miss Belsize mustn't go up to Lord's this morning. She would only spoil her things, and you may tell her from me that there would be no play for an hour after this, even if it stopped this minute, which it won't. Meanwhile let her think that Teddy's weatherbound with the rest of them in the pavilion; but she mustn't come until you hear from me again; and the best way to keep her here is to stay with her yourself.'

'And when may I expect to hear?' asked Mr Garland as Raffles held out his hand.

'Let me see. I shall be at Lord's in less than twenty minutes; another five or ten should polish off Studley; and then I shall barricade myself in the telephone box and ring up every hospital in town! You see, it may be an accident after all, though I don't think so. You won't hear from me on the point unless it is; the fewer messengers flying about the better, if you agree with me as to the wisdom of keeping the matter dark at this end.'

'Oh, yes, I agree with you, Raffles; but it will be a terribly hard task for me!'

'It will, indeed, Mr Garland. Yet no news is always good news, and I promise to come straight to you the moment I have news of any kind.'

With that they shook hands, our host with an obvious reluctance that turned to a less understandable dismay as I also prepared to take my leave of him.

'What!' cried he, 'am I to be left quite alone to hoodwink that poor girl and hide my own anxiety?'

'There's no reason why you should come, Bunny,' said Raffles to me. 'If either of them is a one-man job, it's mine.'

Our host said no more, but he looked at me so wistfully that I could not but offer to stay with him if he wished it; and when at length the drawing-room door had closed upon him and his son's fiancée, I took an umbrella from the stand and saw Raffles through the providential downpour into the brougham.

'I'm sorry, Bunny,' he muttered between the butler in the porch and the coachman on the box. 'This sort of thing is neither in my line nor yours, but it serves us right for straying from the path of candid crime. We should have opened a safe for that seven hundred.'

'But what do you really think is at the bottom of this extraordinary disappearance?'

'Some madness or other, I'm afraid; but if that boy is still in the land of the living, I shall have him before the sun goes down on his insanity.'

'And what about this engagement of his?' I pursued. 'Do you disapprove of it?'

'Why on earth should I?' asked Raffles, rather sharply, as he plunged from under my umbrella into the brougham.

'Because you never told me when he told you,' I replied. 'Is the girl beneath him?'

Raffles looked at me inscrutably with his clear blue eyes.

'You'd better find out for yourself,' said he. 'Tell the coachman to hurry up to Lord's – and pray that this rain may last!'

6

CAMILLA BELSIZE

It would be hard to find a better refuge on a rainy day than the amphibious retreat described by Raffles as a 'country house in Kensington.' There was a good square hall, full of the club comforts so welcome in a home, such as magazines and cigarettes, and a fire when the rain set in. The usual rooms opened off the hall, and the library was not the only one that led on into the conservatory; the drawing-room was another, in which I heard voices as I lit a cigarette among the palms and tree-ferns. It struck me that poor Mr Garland was finding it hard work to propitiate the lady whom Raffles had deemed unworthy of mention overnight. But I own I was in no hurry to take over the invidious task. To me it need prove nothing more; to him, anguish; but I could not help feeling that even as matters stood I was quite sufficiently embroiled in these people's affairs. Their name had been little more than a name to me until the last few hours. Only yesterday I might have hesitated to nod to Teddy Garland at the club, so seldom had we met. Yet here was I helping Raffles to keep the worst about the son from the father's knowledge, and on the point of helping that father to keep what might easily prove worse still from his daughter-in-law to be. And all the time there was the worst of all to be hidden from everybody concerning Raffles and me!

Meanwhile I explored a system of flower-houses and vineries that ran out from the conservatory in a continuous chain – each link with its own temperature and its individual scent – and not a pane but rattled and streamed beneath the timely torrent. It was in a fernery where a playing fountain added its tuneful drop to the noisy deluge that the voices of the drawing-room sounded suddenly at my elbow, and I was introduced to Miss Belsize before I could recover from my surprise. My foolish face must have made her smile in spite of herself, for I did not see quite the same smile again all day; but it made me her admirer on the spot, and I really think she warmed to me for amusing her even for a moment.

So we began rather well; and that was a mercy in the light of poor Mr Garland's cynically prompt departure; but we did not go on quite as well as we had begun. I do not say that Miss Belsize was in a bad temper, but emphatically she was not pleased, and I for one had the utmost sympathy with her displeasure. She was simply but exquisitely dressed, with unostentatious touches of Cambridge blue and a picture hat that really was a picture. Yet on a perfect stranger in a humid rockery she was wasting what had been meant for mankind at Lord's. The only consolation I could suggest was that by this time Lord's would be more humid still.

'And so there's something to be said for being bored to tears under shelter, Miss Belsize.' Miss Belsize did not deny that she was bored.

'But there's plenty of shelter there,' said she.

'Packed with draggled dresses and squelching shoes! You might swim for it before they admitted you to that Pavilion, you know.'

'But if the ground's under water, how can they play today?'

'They can't, Miss Belsize, I don't mind betting.'

That was a rash remark.

'Then why doesn't Teddy come back?'

'Oh, well, you know,' I hedged, 'you can never be quite absolutely sure. It might clear up. They're bound to give it a chance until the afternoon. And the players can't leave till stumps are drawn.'

'I should have thought Teddy could have come home to lunch,' said Miss Belsize, 'even if he had to go back afterwards.'

'I shouldn't wonder if he did come,' said I, conceiving the bare possibility: 'and A.J. with him.'

'Do you mean Mr Raffles?'

'Yes, Miss Belsize; he's the only A.J. that counts!'

Camilla Belsize turned slightly in the basket-chair to which she had confided her delicate frock, and our eyes met almost for the first time. Certainly we had not exchanged so long a look before, for she had been watching the torpid goldfish in the rockery pool, and I admiring her bold profile and the querulous poise of a fine head as I tried to argue her out of all desire for Lord's. Suddenly our eyes met, as I say, and hers dazzled me; they were soft and yet brilliant, tender and yet cynical, calmly reckless, audaciously sentimental – all that and more as I see them now on looking back; but at the time I was merely dazzled.

'So you and Mr Raffles are great friends?' said Miss Belsize, harking back to a remark of Mr Garland's in introducing us.

'Rather!' I replied.

'Are you as great a friend of his as Teddy is?'

I liked that, but simply said I was an older friend. 'Raffles and I were at school together,' I added loftily.

'Really? I should have thought he was before your time.'

'No, only senior to me. I happened to be his fag.'

'And what sort of a schoolboy was Mr Raffles?' inquired Miss Belsize, not by any means in the tone of a devotee. But I reflected that her own devotion was bespoke, and not improbably tainted with some little jealousy of Raffles.

'He was the most Admirable Crichton who was ever at the school,' said I: 'captain of the eleven, the fastest man in the fifteen, athletic champion, and an ornament of the Upper Sixth.'

'And you worshipped him, I suppose?'

'Absolutely.'

My companion had been taking renewed interest in the goldfish; now she looked at me again with the cynical light full on in her eyes.

'You must be rather disappointed in him now!'

'Disappointed! Why?' I asked with much outward amusement. But I was beginning to feel uncomfortable.

'Of course I don't know much about him,' remarked Miss Belsize as though she cared less.

'But does anybody know anything of Mr Raffles except as a cricketer?'

'I do,' said I, with injudicious alacrity.

'Well,' said Miss Belsize, 'what else is he?'

'The best fellow in the world, among other things.'

'But what other things?'

'Ask Teddy!' I said unluckily.

'I have,' replied Miss Belsize. 'But Teddy doesn't know. He often wonders how Mr Raffles can afford to play so much cricket without doing any work.'

'Does he, indeed!'

'Many people do.'

'And what do they say about him?'

Miss Belsize hesitated, watching me for a moment and the goldfish rather longer. The rain sounded louder, and the fountain as though it had been turned on again, before she answered:

'More than their prayers, no doubt!'

'Do you mean,' I almost gasped, 'as to the way Raffles gets his living?'

'Yes.'

'You might tell me the kind of things they say, Miss Belsize!'

'But if there's no truth in them?'

'I'll soon tell you if there is or not.'

'But suppose I don't care either way?' said Miss Belsize with a brilliant smile.

'Then I care so much that I should be extremely grateful to you.'

'Mind, I don't believe it myself, Mr Manders.'

'You don't believe – '

'That Mr Raffles lives by his wits and – his cricket!'

I jumped to my feet.

'Is that all they say about him?' I cried.

'Isn't it enough?' asked Miss Belsize, astonished in her turn at my demeanour.

'Oh, quite enough, quite enough!' said I. 'It's only the most scandalously unfair and utterly untrue report that ever got about – that's all!'

This heavy irony was, of course, intended to convey the impression that one's first explosion of relief had been equally ironical. But I was to discover that Camilla Belsize was never easily deceived; it was unpleasantly apparent in her bold eyes before she opened her firm mouth.

'Yet you seemed to expect something worse,' she said at length.

'What could be worse?' I asked, my back against the wall of my own indiscretion. 'Why, a man like A.J. Raffles would rather be any mortal thing than a paid amateur!'

'But you haven't told me what he *is*, Mr Manders.'

'And you haven't told me, Miss Belsize, why you're so interested in A.J. after all!' I retorted, getting home for once, and sitting down again on the strength of it.

But Miss Belsize was my superior to the last; in the single moment of my ascendency she made me blush for it and for myself. She would be quite frank with me: my friend Mr

Raffles did interest her rather more than she cared to say. It was because Teddy thought so much of him, that was the only reason, and her one excuse for all inquisitive questions and censorious remarks. I must have thought her very rude; but now I knew. Mr Raffles had been such a friend to Teddy; sometimes she wondered whether he was quite a good friend; and there I had 'the whole thing in a nutshell.'

I had indeed! And I knew the nut, and had tasted its bitter kernel too often to make any mistake about it. Jealousy was its other name. But I did not care how jealous Miss Belsize became of Raffles as long as jealousy did not beget suspicion; and my mind was not entirely relieved on that point.

We dropped the whole subject, however, with some abruptness; and the rest of our conversation in the rockery, and in the steaming orchid-house and further vineries which we proceeded to explore together, was quite refreshingly tame. Yet I think it was on this desultory tour, to the still incessant accompaniment of rain on the glasshouses, that Camilla's mother took shape in my mind as the Lady Laura Belsize, an apparently impecunious widow reduced to 'semi-detachment down the river' and suburban neighbours whose manners and customs my companion hit off with vivacious intolerance. She told me how she had shocked them by smoking cigarettes in the back garden, and pronounced a gratuitous conviction that I of all people would have been no less scandalised! That was in the uttermost vinery, and in another minute two Sullivans were in full blast under the vines. I remember discovering that the great brand was not unfamiliar to Miss Belsize, and even gathering that it was Raffles himself who had made it known to her. Raffles, whom she did not 'know much about,' or consider 'quite a good friend' for Teddy Garland!

I was becoming curious to see this antagonistic pair together; but it was the middle of the afternoon before Raffles reappeared, though Mr Garland told me he had received an optimistic note from him by special messenger earlier in the day. I felt I might have been told a little more, considering the intimate part I was already playing as a stranger in a strange house. But I was only too thankful to find that Raffles had so far infected our host with his confidence as to tide us through luncheon with far fewer embarrassments than before; nor did Mr Garland desert us again until the butler with a visitor's card brought about his abrupt departure from the conservatory.

Then my troubles began afresh. It stopped raining at last; if Miss Belsize could have had her way we should all have started for Lord's that minute. I took her into the garden to show her the state of the lawns, coldly scintillant with standing water and rimmed by regular canals. Lord's would be like them, only fifty times worse; play had no doubt been abandoned on that quagmire for the day. Miss Belsize was not so sure about that; why should we not drive over and find out? I said that was the surest way of missing Teddy. She said a hansom would take us there and back in a half-an-hour. I gained time disputing that statement, but said if we went at all I was sure Mr Garland would want to go with us, and that in his own brougham. All this on the crown of a sloppy path, and when Miss Belsize asked me how many more times I was going to change my ground, I could not help looking at her absurd shoes sinking into the softened gravel, and saying I thought it was for her to do that. Miss Belsize took my advice to the extent of turning upon a submerged heel, though with none too complimentary a smile; and then it was that I saw what I had been curious to see all day. Raffles was coming down the path towards us. And I saw Miss Belsize hesitate and stiffen before shaking hands with him.

'They've given it up as a bad job at last,' said he. 'I've just come from Lord's, and Teddy won't be very long.'

'Why didn't you bring him with you?' asked Miss Belsize pertinently.

'Well, I thought you ought to know the worst at once,' said Raffles, rather lamely for him; 'and then a man playing in a Varsity match is never quite his own master, you know. Still, he oughtn't to keep you waiting much longer.'

It was perhaps unfortunately put; at any rate Miss Belsize took it pretty plainly amiss, and I saw her colour rise as she declared she had been waiting in the hope of seeing some cricket. Since that was at an end she must be thinking of getting home, and would just say goodbye to Mr Garland. This sudden decision took me as much by surprise as I believe it took Miss Belsize herself; but having announced her intention, however hot-headedly, she proceeded to action by way of the conservatory and the library door, while Raffles and I went through into the hall the other way.

'I'm afraid I've put my foot in it,' said he to me. 'But it's just as well, since I needn't tell you there's no sign of Teddy up at Lord's.'

'Have you been there all day?' I asked him under my breath.

'Except when I went to the office of this rag,' replied Raffles, brandishing an evening paper that ill deserved his epithet. 'See what they say about Teddy here.'

And I held my breath while Raffles showed me a stupendous statement in the stop-press column: it was to the effect that E.M. Garland (Eton and Trinity) might be unable to keep wicket for Cambridge after all, 'owing to the serious illness of his father.'

'His father!' I exclaimed. 'Why, his father's closeted with somebody or other at this very moment behind the door you're looking at!'

'I know, Bunny. I've seen him.'

'But what an extraordinary fabrication to get into a decent paper! I don't wonder you went to the office about it.'

'You'll wonder still less when I tell you I have an old pal on the staff.'

'Of course you made him take it straight out?'

'On the contrary, Bunny, I persuaded him to put it in!'

And Raffles chuckled in my face as I have known him chuckle over many a more felonious – but less incomprehensible – exploit.

'Didn't you see, Bunny, how bad the poor old boy looked in his library this morning? That gave me my idea; the fiction is at least founded on fact. I wonder you don't see the point; as a matter of fact, there are two points, just as there were two jobs I took on this morning; one was to find Teddy, and the other was to save his face at Lord's. Well, I haven't actually found him yet; but if he's in the land of the living he will see this statement, and when he does see it even you may guess what he will do! Meanwhile, there's nothing but sympathy for him at Lord's. Studley couldn't have been nicer; a place will be kept for Teddy up to the eleventh hour tomorrow. And if that isn't killing two birds with one stone, Bunny, may I never perform the feat!'

'But what will old Garland say, A.J.?'

'He has already said, Bunny. I told him what I was doing in a note before lunch, and the moment I arrived just now he came out to hear what I had done. He doesn't mind what I do so long as I find Teddy and save his face before the world at large and Miss Belsize in particular. Look out, Bunny – here she is!'

The excitement in his whisper was not characteristic of Raffles, but it was less remarkable than the change in Camilla Belsize as she entered the hall through the drawing-room as we had done before her. For one moment I suspected her of eavesdropping; then I saw that all traces of personal pique had vanished from her face, and that some anxiety for another had taken its place. She came up to Raffles and me as though she had forgiven both of us our trespasses of two or three minutes ago.

'I didn't go into the library after all,' she said, looking askance at the library door. 'I am afraid Mr Garland is having a trying interview with somebody. I had just a glimpse of the man's face as I hesitated, and I thought I recognised him.'

'Who was it?' I asked, for I myself had wondered who the rather mysterious visitor might be for whom Mr Garland had deserted us so abruptly in the conservatory, and with whom he was still conferring in the hour of so many issues.

'I believe it's a dreadful man I know by sight down the river,' said Miss Belsize; and hardly had she spoke before the library door opened and out came the dreadful man in the portentous person of Dan Levy, the usurer of European notoriety, our victim of the morning and our certain enemy for life.

7

IN WHICH WE FAIL TO SCORE

Mr Levy sailed in with frock-coat flying, shiny hat in hand; he was evidently prepared for us, and Raffles for once behaved as though we were prepared for Mr Levy. Of myself I cannot speak. I was ready for a terrific scene. But Raffles was magnificent, and to do our enemy justice he was quite as good; they faced each other with a nod and a smile of mutual suavity, shot with underlying animosity on the one side and delightful defiance on the other. Not a word was said or a tone employed to betray the true situation between the three of us; for I took my cue from the two protagonists just in time to preserve the triple truce. Meanwhile Mr Garland, obviously distressed as he was, and really ill as he looked, was not the least successful of us in hiding his emotions; for having expressed a grim satisfaction in the coincidence of our all knowing each other, he added that he supposed Miss Belsize was an exception, and presented Mr Levy forthwith as though he were an ordinary guest.

'You must find a better exception than this young lady!' cried that worthy with a certain *aplomb*. 'I know you very well by sight, Miss Belsize, and your mother, Lady Laura, into the bargain.'

'Really?' said Miss Belsize, without returning the compliment at her command.

'The bargain!' muttered Raffles to me with sly irony. The echo was not meant for Levy's ears, but it reached them nevertheless, and was taken up with adroit urbanity.

'I didn't mean to use a trade term,' explained the Jew, 'though bargains, I confess, are somewhat in my line; and I don't often get the worst of one, Mr Raffles; when I do, the other fellow usually lives to repent it.'

It was said with a laugh for the lady's benefit, but with a gleam of the eyes for ours. Raffles answered the laugh with a much heartier one; the look he ignored. I saw Miss Belsize beginning to watch the pair, and only interrupted by the arrival of the tea-tray, over which Mr Garland begged her to preside. Mr Garland seemed to have an anxious eye upon us all in turn; at Raffles he looked wistfully as though burning to get him to himself for further consultation; but the fact that he refrained from doing so, coupled with a grimly punctilious manner towards the money-lender, gave the impression that his son's whereabouts was no longer the sole anxiety.

'And yet,' remarked Miss Belsize, as we formed a group about her in the firelight, 'you seem to have met your match the other day, Mr Levy?'

'Where was that, Miss Belsize?'

'Somewhere on the Continent, wasn't it? It got into the newspapers, I know, but I forget the name of the place.'

'Do you mean when my wife and I were robbed at Carlsbad?'

I was holding my breath now as I had not held it all day. Raffles was merely smiling into his teacup as one who knew all about the affair.

'Carlsbad it was!' certified Miss Belsize, as though it mattered. 'I remember now.'

'I don't call that meeting your match,' said the money-lender. 'An unarmed man with a frightened wife at his elbow is no match for a desperate criminal with a loaded revolver.'

'Was it as bad as all that?' whispered Camilla Belsize.

Up to this point one had felt her to be forcing the unlucky topic with the best of intentions towards us all; now she was interested in the episode for its own sake, and eager for more details than Mr Levy had a mind to impart.

'It makes a good tale, I know,' said he, 'but I shall prefer telling it when they've got the man. If you want to know any more, Miss Belsize, you'd better ask Mr Raffles; 'e was in our hotel, and came in for all the excitement. But it was just a trifle too exciting for me and my wife.'

'Raffles at Carlsbad?' exclaimed Mr Garland.

Miss Belsize only stared.

'Yes,' said Raffles. 'That's where I had the pleasure of meeting Mr Levy.'

'Didn't you know he was there?' inquired the money-lender of our host. And he looked sharply at Raffles as Mr Garland replied that this was the first he had heard of it.

'But it's the first we've seen of each other, sir,' said Raffles, 'except those few minutes this morning. And I told you I only got back last night.'

'But you never told me you had been at Carlsbad, Raffles!'

'It's a sore subject, you see,' said Raffles, with a sigh and a laugh. 'Isn't it, Mr Levy?'

'You seem to find it so,' replied the moneylender.

They were standing face to face in the firelight, each with a shoulder against the massive chimney-piece; and Camilla Belsize was still staring at them both from her place behind the tea-tray; and I was watching the three of them by turns from the other side of the hall.

'But you're the fittest man I know. Raffles,' pursued old Garland with terrible tact. 'What on earth were you doing at a place like Carlsbad?'

'The cure,' said Raffles. 'There's nothing else to do there – is there, Mr Levy?'

Levy replied with his eyes on Raffles:

'Unless you've got to cope with a *swell mobsman* who steals your wife's jewels and then gets in such a funk that he practically gives them back again!'

The emphasised term was the one that Dan Levy had applied to Raffles and myself in his own office that very morning.

'Did he give them back again?' asked Camilla Belsize, breaking her silence on an eager note.

Raffles turned to her at once.

'The jewels were found buried in the woods,' said he. 'Out there everybody thought the thief had simply hidden them. But no doubt Mr Levy has the better information.'

Mr Levy smiled sardonically in the firelight. And it was at this point I followed the example of Miss Belsize and put in my one belated word.

'I shouldn't have thought there was such a thing as a swell mob in the wilds of Austria,' said I.

'There isn't,' admitted the money-lender readily. 'But your true mobsman knows his whole blooming Continent as well as Piccadilly Circus. His 'ead-quarters are in London, but a week's journey at an hour's notice is nothing to him if the swag looks worth it. Mrs Levy's necklace was actually taken at Carlsbad, for instance, but the odds are that it was marked down at some London theatre – or restaurant, eh, Mr Raffles?'

'I'm afraid I can't offer an expert opinion,' said Raffles very merrily as their eyes met. 'But if the man was an Englishman and knew that you were one, why didn't he bully you in the vulgar tongue?'

'Who told you he didn't?' cried Levy, with a sudden grin that left no doubt about the thought behind it. To me that thought had been obvious from its birth within the last few minutes; but this expression of it was as obvious a mistake.

'Who told me anything about it,' retorted Raffles, 'except yourself and Mrs Levy? Your gospels clashed a little here and there; but both agreed that the fellow threatened you in German as well as with a revolver.'

'We thought it was German,' rejoined Levy, with dexterity. 'It might 'ave been 'Industani or 'Eathen Chinee for all I know! But there was no error about the revolver. I can see it covering me, and his shooting eye looking along the barrel into mine – as plainly as I'm looking into yours now, Mr Raffles.'

Raffles laughed outright.

'I hope I'm a pleasanter spectacle, Mr Levy? I remember your telling me that the other fellow looked the most colossal cut-throat.'

'So he did,' said Levy; 'he looked a good deal worse than he need to have done. His face was blackened and disguised, but his teeth were as white as yours are.'

'Any other little point in common?'

'I had a good look at the hand that pointed the revolver.'

Raffles held out his hands.

'Better have a good look at mine.'

'His were as black as his face, but even yours are no smoother or better kept.'

'Well, I hope you'll clap the bracelets on them yet, Mr Levy.'

'You'll get your wish, I promise you, Mr Raffles.'

'You don't mean to say you've spotted your man?' cried A.J. airily.

'I've got my eye on him!' replied Dan Levy, looking Raffles through and through.

'And won't you tell us who he is?' asked Raffles, returning that deadly look with smiling interest, but answering a tone as deadly in one that maintained the note of persiflage in spite of Daniel Levy.

For Levy alone had changed the key with his last words; to that point I declare the whole passage might have gone for banter before the keenest eyes and the sharpest ears in Europe. I alone could know what a duel the two men were fighting behind their smiles. I alone could follow the finer shades, the mutual play of glance and gesture, the subtle tide of covert battle. So now I saw Levy debating with himself as to whether he should accept this impudent challenge and denounce Raffles there and then. I saw him hesitate, saw him reflect. The crafty, coarse, emphatic face was easily read; and when it suddenly lit up with a baleful light, I felt we might be on our guard against something more malign than mere reckless denunciation.

'Yes!' whispered a voice I hardly recognised. 'Won't you tell us who it was?'

'Not yet,' replied Levy, still looking Raffles full in the eyes. 'But I know all about him now!'

I looked at Miss Belsize; she it was who had spoken, her pale face set, her pale lips trembling. I remembered her many questions about Raffles during the morning. And I began to wonder whether after all I was the only entirely understanding witness of what had passed here in the firelit hall.

Mr Garland, at any rate, had no inkling of the truth. Yet even in that kindly face there was a vague indignation and distress, though it passed almost as our eyes met. Into his there had come a sudden light; he sprang up as one alike rejuvenated and transfigured; there was a quick step in the porch, and next instant the truant Teddy was in our midst.

Mr Garland met him with outstretched hand but not a question or a syllable of surprise; it was Teddy who uttered the cry of joy, who stood gazing at his father and raining questions upon him as though they had the hall to themselves. What was all this in the evening papers? Who had put it in? Was there any truth in it at all?

'None, Teddy,' said Mr Garland, with some bitterness; 'my health was never better in my life.'

'Then I can't understand it,' cried the son, with savage simplicity. 'I suppose it's some rotten practical joke; if so, I would give something to lay hands on the joker!'

His father was still the only one of us he seemed to see, or could bring himself to face in his distress. Not that young Garland had the appearance of one who had been through fresh vicissitudes; on the contrary, he looked both trimmer and ruddier than overnight; and in his sudden fit of passionate indignation, twice the man that one remembered so humiliated and abased.

Raffles came forward from the fireside.

'There are some of us,' said he, 'who won't be so hard on the beggar for bringing you back from Lord's at last! You must remember that I'm the only one here who has been up there at all, or seen anything of you all day.'

Their eyes met; and for one moment I thought that Teddy Garland was going to repudiate this cool *suggestiofalsi*, and tell us all where he had really been; but that was now impossible without giving Raffles away, and then there was his Camilla in evident ignorance of the disappearance which he had expected to find common property. The double circumstance was too strong for him; he took her hand with a confused apology which was not even necessary. Anybody could see that the boy had burst among us with eyes for his father only, and thoughts of nothing but the report about his health; as for Miss Belsize, she looked as though she liked him the better for it, or it may have been for an excitability rare in him and rarely becoming. His pink face burnt like a flame. His eyes were brilliant; they met mine at last, and I was warmly greeted; but their friendly light burst into a blaze of wrath as almost simultaneously they fell upon his bugbear in the background.

'So you've kept your threat, Mr Levy!' said young Garland, quietly enough once he had found his voice.

'I generally do,' remarked the money-lender, with a malevolent laugh.

'His threat!' cried Mr Garland sharply. 'What are you talking about, Teddy?'

'I will tell you,' said the young man. 'And you, too!' he added almost harshly, as Camilla Belsize rose as though about to withdraw. 'You may as well know what I am – while there's time. I got into debt – I borrowed from this man.'

'You borrowed from him?'

It was Mr Garland speaking in a voice hard to recognise, with an emphasis harder still to understand; and as he spoke he glared at Levy with new loathing and abhorrence.

'Yes,' said Teddy; 'he had been pestering me with his beastly circulars every week of my first year at Cambridge. He even wrote to me in his own fist. It was as though he knew something about me and meant getting me in his clutches; and he got me all right in the end, and bled me to the last drop as I deserved. I don't complain so far as I'm concerned. It serves me right. But I did mean to get through without coming to you again, father! I was fool enough to tell him so the other day; that was when he threatened to come to you himself. But I didn't think he was such a brute as to come today!'

'Or such a fool?' suggested Raffles, as he put a piece of paper into Teddy's hands.

It was his own original promissory note, the one we had recovered from Dan Levy in the morning. Teddy glanced at it, clutched Raffles by the hand, and went up to the money-lender as though he meant to take him by the throat before us all.

'Does this mean that we're square?' he asked hoarsely.

'It means that you are,' replied Dan Levy.

'In fact it amounts to your receipt for every penny I ever owed you?'

'Every penny that you owed me, certainly.'

'Yet you must come to my father all the same; you must have it both ways – your money and your spite as well!'

'Put it that way if you like,' said Levy, with a shrug of his massive shoulders. 'It isn't the case, but what does that matter so long as you're 'appy?'

'No,' said Teddy through his teeth; 'nothing matters now that I've come back in time.'

'In time for what?'

'To turn you out of the house if you don't clear out this instant!'

The great gross man looked upon his athletic young opponent, and folded his arms with a guttural chuckle.

'So you mean to chuck me out, do you?'

'By all my gods, if you make me, Mr Levy! Here's your hat; there's the door; and never you dare to set foot in this house again.'

The money-lender took his shiny topper, gave it a meditative polish with his sleeve, and actually went as bidden to the threshold of the porch; but I saw the suppression of a grin beneath the pendulous nose, a cunning twinkle in the inscrutable eyes, and it did not astonish me when the fellow turned to deliver a Parthian shot. I was only surprised at the harmless character of the shot.

'May I ask whose house it is?' were his words, in themselves notable chiefly for the aspirates of undue deliberation.

'Not mine, I know; but I'm the son of the house,' returned Teddy truculently, 'and out you go!'

'Are you so sure that it's even your father's house?' inquired Levy with the deadly suavity of which he was capable when he liked. A groan from Mr Garland confirmed the doubt implied in the words.

'The whole place is his,' declared the son, with a sort of nervous scorn – 'freehold and everything.'

'The whole place happens to be *mine* – "freehold and everything!"' replied Levy, spitting his iced poison in separate syllables. 'And as for clearing out, that'll be your job, and I've given you a week to do it in – the two of you!'

He stood a moment in the open doorway, towering in his triumph, glaring on us all in turn, but at Raffles longest and last of all.

'And you needn't think you're going to save the old man,' came with a passionate hiss, 'like you did the son – *because I know all about you now*!'

8

THE STATE OF THE CASE

Of course I made all decent haste from the distressing scene, and of course Raffles stayed behind at the solicitation of his unhappy friends. I was sorry to desert him in view of one aspect of the case; but I was not sorry to dine quietly at the club after the alarms and excitements of that disastrous day. The strain had been the greater after sitting up all night, and I for one could barely realise all that had happened in the twenty-four hours. It seemed incredible that the same midsummer night and day should have seen the return of Raffles and our orgy at the club to which neither of us belonged; the dramatic douche that saluted us at the Albany; the confessions and conferences of the night, the overthrow of the money-lender in the morning; and then the untimely disappearance of Teddy Garland, my day of it at his father's house, and the rain and the ruse that saved the passing situation, only to aggravate the crowning catastrophe of the money-lender's triumph over Raffles and all his friends.

Already a bewildering sequence to look back upon; but it is in the nature of a retrospect to reverse the order of things, and it was the new risk run by Raffles that now loomed largest in my mind, and Levy's last word of warning to him that rang the loudest in my ears. The apparently complete ruin of the Garlands was still a profound mystery to me. But no mere mystery can hold the mind against impending peril; and I was less exercised to account for the downfall of these poor people than in wondering whether it would be followed by that of their friend and mine. Had his Carlsbad crime really found him out? Had Levy only refrained from downright denunciation of Raffles in order to denounce him more effectually to the police? These were the doubts that dogged me at my dinner, and on through the evening until Raffles himself appeared in my corner of the smoking-room, with as brisk a step and as buoyant a countenance as though the whole world and he were one.

'My dear Bunny! I've never given the matter another thought,' said he in answer to my nervous queries, 'and why the deuce should Dan Levy? He has scored us off quite handsomely as it is; he's not such a fool as to put himself in the wrong by stating what he couldn't possibly prove. They wouldn't listen to him at Scotland Yard; it's not their job, in the first place. And even if it were, no one knows better than our Mr Shylock that he hasn't a shred of evidence against me.'

'Still,' said I, 'he happens to have hit upon the truth, and that's half the battle in a criminal charge.'

'Then it's a battle I should love to fight, if the odds weren't all on Number One! What happens, after all? He recovers his property – he's not a pin the worse off – but because he has a row with me about something else he thinks he can identify me with the Teutonic thief! But not in his heart, Bunny; he's not such a fool as that. Dan Levy's no fool at all, but the most magnificent knave I've been up against yet. If you want to hear all about his tactics, come round to the Albany and I'll open your eyes for you.'

His own were radiant with light and life, though he could not have closed them since his arrival at Charing Cross the night before. But midnight was his hour. Raffles was at his best when the stars of the firmament are at theirs; not at Lord's in the light of day, but at dead of night in the historic chambers to which we now repaired. Certainly he had a congenial subject in the celebrated Daniel, 'a villain after my own black heart, Bunny! A foeman worthy of Excalibur itself.'

And how he longed for the fierce joy of further combat for a bigger stake! But the stake was big enough for even Raffles to shake a hopeless head over it. And his face grew grave as he passed from the fascinating prowess of his enemy to the pitiful position of his friends.

'They said I might tell you, Bunny, but the figures must keep until I have them in black and white. I've promised to see if there really isn't a forlorn hope of getting these poor Garlands out of the spider's web. But there isn't, Bunny, I don't mind telling you.'

'What I can't understand,' said I, 'is how father and son seem to have walked into the same parlour – and the father a business man!'

'Just what he never was,' replied Raffles; 'that's at the bottom of the whole thing. He was born into a big business, but he wasn't born a business man. So his partners were jolly glad to buy him out some years ago; and then it was that poor old Garland lashed out into the place where you spent the day, Bunny. It has been his ruin. The price was pretty stiff to start with; you might have a house in most squares and quite a good place in the country for what you've got to pay for a cross between the two. But the mixture was exactly what attracted these good people; for it was not only in Mrs Garland's time, but it seems she was the first to set her heart upon the place. So she was the first to leave it for a better world – poor soul – before the glass was on the last vinery. And the poor old boy was left to pay the shot alone.'

'I wonder he didn't get rid of the whole show,' said I, 'after that.'

'I've no doubt he felt like it, Bunny, but you don't get rid of a place like that in five minutes; it's neither fish nor flesh;

the ordinary house-hunter, with the money to spend, wants to be nearer in or further out. On the other hand there was a good reason for holding on. That part of Kensington is being gradually rebuilt; old Garland had bought the freehold, and sooner or later it was safe to sell at a handsome profit for building sites. That was the one excuse for his dip; it was really a fine investment, or would have been if he had left more margin for upkeep and living expenses. As it was he soon found himself a bit of a beggar on horseback. And instead of selling his horse at a sacrifice, he put him at a fence that's brought down many a better rider.'

'What was that?'

'South Africans!' replied Raffles succinctly. 'Piles were changing hands over them at the time, and poor old Garland began with a lucky dip himself; that finished him off. There's no tiger like an old tiger that never tasted blood before. Our respected brewer became a reckless gambler, lashed at everything, and in due course omitted to cover his losses. They were big enough to ruin him, without being enormous. Thousands were wanted at almost a moment's notice; no time to fix up an honest mortgage; it was a case of pay, fail, or borrow through the nose! And old Garland took ten thousand of the best from Dan Levy – and had another dip!'

'And lost again?'

'And lost again, and borrowed again, this time on the security of his house; and the long and short of it is that he and every stick, brick and branch he is supposed to possess have been in Dan Levy's hands for months and years.'

'On a sort of mortgage?'

'On a perfectly nice and normal mortgage so far as interest went, only with a power to call in the money after six months. But old Garland is being bled to the heart for iniquitous interest on the first ten thousand, and of course he can't meet the call for another fifteen when it comes; but he thinks it's all right because Levy doesn't press for the dibs. Of course it's all wrong from that moment. Levy has the right to take possession whenever he jolly well likes; but it doesn't suit him to have the place empty on his hands, it might depreciate a rising property, and so poor old Garland is deliberately lulled into a false sense of security. And there's no saying how long that state of things might have lasted if we hadn't taken a rise out of old Shylock this morning.'

'Then it's our fault, A.J.?'

'It's mine,' said Raffles remorsefully. 'The idea, I believe, was altogether mine, Bunny; that's why I'd give my bowing hand to take the old ruffian at his word, and save the governor as we did the boy!'

'But how *do* you account for his getting them both into his toils?' I asked. 'What was the point of lending heavily to the son when the father already owed more than he could pay?'

'There are so many points,' said Raffles. 'They love you to owe more than you can pay; it's not their principal that they care about nearly so much as your interest; what they hate is to lose you when once they've got you. In this case Levy would see how frightfully keen poor old Garland was about his boy – to do him properly and, above all, not to let him see what an effort it's become. Levy would find out something about the boy; that he's getting hard up himself, that he's bound to discover the old man's secret, and capable of making trouble and spoiling things when he does. "Better give him the same sort of secret of his own to keep," says Levy, "then they'll both hold their tongues, and I'll have one of 'em under each thumb till all's blue." So he goes for Teddy till he gets him, and finances father and son in watertight compartments until this libel case comes along and does make things look a bit blue for once. Not blue enough, mind you, to compel the sale of a big rising property at a sacrifice; but the sort of thing to make a man squeeze his small creditors all round, while still nursing his top class. So you see how it all fits in. They say the old blackguard is briefing Mr Attorney himself; that along with all the rest to scale, will run him into thousands even if he wins his case.'

'May he lose it!' said I, drinking devoutly, while Raffles lit the inevitable Egyptian. I gathered that this plausible exposition of Mr Levy's tactics had some foundation in the disclosures of his hapless friends; but his ready grasp of an alien subject was highly characteristic of Raffles. I said I supposed Miss Belsize had not remained to hear the whole humiliating story, but Raffles replied briefly that she had. By putting the words into his mouth, I now learnt that she had taken the whole trouble as finely as I should somehow have expected from those fearless eyes of hers; that Teddy had offered to release her on the spot, and that Camilla Belsize had refused to be released; but when I applauded her spirit, Raffles was ostentatiously irresponsive. Nothing, indeed, could have been more marked than the contrast between his reluctance to discuss Miss Belsize and the captious gusto with which she had discussed him. But in each case the inference was that there was no love lost between the pair; and in each case I could not help wondering why.

There was, however, another subject upon which Raffles exercised a much more vexatious reserve. Had I been more sympathetically interested in Teddy Garland, no doubt I should have sought an earlier explanation of his sensational disappearance, instead of leaving it to the last. My interest in the escapade, however, was considerably quickened by the prompt refusal of Raffles to tell me a word about it.

'No, Bunny,' said he, 'I'm not going to give the boy away. His father knows, and I know – and that's enough.'

'Was it your paragraph in the papers that brought him back?'

Raffles paused, cigarette between fingers, in a leonine perambulation of his cage; and his smile was a sufficient affirmative.

'I mustn't talk about it, really, Bunny,' was his actual reply. 'It wouldn't be fair.'

'I don't think it's conspicuously fair on me,' I retorted, 'to set me to cover up your pal's tracks, to give me a lie like that to act all day, and then not to take one into the secret when he does turn up. I call it trading on a fellow's good-nature – not that I care a curse!'

'Then that's all right, Bunny,' said Raffles genially. 'If you cared I should feel bound to apologise to you for the very rotten way you've been treated all round; as it is I give you my word not to take you in with me if I have another dip at Dan Levy.'

'But you're not seriously thinking of it, Raffles?'

'I am if I see half a chance of squaring him short of wilful murder.'

'You mean a chance of settling his account against the Garlands?'

'To say nothing of my own account against Dan Levy! I'm spoiling for another round with that sportsman, Bunny, for its own sake quite apart from these poor pals of mine.'

'And you really think the game would be worth a candle that might fire the secret mine of your life and blow your character to blazes?'

One could not fraternise with Raffles without contracting a certain facility in fluent and florid metaphor; and this parody of his lighter manner drew a smile from my model. But it was the bleak smile of a man thinking of other things, and I thought he nodded rather sadly. He was standing by the open window; he turned and leant out as I had done that interminable twenty-four hours ago; and I longed to know his thoughts, to guess what it was that I knew he had not told me, that I could not divine for myself. There was something behind his mask of gay pugnacity; nay, there was something behind the good Garlands and their culpably commonplace misfortunes. They were the pretext. But could they be the Cause?

The night was as still as the night before. In another moment a flash might have enlightened me. But, in the complete cessation of sound in the room, I suddenly heard one, soft and stealthy but quite distinct, outside the door.

9

A TRIPLE ALLIANCE

It was the intermittent sound of cautious movements, the creak of a sole not repeated for a great many seconds, the all but inaudible passing of a hand over the unseen side of the door leading into the lobby. It may be that I imagined more than I actually heard of the last detail; nevertheless I was as sure of what was happening as though the door had been plate-glass. Yet there was the outer door between lobby and landing and that I distinctly remembered Raffles shutting behind him when we entered. Unable to attract his attention now, and never sorry to be the one to take the other by surprise, I listened without breathing until assurance was doubly sure, then bounded out of my chair without a word. And there was a resounding knock at the inner door, even as I flung it open upon a special evening edition of Mr Daniel Levy, a resplendent figure with a great stud blazing in a frilled shirt, white waistcoat and gloves, opera-hat and cigar, and all the other insignia of a nocturnal vulgarian about town.

'May I come in?' said he with unctuous affability.

'May you!' I took it upon myself to shout. 'I like that, seeing that you came in long ago! I heard you all right – you were listening at the door – probably looking through the keyhole – and you only knocked when I jumped up to open it!'

'My dear Bunny!' exclaimed Raffles, a reproving hand upon my shoulder. And he bade the unbidden guest a jovial welcome.

'But the outer door was shut,' I expostulated. 'He must have forced it or else picked the lock.'

'Why not, Bunny? Love isn't the only thing that laughs at locksmiths,' remarked Raffles with exasperating geniality.

'Neither are swell mobsmen!' cried Dan Levy, not more ironically than Raffles, only with a heavier type of irony.

Raffles conducted him to a chair. Levy stepped behind it and grasped the back as though prepared to break the furniture on our heads if necessary. Raffles offered him a drink; it was declined with a crafty grin that made no secret of a base suspicion.

'I don't drink with the swell mob,' said the money-lender.

'My dear Mr Levy,' returned Raffles, 'you're the very man I wanted to see, and nobody could possibly be more welcome in my humble quarters; but that's the fourth time today I've heard you make use of an obsolete expression. You know as well as I do that the slap-bang-here-we-are-again type of work is a thing of the past. Where are the jolly dogs of the old song now?'

'"Ere at the Albany!' said Levy. 'Here in your rooms, Mr A.J. Raffles.'

'Well, Bunny,' said Raffles, 'I suppose we must both plead guilty to a hair of the jolly dog that bit him – eh?'

'You know what I mean,' our visitor ground out through his teeth. 'You're cracksmen, magsmen, mobsmen, the two of you; so you may as well both own up to it.'

'Cracksmen? Magsmen? Mobsmen?' repeated Raffles, with his head on one side. 'What does the kind gentleman mean, Bunny? Wait! I have it – thieves! Common thieves!'

And he laughed loud and long in the moneylender's face and mine.

'You may laugh,' said Levy. 'I'm too old a bird for your chaff; the only wonder is I didn't spot you right off when we were abroad.' He grinned malevolently. 'Shall I tell you when I did tumble to it – Mr Ananias J. Raffles?'

'Daniel in the liars" den,' murmured Raffles, wiping the tears from his eyes. 'Oh, yes, do tell us anything you like; this is the best entertainment we've had for a long time, isn't it, Bunny?'

'Chalks!' said I.

'I thought of it this morning,' proceeded the money-lender, with a grim contempt for all our raillery, 'when you played your pretty trick upon me, so glib and smooth, and up to every move, the pair of you! One borrowing the money, and the other paying me back in my very own actual coin!'

'Well,' said I, 'there was no crime in that.'

'Oh, yes, there was,' replied Levy, with a wide wise grin; 'there was the one crime you two ought to know better than ever to commit, if you call yourselves what I called you just now. The crime that you committed was the crime of being found out; but for that I should never have suspected friend Ananias of that other job at Carlsbad; no, not even when I saw his friends so surprised to hear that he'd been out there – a strapping young chap like 'im! Yes,' cried the money-lender, lifting the chair and jobbing it down on the floor; 'this morning was when I thought of it, but this afternoon was when I jolly well knew.'

Raffles was no longer smiling; his eyes were like points of steel, his lips like a steel trap.

'I saw what you thought,' said he, disdainfully. 'And you still seriously think I took your wife's necklace and hid it in the woods?'

'I know you did.'

'Then what the devil are you doing here alone?' cried Raffles. 'Why didn't you bring along a couple of good men and true from Scotland Yard? Here I am, Mr Levy, entirely at your service. Why don't you give me in charge?'

Levy chuckled consumedly – ventriloquously – behind his three gold buttons and his one diamond stud.

'P'r'aps I'm not such a bad sort as you think,' said he. 'An" p'r'aps you two gentlemen are not such bad sorts as *I* thought.'

'Gentlemen once more, eh?' said Raffles. 'Isn't that rather a quick recovery for swell magsmen, or whatever we were a minute ago?'

'P'r'aps I never really thought you quite so bad as all that, Mr Raffles.'

'Perhaps you never really thought I took the necklace, Mr Levy?'

'I know you took it,' returned Levy, his new tone of crafty conciliation softening to a semblance of downright apology. 'But I believe you did put it back where you knew it'd be found. And I begin to think you only took it for a bit o' fun!'

'If he took it at all,' said I. 'Which is absurd.'

'I only wish I had!' exclaimed Raffles, with gratuitous audacity. 'I agree with you, Mr Levy, it would have been more like a bit of fun than anything that came my way on the human rubbish-heap we were both inhabiting for our sins.'

'The kind of fun that appeals to you?' suggested Levy, with a very shrewd glance.

'It would,' said Raffles, 'I feel sure.'

"'Ow would you care for another bit o' fun like it, Mr Raffles?'

'Don't say "another," please.'

'Well, would you like to try your 'and at the game again?'

'Not "again," Mr Levy; and my "prentice" hand, if you don't mind.'

'I beg pardon; my mistake,' said Levy, with becoming gravity.

'How would I like to try my prentice hand on picking and stealing for the pure fun of the thing? Is that it, Mr Levy?'

Raffles was magnificent now; but so was the other in his own way. And once more I could but admire the tact with which Levy had discarded his favourite cudgels, and the surprising play that he was making with the buttoned foil.

'It'd be more picking than stealing,' said he. 'Tricky picking too, Raffles, but innocent enough even for an amatoor.'

'I thank you, Mr Levy. So you have a definite case in mind?'

'I have – a case of recovering a man's own property.'

'You being the man, Mr Levy?'

'I being the man, Mr Raffles.'

'Bunny, I begin to see why he didn't bring the police with him!'

I affected to have seen it for some time; thereupon our friend the enemy protested that in no circumstances could he have taken such a course. By the searchlight of the present he might have detected things which had entirely escaped his notice in the past – incriminating things – things that would put together into a Case. But, after all, what evidence had he against Raffles as yet? Mr Levy himself propounded the question with unflinching candour. He might inform the Metropolitan Police of his strong suspicions; and they might communicate with the Austrian police, and evidence beyond the belated evidence of his own senses be duly forthcoming; but nothing could be done at once, and if Raffles cared to endorse his theory of the practical joke, by owning up to that and nothing more, then, so far as Mr Levy was concerned, nothing should ever be done at all.

'Except this little innocent recovery of your own property,' suggested Raffles. 'I suppose that's the condition?'

'Condition's not the word I should have employed,' said Levy, with a shrug.

'Preliminary, then?'

'Indemnity is more the idea. You put me to a lot of trouble by abstracting Mrs Levy's jewels for your own amusement – '

'So you assert, Mr Levy.'

'Well, I may be wrong; that remains to be seen – or not – as you decide,' rejoined the Jew, lifting his mask for the moment. 'At all events you admit that it's the sort of adventure you would like to try. And so I ask you to amuse yourself by abstracting something else of mine that 'appens to have got into the wrong hands; then, I say, we shall be quits.'

'Well,' said Raffles, 'there's no harm in our hearing what sort of property it is, and where you think it's to be found.'

The usurer leant forward in his chair; he had long been sitting in the one which at first he had seemed inclined to wield as a defensive weapon. We all drew together into a smaller triangle. And I found our visitor looking specially hard at me for the first time.

'I've seen you, too, before today,' said he. 'I thought I had, after you'd gone this morning, and when we met in the afternoon I made sure. It was at the Savoy when me and my wife were dining there and you gentlemen were at the next table.' There was a crafty twinkle in his eye, but the natural allusion to the necklace was not made. 'I suppose,' he continued, 'you are partners in – amusement? Otherwise I should insist on speaking to Mr Raffles alone.'

'Bunny and I are one,' said Raffles airily.

'Though two to one – numerically speaking,' remarked Levy, with a disparaging eye on me. 'However, if you're both in the job, so much the more chance of bringing it off, I daresay. But you'll never 'ave to 'andle a lighter swag, gentlemen!'

'More jewellery?' inquired Raffles, as one thoroughly enjoying the joke.

'No – lighter than that – a letter!'

'One little letter?'

'That's all.'

'Of your own writing, Mr Levy?'

'No, sir!' thundered the money-lender, just when I could have sworn his lips were framing an affirmative.

'I see; it was written to you, not by you.'

'Wrong again, Raffles!'

'Then how can the letter be your property, my dear Mr Levy?'

There was a pause. The money-lender was at visible grips with some new difficulty. I watched his heavy but not unhandsome face, and timed the moment of mastery by the sudden light in his crafty eyes.

'They think it was written by me,' said he. 'It's a forgery, written on my office paper; if that isn't my property, I should like to know what is?'

'It certainly ought to be,' returned Raffles, sympathetically. 'Of course you're speaking of the crucial letter in your case against *Fact*?'

'I am,' said Levy, rather startled; 'but 'ow did you know I was?'

'I am naturally interested in the case.'

'And you've read about it in the papers; they've had a fat sight too much to say about it, with the whole case still *sub judice*.'

'I read the original articles in *Fact*,' said Raffles.

'And the letters I'm supposed to have written?'

'Yes; there was only one of them that struck me as being slap in the wind's eye.'

'That's the one I want.'

'If it's genuine, Mr Levy, it might easily form the basis of a more serious sort of case.'

'But it isn't genuine.'

'Nor would you be the first plaintiff in the High Court of Justice,' pursued Raffles, blowing soft grey rings into the upper air, 'who has been rather rudely transformed into the defendant at the Old Bailey.'

'But it isn't genuine, I'm telling you!' cried Dan Levy with a curse.

'Then what in the world do you want with the letter? Let the prosecution love and cherish it, and trump it up in court for all it's worth; the less it is worth, the more certain to explode and blow their case to bits. A palpable forgery in the hands of Mr Attorney!' cried Raffles, with a wink at me. 'It'll be the best fun of its kind since the late lamented Mr Pigott; my dear Bunny, we must both be there.'

Mr Levy's uneasiness was a sight for timid eyes. He had presented his case to us naked and unashamed; already he was in our hands more surely than Raffles was in his. But Raffles was the last person to betray his sense of an advantage a second too soon: he merely gave me another wink. The usurer was frowning at the carpet. Suddenly he sprang up and burst out in a bitter tirade upon the popular and even the judicial prejudice against his own beneficent calling. No money-lender would ever get justice in a British court of law; easier for the camel to thread the needle's eye. That flagrant forgery would be accepted at sight by our vaunted British jury. The only chance was to abstract it before the case came on.

'But if it can be proved to be a forgery,' urged Raffles, 'nothing could possibly turn the tables on the other side with such complete and instantaneous effect.'

'I've told you what I reckon my only chance,' said Levy fiercely. 'Let me remind you that it's yours as well!'

'If you talk like that,' said Raffles, 'I shan't consider it.'

'You won't in any case, I should hope,' said I.

'Oh, yes, I might; but not if he talks like that.'

Levy stopped talking quite like that.

'Will you do it, Mr Raffles, or will you not?'

'Abstract the – forgery?'

'Yes.'

'Where from?'

'Wherever it may be; their solicitors'' safe, I suppose.'

'Who are the solicitors to *Fact*?'

'Burroughs and Burroughs.'

'Of Gray's Inn Square?'

'That's right.'

'The strongest firm in England for a criminal case,' said Raffles, with a grimace at me. 'Their strong-room is probably the strongest strong-room!'

'I said it was a tricky job,' rejoined the moneylender.

Raffles looked more than dubious.

'Big game for a first shoot, eh, Bunny?'

'Too big by half.'

'And you merely wish to have their letter – withdrawn, Mr Levy?'

'That's the way to put it.'

And the diamond stud sparkled again as it heaved upon the billows of an intestine chuckle.

'Withdrawn – and nothing more?'

'That'll be good enough for me, Mr Raffles.'

'Even though they miss it the very next morning?'

'Let them miss it.'

Raffles joined his finger-tips judicially, and shook his head in serene dissent.

'It would do you more harm than good, Mr Levy. I should be inclined to go one better – if I went into the thing at all,' he added, with so much point that I was thankful to think he was beginning to decide against it.

'What improvement do you suggest?' inquired Dan Levy, who had evidently no such premonition.

'I should take a sheet of your paper with me, and forge the forgery!' said Raffles, a light in his eye and a gusto in his voice that I knew only too well. 'But I shouldn't do my work as perfectly as – the other cove – did his. My effort would look the same as yours – *his* – until Mr Attorney fixed it with his eyeglass in open court. And then the bottom would be out of the defence in five minutes!'

Dan Levy came straight over to Raffles – quivering like a jelly – beaming at every pore.

'Shake!' he cried. 'I always knew you were a man after my own heart, but I didn't know you were a man of genius until this minute.'

'It's no use my shaking,' replied Raffles, the tips of his sensitive fingers still together, 'until I make up my mind to take on the job. And I'm a very long way from doing that yet, Mr Levy.'

I breathed again.

'But you must, my dear friend, you simply must!' said Levy, in a new tone of pure persuasion. I was sorry he forgot to threaten instead. Perhaps it was not forgetfulness; perhaps he was beginning to know his Raffles as I knew mine; if so, I was sorrier still.

'It's a case of *quid pro quo*,' said Raffles calmly. 'You can't expect me to break out into downright crime – however technical the actual offence – unless you make it worth my while.'

Levy became the man I wanted him to be again. 'I fancy it's worth your while not to hear anything more about Carlsbad,' said he, though still with less of the old manner than I could have wished.

'What!' cried Raffles, 'when you own yourself that you've no evidence against me there?'

'Evidence is to be got that may mean five years to you; don't you make any mistake about that.'

'Whereas the evidence of this particular letter against yourself has, on your own showing, already been obtained! It's as you like, of course,' added Raffles, getting up with a shrug. 'But if the Old Bailey sees us both, Mr Levy, I'll back my chance against yours – and your sentence against mine!'

Raffles helped himself to a drink, after a quizzical look at his guest, decanter in hand; the usurer snatched it from him and splashed out half a tumbler. Certainly he was beginning to know his Raffles perilously well.

'There, damn you!' said he, blinking into an empty glass. 'I trust you further than I'd trust any other young blood of your kidney; name your price, and you shall earn it if you can.'

'You may think it a rather long one, Mr Levy.'

'Never mind; you say what you want.'

'Leave that money of yours on the mortgage with Mr Garland; forgive him his other debt as you hope to be forgiven; and either that letter shall be in your hands, or I'll be in the hands of the police, before a week is up!'

Spoken from man to man with equal austerity and resolution, yet in a voice persuasive and conciliatory rather than arbitrary or dictatorial, the mere form and manner of this quixotic undertaking thrilled all my fibres in defiance of its sense. It was like the blare of bugles in a dubious cause; one's blood responded before one's brain; and but for Raffles, little as his friends were to me, and much as I repudiated his sacrifices on their behalf, that very minute I might have led the first assault on their oppressor. In a sudden fury the savage had hurled his empty tumbler into the fireplace, and followed the crash with such a volley of abuse as I have seldom heard from human brute.

'I'm surprised at you, Mr Levy,' said Raffles, contemptuously; 'if we copied your tactics we should throw you through that open window!'

And I stood by for my share in the deed.

'Yes! I know it'd pay you to break my neck,' retorted Levy. 'You'd rather swing than do time, wouldn't you?'

'And you prefer the other alternative,' said Raffles, 'to loosing your grip upon a man who's done you no harm whatever! In interest alone he's almost repaid all you lent him in the first instance; you've first-class security for the rest; yet you must ruin him to revenge yourself upon us. On us, mark you! It's against us you've got your grievance, not against old Garland or his son. You've lost sight of that fact. That little trick this morning was our doing entirely. Why don't you take it out of us? Why refuse a fair offer to spite people who have done you no harm?'

'It's not a fair offer,' growled Levy. 'I made you the fair offer.'

But his rage had moderated; he was beginning to listen to Raffles and to reason, with however ill a grace. It was the very moment which Raffles was the very man to improve.

'Mr Levy,' said he, 'do you suppose I care whether you hold your tongue or not on a matter of mere suspicion, which you can't support by a grain of evidence? You lose a piece of jewellery abroad; you recover it intact; and after many days you get the bright idea that I'm the culprit because I happen to have been staying in your hotel at the time. It never occurred to you there or then, though you interviewed the gentleman face to face, as you were constantly interviewing me. But as soon as I borrow some money from you, here in London in the ordinary way, you say I must be the man who borrowed Mrs Levy's necklace in that extraordinary way at Carlsbad! I should say it to the marines, Mr Levy, if I were you; they're the only force that are likely to listen to you.'

'I do say it, all the same; and what's more you don't deny it. If you weren't the man you wouldn't be so ready for another game like it now.'

'Ready for it?' cried Raffles, more than ready for an undeniable point. 'I'm always your man for a new sensation, Mr Levy, and for years I've taken an academic interest in the very fine art of burglary; isn't that so, Bunny?'

'I've often heard you say so,' I replied without mishap.

'In these piping times,' continued Raffles, 'it's about the one exciting and romantic career open to us. If it were not so infernally dishonest I should have half a mind to follow it myself. And here you come and put up a crib for me to crack in the best interests of equity and justice; not to enrich the wicked cracksman, but to restore his rightful property to the honest financier; a sort of teetotal felony – the very ginger-ale of crime! Is that a beverage to refuse – a chance to miss – a temptation to resist? Yet the risks are just as great as if it were a fine old fruity felony; you can't expect me to run them for nothing, or even for their own exciting sake. You know my terms, Mr Levy; if you don't accept them, it's already two in the morning, and I should like to get to bed before it's light.'

'And if I did accept them?' said Levy, after a considerable pause.

'The letter to which you attach such importance would most probably be in your possession by the beginning of next week.'

'And I should have to take my hands off a nice little property that has tumbled into them?'

'Only for a time,' said Raffles. 'On the other hand, you would be permanently out of danger of figuring in the dock on a charge of blackmail. And you know your profession isn't popular in the courts, Mr Levy; it's in nearly as bad odour as the crime of blackmail!'

A singular docility had descended like a mantle upon Daniel Levy: no uncommon reaction in the case of very passionate men, and yet in this case ominous, sinister, and completely unconvincing so far as I personally was concerned. I longed to tell Raffles what I thought, to put him on his guard against his obvious superior in low cunning. But Raffles would not even catch my eye. And already he looked insanely pleased with himself and his apparent advantage.

'Will you give me until tomorrow morning?' said Levy, taking up his hat.

'If you mean the morning; by eleven I must be at Lord's.'

'Say ten o'clock in Jermyn Street?'

'It's a strange bargain, Mr Levy. I should prefer to clinch it out of earshot of your clerks.'

'Then I will come here.'

'I shall be ready for you at ten.'

'And alone?'

There was a sidelong glance at me with the proviso.

'You shall search the premises yourself and seal up all the doors.'

'Meanwhile,' said Levy, putting on his hat, 'I shall think about it, but that's all. I haven't agreed yet, Mr Raffles; don't you make too sure that I ever shall. I shall think about it – but don't you make too sure.'

He was gone like a lamb, this wild beast of five minutes back. Raffles showed him out, and down into the courtyard, and out again into Piccadilly. There was no question but that he was gone for good; back came Raffles, rubbing his hands for joy.

'A fine night, Bunny! A finer day to follow! But a nice, slow, wicket-keeper's wicket if ever Teddy had one in his life!'

I came to my point with all vehemence.

'Confound Teddy!' I cried from my heart. 'I should have thought you had run risks enough for his sake as it was!'

'How do you know it's for his sake – or anybody's?' asked Raffles, quite hotly. 'Do you suppose I want to be beaten by a brute like Levy, Garlands or no Garlands? Besides, there's far less risk in what I mean to do than in what I've been doing; at all events it's in my line.'

'It's not in your line,' I retorted, 'to strike a bargain with a swine who won't dream of keeping his side.'

'I shall make him,' said Raffles. 'If he won't do what I want he shan't have what he wants.'

'But how could you trust him to keep his word?'

'His word!' cried Raffles, in ironical echo. 'We shall have to carry matters far beyond his word, of course; deeds, not words, Bunny, and the deeds properly prepared by solicitors and executed by Dan Levy before he lays a finger on his own blackmailing letter. You remember old Mother Hubbard in our house at school? He's a little solicitor somewhere in the

City; he'll throw the whole thing into legal shape for us, and ask no questions and tell no tales. You leave Mr Shylock to me and Mother, and we'll bring him up to the scratch as he ought to go.'

There was no arguing with Raffles in such a mood; argue I did, but he paid no attention to what I said. He had unlocked a drawer in the bureau, and taken out a map that I had never seen before. I looked over his shoulder as he spread it out in the light of his reading-lamp. And it was a map of London capriciously sprinkled with wheels and asterisks of red ink; there was a finished wheel in Bond Street, another in Half-Moon Street, one on the site of Thornaby House, Park Lane, and others as remote as St. John's Wood and Peter Street, Campden Hill; the asterisks were fewer, and I have less reason to remember their latitude and longitude.

'What's this, A.J.?' I asked. 'It looks exactly like a war-map.'

'It is one, Bunny,' said he; 'it's the map of one man's war against the ordered forces of society. The spokes are only the scenes of future operations, but each finished wheel marks the field of some past engagement, in which you have usually been the one man's one and only accomplice.'

And he stooped and drew the neatest of blood-red asterisks at the southern extremity of Gray's Inn Square.

10

'MY RAFFLES RIGHT OR WRONG'

The historic sward had just been cleared for action when Raffles and I met at Lord's next day. I blush to own I had been knave and fool enough to suggest that he should smuggle me into the pavilion; but perhaps the only laws of man that Raffles really respected were those of the M.C.C., and it was in Block B. that he joined me a minute or so before eleven. The sun was as strong and the sky as blue as though the disastrous day before had been just such another. But its tropical shower-bath had left the London air as cleanly and as clear as crystal; the neutral tints of every day were splashes of vivid colour, the waiting umpires animated snow-men, the heap of sawdust at either end a pyramid of powdered gold upon an emerald ground. And in the expectant hush before the appearance of the fielding side, I still recall the Yorkshire accent of the Surrey Poet, hawking his latest lyric on some 'Great Stand by Mr Webbe and Mr Stoddart,' and incidentally assuring the crowd that Cambridge was going to win because everybody said Oxford would.

'Just in time,' said Raffles, as he sat down and the Cambridge men emerged from the pavilion, capped and sashed in varying shades of light blue. The captain's colours were bleached by service; but the wicket-keeper's were the newest and the bluest of the lot, and as a male historian I shrink from saying how well they suited him.

'Teddy Garland looks as though nothing had happened,' was what I said at the time, as I peered through my binocular at the padded figure with the pink face and the gigantic gloves.

'That's because he knows there's a chance of nothing more happening,' was the reply. 'I've seen him and his poor old governor up here since I saw Dan Levy.'

I eagerly inquired as to the upshot of the earlier interview, but Raffles looked as though he had not heard. The Oxford captain had come out to open the innings with a player less known to fame; the first ball of the match hurtled down the pitch, and the Oxford captain left it severely alone. Teddy took it charmingly, and almost with the same movement the ball was back in the bowler's hands.

'*He's* all right!' muttered Raffles with a long breath. 'So is our Mr Shylock, Bunny; we fixed things up in no time after all. But the worst of it is I shall only be able to stop – '

He broke off, mouth open as it might have been mine. A ball had been driven hard to extra cover, and quite well fielded; another had been taken by Teddy as competently as the first, but not returned to the bowler. The Oxford captain had played at it, and we heard something even in Block B.

'How's that?' came almost simultaneously in Teddy's ringing voice. Up went the umpire's finger, and down came Raffles's hand upon my thigh.

'He's caught him, Bunny!' he cried in my ear above the Cambridge cheers. 'The best bat on either side, and Teddy's outed him third ball!' He stopped to watch the defeated captain's slow return, the demonstration on the pitch in Teddy's honour; then he touched me on the arm and dropped his voice. 'He's forgotten all his troubles now, Bunny, if you like; nothing's going to worry him till lunch, unless he misses a sitting chance. And he won't, you'll see; a good start means even more behind the sticks than in front of 'em.'

Raffles was quite right. Another wicket fell cheaply in another way; then came a long spell of plucky cricket, a stand not masterly but dogged and judicious, in which many a ball outside the off-stump was allowed to pass unmolested, and a few were unfortunate in just beating the edge of the bat. On the tricky wicket Teddy's work was cut out for him, and beautifully he did it. It was a treat to see his lithe form crouching behind the bails, to rise next instant with the rising ball; his great gloves were always in the right place, always adhesive. Once only he held them up prematurely, and a fine ball brushed the wicket on its way for four byes; it was his sole error all the morning. Raffles sat enchanted; so in truth did I; but between the overs I endeavoured to obtain particulars of his latest parley with Dan Levy, and once or twice extracted a stray detail.

'The old sinner has a place on the river, Bunny, though I have my suspicions of a second establishment nearer town. But I'm to find him at his lawful home all the next few nights, and sitting up for me till two in the morning.'

'Then you're going to Gray's Inn Square this week?'

'I'm going there this morning for a peep at the crib; there's no time to be lost, but on the other hand there's a devil of a lot to learn. I say, Bunny, there's going to be another change of bowling; the fast stuff, too, by Jove!'

A massive youth had taken the ball at the top end, and the wicket-keeper was retiring to a more respectful distance behind the stumps.

'You'll let me know when it's to be?' I whispered, but Raffles only answered, 'I wonder Jack Studley didn't wait till there was more of a crust on the mud pie. That tripe's no use without a fast wicket!'

The technical slang of the modern cricket-field is ever a weariness; at the moment it was something worse, and I resigned myself to the silent contemplation of as wild an over as ever was bowled at Lord's. A shocking thing to the off was sent skipping past point for four. 'Tripe!' muttered Raffles to himself. A very good one went over the bails and thud into Garland's gloves like a round-shot. 'Well bowled!' said Raffles with less reserve. Another delivery was merely ignored, both at the wicket and at my side, and then came a high full-pitch to leg which the batsman hit hard but very late. It was a hit that might have smashed the pavilion palings. But it never reached them; it stuck in Teddy's left glove instead, and none of us knew it till we saw him staggering towards long-leg, and tossing up the ball as he recovered balance.

'That's the worst ball that ever took a wicket in this match!' vowed a reverend veteran as the din died down.

'And the best catch!' cried Raffles. 'Come on, Bunny; that's my *nunc dimittis* for the day. There would be nothing to compare with it if I could stop to see every ball bowled, and I mustn't see another.'

'But why?' I asked, as I followed Raffles into the press behind the carriages.

'I've already told you why,' said he.

I got as close to him as one could in that crowd.

'You're not thinking of doing it tonight, A.J.?'

'I don't know.'

'But you'll let *me* know?'

'Not if I can help it, Bunny; didn't I promise not to drag you any further through this particular mire?'

'But if *I* can help *you*?' I whispered, after a momentary separation in the throng.

'Oh! if I can't get on without you,' said Raffles, not nicely, 'I'll let you know fast enough. But do drop the subject now; here come old Garland and Camilla Belsize!'

They did not see us quite so soon as we saw them, and for a moment one felt a spy; but it was an interesting moment even to a person smarting from a snub. The ruined man looked haggard, ill, unfit to be about, the very embodiment of the newspaper report concerning him. But the spirit beamed through the shrinking flesh, the poor old fellow was alight with pride and love, exultant in spite of himself and his misfortunes. He had seen his boy's great catch; he had heard the cheers, he would hear them till his dying hour. Camilla Belsize had also seen and heard, but not with the same exquisite appreciation. Cricket was a game to her, it was not that quintessence and epitome of life it would seem to be to some of its devotees; and real life was pressing so heavily upon her that the trivial consolation which had banished her companion's load could not lighten hers. So at least I thought as they approached, the man so worn and radiant, the girl so pensive for all her glorious youth and beauty: his was the old head bowed with sorrow, his also the simpler and the younger heart.

'That catch will console me for a lot,' I heard him say quite heartily to Raffles. But Camilla's comment was altogether perfunctory; indeed, I wondered that so sophisticated a person did not affect some little enthusiasm. She seemed more interested, however, in the crowd than in the cricket. And that was usual enough.

Raffles was already saying he must go, with an explanatory murmur to Mr Garland, who clasped his hand with a suddenly clouded countenance. But Miss Belsize only bowed, and scarcely took her eyes off a couple of outwardly inferior men, who had attracted my attention through hers, until they also passed out of the ground.

Mr Garland was on tip-toes watching the game again with mercurial ardour.

'Mr Manders will look after me,' she said to him, 'won't you, Mr Manders?' I made some suitable asseveration, and she added: 'MrGarland's a member, you know, and dying to go into the Pavilion.'

'Only just to hear what they think of Teddy,' the poor old boy confessed; and when we had arranged where to meet in the interval, away he hurried with his keen, worn face.

Miss Belsize turned to me the moment he was gone.

'I want to speak to you, Mr Manders,' she said quickly but without embarrassment. 'Where can we talk?'

'And watch as well?' I suggested, thinking of the young man at his best behind the sticks.

'I want to speak to you first,' she said, 'where we shan't be overheard. It's about Mr Raffles!' added Miss Belsize as she met my stare.

About Raffles again! About Raffles, after all that she had learnt the day before! I did not enjoy the prospect as I led the way past the ivy-mantled tennis-court of those days to the practice-ground, turned for the nonce into a tented lawn.

'And what about Raffles?' I asked as we struck out for ourselves across the grass.

'I'm afraid he's in some danger,' replied Miss Belsize. And she stopped in her walk and confronted me as frankly as though we had the animated scene to ourselves.

'Danger!' I repeated, guiltily enough, no doubt. 'What makes you think that, Miss Belsize?'

My companion hesitated for the first time.

'You won't tell him I told you, Mr Manders?'

'Not if you don't want me to,' said I, taken aback more by her manner than by the request itself.

'You promise me that?'

'Certainly.'

'Then tell me, did you notice two men who passed close to us just after we had all met?'

'There are so many men to notice,' said I to gain time.

'But these were not the sort one expects to see here today.'

'Did they wear bowlers and short coats?'

'You did notice them!'

'Only because I saw you watching them,' said I, recalling the whole scene.

'They wanted watching,' rejoined Miss Belsize dryly. 'They followed Mr Raffles out of the ground!'

'So they did!' I reflected aloud in my alarm.

'They were following you both when you met us.'

'The dickens they were! Was that the first you saw of them?'

'No; the first time was over there at the nets before play began. I noticed those two men behind Teddy's net. They were not watching him; that called my attention to them. It's my belief they were lying in wait for Mr Raffles; at any rate, when he came they moved away. But they followed us afterwards across the ground.'

'You are sure of that?'

'I looked round to see,' said Miss Belsize, avoiding my eyes for the first time.

'Did you think the men – detectives?'

And I forced a laugh.

'I was afraid they might be, Mr Manders, though I have never seen one off the stage.'

'Still,' I pursued, with painfully sustained amusement, 'you were ready to find A.J. Raffles being shadowed here at Lord's of all places in the world?'

'I was ready for anything, anywhere,' said Miss Belsize, 'after all I heard yesterday afternoon.'

'You mean about poor Mr Garland and his affairs?'

It was an ingenuously disingenuous suggestion; it brought my companion's eyes back to mine, with something of the scorn that I deserved.

'No, Mr Manders, I meant after what we all heard between Mr Levy and Mr Raffles; and you knew very well what I meant,' added Miss Belsize severely.

'But surely you didn't take all that seriously?' said I, without denying the just impeachment.

'How could I help it? The insinuation was serious enough, in all conscience!' exclaimed Camilla Belsize.

'That is,' said I, since she was not to be wilfully misunderstood, 'that poor old Raffles had something to do with this jewel robbery at Carlsbad?'

'If it was a robbery.'

She winced at the word.

'Do you mean it might have been a trick?' said I, recalling the victim's own make-believe at the Albany. And not only did Camilla appear to embrace that theory with open arms; she had the nerve to pretend that it really was what she had meant.

'Obviously!' says she, with an impromptu superiority worthy of Raffles himself. 'I wonder you never thought of that, Mr Manders, when you know what a trick you both played Mr Levy only yesterday. Mr Raffles himself told us all about that; and I'm very grateful to you both; you must know I am – for Teddy's sake,' added Miss Belsize, with one quick remorseful glance towards the great arena. 'Still it only shows what Mr Raffles is – and – and it's what I meant when we were talking about him yesterday.'

'I don't remember,' said I, remembering fast enough.

'In the rockery,' she reminded me. 'When you asked what people said about him, and I said that about living on his wits.'

'And being a paid amateur!'

'But the other was the worst.'

'I'm not so sure,' said I. 'But his wits wouldn't carry him very far if he only took necklaces and put them back again.'

'But it was all a joke,' she reminded us both with a bit of a start. 'It must have been a joke, if Mr Raffles did it at all. And it would be dreadful if anything happened to him because of a wretched practical joke!'

There was no mistake about her feeling now; she really felt that it would be 'dreadful if anything happened' to the man whom yesterday she had seemed both to dislike and to distrust. Her voice vibrated with anxiety. A bright film covered the fine eyes, and they were finer than ever as they continued to face me unashamed; but I was fool enough to speak my mind, and at that they flashed themselves dry.

'I thought you didn't like him?' had been my remark, and 'Who says I do?' was hers. 'But he has done a lot for Teddy,' she went on, 'and never more than yesterday,' with her hand for an instant on my arm, 'when you helped him! I am dreadfully sorry for Mr Garland, sorrier than I am for poor Teddy. But Mr Raffles is more than sorry. I know he means to do what he can. He seems to think there must be something wrong; he spoke of bringing that brute to reason – if not to justice. It would be too dreadful if such a creature could turn the tables on Mr Raffles by trumping up any charge against him!'

There was an absolute echo of my own tone in 'trumping up any charge,' and I thought the echo sounded even more insincere. But at least it showed me where we were. Miss Belsize was not deceived; she only wanted me to think she was. Miss Belsize had divined what I knew, but neither of us would admit to the other that the charge against Raffles would be true enough.

'But why should these men follow him?' said I, really wondering why they should. 'If there were anything definite against old Raffles, don't you think he would be arrested?'

'Oh! I don't know,' was the slightly irritable answer. 'I only think he should be warned that he is being followed.'

'Whatever he has done?' I ventured.

'Yes!' said she. 'Whatever he has done – after what he did for Teddy yesterday!'

'You want me to warn him?'

'Yes – but not from me!'

'And suppose he really did take Mrs Levy's necklace?'

'That's just what we are supposing.'

'But suppose it wasn't for a joke at all?'

I spoke as one playfully plumbing the abysmally absurd; what I did desire to sound was the loyalty of this new, unexpected, and still captious ally. And I thought myself strangely successful at the first cast; for Miss Belsize looked me in the face as I was looking her, and I trusted her before she spoke.

'Well, after yesterday,' she said, 'I should warn him all the same!'

'You would back your Raffles right or wrong?' I murmured, perceiving that Camilla Belsize was, after all, like all the rest of us.

'Against a vulgar extortioner, most decidedly!' she returned, without repudiating the possessive pronoun. 'It doesn't follow that I think anything of him – apart from what you did between you for Teddy yesterday.'

We had continued our stroll some time ago, and now it was I who stood still. I looked at my watch. It still wanted some minutes to the luncheon interval.

'If Raffles took a cab to his rooms,' I said, 'he must be nearly there and I must telephone to him.'

'Is there a call-office on the ground?'

'Only in the pavilion, I believe, for the use of the members.'

'Then you must go to the nearest one outside.'

'And what about you?'

Miss Belsize brightened with her smile of perfect and unconscious independence.

'Oh, I shall be all right,' she said. 'I know where to find Mr Garland, even if I don't pick up an escort on the way.'

But it was she who escorted me to the tall turnstile nearest Wellington Road.

'And you do see why I want to put Mr Raffles on his guard?' she said pointedly as we shook hands. 'It's only because you and he have done so much for Teddy!'

And because she did not end by reminding me of my promise, I was all the more reluctantly determined to keep it to the letter, even though Raffles should think as ill as ever of one who was at least beginning to think better of him.

11

A DASH IN THE DARK

In a few lines which I found waiting for me at the club, and have somewhat imprudently preserved, Raffles professes to have known he was being shadowed even before we met at Lord's: 'but it was no use talking about it until the foe were in the cart.' He goes on to explain the simple means by which he reduced the gentlemen in billycocks to the pitch of discomfiture implied in his metaphor. He had taken a hansom to the Burlington Gardens entrance to the Albany, and kept it waiting while he went in and changed his clothes; then he had sent Barraclough to pay off the cab, and himself marched out into Piccadilly, what time the billycock brims were still shading watchful eyes in Burlington Gardens. There, to be sure, I myself had spotted one of the precious pair when I drove up after vain exertions at the call-office outside Lord's; but by that time his confederate was on guard at the Piccadilly end, and Raffles had not only shown a clean pair of wings, but left the poor brutes to watch an empty cage. He dismisses them not unfairly with the epithet 'amateurish'. Thus I was the more surprised, but not the less relieved, to learn that he was 'running down into the country for the weekend, to be out of their way'; but he would be back on the Monday night, 'to keep an engagement you wot of, Bunny. And if you like you may meet me under the clock at Waterloo (in flannel kit and tennis-shoes for choice) at the witching hour of twelve sharp.'

If I liked! I had a premature drink in honour of an invitation more gratifying to my vanity than any compliment old Raffles had paid me yet; for I could still hear his ironical undertaking to let me know if he could not do without me, and there was obviously no irony in this delightfully early intimation of that very flattering fact. It altered my whole view of the case. I might disapprove of the risks Raffles was running for his other friends, but the more I was allowed to share in them the less critical I was inclined to be. Besides I was myself clearly implicated in the issue as between my own friend and the common enemy; it was no more palatable to me than it was to Raffles, to be beaten by Dan Levy after our initial victory over him. So I drank like a man to his destruction, and subsequently stole forth to spy upon his foolish myrmidons, who flattered themselves that they were spying on Raffles. The imbeciles were at it still! The one hanging about Burlington Gardens looked unutterably bored, but with his blots of whisker and his grimy jowl, as flagrant a detective officer as ever I saw, even if he had not so considerately dressed the part. The other bruiser was an equally distinctive type, with a formidable fighting face and a chest like a barrel; but in Piccadilly he seemed to me less occupied in taking notice than in avoiding it. In innocuous futility one could scarcely excel the other; and between them they raised my spirits to the zenith.

I spent the rest of the afternoon at their own game, dogging Miss Belsize about Lord's until at last I had an opportunity of informing her that Raffles was quite safe. It may be that I made my report with too much gusto when my chance came; at any rate, it was only the fact that appeared to interest Miss Belsize; the details, over which I gloated, seemed to inspire in her a repugnance consistent with the prejudice she had displayed against Raffles yesterday, but not with her grateful solicitude on his behalf as revealed to me that very morning. I could only feel that gratitude was the beginning and the end of her new regard for him. Raffles had never fascinated this young girl as he did the rest of us; ordinarily engaged to an ordinary man, she was proof against the glamour that dazzled us. Nay, though she would not admit it even to me his friend, though like Levy she pretended to embrace the theory of the practical joke, making it the pretext for her anxiety, I felt more certain than ever that she now guessed, and had long suspected, what manner of man Raffles really was, and that her natural antipathy was greater even than before. Still more certain was I that she would never betray him by word or deed; that, whatever harm might come of his present proceedings, it would not be through Camilla Belsize.

But I was now determined to do my own utmost to minimise the dangers, to be a real help to Raffles in the act of altruistic depravity to which he had committed himself, and not merely a fifth wheel to his dashing chariot. Accordingly I went into solemn training for the event before us: a Turkish bath on the Saturday, a quiet Sunday between Mount Street and the club, and most of Monday lying like a log in cold-blooded preparation for the night's work. And when night fell I took it upon me to reconnoitre the ground myself before meeting Raffles at Waterloo.

Another cool and starry evening seemed to have tempted all the town and his wife into the streets. The great streams of traffic were busier than ever, the backwaters emptier, and Gray's Inn a basin drained to the last dreg of visible humanity. In one moment I passed through gateway and alley from the voices and lights of Holborn into a perfectly deserted square of bare ground and bright stars. The contrast was altogether startling, for I had never been there before; but for the same reason I had already lost my bearings, believing myself to be in Gray's Inn Square when I was only in South Square, Gray's Inn. Here I entered upon a hopeless search for the offices of Burroughs and Burroughs. Door after door had I tried in vain, and was beginning to realise my mistake, when a stray molecule of the population drifted in from Holborn as I had done, but with the quick step of the man who knows his way. I darted from a doorway to inquire mine, but he was across the square before I could cut him off, and as he passed through the rays of a lamp beside a second archway, I fell back thanking Providence and Raffles for my rubber soles. The man had neither seen nor heard me, but at the last moment I had recognised him as the burlier of the two blockheads who had shadowed Raffles three days before.

He passed under the arch without looking round. I flattened myself against the wall on my side of the arch; and in so standing I was all but eye-witness of a sudden encounter in the square beyond.

The quick steps stopped, and there was a 'Here you are!' on one side, and a 'Well! Where is he?' on the other, both very eager and below the breath.

'On the job,' whispered the first voice. 'Up to the neck!'

'When did 'e go in?'

'Nearly an hour ago; when I sent the messenger.'

'Which way?'

'Up through number seventeen.'

'Next door, eh?'

'That's right.'

'Over the roof?'

'Can't say; he's left no tracks. I been up to see.'

'I suppose there's the usual ladder and trapdoor?'

'Yes, but the ladder's hanging in its proper place. He couldn't have put it back there, could he?'

The other grunted; presently he expressed a doubt whether Raffles (and it thrilled me to hear the very name) had succeeded in breaking into the lawyer's office at all. The first man on the scene, however, was quite sure of it – and so was I.

'And we've got to hang about,' grumbled the newcomer, 'till he comes out again?'

'That's it. We can't miss him. He must come back into the square or through into the gardens, and if he does that he'll have to come over these here railings into Field Court. We got him either way, and there's a step just here where we can sit and see both ways as though it had been made for us. You come and try ... a door into the old hall ...'

That was all I heard distinctly; first their footsteps, and then the few extra yards, made the rest unintelligible. But I had heard enough. 'The usual ladder and trap-door!' Those blessed words alone might prove worth their weight in great letters of solid gold.

Now I could breathe again; now I relaxed my body and turned my head, and peered through the arch with impunity, and along the whole western side of Gray's Inn Square, with its dusky fringe of plane-trees and its vivid line of lamps, its strip of pavement, and its wall of many-windowed houses under one unbroken roof. Dim lights smouldered in the column of landing windows over every door; otherwise there was no break in the blackness of that gaunt façade. Yet in some dark room or other behind those walls I seemed to see Raffles at work as plainly as I had just heard our natural enemies plotting his destruction. I saw him at a safe. I saw him at a desk. I saw him leaving everything as he had found it, only to steal down and out into the very arms of the law. And I felt that even that desperate *dénouement* was little more than he deserved for letting me think myself accessory before the fact, when all the time he meant me to have nothing whatever to do with it! Well, I should have everything to do with it now; if Raffles was to be saved from the consequences of his own insanity, I and I alone must save him. It was the chance of my life to show him my real worth. And yet the difficulty of the thing might have daunted Raffles himself.

I knew what to do if only I could gain the house which he had made the base of his own operations; at least I knew what to attempt, and what Raffles had done I might do. So far the wily couple within earshot had helped me out of their own mouths. But they were only just round the corner that hid them from my view; stray words still reached me; and they knew me by sight, would recognise me at a glance, might pounce upon me as I passed. Unless –

I had it!

The crowd in Holborn seemed strange and unreal as I jostled in its midst once more. I was out of it in a moment, however, and into a bus, and out of the bus in a couple of minutes by my watch. One more minute and I was seeing how far back I could sit in a hansom bound for Gray's Inn Square.

'I forget the number,' I had told the cabman, 'but it's three or four doors beyond Burroughs and Burroughs, the solicitors.'

The gate into Holborn had to be opened for me, but the gate-keeper had not seen me on my previous entrance and exit afoot through the postern. It was when we drove under the further arch into the actual square that I pressed my head hard against the back of the hansom, and turned my face towards Field Court. The enemy might have abandoned their position, they might meet me face to face as I landed on the pavement; that was my risk, and I ran it without disaster. We passed the only house with an outer door to it in the square (now there is none), and on the plate beside it I read BURROUGHS AND BURROUGHS with a thrill. Up went my stick; my shilling (with a peculiarly superfluous sixpence for luck) I thrust through the trap with the other hand; and I was across the pavement, and on the stairs four clear doors beyond the lawyer's office, before the driver had begun to turn his horse.

They were broad bare stairs, with great office doors right and left on every landing, and in the middle the landing window looking out into the square. I waited well within the window on the first floor; and as my hansom drove out under the arch, the light of its near lamp flashed across two figures lounging on the steps of that entrance to the hall; but there was no stopping or challenging the cabman, no sound at all but those of hoofs and bell, and soon only that of my own heart beating as I fled up the rest of the stairs in my rubber soles.

Near the top I paused to thank my kindly stars; sure enough there was a long step-ladder hanging on a great nail over the last half-landing, and a square trap-door right over the landing proper! I ran up just to see the names on the two top doors; one was evidently that of some pettifogging firm of solicitors, while the other bespoke a private resident, whom I judged to be out of town by the congestion of postal matter that met my fingers in his letter-box. Neither had any terrors for me. The step-ladder was unhooked without another moment's hesitation. Care alone was necessary to place it in position without making a noise; then up I went, and up went the trapdoor next, without mishap or hindrance until I tried to stand up in the loft, and caught my head a crack against the tiles instead.

This was disconcerting in more ways than one, for I could not leave the ladder where it was, and it was nearly twice my height. I struck a match and lit up a sufficient perspective of lumber and cobwebs to reassure me. The loft was long enough, and the trap-door plumb under the apex of the roof, whereas I had stepped sideways off the ladder. It was to be got up, and I got it up, though not by any means as silently as I could have wished. I knelt and listened at the open trap-door for a good minute before closing it with great caution, a squeak and a scuttle in the loft itself being the only sign that I had disturbed a living creature.

There was a grimy dormer window, not looking down into the square, but leading like a companion hatchway into a valley of once red tiles, now stained blue-black in the starlight. It was great to stand upright here in the pure night air out of sight of man or beast. Smokeless chimney-stacks deleted whole pages of stars, but put me more in mind of pollards rising out of these rigid valleys, and sprouting with telephone wires that interlaced for foliage. The valley I was in ended fore and aft in a similar slope to that at either side; the length of it doubtless tallied with the frontage of a single house; and when I had clambered over the southern extremity into a precisely similar valley I saw that this must be the case. I had entered the fourth house beyond Burroughs and Burroughs's, or was it the fifth? I threaded three valleys, and then I knew.

In all three there had been dormer windows on either hand, that on the square side leading into the loft; the other, or others, forming a sort of skylight to some top-floor room. Suddenly I struck one of these standing very wide open, and trod upon a rope's end curled like a snake on the leads. I stooped down, and at a touch I knew that I had hold of Raffles's favourite Manila, which united a silken flexibility with the strength of any hawser. It was tied to the window-post, and it dangled into a room in which there was a dull red glow of fire: an inhabited room if ever I put my nose in one! My body must follow, however, where Raffles had led the way; and when it did I came to ground sooner than I expected on something less secure. The dying firelight, struggling through the bars of a kitchen range, showed my tennis-shoes in the middle of the kitchen table. A cat was stretching itself on the hearth-rug as I made a step of a wooden chair, and came down like a cat myself.

I found the kitchen door, found a passage so dark that the window at the end hung like a picture slashed across the middle. Yet it only looked into the square, for I peered out when I had crept along the passage, and even thought I both heard and saw the enemy at their old post. But I was in another enemy's country now; at every step I stopped to listen for the thud of feet bounding out of bed. Hearing nothing, I had the temerity at last to strike a match upon my trousers, and by its light I found the outer door. This was not bolted nor yet shut; it was merely ajar, and so I left it.

The rooms opposite appeared to be an empty set; those on the second and first floors were only partially shut off by swing doors leading to different departments of the mighty offices of Burroughs and Burroughs. There were no lights upon these landings, and I gathered my information by means of successive matches, whose tell-tale ends I carefully concealed about my person, and from copious legends painted on the walls. Thus I had little difficulty in groping my way to the private offices of Sir John Burroughs, head of the celebrated firm; but I looked in vain for a layer of light under any of the massive mahogany doors with which this portion of the premises was glorified. Then I began softly trying doors that proved to be locked. Only one yielded to my hand; and when it was a few inches open, all was still black; but the next few brought me to the end of my quest, and the close of my solitary adventures.

12

A MIDSUMMER NIGHT'S WORK

The dense and total darkness was broken in one place, and one only, by a plateful of light proceeding from a tiny bulb of incandescence in its centre. This blinding atom of white heat lit up a hand hardly moving, a pen continually poised, over a disc of snowy paper; and on the other side, something that lay handy on the table, reflecting the light in its plated parts. It was Raffles at his latest devilry. He had not heard me, and he could not see; but for that matter he never looked up from his task. Sometimes his face bent over it, and I could watch its absolute concentration. The brow was furrowed, and the mouth pursed, yet there was a hint of the same quiet and wary smile with which Raffles would bowl an over or drill holes in a door.

I stood for some moments fascinated, entranced, before creeping in to warn him of my presence in a whisper. But this time he heard my step, snatched up electric torch and glittering revolver, and covered me with the one in the other's light.

'A.J.!' I gasped.

'Bunny!' he exclaimed in equal amazement and displeasure. 'What the devil do you mean by this?'

'You're in danger,' I whispered. 'I came to warn you!'

'Danger? I'm never out of it. But how did you know where to find me, and how on God's earth did *you* get here?'

'I'll tell you some other time. You know those two brutes you dodged the other day?'

'I ought to.'

'They're waiting below for you at this very moment.'

Raffles peered a few moments through the handful of white light between our faces.

'Let them wait!' said he, and replaced the torch upon the table and put down his revolver for his pen.

'They're detectives!' I urged.

'Are they, Bunny?'

'What else could they be?'

'What, indeed!' murmured Raffles, as he fell to work again with bent head and deliberate pen.

'You gave them the slip on Friday, but they must have known your game and lain in wait for you here, one or other of them, ever since. It's my belief Dan Levy put them up to it, and the yarn about the letter was just to tempt you into this trap and get you caught in the act. He didn't want a copy one bit; for God's sake, don't stop to finish it now!'

'I don't agree with you,' said Raffles without looking up, 'and I don't do things by halves, Your precious detectives must have patience, Bunny, and so must you.' He held his watch to the bulb. 'In about twenty minutes there'll be real danger, but we couldn't be safer in our beds for the next ten. So perhaps you'll let me finish without further interruption, or else get out by yourself as you came in.'

I turned away from Raffles and his light, and blundered back to the landing. The blood boiled in my veins. Here had I fought and groped my way to his side, through difficulties it might have taxed even him to surmount, as one man swims ashore with a rope from the wreck, at the same mortal risk, with the same humane purpose. And not a word of thanks, not one syllable of congratulation, but 'get out by yourself as you came in!' I had more than half a mind to get out, and for good; nay, as I stood and listened on the landing, I could have found it in my outraged heart to welcome those very sleuthhounds from the square, with a cordon of police behind them.

Yet my boiling blood ran cold when warm breath smote my cheek and a hand my shoulder at one and the same awful moment.

'Raffles!' I cried in a strangled voice.

'Hush, Bunny!' he chuckled in my ear. 'Didn't you know who it was?'

'I never heard you; why did you steal on me like that?'

'You see you're not the only one who can do it, Bunny! I own it would have served me right if you'd brought the square about our ears.'

'Have you finished in there?' I asked gruffly.

'Rather!'

'Then you'd better hurry up and put everything as you found it.'

'It's all done, Bunny; red tape tied on such a perfect forgery that the crux will be to prove it is one; safe locked up, and every paper in its place.'

'I never heard a sound.'

'I never made one,' said Raffles, leading me upstairs by the arm. 'You see how you put me on my mettle, Bunny, old boy!'

I said no more till we reached the self-contained flat at the top of the house; then I begged Raffles to be quiet in a lower whisper than his own.

'Why, Bunny? Do you think there are people inside?'

'Aren't there?' I cried aloud in my relief.

'You flatter me, Bunny!' laughed Raffles, as we groped our way in. 'This is where they keep their John Bulldog, a magnificent figure of a commissionaire with the V.C. itself on his manly bosom. Catch me come when he was at home; one of us would have had to die, and it would have been a shame either way. Poor pussy, then, poor puss!'

We had reached the kitchen and the cat was rubbing itself against Raffles's legs.

'But how on earth did you get rid of him for the night?'

'Made friends with him when I called on Friday; didn't I tell you I had an appointment with the bloated head of this notorious firm when I cleared out of Lord's? I'm about to strengthen his already unrivalled list of clients; you shall hear all about that later. We had another interview this afternoon, when I asked my V.C. if he ever went to the theatre; you see he had spotted Tom Fool, and told me he never had a chance of getting to Lord's. So I got him tickets for "Rosemary" instead, but of course I swore they had just been given to me and I couldn't use them. You should have seen how the hero beamed! So that's where he is, he and his wife – or was, until the curtain went down.'

'Good Lord, Raffles, is the piece over?'

'Nearly ten minutes ago, but it'll take 'em all that unless they come home in a cab.'

And Raffles had been sitting before the fire, on the kitchen table, encouraging the cat, when this formidable V.C. and his wife must be coming every instant nearer Gray's Inn Square!

'Why, my dear Bunny, I should back myself to swarm up and out without making a sound or leaving a sign, if I heard our hero's key in the lock this moment. After you, Bunny.'

I climbed up with trembling knees, Raffles holding the rope taut to make it easier. Once more I stood upright under the stars and the telephone wires, and leaned against a chimney-stack to wait for Raffles. But before I saw him, before I even heard his unnecessarily noiseless movements, I heard something else that sent a chill all through me.

It was not the sound of a key in the lock. It was something far worse than that. It was the sound of voices on the roof, and of footsteps drawing nearer through the very next valley of leads and tiles.

I was crouching on the leads outside the dormer window as Raffles climbed into sight within.

'They're after us up here!' I whispered in his face. 'On the next roof! I hear them!'

Up came Raffles with his hands upon the sill, then with his knees between his hands, and so out on all-fours into the narrow rivulet of lead between the sloping tiles. Out of the opposite slope, a yard or two on, rose a stout stack of masonry, a many-headed monster with a chimney-pot on each, and a full supply of wires for whiskers. Behind this Gorgon of the house-tops Raffles hustled me without a word, and himself took shelter as the muffled voices on the next roof grew more distinct. They were the voices that I had overheard already in the square, the voices but not the tones. The tones – the words – were those of an enemy divided against itself.

'And now we've gone and come too far!' grumbled the one who had been last to arrive upon the scene below.

'We did that,' the other muttered, 'the moment we came in after 'em. We should've stopped where we were.'

'With that other cove driving up and going in without ever showing a glim?'

Raffles nudged me, and I saw what I had done. But the weakling of the pair still defended the position he had reluctantly abandoned on *terra firma*; he was all for returning while there was time; and there were fragments of the broken argument that were beginning to puzzle me when a soft oath from the man in front proclaimed the discovery of the open window and the rope.

'We got 'em,' he whispered, stagily, 'like rats in a trap!'

'You forget what it is we've got to get.'

'Well, we must first catch our man, mustn't we? And how d'ye know his pal hasn't gone in to warn him where we were? If he has, and we'd stopped there, they'd do us easy.'

'They may do us easier down there in the dark,' replied the other, with a palpable shiver. 'They'll hear us and lie in wait. In the dark! We shan't have a dog's chance.'

'All right! You get out of it and save your skin. I'd rather work alone than with a blessed funk!'

The situation was identical with many a one in the past between Raffles and me. The poor brute in my part resented the charge against his courage as warmly as I had always done. He was merely for the better part of valour, and how right he was Raffles and I only knew. I hoped the lesson was not lost upon Raffles. Dialogue and action alike resembled one of our own performances far more than ordinary police methods as we knew them. We heard the squeeze of the leader's clothes and the rattle of his buttons over the window ledge. 'It's like old times,' we heard him mutter; and before many moments the weakling was impulsively whispering down to know if he should follow.

I felt for that fellow at every stage of his unwilling proceedings. I was to feel for him still more. Raffles had stepped down like a cat from behind our cover; grasping an angle of the stack with either hand, I put my head round after him. The wretched player of my old part was on his haunches at the window, stooping forward, more in than out. I saw Raffles grinning in the starlight, saw his foot poised and the other poor devil disappear. Then a dull bump, then a double crash and such a cursing as left no doubt that the second fellow had fallen plumb on top of the first. Also from his language I fancied he would survive the fall.

But Raffles took no peep at his handiwork; hardly had the rope whipped out at my feet than he had untied the other end.

'Like lamplighters, Bunny!'

And back we went helter-skelter along the valleys of lead and over the hills of tile... The noise in the kitchen died away as we put a roof or two between us and that of Burroughs and Burroughs.

'This is where I came out,' I called to Raffles as he passed the place. 'There's a ladder here where I left it in the loft!'

'No time for ladders!' cried Raffles over his shoulder, and not for some moments did he stop in his stride. Nor was it I who stopped him then; it was a sudden hubbub somewhere behind us, somewhere below; the blowing of a police whistle, and the sound of many footsteps in the square.

'That's for us!' I gasped. 'The ladder! The ladder!'

'Ladder be damned!' returned Raffles, roughly. 'It isn't for us at all; it's my pal the V.C. who has come home and bottled the other blighters.'

'Thinking they're thieves?'

'Thinking any rot you like! Our course is over the rest of the roofs on this side, over the whole lot at the top end, and, if possible, down the last staircase in the corner. Then we only have to show ourselves in the square for a tick before we're out by way of Verulam Buildings.'

'Is there another gate there?' I asked as he scampered on with me after him.

'Yes; but it's closed and the porter leaves at twelve, and it must be jolly near that now. Wait, Bunny! Some one or other is sure to be looking out of the top windows across the square; they'll see us if we take our fences too freely!'

We had come to one of the transverse tile-slopes, which hitherto we had run boldly up and down in our helpful and noiseless rubber soles; now, not to show ourselves against the stars, to a stray pair of eyes on some other high level, we crept up on all fours and rolled over at full length. It added considerably to our time over more than a whole side of the square. Meanwhile the police whistles had stopped, but the company in the square had swollen audibly.

It seemed an age, but I suppose it was not many minutes, before we came to the last of the dormer windows, looking into the last vale of tiles in the north-east angle of the square.

Something gleamed in the starlight, there was a sharp little sound of splitting wood, and Raffles led me on hands and knees into just such a loft as I had entered before by ladder. His electric torch discovered the trapdoor at a gleam. Raffles opened it and let down the rope, only to whisk it up again so smartly that it struck my face like a whiplash.

A door had opened on the top landing. We listened over the open trap-door, and knew that another stood listening on the invisible threshold underneath; then we saw him running downstairs, and my heart leapt for he never once looked up. I can see him still, foreshortened by our bird's-eye view into a Turkish fez and a fringe of white hair and red neck, a billow of dressing-gown, and bare heels peeping out of bedroom slippers at every step that we could follow; but no face all the way down, because he was a bent old boy who never looked like looking up.

Raffles threw his rope aside, gave me his hand instead, and dropped me on the landing like a feather, dropping after me without a moment's pause. In fact, the old fellow with the fez could hardly have completed his descent of the stairs when we began ours. Yet through the landing window we saw him charging diagonally across the square, shouting and gesticulating in his flight to the gathering crowd near the far corner.

'He spotted us, Bunny!' exclaimed Raffles, after listening an instant in the entrance. 'Stick to me like my shadow, and do every blessed thing I do.'

Out he dived, I after him, and round to the left with the speed of lightning, but apparently not without the lightning's attribute of attracting attention to itself. There was a hullabaloo across the square behind us, and I looked round to see the crowd there breaking in our direction, as I rushed after Raffles under an arch and up the alley in front of Verulam Buildings.

It was striking midnight as we made our sprint along this alley, and at the far end the porter was preparing to depart, but he waited to let us through the gate into Gray's Inn Road, and not until he had done so can the hounds have entered the straight. We did not hear them till the gate had clanged behind us, nor had it opened again before we were high and dry in a hansom.

'King's Cross!' roared Raffles for all the street to hear; but before we reached Clerkenwell Road he said he meant Waterloo, and round we went to the right along the tram-lines. I was too breathless to ask questions, and Raffles offered no explanations until he had lit a Sullivan. 'That little bit of wrong way may lose us our train,' he said as he puffed the first cloud. 'But it'll shoot the whole field to King's Cross as sure as scent is scent; and if we do catch our train, Bunny, we shall have it to ourselves as far as this pack is concerned. Hurrah! Blackfriar's Bridge and a good five minutes to go!'

'You're going straight down to Levy's with the letter?'

'Yes; that's why I wanted you to meet me under the clock at twelve.'

'But why in tennis-shoes?' I asked, recalling the injunctions in his note, and the meaning that I had naturally read into them.

'I thought we might possibly finish the night on the river,' replied Raffles, darkly. 'I think so still.'

'And *I* thought you meant me to lend you a hand in Gray's Inn!'

Raffles laughed.

'The less you think, my dear old Bunny, the better it always is! Tonight, for example, you have performed prodigies on my account; your unselfish audacity has only been equalled by your resource; but, my dear fellow, it was a sadly unnecessary effort.'

'Unnecessary to tell you those brutes were waiting for you down below?'

'Quite, Bunny. I saw one of them and let him see me. I knew he'd send off for his pal.'

'Then I don't understand your tactics or theirs.'

'Mine were to walk out the very way we did, you and I. They would never have seen me from the opposite corner of the square, or dreamt of going in after me if they hadn't spotted your getting in before them to put me on my guard. The place would have been left exactly as I found it, and those two numskulls as much in the lurch as I left them last week outside the Albany.'

'Perhaps they were beginning to fear that,' said I, 'and meant ferreting for you in any case if you didn't show up.'

'Not they,' said Raffles. 'One of them was against it as it was; it wasn't their job at all.'

'Not to take you in the act if they could?'

'No; their job was to take the letter from me as soon as I got back to earth. That was all. I happen to know. Those were their instructions from old Levy.'

'Levy!'

'Did it never occur to you that I was being dogged by his creatures?'

'His creatures, Raffles?'

'He set them to shadow me from the hour of our interview on Saturday morning. Their instructions were to bag the letter from me as soon as I got it, but to let me go free to the devil!'

'How can you know, A.J.?'

'My dear Bunny, where do you suppose I've been spending the week-end? Did you think I'd go in with a sly dog like old Shylock without watching him and finding out his real game? I should have thought it hardly necessary to tell you I've been down the river all the time; down the river,' added Raffles, chuckling, 'in a Canadian canoe and a torpedo beard! I was cruising near the foot of the old brute's garden on Friday evening when one of the precious pair came down to tell him they had let me slip already. I landed and heard the whole thing through the window of the room where we shall find him tonight. It was Levy who set them to watch the crib since they'd lost the cracksman; he was good enough to reiterate all his orders for my benefit. You will hear me take him through them when we get down there, so it's no use going over the same ground twice.'

'Funny orders for a couple of Scotland Yard detectives!' was my puzzled comment as Raffles produced an inordinate cab-fare.

'Scotland Yard?' said he. 'My good Bunny, those were no limbs of the law; they're old thieves set to catch a thief, and they've been caught themselves for their pains!'

Of course they were! Every detail of their appearance and their behaviour confirmed the statement in the flash that brought them all before my mind! And I had never thought of it, never but dreamt that we were doing battle with the archenemies of our class. But there was no time for further reflection, nor had I recovered breath enough for another word, when the hansom clattered up the cobbles into Waterloo Station. And our last sprint of that athletic night ended in a simultaneous leap into separate carriages as the platform slid away from the 12:10 train.

13

KNOCKED OUT

But it was hardly likely to be the last excitement of the night, as I saw for myself before Raffles joined me at Vauxhall. An arch-traitor like Daniel Levy might at least be trusted to play the game out with loaded dice; no single sportsman could compete against his callous machinations; and that was obviously where I was coming in. I only wished I had not come in before! I saw now the harm that I had done by my rash proceedings in Gray's Inn, the extra risk entailed already and a worse one still impending. If the wretches who had shadowed him were really Levy's mercenaries, and if they really had been taken in their own trap, their first measure of self-defence would be the denunciation of Raffles to the real police. Such at least was my idea, and Raffles himself made light enough of it; he thought they could not expose him without dragging in Levy, who had probably made it worth their while not to do that on any consideration. His magnanimity in the matter, which he flatly refused to take as seriously as I did, made it difficult for me to press old Raffles, as I otherwise might have done, for an outline of those further plans in which I hoped to atone for my blunders by being of some use to him after all. His nonchalant manner convinced me that they were cut-and-dried; but I was left perhaps deservedly in the dark as to the details. I merely gathered that he had brought down some document for Levy to sign in execution of the verbal agreement made between them in town; not until that agreement was completed by his signature was the harpy to receive the precious epistle he pretended never to have written. Raffles, in fine, had the air of a man who has the game in his hands, who is none the less prepared for foul play on the other side, and by no means perturbed at the prospect.

We left the train at a sweet-smelling platform, on which the lights were being extinguished as we turned into a quiet road where bats flew over our heads between the lamp-posts, and a policeman was passing a disc of light over a jerry-built abuse of the name of Queen Anne. Our way led through quieter roads of larger houses standing further back, until at last we came to the enemy's gates. They were wooden gates without a lodge, yet the house set well beyond them, on the river's brim, was a mansion of considerable size and still greater peculiarity. It was really two houses, large and small, connected by a spine of white posts and joists and glimmering glass. In the more substantial building no lights were to be seen from the gates, but in the annex a large French window made a lighted square at right angles with the river and the road. We had set foot in the gravel drive; with a long line of poplars down one side, and on the other a wide lawn dotted with cedars and small shrubs, when Raffles strode among these with a smothered exclamation, and a wild figure started from the ground.

'What are you doing here?' demanded Raffles, with all the righteous austerity of a law-abiding citizen.

'Nutting, sare!' replied an alien tongue, a gleam of good teeth in the shadow of his great soft hat. 'I been see Mistare Le-vie in ze 'ouse, on ze beezness, shentlemen.'

'Seen him, have you? Then if I were you I should make a decent departure,' said Raffles, 'by the gate – ' to which he pointed with increased severity of tone and bearing.

The weird figure uncovered a shaggy head of hair, made us a grotesque bow with his right hand melodramatically buried in the folds of a voluminous cape, and stalked off in the starlight with much dignity. But we heard him running in the road before the gate had clicked behind him.

'Isn't that the fellow we saw in Jermyn Street last Thursday?' I asked Raffles in a whisper.

'That's the chap,' he whispered back. 'I wonder if he spotted us, Bunny? Levy's treated him scandalously, of course; it all came out in a torrent the other morning. I only hope he hasn't been serving Dan Levy as Jack Rutter served old Baird! I could swear that was a weapon of sorts he'd got under his cloak.'

And as we stood together under the stars, listening to the last of the runaway footfalls, I recalled the killing of another and a less notorious usurer by a man we both knew, and had even helped to shield from the consequences of his crime. Yet the memory of our terrible discovery on that occasion had not the effect of making me shrink from such another now; nor could I echo the hope of Raffles in my heart of hearts. If Dan Levy also had come to a bad end – well, it was no more than he deserved, if only for his treachery to Raffles, and, at any rate, it would put a stop to our plunging from bad to worse in an adventure of which the sequel might well be worst of all. I do not say that I was wicked enough absolutely to desire the death of this sinner for our benefit; but I saw the benefit at least as plainly as the awful possibility, and it was not with unalloyed relief that I beheld a great figure stride through the lighted windows at our nearer approach.

Though his back was to the light before I saw his face, and the whole man might have been hacked out of ebony, it was every inch the living Levy who stood peering in our direction, one hand hollowed at an ear, the other shading both eyes.

'Is that you, boys?' he croaked in sepulchral salute.

'It depends which boys you mean,' replied Raffles, marching into the zone of light. 'There are so many of us about tonight!'

Levy's arms dropped at his sides, and I heard him mutter 'Raffles!' with a malediction. Next moment he was inquiring whether we had come down alone, yet peering past us into the velvet night for his answer.

'I brought our friend Bunny,' said Raffles, 'but that's all.'

'Then what do you mean by saying there are so many of you about?'

'I was thinking of the gentleman who was here just before us.'

'Here just before you? Why, I haven't seen a soul since my 'ousehold went to bed.'

'But we met the fellow just this minute within your gates: a little foreign devil with a head like a mop and the cloak of an operatic conspirator.'

'That beggar!' cried Levy, flying into a high state of excitement on the spot. 'That blessed little beggar on my tracks down here! I've 'ad him thrown out of the office in Jermyn Street; he's threatened me by letter and telegram; so now he thinks he'll come and try it on in person down 'ere. Seen me, eh? I wish I'd seen *'im*! I'm ready for biters like that, gentlemen. I'm not to be caught on the 'op down here!'

And a plated revolver twinkled and flashed in the electric light as Levy drew it from his hip pocket and flourished it in our faces; he would have gone prowling through the grounds with it if Raffles had not assured him that the foreign foe had fled on our arrival. As it was the pistol was not put back in his pocket when Levy at length conducted us indoors; he placed it on an occasional table beside the glass that he drained on entering; and forthwith set his back to a fire which seemed in keeping with the advanced hour, and doubly welcome in an apartment so vast that the billiard table was a mere item at one end, and sundry trophies of travel and the chase a far more striking and unforeseen feature.

'Why, that's a better grisly than the one at Lord's!' exclaimed Raffles, pausing to admire a glorious fellow near the door, while I mixed myself the drink he had declined.

'Yes,' said Levy, 'the man that shot all this lot used to go about saying he'd shoot *me* at one time; but I need 'ardly tell you he gave it up as a bad job, and went an" did what some folks call a worse instead. He didn't get much show 'ere, *I* can tell you; that little foreign snipe won't either, nor yet any other carrion that think they want my blood. I'd empty this shooter o' mine into their in'ards as soon as look at 'em, I don't give a curse who they are! Just as well I wasn't brought up to your profession, eh, Raffles?'

'I don't quite follow you, Mr Levy.'

'Oh yes you do!' said the money-lender, with his gastric chuckle. 'How've you got on with that little bit o' burgling?'

And I saw him screw up his bright eyes, and glance through the open windows into the outer darkness, as though there was still a hope in his mind that we had not come down alone. I formed the impression that Levy had returned by a fairly late train himself, for he was in morning dress, in dusty boots, and there was an abundant supply of sandwiches on the table with the drinks. But he seemed to have confined his own attentions to the bottle, and I liked to think that the sandwiches had been cut for the two emissaries for whom he was welcome to look out for all night.

'How did you get on?' he repeated when he had given them up for the present.

'For a first attempt,' replied Raffles, without a twinkle, 'I don't think I've done so badly.'

'Ah! I keep forgetting you're a young beginner,' said Levy, catching the old note in his turn.

'A beginner who's scarcely likely to go on, Mr Levy, if all cribs are as easy to crack as that lawyers" office of yours in Gray's Inn Square.'

'As easy?'

Raffles recollected his pose.

'It was enormous fun,' said he. 'Of course one couldn't know that there would be no hitch. There was an exciting moment towards the end. I have to thank you for quite a new thrill of sorts. But, my dear Mr Levy, it was as easy as ringing the bell and being shown in; it only took rather longer.'

'What about the caretaker?' asked the usurer, with a curiosity no longer to be concealed.

'He obliged me by taking his wife to the theatre.'

'At your expense?'

'No, Mr Levy, the item will be debited to you in due course.'

'So you got in without any difficulty?'

'Over the roof.'

'And then?'

'I hit upon the right room.'

'And then, Raffles?'

'I opened the right safe.'

'Go on, man!'

But the man was only going on at his own rate, and the more Levy pressed him, the greater his apparent reluctance to go on at all.

'Well, I found the letter all right. Oh, yes, I made a copy of it. Was it a good copy? Almost too good, if you ask me.' Thus Raffles under increasing pressure.

'Well? Well? You left that one there, I suppose? What happened next?'

There was no longer any masking the moneylender's eagerness to extract the *dénouement* of Raffles's adventure; that it required extracting must have seemed a sufficient earnest of the ultimate misadventure so craftily plotted by Levy himself. His great nose glowed with the imminence of victory. His strong lips loosened their habitual hold upon each other, and there was an impressionist daub of yellow fang between. The brilliant little eyes were reduced to sparkling pinheads of malevolent glee. This was not the fighting face I knew better and despised less, it was the living epitome of low cunning and foul play.

'The next thing that happened,' said Raffles, in his most leisurely manner, 'was the descent of Bunny like a bolt from the blue.'

'Had he gone in with you?'

'No; he came in after me as bold as blazes to say that a couple of common, low detectives were waiting for me down below in the square!'

'That was very kind of 'im,' snarled Levy, pouring a murderous fire upon my person from his little black eyes.

'Kind!' cried Raffles. 'It saved the whole show.'

'It did, did it?'

'I had time to dodge the limbs of the law by getting out another way, and never letting them know that I had got out at all.'

'Then you left them there?'

'In their glory!' said Raffles, radiant in his own.

Though I must confess I could not see them at the time, there were excellent reasons for not stating there and then the delicious plight in which we had really left Levy's myrmidons. I myself would have driven home our triumph and his treachery by throwing our winning cards upon the table and simultaneously exposing his false play. But Raffles was right, and I should have been wrong, as I was soon enough to see for myself.

'And you came away, I suppose,' suggested the money-lender, ironically, 'with my original letter in your pocket?'

'Oh, no, I didn't,' replied Raffles, with a reproving shake of the head.

'I thought not!' cried Levy in a gust of exultation.

'I came away,' said Raffles, 'if you'll pardon the correction, with the letter you never dreamt of writing, Mr Levy!'

The Jew turned a deeper shade of yellow; but he had the wisdom and the self-control otherwise to ignore the point against him. 'You'd better let me see it,' said he, and flung out his open hand with a gesture of authority which it took a Raffles to resist.

Levy was still standing with his back to the fire, and I was at his feet in a saddle-bag chair, with my yellow beaker on the table at my elbow. But Raffles remained aloof upon his legs, and he withdrew still further from the fire as he unfolded a large sheet of office paper, stamped with the notorious address in Jermyn Street, and displayed it on high like a phylactery.

'You may see, by all means, Mr Levy,' said Raffles, with a slight but sufficient emphasis on his verb.

'But I'm not to touch – is that it?'

'I'm afraid I must ask you to look first,' said Raffles, smiling. 'I should suggest, however, that you exercise the same caution in showing me that part of your *quid pro quo* which you have doubtless in readiness; the other part is in my pocket ready for you to sign; and after that, the three little papers can change hands simultaneously.'

Nothing could have excelled the firmness of this intimation, except the exggravating delicacy with which it was conveyed. I saw Levy clench and unclench his great fists, and his canine jaw working protuberantly as he ground his teeth. But not a word escaped him, and I was admiring the monster's self-control when of a sudden he swooped upon the table at my side, completely filled his empty glass with neat whiskey, and, spluttering and blinking from an enormous gulp, made a lurch for Raffles with his drink in one hand and his plated pistol in the other.

'Now I'll have a look,' he hiccoughed, 'an" a good look, unless you want a lump of lead in your liver!'

Raffles awaited his uncertain advance with a contemptuous smile.

'You're not such a fool as all that, Mr Levy, drunk or sober,' said he; but his eye was on the waving weapon, and so was mine; and I was wondering how a man could have got so very suddenly drunk, when the nobbler of crude spirit was hurled with most sober aim, glass and all, full in the face of Raffles, and the letter plucked from his grasp and flung upon the fire, while Raffles was still reeling in his blindness, and before I had struggled to my feet.

Raffles, for the moment, was absolutely blinded; as I say, his face was streaming with blood and whiskey, and the prince of traitors already crowing over his vile handiwork. But that was only for a moment, too; the blackguard had been fool enough to turn his back on me; and, first jumping upon my chair, I sprang upon him like any leopard, and brought him down with my ten fingers in his neck, and such a crack on the parquet with his skull as left it a deadweight on my hands. I remember the rasping of his bristles as I disengaged my fingers and let the leaden head fall back; it fell sideways now, and if it had but looked less dead I believe I should have stamped the life out of the reptile on the spot.

I know that I rose exultant from my deed...

14

CORPUS DELICTI

Raffles was still stamping and staggering with his knuckles in his eyes, and I heard him saying, 'The letter, Bunny, the letter!' in a way that made me realise all at once that he had been saying nothing else since the moment of the foul assault. It was too late now and must have been from the first; a few filmy scraps of blackened paper, stirring on the hearth, were all that remained of the letter by which Levy had set such store, for which Raffles had risked so much.

'He's burnt it,' said I. 'He was too quick for me.'

'And he's nearly burnt my eyes out,' returned Raffles, rubbing them again. 'He was too quick for us both.'

'Not altogether,' said I, grimly. 'I believe I've cracked his skull and finished him off!'

Raffles rubbed and rubbed until his bloodshot eyes were blinking out of a blood-stained face into that of the fallen man. He found and felt the pulse in a wrist like a ship's cable.

'No, Bunny, there's some life in him yet! Run out and see if there are any lights in the other part of the house.'

When I came back Raffles was listening at the door leading into the long glass passage.

'Not a light!' said I.

'Nor a sound,' he whispered. 'We're in better luck than we might have been; even his revolver didn't go off.' Raffles extracted it from under the prostrate body. 'It might just as easily have gone off and shot him, or one of us.' And he put the pistol in his own pocket.

'But have I killed him, Raffles?'

'Not yet, Bunny.'

'But do you think he's going to die?'

I was overcome by reaction now; my knees knocked together, my teeth chattered in my head; nor could I look any longer upon the great body sprawling prone, or the insensate head twisted sideways on the parquet floor.

'He's all right,' said Raffles, when he had knelt and felt and listened again. I whimpered a pious but inconsistent ejaculation. Raffles sat back on his heels, and meditatively wiped a smear of his own blood from the polished floor. 'You'd better leave him to me,' he said, looking and getting up with sudden decision.

'But what am I to do?'

'Go down to the boathouse and wait in the boat.'

'Where is the boathouse?'

'You can't miss it if you follow the lawn down to the water's edge. There's a door on this side; if it isn't open, force it with this.'

And he passed me his pocket jimmy as naturally as another would have handed over a bunch of keys.

'And what then?'

'You'll find yourself on the top step leading down to the water; stand tight, and lash out all round until you find a windlass. Wind that windlass as gingerly as though it were a watch with a weak heart; you will be raising a kind of portcullis at the other end of the boathouse, but if you're heard doing it at dead of night we may have to run or swim for it. Raise the thing just high enough to let us under in the boat, and then lie low on board till I come.'

Reluctant to leave that ghastly form upon the floor, but now stricken helpless in its presence, I was softer wax than ever in the hands of Raffles, and soon found myself alone in the dew upon an errand in which I neither saw nor sought for any point. Enough that Raffles had given me something to do for our salvation; what part he had assigned to himself, what he was about indoors already, and the nature of his ultimate design, were questions quite beyond me for the moment. I did not worry about them. Had I killed my man? That was the one thing that mattered to me, and I frankly doubt whether even it mattered at the time so supremely as it seemed to have mattered now. Away from the *corpus delicti*, my horror was already less of the deed than of the consequences, and I had quite a level view of those. What I had done was barely even manslaughter at the worst. But at the best the man was not dead. Raffles was bringing him to life again. Alive or dead, I could trust him to Raffles, and go about my own part of the business, as indeed I did in a kind of torpor of the normal sensibilities.

Not much do I remember of that dreamy interval, until the dream became the nightmare that was still in store. The river ran like a broad road under the stars, with hardly a glimmer and not a floating thing upon it. The boathouse stood at the foot of a file of poplars, and I only found it by stooping low and getting everything over my own height against the stars. The door was not locked; but the darkness within was such that I could not see my own hand as it wound the windlass inch by inch. Between the slow ticking of the cogs I listened jealously for foreign sounds, and heard at length a gentle dripping across the breadth of the boathouse; that was the last of the 'portcullis,' as Raffles called it, rising out of the river; indeed, I could now see the difference in the stretch of stream underneath, for the open end of the boathouse was much less dark than mine; and when the faint band of reflected starlight had broadened as I thought enough, I ceased winding and groped my way down the steps into the boat.

But inaction at such a crisis was an intolerable state, and the last thing I wanted was time to think. With nothing more to do I must needs wonder what I was doing in the boat, and then what Raffles could want with the boat if it was true that Levy was not seriously hurt. I could see the strategic value of my position if we had been robbing the house, but Raffles was not out for robbery this time; and I did not believe he would suddenly change his mind. Could it be that he had never been quite confident of the recovery of Levy, but had sent me to prepare this means of escape from the scene of a tragedy? I cannot have been long in the boat, for my thwart was still rocking under me, when this suspicion shot me ashore in a cold sweat. In my haste I went into the river up to one knee, and ran across the lawn with that boot squelching. Raffles came out of the lighted room to meet me, and as he stood like Levy against the electric glare, the first thing I noticed was that he was wearing an overcoat that did not belong to him, and that the pockets of this overcoat were bulging grotesquely. But it was the last thing I remembered in the horror that was to come.

Levy was lying where I had left him, only straighter, and with a cushion under his head, as though he were not merely dead, but laid out in his clothes where he had fallen.

'I was just coming for you, Bunny,' whispered Raffles before I could find my voice. 'I want you to take hold of his boots.'

'His boots!' I gasped, taking Raffles by the sleeve instead. 'What on earth for?'

'To carry him down to the boat!'

'But is he – is he still – '

'Alive?' Raffles was smiling as though I amused him mightily. 'Rather, Bunny! Too full of life to be left, I can tell you; but it'll be daylight if we stop for explanations now. Are you going to lend a hand, or am I to drag him through the dew myself?'

I lent every fibre, and Raffles raised the lifeless trunk, I suppose by the armpits, and led the way backward into the night, after switching off the lights within. But the first stage of our revolting journey was a very short one. We deposited our poor burden as charily as possible on the gravel, and I watched over it for some of the longest minutes of my life, while Raffles shut and fastened all the windows, left the room as Levy himself might have left it, and finally found his way out by one of the doors. And all the while not a movement or a sound came from the senseless clay at my feet; but once, when I bent over him, the smell of whiskey was curiously vital and reassuring.

We started off again, Raffles with every muscle on the strain, I with every nerve; this time we staggered across the lawn without a rest, but at the boathouse we put him down in the dew, until I took off my coat and we got him lying on that while we debated about the boathouse, its darkness, and its steps. The combination beat us on a moment's consideration; and again I was the one to stay, and watch, and listen to my own heart beating; and then to the water bubbling at the prow and dripping from the blades as Raffles sculled round to the edge of the lawn.

I need dwell no more upon the difficulty and the horror of getting that inanimate mass on board; both were bad enough, but candour compels me to admit that the difficulty dwarfed all else until at last we overcame it. How near we were to swamping our craft, and making sure of our victim by drowning, I still shudder to remember; but I think it must have prevented me from shuddering over more remote possibilities at the time. It was a time, if ever there was one, to trust in Raffles and keep one's powder dry; and to that extent I may say I played the game. But it was his game, not mine, and its very object was unknown to me. Never, in fact, had I followed my inveterate leader quite so implicitly, so blindly, or with such reckless excitement. And yet, if the worst did happen and our mute passenger was never to open his eyes again, it seemed to me that we were well on the road to turn manslaughter into murder in the eyes of any British jury: the road that might easily lead to destruction at the hangman's hands.

But a more immediate menace seemed only to have awaited the actual moment of embarkation, when, as we were pushing off, the rhythmical plash and swish of a paddle fell suddenly upon our ears, and we clutched the bank while a canoe shot down-stream within a length of us. Luckily the night was as dark as ever, and all we saw of the paddler was a white shirt fluttering as it passed. But there lay Levy with his heavy head between my shins in the stern-sheets, with his waistcoat open, and *his* white shirt catching what light there was as greedily as the other; and his white face as conspicuous to my guilty mind as though we had rubbed it with phosphorus. Nor was I the only one to lay this last peril to heart. Raffles sat silent for several minutes on his thwart; and when he did dip his sculls it was to muffle his strokes so that even I could scarcely hear them, and to keep peering behind him down the Stygian stream.

So long had we been getting under way that nothing surprised me more than the extreme brevity of our actual voyage. Not many houses and gardens had slipped behind us on the Middlesex shore, when we turned into an inlet running under the very windows of a house so near the river itself that even I might have thrown a stone from any one of them into Surrey. The inlet was empty and ill-smelling; there was a crazy landing-stage, and the many windows overlooking us had the black gloss of empty darkness within. Seen by starlight with a troubled eye, the house had one salient feature in the shape of a square tower, which stood out from the facade fronting the river, and rose to nearly twice the height of the main roof. But this curious excrescence only added to the forbidding character of as gloomy a mansion as one could wish to approach by stealth at dead of night.

'What's this place?' I whispered as Raffles made fast to a post.

'An unoccupied house, Bunny.'

'Do you mean to occupy it?'

'I mean our passenger to do so – if we can land him alive or dead!'

'Hush, Raffles!'

'It's a case of heels first, this time – '

'Shut up!'

Raffles was kneeling on the landing-stage – luckily on a level with our rowlocks – and reaching down into the boat.

'Give me his heels,' he muttered; 'you can look after his business end. You needn't be afraid of waking the old hound, nor yet hurting him.'

'I'm not,' I whispered, though mere words had never made my blood run colder. 'You don't understand me. Listen to that!'

And as Raffles knelt on the landing-stage, and I crouched in the boat, with something desperately like a dead man stretched between us, there was a swish and a dip outside the inlet, and a flutter of white on the river beyond.

'Another narrow squeak!' he muttered with grim levity when the sound had died away. 'I wonder who it is paddling his own canoe at dead of night?'

'I'm wondering how much he saw.'

'Nothing,' said Raffles, as though there could be no two opinions on the point. 'What did we see to swear to between a sweater and a pocket-handkerchief? Only something white, and we were looking out, and it's far darker in here than out there on the main stream. But it'll soon be getting light, and we really may be seen unless we land our big fish first.'

And without more ado he dragged the lifeless Levy ashore by the heels, while I alternately grasped the landing-stage to steady the boat, and did my best to protect the limp members and the leaden head from actual injury. All my efforts could not avert a few hard knocks, however, and these were sustained with such a horrifying insensibility of body and limb, that my worst suspicions were renewed before I crawled ashore myself, and remained kneeling over the prostrate form.

'Are you certain, Raffles?' I began, and could not finish the awful question.

'That he's alive?' said Raffles. 'Rather, Bunny, and he'll be kicking below the belt again in a few more hours!'

'A few more *hours*, A.J.?'

'I give him four or five.'

'Then it's concussion of the brain!'

'It's the brain all right,' said Raffles. 'But for "concussion" I should say "coma," if I were you.'

'What have I done!' I murmured, shaking my head over the poor old brute.

'You?' said Raffles. 'Less than you think, perhaps!'

'But the man's never moved a muscle.'

'Oh, yes, he has, Bunny!'

'When?'

'I'll tell you at the next stage,' said Raffles. 'Up with his heels and come this way.'

And we trailed across a lawn so woefully neglected that the big body sagging between us, though it cleared the ground by several inches, swept the dew from the rank growth until we got it propped up on some steps at the base of the tower, and Raffles ran up to open the door. More steps there were within, stone steps allowing so little room for one foot and so much for the other as to suggest a spiral staircase from top to bottom of the tower. So it turned out to be; but there were landings communicating with the house, and on the first of them we laid our man and sat down to rest.

'How I love a silent, uncomplaining, stone staircase!' sighed the now quite invisible Raffles. 'So of course we find one thrown away upon an empty house. Are you there, Bunny?'

'Rather! Are you quite sure nobody else is here?' I asked, for he was scarcely troubling to lower his voice.

'Only Levy, and he won't count till all hours.'

'I'm waiting to hear how you know.'

'Have a Sullivan, first.'

'Are we as safe as all that?'

'If we're careful to make an ash-tray of our own pockets,' said Raffles, and I heard him tapping his cigarette in the dark. I refused to run any risks. Next moment his match revealed him sitting at the bottom of one flight, and me at the top of the flight below; either spiral was lost in shadow; and all I saw besides was a cloud of smoke from the blood-stained lips of Raffles, more clouds of cobwebs, and Levy's boots lying over on their uppers, almost in my lap. Raffles called my attention to them before he blew out his match.

'He hasn't turned his toes up yet, you see! It's a hog's sleep, but not by any means his last.'

'Did you mean just now that he woke up while I was in the boathouse?'

'Almost as soon as your back was turned, Bunny – if you call it waking up. You had knocked him out, you know, but only for a few minutes.'

'Do you mean to tell me that he was none the worse?'

'Very little, Bunny.'

My feeble heart jumped about in my body.

'Then what knocked him out again, A.J.?'

'I did.'

'In the same way?'

'No, Bunny, he asked for a drink and I gave him one.'

'A doctored drink!' I whispered with some horror; it was refreshing to feel once more horrified at some act not one's own.

'So to speak,' said Raffles, with a gesture that I followed by the red end of his cigarette; 'I certainly touched it up a bit, but I always meant to touch up his liquor if the beggar went back on his word. He did a good deal worse – for the second time of asking – and you did better than I ever knew you do before, Bunny! I simply carried on the good work. Our friend is full of a judicious blend of his own whiskey and the stuff poor Teddy had the other night. And when he does come to his senses I believe we shall find him damned sensible.'

'And if he isn't, I suppose you'll keep him here until he is?'

'I shall hold him up to ransom,' said Raffles, 'at the top of this ruddy tower, until he pays through both nostrils for the privilege of climbing down alive.'

'You mean until he stands by his side of your bargain?' said I, only hoping that was his meaning, but not without other apprehensions which Raffles speedily confirmed.

'And the rest!' he replied, significantly. 'You don't suppose the skunk's going to get off as lightly as if he'd played the game, do you? I've got one of my own to play now, Bunny, and I mean to play it for all I'm worth. I thought it would come to this!'

In fact, he had foreseen treachery from the first, and the desperate device of kidnapping the traitor proved to have been as deliberate a move as Raffles had ever planned to meet a probable contingency. He had brought down a pair of handcuffs as well as a sufficient supply of Somnol. My own deed of violence was the one entirely unforeseen effect, and Raffles vowed it had been a help. But when I inquired whether he had ever been over this empty house before, an irritable jerk of his cigarette end foretold the answer.

'My good Bunny, is this a time for rotten questions? Of course I've been over the whole place; didn't I tell you I'd been spending the week-end in these parts? I got an order to view the place, and have bribed the gardener not to let anybody else see over it till I've made up my mind. The gardener's cottage is on the other side of the main road, which runs flush with the front of the house; there's a splendid garden on that side, but it takes him all his time to keep it up, so he's given up bothering about this bit here. He only sets foot in the house to show people over; his wife comes in sometimes to open the downstairs windows; the ones upstairs are never shut. So you perceive we shall be fairly free from interruption at the top of this tower, especially when I tell you that it finishes in a room as soundproof as old Carlyle's crow's-nest in Cheyne Row.'

It flashed across me that another great man of letters had made his local habitation if not his name in this part of the Thames Valley; and when I asked if this was that celebrity's house, Raffles seemed surprised that I had not recognised it as such in the dark. He said it would never let again, as the place was far too good for its position, which was now much too near London. He also told me that the idea of holding Dan Levy up to ransom had occurred to him when he found himself being followed about town by Levy's 'mamelukes,' and saw what a traitor he had to cope with.

'And I hope you like the idea, Bunny,' he added, 'because I was never caught kidnapping before, and in all London there wasn't a bigger man to kidnap.'

'I love it,' said I (and it was true enough of the abstract idea), 'but don't you think he's just a bit too big? Won't the country ring with his disappearance?'

'My dear Bunny, nobody will dream he's disappeared!' said Raffles, confidently. 'I know the habits of the beast; didn't I tell you he ran another show somewhere? Nobody seems to know where, but when he isn't here, that's where he's supposed to be, and when he's there he cuts town for days on end. I suppose you never noticed I've been wearing an overcoat all this time, Bunny?'

'Oh, yes, I did,' said I. 'Of course it's one of his?'

'The very one he'd have worn tonight, and his soft hat from the same peg is in one of the pockets; their absence won't look as if he'd come out feet first, will it, Bunny? I thought his stick might be in the way, so instead of bringing it too, I stowed it away behind his books. But these things will serve a second turn when we see our way to letting him go again like a gentleman.'

The red end of the Sullivan went out sizzling between a moistened thumb and finger, and no doubt Raffles put it carefully in his pocket as he rose to resume the ascent. It was still perfectly dark on the tower stairs; but by the time we reached the sanctum at the top we could see each other's outlines against certain ovals of wild grey sky and dying stars. For there was a window more like a porthole in three of the four walls; in the fourth wall was a cavity like a ship's bunk, into which we lifted our still unconscious prisoner as gently as we might. Nor was that the last that was done for him, now that some slight amends were possible. From an invisible locker Raffles produced bundles of thin, coarse stuff, one of which he placed as a pillow under the sleeper's head, while the other was shaken out into a covering for his body.

'And you asked me if I'd ever been over the place!' said Raffles, putting a third bundle in my hands. 'Why, I slept up here last night, just to see if it was all as quiet as it looked; these were my bed-clothes, and I want you to follow my example.'

'I go to sleep?' I cried. 'I couldn't and wouldn't for a thousand pounds, Raffles!'

'Oh, yes, you could!' said Raffles, and as he spoke there was a horrible explosion in the tower. Upon my word, I thought one of us was shot, until there came the smaller sounds of froth pattering on the floor and liquor bubbling from a bottle.

'Champagne!' I exclaimed, when he had handed me the metal cap of a flask, and I had taken a sip. 'Did you hide that up here as well?'

'I hid nothing up here except myself,' returned Raffles, laughing. 'This is one of a couple of pints from the cellarette in Levy's billiard den; take your will of it, Bunny, and perhaps the old man may have the other when he's a good boy. I fancy we shall find it a stronger card than it looks. Meanwhile let sleeping dogs lie and lying dogs sleep! And you'd be far more use to me later, Bunny, if only you'd try to do the same.'

I was beginning to feel that I might try, for Raffles was filling up the metal cup every minute, and also plying me with sandwiches from Levy's table, brought hence (with the champagne) in Levy's overcoat pocket. It was still pleasing to reflect that they had been originally intended for the rival bravos of Gray's Inn. But another idea that did occur to me, I dismissed at the time, and so justly that I would disabuse any other suspicious mind of it without delay. Dear old Raffles was scarcely more skilful and audacious as amateur cracksman than as amateur anaesthetist, nor was he ever averse from the practice of his uncanny genius at either game. But, sleepy as I soon found myself at the close of our very long night's work, I had no subsequent reason to suppose that Raffles had given *me* drop or morsel of anything but sandwiches and champagne.

So I rolled myself up on the locker, just as things were beginning to take visible shape even without the tower windows behind them, and I was almost dropping off to sleep when a sudden anxiety smote my mind.

'What about the boat?' I asked.

There was no answer.

'Raffles!' I cried. 'What are you going to do about the beggar's boat?'

'You go to sleep,' came the sharp reply, 'and leave the boat to me.'

And I fancied from his voice that Raffles also had lain him down, but on the floor.

15

TRIAL BY RAFFLES

When I awoke it was dazzling daylight in the tower, and the little scene was quite a surprise to me. It had felt far larger in the dark. I suppose the floor-space was about twelve feet square, but it was contracted on one side by the well and banisters of a wooden staircase from the room below, on another by the ship's bunk, and opposite that by the locker on which I lay. Moreover, the four walls, or rather the four triangles of roof, sloped so sharply to the apex of the tower as to leave an inner margin in which few grown persons could have stood upright. The port-hole windows were shrouded with rags of cobweb spotted with dead flies. They had evidently not been opened for years; it was even more depressingly obvious that we must not open them. One was thankful for such modicum of comparatively pure air as came up the open stair from the floor below; but in the freshness of the morning one trembled to anticipate the atmosphere of this stale and stuffy eyrie through the heat of a summer's day. And yet neither the size nor the scent of the place, nor any other merely scenic feature, was half so disturbing or fantastic as the appearance of my two companions.

Raffles, not quite at the top of the stairs, but near enough to loll over the banisters, and Levy, cumbering the ship's bunk, were indeed startling figures to an eye still dim with sleep. Raffles had an ugly cut from the left nostril to the corner of the mouth; he had washed the blood from his face, but the dark and angry streak remained to heighten his unusual pallor. Levy looked crumpled and debauched, flabbily and feebly senile, yet with his vital forces making a last flicker in his fiery eyes. He was grotesquely swathed in scarlet bunting, from which his doubled fists protruded in handcuffs; a bit of thin rope attached the handcuffs to a peg on which his coat and hat were also hanging, and a longer bit was taken round the banisters from the other end of the bunting, which I now perceived to be a tattered and torn Red Ensign. This led to the discovery that I myself had been sleeping in the Union Jack, and it brought my eyes back to the ghastly face of Raffles, who was already smiling at mine.

'Enjoyed your night under canvas, Bunny? Then you might get up and present your colours to the prisoner in the bunk. You needn't be frightened of him, Bunny; he's such a devilish tough customer that I've had to clap him in irons, as you see. Yet he can't say I haven't given him rope enough; he's got lashings of rope – eh, Bunny?'

'That's right!' said Levy, with a bitter snarl. 'Get a man down by foul play, and then wipe your boots on him! I'd stick it like a lamb if only you'd give me that drink.'

And then it was, as I got to my feet, and shook myself free from the folds of the Union Jack, that I saw the unopened pint of champagne standing against the banisters in full view of the bunk. I confess I eyed it wistfully myself; but Raffles was adamant alike to friend and foe, and merely beckoned me to follow him down the wooden stair, without answering Levy at all. I certainly thought it a risk to leave that worthy unwatched for a moment, but it was scarcely for more. The room below was fitted with a bath and a lavatory basin, which Raffles pointed out to me without going all the way down himself. At the same time he handed me a stale remnant of the sandwiches removed with Levy from his house.

'I'm afraid you'll have to wash these down at that tap,' said he. 'The poor devil has finished what you left at daybreak, besides making a hole in my flask; but he can't or won't eat a bite, and if only he stands his trial and takes his sentence like a man, I think he might have the other pint to his own infernal cheek.'

'Trial and sentence!' I exclaimed. 'I thought you were going to hold him up to ransom?'

'Not without a fair trial, my dear Bunny,' said Raffles in the accents of reproof. 'We must hear what the old swab has to say for himself, when he's heard what I've got to say to him. So you stick your head under the tap when you've had your snack, Bunny; it won't come up to the swim I had after I'd taken the boat back, when you and Shylock were fast asleep, but it's all you've time for if you want to hear me open my case.'

And open it he did before himself, as judge and counsel in one, sitting on the locker as on the bench, the very moment I reappeared in court.

'Prisoner in the bunk, before we formulate the charge against you we had better deal with your last request for drink, made in the same breath as a preposterous complaint about foul play. The request has been made and granted more than once already this morning. This time it's refused. Drink has been your undoing, prisoner in the bunk; it is drink that necessitates your annual purification at Carlsbad, and yet within a week of that chastening experience you come before me without knowing where you are or how you got here.'

'That wasn't the whisky,' muttered Levy with a tortured brow. 'That was something else, which you'll hear more about; foul play it was, and you'll pay for it yet. There's not a headache in a hogshead of my whisky.'

'Well,' resumed Raffles, 'your champagne is on the same high level, and here's a pint of the best which you can open for yourself if only you show your sense before I've done with you. But you won't advance that little millennium by talking about foul play as though it were all on one side and the foulest of the foul not on yours. You will only retard the business of the court. You are indicted with extortion and sharp practice in all your dealings, with cheating and misleading your customers, attempting to cheat and betray your friends, and breaking all the rules of civilised crime. You are not invited to plead either way, because this court would not attach the slightest value to your plea; but presently you will get an opportunity of addressing the court in mitigation of your sentence. Or, if you like,' continued Raffles, with a wink at me, 'you may be represented by counsel. My learned friend here, I'm sure, will be proud to undertake your defence as a "docker"; or – perhaps I should say a "bunker," Mr Bunny?'

And Raffles laughed as coyly as a real judge at a real judicial joke, whereupon I joined in so uproariously as to find myself degraded from the position of leading counsel to that of the general public in a single flash from the judge's eye.

'If I hear any more laughter,' said Raffles, 'I shall clear the court. It's perfectly monstrous that people should come here to a court of justice and behave as though they were at a theatre.'

Levy had been reclining with his yellow face twisted and his red eyes shut; but now these burst open as with flames, and the dry lips spat a hearty curse at the judge upon the locker.

'Take care!' said Raffles. 'Contempt of court won't do you any good, you know!'

'And what good will all this foolery do you? Say what you've got to say against me, and be damned to you!'

'I fear you're confusing our functions sadly,' said Raffles, with a compassionate shake of the head. 'But so far as your first exhortation goes, I shall endeavour to take you at your word. You are a money-lender trading, among other places, in Jermyn Street, St. James's, under the style and title of Daniel Levy.'

'It 'appens to be my name.'

'That I can well believe,' rejoined Raffles; 'and if I may say so, Mr Levy, I respect you for it. You don't call yourself MacGregor or Montgomery. You don't sail under false colours at all. You fly the skull and crossbones of Daniel Levy, and it's one of the points that distinguish you from the ruck of money-lenders and put you in a class by yourself. Unfortunately, the other points are not so creditable. If you are more brazen than most you are also more unscrupulous; if you fly at higher game, you descend to lower dodges. You may be the biggest man alive at your job; you are certainly the biggest villain.'

'But I'm up against a bigger now,' said Levy, shifting his position and closing his crimson eyes.

'Possibly,' said Raffles, as he produced a long envelope and unfolded a sheet of foolscap; 'but permit me to remind you of a few of your own proven villainies before you take any more shots at mine. Last year you had three of your great bargains set aside by the law as hard and unconscionable; but every year you have these cases, and at best the terms are modified in favour of your wretched client. But it's only the exception who will face the music of the law-courts and the Press, and you figure on the general run. You prefer people like the Lincolnshire vicar you hounded into an asylum the year before last. You cherish the memory of the seven poor devils that you drove to suicide between 1890 and 1894; that sort pay the uttermost farthing before the debt to nature! You set great store by the impoverished gentry and nobility who have you to stay with them when the worst comes to the worst, and secure a respite in exchange for introductions to their pals. No fish is too large for your net, and none is too small, from his highness of Hathipur to that poor little builder at Bromley, who cut the throats – '

'Stop it!' cried Levy, in a lather of impotent rage.

'By all means,' said Raffles, restoring the paper to its envelope. 'It's an ugly little load for one man's soul, I admit; but you must see it was about time somebody beat you at your own beastly game.'

'It's a pack of blithering lies,' retorted Levy, 'and you haven't beaten me yet. Stick to facts within your own knowledge, and then tell me if your precious Garlands haven't brought their troubles on themselves?'

'Certainly they have,' said Raffles. 'But it isn't your treatment of the Garlands that has brought you to this pretty pass.'

'What is it, then?'

'Your treatment of me, Mr Levy.'

'A cursed crook like you!'

'A party to a pretty definite bargain, however, and a discredited person only so far as that bargain is concerned.'

'And the rest!' said the money-lender, jeering feebly. 'I know more about you than you guess.'

'I should have put it the other way round,' replied Raffles, smiling. 'But we are both forgetting ourselves, prisoner in the bunk. Kindly note that your trial is resumed, and further contempt will not be allowed to go unpurged. You referred a moment ago to my unfortunate friends; you say they were the engineers of their own misfortunes. That might be said of all who ever put themselves in your clutches. You squeeze them as hard as the law will let you, and in this case I don't see how the law is to interfere. So I interfere myself – in the first instance as disastrously as you please.'

'You did so!' exclaimed Levy, with a flicker of his inflamed eyes. 'You brought things to a head; that's all *you* did.'

'On the contrary, you and I came to an agreement which still holds good,' said Raffles, significantly. 'You are to return me a certain note of hand for thirteen thousand and odd pounds, taken in exchange for a loan of ten thousand, and you are also to give an understanding to leave another fifteen thousand of yours on mortgage for another year at least, instead of foreclosing, as you threatened and had a right to do this week. That was your side of the bargain.'

'Well,' said Levy, 'and when did I go back on it?'

'My side,' continued Raffles, ignoring the interpolation, 'was to get you by hook or crook a certain letter which you say you never wrote. As a matter of fact it was only to be got by crook – '

'Aha!'

'I got hold of it, nevertheless. I brought it to you at your house last night. And you instantly destroyed it after as foul an attack as one man ever made upon another!'

Raffles had risen in his wrath, was towering over the prostrate prisoner, forgetful of the mock trial, dead even to the humour which he himself had infused into a sufficiently lurid situation, but quite terribly alive to the act of treachery and violence which had brought that situation about. And I must say that Levy looked no less alive to his own enormity; he quailed in his bonds with a guilty fearfulness strange to witness in so truculent a brute; and it was with something near a quaver that his voice came next.

'I know that was wrong,' the poor devil owned. 'I'm very sorry for it, I'm sure! But you wouldn't trust me with my own property, and that and the drink together made me mad.'

'So you acknowledge the alcoholic influence at last?'

'Oh, yes! I must have been as drunk as an owl.'

'You know you've been suggesting that we drugged you?'

'Not seriously, Mr Raffles. I knew the old stale taste too well. It must have been the best part of a bottle I had before you got down.'

'In your anxiety to see me safe and sound?'

'That's it – with the letter.'

'You never dreamt of playing me false until I hesitated to let you handle it?'

'Never for one moment, my dear Raffles!'

Raffles was still standing up to his last inch under the apex of the tower, his head and shoulders the butt of a climbing sunbeam full of fretful motes. I could not see his expression from the banisters, but only its effect upon Dan Levy, who first held up his manacled hands in hypocritical protestation, and then dropped them as though it were a bad job.

'Then why,' said Raffles, 'did you have me watched almost from the moment that we parted company at the Albany last Friday morning?'

'*I* have you watched!' exclaimed the other in real horror. 'Why should I? It must have been the police.'

'It was not the police, though the blackguards did their best to look as if they were. I happen to be too familiar with both classes to be deceived. Your fellows were waiting for me up at Lord's, but I had no difficulty in shaking them off when I got back to the Albany. They gave me no further trouble until last night, when they got on my tracks at Gray's Inn in the guise of the two common, low detectives whom I believe I have already mentioned to you.'

'You said you left them there in their glory.'

'It was glorious from my point of view rather than theirs.'

Levy struggled into a less recumbent posture.

'And what makes you think,' said he, 'that I set this watch upon you?'

'I don't think,' returned Raffles. 'I know.'

'And how the devil do you know?'

Raffles answered with a slow smile, and a still slower shake of the head: 'You really mustn't ask me to give everybody away, Mr Levy!'

The money-lender swore an oath of sheer incredulous surprise, but checked himself at that and tried one more poser.

'And what do you suppose was my object in having you watched, if it wasn't to ensure your safety?'

'It might have been to make doubly sure of the letter, and to cut down expenses at the same swoop, by knocking me on the head and abstracting the treasure from my person. It was a jolly cunning idea – prisoner in the bunk! I shouldn't be upset about it just because it didn't come off. My compliments especially on making up your varlets in the quite colourable image of the true detective. If they had fallen upon me, and it had been a case of my liberty or your letter, you know well enough which I should let go.'

But Levy had fallen back upon his pillow of folded flag, and the Red Ensign over him bubbled and heaved with his impotent paroxysms.

'They told you! They must have told you!' he ground out through his teeth. 'The traitors – the blasted traitors!'

'It's a catching complaint, you see, Mr Levy,' said Raffles, 'especially when one's elders and betters themselves succumb to it.'

'But they're such liars!' cried Levy, shifting his ground again. 'Don't you see what liars they are? I did set them to watch you, but for your own good, as I've just been telling you. I was so afraid something might 'appen to you; they were there to see that nothing did. Now do you spot their game? I'd got to take the skunks into the secret, more or less, an'' they've played it double on us both. Meant bagging the letter from you to blackmail me with it; that's what they meant! Of course, when they failed to bring it off, they'd pitch any yarn to you. But that was their game all right. You must see for yourself it could never have been mine, Raffles, and – and let me out o' this, like a good feller!'

'Is this your defence?' asked Raffles as he resumed his seat on the judicial locker.

'Isn't it your own?' the other asked in his turn, with an eager removal of all resentment from his manner. '"Aven't we both been got at by those two jackets? Of course I was sorry ever to 'ave trusted 'em an inch, and you were quite right to serve me as you did if what they'd been telling you 'ad been the truth; but, now you see it was all a pack of lies it's surely about time to stop treating me like a mad dog.'

'Then you really mean to stand by your side of the original arrangement?'

'Always did,' declared our captive; 'never 'ad the slightest intention of doing anything else.'

'Then where's the first thing you promised me in fair exchange for what you destroyed last night? Where's Mr Garland's note of hand?'

'In my pocket-book, and that's in my pocket.'

'In case the worst comes to the worst,' murmured Raffles in sly commentary, and with a sidelong glance at me.

'What's that? Don't you believe me? I'll 'and it over this minute, if only you'll take these damned things off my wrists. There's no excuse for 'em now, you know!'

Raffles shook his head.

'I'd rather not trust myself within reach of your raw fists yet, prisoner. But my marshal will produce the note from your person if it's there.'

It was there, in a swollen pocket-book which I replaced otherwise intact while Raffles compared the signature on the note of hand with samples which he had brought with him for the purpose.

'It's genuine enough,' said Levy, with a sudden snarl and a lethal look that I intercepted at close quarters.

'So I perceive,' said Raffles. 'And now I require an equally genuine signature to this little document which is also a part of your bond.'

The little document turned out to be a veritable Deed, engrossed on parchment, embossed with a ten-shilling stamp, and duly calling itself an INDENTURE, in fourteenth century capitals. So much I saw as I held it up for the prisoner to read over. The illegally legal instrument is still in existence, with its unpunctuated jargon about 'hereditaments' and 'fee simple,' its 'and whereas the said Daniel Levy' in every other line, and its eventual plain provision for 'the said sum of £15,000 to remain charged upon the security of the hereditaments in the said recited Indenture ... until the expiration of one year computed from – ' that summer's day in that empty tower! The whole thing had been properly and innocently prepared by old Mother Hubbard, the 'little solicitor' whom Raffles had mentioned as having been in our house at school, from a copy of the original mortgage deed supplied in equal innocence by Mr Garland. I sometimes wonder what those worthy citizens would have said, if they had dreamt for a moment under what conditions of acute duress their deed was to be signed!

Signed it was, however, and with less demur than might have been expected of so inveterate a fighter as Dan Levy. But his one remaining course was obviously the line of least resistance; no other would square with his ingenious repudiation of the charge of treachery to Raffles, much less with his repeated protestations that he had always intended to perform his part of their agreement. It was to his immediate interest to convince us of his good faith, and up to this point he might well have thought he had succeeded in so doing. Raffles had concealed his full knowledge of the creature's duplicity, had enjoyed leading him on from lie to lie, and I had enjoyed listening almost as much as I now delighted in the dilemma in which Levy had landed himself; for either he must sign and look pleasant, or else abandon his innocent posture altogether; and so he looked as pleasant as he could, and signed in his handcuffs, with but the shadow of a fight for their immediate removal.

'And now,' said Levy, when I had duly witnessed his signature, 'I think I've about earned that little drop of my own champagne.'

'Not quite yet,' replied Raffles, in a tone like thin ice. 'We are only at the point we should have reached the moment I arrived at your house last night; you have now done under compulsion what you had agreed to do of your own free will then.'

Levy lay back in the bunk, plunged in billows of incongruous bunting, with fallen jaw and fiery eyes, an equal blend of anger and alarm. 'But I told you I wasn't myself last night,' he whined. 'I've said I was very sorry for all I done, but can't 'ardly remember doing. I say it again from the bottom of my 'eart.'

'I've no doubt you do,' said Raffles. 'But what you did after our arrival was nothing to what you had already done; it was only the last of those acts of treachery for which you are still on your trial – prisoner in the bunk!'

'But I thought I'd explained all the rest?' cried the prisoner, in a palsy of impotent rage and disappointment.

'You have,' said Raffles, 'in the sense of making your perfidy even plainer than it was before. Come, Mr Levy! I know every move you've made, and the game's been up longer than you think; you won't score a point by telling lies that contradict each other and aggravate your guilt. Have you nothing better to say why the sentence of the court should not be passed upon you?'

A sullen silence was broken by a more precise and staccato repetition of the question. And then to my amazement, I beheld the gross lower lip of Levy actually trembling, and a distressing flicker of the inflamed eyelids.

'I felt you'd swindled me,' he quavered out 'And I thought – I'd swindle – you.'

'Bravo!' cried Raffles. 'That's the first honest thing you've said; let me tell you, for your encouragement, that it reduces your punishment by twenty-five per cent. You will, nevertheless, pay a fine of fifteen hundred pounds for your latest little effort in low treason.'

Though not unprepared for some such ultimatum, I must own I heard it with dismay. On all sorts of grounds, some of them as unworthy as itself, this last demand failed to meet with my approval; and I determined to expostulate with Raffles before it was too late. Meanwhile I hid my feelings as best I could, and admired the spirit with which Dan Levy expressed his.

'I'll see you damned first!' he cried. 'It's blackmail!'

'Guineas,' said Raffles, 'for contempt of court.'

And more to my surprise than ever, not a little indeed to my secret disappointment, our captive speedily collapsed again, whimpering, moaning, gnashing his teeth, and clutching at the Red Ensign, with closed eyes and distorted face, so much as though he were about to have a fit that I caught up the half-bottle of champagne, and began removing the wire at a nod from Raffles.

'Don't cut the string just yet,' he added, however, with an eye on Levy – who instantly opened his.

'I'll pay up!' he whispered, feebly yet eagerly. 'It serves me right. I promise I'll pay up!'

'Good!' said Raffles. 'Here's your own cheque-book from your own room, and here's my fountain pen.'

'You won't take my word?'

'It's quite enough to have to take your cheque; it should have been hard cash.'

'So it shall be, Raffles, if you come up with me to my office!'

'I dare say.'

'To my bank, then!'

'I prefer to go alone. You will kindly make it an open cheque payable to bearer.'

The fountain pen was poised over the chequebook, but only because I had placed it in Levy's fingers, and was holding the cheque-book under them.

'And what if I refuse?' he demanded, with a last flash of his native spirit.

'We shall say goodbye, and give you until tonight.'

'All day to call for help in!' muttered Levy, all but to himself.

'Do you happen to know where you are?' Raffles asked him.

'No, but I can find out.'

'If you knew already you would also know that you might call till you were black in the face; but to keep you in blissful ignorance you will be bound a good deal more securely than you are at present. And to spare your poor voice you will also be very thoroughly gagged.'

Levy took remarkably little notice of either threat or gibe.

'And if I give in and sign?' said he, after a pause.

'You will remain exactly as you are, with one of us to keep you company, while the other goes up to town to cash your cheque. You can't expect me to give you a chance of stopping it, you know.'

This, again, struck me as a hard condition, if only prudent when one came to think of it from our point of view; still, it took even me by surprise, and I expected Levy to fling away the pen in disgust. He balanced it, however, as though also weighing the two alternatives very carefully in his mind, and during his deliberations his bloodshot eyes wandered from Raffles to me and back again to Raffles. In a word, the latest prospect appeared to disturb Mr Levy less than, for obvious reasons, it did me. Certainly for him it was the lesser of the two evils, and as such he seemed to accept it when he finally wrote out the cheque for fifteen hundred guineas (Raffles insisting on these), and signed it firmly before sinking back as though exhausted by the effort.

Raffles was as good as his word about the champagne now: dram by dram he poured the whole pint into the cup belonging to his flask, and dram by dram our prisoner tossed it off, but with closed eyes, like a delirious invalid, and towards the end, with a head so heavy that Raffles had to raise it from the rolled flag, though foul talons still came twitching out for more. It was an unlovely process, I will confess; but what was a pint, as Raffles said? At any rate I could bear him out that these potations had not been hocussed, and Raffles whispered the same for the flask which he handed me with Levy's revolver at the head of the wooden stairs.

'I'm coming down,' said I, 'for a word with you in the room below.'

Raffles looked at me with open eyes, then more narrowly at the red lids of Levy, and finally at his own watch.

'Very well, Bunny, but I must cut and run for my train in about a minute. There's a 9.24 which would get me to the bank before eleven, and back here by one or two.'

'Why go to the bank at all?' I asked him point-blank in the lower room.

'To cash his cheque before he has a chance of stopping it. Would you like to go instead of me, Bunny?'

'No, thank you!'

'Well, don't get hot about it; you've got the better billet of the two.'

'The softer one, perhaps.'

'Infinitely, Bunny, with the old bird full of his own champagne, and his own revolver in your pocket or your hand! The worst he can do is to start yelling out, and I really do believe that not a soul would hear him if he did. The gardeners are always at work on the other side of the main road. A passing boatload is the only danger, and I doubt if even they would hear.'

'My billet's all right,' said I, valiantly. 'It's yours that worries me.'

'Mine!' cried Raffles, with an almost merry laugh. 'My dear, good Bunny, you may make your mind easy about my little bit! Of course, it'll take some doing at the bank. I don't say it's a straight part there. But trust me to play it on my head.'

'Raffles,' I said, in a low voice that may have trembled, 'it's not a part for you to play at all! I don't mean the little bit at the bank. I mean this whole blackmailing part of the business. It's not like you, Raffles. It spoils the whole thing!'

I had got it off my chest without a hitch. But so far Raffles had not discouraged me. There was a look on his face which even made me think that he agreed with me in his heart. Both hardened as he thought it over.

'It's Levy who's spoilt the whole thing,' he rejoined obdurately in the end. 'He's been playing me false all the time, and he's got to pay for it.'

'But you never meant to make anything out of him, A.J.!'

'Well, I do now, and I've told you why. Why shouldn't I?'

'Because it's not your game!' I cried, with all the eager persuasion in my power. 'Because it's the sort of thing Dan Levy would do himself – it's *his* game, all right – it simply drags you down to his level – '

But there he stopped me with a look, and not the kind of look I often had from Raffles. It was no new feat of mine to make him angry, scornful, bitterly cynical or sarcastic. This, however, was a look of pain and even shame, as though he had suddenly seen himself in a new and peculiarly unlovely light.

'Down to it!' he exclaimed, with an irony that was not for me. 'As though there could be a much lower level than mine! Do you know, Bunny, I sometimes think my moral sense is ahead of yours?'

I could have laughed outright; but the humour that was the salt of him seemed suddenly to have gone out of Raffles.

'I know what I am,' said he, 'but I'm afraid you're getting a hopeless villain-worshipper!'

'It's not the villain I care about,' I answered, meaning every word. 'It's the sportsman behind the villain, as you know perfectly well.'

'I know the villain behind the sportsman rather better,' replied Raffles, laughing when I least expected it. 'But you're by way of forgetting his existence altogether. I shouldn't wonder if some day you wrote me up into a heavy hero, Bunny, and made me turn in my quicklime! Let this remind you what I always was and shall be to the end.'

And he took my hand, as I fondly hoped in surrender to my appeal to those better feelings which I knew I had for once succeeded in quickening within him.

But it was only to bid me a mischievous goodbye, ere he ran down the spiral stair, leaving me to listen till I lost his feathery foot-falls in the base of the tower, and then to mount guard over my tethered, handcuffed, somnolent, and yet always formidable prisoner at the top.

16

WATCH AND WARD

I well remember, as I set reluctant foot upon the wooden stair, taking a last and somewhat lingering look at the dust and dirt of the lower chamber, as one who knew not what might happen before he saw it again. The stain as of red rust in the lavatory basin, the gritty deposit in the bath, the verdigris on all the taps, the foul opacity of the windows, are among the trivialities that somehow stamped themselves upon my mind. One of the windows was open at the top, had been so long open that the aperture was curtained with cobwebs at each extremity, but in between I got quite a poignant picture of the Thames as I went upstairs. It was only a sinuous perspective of sunlit ripples twinkling between wooded gardens and open meadows, a fisherman or two upon the tow-path, a canoe in mid-stream, a gaunt church crowning all against the sky. But inset in such surroundings it was like a flash from a magic-lantern in a coal-cellar. And very loth was I to exchange that sunny peep for an indefinite prospect of my prisoner's person at close quarters.

Yet the first stage of my vigil proved such a sinecure as to give me some confidence for all the rest. Dan Levy opened neither his lips nor his eyes at my approach, but lay on his back with the Red Ensign drawn up to his chin, and the peaceful countenance of profound oblivion. I remember taking a good look at him, and thinking that his face improved remarkably in repose, that in death he might look fine. The forehead was higher and broader than I had realised, the thick lips were firm enough now, but the closing of the crafty little eyes was the greatest gain of all. On the whole, not only a better but a stronger face than it had been all the morning, a more formidable face by far. But the man had fallen asleep in his bonds, and forgotten them; he would wake up abject enough; if not, I had the means to reduce him to docility. Meanwhile, I was in no hurry to show my power, but stole on tiptoe to the locker, and took my seat by inches.

Levy did not move a muscle. No sound escaped him either, and somehow or other I should have expected him to snore; indeed, it might have come as a relief, for the silence of the tower soon got upon my nerves. It was not a complete silence; that was (and always is) the worst of it. The wooden stairs creaked more than once; there were little rattlings, faint and distant, as of a dried leaf or a loose window, in the bowels of the house; and though nothing came of any of these noises, except a fresh period of tension on my part, they made the skin act on my forehead every time. Then I remember a real anxiety over a blue-bottle, that must have come in through the open window just below, for suddenly it buzzed into my ken and looked like attacking Levy on the spot. Somehow I slew it with less noise than the brute itself was making; and not until after that breathless achievement did I realise how anxious I was to keep my prisoner asleep. Yet I had the revolver, and he lay handcuffed and bound down! It was in the next long silence that I became sensitive to another sound which indeed I had heard at intervals already, only to dismiss it from my mind as one of the signs of extraneous life which were bound to penetrate even to the top of my tower. It was a slow and regular beat, as of a sledge-hammer in a distant forge, or some sort of machinery only audible when there was absolutely nothing else to be heard. It could hardly be near at hand, for I could not hear it properly unless I held my breath. Then, however, it was always there, a sound that never ceased or altered, so that in the end I sat and listened to it and nothing else. I was not even looking at Levy when he asked me if I knew what it was.

His voice was quiet and civil enough, but it undoubtedly made me jump, and that brought a malicious twinkle into the little eyes that looked as though they had been studying me at their leisure. They were perhaps less violently bloodshot than before, the massive features calm and strong as they had been in slumber or its artful counterfeit.

'I thought you were asleep?' I snapped, and knew better for certain before he spoke.

'You see, that pint o' pop did me prouder than intended,' he explained. 'It's made a new man o' me, you'll be sorry to 'ear.'

I should have been sorrier to believe it, but I did not say so, or anything else just then. The dull and distant beat came back to the ear. And Levy again inquired if I knew what it was.

'Do you?' I demanded.

'Rather!' he replied, with cheerful certitude. 'It's the clock, of course.'

'What clock?'

'The one on the tower, a bit lower down, facing the road.'

'How do *you* know?' I demanded, with uneasy credulity.

'My good young man,' said Dan Levy, 'I know the face of that clock as well as I know the inside of this tower.'

'Then you do know where you are!' I cried, in such surprise that Levy grinned in a way that ill became a captive.

'Why,' said he, 'I sold the last tenant up, and nearly took the 'ouse myself instead o' the place I got. It was what first attracted me to the neighhour'ood.'

'Why couldn't you tell us the truth before?' I demanded, but my warmth merely broadened his grin.

'Why should I? It sometimes pays to seem more at a loss than you are.'

'It won't in this case,' said I through my teeth. But for all my austerity, and all his bonds, the prisoner continued to regard me with quiet but most disquieting amusement.

'I'm not so sure of that,' he observed at length. 'It rather paid, to my way of thinking, when Raffles went off to cash my cheque, and left you to keep an eye on me.'

'Oh, did it!' said I, with pregnant emphasis, and my right hand found comfort in my jacket pocket, on the butt of the old brute's own weapon.

'I only mean,' he rejoined, in a more conciliatory voice, 'that you strike me as being more open to reason than your flash friend.'

I said nothing to that.

'On the other 'and,' continued Levy, still more deliberately, as though he really was comparing us in his mind; 'on the other *hand*' stooping to pick up what he had dropped, 'you don't take so many risks. Raffles takes so many that he's bound to land you both in the jug some day, if he hasn't done it this time. I believe he has, myself. But it's no use hollering before you're out o' the wood.'

I agreed, with more confidence than I felt.

'Yet I wonder he never thought of it,' my prisoner went on as if to himself.

'Thought of what?'

'Only the clock. He must've seen it before, if you never did; you don't tell me this little bit o' kidnapping was a sudden idea! It's all been thought out and the ground gone over, and the clock seen, as I say. Seen going. Yet it never strikes our flash friend that a going clock's got to be wound up once a week, and it might be as well to find out which day!'

'How do you know he didn't?'

'Because this 'appens to be the day!'

And Levy lay back in the bunk with the internal chuckle that I was beginning to know so well, but had little thought to hear from him in his present predicament. It galled me the more because I felt that Raffles would certainly not have heard it in my place. But at least I had the satisfaction of flatly and profanely refusing to believe the prisoner's statement.

'That be blowed for a bluff!' was more or less what I said. 'It's too much of a coincidence to be anything else.'

'The odds are only six to one against it,' said Levy, indifferently. 'One of you takes them with his eyes open. It seems rather a pity that the other should feel bound to follow him to certain ruin. But I suppose you know your own business best.'

'At all events,' I boasted, 'I know better than to be bluffed by the most obvious lie I ever heard in my life. You tell me how you know about the man coming to wind the clock, and I may listen to you.'

'I know because I know the man; little Scotchman he is, nothing to run away from – though he looks as hard as nails – what there is of him,' said Levy, in a circumstantial and impartial flow that could not but carry some conviction. 'He comes over from Kingston every Tuesday on his bike; some time before lunch he comes, and sees to my own clocks on the same trip. That's how I know. But you needn't believe me if you don't like.'

'And where exactly does he come to wind this clock? I see nothing that can possibly have to do with it up here.'

'No,' said Levy; 'he comes no higher than the floor below.' I seemed to remember a kind of cupboard at the head of the spiral stair. 'But that's near enough.'

'You mean that we shall hear him?'

'And he us!' added Levy, with unmistakable determination.

'Look here, Mr Levy,' said I, showing him his own revolver, 'if we do hear anybody, I shall hold this to your head, and if he does hear us I shall blow out your beastly brains!'

The mere feeling that I was, perhaps, the last person capable of any such deed enabled me to grind out this shocking threat in a voice worthy of it, and with a face, I hoped, not less in keeping. It was all the more mortifying when Dan Levy treated my tragedy as farce; in fact, if anything could have made me as bad as my word, it would have been the guttural laugh with which he greeted it.

'Excuse me,' said he, dabbing his red eyes with the edge of the red bunting, 'but the thought of your letting that thing off in order to preserve silence – why, it's as droll as your whole attempt to play the cold-blooded villain – *you*!'

'I shall play him to some purpose,' I hissed, 'if you drive me to it. I laid you out last night, remember, and for two pins I'll do the same thing again this morning. So now you know.'

'That wasn't in cold blood,' said Levy, rolling his head from side to side; 'that was when the lot of us were brawling in our cups. I don't count that. You're in a false position, my dear sir. I don't mean last night or this morning – though I can see that you're no brigand or blackmailer at bottom – and I shouldn't wonder if you never forgave Raffles for letting you in for this partic'lar part of this partic'lar job. But that isn't what I mean. You've got in with a villain, but you ain't one yourself; that's where you're in the false position. He's the magsman, you're only the swell. *I* can see that. But the judge won't. You'll both get served the same, and in your case it'll be a thousand shames!'

He had propped himself on one elbow, and was speaking eagerly, persuasively, with almost a fatherly solicitude; yet I felt that both his words and their effect on me were being weighed and measured with meticulous discretion. And I encouraged him with a countenance as deliberately rueful and depressed, to an end which had only occurred to me with the significance of his altered tone.

'I can't help it,' I muttered. 'I must go through with the whole thing now.'

'Why must you?' demanded Levy. 'You've been led into a job that's none of your business, on be'alf of folks who're no friends of yours, and the job's developed into a serious crime, and the crime's going to be found out before you're an hour older. Why go through with it to certain quod?'

'There's nothing else for it,' I answered, with a sulky resignation, though my pulse was quick with eagerness for what I felt was coming.

And then it came.

'Why not get out of the whole thing,' suggested Levy, boldly, 'before it's too late?'

'How can I?' said I, to lead him on with a more explicit proposition.

'By first releasing me, and then clearing out yourself!'

I looked at him as though this was certainly an idea, as though I were actually considering it in spite of myself and Raffles; and his eagerness fed upon my apparent indecision. He held up his fettered hands, begging and cajoling me to remove his handcuffs, and I, instead of telling him it was not in my power to do so until Raffles returned, pretended to hesitate on quite different grounds.

'It's all very well,' I said, 'but are you going to make it worth my while?'

'Certainly!' cried he. 'Give me my chequebook out of my own pocket, where you were good enough to stow it before that blackguard left, and I'll write you one cheque for a hundred now, and another for another hundred before I leave this tower.'

'You really will?' I temporised.

'I swear it!' he asseverated; and I still believe he might have kept his word about that. But now I knew where he *had* been lying to me, and now was the time to let him know I knew it.

'Two hundred pounds,' said I, 'for the liberty you are bound to get for nothing, as you yourself have pointed out, when the man turns up to wind the clock? A couple of hundred to save less than a couple of hours?'

Levy changed colour as he saw his mistake, and his eyes flashed with sudden fury; otherwise his self-command was only less admirable than his presence of mind.

'It wasn't to save time,' said he; 'it was to save my face in the neighbourhood. The well-known money-lender found bound and handcuffed in an empty house! It means the first laugh at my expense, whoever has the last laugh. But you're quite right; it wasn't worth two hundred golden sovereigns. Let them laugh! At any rate you and your flash friend'll be laughing on the wrong side of your mouths before the day's out. So that's all there is to it, and you'd better start screwing up your courage if you want to do me in! I did mean to give you another chance in life – but by God I wouldn't now if you were to go down on your knees for one!'

Considering that he was bound and I was free, that I was armed and he defenceless, there was perhaps more humour than the prisoner saw in his picture of me upon my knees to him. Not that I saw it all at once myself. I was too busy wondering whether there could be anything in his clock-winding story after all. Certainly it was inconsistent with the big bribe offered for his immediate freedom; but it was with something more than mere adroitness that the money-lender had reconciled the two things. In his place I should have been no less anxious to keep my humiliating experience a secret from the world; with his means I could conceive myself prepared to pay as dearly for such secrecy. On the other hand, if his idea was to stop the huge cheque already given to Raffles, then there was indeed no time to be lost, and the only wonder was that Levy should have waited so long before making overtures to me.

Raffles had now been gone a very long time, as it seemed to me, but my watch had run down, and the clock on the tower did not strike. Why they kept it going at all was a mystery to me; but now that Dan Levy was lying still again, with set teeth and inexorable eyes, I heard it beating out the seconds more than ever like a distant sledgehammer, and sixty of these I counted up into a minute of such portentous duration that what had seemed many hours to me might easily have been less than one. I only knew that the sun, which had begun by pouring in at one port-hole and out at the other, which had bathed the prisoner in his bunk about the time of his trial by Raffles, now crowned me with fire if I sat upon the locker, and made its varnish sticky if I did not. The atmosphere of the place was fast becoming unendurable in its unwholesome heat and sour stagnation. I sat in my shirt-sleeves at the top of the stairs, where one got such air as entered by the open window below. Levy had kicked off his covering of scarlet bunting, with a sudden oath which must have been the only sound within the tower for an hour at least; all the rest of the time he lay with fettered fists clenched upon his breast, with fierce eyes fixed upon the top of the bunk, and something about the whole man that I was forced to watch, something indomitable and intensely alert, a curious suggestion of smouldering fires on the point of leaping into flame.

I feared this man in my heart of hearts. I may as well admit it frankly. It was not that he was twice my size, for I had the like advantage in point of years; it was not that I had any reason to distrust the strength of his bonds or the efficacy of the weapon in my possession. It was a question of personality, not of material advantage or disadvantage, or of physical fear at all. It was simply the spirit of the man that dominated mine. I felt that my mere flesh and blood would at any moment give a good account of his, as well they might with the odds that were on my side. Yet that did not lessen the sense of subtle and essential inferiority, which grew upon my nerves with almost every minute of that endless morning, and made me long for the relief of physical contest even on equal terms. I could have set the old ruffian free, and thrown his revolver out of the window, and then said to him, 'Come on! Your weight against my age, and may the devil take the worse man!' Instead, I must sit glaring at him to mask my qualms. And after much thinking about the kind of conflict that could never be, in the end came one of a less heroic but not less desperate type, before there was time to think at all.

Levy had raised his head, ever so little, but yet enough for my vigilance. I saw him listening. I listened too. And down below in the core of the tower I heard, or thought I heard, a step like a feather, and then after some moments another. But I had spent those moments in gazing instinctively down the stair; it was the least rattle of the handcuffs that brought my eyes like lightning back to the bunk; and there was Levy with hollow palms about his mouth, and his mouth wide open for the roar that my own palms stifled in his throat.

Indeed, I had leapt upon him once more like a fiend, and for an instant I enjoyed a shameful advantage; it can hardly have lasted longer. The brute first bit me through the hand, so that I carry his mark to this day; then, with his own hands, he took me by the throat, and I thought that my last moments were come. He squeezed so hard that I thought my windpipe must burst, thought my eyes must leave their sockets. It was the grip of a gorilla, and it was accompanied by a spate of curses and the grin of a devil incarnate. All my dreams of equal combat had not prepared me for superhuman power on his part, such utter impotence on mine. I tried to wrench myself from his murderous clasp, and was nearly felled by the top of the bunk. I hurled myself out sideways, and out he came after me, tearing down the peg to which his handcuffs were tethered; that only gave him the better grip upon my throat, and he never relaxed it for an instant, scrambling to his feet when I staggered to mine, for by them alone was he fast now to the banisters.

Meanwhile I was feeling in an empty pocket for his revolver, which had fallen out as we struggled on the floor. I saw it there now with my starting eyeballs, kicked about by our shuffling feet. I tried to make a dive for it, but Levy had seen it also, and he kicked it through the banisters without relaxing his murderous hold. I could have sworn afterwards that I heard the weapon fall with a clatter on the wooden stairs. But what I still remember hearing most distinctly (and feeling hot upon my face) is the stertorous breathing that was unbroken by a single syllable after the first few seconds.

It was a brutal encounter, not short and sharp like the one over-night, but horribly protracted. Nor was all the brutality by any means on one side; neither will I pretend that I was getting much more than my deserts in the defeat that threatened to end in my extinction. Not for an instant had my enemy loosened his deadly clutch, and now he had me penned against the banisters, and my one hope was that they would give way before our united weight, and precipitate us both into the room below. That would be better than being slowly throttled, even if it were only a better death. Other chance there was none, and I was actually trying to fling myself over, beating the air with both hands wildly, when one of them closed upon the butt of the revolver that I thought had been kicked into the room below!

I was too far gone to realise that a miracle had happened – to be so much as puzzled by it then. But I was not too far gone to use that revolver, and to use it as I would have done on cool reflection. I thrust it under my opponent's armpit, and I fired through into space. The report was deafening. It did its work. Levy let go of me, and staggered back as though I had really shot him. And that instant I was brandishing his weapon in his face.

'You tried to shoot me! You tried to shoot me!' he gasped twice over through a livid mask.

'No, I didn't!' I panted. 'I tried to frighten you, and I jolly well succeeded! But I'll shoot you like a dog if you don't get back to your kennel and lie down.'

He sat and gasped upon the side of the bunk. There was no more fight in him. His very lips were blue. I put the pistol back in my pocket, and retracted my threat in a sudden panic.

'There! It's your own fault if you so much as see it again,' I promised him, in a breathless disorder only second to his own.

'But you jolly nearly strangled me. And now we're a pretty pair!'

His hands grasped the edge of the bunk, and he leant his weight on them, breathing very hard. It might have been an attack of asthma, or it might have been a more serious seizure, but it was a case for stimulants if ever I saw one, and in the nick of time I remembered the flask that Raffles had left with me. It was the work of a very few seconds to pour out a goodly ration, and of but another for Daniel Levy to toss off the raw spirit like water. He was begging for more before I had helped myself. And more I gave him in the end; for it was no small relief to me to watch the leaden hue disappearing from the flabby face, and the laboured breathing gradually subside, even if it meant a renewal of our desperate hostilities.

But all that was at an end; the man was shaken to the core by his perfectly legitimate attempt at my destruction. He looked dreadfully old and hideous as he got bodily back into the bunk of his own accord. There, when I had yielded to his further importunities, and the flask was empty, he fell at length into a sleep as genuine as the last was not; and I was still watching over the poor devil, keeping the flies off him, and sometimes fanning him with a flag, less perhaps from humane motives than to keep him quiet as long as possible, when Raffles returned to light up the tableau like a sinister sunbeam.

Raffles had had his own adventures in town, and I soon had reason to feel thankful that I had not gone up instead of him. It seemed he had foreseen from the first the possibility of trouble at the bank over a large and absolutely open cheque. So he had gone first to the Chelsea studio in which he played the painter who never painted but kept a whole wardrobe of disguises for the models he never hired. Thence he had issued on this occasion in the living image of a well-known military man about town who was also well known to be a client of Dan Levy's. Raffles said the cashier stared at him, but the cheque was cashed without a word. The unfortunate part of it was that in returning to his cab he had encountered an acquaintance both of his own and of the spendthrift soldier, and had been greeted evidently in the latter capacity.

'It was a jolly difficult little moment, Bunny. I had to say there was some mistake, and I had to remember to say it in a manner equally unlike my own and the other beggar's! But all's well that ends well; and if you'll do exactly what I tell you I think we may flatter ourselves that a happy issue is at last in sight.'

'What am I to do now?' I asked with some misgiving.

'Clear out of this, Bunny, and wait for me in town. You've done jolly well, old fellow, and so have I in my own department of the game. Everything's in order, down to those fifteen hundred guineas which are now concealed about my person in as hard cash as I can carry. I've seen old Garland and given him back his promissory note myself, with Levy's undertaking about the mortgage. It was a pretty trying interview, as you can understand; but I couldn't help wondering what the poor old boy would say if he dreamt what sort of pressure I've been applying on his behalf! Well, it's all over now except our several exits from the surreptitious stage. I can't make mine without our sleeping partner, but you would really simplify matters, Bunny, by not waiting for us.'

There was a good deal to be said for such a course, though it went not a little against my grain. Raffles had changed his clothes and had a bath in town, to say nothing of his luncheon. I was by this time indescribably dirty and dishevelled, besides feeling fairly famished now that mental relief allowed a thought for one's lower man. Raffles had foreseen my plight, and had actually prepared a way of escape for me by the front door in broad daylight. I need not recapitulate the elaborate story he had told the caretaking gardener across the road; but he had borrowed the gardener's keys as a probable purchaser of the property, who had to meet his builder and a business friend at the house during the course of the afternoon. I was to be the builder, and in that capacity to give the gardener an ingenious message calculated to leave Raffles and Levy in uninterrupted possession until my return. And of course I was never to return at all.

The whole thing seemed to me a super-subtle means to a far simpler end than the one we had achieved by stealth in the dead of the previous night. But it was Raffles all over and I ultimately acquiesced, on the understanding that we were to meet again in the Albany at seven o'clock, preparatory to dining somewhere in final celebration of the whole affair.

But much was to happen before seven o'clock, and it began happening. I shook the dust of that derelict tower from my feet; for one of them trod on something at the darkest point of the descent; and the thing went tinkling down ahead on its own account, until it lay shimmering in the light on a lower landing, where I picked it up.

Now I had not said much to Raffles about my hitherto inexplicable experience with the revolver, when I thought it had gone through the banisters, but found it afterwards in my hand. Raffles said it would not have gone through, that I must have been all but over the banisters myself when I grasped the butt as it protruded through them on the level of the floor. This he said (like many another thing) as though it made an end of the matter. But it was not the end of the matter in my own mind; and now I could have told him what the explanation was, or at least to what conclusion I had jumped. I had half a mind to climb all the way up again on purpose to put him in the wrong upon the point. Then I remembered how anxious he had seemed to get rid of me, and for other reasons also I decided to let him wait a bit for his surprise.

Meanwhile my own plans were altered, and when I had delivered my egregious message to the gardener across the road, I sought the nearest shops on my way to the nearest station; and at one of the shops I got me a clean collar, at another a tooth-brush; and all I did at the station was to utilise my purchases in the course of such scanty toilet as the lavatory accommodation would permit.

A few minutes later I was inquiring my way to a house which it took me another twenty or twenty-five to find.

17

A SECRET SERVICE

This house also was on the river, but it was very small bricks-and-mortar compared with the other two. One of a semi-detached couple built close to the road, with narrow strips of garden to the river's brim, its dingy stucco front and its green Venetian blinds conveyed no conceivable attraction beyond that of a situation more likely to prove a drawback three seasons out of the four. The wooden gate had not swung home behind me before I was at the top of a somewhat dirty flight of steps, contemplating blistered paint and ground glass fit for a bathroom window, and listening to the last reverberations of an obsolete type of bell. There was indeed something oppressively and yet prettily Victorian about the riparian retreat to which Lady Laura Belsize had retired in her impoverished widowhood.

It was not for Lady Laura that I asked, however, but for Miss Belsize, and the almost slatternly maid really couldn't say whether Miss Belsize was in or whether she wasn't. She might be in the garden, or she might be on the river. Would I step inside and wait a minute? I would and did, but it was more minutes than one that I was kept languishing in an interior as dingy as the outside of the house. I had time to take the whole thing in. There were massive remnants of deservedly unfashionable furniture. The sofa I can still see in my mind's eye, and the steel fire-irons, and the crystal chandelier. An aged and gigantic Broadwood occupied nearly half the room; and in a cheap frame thereon, inviting all sorts of comparisons and contrasts, stood a full-length portrait of Camilla Belsize resplendent in contemporary court kit.

I was still studying that frankly barbaric paraphernalia – the feather, the necklace, the coiled train – and wondering what noble kinsman had come to the rescue for the great occasion, and why Camilla should have looked so bored with her finery, when the door opened and she herself entered – not even very smartly dressed – and looking anything but bored, although I say it.

But she did seem astonished, anxious, indignant, reproachful, and to my mind still more nervous and distressed, though this hardly showed through the loopholes of her pride. And as for her white serge coat and skirt, they looked as though they had seen considerable service on the river, and I immediately perceived that one of the large enamel buttons was missing from the coat.

Up to that moment, I may now confess, I had been suffering from no slight nervous anxiety of my own. But all qualms were lost in sheer excitement when I spoke.

'You may well wonder at this intrusion,' I began. 'But I thought this must be yours, Miss Belsize.'

And from my waistcoat pocket I produced the missing button of enamel.

'Where did you find it?' inquired Miss Belsize, with an admirably slight increase of astonishment in voice and look. 'And how did you know it was mine?' came quickly in the next breath.

'I didn't know,' I answered. 'I guessed. It was the shot of my life!'

'But you don't say where you found it?'

'In an empty house not far from here.'

She had held her breath; now I felt it like the lightest zephyr. And quite unconsciously I had retained the enamel button.

'Well, Mr Manders? I'm very much obliged to you. But may I have it back again?'

I returned her property. We had been staring at each other all the time. I stared still harder as she repeated her perfunctory thanks.

'So it was you!' I said, and was sorry to see her looking purposely puzzled at that, but thankful when the reckless light outshone all the rest in those chameleon eyes of hers.

'Who did you think it was?' she asked me with a frosty little smile.

'I didn't know if it was anybody at all. I didn't know what to think,' said I, quite candidly. 'I simply found his pistol in my hand.'

'Whose pistol?'

'Dan Levy's.'

'Good!' she said grimly. 'That makes it all the better.'

'You saved my life.'

'I thought you had taken his – and I'd collaborated!'

There was not a tremor in her voice; it was cautious, eager, daring, intense, but absolutely her own voice now.

'No,' I said, 'I didn't shoot the fellow, but I made him think I had.'

'You made me think so too, until I heard what you said to him.'

'Yet you never made a sound yourself.'

'I should think not! I made myself scarce instead.'

'But, Miss Belsize, I shall go perfectly mad if you don't tell me how you happened to be there at all!'

'Don't you think it's for you to tell me that about yourself and – all of you?'

'Oh, I don't mind which of us fires first!' said I, excitedly.

'Then I will,' she said at once, and took me to the dreadful sofa at the inner end of the room, and sat down as though it were the most ordinary experience she had to relate. Nor could I believe the things that had really happened, and all so recently, as we talked them over in that commonplace environment of faded gentility. There was a window behind us, overlooking the ribbon of lawn and the cord of gravel, and the bunch of willows that hedged them from the Thames. It all looked unreal to me, unreal in its very realism as the scene of our incredible conversation.

'You know what happened the other afternoon – I mean the day they couldn't play,' began Miss Belsize, 'because you were there; and though you didn't stay to hear all that came out afterwards, I expect you know everything now. Mr Raffles would be sure to tell you; in fact, I heard poor dear Mr Garland give him leave. It's a dreadful story from every point of view. Nobody comes out of it with flying colours, but what nice person could cope with a horrid money-lender? Mr Raffles, perhaps – if you call him nice!'

I said that was about the worst thing I called him. I mentioned some of the other things. Miss Belsize listened to them with exemplary patience.

'Well,' she resumed, 'he was quite nice about this. I will say that for him. He said he knew Mr Levy pretty well, and would see what could be done. But he spoke like an executioner who was going to see what could be done with the condemned man! And all the time I was wondering what had been done already at Carlsbad – what exactly that horrid creature meant when he was talking *at* Mr Raffles before us all. Well, of course, I knew what he meant us to think he meant; but was there, could there be, anything in it?'

Miss Belsize looked at me as though she expected an answer, only to stop me the moment I opened my mouth to speak.

'I don't want to know, Mr Manders! Of course you know all about Mr Raffles' – there was a touch of feeling in this – 'but it's nothing to me, though in this case I should certainly have been on his side. You said yourself that it could only have been a practical joke, if there was anything in it at all, and so I tried to think in spite of those horrid men who were following him about at Lord's, even in spite of the way he vanished with them after him. But he never came near the match again – though he had travelled all the way from Carlsbad to see it! Why had he ever been there? What had he really done there? And what could he possibly do to rescue anybody from Mr Levy, if he himself was already in Levy's power?'

'You don't know Raffles,' said I, promptly enough this time. 'He never was in any man's power for many minutes. I would back him to save the most desperate situation you could devise.'

'You mean by some desperate deed? That's what I feared,' declared Miss Belsize, rather strenuously. 'Something really had happened at Carlsbad; something worse was by way of happening next. For Teddy's sake,' she whispered, 'and his poor father's!'

I agreed that old Raffles stuck at nothing for his friends, and Miss Belsize again said that was what she had feared. Her tone had completely altered about Raffles, as well it might. I thought it would have broken with gratitude when she spoke of the unlucky father and son.

'And I was right!' she exclaimed, with that other kind of feeling to which I found it harder to put a name. 'I came home miserable from the match on Saturday – '

'Though Teddy had done so well!' I was fool enough to interject.

'I couldn't help thinking about Mr Raffles,' replied Camilla, with a flash of her frank eyes, 'and wondering, and wondering, what had happened. And then on Sunday I saw him on the river.'

'He didn't tell me.'

'He didn't know I recognised him; he was disguised – absolutely!' said Camilla Belsize under her breath. 'But he couldn't disguise himself from me,' she added as though glorying in her perspicacity.

'Did you tell him so, Miss Belsize?'

'Not I, indeed! I didn't speak to him; it was no business of mine. But there he was, at the bottom of Mr Levy's garden, having a good look at the boathouse when nobody was about. Why? What could his object be? And why disguise himself? I thought of the affair at Carlsbad, and I felt certain that something of the kind was going to happen again!'

'Well?'

'What could I do? Should I do anything at all? Was it any business of mine? You may imagine the way I cross-questioned myself, and you may imagine the crooked answers I got! I won't bore you with the psychology of the thing; it's pretty obvious after all. It was not so much a case of doing the best as of knowing the worst. All day yesterday there were no developments of any sort, and there was no sign of Mr Raffles; nothing had happened in the night, or we should have heard of it; but that made me all the more certain that something or other would happen last night. The week's grace was nearly up – you know what I mean – their last week at their own house. If anything was to be done, it was about time, and I knew Mr Raffles was going to do something. I wanted to know what – that was all.'

'Quite right, too!' I murmured. But I doubt if Miss Belsize heard me; she was in no need of my encouragement or my approval. The old light – her own light – the reckless light – was burning away in her brilliant eyes!

'The night before,' she went on, 'I hardly slept a wink; last night I preferred not to go to bed at all. I told you I sometimes did weird things that astonished the natives of these suburban shores. Well, last night, if it wasn't early this morning, I made my weirdest effort yet. I have a canoe, you know; just now I almost live in it. Last night I went out unbeknowns after midnight, partly to reassure myself, partly – I beg your pardon, Mr Manders?'

'I didn't speak.'

'Your face shouted!'

'I'd rather you went on.'

'But if you know what I'm going to say?'

Of course I knew, but I dragged it from her none the less. The nebulous white-shirted figure in the canoe, that had skimmed past Dan Levy's frontage as we were trying to get him aboard his own pleasure-boat, and again past the empty house when we were in the act of disembarking him there, that figure was the trim and slim one now at my side. She had seen us – searched for us – each time. Our voices she had heard and recognised; only our actions, or rather that midnight deed of ours, had she misinterpreted. She would not admit it to me, but I still believe she feared it was a dead body that we had shipped at dead of night to hide away in that desolate tower.

Yet I cannot think she thought it in her heart. I rather fancy (what she indeed averred) that some vague inkling of the truth flashed across her at least as often as that monstrous hypothesis. But know she must; therefore, after boldly ascertaining that nothing was known of the master's whereabouts at Levy's house, but that no uneasiness was entertained on his account, this young woman, true to the audacity which I had seen in her eyes from the first, had taken the still bolder step of landing on the rank lawn and entering the empty tower to discover its secret, for herself. Her stealthy step upon the spiral stair had been the signal for my mortal struggle with Dan Levy. She had heard the whole, and even seen a little of that; in fact, she had gathered enough from Levy's horrible imprecations to form later a rough but not incorrect impression of the situation between him and Raffles and me. As for the moneylender's language, it was with a welcome gleam of humour that Miss

Belsize assured me she had 'gone too straight to hounds' in her time to be as completely paralysed by it as her mother's neighbours might have been. And as for the revolver, it had fallen at her feet, and first she thought I was going to follow it over the banisters, and before she could think again she had restored the weapon to my wildly clutching hand!

'But when you fired I felt a murderess,' she said. 'So you see I misjudged you for the second time.'

If I am conveying a dash of flippancy in our talk, let me earnestly declare that it was hardly even a dash. It was but a wry and rueful humour on the girl's part, and that only towards the end, but I can promise my worst critic that I was never less facetious in my life. I was thinking in my heavy way that I had never looked into such eyes as these, so bold, so sad, so merry with it all! I was thinking that I had never listened to such a voice, or come across recklessness and sentiment so harmonised, save also in her eyes! I was thinking that there never was a girl to touch Camilla Belsize, or a man either except A.J. Raffles! And yet –

And yet it was over Raffles that she took all the wind from my sails, exactly as she had done at Lord's, only now she did it at parting, and sent me off into the dusk a slightly puzzled and exceedingly exasperated man.

'Of course,' said Camilla at her garden gate, 'of course you won't repeat a word of what I've told you, Mr Manders?'

'You mean about your adventures last night and today?' said I, somewhat taken aback.

'I mean every single thing we've talked about!' was her sweeping reply. 'Not a syllable must go an inch further; otherwise I shall be very sorry I ever spoke to you.'

As though she had come and confided in me of her own accord! But I passed that, even if I noticed it at the time.

'I won't tell a soul, of course,' I said, and fidgeted. 'That is – except – I suppose you don't mind – '

'I do! There must be no exceptions.'

'Not even old Raffles?'

'Mr Raffles least of all!' cried Camilla Belsize, with almost a forked flash from those masterful eyes. 'Mr Raffles is the last person in the world who must ever know a single thing.'

'Not even that it was you who absolutely saved the situation for him and me?' I asked, wistfully; for I much wanted these two to think better of each other; and it had begun to look as though I had my wish, so far as Camilla was concerned, while I had only to tell Raffles everything to make him her slave for life. But now she was adamant on the point, adamant heated in some hidden flame.

'It's rather hard lines on me, Mr Manders, if because I go and get excited, and twist off a button in my excitement, as I suppose I must have done – unless it's a judgment on me – it's rather hard lines if you give me away when I never should have given myself away to you!'

This was unkind. It was still more unfair in view of the former passage between us to the same tune. I was evidently getting no credit for my very irksome fidelity. I helped myself to some at once.

'You gave yourself away to me at Lord's all right,' said I, cheerfully. 'And I never let out a word of that.'

'Not even to Mr Raffles?' she asked, with a quick unguarded intonation that was almost wistful.

'Not a word,' was my reply. 'Raffles has no idea you noticed anything, much less how keen you were for me to warn him.'

Miss Belsize looked at me a moment with civil war in her splendid eyes. Then something won – I think it was only her pride – and she was holding out her hand.

'He must never know a word of this either,' said she, firmly as at first. 'And I hope you'll forgive me for not trusting you quite as I always shall for the future.'

'I'll forgive you everything, Miss Belsize, except your dislike of dear old Raffles!'

I had spoken quite earnestly, keeping her hand; she drew it away as I made my point.

'I don't dislike him,' she answered in a strange tone; but with a stranger stress she added, 'I don't *like* him either.'

And even then I could not see what the verb should have been, or why Miss Belsize should turn away so quickly in the end, and snatch her eyes away quicker still.

I saw them, and thought of her, all the way back to the station, but not an inch further. So I need no sympathy on that score. If I did, it would have been just the same that July evening, for I saw somebody else and had something else to think about from the moment I set foot upon the platform. It was the wrong platform. I was about to cross by the bridge when a down train came rattling in, and out jumped a man I knew by sight before it stopped.

The man was Mackenzie, the incorrigibly Scotch detective whom we had met at Milchester Abbey, who I always thought had kept an eye on Raffles ever since. He was across the platform before the train pulled up, and I did what Raffles would have done in my place. I ran after him.

'Ye ken Dan Levy's hoose by the river?' I heard him babble to his cabman, with wilful breadth of speech. 'Then drive there, mon, like the deevil himsel'!'

18

THE DEATH OF A SINNER

What was I to do? I knew what Raffles would have done; he would have outstripped Mackenzie in his descent upon the moneylender, beaten the cab on foot most probably, and dared Dan Levy to denounce him to the detective. I could see a delicious situation, and Raffles conducting it inimitably to a triumphant issue. But I was not Raffles, and what was more I was due already at his chambers in the Albany. I must have been talking to Miss Belsize by the hour together; to my horror I found it close upon seven by the station clock; and it was some minutes past when I plunged into the first up train. Waterloo was reached before eight, but I was a good hour late at the Albany, and Raffles let me know it in his shirt-sleeves from the window.

'I thought you were dead, Bunny!' he muttered down as though he wished I were. I scaled his staircase at two or three bounds, and began all about Mackenzie in the lobby.

'So soon!' says Raffles, with a mere lift of the eyebrows. 'Well, thank God, I was ready for him again.'

I now saw that Raffles was not dressing, though he had changed his clothes, and this surprised me for all my breathless preoccupation. But I had the reason at a glance through the folding-doors into his bedroom. The bed was cumbered with clothes and an open suit-case. A Gladstone bag stood strapped and bulging; a travelling rug lay ready for rolling up, and Raffles himself looked out of training in his travelling tweeds.

'Going away?' I ejaculated.

'Rather!' said he, folding a smoking jacket. 'Isn't it about time after what you've told me?'

'But you were packing before you knew!'

'Then for God's sake go and do the same yourself!' he cried, 'and don't ask questions now. I was beginning to pack enough for us both, but you'll have time to shove in a shirt and collar of your own if you jump straight into a hansom. I'll take the tickets, and we'll meet on the platform at five to nine.'

'What platform, Raffles?'

'Charing Cross. Continental train.'

'But where the deuce do you think of going?'

'Australia, if you like! We'll discuss it in our flight across Europe.'

'Our flight!' I repeated. 'What has happened since I left you, Raffles?'

'Look here, Bunny, you go and pack!' was all my answer from a savage face, as I was fairly driven to the door. 'Do you realise that you were due here one golden hour ago, and have I asked what happened to you? Then don't you ask rotten questions that there's no time to answer. I'll tell you everything in the train, Bunny.'

And my name at the end in a different voice, and his hand for an instant on my shoulder as I passed out, were my only consolation for his truly terrifying behaviour, my only comfort and reassurance of any kind, until we really were off by the night mail from Charing Cross.

Raffles was himself again by that time, I was thankful to find, nor did he betray that dread or expectation of pursuit which would have tallied with his previous manner. He merely looked relieved when the Embankment lights ran right and left in our wake. I remember one of his remarks, that they made the finest necklace in the world when all was said, and another that Big Ben was the Koh-i-noor of the London lights. But he had also a quizzical eye upon the paper bag from which I was endeavouring to make a meal at last. And more than once he wagged his head with a humorous admixture of reproof and sympathy; for with shamefaced admissions and downcast pauses I was allowing him to suppose I had been drinking at some riverside public-house instead of hurrying up to town, but that the *rencontre* with Mackenzie had served to sober me.

'Poor Bunny! We won't pursue the matter any further; but I do know where we both should have been between seven and eight. It was as nice a little dinner as I ever ordered in my life. And to think that we never turned up to eat a bite of it!'

'Didn't *you*?' I queried, and my sense of guilt deepened to remorse as Raffles shook his head.

'No fear, Bunny! I wanted to see you safe and sound. That was what made me so stuffy when you did turn up.'

Loud were my lamentations, and earnest my entreaties to Raffles to share the contents of my paper bag; but not he. To replace such a feast as he had ordered with sandwiches and hard-boiled eggs would be worse than going healthily hungry for once; it was all very well for me who knew not what I had missed. Not that Raffles was hungry by his own accounts; he had merely fancied a little dinner, more after my heart than his, for our last on British soil.

This, and the way he said it, brought me back to the heart of things; for beneath his frothy phrases I felt that the wine of life was bitter to his taste. His gayety now afforded no truer criterion to his real feelings than had his petulance at the Albany. What had happened since our parting in that fatal tower, to make this wild flight necessary without my news, and whither in all earnest were we to fly?

'Oh, nothing!' said Raffles, in unsatisfactory answer to my first question. 'I thought you would have seen that we couldn't clear out too soon after restoring poor Shylock, like our brethren in the song, "to his friends and his relations".'

'But I thought you had something else for him to sign?'

'So I had, Bunny.'

'What was that?'

'A plain statement of all he had suborned me to do for him, and what he had given me for doing it,' said Raffles, as he lit a Sullivan from his last easeful. 'One might almost call it a receipt for the letter I stole and he destroyed.'

'And did he sign that?'

'I insisted on it for our protection.'

'Then we are protected, and yet we cut and run?'

Raffles shrugged his shoulders as we hurtled between the lighted platforms of Herne Hill.

'There's no immunity from a clever cove like that, Bunny, unless you send him to another world or put the thick of this one between you. He may hold his tongue about the last twenty-four hours – I believe he will – but that needn't prevent him from setting old Mackenzie to watch us day and night. So we are not going to stay to be watched. We are starting off round the world for a change. Before we get very far Mr Shylock may be in the jug himself; that accursed letter won't be the only incriminating thing against him, you take my word. Then we can come back trailing clouds of glory, and blowing clouds of Sullivan. Then we can have our *secondes noces* – meaning second knocks, Bunny, and more power to our elbows when we get them!'

But I was not convinced. There was something else at the bottom of this sudden impulse and its inconceivably sudden execution. Why had he never told me of this plan? Well, because it had never become one until after the morning's work at Levy's bank, in itself a reason for being out of the way, as I myself admitted. But he would have told me if only I had turned up at seven: he had never meant to give me time for much packing, added Raffles, as he was anxious that neither of us should leave the impression that we had gone far afield.

I thought this was childish, and treating me like a child, to which, however, I was used; but more than ever did I feel that Raffles was not being frank with me, that he for one was making good his escape from something or somebody besides Dan Levy. And in the end he admitted that this was so. But we had not dashed through Sitting-bourne and Faversham before I wormed my way to about the last discovery that I expected to make concerning A.J. Raffles.

'What an inquisitor you are, Bunny!' said he, putting down an evening paper that he had only just taken up. 'Can't you see that this whole show has been no ordinary one for me? I've been fighting for a crowd I rather love. Their battle has got on my nerves as none of my own ever did; and now it's won I honestly funk their gratitude as much as anything.'

That was another hard saying to swallow; and yet, as Raffles said it, I knew it to be true. He was looking me full in the face in the ample light of the first-class compartment, which we of course had to ourselves. Some softening influence seemed to have been at work upon him; he looked resolute as ever, but full of regret, than which nothing was rarer in A.J.

'I suppose,' said I, 'that poor old Garland has treated you to a pretty good dose already?'

'Yes, Bunny; that he has.'

'And well he may, and well may Teddy and Camilla Belsize!'

'But I couldn't do with it from them,' said Raffles, with quite a bitter little laugh. 'Teddy wasn't there, of course; he's up north for that rotten match the team play nowadays against Liverpool. But the game's fizzling, he'll be home tomorrow, and I simply can't face him and his Camilla. He'll be a married man before we see him again,' added Raffles, getting hold of his evening paper once more.

'Is that to come off so soon?'

'The sooner the better,' said Raffles, strangely.

'You're not quite happy about it,' said I, with execrable tact, I know, and yet deliberately, because his view of this marriage had always puzzled me.

'I'm happy as long as they are,' responded Raffles, not without a laugh at his own meritorious sentiment. 'I only wish,' he sighed, 'that they were both absolutely worthy of each other!'

'And you don't think they are?'

'No, I don't.'

'You think such a lot of young Garland?'

'I'm very fond of him, Bunny.'

'But you see his faults?'

'I've always seen them; they're not full-fathom-five like mine!'

'Yet you think she's not good enough for him?'

'Not good enough – she?' and he stopped himself at that. But his voice was enough for me; the unspoken antithesis was stronger than words could have made it. Scales fell from my eyes. 'Where on earth did you get that idea?'

'I thought it was yours, A.J.'

'But why?'

'You seemed to disapprove of the engagement from the first.'

'So I did, after what poor Teddy had been up to in his extremity! I may as well be honest about that now. It was all right in a pal of ours, Bunny, but all wrong in the man who dreamt of marrying Camilla Belsize.'

'Yet you have just been moving heaven and hell to make it possible for them to marry after all!'

Raffles made another attempt upon his paper. I marvel now that he let me catechise him as I was doing. But the truth had just dawned upon me, and I simply had to see it whole as the risen sun, whereas Raffles seemed under no such passionate necessity to keep it to himself.

'Teddy's all right,' said he, inconsistently. 'He'll never try anything of the kind again; he's had a lesson for life. Besides, I don't often take my hand from the plough, as you ought to know. Bunny. It was I who brought those two together. But it was none of my mundane business to put them asunder again.'

'It was you who brought them together?' I repeated insidiously.

'More or less, Bunny. It was at some cricket week, if it wasn't two weeks running; they were pals already, but she and I were greater pals before the first week was over.'

'And yet you didn't cut him out!'

'My dear Bunny, I should hope not.'

'But you might have done, A.J.; don't tell me you couldn't if you'd tried.'

Raffles played with his paper without replying. He was no coxcomb. But neither would he ape an alien humility.

'It wouldn't have been the game, Bunny – won or lost – Teddy or no Teddy: And yet,' he added, with pensive candour, 'we were getting on like a semi-detached house on fire! I burnt my fingers, I don't mind telling you; if I hadn't been what I am, Bunny, I might have taken my courage in all ten of 'em, and "put it to the touch, to win or lose it all."'

'I wish you had,' I whispered, as he studied his paper upside down.

'Why, Bunny? What rot you do talk!' he cried, but only with the skin-deep irritation of a half-hearted displeasure.

'She's the only woman I ever met,' I went on unguardedly, 'who was your mate at heart – in pluck – in temperament!'

'How the devil do you know?' cried Raffles, off his own guard now, and staring in my guilty face.

But I have never denied that I could emulate his presence of mind upon occasion.

'You forget what a lot we saw of each other last Thursday in the rain.'

'Did she talk about me then?'

'A little.'

'Had she her knife in me, Bunny?'

'Well – yes – a little!'

Raffles smiled stoically: it was a smile of duty done and odds well damned.

'Up to the hilt, Bunny, up to the hilt is what you mean. I stuck it in for her. It's easily done, and it needed doing, for my sake if not for hers. Sooner or later I should have choked her off, so the sooner the better. You play them false, you cut a dance, you let them down over something that doesn't matter, and they'll never give you a dog's chance over anything that does! I got her to write and never answered. What do you think of that for a cavalier swine? I said I'd call before I went abroad, and only wired to say sorry I couldn't. I don't say it would or could have been all right otherwise; but you see it was all right for Teddy before I got back! Which was as it was to be. She would hardly look at me at first last week; but, Bunny, she wasn't above looking when that old Shylock was playing at giving me away before them all. She looked at him, and she looked at me, and I've got one of the looks she gave him, and another that she never meant me to see, bottled in my blackguard heart forever!'

Raffles looked dim to me across the narrow compartment; but there was no nonsense in his look or voice. I longed to tell him all I knew, all that she had said to me and he had unwittingly interpreted; that she loved him, as now at last I knew she did; but I had given her my word, and after all it was a word to keep for both their sakes as well as for its own.

'You were made for each other, you two!'

That was all I said, and Raffles only laughed.

'All the more reason to hook it round the world, Bunny, before there's a dog's chance of our meeting again.'

He opened his paper the proper way up at last. The train rushed on with flying sparks, and flying lights along the line. We were getting nearer Dover now. My next brilliant remark was that I could 'smell the sea'. Raffles let it pass; he had been talking of the close-of-play scores in the stop-press column, and I thought he was studying them rather silently. Or perhaps he was not studying them at all, but still thinking of Camilla Belsize, and the look from those brave bright eyes that she had never meant him to see. Then, suddenly, I perceived that his forehead was glistening white and wet in the lamplight.

'What is it, Raffles? What's the matter?'

He reversed his paper with a shaky hand, and thrust it upon me without a word, merely pointing out four or five ill-printed lines of latest news. This was the item that danced before my eyes:

TRAGIC DEATH OF FAMOUS MONEYLENDER

Mr Daniel Levy, the financier, reported shot dead at front gates of his residence in Thames Valley at 5.30 this afternoon, by unknown man who made good his escape.

I looked up into a ghastly face.

'It was half-past five when I left him, Bunny!'

'You left him – '

I could not ask it. But the ghastly face had given me a ghastlier thought.

'As well as you are, Bunny!' so Raffles completed my sentence. 'Do you think I'd leave him for dead at his own gates?'

Of course I denied the thought; but it had come to haunt me none the less; for if I had sailed so near such a deed, what about Raffles under equal provocation? And what such motive for the very flight that we were making with but a moment's preparation? It all fitted in, except the face and voice of Raffles as they had been while he was speaking of Camilla Belsize;

but again, the fatal act would indeed have made him feel that he had lost her, and loosened his tongue upon his loss as something had done without doubt; and as for voice and face, there was no longer in either any lack of the mad excitement of the hunted man.

'But what were you doing at his gates, A.J.?'

'I saw him home. It was on my way. Why not?'

'And you say you left him at half-past five?'

'I swear it. I looked at my watch, thinking of my train, and my watch is plumb right.'

'And you heard no shot as you went on?'

'No – I was hurrying. I even ran. I must have been seen running! And now I'm like Charley's Aunt,' he went on with his sardonic laugh, 'and bound to stick to it until they catch me by the leg. Now you know what Mackenzie was doing down there! The old hound may be on my track already. There's no going back now.'

'Not for an innocent man?'

'Not for such dubious innocence as mine, Bunny! Remember all we've been up to with poor old Levy for the last twenty-four hours.'

He paused, remembering everything himself, as I could see; and the human compassion in his face should have been sufficient answer to my vile misgivings. But there was contrition in his look as well, and that was a much rarer sign in Raffles. Rarer still was a glance of alarm almost akin to panic, alike without precedent in my experience of my friend and beyond belief in my reading of his character. But through all there peeped a conscious enjoyment of these new sensations, a very zest in the novelty of fear, which I knew to be at once signally characteristic, and yet compatible either with his story or with my own base dread.

'Nobody need ever know about that,' said I, with the certainty that nobody ever would know through the one other who knew already. But Raffles threw cold water upon that poor little flicker of confidence and good hope.

'It's bound to come out, Bunny. They'll start accounting for his last hours on earth, and they'll stick ominously in the first five minutes working backwards. Then I am described as bolting from the scene, then identified with myself, then found to have fled the country! Then Carlsbad, then our first row with him, then yesterday's big cheque; my heavy double finds he was impersonated at the bank; it all comes out bit by bit, and if I'm caught it means that dingy Old Bailey dock on the capital charge!'

'Then I'll be with you,' said I, 'as accessory before and after the fact. That's one thing!'

'No, no, Bunny! You must shake me off and get back to town. I'll push you out as we slow down through the streets of Dover, and you can put up for the night at the Lord Warden. That's the sort of public place for the likes of us to lie low in, Bunny. Don't forget all my rules when I'm gone.'

'You're not going without me, A.J.'

'Not even if I did it, Bunny?'

'No; less than ever then!'

Raffles leant across and took my hand. There was a flash of mischief in his eyes, but a very tender light as well.

'It makes me almost wish I were what I do believe you thought I was,' said he, 'to see you stick to me all the same! But it's about time that we were making the lights of Dover,' he added, beating an abrupt retreat from sentiment, even to the length of getting up and looking out as we clattered through a country station. His head was in again before the platform was left behind, a pale face peering into mine, real panic flaring in those altered eyes, like blue lights at sea. 'My God, Bunny!' cried Raffles. 'I believe Dover's as far as I shall ever get!'

'Why? What's the matter now?'

'A head sticking out of the next compartment but one!'

'Mackenzie's?'

'Yes!'

I had seen it in his face.

'After us already?'

'God knows! Not necessarily; they watch the ports after a big murder.'

'Swagger detectives from Scotland Yard?'

Raffles did not answer; he had something else to do. Already he was turning his pockets inside out. A false beard rolled off the seat.

'That's for you,' he said as I picked it up. 'I'll finish making you up.' He was busy on himself in one of the oblong mirrors, kneeling on the cushions to be near his work. 'If it's a scent at all it must be a pretty hot one, Bunny, to have landed him in the very train and coach! But it mayn't be as bad as it looked at first sight. He can't have much to go upon yet. If he's only going to shadow us while they find out more at home, we shall give him the slip all right.'

'Do you think he saw you?'

'Looking out? No, thank goodness, he was looking toward Dover too.'

'But before we started?'

'No, Bunny, I don't believe he came aboard before Cannon Street. I remember hearing a bit of a fuss there. But our blinds were down, thank God!'

They were all down now, but by our decreasing speed I felt that we were already gliding over level crossings to the admiration of belated townsfolk waiting at the gates. Raffles turned from his mirror, and I from mine, simultaneously; and even to my initiated eye it was not Raffles at all, but another noble scamp who even in those days before the war was the observed of all observers about town.

'It's ever so much better than anonymous disguises,' said Raffles, as he went to work upon me with his pocket make-up box and his lightning touch. 'I was always rather like him, and I tried him on yesterday with such success at the bank that I certainly can't do better tonight. As for you, Bunny, if you slouch your hat and stick your beard in your bread basket, you ought to pass for a poor relation or a disreputable dun. But here we are, my lad, and now for Meester Mackenzie o' Scoteland Yarrd!'

The gaunt detective was in fact the first person we beheld upon the pier platform; raw-boned, stiff-jointed, and more than middle-aged, he must nevertheless have jumped out once again before the train stopped, and that almost on top of a diminutive telegraph boy, who was waiting while the old hound read his telegram with one eye and watched emerging passengers with both. Whether we should have passed him unobserved I cannot say. We could but have tried; but Raffles preferred to grasp the nettle and salute Mackenzie with a pleasant nod.

'Good evening, my lord!' says the Scotchman with a canny smirk.

'I can guess why you're down here,' says Raffles, actually producing a palpable Sullivan under the nose of the law.

'Is that a fact?' inquires the other, oiling the rebuff with deferential grin.

'And I mustn't stand between you and poor Dan Levy's murderer,' adds my lord, nodding finally, when Mackenzie steps after him to my horror. But it is only to show Raffles his telegram. And he does not follow us on board.

Neither did our disguises accompany our countenances across the Channel. It was at dead of night on the upper deck (whence all but us had fled) that Raffles showed me how to doff my beard and still look as though I had merely buttoned it inside my overcoat; meanwhile his own moustachios and imperial were disappearing by discreet degrees; and at last he told me why, though not by any means without pressing.

'I'm only afraid you'll want to turn straight back from Calais, Bunny!'

'Oh, no, I shan't.'

'You'll come with me round the world, so to speak?'

'To its uttermost ends, A.J.!'

'You do know now who it really is that I don't want to see again just yet?'

'Yes. I know. Now tell me what Mackenzie told you.'

'It was all in the wire he showed me,' said Raffles. 'The wire was to say that the murderer of Dan Levy had given himself up to the police!'

Profane expletives flew from my lips; those of much holier men might have been no less unguardedly emphatic in the self-same circumstances.

'But who was it?'

'I could have told you all along if you hadn't suspected me.'

'It wasn't a suspicion, Raffles. It was never more than a dread, and I didn't even dread it in my heart of hearts. Do tell me now.'

Raffles watched the red end of a ruined Sullivan make a fine trajectory as it flew to leeward between sea and stars.

'It was that poor unlucky little alien who was waiting for him the other morning in Jermyn Street, and again last night near his own garden gate. That's where he got him in the end. But it wasn't a shooting case at all, Bunny; that's why I never heard anything. It was a case of stabbing in accordance with the best traditions of the Latin races.'

'God forgive both poor devils!' said I at last.

'And other two,' said Raffles, 'who have rather more to be forgiven.'

19

APOLOGIA

On one of the worst days of last year, to wit the first day of the Eton and Harrow match, I had turned into the Hamman, in Jermyn Street, as the best available asylum for wet boots that might no longer enter any club. Mine had been removed by a little pinchbeck oriental in the outer courts, and I wandered within unpleasantly conscious of a hole in one sock, to find myself by no means the only obvious refugee from the rain. The bath was in fact inconveniently crowded. But at length I found a divan to suit me in an upstairs alcove. I had the choice indeed of more than one; but in spite of my antecedents I am fastidious about my cooling companions in a Turkish bath, and it was by no accident that I hung my clothes opposite to a newer morning coat and a pair of trousers more decisively creased than my own.

But the coincidence in pickle was no less remarkable. In ensuing stages of physical devastation one had dim glimpses of a not unfamiliar, reddish countenance; but with the increment of years it has been my lot to contract short sight as well as incipient obesity, and in the hot rooms my glasses lose their grip upon my nose. So it was not until I lay swathed upon my divan that I recognised E.M. Garland in the fine fresh-faced owner of the nice clothes opposite mine. A tawny moustache rather spoilt him as Phoebus, and there was a hint of old gold about the shaven jaw and chin; but I never saw better looks of the unintellectual order; and the amber eye was as clear as ever, the great strong wicket-keeper's hand unexpectedly hearty, when recognition dawned on Teddy in his turn.

He spoke of Raffles without hesitation or reserve, and of me and my Raffles writings as though there was nothing reprehensible in one or the other, displaying indeed a flattering knowledge of those pious memorials.

'But of course I take them with a grain of salt,' said Teddy Garland; 'you don't make me believe you were either of you such desperate dogs as all that. I can't see you climbing ropes or squirming through scullery windows – even for the fun of the thing!' he added with somewhat tardy tact.

It is certainly rather hard to credit now. I felt that after all there was something to be said for being too fat at forty, and that Teddy Garland had said it excellently.

'Now,' he continued, 'if only you would give us the row between Raffles and Dan Levy, I mean the whole battle royal that A.J. fought and won for me and my poor father, that would be something like! The world would see the sort of chap he really was.'

'I am afraid it would have to see the sort of chaps we all were just then,' said I, as I still think with exemplary delicacy; but Teddy lay silent and florid for some time. These athletes have their vanity. But this one rose superior to his.

'Manders,' said he, leaving his divan and coming and sitting on the edge of mine, 'you have my free leave to give me and mine away to the four winds, if you will tell the truth about that duel, and what Raffles did for the lot of us!'

'Perhaps he did more than you ever knew.'

'Put it all in.'

'It was a longer duel than you think. He once called it a guerilla duel.'

'Then make a book of it.'

'But I've written my last word about the old boy.'

'Then by George I've a good mind to write it myself!'

This was an awful threat. Happily he lacked the materials, and so I told him. 'I haven't got them all myself,' I added, only to be politely but openly disbelieved. 'I don't know where you were,' said I, 'all that first day of the match, when it rained.'

Garland was beginning to smile when the surprise of my statement got home and changed his face.

'Do you mean to say A.J. never told you?' he cried, still incredulously.

'No; he wouldn't give you away.'

'Not even to you – his pal?'

'No. I was naturally curious on the point. But he refused to tell me.'

'What a chap!' murmured Teddy, with a tender enthusiasm that made me love him. 'What a friend for a fellow! Well, Manders, if you don't write all this I certainly shall. So I may as well tell you where I was.'

'I must say it would interest me to know.'

My companion resumed his smile where he had left it off. 'I wonder if you would ever guess?' he speculated, looking down into my face.

'I don't suppose I should.'

'No more do I; not in a month of Sundays; for I spent that day on the very sofa I was on a minute ago!'

I looked at the striped divan opposite. I looked at Teddy Garland sitting on mine. His smile was a little wry with the remnant of his bygone shame; he hurried on before I could find a word.

'You remember that drug I had? Somnol I think it was. That was a risky game to play with any head but one's own; still A.J. was right in thinking I should have been worse without any sleep at all. I should,' said Teddy, 'but I should have rolled up at Lord's! The beastly stuff put me asleep all right, but it didn't keep me asleep long enough! I was awake before four, heard you both talking in the next room, remembered everything in a flash! But for that flash I should have dropped off again in a minute; but if you remember all I had to remember, Manders, you won't wonder that I lay madly awake all the rest of the night. My head was rotten with sleep, but my heart was in such hell as I couldn't describe to you if I tried.'

'I've been there,' said I, briefly.

'Well, then, you can imagine my frightful thoughts. Suicide was one; but to get out of that came first, to get away without looking either of you in the face in broad daylight. So I shammed sleep when Raffles looked in, and when you both went out I dressed in five minutes and slunk out too. I had no idea where I was going. I don't remember what brought me down into this street. It may have been my debt to Dan Levy. All I remember is finding myself opposite this place, my head splitting, and the sudden idea that a bath might freshen me up and couldn't make me worse. I remembered A.J. telling me he had once taken six wickets after one. So in I came. I had my bath, and some tea and toast in the hot-rooms; we were all to have a late breakfast together, if you recollect. I felt I should be in plenty of time for that and Lord's – if only I hadn't boiled all the cricket out of me. So I came up here and lay down there. But what I hadn't boiled out was that beastly drug. It got back on me like a boomerang. I closed my eyes for a minute – and it was well on in the afternoon when I awoke!'

Here Teddy interrupted himself to order whiskies and soda of a metropolitan Bashi–Bazouk who happened to pass along the gallery; and to go stumbling over to his pockets, in his swaddling towels, for cigarettes and matches. And the rest of his discourse was less coherent.

'Then I did feel it was a toss-up between my razor and a charge of shot! I had no idea it was raining; if you look up at that coloured skylight, you can't say if it's raining now. There's another sort of hatchway on top of it. Then you hear that fountain tinkling all the time; you don't hear any rain, do you? – It was after three, but I lay till nearly four simply cursing my luck; there was no hurry then. At last I wondered what the papers had to say about me – who was playing in my place, who'd won the toss and all the rest of it. So I had the nerve to send out for one, and what should I see? "No play at Lord's" – and sudden illness of my poor old father! You know the rest, Manders, because in less than twenty minutes after that we met.'

'And I remember thinking how fit you looked,' said I. 'It was the bath, of course, and the sleep on top of it. But I wonder they let you sleep so long.'

'How could they know what I'd been up to?' said Teddy. 'I mightn't have had any sleep for a week; it was their business to let me be. But to think of the rain coming on and saving me – for even Raffles couldn't have done it without the rain. That was the great slice of luck – while I was lying right there! And that's why I like to lie there still – for luck rather than remembrance!'

The drinks came; we smoked and sipped. I regretted to find that Teddy was no longer faithful to the only old cigarette. But his loyalty to Raffles won my heart as he had never won it in his youth.

'Give us away to your heart's content,' said he; 'but give the dear old devil his due at last.'

'But who exactly do you mean by "us"?'

'My father not so much, perhaps, because he's dead and gone; but self and wife as much as ever you like.'

'Are you sure Mrs Garland won't mind?'

'Mind! It was for her he did it all; didn't you know that?'

I didn't know Teddy knew it, and I began to think him a finer fellow than I had supposed.

'Am I to say all I know about that too?' I asked.

'Rather! Camilla and I will both be delighted – so long as you change our names – for we both loved him!' said Teddy Garland.

I wonder if they both forgive me for taking him entirely at his word?

Appendix

GEORGE ORWELL
RAFFLES AND MISS BLANDISH

Nearly half a century after his first appearance, Raffles, 'the amateur cracksman', is still one of the best-known characters in English fiction. Very few people would need telling that he played cricket for England, had bachelor chambers in the Albany and burgled the Mayfair houses which he also entered as a guest. Just for that reason he and his exploits make a suitable background against which to examine a more modern crime story such as *No Orchids for Miss Blandish*. Any such choice is necessarily arbitrary — I might equally well have chosen *Arsène Lupin* for instance — but at any rate *No Orchids* and the Raffles books have the common quality of being crime stories which play the limelight on the criminal rather than the policeman. For sociological purposes they can be compared. *No Orchids* is the 1939 version of glamorized crime, *Raffles* the 1900 version. What I am concerned with here is the immense difference in moral atmosphere between the two books, and the change in the popular attitude that this probably implies.

At this date, the charm of *Raffles* is partly in the period atmosphere and partly in the technical excellence of the stories. Hornung was a very conscientious and on his level a very able writer. Anyone who cares for sheer efficiency must admire his work. However, the truly dramatic thing, about Raffles, the thing that makes him a sort of byword even to this day (only a few weeks ago, in a burglary case, a magistrate referred to the prisoner as 'a Raffles in real life'), is the fact that he is *a gentleman*. Raffles is presented to us and this is rubbed home in countless scraps of dialogue and casual remarks — not as an honest man who has gone astray, but as a public-school man who has gone astray. His remorse, when he feels any, is almost purely social; he has disgraced 'the old school', he has lost his right to enter 'decent society', he has forfeited his amateur status and become a cad. Neither Raffles nor Bunny appears to feel at all strongly that stealing is wrong in itself, though Raffles does once justify himself by the casual remark that 'the distribution of property is all wrong anyway'. They think of themselves not as sinners but as renegades, or simply as outcasts. And the moral code of most of us is still so close to Raffles' own that we do feel his situation to be an especially ironical one. A West End club man who is really a burglar! That is almost a story in itself, is it not? But how if it were a plumber or a greengrocer who was really a burglar? Would there be anything inherently dramatic in that? No although the theme of the 'double life', of respectability covering crime, is still there. Even Charles Peace in his clergyman's dog-collar, seems somewhat less of a hypocrite than Raffles in his Zingari blazer.

Raffles, of course, is good at all games, but it is peculiarly fitting that his chosen game should be cricket. This allows not only of endless analogies between his cunning as a slow bowler and his cunning as a burglar, but also helps to define the exact nature of his crime. Cricket is not in reality a very popular game in England — it is nowhere so popular as football, for instance — but it gives expression to a well-marked trait in the English character, the tendency to value 'form' or 'style' more highly than success. In the eyes of any true cricket-lover it is possible for an innings of ten runs to be 'better' (*i. e.* more elegant) than an innings of a hundred runs: cricket is also one of the very few games in which the amateur can excel the professional. It is a game full of forlorn hopes and sudden dramatic changes of fortune, and its rules are so defined that their interpretation is partly an ethical business. When Larwood, for instance, practised bodyline bowling in Australia he was not actually breaking any rule : he was merely doing something that was 'not cricket'. Since cricket takes up a lot of time and is rather an expensive game to play, it is predominantly an upper-class game, but for the whole nation it is bound up with such concepts as 'good form', 'playing the game', etc., and it has declined in popularity just as the tradition of 'don't hit a man when he's down' has declined. It is not a twentieth-century game, and nearly all modern-minded people dislike it. The Nazis, for instance, were at pains to discourage cricket, which had gained a certain footing in Germany before and after the last war. In making Raffles a cricketer as well as a burglar, Hornung was not merely providing him with a plausible disguise; he was also drawing the sharpest moral contrast that he was able to imagine.

Raffles, no less than *Great Expectations* or *Le Rouge et le Noir*, is a story of snobbery, and it gains a great deal from the precariousness of Raffles's social position. A cruder writer would have made the 'gentleman burglar' a member of the peerage, or at least a baronet. Raffles, however, is of upper-middle-class origin and is only accepted by the aristocracy because of his personal charm. 'We were in Society but not of it', he says to Bunny towards the end of the book; and 'I was asked about for my cricket'. Both he and Bunny accept the values of 'Society' unquestioningly, and would settle down in it for good if only they could get away with a big enough haul. The ruin that constantly threatens them is all the blacker because they only doubtfully 'belong'. A duke who has served a prison sentence is still a duke, whereas a mere man about town, if once disgraced, ceases to be 'about town' for evermore. The closing chapters of the book, when Raffles has been exposed and is living under an assumed name, have a twilight of the gods feeling, a mental atmosphere rather similar to that of Kipling's poem, 'Gentleman Rankers':

> Yes, a trooper of the forces —
> Who has run his own six horses! *etc.*

Raffles now belongs irrevocably to the 'cohorts of the damned'. He can still commit successful burglaries, but there is no way back into Paradise, which means Piccadilly and the M.C.C. According to the public-school code there is only one means of rehabilitation: death in battle. Raffles dies fighting against the Boers (a practised reader would foresee this from the start), and in the eyes of both Bunny and his creator this cancels his crimes.

Both Raffles and Bunny, of course, are devoid of religious belief, and they have no real ethical code, merely certain rules of behaviour which they observe semi-instinctively. But it is just here that the deep moral difference between *Raffles* and *No Orchids* becomes apparent. Raffles and Bunny, after all, are gentlemen, and such standards as they do have are not to be violated. Certain things are 'not done', and the idea of doing them hardly arises. Raffles will not, for example, abuse hospitality. He will commit a burglary in a house where he is staying as a guest, but the victim must be a fellow-guest and not the host. He will not commit murder(2), and he avoids violence wherever possible and prefers to carry out his robberies unarmed. He regards friendship as sacred, and is chivalrous though not moral in his relations with women. He will take extra risks in the name of 'sportsmanship', and sometimes even for aesthetic reasons. And above all, he is intensively patriotic.

He celebrates the Diamond Jubilee ('For sixty years, Bunny, we've been ruled over by absolutely the finest sovereign the world has ever seen') by dispatching to the Queen, through the post, an antique gold cup which he has stolen from the British Museum. He steals, from partly political motives, a pearl which the German Emperor is sending to one of the enemies of Britain, and when the Boer War begins to go badly his one thought is to find his way into the fighting line. At the front he unmasks a spy at the cost of revealing his own identity, and then dies gloriously by a Boer bullet. In this combination of crime and patriotism he resembles his near-contemporary Arsène Lupin, who also scores off the German Emperor and wipes out his very dirty past by enlisting in the Foreign Legion.

It is important to note that by modern standards Raffles's crimes are very petty ones. Four hundred pounds worth of jewellery seems to him an excellent haul. And though the stories are convincing in their physical detail, they contain very little sensationalism — very few corpses, hardly any blood, no sex crimes, no sadism, no perversions of any kind. It seems to be the case that the crime story, at any rate on its higher levels, has greatly increased in blood-thirstiness during the past twenty years. Some of the early detective stories do not even contain a murder. The Sherlock Holmes stories, for instance, are not all murders, and some of them do not even deal with an indictable crime. So also with the John Thorndyke stories, while of the Max Carrados stories only a minority are murders. Since 1918, however, a detective story not containing a murder has been a great rarity, and the most disgusting details of dismemberment and exhumation are commonly exploited. Some of the Peter Wimsey stories, for instance, display an extremely morbid interest in corpses. The Raffles stories, written from the angle of the criminal, are much less anti-social than many modern stories written from the angle of the detective. The main impression that they leave behind is of boyishness. They belong to a time when people had standards, though they happened to be foolish standards. Their key-phrase is 'not done'. The line that they draw between good and evil is as senseless as a Polynesian taboo, but at least, like the taboo, it has the advantage that everyone accepts it.

So much for *Raffles*. Now for a header into the cesspool. *No Orchids for Miss Blandish*, by James Hadley Chase, was published in 1939, but seems to have enjoyed its greatest popularity in 1940, during the Battle of Britain and the blitz. In its main outlines its story is this:

Miss Blandish, the daughter of a millionaire, is kidnapped by some gangsters who are almost immediately surprised and killed off by a larger and better organized gang. They hold her to ransom and extract half a million dollars from her father. Their original plan had been to kill her as soon as the ransom-money was received, but a chance keeps her alive. One of the gang is a young man named Slim, whose sole pleasure in life consists in driving knives into other people's bellies. In childhood he has graduated by cutting up living animals with a pair of rusty scissors. Slim is sexually impotent, but takes a kind of fancy to Miss Blandish. Slim's mother, who is the real brains of the gang, sees in this the chance of curing Slim's impotence, and decides to keep Miss Blandish in custody till Slim shall have succeeded in raping her. After many efforts and much persuasion, including the flogging of Miss Blandish with a length of rubber hosepipe, the rape is achieved. Meanwhile Miss Blandish's father has hired a private detective, and by means of bribery and torture the detective and the police manage to round up and exterminate the whole gang. Slim escapes with Miss Blandish and is killed after a final rape, and the detective prepares to restore Miss Blandish to her family. By this time, however, she has developed such a taste for Slim's caresses(3) that she feels unable to live without him, and she jumps, out of the window of a sky-scraper.

Several other points need noticing before one can grasp the full implications of this book. To begin with, its central story bears a very marked resemblance to William Faulkner's novel, *Sanctuary*. Secondly, it is not, as one might expect, the product of an illiterate hack, but a brilliant piece of writing, with hardly a wasted word or a jarring note anywhere. Thirdly, the whole book, *récit* as well as dialogue, is written in the American language; the author, an Englishman who has (I believe) never been in the United States, seems to have made a complete mental transference to the American underworld. Fourthly, the book sold, according to its publishers, no less than half a million copies.

I have already outlined the plot, but the subject-matter is much more sordid and brutal than this suggests. The book contains eight full-dress murders, an unassessable number of casual killings and woundings, an exhumation (with a careful reminder of the stench), the flogging of Miss Blandish, the torture of another woman with red-hot cigarette-ends, a strip-tease act, a third-degree scene of unheard-of cruelty and much else of the same kind. It assumes great sexual sophistication in its readers (there is a scene, for instance, in which a gangster, presumably of masochistic tendency, has an orgasm in the moment of being knifed), and it takes for granted the most complete corruption and self-seeking as the norm of human behaviour. The detective, for instance, is almost as great a rogue as the gangsters, and actuated by nearly the same motives. Like them, he is in pursuit of 'five hundred grand'. It is necessary to the machinery of the story that Mr. Blandish should be anxious to get his daughter back, but apart from this, such things as affection, friendship, good nature or even ordinary politeness simply do not enter. Nor, to any great extent does normal sexuality. Ultimately only one motive is at work throughout the whole story: the pursuit of power.

It should be noticed that the book is not in the ordinary sense pornography. Unlike most books that deal in sexual sadism, it lays the emphasis on the cruelty and not on the pleasure. Slim, the ravisher of Miss Blandish, has 'wet slobbering lips': this is disgusting, and it is meant to be disgusting. But the scenes describing cruelty to women are comparatively perfunctory. The real high-spots of the book are cruelties committed by men upon other men; above all, the third-degreeing of the gangster, Eddie Schultz, who is lashed into a chair and flogged on the windpipe with truncheons, his arms broken by fresh blows as he breaks loose. In another of Mr. Chase's books, *He Won't Need It Now*, the hero, who is intended to be a sympathetic and perhaps even noble character, is described as stamping on somebody's face, and then, having crushed the man's mouth in, grinding his heel round and round in it. Even when physical incidents of this kind are not occurring, the mental atmosphere of these books is always the same. Their whole theme is the struggle for power and the triumph of the strong over the weak. The big gangsters wipe out the little ones as mercilessly as a pike gobbling up the little fish in a pond; the police kill off the criminals as cruelly as the angler kills the pike. If ultimately one sides with the police against the gangsters, it is merely because they are better organized and more powerful, because, in fact, the law is a bigger racket than crime. Might is right: *vae victis.*

As I have mentioned already, *No Orchids* enjoyed its greatest vogue in 1940, though it was successfully running as a play till some time later. It was, in fact, one of the things that helped to console people for the boredom of being bombed. Early in the war the *New Yorker* had a picture of a little man approaching a news-stall littered with paper with such headlines as 'Great Tank Battles in Northern France', 'Big Naval Battle in the North Sea', 'Huge Air Battles over the Channel', etc., etc. The little man is saying '*Action Stories*, please'. That little man stood for all the drugged millions to whom the world of the gangster and the prize-ring is more 'real', more 'tough', than such things as wars, revolutions, earthquakes, famines and pestilences. From the point of view of a reader of *Action Stories*, a description of the London blitz, or of the struggles of the European underground parties, would be 'sissy stuff'. On the other hand, some puny gun-battle in Chicago, resulting in perhaps half a dozen deaths, would seem genuinely 'tough'. This habit of mind is now extremely widespread. A soldier sprawls in a muddy trench, with the machine-gun bullets crackling a foot or two overhead, and whiles away his intolerable boredom by reading an American gangster story. And what is it that makes that story so exciting? Precisely the fact that people are shooting at each other with machine-guns! Neither the soldier nor anyone else sees anything curious in this. It is taken for granted that an imaginary bullet is more thrilling than a real one.

The obvious explanation is that in real life one is usually a passive victim, whereas in the adventure story one can think of oneself as being at the centre of events. But there is more to it than that. Here it is necessary to refer again to the curious fact of *No Orchids* being written — with technical errors, perhaps, but certainly with considerable skill — in the American language.

There exists in America an enormous literature of more or less the same stamp as *No Orchids*. Quite apart from books, there is the huge array of 'pulp magazines', graded so as to cater for different kinds of fantasy, but nearly all having much the same mental atmosphere. A few of them go in for straight pornography, but the great majority are quite plainly aimed at sadists and masochists. Sold at threepence a copy under the title of Yank Mags(4), these things used to enjoy considerable popularity in England, but when the supply dried up owing to the war, no satisfactory substitute was forthcoming. English imitations of the 'pulp magazine' do now exist, but they are poor things compared with the original. English crook films, again, never approach the American crook film in brutality.

And yet the career of Mr. Chase shows how deep the American influence has already gone. Not only is he himself living a continuous fantasy-life in the Chicago underworld, but he can count on hundreds of thousands of readers who know what is meant by a 'clipshop' or the 'hotsquat', do not have to do mental arithmetic when confronted by 'fifty grand', and understand at sight a sentence like 'Johnny was a rummy and only two jumps ahead of the nut-factory'. Evidently there are great numbers of English people who are partly americanized in language and, one ought to add, in moral outlook. For there was no popular protest against *No Orchids*. In the end it was withdrawn, but only retrospectively, when a later work, *Miss Callaghan Comes to Grief*, brought Mr. Chase's books to the attention of the authorities. Judging by casual conversations at the time, ordinary readers got a mild thrill out of the obscenities of *No Orchids*, but saw nothing undesirable in the book as a whole. Many people, incidentally, were under the impression that it was an American book reissued in England.

The thing that the ordinary reader *ought* to have objected to — almost certainly would have objected to, a few decades earlier — was the equivocal attitude towards crime. It is implied throughout *No Orchids* that being a criminal is only reprehensible in the sense that it does not pay. Being a policeman pays better, but there is no moral difference, since the police use essentially criminal methods. In a book like *He Won't Need It Now* the distinction between crime and crime-prevention practically disappears. This is a new departure for English sensational fiction, in which till recently there has always been a sharp distinction between right and wrong and a general agreement that virtue must triumph in the last chapter. English books glorifying crime (modern crime, that is — pirates and highwaymen are different) are very rare. Even a book like *Raffles*, as I have pointed out, is governed by powerful taboos, and it is clearly understood that Raffles's crimes must be expiated sooner or later. In America, both in life and fiction, the tendency to tolerate crime, even to admire the criminal so long as he is success, is very much more marked. It is, indeed, ultimately this attitude that has made it possible for crime to flourish upon so huge a scale. Books have been written about Al Capone that are hardly different in tone from the books written about Henry Ford, Stalin, Lord Northcliffe and all the rest of the 'log cabin to White House' brigade. And switching back eighty years, one finds Mark Twain adopting much the same attitude towards the disgusting bandit Slade, hero of twenty-eight murders, and towards the Western desperadoes generally. They were successful, they 'made good', therefore he admired them.

In a book like *No Orchids* one is not, as in the old-style crime story, simply escaping from dull reality into an imaginary world of action. One's escape is essentially into cruelty and sexual perversion. *No Orchids* is aimed at the power-instinct, which *Raffles* or the Sherlock Holmes stories are not. At the same time the English attitude towards crime is not so superior to the American as I may have seemed to imply. It too is mixed up with power-worship, and has become more noticeably so in the last twenty years. A writer who is worth examining is Edgar Wallace, especially in such typical books as *The Orator* and the Mr. J. G. Reeder stories. Wallace was one of the first crime-story writers to break away from the old tradition of the private detective and make his central figure a Scotland Yard official. Sherlock Holmes is an amateur, solving his problems without the help and even, in the earlier stories, against the opposition of the police. Moreover, like Lupin, he is essentially an intellectual, even a scientist. He reasons logically from observed fact, and his intellectuality is constantly contrasted with the routine methods of the police. Wallace objected strongly to this slur, as he considered it, on Scotland Yard, and in several newspaper articles he went out of his way to denounce Holmes byname. His own ideal was the detective-inspector who catches criminals not because he is intellectually brilliant but because he is part of an all-powerful organi- zation. Hence the curious fact that in Wallace's most characteristic stories the 'clue' and the 'deduction' play no part. The criminal is always defeated by an incredible coincidence, or because in some unexplained manner the police know all about the crime beforehand. The tone of the stories makes it quite clear that Wallace's admiration for the police is pure bully-worship. A Scotland Yard detective is the most powerful kind of being that he can imagine, while the criminal figures in his mind as an outlaw against whom anything is permissible, like the condemned slaves in the Roman arena. His policemen behave much more brutally than British policemen do in real life — they hit people with out provocation, fire revolvers past their ears to terrify them and so on — and some of the stories exhibit a fearful intellectual sadism. (For instance, Wallace likes to arrange things so that the villain is hanged on the same day as the heroine is married.) But it is sadism after the English fashion: that is to say, it is unconscious, there is not overtly any sex in it, and it keeps within the bounds of the law. The British public tolerates a harsh criminal law and gets a kick out of monstrously unfair murder trials: but still that is better, on any account, than tolerating or admiring crime. If one must worship a bully, it is better that he should be a policeman than a gangster. Wallace is still governed to some extent by the concept of 'not done'. In *No Orchids* anything is 'done' so long as it leads on to power. All the barriers are down, all the motives are out in the open. Chase is a worse symptom than Wallace, to the extent that all-in wrestling is worse than boxing, or Fascism is worse than capitalist democracy.

In borrowing from William Faulkner's *Sanctuary*, Chase only took the plot; the mental atmosphere of the two books is not similar. Chase really derives from other sources, and this particular bit of borrowing is only symbolic. What it symbolizes is the vulgarization of ideas which is constantly happening, and which probably happens faster in an age of print. Chase has been described as 'Faulkner for the masses', but it would be more accurate to describe him as Carlyle for the masses. He is a popular writer — there are many such in America, but they are still rarities in England — who has caught up with what is now fashionable to call 'realism', meaning the doctrine that might is right. The growth of 'realism' has been the great feature of the intellectual history of our own age. Why this should be so is a complicated question. The interconnexion between sadism, masochism, success-worship, power-worship, nationalism, and totalitarianism is a huge subject whose edges have barely been scratched, and even to mention it is considered somewhat indelicate. To take merely the first example that comes to mind, I believe no one has ever pointed out the sadistic and masochistic element in Bernard Shaw's work, still less suggested that this probably has some connexion with Shaw's admiration for dictators. Fascism is often loosely equated with sadism, but nearly always by people who see nothing wrong in the most slavish worship of Stalin. The truth is, of course, that the countless English intellectuals who kiss the arse of Stalin are not different from the minority who give their allegiance to Hitler or Mussolini, nor from the efficiency experts who preached 'punch', 'drive', 'personality' and 'learn to be a Tiger man' in the nineteen-twenties, nor from that older generation of intellectuals, Carlyle, Creasey and the rest of them, who bowed down before German militarism. All of them are worshipping power and successful cruelty. It is important to notice that the cult of power tends to be mixed up with a love of cruelty and wickedness for *their own sakes*. A tyrant is all the more admired if he happens to be a bloodstained crook as well, and 'the end justifies the means' often becomes, in effect, 'the means justify themselves provided they are dirty enough'. This idea colours the outlook of all sympathizers with totalitarianism, and accounts, for instance, for the positive delight with which many English intellectuals greeted the Nazi-Soviet pact. It was a step only doubtfully useful to the U.S.S.R., but it was entirely unmoral, and for that reason to be admired; the explanations of it, which were numerous and self-contradictory, could come afterwards.

Until recently the characteristic adventure stories of the English-speaking peoples have been stories in which the hero fights *against odds*. This is true all the way from Robin Hood to Pop-eye the Sailor. Perhaps the basic myth of the Western world is Jack the Giant-killer, but to be brought up to date this should be renamed Jack the Dwarf-killer, and there already exists a considerable literature which teaches, either overtly or implicitly, that one should side with the big man against the little man. Most of what is now written about foreign policy is simply an embroidery on this theme, and for several decades such phrases as 'Play the game', 'Don't hit a man when he's down' and 'It's not cricket' have never failed to draw a snigger from anyone of intellectual pretensions. What is comparatively new is to find the accepted pattern, according to which (*a*) right is right and wrong is wrong, whoever wins, and (*b*) weakness must be respected, disappearing from popular literature as well. When I first read D. H. Lawrence's novels, at the age of about twenty, I was puzzled by the fact that there did not seem to be any classification of the characters into 'good' and 'bad'. Lawrence seemed to sympathize with all of them about equally, and this was so unusual as to give me the feeling of having lost my bearings. Today no one would think of looking for heroes and villains in a serious novel, but in lowbrow fiction one still expects to find a sharp distinction between right and wrong and between legality and illegality. The common people, on the whole, are still living in the world of absolute good and evil from which the intellectuals have long since escaped. But the popularity of *No Orchids* and the American books and magazines to which it is akin shows how rapidly the doctrine of 'realism' is gaining ground.

Several people, after reading *No Orchids*, have remarked to me, 'It's pure Fascism'. This is a correct description, although the book has not the smallest connexion with politics and very little with social or economic problems. It has merely the same relation to Fascism as, say Trollope's novels have to nineteenth-century capitalism. It is a daydream appropriate to a totalitarian age. In his imagined world of gangsters Chase is presenting, as it were, a distilled version of the modern political scene, in which such things as mass bombing of civilians, the use of hostages, torture to obtain confessions, secret prisons, execution without trial, floggings with rubber truncheons, drownings in cesspools, systematic falsification of records and statistics, treachery, bribery, and quislingism are normal and morally neutral, even admirable when they are done in a large and bold way. The average man is not directly interested in politics, and when he reads, he wants the current struggles of the world to be translated into a simple story about individuals. He can take an interest in Slim and Fenner as he could not in the G.P.U. and the Gestapo. People worship power in the form in which they are able to understand it. A twelve-year-old boy worships Jack Dempsey. An adolescent in a Glasgow slum worships Al Capone. An aspiring pupil at a business college worships Lord Nuffield. A *New Statesman* reader worships Stalin. There is a difference in intellectual maturity, but none in moral outlook. Thirty years ago the heroes of popular fiction had nothing in common with Mr. Chase's gangsters and detectives, and the idols of the English liberal intelligentsia were also comparatively sympathetic figures. Between Holmes and Fenner on the one hand, and between Abraham Lincoln and Stalin on the other, there is a similar gulf.

One ought not to infer too much from the success of Mr. Chase's books. It is possible that it is an isolated phenomenon, brought about by the mingled boredom and brutality of war. But if such books should definitely acclimatize themselves in England, instead of being merely a half-understood import from America, there would be good grounds for dismay. In choosing *Raffles* as a background for *No Orchids* I deliberately chose a book which by the standards of its time was morally equivocal. Raffles, as I have pointed out, has no real moral code, no religion, certainly no social consciousness. All he has is a set of reflexes the nervous system, as it were, of a gentleman. Give him a sharp tap on this reflex or that (they are called 'sport', 'pal', 'woman', 'king and country' and so forth), and you get a predictable reaction. In Mr. Chase's books there are no gentlemen and no taboos. Emancipation is complete. Freud and Machiavelli have reached the outer suburbs. Comparing the schoolboy atmosphere of the one book with the cruelty and corruption of the other, one is driven to feel that snobbishness, like hypocrisy, is a check upon behaviour whose value from a social point of view has been underrated.

1944

A fan of Sherlock Holmes?
Then meet Solar Pons

The original fan fiction from the great August Derleth—the Sherlock Holmes of Praed Street.

"the best substitutes for Sherlock Holmes known."
– Vincent Starrett

"an excellent series of adventures in detection in their own right." – *The Chicago Tribune*

For more details and a full list of titles:
visit https://www.hachetteindia.com/home/yellowbacks